THE FAV

Philippa Gregory is an established writer and broadcaster for radio and television. She holds a PhD in eighteenth-century literature from the University of Edinburgh. She has been widely praised for her historical novels, including *Earthly Joys* and *A Respectable Trade* (which she adapted for BBC Television), as well as her works of contemporary suspense. *The Other Boleyn Girl* won the Parker Romantic Novel of the Year Award in 2002 and it has recently been adapted for BBC Television. Philippa Gregory lives in the North of England with her family.

Visit www.PhilippaGregory.com for more information and www.AuthorTracker.co.uk for exclusive updates about Philippa Gregory.

PHILIPPA GREGORY

The Favoured Child

HARPER

Harper
An imprint of HarperCollins*Publishers*
77–85 Fulham Palace Road,
Hammersmith, London W6 8JB

www.harpercollins.co.uk

This production 2013

First published in Great Britain by
Viking 1989

A catalogue record for this book is
available from the British Library

ISBN 978 0 00 793271 9

Set in Plantin

Printed and bound in Great Britain by
Clays Ltd, St Ives plc

MIX
Paper from
responsible sources
FSC C007454

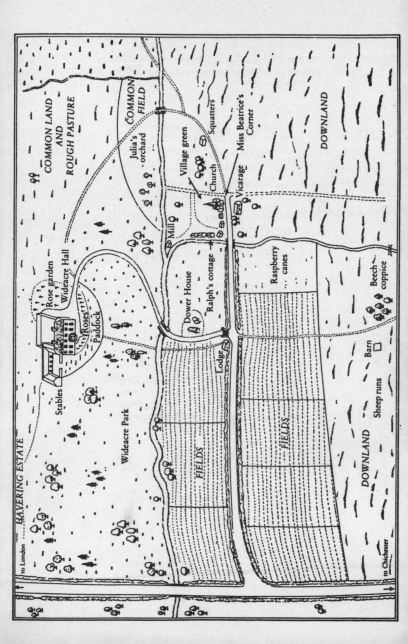

THE DREAM

*B*efore there was anything, there was the dream. Before Richard, before I even knew the hills around Wideacre, the sweet rolling green downs which encircle and guard my home – there was the dream. As far back as I can remember, the dream is there. Was always there.

And it is not the dream of a child. It is not my dream. It belongs to someone else. But I do not know whose dream it is.

In the dream I am hurt – hurt and heartbroken with a pain that I hope has never been felt in real life. My feet are sore from walking far on stony cold ground, and they are wet with mud, Wideacre mud, and with blood from a hundred cuts from the sharp chalk and flint stones. I am stumbling in midnight darkness through the woods near our house towards the river, the River Fenny, and I can hear the roar of its winter-deep waters, louder even than the howling and tossing of the wind in the treetops. It is too dark for me to see my way and I stumble in the blackness between the shattering blasts of lightning.

I could walk easier but for my burden. The only warm dry part about me is the little bundle of a new-born baby which I am holding tight to my heart under my cape. I know that this baby is my responsibility. She is mine. She belongs to me; and yet I must destroy her. I must take her down to the river and hold that tiny body under the turbulent waters. Then I can let her go, and the little body in the white shawl will be rolled over and over by the rushing flood, away from my empty hands. I must let her go.

The roaring noise of water gets louder as I struggle down the muddy footpath, and then I catch my breath with fear when I see the river – broader than it has ever been before, buffeting the trunks

1

of the trees high on the banks, for it has burst out of its course. The fallen tree across the river which we use as a bridge is gone, hidden by boiling depths of rushing water. I give a little cry, which I cannot even hear above the noise of the storm, for I do not now know how I am to get the baby into the river. And she must be drowned. I have to drown her. It is my duty as a Lacey.

This is too much for me, this fresh obstacle on top of my tears and the pain in my heart and the pain in my feet, and I start to struggle to wake. I cannot see how I can get this warm soft sleeping baby to the cold dashing river water, and yet I have to do it. I am stumbling forward, sobbing, towards the river, which is boiling like a cauldron in hell. But at the same time a part of my mind knows this is a dream — the dream which I always have. I struggle to be free of it, but it holds me. It is living its life in my mind. It is as if I have split into two people. One of them is a little girl struggling to wake from a nightmare, tossing in her bed in the little room and crying for her mama to come. And the other is this woman with a baby warm under her cloak and an utter determination to drown her like an inbred puppy in the cold waters of the river which rushes from the slopes of the downs and through Wideacre and away.

I am an old woman now. In my heart I am an old woman, tired, and ready for my death. But when I was a child, I was a girl on Wideacre. A girl who knew everything, and yet knew nothing. A girl who could see the past all around as she walked on the land – dimly, like firelit smoke. And could see the future in bright glimpses – like moonlight through storm-torn clouds. The unstoppable hints of past and future moulded my childhood like drips of water on a tortuous limestone stalactite that grows and grows into a strange racked shape, knowing nothing.

Oh! I know now. I have been a fool. I was a fool over and over in the years when I learned to be a woman. But I am no fool now. I had to shed the shell of lies and half-truths like a summer-time adder coming out of a sloughed skin. I had to scrape the scales of lies off my very eyes so that I blinked in the strong light of the truth at last; and was a fool no more. In the end I was the only one that dared to face the truth. In the end I was quite alone. In the end there was only me. Only me and the land.

It is no ordinary land – that is our explanation and our excuse. This is Wideacre, set on the very chalk backbone of southern England, as beautiful and as rich as a garden, as the very first garden of Eden. The South Downs enclose the valley of the River Fenny like a cupped hand. High chalk downs, sweet with short-cropped grass and rare meadow flowers, dizzy in summer with tiny blue butterflies. These hills were my horizon. My little world was held inside them. And its centre was the hall, Wideacre Hall. A smoke-blackened ruin at the head of the chalk-mud and flint-stone drive, tumbling down amid an overgrown rose garden where no one walks. In the old days the carriages would roll past the front door and down the drive, passing fertile fields, passing the little square sandstone Dower House, stopping at the great iron gates at the head of the drive for the lodge-keeper to swing them open for a tossed coin or a nod. To the left is the village of Acre – a lane lined with tradesmen's cottages, a whitewashed vicarage, a church with a pretty rounded spire; to the right is the lane which runs to the London road, meeting it at the corner where the stage-coach stops on its way north to Midhurst and beyond.

I was born Julia Lacey, the daughter of the squire of Wideacre and his wife, Celia, of Havering Hall. I was their only child, the only heir. I was raised with my cousin Richard, the son of Beatrice, my father's sister. Those two – my papa and his sister – made my cousin and me joint heirs to Wideacre. They changed the entail on the estate so that we two could jointly inherit. We always knew that we were to run Wideacre together.

Those are the facts. But there is also the truth. The truth that Beatrice was desperate to own her brother's estate, that she lied and schemed and ruined the land and murdered – oh, yes, the Laceys have always been killers. She stopped at nothing to put herself in the squire's chair. She enclosed fields and shut footpaths, she raised rents and planted wheat everywhere to pay for her plans. She drove her husband half mad and stole his fortune. She dominated her brother in every way a woman can. And she outran her destiny for season after season until the village which had once adored her came against her with torches in their hands and a leader on a black horse riding before them.

They killed her.

They killed her. They burned down the house. They ruined the Lacey family. And they put themselves outside the law for ever.

My papa, the squire, died of a weak heart. Beatrice's husband, Dr John MacAndrew, went away to India, swearing to repay her creditors. And then there were only the three of us left: my mama, my cousin Richard and me in the square little box of a house, half-way down the drive from Wideacre Hall with the great trees of the Wideacre parkland leaning over the roof and pressing close to the windows. Three of us, two servants, and a whole world of ghosts.

I could name them all. I saw them all. Not very clearly. Not well enough to understand with my child's imagination. But at night when I was asleep, I sometimes heard a voice, a word or an echo of a word. Or once, very clearly, the ripple of a joyous laugh. And once I had a dream so intense that I awoke, in a start of terror, my bedroom windows bright with the reflection of flames from a fire as big as a house, the fire which burned down Wideacre Hall, my house. And killed the squire, my papa. And left three survivors in this house: the three of us and a family of ghosts.

In real life there was my mama. Her face was heart-shaped, pale like a cream rose, her eyes pansy-brown. Her hair was fair when she was young but went grey – long ageing streaks of dullness among the gold, as if her sorrow and her worry had laid fingers on her smooth head. She was widowed when I was only two years old, so I cannot remember her wearing any colour other than purple or sage or black. I cannot remember the hall as anything but a ruin. When we were little children, she would revile the dull colours and swear she would marry a great merchant for his stocks of pink shot silk. But as we grew and no merchant arrived, no geese laid golden eggs and no trees grew diamonds, she laughed no more about her old dark gowns, shiny at the seams and worn at the hems.

And there was Richard. My cousin Richard. My dearest friend, my little tyrant, my best ally, my worst enemy, my fellow conspirator, my betrayer, my playmate, my rival, my betrothed. I cannot remember a time before I loved him. I cannot remember a time before I loved Wideacre. He was as much a part of me, of my childhood, as the downland and common land, as the tall trees of Wideacre woods. I never made a choice about loving him, I never made a choice about loving the land. I loved land and boy because they were at the very heart of me. I could not imagine myself without my love for Richard. I could not imagine myself with any other home than Wideacre, with any other name than Lacey.

I was blessed in my loves. For Richard, my cousin, was the sweetest of boys, as dear to me as a brother, one of those special children who draw in love as easily as green grass growing. People would turn to smile at him in the streets of Chichester, smile at his light-footed stride, his mop of black curls, his startlingly bright blue eyes, and the radiance of his smile. And anyone who heard him sing would have loved him for that alone. He had one of those innocent boyish voices which soar and soar higher than you can imagine anyone can sing, and the clear purity of each note could make me shiver like a breeze sighing out of the sky from heaven itself. I loved so much to hear him sing that I would volunteer for hours of pianoforte practice and for the discomfort of constantly learning new pieces so that I could play while he sang.

He loved duets, but neither threats nor blandishments could make me hold a tune. 'Listen, Julia! Listen!' he would cry at me, singing a note as pure as spring water, but I could not copy it. Instead I would strum the accompaniment as well as I was able, and sometimes in the evening Mama would hum the lower part while Richard's voice soared and filled the whole of the tiny parlour and drifted out of the half-open window to rival the birdsong in the twilit woods.

And then, when Richard was singing and the house was still, I could feel them. The ghosts who were always around us, as palpable as the evening mist filtering through the trees from the River Fenny. They were always near, though only I could feel them, and only at certain times. But I knew they were always near, those two – Richard's mama, Beatrice, and my papa, the squire, who were partners in the flowering and destruction of the Laceys in the short years when they made and wrecked Wideacre.

And when Richard was singing and my hands were stumbling but picking out the tune and Mama dropped her sewing unnoticed in her lap to listen to that high sweet tone, I knew that they were waiting. Waiting almost like the three of us. For something to happen.

For something to happen on Wideacre again.

I was older by a year; but Richard was always bigger than me. I was the daughter of the squire and the only surviving Lacey; but Richard was a boy and the natural master. We were raised as country children, but we were not allowed into the village. We were isolated in threadbare gentility, hidden in the overgrown woods of the Wideacre parkland like a pair of enchanted children in a fairytale, waiting for the magic to set us free.

Richard was the leader. It was he who ordered the games and devised the rules; it was I who offended against them. Then Richard would be angry with me and set himself up as judge, jury and executioner, and I would go white-faced and tearful to my mama and complain that Richard had been mean to me, gaining us both a reliably even-handed punishment. We were often in trouble with my mama, for we were a bad team of petty sinners. Richard was often naughty – and I could not resist confession.

I once earned us a scolding from Mama, who had spotted my stained pinafore and taxed me with stealing bottled fruit from the larder. Richard would have brazened it out, blue eyes persuasively wide, but I confessed at once, not only to the theft of the bottle of fruit, but also to stealing a pot of jam days before, which had not even been missed.

Richard said nothing as we left Mama's parlour, our eyes on the carpet, uncomfortably guilty. Richard said nothing all day. But later that afternoon we were playing by the river and he was paddling in midstream when he suddenly said, 'Hush!' and urgently beckoned me in beside him. He said there was a kingfisher's nest, but when I tucked my skirts up and paddled in alongside him, I could not see it.

'There!' he said, pointing to the bank. 'There!' But I could see nothing. As I turned, he took both my hands in a hard grip and his face changed from smiles to his darkest scowl. He pulled me closer to him and held me tight so I could not escape and hissed, 'There are water-snakes in this river, Julia, and they are sliding out of their holes to come for you.'

He needed to do no more. The ripples in the river were at once the bow waves from the broad heads of brown water-snakes. The touch of a piece of weed against my ankle was its wet body coiling around my bare foot. The splash of a piece of driftwood in the flow was a venomous dark-eyed snake slithering in the river towards me. Not until I was screaming with terror, my cheeks wet with tears and my wrists red from trying to pull away, would the little tyrant let me go, so that I could scramble for the bank and fling myself out of the water in a frenzy of fear.

And then, as if my tears were a salve for his rage, he forgave me. He took my handkerchief out of my pocket and dried my eyes. He put his arm around me and talked to me in a tender voice, and petted me, and called me sweet little names. And finally, irresistibly, he sang for me my favourite folk-songs about shepherds and farming and the land and crops growing ripely and easily, and I forgot to cry, I forgot my tears, I forgot my terror. I even forgot that Richard had been bullying me at all. I nuzzled my head into his neck and let him stroke my hair with his muddy hand, and I sat on his lap and listened to all the songs he could remember until he was tired of singing.

When we splashed home in the golden sunlight of the summer evening and Mama exclaimed at my dress, my pinafore, my hair all wet and muddy, I told her that I had fallen in the river and bore her reproaches without one murmur. For that I had my reward. Richard came to my bedroom later in the night when Mama was sitting downstairs trying to work by the light of only two candles. He came with his hands full of sweet things begged or stolen from Mrs Gough, the cook. And he sat beside me on my bed and gave me the best, the very best, of his haul.

'I love you when you are good, Julia,' he said, holding a cherry to my lips so I turned up my face like a questing lap-dog.

'No,' I said sadly, as I spat out the cherry stone into his warm little palm. 'You love me when I am bad. For lying to Mama is not good, but if I had told her about you and the water-snakes, she would have had you whipped.'

And Richard laughed carelessly, seeming much older than me, not a year younger.

'Shhh!' I said suddenly. I had heard a floorboard in the un-carpeted parlour creak and the scrape of her chair.

Richard gathered the remains of our feast in his hands and slid like a ghost in his nightgown towards the bedroom door. Mama came slowly, slowly up each step as if she were very tired, and Richard melted up the stairs to his attic bedroom at the top of the house. I saw the ribbon of light from Mama's night-time candle widen as she pushed open my bedroom door. I had my eyes shut tight, but I could never deceive her.

'Oh, Julia,' she said lovingly. 'You will be so tired tomorrow if you don't go to sleep at the proper time.'

I sat up in bed and stretched my arms to her for a goodnight hug. She smelled faintly of lilies and clean linen. Her fair hair was full of silver and there were lines around her brown eyes. I could tell by the weariness on her face that she had been worrying about money again. But she smiled tenderly at me and the love in her face made her beautiful. There might be a darn on her collar, and her dark dress might be shiny with wear, but just the smell of Mama and the way she walked told you she was Quality born and bred. I sniffed appreciatively and hugged her tight.

'Were you writing to Uncle John?' I asked as she pulled up my bedclothes and tucked them securely around me.

'Yes,' she said.

'Did you tell him that Richard wants singing lessons?' I asked.

'Yes,' she said, smiling, but I saw her eyes were grave.

'Do you think he will send the money?' I asked, my concern for Richard making me press her.

'I doubt it very much,' she said levelly. 'There are more import-ant bills to pay first, Julia. There are the Lacey creditors to repay. And we have to save for Richard's schooling. There is not a lot of money to spare.'

Indeed there was not. Mrs Gough and Stride worked for love,

loyalty and a pittance paid monthly in arrears. The food on the table was game from the Havering estate or fish from the Fenny. The vegetables were grown in the kitchen garden, the fruit came from Grandmama at Havering Hall and wine was a rare luxury. My dresses were hand-me-downs from my distant Havering cousins, and Richard's shirt collars were turned and turned and turned again until there was neither shirt nor collar left. Mama would accept clothes and food from her mama, my Grandmama Havering. But she never applied to her for money. She was too proud. And anyway the Havering estate, our nearest neighbour, was itself derelict through neglect.

'Go to sleep, Julia,' Mama said softly, taking up her candle and going to the door.

'Goodnight,' I said and obediently shut my eyes. But I lay half wakeful, listening as the house settled for the night. I heard Mama's footsteps in her room and the creak of her bed as she sprang in quickly, for the floorboards were icy to bare feet; the night-time noises of Stride bolting the back door, checking the front door – as if there were anything to steal! – and then his heavy tread up the back stairs to his bedroom at the top of the house.

Then the outside noises: a trailing creeper tapping at a window-pane, the distant call of a barn owl flying low across a dark field and away in the woods the abrupt bark of a dog fox. I imagined myself, high as the owl, flying over the sleeping fields, seeing below me the huddle of cottages that is Acre village, with no lights showing, like a pirate ship in a restless sea, seeing the breast of the common behind the village with the sandy white tracks luminous in the darkness and a herd of deer silent as deep-sea fish, winding across it. Then, if I were an owl, I would fly to the west wall of the hall of Wideacre, which is the only one left standing. If I were an owl I would fly to the gable head of it, where the proud roof timbers once rested, where it is scorched and blackened by the fire that burned out the Laceys, that wrecked the house and the family. I would sit there and look with round wide eyes at the desolate fields and the woods growing wild and call, 'Whoo! Whooo! Whoooo!' for the waste and the folly and the loss of the land.

I knew, even then, that there is a balance of needs on a land like ours. The masters take so much, the men take so much, and they both keep the poor. The land has its rights too: even fields must rest. My Aunt Beatrice was once the greatest farmer for miles around, but somehow, and no one would ever tell me quite how, it all went bad. When my Aunt Beatrice died and my papa died in the same night, the night of the fire, the Laceys were already ruined.

After that day nothing went right on Wideacre: not in the village, where they were as dirty as gypsies and as poor, and not for the Laceys. Mama and I were the only survivors of the great Lacey family, and we went in darned gowns and had no carriage. Worse than that, for Mama, we had no power. Oh, not in the way that many landowners have power. I don't think she would ever have missed the power to order men as if they were all servants. But when things were wrong in the village, she had no power to intervene. No one could help Acre now it was in the hands of the Poor Law authorities. Not even Dr Pearce, who came riding up the drive with his fat bay cob actually sweating at the neck and withers one hot day in summer when I was ten. He asked to see Mama urgently and came into the parlour on Stride's heels. I was seated by the open window, trying to get some air while I transposed a score Richard wanted to sing. Richard was idly fingering chords on the pianoforte. Mama was darning.

'Forgive this intrusion, Lady Lacey,' Dr Pearce said, his breath coming in pants from his hurried ride. 'There are dreadful doings in Acre. They are taking the children.'

'What?' Mama said. She cast one fearful glance towards the window, and I shrank too, afraid – like a child – of being 'taken', whatever that meant.

Dr Pearce stripped off his riding gloves, and then, uselessly, put them back on again. 'It's the parish overseer from Chichester,' he said, half stammering in his haste. 'He has an order from some manufacturing gentlemen in the north. They want able-bodied pauper children for apprenticeships.'

Mama nodded.

Dr Pearce pulled his glove off one hand. 'It is a slavery!' he exclaimed. 'Lady Lacey! They are taking them without consent! Any child whose parents cannot support them can be taken. That is all of Acre, for none of them are in regular work. They have a great carriage and they are going through Acre and taking the pick of the healthiest largest children. They had chosen three when I came here to you.'

I looked up at my mama's face. She had risen to stand by the empty hearth. Her face was so white she looked sallow in the bright summer light. 'Why did you come to me?' she asked, her voice low.

Dr Pearce pulled off his other glove and slapped them in his hand. 'I thought you would know what to do!' he said. 'I thought you would stop them!'

Mama made a slow gesture with one stiff hand, which took in the bare parlour, the chipped table, the old pianoforte and the single rug before the fire. 'I am a woman of neither means nor influence,' she said slowly.

'You are the squire's widow!' Dr Pearce exclaimed.

Mama grimaced. 'And you are the parson,' she said bitterly. 'But neither of us is able to stop what is happening down there.'

'Your father? Lord Havering?' Dr Pearce suggested.

Mama sat down in her chair again. 'He says it is a village of outlaws,' she said. 'He would not lift a hand if the whole village were to be moved. Besides, he believes in these new factories. He has invested in them.'

Dr Pearce slumped down into a chair without invitation and rolled his gloves into a tight ball. 'We do nothing?' he asked helplessly.

My mama lifted her work to the light and started again to sew. 'I can do nothing to stop this,' she said. 'Is it being done legally?'

'Legally, yes!' Dr Pearce said. 'But morally?'

'Then I can do nothing,' Mama said again. 'Perhaps you could ensure that the parents have the addresses of where the children are sent? So that they can bring them home when times improve.'

'When times improve,' Dr Pearce repeated. He got to his feet.

Mama looked up at him. Her face was stony, but her eyes were filled with tears. 'When times improve,' she said.

He took her hand and bowed over it as though she were a great lady receiving a courtier. 'I'll go back, then,' he said. 'The mood in the village is going to be very ugly. But I'll do what I can.'

'Will they listen to you?' Mama asked.

Dr Pearce pulled his gloves on, and for the first time that day he smiled his sweet helpless smile. 'I doubt it,' he said wryly. 'They have never done so before. But I will do what I can.'

He was right in thinking there was little he could do. The quicker parents had hidden their children as soon as the carriage had come into the village. In the end only six children were taken, taken away to work in the mills in the north. The roundsman said that they would serve a proper apprenticeship and be able to send home good wages. They would have an education and a religious upbringing. They would probably be home in a few years, a credit to their parents and to their employers. Acre heard that out in silence, and let the children go.

My grandmother took us to Chichester Cathedral in her carriage every Sunday for a month. Mama did not want to go to Acre church. But then Dr Pearce wrote her a note to say that there was no cause for concern in Acre, we could come and go quite safely. It was as it had been before.

Only I noticed that it was not as it had been before.

The children who sometimes used to come and peep through our front gate came no more. The girls who would bob a curtsy to Mama as we went down the aisle from church no longer looked at her or grinned impertinently at me. The whole village became as quiet as if every child had been stolen away by some malevolent Pied Piper. And every child learned to run like the wind up to the common and hide if they saw a strange coach come down the lane.

There were only six children lost, but it was not as it had been before.

It stayed hot all that summer. Hot, and quiet. Mama was ill

with headaches and weariness; she trusted us to go no further than the common and the Wideacre estate and let us roam. Not for the first time I asked her where the money had gone, and why the hall had been burned, and why she – who was all powerful in my little world – could do nothing in the wider world of Acre and Chichester. And not for the first time her face took on that frozen look which both Richard and I had learned to dread, and she said softly, 'Not now, darling. I will explain it all to you when you are old enough to understand it. But I will not tell you now.'

And with that Richard and I were content. We had only the casual curiosity of children. Having seen the hall in ruins and the land idle all our lives, we could hardly imagine a time when it had been whole any more than we could imagine a time when we were not there. Left to ourselves for that hot summer, we walked, and lazed, and dreamed, and played, and talked.

'I wish I were a Lacey,' Richard said to me, as we lay sprawled in the bracken of the common, looking up at the blue sky rippled with white clouds.

'Why?' I asked, as idle as he. I had a grass stalk between my thumbs and I was blowing and blowing, producing the most painful shrieks from it.

'To be a Lacey of Wideacre,' he said. 'To be known as the owner of Wideacre. To have been landowners for so many years that no one could ever challenge you . . .'

I dropped my grass stalk and rolled over beside him, my head butting companionably against his skinny chest. 'When we are married, you can take my name,' I offered. 'Then you'll be a Lacey, if you like.'

'Yes,' he said, pleased. 'And we can rebuild the hall and make it all just as it was. And I shall be the squire as my mama wanted me to be.'

I nodded. 'Let's go to the hall on our way home,' I said.

I pulled Richard to his feet and we went in single file down the narrow sandy path that leads to the back of Wideacre woods from the common. There were gaps all around the smooth perimeter of the park wall, and rabbits, deer and foxes and the two of us could pass freely from common land to parkland, as if there were no ownership of land or game at all.

The poachers from Acre could go where they wished. Bellings, the man who used to be gamekeeper, was as bad as any of them. But they avoided the ruined hall. It was a place still owned exclusively by the Laceys. I went there with Richard, but apart from us the roofless half-walls echoed only to the sound of the Lacey ghosts.

'Let's be Saracens,' said Richard with the abruptness of a child, and we both broke stick swords from the hazel bushes and held them before us. Richard made a quick gesture and we dropped to our bellies in a well-practised dive as we sighted the house. Wriggling like worms we came through the overgrown kitchen garden – meadowsweet and gypsy's lace as tall as a jungle and brambles everywhere – and then Richard gave the order to charge and we thundered around the back of the stable block and tumbled into the yard with a triumphant shout.

The grass was thick between the cobbles, the pump rusted with its handle up, the water stagnant in the trough beneath the spout.

'Lacey squires,' Richard said, changing the game and offering me his arm with a courtly bow. I swept him a curtsy, holding my mud-stained muslin dress wide, and came up with a simper to take his arm. We processed, heads high, around to the front of the house, play-acting the people we should have been.

'Damned good run with that fox!' Richard said.

'Damned good,' I echoed, as daring as he.

And then we faced the house and ceased the play to look up at it. The house stared blankly at us, its honey-yellow sandstone colour streaked and black with the smoke of that long-ago fire, a buddleia plant, like a plume on a hat, growing from the crumbling wall near the top of the house. When the wooden floors and beams were burned, they crashed down, and the east wall, over the rose garden, collapsed. The façade of the house was still holding, but people came in secret and quarried away at it for the stone. It stared like a sightless giant over the nettles and rose-bay willow-herb in the rose garden and over the paddock, all dry and self-seeded. The great front door was gone, either burned out or stolen for the wood. The terrace, where Mama had taught me to walk, was chipped; and the cracks between the stones sprouted groundsel and dandelions.

That was our legacy. The ruin, a ledgerful of debts and a handful of fields which we could neither rent nor farm. The Wideacre woods were still ours, but Uncle John would not sell the timber yet. We still owned a few farms. But the tenants were dilatory with the rent and Mama could not force them to pay. All we owned, all that we were certain of, was the smoke-smudged ruin and the ground beneath our feet where we stood in the weed-strewn garden.

And it gave me such joy!

From babyhood, I think, I loved this place. Whatever else might happen in my life, I knew I must wake every morning to see that high forehead of the downs and to smell the heather and the bracken on the common. When my feet were on Wideacre earth, I knew who I was. When my face was turned to that sweet salt-stained wind from the south, I feared nothing. And when I put my hand to one of our great grey-barked beech trees or put my cheek to the turf, I could feel the pulse of Wideacre, feel the great secret heart of the land beating in time with mine.

Then I looked at the sun dipping down towards the common and realized we were late for dinner again. We trotted side by side down the drive at the steady pace we had learned almost in infancy. Richard might be skinny as a poor boy and I might be tall 'and narrer as a broom handle' as Mrs Gough would say disapprovingly, but we could run like poachers' dogs; and we loped for home without needing to stop once to catch our breaths. With a wary eye on the parlour window, we ran around to the back of the house to the garden and tumbled in the back door to find the kitchen scorching from the heat of the oven and Mrs Gough hot and cross.

'Late again, you two,' she said, her arms akimbo, floured to the elbows. 'Mr Stride is just about to announce dinner and here you two are looking like a pair of paupers.'

I sidled past her like a stable cat, anxious to get to my room and change before dinner. But Richard could always rely on his charm.

'Oh, Mrs Gough, Mrs Gough,' he said winningly, and slid his little arm half-way around her broad waist. 'We forgot the time and I was so looking forward to your pheasant pie! Don't tell me it will spoil if Stride waits just a few minutes until we are dressed for dinner.'

'Waits long enough for you to change so you can pretend to your mama you've been home all this while,' Mrs Gough said as she bridled.

Richard gleamed at her. 'Yes,' he said candidly. 'You wouldn't get me into trouble, would you, Mrs Gough?'

'Be off with you,' she said, giving him a little push towards the door, her smiles all for him. 'Be off with you, Master Richard, and try and get a comb through that mop of black curls of yours. You look like a tatty-bogle. I can keep dinner hot for ten minutes without it spoiling, so you be quick, both of you.'

We did not need telling twice and were up the stairs, washed and changed and down in the parlour seconds before Stride came to announce dinner.

Mrs Gough was always easy on Richard. He could charm her with one upturned roguish smile. He was the boy of the household. It was natural for him to be indulged. But Richard was more than that: he was the only hope for the Laceys, the only hope for the Wideacre estate. He and I were joint heirs of the ruin, but it was on Richard that all the hopes rested. We were as poor as tenants, but Richard must be educated and prepared for the future he would have when his papa came home. And then, however long it took, Richard would rebuild the great house of Wideacre, take the great Wideacre estate back in hand, and there would be money in Acre and work for the men and the women, and it would be paradise regained for this little corner of Sussex. And Richard would marry me.

Mama was against our childish betrothal. She never told us why it could not be; we were just aware – in that simple way of children – that she did not like the idea, that she did not like to hear us speak of it. And in the simple way of children, we did not challenge her judgement or lie to her. We just kept our promise and our plans to ourselves.

She explained only once, when I was seven and we were still allowed to bathe together before the fire in the great wooden tub Stride carried up from the kitchen. Mama had left us to play and, when she came back, I was in my white nightdress with a white towel on my head and a curtain ring on my finger. Richard, naked with a small towel twisted on his head like a turban, was playing the bridegroom.

Mama had laughed when she had seen us – Richard's brown limbs gleaming in the firelight and my little face so grave. But when she had heard we were playing at weddings, she had frowned.

'There are good reasons why you two cannot marry,' she had said solemnly. 'In very old families, in very noble families such as the Laceys, there is too much marrying, cousin with cousin. You are too young to understand now, and I shall explain more when you are older. But there are some sorts of Lacey behaviour which could do with diluting – with new blood. The Lacey passion for the land has not always been a happy one. Both Harry and Beatrice loved this land very dearly. But their judgement was not always sound. Your Uncle John and I have agreed that you two should never marry. Do not play at getting married, and do not think of it. It is better that you both marry outside the Lacey family. You will marry people who do not have the Lacey blood, and the Lacey weakness.'

We had nodded at that, and ceased our game to please her. Richard climbed into her lap and demanded kisses and cuddles as he was dried. 'And dry my special mark,' he commanded, and Mama took the towel and softly patted the little circular scar at his throat. 'And tell me the story about it,' he said, snuggling into her lap. I wrapped the warm towel around my skinny little body and sat at my mama's feet and put my head against her knees. Richard's bare feet kicked me gently away, matching the rhythm of Mama's voice.

'It was when you were a little tiny one, new born,' she said softly, using the same words as always. 'Your papa and I were with Dr Pearce at the vicarage. It was during the hard times in Acre, and your papa and the vicar and I were trying to find some way to feed the people. Your mama, Beatrice, was driving you in the sunshine. You were held by your nurse. Suddenly your mama saw that you had swallowed the bell of your little silver rattle!'

'Yes!' Richard said, his face intent.

'As fast as she could, she drove towards the village to find your papa! And your mama was a very good horsewoman. She certainly drove fast!'

'Yes,' Richard said. We both knew this story as well as Mama.

'She snatched you up and ran into the vicar's parlour. And there, on the desk, your papa took a sharp knife and cut open your little throat, and took my crochet hook and pulled out the bell so that you could breathe!'

Richard and I sighed with satisfaction at the end of the story. But my mama was not looking at us. She was looking over Richard's mop of damp curls into the red embers of the fire as if she could see the vicar's parlour in the red caverns of the logs, and the man with steady hands who had the courage to cut open a baby's throat to save his life. 'It was the most wonderful thing I had ever seen,' she said. 'Even more of a miracle than birth – in a way.'

'And did you feed the poor?' I asked.

The closed look came over her face at once, and I could have bitten off my tongue in vexation at having interrupted her when she was, so rarely, telling us of how things had been.

'No,' she said slowly. 'Not very well. It was a hard year for Acre that year.'

'And was that the year of the riot and the fire?' I pressed her. 'Because they were poor?'

'Yes,' she said shortly. 'But that was all long ago, and besides, you two should be getting ready for bed.'

'I don't care about the bad past,' Richard said, butting his head into her shoulder. 'Will you tell me about the day I was born?'

'In bed I will,' Mama said firmly, and pulled his nightgown over his head. 'But I'll put Julia to bed first.'

I smiled at her. I loved Richard so well I did not even have to make an effort to put him first. 'I'll wait,' I said.

My love for him served us all well. It kept the peace in that cramped little household. I watched his love for my mama, and hers for him, and I never worried if she had a preference. Her love warmed us both equally – she could have had ten children and we would all have felt equally precious. I don't think I was envious for any moment in our childhood up till the time when he was eleven and started lessons with Dr Pearce in his well-stocked library. I had asked Mama if I could go too, and when she said there was not enough money to teach us both, I remember that I scowled.

'It is not possible, Julia,' she said. 'I know how much you love learning, and indeed, my dear, you are so bright and clever that I wish I had learned Latin so that I could have helped you to teach yourself. But it is just an amusement for ladies. For gentlemen, for Richard, it is essential.'

'He doesn't even want an education, Mama! All he wants is a music master and to be taught how to sing!' I started, but the sight of her frown silenced me.

'All the more credit to him for being prepared to go,' she said gently. 'And if he is prepared to go over his work with you in the evening, you may well learn a lot that way. But you must not tease him to teach you, Julia. John is sending money from his salary for Richard's education, not yours.'

In the event I did very well. Richard was generous with his homework and shared it with me. When he came home with his books – old primers once used by Dr Pearce – he let me stand at his elbow in respectful silence while he tried to puzzle out the verbs and declensions.

'What a bother it is,' he would say impatiently and push the book towards me. 'Here, Julia, see if you can make head or tail of this. I have to translate it somehow and I cannot make out what they're saying.'

Trembling with excitement I would take the book and turn to the back for the translated words and scribble them down in any order.

'Here, let me see,' Richard would say, repossessing his goods with brutal suddenness. 'I think I know what to do now.' And then he would complete the sentence in triumph and we would beam at each other with mutual congratulation.

Mama was glad to see us content, to see the different treatment of us so well resolved. She tried very hard to treat us fairly, to treat us alike. But she could not help favouring Richard, because he needed so much more. He took the best cuts of meat and the largest helpings, because he was growing so fast and was always hungry. He had new clothes; Mama could always cut down and turn her gowns for me, but she could not tailor jackets, so Richard's clothes were made new. He had new boots more often as he grew quicker, and then he had proper schooling. If I had loved him any less, if I had not tried to be as good as a sister to him, I think I would have envied him. But I only ever begrudged him one thing for more than a moment, the only thing he ever had which I desired, which I could not help desiring: Scheherazade.

She was Richard's horse – the horse we had both been promised off and on since we were children by my Grandpapa Havering, that feckless charming rogue who breezed into the county half a dozen times a year on a repairing lease from London. On one of his visits, in June, when I was twelve and Richard eleven, he finally got around to honouring his promise. I first learned of it when he sent a message to my mama. She opened it in the parlour while I sat at her feet, my head leaning against her knees, idly gazing out of the window at the tossing trees which crowd so close around the little sandstone box of a house, waiting for Richard to come home from his lessons. Mama broke the seal on the note and then paused. 'What is that singing?' she asked Stride.

He cleared his throat, embarrassed. 'It's Master Richard,' he said. 'He came in by the kitchen door, and Mrs Gough stopped him and asked him for a song. She loves to hear him sing.'

Mama nodded and listened in silence. The clear pure arc of sound swept unstoppably through the house. Richard was singing an Italian song – one he had despaired of teaching me to play aright – but I had guessed at an English version of the words for him, and he was singing them. His high sweet voice had a more tremulous tone than usual: 'If there is ever a favourite – then let it be me,' came the chorus. And then more quietly, more entreatingly, to the cruel gods who are never just to needy mortals: 'If there is ever a favourite – oh, let it be me!'

Stride, Mama and I were as still as statues until the last echo of the last note had died, then Stride recollected the dinner table not yet laid and left the room, closing the door behind him.

'It is a great gift,' Mama said. 'Richard is fortunate.'

'Does Uncle John realize how good Richard is?' I asked. 'If he really understood, surely he would find the money from somewhere for Richard to have a music master?'

Mama shook her head and spread out the note on her knee. 'Music is a luxury we cannot afford, my darling. Richard has to enter the university and obtain the degree he will need to make his way in the world. That must come before the polishing of an amateur gift.'

'If he could give concerts, he could earn enough money so that Uncle John could come home,' I said stoutly.

Mama smiled. 'If everyone was as readily pleased as you and I and Mrs Gough, we would be wealthy in no time,' she said. 'But Richard would need a long training before he could give a concert. And neither his papa nor I would wish it. Singing in the parlour is one thing, Julia, but no gentleman would ever go on a stage.'

I paused. I wanted to pursue the matter further. 'He could sing in church,' I suggested. 'He could train with a choir.'

My mama dropped her sewing in her lap and put her hand down to my head and turned my cheek so that I looked up and met her eyes. 'Listen, Julia,' she said earnestly, 'I love him dearly and so do you. But we should not let our affections blind us to nature. Richard has a lovely voice, but he plays at music as if it were a toy. He is skilled in drawing, but he takes it up and puts it down as a hobby. He is like his uncle, your own papa, who had many fine talents but lacked the greatest gift of concentration. Richard would never work and struggle and strive in the way that a great musician has to do. Richard likes things to be easy for him. Of the two of you, it is you who works hardest at music – you practise longer hours than he does so that you can accompany him. If Richard had the dedication of a true musician, he would sing all the time – not when it suits him.'

I scanned her face, considering what she had said, and hearing also an old judgement made years ago on my papa, the man who liked to play at farming while his sister ran the land.

Then the door opened and Richard came in, his eyes bright blue and his cheeks rosy with the praise he had received in the kitchen. 'Did you hear me singing even in here?' he asked. 'Stride said you did. Yet the kitchen door and the baize door were tight shut. Fancy!'

'Yes, we did,' Mama said and she smiled kindly at his bright face. 'It was lovely singing, Richard, I should like to hear it again after dinner. But now go and wash your hands, my darling, while I read this note from Julia's grandpapa.'

We went from the room together, and not until dinner did she tell us what the note said, and then it was the last thing we expected.

'I have had a note from Havering,' she said while Stride served the thin soup. 'Lord Havering writes that he has a horse which might suit the two of you.'

Richard's head jerked up from his plate, his eyes bright on her face. She smiled at him. 'I said we would all go over tomorrow so that you could try its paces,' she said. 'You may ride in your ordinary boots, Richard.'

'Oh, yes,' said Richard. 'Oh, yes.'

'But we have no habit for you, Julia,' Mama said, turning to me. 'I dare say you would have liked to learn, but I cannot see how to contrive it.'

'It is all right, Mama,' I said, my voice strained. 'It doesn't matter. Richard wants to ride so much more than I do. He can learn now, and perhaps I will learn later.'

I had a warm smile from my mama for that little piece of generosity, but Richard scarcely noticed it.

'Is it a mare or a gelding, Aunt Celia?' he asked. 'Did Lord Havering say how old it is?'

'No,' my mother laughed. 'I know no more than I have told you. You will have to wait until tomorrow. But I do know that my step-papa is a great judge of horses. I think you may be certain that it is a good animal.'

'Yes,' Richard nodded. 'I'll wager it's a mare.'

'Perhaps,' Mama said and nodded to Stride to clear the dishes, and then she turned to me and asked me what I had been doing in the afternoon while she had been writing her letters.

While I spoke, I could see Richard fidgeting like a cur with fleas, and all through dinner he could scarce sit still. I was not at all surprised when he drew me aside while Mama went to take tea in the parlour and said, 'Julia, I cannot wait until tomorrow. I have to go and see the horse now. Come with me! We can be back by supper-time.'

'Mama said . . .' I started.

'Mama said . . .' he echoed cruelly. 'I am going, are you going to come too? Or stay at home?'

I went. It was a pattern I could not break, like a phrase of music which you hum even when you do not know you are singing. When Richard called to me, I went. I always went.

'We should tell Mama,' I said, hanging back. 'She may ask for me.'

'Tell her what you like,' Richard said carelessly, shrugging on his jacket and heading for the door to the kitchen.

'Wait for me!' I said, but the door was already swinging and I only paused to catch up a shawl and run after him.

Stride was sitting at the kitchen table. He looked at Richard without approval. 'Where do you think you're going, Master Richard?' he asked. The remains of his dinner were before him, a half-pint of small beer beside the plate. Mrs Gough had Mama's tea-tray laid and a kettle on the boil.

'We are taking the air,' Richard said grandly. 'There is no need to open the door for us.' And he swept towards the door with as good an imitation of Grandpapa Havering's arrogance as an eleven-year-old boy could manage.

I followed in his wake and peeped a look at Stride as I went. He shook his head reprovingly at me, but he said nothing.

Outside, I forgot I had ever hesitated. The magic of the land caught me. I could feel it take me; anyone watching my face could have seen it take me.

My mama once commissioned an artist – a poor travelling painter – to make a sketch of us when I was just seven and Richard was six years old. She wanted a parlour picture: the two of us seated on a blue velvet sofa in the drawing-room of the Dower House, the only piece of respectable furniture in the only properly furnished room. I can imagine the picture she saw in her mind. The two little children wide-eyed and formal, seated side by side. And even at the age of seven, as a little girl, I should have liked to have pleased my mama by posing for a picture like that.

But the painter was a man with seeing eyes, and before he made his sketch, he asked Richard and me to show him a little of the estate. He walked with us in the woods of Wideacre and he saw how we could move as silently as deer under the trees so that the birds stayed in the branches even when we passed directly beneath them. And he felt that we trod the land as a living thing. And he sensed that Richard and the land and I belonged together in some unbreakable triangle of need and love and longing.

So he made his picture in the woods of Wideacre, and Mama had it framed and hung on the chimney-breast of the Dower House drawing-room. It showed me, just a little girl in a sprigged muslin dress tied with a blue sash, with my hat off and my hair tumbling down, seated beneath one of the great flowering chestnut trees of Wideacre. It was May and the tree was in bloom with thick candles of red flowers, and all around me were drifts of petals as scarlet as blood; the sunlight on my light-brown hair turned it golden. My cousin Richard was standing behind me, looking down on me, posed like a little hero, half an eye on the effect he was creating. But my eyes were hazy grey and I was looking out of the picture. Away, past the painter, out of the frame of the picture, out of the little world of childhood, away from the safety of our little home.

Richard stood like a small cavalier for the picture, because he had the knack of being what people desired. Mama wanted a formal picture, and there Richard was, behind me, one little fist on his hip, his shoulders squared. Unlike him, I looked fey and wild and dreamy in the picture, because I was seated under a blood-red chestnut tree. Wideacre brought out the wildness in me and I could not help myself.

I heard a humming in my head and I longed to be running free on the land. When I had to stay indoors with my sampler or read aloud to my mama, my book or my work would fall into my lap and I would rest my head against the cold glass of the window and look away. I looked away from my home, away from the little house, away from the penny-pinching shabby gentility and the worry, from the false appearances and the cut-down gowns. I looked away to Wideacre. And I wished that I could own and run the land.

It distressed my mama. She saw it in me early on, and she tried with her love and her persevering gentle discipline to make me into a child in her own image. A child who could sit still, who could stay in clean clothes, who could sit in a small room without fretting for the smell of the South Downs' wind in her face.

She failed. When the ground was covered with the thin white of a hoar-frost, or when the spring winds were blowing, I could not stay indoors, I had to go. I had to go, but the fine lines of worry around my mama's eyes made me pause.

'I know you long to be out, Julia,' she said to me gently. 'But young ladies cannot always do exactly as they wish. There is your sampler, which you have not touched this week, and some darning to be done as well. You may have a little walk this afternoon.'

'It is not a walk that I want, Mama,' I replied, forced into words by the sound of birdsong, so temptingly close in the woods outside the closed window. 'I need to be out there, out on the land. The spring is here and I have hardly seen it this year. I have only been in the garden and the woods. But there is the common, and the downs. I have not seen the bracken coming out, nor the spring flowers on the downs.' Then I stopped, for I saw her looking at me oddly as if she could not understand me, looking at me sadly as if my love for my home somehow distressed her.

'I know,' she had said gently and put her hand on my skinny shoulder. 'I know that you love the land. But it is a wasted love, Julia. You would do better to love God and love those that love you. Loving land brings little pleasure and can bring much pain.'

I nodded, and tried to look obedient. I lowered my eyes so that she should not be hurt by my immediate contradiction of her good sense. I could no more help loving the land than I could help loving my cousin Richard. I could never be free of my love for them. I would never want to be free of my love for them.

But I knew that my mama was right about wasted love! When I saw the cornfields of Wideacre self-seeded and the meadowlands grown high since there was no stock to graze them and no haymaking, I knew then that a love for the land without money and good sense behind it was worthless love indeed. And when Richard tormented me to tears and back again, I felt that my love for him was wasted too, for it brought more pain than pleasure.

But there was no other land but Wideacre.

And there was no one else but Richard.

So when Richard called me, I went. Even when I knew I should not. And he was so certain of this, so certain of my love for him, that he could trot down the drive without even troubling to look back, certain that he would hear my boots pattering along behind him.

It was a long way to Havering Hall, even going cross-country and splashing through the Fenny at the boundary of the two estates. When we arrived at the stables, breathless and sweating from our run, Lord Havering was looking over his horses before going to his supper.

'Good Lord,' he said in his rich voice, warm as port, thick as cigar smoke. 'Look what the wind has blown our way, Dench.'

The Havering chief groom looked over the half-door of the loose box and smiled to see us. 'Come to see the new mare?' he asked Richard softly in his Sussex drawl.

'Yes, if I may,' Richard said, beaming. You would have thought him a boy utterly incapable of disobedience. 'Mama told me of her at dinner, Lord Havering, and I am ashamed to say I could not wait until tomorrow.'

My grandpapa chuckled indulgently at his favourite, Richard. 'Bring her out,' he said to Dench and bent down to me. 'And you? Little Miss Julia? Came in Richard's shadow as usual, did you?'

I blushed and said nothing. I lacked Richard's ease with adults. I wanted to explain that I too had come because I wanted to see the horse. I had wanted the hard steady run from one side of the estate to the other. And I wanted to tell my grandpapa that Richard was not to be blamed for my coming. But not one of these things did I say. I just shuffled my feet and looked silly, and kept my eyes down.

Dench brought the mare clattering on the cobbles out of her stable at the end of the row. She was a lovely animal, a rich russet chestnut with a mane and tail of a darker shade of un-polished copper. She had a white blaze down her nose and deep brown eyes. Dench had a firm hand on her head collar, but she stood gently beside him and looked at us.

Her eyes, as warm as melted chocolate, seemed to invite me to her side and, without waiting for Richard to approach her, I went straight past my grandfather, straight past Richard, and put my hand up to her.

She whickered softly as I came close and bent her head to nuzzle at my pocket. I had nothing for her, but Dench slipped me a handful of oats out of his own capacious breeches. Her lips on my flattened hand were discriminating, gentle, as if she were taking care not to nip my thin fingers. I reached up a shy hand and rubbed her behind the ears, where mares nuzzle their foals. She blew out of her nostrils at my touch and sniffed at the front of my dress. Without thinking what I was doing, I dropped my face down and sniffed rapturously at her damp oat-smelling breath, and blew gently back. It was love at first sight for me.

'Make haste, Richard, or you'll lose your horse,' said Grandpapa, who had been watching me with appreciation. 'Your cousin is there before you. You seem to have the Lacey magic with horses, m'dear,' he said genially. 'Your Aunt Beatrice could charm a horse out of the field, and your papa was a grand rider too. And your grandpapa and I had some rides together which I still have nightmares about! Laceys have always been horse-mad.'

I stepped back and let Richard get to his horse. 'What's she called?' I asked, finding my voice for once.

'Scheherazade,' my grandpapa said in tones of deep disgust. 'I call her Sally.'

'Scheherazade,' I whispered to myself. 'A princess from the Arabian Nights.'

'She may have a touch of Arab in her,' my grandpapa said, mishearing my awed murmur. 'Good hunting stock, though. I chose her myself from poor old Tiley's sale. His daughter used to ride her, so she's used to novices. She's used to a lady's saddle too!' he said as the thought struck him. 'No reason why I should not teach you to ride at the same time as Richard, m'dear.'

'Julia doesn't have a habit,' Richard said firmly. He was trying to offer Scheherazade a couple of green apples he had picked from the Wideacre orchard, holding them outstretched at the full length of his arm. Not close to the horse at all. 'Julia's mama would not let her ride without a habit.'

'No,' said my grandpapa. 'Pity. Still, I expect we can find one for you if you'd like to try, missy.'

Richard shot me a look. Just one look.

'No,' I said regretfully. 'No, thank you, Grandpapa.'

I said nothing more. I had no quick excuse or explanation. But my grandpapa did not question my refusal. He raised a disdainful eyebrow at my rejection of his offer and went towards Richard, and Richard's lovely horse, and held her head while Dench gave Richard a leg-up on to her back.

'How's that?' Grandpapa shouted, and led Richard around the stable yard, Richard clinging tightly to the copper mane, Scheherazade mincing over the cobbles.

'Wonderful!' Richard said, but his face was white.

We would have stayed for Richard's first lesson, but my grandpapa caught sight of the stable clock on Richard's second circuit of the yard.

'Your mama will be after me,' he said ruefully. 'Dench, get out the little trap and take these two home. They shouldn't have come without permission in the first place. If they're out after dark, Celia will have me skinned alive.'

Dench pulled Richard down without ceremony and took Scheherazade back to the stable. I trailed along behind, unwilling to see her go, and wanting to see her stable and smell the straw and the sweet grassy scent of hay.

'When will you learn then, Miss Julia?' Dench asked me, his brown eyes bright with curiosity. He had seen my face when she fed from my hand, he had seen how she dipped her head for my caress.

'When Richard has learned,' I said certainly. I knew Richard would claim the lovely Scheherazade as his own, and I longed to see him ride her. But I knew also that if I did not challenge him and awaited my turn, there would be no one in the world more generous and thoughtful than Richard. We always shared our playthings, and if I was quick to return them and always gave Richard first turn, then we never quarrelled. He would give me unending rides on Scheherazade providing we both knew that she was his horse.

Dench nodded and flung long reins and a bridle over the carriage horse in the stall next door. 'Master Richard first, eh?' he said, shooting a look at me. 'And you don't mind, Miss Julia?'

'Oh, no!' I said, and the smile I gave him was as clear as my thoughts. 'I want to see Richard ride. I have been looking forward to it for months.'

Dench said something under his breath, perhaps to the horse, and then led her out of the stable and backed her into the shafts of the trap in the carriage-house. Richard and I sat either side of him on the little bench seat and my grandpapa waved his cigar in farewell.

'See you tomorrow,' he said jovially. 'And mind you make your apologies to your mama!'

We did not have to confess. Mama had guessed at once where we had gone and was sitting down to her supper in solitary splendour when the trap came trotting up to the garden gate in the dusk. Before her was a plate of toast and a little jar of potted meat, and she did not look up from buttering her toast when we crept into the dining-room. 'Your supper is in the kitchen,' she said, her voice cool. 'Children who run off like stable lads should eat in the kitchen.'

There was nothing we could say. I curtsied low – a placatory gesture – and backed out of the room in silence. But Richard stepped forward and laid a single red rose, openly thieved from the Havering garden, beside her plate.

Her face softened at once. 'Oh, Richard!' she said lovingly. 'You are so naughty! Now go and eat your suppers and have your baths and go to bed or there will be no riding for you tomorrow, new horse or not!'

And then I let out a sigh of relief for I knew we were forgiven, I could sleep sound in my bed that night, since the two people I loved most dearly in the whole of the unsafe uncertain world were under the same roof as I, and neither of them was angry with me.

'You shall have a riding habit,' Mama said softly to me when she kissed me goodnight. 'I shall find an old gown of my sisters' at Havering Hall. Or I shall make you a new one.'

'You shall learn to ride,' Richard promised me on the stairs as we went up to bed, our candle-flames bobbing in the draughts which came up the stairwell and through the gaps in the bare floorboards. 'As soon as I have learned, I shall teach you, dear little Julia.'

'Oh, thank you,' I said and turned my face to him for his goodnight kiss. For once, instead of a token buss on the cheek, he kissed me tenderly on the lips.

'Good Julia,' he said sweetly, and I knew my refusal of lessons from my grandpapa had been seen and was being rewarded. Plentifully rewarded; for I would rather have had Richard's love than anything else in the world.

2

Richard's long-awaited first riding lesson was tedious for my grandfather, humiliating for Richard and two long hours of agony for me. At first I could not understand what was wrong.

When Richard went to mount the horse in the stable yard in the warm end-of-summer sunlight, I saw that his face was so white that the freckles on his nose were as startling as spots in an illness. His eyes were brilliant blue with a sheen on them like polished crystal. I thought he was excited. I thought he was brittle with excitement at the prospect of his first proper ride on a horse of his own.

Scheherazade knew better. She would not stand still when he put his foot to the stirrup, she wheeled in a nervous circle, her hooves sliding on the cobbles. She pulled at the bit while Dench was holding the reins, trying to steady her. She threw up her head and snorted. Richard, one foot up in the stirrup, one foot on the ground, hopped around trying to get up.

Grandpapa gave an unsympathetic 'Tsk!' under his breath and called to Dench, 'Throw Master Richard up!'

Dench clapped two dirty hands under Richard's hopping leg and threw him up with as little ceremony as if Richard were a sack of meal.

My grandpapa was mounted on his hunter, a beautiful dappled grey gelding which stood rock steady, like a statue of a horse in pale marble against the background of the green paddock and the rich whispering trees of the Havering–Wideacre woods.

'Remember her mouth is soft,' Grandpapa told Richard. 'Think of the reins like silk ribbons. You must not pull too hard or you will break them. Use them to remind her what you want, but don't pull. I said, "*Don't* pull!"' he snapped as Scheherazade side-stepped nervously on the cobblestones and Richard jabbed at her mouth.

Dench put a hand out and held her above the bit without a word of prompting. I watched uncritically. I had never seen a novice rider before and I thought Richard looked as grand as a Sussex huntsman, as gallant as one of Arthur's knights. I watched him with eyes glowing with adoration. Richard on his own could do no ill in my eyes; Richard on Scheherazade was a demigod.

'Let's walk out into the paddock,' said my grandpapa. There was an edge to his voice.

Dench led Richard out behind Grandpapa, his steady hand on the reins. He was talking to Scheherazade as they went past me, and I sensed that Scheherazade was anxious and felt uneasy. Richard on her back felt insecure. His touch on the reins fidgeted her.

I waited until they were some paces ahead of me before following. I did not want Scheherazade unsettled by footsteps behind her. It was Richard's first riding lesson and I wanted everything to be perfect for him.

But it was not. I sat on the ramshackle fence and watched my grandpapa riding his hunter around at a walk and a trot in a steady assured loop and circle, and then calling to Richard to follow him.

But Scheherazade would not go. When Dench released her she threw up her head as if Richard's hands were heavy on the reins. When he squeezed her with his legs, she sidled, uneasy. When he touched, just touched, her flank with his whip, she backed infuriatingly, while Richard's pallor turned to a scarlet flush with his rising temper. But she would not do as she was bid.

My grandpapa reined in his hunter and called instructions to Richard. 'Be gentle with her! Gentle hands! Don't touch her mouth! Squeeze with your legs, but don't pull her back! No! Not like that! Relax your hands, Richard! Sit down deeper in the saddle! Be more certain with her! *Tell* her what you want! Oh, hell and damnation!'

He jumped down from his hunter then and strode towards Richard and Scheherazade, tugging his own horse behind him. He tossed his own reins to Dench, who stood stoical, his face showing nothing. Grandpapa pulled Richard down from Scheherazade like an angry landowner taking a village child out of an apple tree, and, spry as a young man, swung himself into the saddle.

'Now, you listen here, Sally-me-girl,' he said, his voice suddenly tender and warm again. 'I won't have this.' And Scheherazade's ears, which had been pointy and laid back, making her head all bony and ugly, suddenly swivelled around to face front again and her eyes glowed brown and stopped showing white rims.

'Now, Richard,' said Grandpapa, keeping his voice even. 'Like I told you in the yard, if you pull on the reins, you mean "stop" or "back".' He lifted his hands a fraction and Scheherazade moved forward. He pulled his hands a shade back towards his body, and she stopped as soon as she felt the tension on the reins. He drew the reins towards him again and she placed one hoof behind the other, as pretty as a dancer, and backed for three or four steps.

'If you squeeze her with your legs, that means "forward",' Grandpapa said. He dropped his hands and invisibly tensed his muscles. At once Scheherazade flowed forward in a smooth elegant gait. She was as lovely as a fountain in sunlight. She rippled over the ground in a wave of copper. I clasped my hands under my chin and watched her. I ached with love for her. She was the most beautiful thing I had ever seen in my life.

'But if you tell her to stop and go at once, then you will muddle her,' Grandpapa said, letting her walk the circle while he spoke. 'She feels you telling her to stop, and she feels you telling her to go. That upsets her. You should always be clear with animals – with people too!' he said with a wry grin, taking his attention from her for a fraction of a moment. 'She's got a lovely pace,' he said. 'She's a sweet goer. But she needs gentleness. Sit down deep in the saddle so that she can feel you there. And tell her clearly what you want. She'll do anything in the world for you if you treat her well.'

He brought Scheherazade up to a mincing halt beside Richard and swung himself down from the saddle. 'Up you go, lad,' he said gently. 'She knows her business. But you have to learn yours.'

He helped Richard into the saddle, and Richard got one foot into the stirrup, but he could not find the stirrup on the far side. He dug for it with his toe, trying to get his foot into the metal loop. Scheherazade at once side-stepped and bumped my grandpapa, who swore.

'Calm down!' he said to horse and rider. 'You two will have to learn to calm down together. You are like a pair of violin strings wound too tight. What the hell's the matter with your stirrup, Richard?'

'Nothing, sir,' Richard said; his voice was thin. It was the first thing I had heard him say since he had mounted, and with a shock I realized his voice was strained and he sounded afraid. 'I could not find it at first,' he said, 'but I have it now.'

'Well, learn to find it without digging your toe into her,' Grandpapa said unsympathetically. 'Don't bother the animal. She needs to be gentled. Not kicked about.' He twitched the reins out of Dench's hands and a look passed between them which I was too far away to read. Dench turned and came towards me, his face as expressive as a lump of chalk.

'Now,' said Grandpapa, back in his own saddle. 'Ride towards me.'

Richard dropped his hands in a stiff motion and Scheherazade minced forward. She walked as if she feared the earth were hollow, as if it might open up underneath her hooves. Seeing her gait, I sensed her unease and found I was clenching my hands in two fists under my chin, as wary as she was.

She did not like Richard.

That was the reason for the look between my grandpapa and Dench. That was why Scheherazade flinched when Richard was in the saddle. That was why Richard sat awkwardly and his face was white. Something about him bothered the animal. She was as irritable as a cat with its fur rubbed up the wrong way from head to toe. She was sparky with her dislike. She was not easy, and I could smell her sweat, sharp with fear.

I could watch no more. When Richard stopped her with a short jab on the mouth and my grandpapa leaned over from his mount and loosened the reins between Richard's fingers, I flinched in sympathy. When Scheherazade followed my grandpapa's lead around the field, with Richard sitting stiffly on top of her, as awkward as though he were on a cart seat, I could feel my own shoulders slump as I willed him to be easy with her, to sink into the saddle so that she might feel his weight.

Then I could not stand to see any more of it. Richard's face had lost its flush of temper and was pale again, his eyes narrowed with concentration, his face set. He did not look like a knight from a story book any more. He made me uneasy. I slid down from the fence, careful to guard my muslin dress from the splinters of the rotting timbers, and went back to the house, to the parlour, where ladies, in any case, should be.

I knew that Richard's much heralded first lesson had not been a success, because I had seen it, but I would never have known it from Richard. When he came in for dinner, changed and washed, his smile was bright and his answers to Mama were confident. She believed him delighted with the mare, and I thought perhaps things had gone better after I had left my seat on the fence.

'He's heavy-handed,' Grandpapa said dourly to Mama's inquiry. 'But riding's in his blood. He should do well enough. And Harry Lacey – the old squire – had hands like mutton chops too. We used to laugh about it! I'd never let him touch one of my horses. But he taught Beatrice, y'know, and Harry. And Beatrice had the best pair of hands I've ever seen in this country. None to match 'em.' He broke off, his smile reminiscent; perhaps he could see on the faded wallpaper of the parlour a bright red-headed girl who could whisper a horse out of a field. 'She was a rider!' he said. 'Odd that her son's so awkward.' He glanced over at Richard, who was straining to hear the conversation while he talked with Grandmama. 'He'll get accustomed,' he said.

But Richard did not get accustomed. He had a round dozen of lessons from my grandpapa at Havering Hall and rode out with him in the Havering woods and up over the common. But he was never easy with Scheherazade. He sat on her back as if she were a tinder-box which might accidentally burst into flames. He and Scheherazade simply could not deal together. I saw it, and I wondered at it, but I could not have described it. Grandpapa was brutally frank.

'Scots blood,' he said to Mama. We were in the back garden of the Dower House, and Richard and Grandpapa had ridden over from the hall. Grandpapa judged that Richard might now keep his horse in the Dower House and ride without supervision whenever he wished. In any case, my grandpapa had wearied of teaching and was happy to hand over the job of coaching Richard to our groom Jem, or to Dench, the Havering man. Grandpapa was off back to London. He felt he had rusticated long enough.

'Scots blood,' he said ominously. 'His papa, John MacAndrew, rides well enough, I grant you. But they're not a nation of horsemen. No cavalry, damn small animals. No breeding, m'dear. On the distaff side he's a Lacey, and there was never one of them who was not at home in a saddle; but he does not have the heart for it. He does not have the hands for it. He's a good jobbing rider and he can get around safe enough. But he'll never match his mama, Beatrice. God rest her soul!'

'Well, I cannot regret that,' my mama said in her soft voice, her face turned towards the orchard where Richard was trotting backwards and forwards. Scheherazade's pace was steady and smooth, but her ears flickered warily. 'Beatrice may have been a joy to watch on the hunting field, but she scared her family half to death with the horses she rode. And I cannot forget that her father died in a riding accident.'

'Oh, nonsense!' said Grandpapa impatiently. 'You're safer on horseback than walking down those damned uncarpeted stairs of yours, Celia. But have it as you will. The boy will never be a neck-or-nothing rider, he'll never cut a dash. But I've done what I can for him. I've started him off and I'll pay for his stabling.'

'Yes,' said Mama gratefully. 'And we both thank you.'

Grandpapa nodded and blew a perfect circle of smoke out into the still afternoon air. 'What about little missy?' he asked. I was standing with my back to them at the orchard fence. And I gripped the paling of the fence post waiting for Mama's answer.

'I think we should leave it until she is older,' she said. 'She has no habit and we have no side-saddle.'

Grandpapa waved a careless hand. 'Soon right that,' he said.

Mama lowered her voice, but I could still hear her. 'Julia has been raised too wild and too free,' she said softly. 'She is twelve now and she has to learn to be a young lady before she needs to learn to ride. I am happy that she should stay indoors with me.'

I said nothing, I did not turn my head. I felt my colour rising and I had a pain where my heart was thudding. Unless Grandpapa insisted, I should not be able to ride Scheherazade. Unless he declared that I was a Lacey and riding was in my blood and I must be taught to ride, I should be confined to the parlour and my only pleasure from Scheherazade would be to see Richard's growing confidence with her. I was glad for Richard, of course, of course I was – but some little rebellious spark inside me said, 'Not fair, Mama! Not fair!'

'As you wish,' said Grandpapa. And the decision against me was taken.

I lost my chance of being a rider, and I had to wait for Richard's bounty. But as that summer turned into autumn, slowly but surely Richard suffered a greater loss. A greater loss than I could imagine. His voice started going.

It was like a new game for him at first. Sometimes it would be high – his familiar clear golden notes – and sometimes he could make it low and husky. One evening in the parlour he created an entertainment as good as a play, telling the adventures of a butterfly exactly in the style of the novel *Chrysal; or the Adventures of a Guinea*. The butterfly he did in a high squeaky voice, and the villains which it encountered on its journey through London thundered with his deepest bass. I played rippling chords and imposing fanfares for when the butterfly was received at court, and Mama laughed so much that the tears poured down her face.

She laughed a good deal less when she discovered that we knew the novel because Richard had ordered it from Grandmama Havering's circulating library. My name was on the order, and my morals were the ones most likely to be corrupted from reading fiction. I took the blame; and Richard took the credit for his wit and imagination. He played with his surprising new voice and I believe he never thought – and I never knew – that his voice was altering for ever.

Its range was not always steady. It was not always controllable. Sometimes in mid-sentence it would suddenly go high or suddenly break and become husky. Richard ceased to find it amusing and snapped at me when I laughed. Then, worst of all – while he was singing a simple high sweet song and I played a lilting harmony on the pianoforte – his voice broke.

He frowned as if something small and trivial had happened, like a doorknob coming off in his hand. 'Play it again, Julia!' he said. 'This stupid voice of mine . . .'

I played it, but my fingers had lost their confidence and I hit a shower of wrong notes. He did not even reproach me. It was only a high G, and he could not hit it. Three times we tried, my piano part sounding worse and worse all the time. Richard did not even complain. He just looked at me in great perplexity and then turned his face to look out of the window at the grey sky and the heaped clouds.

'It seems to have gone,' he said, very puzzled. 'I can't do it.'

He went from the room slowly, with none of his usual swinging stride. As he went up the stairs to his room, I could hear him clearly, all the way up the first flight of stairs, singing the phrase over and over again. And over and over again the leap to the high G quavered and broke. He had lost the high aerial reaches of his wonderful voice. His gift, his very very special gift, was being reclaimed.

After dinner, when we were in the parlour, he said confidently, 'I'd like to try that song again, Julia. The one we were doing this morning. I had a frog in my throat this morning, I think! I couldn't hit the note at all. I can do it now, I know.'

I fetched the sheet of music and propped it on the stand. I bungled the introduction badly, and the ripple of arpeggio that should have been smooth was as lumpy as an apple crumble.

'Really, Julia,' Mama said with a frown. And then she turned to Richard and smiled.

He was sitting in the window-seat, looking out towards the trees, as beautiful as a black-headed cherub, utterly unchanged. He drew a breath ready to sing, and I hit the right chord for once.

The note was wrong.

Richard snapped it off short.

And tried again.

My hands dropped from the keys. I could not think of what to say or do. For a second Richard's pure lovely voice was there, but then it quavered and broke and was gone. Richard looked at me in utter bewilderment, and then at Mama.

'Your voice has broken, Richard,' she said, smiling. 'You are becoming a man.'

Richard looked at her as if he could not understand her.

'Early,' she said. 'You're an early starter, Richard, at only eleven. But your voice is definitely breaking. You will not be able to sing soprano again.'

'His voice will go low?' I asked. I had never thought about such a process. Richard's golden voice seemed such a part of him that I could not think of him without it. By the stunned look on his face, he could not imagine himself without it either.

'Of course,' Mama said smiling. 'He would not make much of a man with a voice like a choirboy all his life, would he?'

'But what shall I sing?' Richard asked. He looked almost ready to cry. His colour had rushed into his cheeks and his eyes were dark with disappointment. 'What shall I sing now?'

'Tenor parts,' Mama said equably. 'Julia will be the soprano of the household now.'

'Julia!' Richard spat out my name in his temper. 'Julia cannot

41

sing. She sings like she was calling cows home. Julia cannot sing soprano.'

Mama frowned at his words, but remained calm. 'Hush, Richard,' she said gently. 'I agree, none of us have your talent for music. But there are many good tenor parts you will enjoy singing. Your uncle, Julia's papa, had a wonderful voice. He used to sing all the tenor parts when we sang together. I still probably have some of the music at Havering. I will look them out for you when we are next there.'

'I don't want them!' Richard cried out in passion. 'I don't want to be a tenor. I will never sing a tenor part. It's such an *ordinary* voice! I don't want an *ordinary* voice. If I cannot have my proper voice, I won't sing at all! My voice is special. No one in the county sings like I do! I won't become an ordinary tenor!' He stormed from the room in a fury, slamming the door. I heard his boots pound upstairs, loud on the bare floorboards. There was a shocked silence in the little parlour. I closed the lid of the pianoforte softly. Mama snipped a thread.

'It was never music for Richard,' she said sadly. 'He just wanted to be exceptional.' I said nothing. 'Poor boy,' Mama said with a great deal of pity in her voice. 'Poor boy.'

Richard did sing again in public. There was an experimental service with harvest hymns at Chichester Cathedral. Grandmama Havering took the two of us, and Richard joined in with a clear light tenor. An unexceptional voice. We both remembered the times when he had sung with a voice as bright as a choirboy and people in the pews all around us had craned their necks to see Richard, with his eyes on the altar, singing like the angel Gabriel. No one turned their heads at Richard's pleasant tones now. Only I looked at him with a little glance which I was careful to keep neutral. If he had thought I pitied him, he would have been most angry.

I said nothing at all until we were home and Mama had gone upstairs to take off her hat. Richard was idling in the parlour. I went to the pianoforte and opened the lid.

'Let's sing something!' I said as lightly as I could manage it. I brought my hands down in a ringing chord and for a mercy hit all the right notes. But when I looked up, Richard's face was sombre.

'No,' he said softly, 'I shall never sing again. Oh, I may groan on a little in church like I did today. But I shall never sing in the parlour, or in the kitchen, or even in my bathtub. I had the voice I liked, but now it has gone. And I'll never get it back.'

'Your voice now is very nice, Richard . . .' I offered hesitantly.

'Nice!' he shouted. But then at once he had himself under control. 'Yes,' he said. 'It is very nice, isn't it? Before it broke I had a voice which was probably as good as anyone's in Europe. But they would not let me use it, or train it, or even see good music teachers. Now it is gone, and all I have instead is a powerless tenor which you tell me is very nice. Well, as far as I am concerned, that is the same as having no voice at all.'

'What will you do, Richard?' I asked. I found my lips were trembling as if Richard were telling me of some mortal wound. In a way, I suppose, he was.

'I shall do nothing,' he said quietly. 'I shall forget the voice I had, and very soon so will everyone else. I shall forget that I wanted to be a musician. I shall forget the plans I had to fill Wideacre Hall with music. I shall concentrate instead on learning to be the squire. The squire of Wideacre. Now it is all I have left. It is the only thing special about me now.'

Richard said no more, and I never asked him to sing with me again. My pianoforte lessons from my mama continued with even less motive or effect, and Richard seemed to think of nothing but his last route to being, as he said, 'special' – being the heir to Wideacre. So while I was kept indoors as much as ever, Richard rode out every day, trying to conquer his fear of the horse and trying to learn his way round the land. The land, his land, the only thing he had left which made him anything other than an ill-educated lad growing out of his clothes.

He might never be truly easy with Scheherazade; but she was a beautifully mannered mare, and once Richard had gained enough confidence to give her clear instructions, she obeyed him. Dench's young nephew, Jem, was in charge of our one-horse stables and he advised that Scheherazade be exercised every day so that she did not become too frisky. Each afternoon that autumn was frosty and inviting, so Richard went out early and stayed out late.

Sometimes Mama and I would sit in the parlour and I would read to her while she sewed. Outside, the leaves on the copper-beech tree turned a lovely purple and the fronded chestnut leaves went as yellow as summer silks. I read two volumes of poetry from cover to cover in those afternoons, while Mama sewed for the poor-box, and I sat with my back to the window to catch the light on the page in that gloomy parlour; and so that the sight of those burning colours would not make my heart ache to be out.

Sometimes we went over to Havering Hall in a little gig we borrowed with a pony, with Jem driving. The frosty air whipped our faces pink, and the sound of hooves on the hard road made my heart leap as if I expected some great treat. But at the end of the drive there was only Grandmama Havering – left alone at the hall now the London season had begun, splendid in her solitary state, creating some kind of stark beauty out of the emptiness of her days.

She invited me to stay with her, and, weary with the quiet Dower House, I consented, and then enjoyed myself more than I had thought possible. It was pleasant to be the only child in the house. It was pleasant to live without having to consider Richard's preferences. My grandmama had created an air of disciplined peace at Havering Hall, which a woman can do if she has the courage to live by her own standards. I learned a lot from her that autumn. I learned that it is possible to look at a bleak past without reproach and at a joyless future without complaint. And the way to do that, without failing and without an inner plaint, is to keep one little part of oneself untouched, and free, and brave.

In the morning we spoke to the housekeeper or the butler, and then we took our walk in the garden. The grounds were horribly dilapidated, as bad as the ruined garden of Wideacre, but Grandmama walked among them like a queen at Versailles. With one hand on my shoulder and the other holding a basket for the flowers she hoped to find among the weeds, she paced down the gravel paths, oblivious to the nettles blowing around us, the ungainly grass scattering seeds over the paths and the burrs catching the flounces of our walking dresses. The flowers which had managed to survive years of neglect in this enclosed wilderness were to be cut and taken indoors, where Grandmama taught me about the elegance of a single bloom or two in a vase against a sparse background of leaves.

'The art of happiness is in being content with what you have,' she would say, looking with apparent satisfaction out of the dusty windows at the garden, yellowing like an uncut hayfield in the October sunshine. 'And good manners depend entirely on appearing content with what you have.'

And I, innately polite and content (for what child of my gentle mama's could be other?), would nod sagely and split a chrysanthemum stem for Grandmama to place precisely in a crystal vase.

My grandmama taught me more than the outward show of ladylike behaviour that autumn. She taught me an inner quietness which comes from knowing your strengths and your weaknesses – and the job you have to do. She taught me – without possibility of contradiction – that I was no longer a wild child. I would be a young lady. And it was I, and no one else, who would have to learn the self-control I would need to fulfil that role. So I learned to discipline myself, while Richard learned to ride.

And I think I had the better bargain of the two of us.

For Richard was afraid. He had learned that now, learned what I had seen when his face had gone white in the stable yard and Scheherazade had sidled away at his approach. She was not an old hack to tease in the meadow with a handful of stones thrown at her back hooves. She was not a bow-backed carriage horse that would strain for a carrot hung out of reach. She was a high-bred hunter, and when Richard and she were out alone on the common or the downs, he feared her. He was afraid of falling, he was afraid of being kicked. But more than that, he was afraid of all of her – of her bright colour, her brown eyes, her wide nostrils.

I spent three weeks at Grandmama's and came home only when Grandpapa was expected again. Neither Grandmama nor Mama wanted me at Havering Hall when Grandpapa and his cronies from the London clubs fell out of their chaises swearing at the roads and lugging their cases of port.

Grandmama helped me pack, and sent me home with a bolt of muslin for a brand new gown as a farewell present.

'You may be a Lacey,' my grandmama said as she stood at the front door with me, watching Dench put my little box under the seat of the gig, 'but you are also my granddaughter.' She made it sound as though being a Lacey and a granddaughter of hers were positions of equal importance, of vast significance in an admiring world. 'Lacey, or Havering, or married to someone with no name at all, I trust you will always remember you are first and foremost a lady.'

I nodded. I tried to concentrate, but I was only a twelve-year-old child and all I could think was that I was returning home to Richard and my mama, and maybe Richard would allow me to ride Scheherazade. I hardly heard my grandmama telling me that there was more to life than a name and an estate, more to life than the man one might marry. More to life, even, than love. More important than all these things was the retention of one's pride, of a tenacious little scrap of dignity, whatever one's name, whoever one's relations.

'You are anxious to go home to your mama,' she said gently.

'Yes, Grandmama,' I said.

'And Richard?' she queried. Under her searching look, I coloured and my eyes fell.

'That is quite suitable,' she said equably. 'You are joint heirs of Wideacre, and cousins. I can imagine no easier way of reconciling the problem of joint shares than to make the estate one again under Richard's ownership. And he is a charming boy. Does he treat you kindly?'

I beamed, our childhood squabbles forgotten. 'Oh, yes!' I said emphatically. 'And he has said ever since we were little children that we should marry and rebuild Wideacre together.'

My grandmama nodded. 'If John MacAndrew returns home wealthy, it would indeed be a most suitable match,' she said. But then she looked at me more closely and her face softened. 'He's not going to grow into a man who will stomach petticoat rule,' she said gently. 'He has been indulged by your mama and he is used to ruling you. He will be the master in his house, and you will have to obey him, Julia.'

I nodded. I could have told her, but I did not, that I had already served a hard apprenticeship in giving way to Richard. It had been my choice to obey him since we had been small children. I could envisage no change. I did not even want a change.

'It is not always easy, obeying one's husband,' my grandmama said, her words stilted. She gave a little sigh which should have told me of a lifetime of self-discipline, of temper bitten back and never expressed. Of complaints, and slights, and accidental cruelties. 'They will tell you in church that marriage is a sacrament. But it is also a binding legal contract, Julia.'

Dench had stowed my box and was standing at the horse's head, waiting out of earshot, patient.

Grandmama tutted under her breath. 'You may marry for love, my dear; but I would want you to remember that marriage is a business contract, and after the love has gone you are still forced to keep your side of the bargain.'

I looked at her uncomprehendingly, my child's eyes wide.

'When love has gone, when liking has gone, you are still married,' she said sternly. 'There is no escaping that. And the services you performed out of love, you have still to do out of duty. *That* is when you are glad you can say, "I am a lady", or "I am a Lacey", or anything which reminds you in your heart that you are a person in your own right, even if you lead the life of a bondsman.'

I shivered although the sunlight was bright. It sounded ominous, a bleak prophecy. But I knew in my loving, trusting heart that she was wrong. She had married fifty years ago in obedience to her father and, when widowed, married again to win a home for herself and her child. Of course marriage seemed to her a contract – and one which carried severe penalties. But Richard and I were quite different. Our marriage would be a natural extension of our childhood love. When the dream of a rebuilt Wideacre became finally true, I knew I would never have to search my heart for a sense of my own individual pride to bear me up through shame and pain. All I ever needed to define myself was the knowledge that I loved Richard and that I was Richard's love. I would never need anything more.

Something of this certainty must have shown in my face, for my grandmama gave a harsh laugh and bent and kissed me once more. 'There's no telling anyone,' she said, resigned. 'Everyone has to learn their own way. Goodbye, my darling, and don't forget to give those receipts to your mama.'

I nodded, and hugged her, and jumped up the step to the seat of the gig while Dench swung himself in beside me. Then I waved to her and smiled at her with love. I knew that she was a fine woman, a brave woman. But I had no thought that I would ever wonder where her courage came from; that I would ever need that courage for myself.

'Home, then?' Dench said.

'Yes,' I said. Sitting high in the gig beside Dench was comfortable. I could see over the hedges to where the self-seeded fields of Wideacre blew in a rippling autumn wind. I liked Dench, I liked the drawl of his downs accent and the way his face stayed still so that if you did not know him you might think he was cross, but then his eyes twinkled. And I knew, in the way that children always know, that he liked me.

'Glad to be going back to your mama?' he asked kindly.

'Yes,' I said. 'And my cousin Richard too. Is he riding much, do you know, Dench?'

'Aye,' he said. He gathered the reins in one hand as we turned left down the lane towards Acre. 'But Jem tells me his hands are as heavy as ever. He'll ruin that mare's mouth. I don't know what m'lord was thinking of.'

'She's his horse!' I said, instantly on the defence.

'Aye,' Dench said, wilfully misunderstanding me. 'You don't get a chance, do you, Miss Julia?'

'Ladies often don't learn to ride until they are married and their husbands teach them,' I said, quoting the wisdom of my mama without much conviction.

'Ever sat on her back at all?' Dench asked me with a swift sideways glance. 'Not sneaked into her stable and climbed on from the door?'

'Yes,' I said, incurably truthful. 'But Richard caught me.'

'Oh, aye?' Dench said invitingly, and waited for me to go on. But I did not.

Richard had come into the stable just as I had swung a leg over Scheherazade's back, having lured her to the door with two wind-fall apples in a bucket. She had thrown her head up and moved back when I had launched myself from the half-door on to her back. But once she had felt my weight she had dipped her head to the bucket again. My skirts up, sitting astride, I was a proper hoyden and I knew it. But, oh! the delight of feeling that smooth warm skin and the fretwork of muscles beneath it. And to be so high in the stable! And when she lifted her head, I saw her column of neck and that great wave of her mane! I adored her. I dropped my face into her mane and hugged her neck in passion.

I did not hear the footsteps come across the yard. I did not even hear the stable door open and close.

'Get down.' Richard's tone was icy. I sat up and looked around wildly. Richard had come into the stable and closed the door behind him. He was standing at the back of the stable in the shadows, the saddle and bridle held before him, his riding crop stuck under the stirrup leather.

'Get down,' he said again. His voice was light, but I am no fool. I saw his eyes were blazing; even in the darkness of the stable I could see the heat behind them.

I clung to the mane and swung my leg over and slid down Scheherazade's smooth flank, loving the touch of her shoulder against my cheek.

As soon as I dropped on the straw, I turned to face him. 'Richard . . .' I said apologetically.

He had put down the saddle and bridle while I was dismounting and he dragged me away from the shelter of Scheherazade's side. He held my wrist in one hard unforgiving hand and pulled me into the corner of the stable. Scheherazade threw her head up and shifted uneasily, and Richard gave a little gasp and swung us around so that I was between him and the restless animal.

'Scheherazade is *my* horse,' he hissed, his face very close to mine. 'Lord Havering gave her to *me*. He taught me to ride on her. You may be a Lacey, but it is my papa who pays the bills here. Lord Havering may be your grandpapa, and not mine, but he gave the horse to me. And I warned you not to touch her, didn't I?'

My lips were trembling so much that I could not speak. It was worse than the pretend water-snakes in the river all those years ago in childhood. It was the worst it had ever been. 'Richard . . . please . . .' I said pitifully.

'*Didn't* I?' he insisted.

'Y-Yes,' I said. 'But Richard . . .'

'I warned you, Julia,' he said authoritatively. 'I told you that you would learn to ride when I was ready to teach you. And I told you to keep away from my horse.'

I could not stop the tears from coming, and they rolled down my face, making my cheeks as wet as if I were out in a rainstorm, while I looked and looked at Richard, hoping he would see them and release the hard grip on my wrist and catch me up to him, and kiss me kindly, as he always did.

'*Didn't* I warn you?' he shouted.

'Yes! Yes!' I sobbed. There seemed nothing I could do to break the spell of this shadowed misery. Mama was far away in the house, Jem was cleaning tack in the tack room or sitting in the kitchen. Richard had me at his mercy, and he had no mercy. He had indeed warned me. He had told me not to touch his horse and I had disobeyed him. He had warned me that if I did, he would be angry. And I had foolishly, irresistibly gone to

Scheherazade and now I had to face Richard's blazing blue-eyed wrath. Then, suddenly, my own temper went.

'You don't even like her!' I said. 'You never did like her as much as me! You promised you'd teach me to ride her, but I don't believe you ever will. All you ever cared about was your stupid singing! You can't do that any more! And you can't ride either!'

Richard grabbed me and spun me around, his full weight throwing me against the stable wall. 'I'll kill you!' he said in the total rage of a child.

I had both hands braced against the wall. For a moment I was literally too frightened to move. He took advantage of that second's immobility to snatch up his riding crop from the floor beside his saddle, and then he grabbed me in a hard one-armed embrace and brought the twangy well-sprung crop down with all his strength on my back.

He meant to cane me – as Stride very occasionally was ordered to beat him. But I twisted in his grip and the blow fell on my side. Even through my jacket it stung, and I screamed with the shock of it, and the hurt of it. Three times he whipped me, before I wriggled free from his hold and dashed to the shelter of Scheherazade's side. She was frightened, her hooves shifting nervously, her eyes rolling and showing their whites. Without a second's thought I dived under her belly and came up on the other side so that she was between Richard and me, and I peeped at him from under her tossing neck.

The rage had gone from Richard's face; he looked ready to weep. 'Oh, Julia!' he said, his voice choked.

But I was beyond reconciliation. Shielded by the horse, I turned for the stable door, struggled with the lock and dashed out of the stable, banging the door behind me.

I did not go to the house, though I could see the light from the parlour window spilling out over the drive. I ran instead to where I could be alone, to the hayloft above the stables where the few bales of hay were stored. I flung myself face down on one of them and wept as if I could not stop; I wept for the pain and the humiliation, and for the fright that my own anger had given me, that had made me taunt Richard and had made him wish me dead.

I gave little screaming sobs, muffled by a fist pressed against my mouth, for I wanted no one to hear me. He had hurt me so! And he could not love me at all if he could treat me thus! And the flame of my own anger burned inside me and said that I should not love him, not ever, not ever again. That we should not even be friends. He had bullied me long enough. This wicked attack would be the last time he would ever make me cry.

The hay scratched my cheek and grew hot and damp while I wept my heart out into its tickly dryness . . . and then I felt the sweetest touch in all the world – Richard's hand upon my shaking shoulder.

He pulled me up, gently, oh, so gently, and he turned me around towards him. 'Oh, little Julia,' he said in a voice of such tenderness and pity; then he cupped his hands either side of my cheeks and kissed every inch of my wet flushed face, so that my cheeks were dried with his kisses.

And I sobbed again and said, 'Richard, you should not treat me so!' I could hardly get the words out. 'You should not, Richard! I will not love you if you bully me like that. You are wrong to treat me so, Richard.'

'I know,' he said remorsefully. 'I know I should not do it. But, Julia, you *must* forgive me. You know I do not mean any harm. It is just an accident.'

'An accident!' I exclaimed. 'Richard, that was no accident! You beat me as hard as you could! Three blows! Not even my own mama has ever beaten me like that! And you said you would kill me!'

'I know,' he said again, his voice warm with his charm. Richard's easy charm. 'I beg your pardon, Julia, and I swear I will never hurt you again.' He knelt beside me on the straw. 'Look!' he said. 'I am on my knees to you, begging you to forgive me.'

I hesitated. The pain was fading and Richard's appealing, worried face was too much for me.

'Say you forgive me!' he entreated in a low whisper, his arms out to me.

'I won't,' I said sullenly. 'You are cruel, Richard, and I had done nothing but sit on her in the stable.'

He was silent at that for a moment, still kneeling at my feet. 'A true lady accepts an apology,' he observed. 'I have said that I am sorry, Julia. And I *am* sorry. I am offering you an apology.'

My mama's training, the lessons of my grandmama, the world we lived in and my own loving heart were too much for my sense of grievance. 'Oh, Richard, all right!' I said and I burst into tears afresh for no reason at all and he threw his arms around me and hugged me and kissed my wet cheeks and dried my eyes on his own white linen handkerchief.

We sat in silence then, in the shadowy hayloft, while the night air grew colder and the first pinpricks of stars came out like sparkles of frost in the autumn sky. And Richard said softly, reasonably, 'I just don't like people taking my things, Julia.'

And I had said – for in a way it *was* all my fault – 'I know you do not, Richard. And I promise I will never sit on Scheherazade again.'

I would have promised more, but a slim new moon came out from behind a wisp of dark cloud and its light shone in my eyes, and I heard a sweet high singing which I always think of as the music of the very heart of Wideacre, which used to ring through Richard's voice. This night it was not thin and peaceful, but somehow ominous. For some reason, I did not know why, it seemed like a warning, as if the moon were telling me that Richard's expectations and Richard's need to own things outright were not good qualities in a young boy, that I should not concede everything to him.

Then the moment passed, and I was just a tearful girl in a hayloft with a loving bullying playmate.

'Master Richard don't like you to even touch his horse, then?' Dench said curiously.

'No,' I said, coming out of my reverie. I had not touched Scheherazade again, and Richard had forgotten his anger. He had taken to riding every day after that evening, and I had seen little of him.

'Dog i' the manger,' said Dench briefly. 'I reckon you'd ride well enough without teaching, Miss Julia. You're the true-bred Lacey, after all.'

'No,' I said. I sat straighter on the seat beside Dench. 'I do not wish to learn until I am grown-up, Dench.'

'Oh, aye,' he said, hearing the reproof in my voice and taking little heed. Then he clicked to the horse to lengthen its stride and we bowled under the great trees of the Wideacre woods.

'Want to take the reins?' Dench said casually.

'Oh, yes!' I said. Jem had let me drive our solitary ageing carriage horse, but this was the first time I had ever been in control of one of the smooth-paced Havering horses.

'Here, y'are,' Dench said generously, and handed the double reins into my small hands. 'Hold them lightly.' He watched as I clicked confidently to the horse as I had heard him do, and saw how my little hands held the fistfuls of leather as if they were precious ribbons.

'Good hands,' he said approvingly. 'You have Miss Beatrice's hands.'

I nodded, but I hardly heard him. The sunlight was dappled on my face as we drove under the branches of the woods. The wind, as sweet as birdsong, blew in my face. A great flock of starlings was chattering in a hundred tones in the hedge to our right, and over the derelict wheatfield the rooks were flapping like dusters and calling hoarsely.

'No need to go straight home,' Dench said, observing my rapt face. 'We can take the gig around by the mill and home through the woods if you wish. The ground is hard enough for the wheels.'

I hesitated. We would have to drive through Acre and I was still afraid of the barely understood story of the 'taking' of the children. But Richard went to Acre for his lessons, and Mama had never specifically told me *not* to go there alone.

'All right,' I said and we went on down the lane past the

Wideacre gates, which stood drunkenly open, rusting on their hinges, and whirled away towards Acre. The village street was deserted, the front doors closed against the wind. There were white faces at a few unglazed windows as we trotted by, and Dench raised a careless hand to the smith's cottage and to the cobbler who sat idle before an empty last in his window. Then we turned left at the church down the smooth grassy lane towards the common land, past the idle mill with weed greening the water wheel, and deeper and deeper into the woods, into the very heart of Wideacre.

'We can canter here if you like,' Dench said, eyeing the smooth turf of the track, and without thinking I lightened my touch on the reins and felt the carriage leap forward as the rhythm of the hooves speeded up and the bars of sunlight on the grass came flickering over me.

'Like it?' Dench said, his voice raised over the rush of the wind and the jingle and creak of the carriage and tack.

'Oh, yes!' I yelled, and my voice was like a sweet call to the horse to go faster, and he pricked his ears, blew air out in a snort and plunged forward.

'Woah!' Dench yelled in sudden alarm and grabbed the reins from me. He nearly knocked me from my seat with his desperate lunge, and elbowed me hard to hold me in.

'What . . .?' I said as he hauled roughly and the horse and gig skidded to a slithering standstill. Dench abruptly backed the horse, and I saw what he had seen down one of the grassy rides to our left: Scheherazade, loose in the woods, her saddle askew, her reins broken. When she saw the carriage, she raised her head to whinny at the horse and came trotting towards us.

'Damnation,' said Dench levelly. 'Where's that cow-handed youngster?'

I tumbled from the gig and caught one trailing rein. Scheherazade whickered and snuffed at me. 'Richard!' I called into the woodland. 'Richard! Where are you?'

There was no reply. A jay called harshly and a woodpecker whooped as it flew dipping up and down, away from us. The wood-pigeons cooed as if all were well. But there was no answering call from Richard.

I glanced back at the gig for guidance. Dench was scowling.

'Cow-handed,' he said, making it sound like an oath. I led Scheherazade back to the gig. He glanced briefly at her, a comprehensive raking survey. 'Not hurt,' he said. 'So chances are he fell off all on his own.' He paused for a moment. 'Where does he usually ride?'

'I don't know,' I said helplessly. 'The common, up on the downs. In the woods. Different places.'

'Could be anywheres,' Dench said sourly, scowling at the ragged field to our right and the hill of purple heather of the common land beyond. 'Could have gone home, walked home. Picked himself up and walked home,' he said more cheerfully. Then his face lowered again. 'Cow-handed,' he said under his breath. He turned abruptly and swung down from the seat of the gig and went to the carriage horse. He started undoing its tack and took the horse from the shafts.

'Hold him,' he said briefly to me, and he took Scheherazade's reins from me. He knotted the break in her reins and pulled her saddle aright. He glanced at me and shortened the stirrups, Richard's stirrups, by guess. Then he brought Scheherazade to me, where I was standing by the carriage horse's head.

'You're to ride home,' he said. 'Stop at the mill on the way, see if there's anyone there and tell 'em Richard had a fall and they're to turn out and look for him. Stop at Acre and tell Ned the smith, he'll know what to do. I'll ride towards the Dower House along the bridle-track and see if he's walking home or if he fell there.'

I gaped at him. 'I cannot ride,' I said. 'I told you! Richard never taught me!'

Dench swore under his breath and motioned to me to put one foot up so he could heave me into the saddle like a stable lad. I went astride, my gown bunched around me, my ankles and even my calves exposed.

'Course you can ride,' Dench said. 'You're a Lacey.'

He tossed the reins up to me and turned his back as if he need say no more and had no interest in watching for my safety. I sat as though frozen. But Scheherazade's ears were forward and she felt solid beneath me. The ground was very far away, but I knew she was gentle, well mannered. I felt her at peace with me on her back, alert for my bidding. I leaned over and tugged my skirts down to cover my legs as well as I could, and then I straightened up and squeezed gently. Scheherazade moved forward with her smooth rolling walk back down the lane towards Acre. I felt completely at ease. I felt I had come home.

And I knew how to ride her. I knew it as easily and as sweetly as I had known how to hold the reins to drive the carriage horse. It might have been that I had listened so intently to Richard's lessons that I had learned to ride sitting on the fence. But when Scheherazade moved and I went with her, as smoothly as perfectly matched dancers, I knew it was something else. I came from a long line of famous horse riders, and to be on horseback in the Wideacre woods was my natural place. Driving a horse on Wideacre had been bliss indeed, but riding Scheherazade up a grassy track with the afternoon sun on my cheek was a most earthly paradise.

Except that Richard . . . with a sudden gasp I remembered that Richard was missing, perhaps lying somewhere hurt. Without meaning to signal to the horse, I had tensed, and instantly obedient Scheherazade broke into a trot, a springy pace which nearly unseated me. I grabbed on to the pommel of the saddle and gritted my teeth as I banged up and down in the saddle, sliding hopelessly from one side to another and trying to right myself. I could remember Grandpapa bellowing to Richard to rise and sit with the trot, and I tried, without much hope, to rise in the stirrups and to sit down again. Almost at once I caught the rhythm. Scheherazade was long-legged and her pace steady. The awful teeth-rattling bumping stopped and I felt safe again. We were travelling fast, too, and were nearly at the gate to the mill, and I sat down in the saddle and gently tightened the reins. Scheherazade slowed at once, and stopped at the garden gate of the miller's house.

'Miller Green! Miller Green!' I called, giving him his title, though he had ground no wheat in ten years, not since the night when the hall had been burned and looters had robbed the grain wagons stored in his yard.

The door opened slowly. Old Mrs Green put her head out. 'Not here,' she said, surly. 'They're all at the fair, looking for work.'

She had been a proud woman once, mistress of the mill with her own pew in the church. The loss of their livelihood had broken her spirit. Four big sons in the house and a husband to feed, and no money coming in from any of them. A river flowed past the garden to turn the mill wheel, but there was no wheat to grind. Not one of them had seen farm meat on the table for ten years, nor fresh fruit except the wild berries in season, nor white flour once they had scraped the millstone clean of dust.

'There's been an accident,' I called to her. 'My cousin Richard may be lying hurt in the woods, or on the common. When your men come home, will you send them out to look for Richard, Mrs Green?'

She looked at me dully. 'Miss Beatrice's son?' she asked me, and then she scowled. 'Nay,' she said with grim satisfaction. 'I won't do that. I wouldn't send my men out to do a favour for the Laceys. Least of all when they come home tired after a day on the tramp looking for work, when there's no work to be had.'

I stared at her blankly, with growing fright. If Richard was injured, perhaps with broken bones, he should be found at once. If Mrs Green would not help, if Acre would not help, it might take hours to find him. Without thinking of anything except the desperate need to get help to Richard, I dropped down from Scheherazade's high back and looped her reins over the gate. Mrs Green was old, stooped, and I was lanky and growing tall for my age. I went up to her and she was barely a head taller than me. She looked down into my child's face and saw an unchildlike determination.

'He may be Beatrice's son,' I said, 'but he's my cousin. And I love him more than anything else in the world. Please help him.'

Some of the hardness went out of her face when she saw me – not a Lacey on horseback, but a girl at her cottage door, white-faced, begging for aid.

'Eh, well,' she said resignedly. 'They'll be back within the hour. I dare say they'll turn out for him then.'

I felt my eyes suddenly fill with tears of relief. 'Thank you,' I said huskily. Then I turned and walked down the little path and used her tumbledown garden wall as a mounting block to reach Scheherazade's saddle high above me. I trotted back down the track to Acre and I knew she was watching and that the incomprehensible hardness had gone from her face.

Without thinking of it, I had been riding easily, confidently, and as we rounded the corner to Acre I sat down deeper in the saddle and let Scheherazade canter. We moved together, and I felt not a trace, not a flicker of fear, but only a delight in the rush of the wind and the thudding of her hooves and the sense of speed. We thundered up Acre lane like a regiment of cavalry, and I pulled her up at the smith's yard with a yell of pure elation.

'Ned Smith!' I called, and he came out, throwing on his tattered apron, his thin face lit-up, hoping for work.

'There's no shoeing needed,' I said quickly. 'I am sorry. But there has been an accident, and Richard has come off his horse. John Dench is looking for him and he said you would help.'

The smith pulled his apron off again and tossed it over the empty anvil by the cold forge. 'Aye,' he said dully. 'Some of the men will come out if they're promised a penny for it.'

'Yes,' I said. Then I added awkwardly, 'I am sorry there was no work for you today. I am sorry you heard the hooves and must have been hopeful. I am sorry we can pay no more than a penny a man.'

That brought his eyes up to my face. 'Why should you care?' he demanded coldly.

'I am a Lacey,' I said; and then, challenged by his stare, I went on, 'I know it is all wrong now, but we were squires here. It is all wrong for the Laceys, and for Acre too, and I am sorry.'

His face warmed, but he did not smile. It was as though he

had forgotten how to smile. 'Eh,' he sighed, like a man grieving. But then he was generous to me. 'You were a babe in arms,' he said. 'No blame for you. I'll get the men out for you, and we'll find your cousin. Don't fret.'

I nodded. 'Thank you,' I said.

'Are you all right on that mare?' he asked as he suddenly noticed me riding astride with shortened stirrups.

I beamed at him. 'Yes!' I said triumphantly. 'I have trotted and cantered. But I shall go carefully home.'

'You ride like Miss Beatrice did,' he said, half to himself. 'And you have her smile too. For a moment, seeing you up there, smiling like that, it was like the old days, before she went bad.'

'Before she went bad.' I heard his words over again in my head, and they sounded like a spell which might make everything suddenly clear to me. 'She went bad,' I repeated aloud. 'What do you mean? My Aunt Beatrice was never bad.'

He gave me an ironic glance from under heavy dark brows. 'No,' he said. 'That's what they would have taught you, I dare say. We see it differently in Acre. But it's an old tale, and little worth the telling.'

'How do you see it in Acre?' I asked. I was leaning forward in the saddle, staring at him as if he could explain so much. As if that one sentence about Beatrice's smile before she went bad might tell me why we were so poor in the Dower House, and why the land around us had turned sour and grew nothing but weeds.

'Not now,' he said briefly, but I saw the closed-in look on his face which I saw on my mama when I asked her what went wrong with the Laceys and what caused the fire that night, all those years ago. 'You've your cousin to think of now.'

I nodded. He was right. I shook my head to clear it of the mystery, and then I used my heel and the lightest of touches on the reins to turn Scheherazade and head for home.

The Acre lane is hard-packed mud, no good for cantering, and we took it at a brisk exhilarating trot. But the drive to Wideacre Hall is seldom used and is overgrown and grassy, and I could loosen her reins a little and let her stride lengthen into a smooth canter again. I did not check her until I saw the garden gate and Mama standing in the front garden; I thundered up, my hat tumbled behind me, my hair flying out over my shoulders, my eyes bright.

'Julia!' she exclaimed in horror. 'What on earth . . .?'

'Dench was driving me home when we found Scheherazade,' I said breathlessly. 'He took the carriage horse to ride and look for Richard and sent me to Acre to turn out the men, and then come home to you. Richard's not here, is he? He didn't walk home, did he?'

'No, I was starting to worry,' Mama said. 'Oh! How dreadful if he should be badly hurt. But, Julia! You riding! How do you know how?'

'I just did it, Mama!' I said triumphantly. 'As soon as I was on her back, I just knew how to do it! And she is so good, she is so gentle. I knew I would not come to any harm!'

'But the men from Acre . . .' said Mama, distressed. 'Whoever did you speak to in Acre?'

'Mrs Green at the mill, and then Ned Smith,' I said. 'They both said they'd help.'

'Oh, dear,' said Mama, overwhelmed by the sight of me thundering down the drive, riding like a poor girl with my skirts bunched up and straddling the horse, and by the impropriety of my giving orders in Acre, but most of all by her rising fear for Richard.

But then I saw her shoulders go back and her voice grow firm as she took command. 'Take the horse to the stables and tell Jem to ride over to Havering,' she said. 'Tell him to tell her ladyship that Richard may be hurt and ask if we may borrow the carriage. You come inside at once.'

She ran up the path to the house and I heard her ring the bell for Stride. Then I just leaned forward slightly, and lovely Scheherazade knew what I wanted and walked towards the stable, her ears pricked for her stall. In the stable yard I swung down from her back and meant to land lightly on my feet. But as soon as my feet touched the paving slabs my knees turned to water and buckled under me so that, instead of confidently handing the reins to Jem, I could only slump in a crumpled heap at his feet, half laughing and half crying with the pain. Jem scooped me up and sat me on the mounting block, then lengthened Scheherazade's stirrups so he could ride her over to the hall.

'Will you be all right?' he said, eyeing me. 'Maybe I should see you into the house.'

'I'm all right,' I lied. In truth my arms and legs felt like pounded jelly. I ached in every bone, and my skin, where I had sat on the saddle, was scalding as if I had been burned. Jem rode Scheherazade up to the gate to the back garden and yelled through the archway for Mrs Gough. While his back was turned, I cautiously pulled up my skirt to see my legs. I felt I was bleeding, as if my legs were rubbed raw, but there were only a couple of red stripes where the saddle and the leathers had chafed me, and some wicked little red blood bruises where the soft skin had been trapped and pinched.

'Gracious me!' said Mrs Gough, standing over me, arms akimbo. 'What a state you're in, Miss Julia! Come inside this minute.'

I tried to rise to obey her, but as I did so, my knees gave way again, the ground beneath me looked like a series of steps, one level melting into another level. I looked up at Mrs Gough's disapproving face and held out my hands to her. 'I don't feel very well,' I said deprecatingly, and I dropped at her feet in a dead faint.

That was the end of my adventures for that day. Mrs Gough might be unsympathetic, but she was efficient. She had Stride carry me up the stairs to my bedroom, and sent up a bowl of soup with a dash of sherry in it, and a little bread. Despite my anxiety for Richard, I could not keep my eyes open and fell fast asleep.

And then I dreamed. A funny dream, all the events of the day mixed up and misunderstood, but with some feeling about them as if they were not me in the dream at all. A girl very like me. A girl like me but more firmly rooted in Wideacre than I. A girl who would never have tolerated a bullying playmate, a girl who was afraid of nothing. Not a quiet girl, not a shy girl. Not a good indoors girl at all. A girl that I would have been if I had not been my mama's child. Like me, but with none of the wildness stolen from her.

She was on horseback, on a bay pony, but his bright summer coat was like Scheherazade's had been in the autumn sunlight. And she was riding not in the woods where I had been that day but up along the little bridle-track to the slopes of the downs. She was me, and when she urged her pony fast up the pale muddy track, it was my laugh I heard, and when they broke out of the trees at the top of the downs, it was my sigh of delight. I looked to my right and there was a flock of sheep which I knew were my sheep, with a shepherd raising a hand in a lazy greeting, and I rode over to him and told him that the sheep were to be washed in the Fenny this afternoon and he smiled and pulled his cap to me as though I were the squire himself and able to order things on the land as I pleased.

I squinted up at the bright cold sky and looked at the horizon as if I owned it and I said to him, 'It will rain later', and he nodded as if there could be no doubt that I was right. He smiled and said, 'Yes, Miss Beatrice', and waved to me as I rode away.

I turned over in my bed in my sleep, and I heard a voice in my sleep saying, 'The favoured child. The favoured child. She always was the favoured child.'

I opened my eyes then and blinked, as confused as a barn owl wakened at midday. I looked around the bare sunny bedroom. The blank walls reassured me that it was nothing but a meaningless dream. The shadows on the pale plaster showed me that I had only been asleep for a few minutes. I put out a hand and touched the empty soup bowl. It was still warm. I thought of Richard and made to rise from the bed to see if he was safe home, but my head was so swimmy I lay back on the pillow again until the room should steady. And while I waited for my head to clear, I dropped off to sleep again like an exhausted child.

I slept until mid-afternoon, and so I missed all the excitement of Richard's return home. Dench had found him and brought him into Acre, slumped across the carriage horse, with Dench leading. He had broken a collar-bone and his left arm, and Dench had torn up his own shirt to make a temporary sling. Mama had sent the Havering carriage to Acre, and Ned the Smith and one of the Green lads had lifted Richard into it, tucked him up under one of the carriage rugs and sent him home. He was not in pain on the jolting journey, because Dench had given him some laudanum. Mrs Green had run out with the tiny precious phial as they walked past the mill. She had saved it from the bailiffs, resisted the temptation to sell it for food; and then given it away.

They put Richard to bed and called the surgeon from Midhurst, who praised Dench's rough strapping, set the arm and the collar-bone and ordered Richard to stay abed for at least a week.

We had a peaceful few days then, Richard and I. He had a fever at first, and I sat with him and sponged his head with vinegar and water to cool him, and read him stories to divert him. By the fourth day he was well enough to talk and he asked me what had happened. I told him about Mrs Green, about Ned Smith, about Dench's sudden decision in the sunlit wood to take the carriage horse and leave me to alert the village.

'How did you get to Acre?' Richard asked. He was lying back on a bank of white pillows and his face was still pale. His freckles stood out, dark as flecks of chocolate, on his creamy skin, and his gaze was down, his eyes veiled by his long eyelashes.

'I rode,' I said, and as I spoke the two words, my heart suddenly thudded in foreboding. I was sitting by the window to catch the wintry morning light, a book open on my knees. As I said the words 'I rode', it struck me for the first time that Richard might object to my having ridden – even in that emergency.

I could tell nothing of Richard's mood from the untroubled curve of his mouth, from the dark lashes on his cheek. 'Dench told me to take Scheherazade while he searched the wood for you. It seemed the only way to do it, Richard.'

Richard's gaze stayed on the counterpane. 'Dench told you to ride my horse,' he said softly. 'But, Julia,' he said and then paused. 'You do not know how to ride.'

'I know!' I said with a nervous laugh. 'I know I do not!' I said again. 'But Dench threw me up into the saddle, and Scheherazade was so good! It must have been all that schooling you have given her, Richard!' I shot a look at him, but his face was still impassive. 'She knew her way home, of course,' I said. 'I just sat on her. It was not proper riding, Richard. Not proper riding like you do.'

'No,' he said softly. 'Did you just walk?'

'Not all the way,' I said hesitantly.

'Not all the way,' he repeated as slowly as if he were writing down my answer in a copy-book. 'She did not walk all the way. So, Julia, did you trot?'

'Yes,' I said quickly. Too quickly. 'I trotted her a little.'

'You trotted,' he repeated again. 'Your first time on horseback and you trotted? A rising trot, Julia? Or did you just bump about, clinging on and hoping for the best?'

'I trotted properly!' I said, stung. 'And I cantered too!'

Richard's head snapped up. His eyes were as black as the centre of a thundercloud.

'You took my horse without my permission and you cantered her?'

'Richard!' I said desperately. 'I had to! I *had* to! Dench told me to! He had to look for you and I had to call out Acre and come home and tell Mama. I could not refuse to go. Dench knew what to do and he ordered me!'

There was an utter silence.

'Dench, was it?' Richard asked.

'Yes,' I said.

'You should have refused,' Richard said, a little frown on his face.

'I didn't know what to do!' I said. 'I didn't know what to do, Richard. Dench seemed to know what had to be done, so I did as he told me.'

'He never liked me,' Richard said, gazing at the blank wall at the foot of the bed, seeming to see Dench's impassive face on the pale lime-wash. He was seeing again in his mind Dench's stony face as he watched Richard struggling to learn to ride, and Grandpapa's impatience. 'Not from the first riding lesson. Not before. He never liked me. He wanted you to have Scheherazade from the start,' he said reflectively, reviewing the scene in the stable yard and remembering Dench's smile as I walked towards the mare. 'Then he used the excuse of my accident to get you on her.'

I said nothing. I knew it was none of it true. But the threat of Richard's rage seemed to be passing away from me. I felt icy cold inside, and the thudding in my head, behind my eyes, warned me that I would have a dizzy nauseous headache unless I could get away at once from this stuffy room. I sat in silence on the window-seat, the cold pane of glass chilling my back, fearful to make a move in case Richard's rage should come back towards me.

'It's Dench's fault,' he said.

'Yes. Yes,' I said, thinking only of my need to get away. Richard said nothing more, and I sat frozen.

He turned and looked at me and I saw with relief that his eyes were a hazy blue, as if he were daydreaming, as if he were happy. He smiled at me, smiled as sweetly as the dearest of friends. 'Don't look so terrified, Julia,' he said as if it were rather funny. 'I'm not angry with you any more. I thought it was your fault. But I see now that it was Dench's.'

I smiled back, still wary.

'You're sure he ordered you?' he asked. 'You're *sure* it was he who made you ride my horse? You didn't think you would seize the chance selfishly for yourself?'

'No! No!' I said hastily. 'It was all his idea.'

'Good,' Richard said, and smiled his seraphic smile at me. He put his right hand out to me and I reached forward and took it in my icy fingers. Obedient to his tug, I slid forward to kneel at his bedside and he put his hand to my face and stroked my cheek as gentle as a lover. Then he kissed my forehead, just where the headache was starting to thud, and at his touch I could feel my fear and strain melting away, and the beat of the pulse behind my eyes grow quiet again.

'That's better now, isn't it?' he asked.

'Yes,' I said softly.

'I hate it when we quarrel,' he said, his voice low. 'There is nothing worse in the world for me than when I think you have been selfish and ugly. You must love me like a true lady, Julia. You must be pure and unselfish.'

I blinked back the tears in my eyes. 'I do try,' I said humbly. 'I try all the time, Richard.'

Richard smiled, his eyes warm. 'I know,' he said sweetly. 'That is how it should be.'

Then I laid my head on his pillow and smelled the sweet nutty smell of his warm body and his dark curly hair and felt such a peace between us.

Richard was angry with me no more.

3

Richard's convalescence from the fever and the mending of his collar-bone and arm progressed without any problems. The surgeon came from Midhurst again to make sure the break was healing and he told Mama he would not need to call again. Richard was irritable during the days when he was cooped up in his tiny low-ceilinged bedroom, but once he could come downstairs for his meals – looking very grand in Grandpapa's old jacket for a dressing-gown – he became his old sweet-tempered self. I thought that his short temper over Scheherazade had come from the fever and the pain and the very great blow it had been to his pride that I should be seen riding a horse which had just thrown him.

Bearing that in mind, I was discreet in my visits to the stables with crusts of stale bread for Scheherazade. I did not dream of riding her again, and I scowled at Dench when I met him chatting with his nephew Jem in our stable yard and he told me of a ladies' saddle he had found which was being sold cheap.

'I am not allowed to ride her,' I said as I might have said, 'Get thee behind me' to my greatest temptation. 'She is Richard's horse, not mine.'

'He can't ride her,' he said frankly. 'He was always afraid of her, she was always unsettled with him. Tell him that you'll ride her for him while his arm's mending. Jem'll give you a few hints on how to manage her.' Jem beamed at me and nodded. 'She needs exercising,' Dench said. He made it sound as if I would be doing Richard a favour instead of giving myself the greatest joy I could imagine. 'No horse likes to be neglected. She'll get bored and fretty locked up in the stable all the time. Tell Master

Richard that she needs to go out. He can watch you ride himself if it makes him feel any better.'

'I'll tell Mama she needs exercising,' I said. 'But I don't know if I'll be allowed to ride her.'

'Pity,' he said succinctly.

Jem nodded. 'You should stand up for yourself, Miss Julia,' he said. 'You're the Lacey, after all.'

I said nothing.

'D'you want to lead her down to the orchard?' Jem suggested.

'Oh yes!' I said. Jem turned to fetch her from the loose box and she came out in a rush. Dench stepped quickly aside and put a hand up for her head collar, but I stayed still. She stopped before me, as though it were me she had been in a hurry to see, and she dropped her lovely huge chestnut head to sniff at the front of my gown. I held her soft nose and laid my cheek along it.

Then I saw a movement at the library window, and I froze. Richard was watching me. As soon as I saw him, I moved, instinctively, away from the horse, ashamed as if he had caught me rifling his possessions or reading his private letters. I lifted my hand in a little wave, but Richard did not respond. He stepped back from the window before Jem and Dench had turned to see who was there.

'Richard was watching,' I said feebly. 'I won't take her to the orchard, Jem. You do it.'

Jem made a hissing noise through his teeth and clipped a rope on to the head collar. He and Dench exchanged one sour look, but said nothing.

'I must go,' I said, and turned away from the horse, the lovely horse, and went back to the parlour.

It was a quiet day, like all the other days, and the only excitement of the afternoon came when Richard and I were playing piquet at the parlour table and I won one hundred and fourteen pounds in buttons. Richard declared himself bankrupt and ruined and tossed down the cards. He glanced across at my mama, sitting at the fireside, and asked her, as if he had just thought of the question, 'Mama-Aunt, what is Lord Havering going to do about Dench?'

'Dench?' my mama repeated in surprise. 'What about Dench?'

Richard looked blank. 'Surely he has been reprimanded,' he said, bewildered. 'After taking such dreadful risks with Julia's safety that day?'

Mama paused. 'I was very shocked at the time,' she said. 'But when he brought you home, I was so relieved to have you safe that I said nothing. It was all such a rush!'

'I would have expected you to be more concerned about Julia,' Richard said, still surprised. 'Didn't she faint when she got home?'

'Yes . . .' Mama said.

'If she had fainted on horseback, she could have fallen and broken her neck,' Richard interrupted. 'Dench should never have put her on Scheherazade. She could have been badly thrown. Scheherazade had just thrown me, and I had been well taught and riding for months.'

Mama looked appalled. 'I should have thought . . .' she said guiltily. Then she turned to me. 'But you seemed so confident,' she said, 'and you rode her so well! You could obviously control her. I just assumed you had been riding her around the paddock when Richard's back was turned!'

'No!' I said at once. 'I never did that. I had never ridden her before. Dench told me to get on her, so I did.'

'It was very wrong to send Julia off on a big dangerous horse for her first ride alone,' said Richard. 'Astride too . . . and through Acre!'

Mama frowned. 'I have been careless,' she said. 'I did not think about it once I had you both safe home, but you are right, Richard. I shall speak to Mama about it.'

She shook her head with worry and bent to snip a thread from her sewing. When she looked up, she smiled at Richard in gratitude. 'What a good head of the household you are, Richard!' she said. 'You are quite right!'.

I smiled too at the praise for Richard, and Richard sat back in his chair and beamed at us both with confident masculine authority.

We saw Lady Havering the next day when she called on her way to Chichester to see if we needed any purchases. I saw Mama talking long and earnestly at the carriage window and I knew that Lady Havering would strongly disapprove of Dench for being careless with my safety; that she would be appalled to learn that I had been riding astride with my skirts pulled up, and through Acre too! I only hoped Dench had nothing worse to face than one of my grandpapa's bawled tirades. I knew he would be utterly untroubled by that.

But everything went wrong. Grandpapa was not at home, and in his absence Lady Havering ruled at the hall. She did not go to Chichester after hearing Mama's complaint; instead she drove straight home to the hall, stiff-backed with ill-founded outrage. She drove straight to the hall and into the stable yard and turned Dench off. She gave him a week's wages and no reference, and she would not hear one word from him.

He packed his bags and left the room above the stables where he had lived for twenty years. He walked the long way back to Acre village, where his brother and his family lived, dirt poor. Then after dinner – rye bread and gruel – he walked up to the Dower House, where only recently he had driven the Havering carriage with Richard inside, and Mama had cried and blessed him.

Stride was out, so Mrs Gough came to the parlour and told us that Dench was at the back door. Mama looked indecisive.

'I hope he isn't drunk and rowdy,' Richard said apprehensively.

That tilted the balance for Mama, and she went to her writing-box and wrapped a florin in a twist of paper. 'Tell him that I am sorry he has been turned off, but that I can do nothing about my step-papa's household,' she said awkwardly. 'Give him this from me.'

'I'll tell him,' Mrs Gough said truculently. 'The idea of

dunning you in your own house!' She stumped from the room, the coin clutched in her hand.

Although the baize door to the kitchen was shut, we could hear her voice raised, berating Dench, and his voice shouting in reply. I looked at Mama. Her face was ashen and I realized she was afraid.

'It's nothing, Mama,' I said gently. 'Mrs Gough has a sharp tongue, and I dare say Dench is just giving as good as he gets. It's nothing more than that.'

'He's a bitter man,' Richard contradicted me. 'I hope this matter ends here. I do not like the thought of him coming to the house, nor hanging around the village making trouble against us. Lord Havering says that Acre is a powder-keg of trouble-makers. Dench is just another one to add to the fuel.'

The kitchen door banged loudly and I saw my mama flinch. But I was thinking of Dench, who had done nothing so very wrong and was now out of a job. He had to walk home again, all the way down the drive and the lane towards Acre, with his head down, watching the toes of his boots which would not last for ever with the walking he would have to do to find work.

I excused myself from the room and slipped out into the hall. The front door was unlocked, and I threw on my cloak and let myself out. I could dimly see Dench ahead of me down the drive, walking back to Acre. Even at that distance I could see that his shoulders were slumped. His stride had lost its swing. I ran after him.

'Dench, I am so sorry!' I exclaimed. He had stopped when he heard me running after him, but at those words he turned homeward again and trudged on. I fell into step beside him. 'When my grandpapa comes home, I shall tell him I was in no danger,' I said. 'My grandmama misunderstood what happened, and you know how strict she is about me.'

He nodded. 'No need for you to say nothing,' he said fairly. 'I'd never put you in the least danger. Your grandpa knows that. Her la'ship is right, I did not think about you riding astride. And I did not think about Acre. I'm damned if I know what she would have had me do. But I had no chance to ask that. No chance to tell her that I was anxious only to get them searching for Master Richard . . .' He broke off. 'When his lordship comes home, he'll find me a place,' he said. 'But it's a poor return for twenty years' work.'

'I am sorry,' I said again. 'It isn't fair.'

'Aye,' he said, the first edge of bitterness in his voice that I had ever heard. 'It's never fair for those at the bottom. I know who I have to thank for this. I'd rather that horse had dropped dead when Master Richard took his tumble than all this bother. And my sister having to feed me with a houseful of hungry mouths of her own . . . You'd not understand,' he said. 'Go home, Miss Julia. I don't blame you.'

I stared at him and had no answer. Then I nodded, unsmiling, and turned back for my home, and the candlelit parlour, and the card game.

But I did not forget that he and Jem had said that Scheherazade needed exercise, and when Richard and I were on our way to our beds that night, I stopped him at the foot of the flight of the stairs which led to his bedroom.

'Richard, would you mind if I asked Mama if I might walk Scheherazade in the paddock and perhaps down the drive and in the woods a little? Not proper riding, of course, just walking her. Jem said this morning that she would need to be walked out until you are ready to ride her again.'

Richard's face was shadowy in the candlelight. 'Would you like that?' he asked.

'Oh, yes,' I said, but I was cautious. 'If you would not mind. Not otherwise.'

'Would you like to learn to ride her properly, perhaps? I could teach you while my arm is getting better.'

'Richard! Would you?' I exclaimed, and I grabbed his sound hand so the candle bobbed and the shadows grew and shrank wildly. 'Oh! I should so love that! Oh, Richard! I *knew* you would let me ride her! Oh, Richard! you are such a darling, darling, darling to me! And when your arm is better, perhaps my grandpapa will find us a pony for me to ride and we can go out riding together every day. And we can learn to jump! And . . . oh, Richard! . . . perhaps he would take us riding to hounds! And we could be famous as neck-or-nothing riders like your mama!'

Richard laughed, but his voice was strained. 'All right! All right! No need to set the house afire!' he said. 'And mind my bad arm! Don't hug me, whatever you do!'

I stepped back and did a little dance on the spot in delight. 'Oh, sorry!' I said. 'But, oh! Richard!'

'There,' he said. 'I knew you wanted to ride her all along.'

'You are the best of cousins,' I told him exuberantly. But then we heard Mama's tread in the parlour coming towards the hall and the stairs, and we fled to our bedrooms.

I could hardly sleep for excitement, and my sleep was light. Something awoke me in the earliest hours of the morning, just before it grew light. I heard someone on the stairs outside my room and I called out, 'Who's there?'

'Shh,' said Richard, pushing open my door. 'It's me. There's someone prowling around the stables. I heard a noise and went down and saw him from the library window.'

'Who?' I said, muddled with sleep.

'Too dark to see,' Richard said. 'I opened the window and called out and he ran off, whoever he was.'

'Whoever could it be, and what could he want in the stables?' I asked. 'Oh, Richard! The horses are all right, are they? Should we wake Mama?'

'I could see their heads over the doors of the loose boxes,' Richard said reassuringly. 'The only person I could think of was Dench. The figure I saw had the look of him. He could have been visiting Jem and run off when he heard me call. He'd know that he'd not be welcome here after that scene he made yesterday afternoon.'

'What shall we do?' I asked. I was warm and cosy in bed and I did not relish the thought of getting out. As long as Scheherazade was safe, I had little interest in midnight prowlers.

Richard yawned mightily. 'Go back to sleep, I think,' he said.

'There's no harm done that I can see. It did indeed look like Dench, but he certainly ran off out of the stable yard. I'll tell Mama-Aunt in the morning; there's no point waking her now.'

'And in the morning I can go riding!' I said in sleepy delight. 'Will you come out and teach me first thing, Richard?'

'Yes, of course,' he said indulgently. 'First thing. Until then, little Julia.'

I slid back into sleep immediately, but my excitement about riding Scheherazade woke me early. At once I jumped out of bed and threw on my oldest gown and pattered down the stairs. Mrs Gough was already up, making our morning chocolate. I said I would be straight back for mine, but I had to see Scheherazade first.

Mrs Gough eyed me dourly, but I paid no heed to her and slid out of the kitchen door, scampered to the orchard for a windfall apple and ran back to the stable. I called, 'Scheherazade!' as soon as I got to the stable yard, but her head did not come over the half-door at my voice as it usually did. I called her again and felt suddenly uneasy that I did not hear her moving.

'Scheherazade?' I said uncertainly. And then I looked over the stable door.

She was lying on the straw. For a moment I thought she must be ill, for she scrabbled with her forelegs like a foal trying to rise when she saw me. But then my eyes adjusted to the gloom and I saw the blood on the straw. The silly thing had cut herself.

'Oh, Scheherazade!' I said reproachfully, and I flung open the door and bent under the pole which slides across the entrance. She scrabbled again, pulling her front half up, but her back legs seemed useless. I realized her injury was serious. Her straw was fouled with urine from where she had lain and it was all red, horribly red, in the bright morning light. She must have been bleeding steadily for most of the night. Her beautiful streaming copper tail was all matted with dried blood. Then she heaved herself up again and I caught sight of her wounds. At the side of each back leg was a clean smooth slash.

She looked as if she had been cut with a knife.

I gazed around wildly, looking for a sharp metal feeding bucket, a mislaid ploughshare, something which could have caused two matched injuries. She looked exactly as if she had been cut with a knife. Two neat small cuts, each severing the proud line of tendons on each leg.

She looked as if she had been cut by a knife.

She *had* been cut with a knife.

Someone had come into this stable and cut Richard's most beautiful horse with a knife, so that he would never be able to ride her again.

I was dry-eyed; but I gave a great shuddering sob to see her so injured. Then I went, slowly, lagging, back to the house. Some-one would have to tell Richard that his horse, his most lovely horse, was quite lame. And I loved Richard so dearly that even in my own grief and horror I knew it had to be no one but me.

Dench had done it.

Richard said it at once. 'It was Dench.'

Dench who knew that life was unfair.

I could not understand how a man who had spent all his life caring for horses could do such a thing to such a flawless animal. But Mama, her face white and pinched, said that poverty did strange and dreadful things to the minds of the poor and filled men with hatred.

He had been hanging around the stables last night, as Richard said. He had a grievance against the Haverings and against us. He had cursed us in our very own kitchen. Even I had to agree that he was a bitter man.

Mama sent Jem with a message to Ned Smith in Acre, and he came to the bloodstained stables and said that the tendons would not heal and she would never be able to flex her feet again. She would be lame for ever.

'Best kill her, your la'ship,' he said, standing awkwardly in the hall, his dirty boots making prints on the shiny floorboards.

'No!' Richard said suddenly, too quick for thought. 'No! She should not be killed. I know she is lamed, but she should not be killed!'

Ned's broad dark face was flinty as he turned to Richard. 'She's good for nothing,' he said, his voice hard. 'She's a working animal, not a pet. If you can't ride her, then you'd best not keep her. Since she's ruined, she's better off dead.'

'No!' Richard said again, an edge of panic in his voice. 'I don't want that! She's my horse. I have a right to decide whether she lives or dies.'

Mama shook her head gently and took Richard by his sound arm and led him towards the parlour. 'The smith is right, Richard,' she said softly, and she nodded at Ned over her shoulder. 'She will have to be put down.'

She took Richard into the parlour, but I stayed standing in the hall. Ned the smith gave me one dark glance. 'I'm sorry, Miss Julia,' he said gently.

'She's not my horse,' I said miserably. 'I only rode her the once.'

'Aye,' he said. 'But I know you loved her well. She was a bonny horse.'

He went, clumsy in his big boots, towards the front door and hefted the mallet he had left outside. He went to her loose box, where she lay like a new-born weak foal in the straw, and he killed her with a great blow from the mallet between her trusting brown eyes, and some men from Acre came and loaded the big awkward body on a cart and drove her away.

'What will they do with her?' I asked. I was in the parlour window-seat and could not drag myself from the window. It seemed I had to see the heavily laden cart rocking down the lane. I had to see the awkward body and the legs sticking out.

Mama's face was grim. 'In that village, I dare say they will eat her,' she said, loathing in her voice.

I gave a cry of horror and turned away. Then I went in silence from the parlour, up to my room, to lie on my bed and gaze blankly at the ceiling. I would have gone to Richard, but I knew he wanted to be alone. He was in the library, sitting in the empty room, in the only chair in the room. Sitting with his back to the window which overlooks the yard and the empty stable so that he could not see Jem mucking-out the empty stall and washing it down.

But in Acre there was no sign of Dench.

Ned said so when he came to the back door to wash his hands and get his pay. I supposed that proved his guilt, but I still could not understand it. Ned told Mrs Gough that Dench had disappeared once he heard that the horse was to be killed.

'He knew where the blame 'ud fall,' he said.

'Well, who else would have done it?' asked Mrs Gough, truculently. 'No one else in all the county has a grievance against that blessed boy. It's fair broke his heart. And where'll he get another horse from? I don't know! He can't be a gentleman without a horse to ride, can he?'

'Can't be a gentleman if he can't stay on!' Ned said, irritated.

'Now, get you out of my kitchen!' said Mrs Gough, her brittle temper snapping. 'You and your spiteful tongue. Get you back to Acre with the rest of 'em. Trouble-makers every one of you! Rick-burners! Horse-maimers!'

And Ned turned away with a sour smile and went back to the village which my grandpapa had called a village of outlaws – just one and a half miles down the lane from where we lived, lonely in the woods.

Grandpapa Havering swore out loud before us all when he finally came home and Mama told him the whole story. Then he turned kindly to Richard and promised him that as soon as Richard's arm was strong again, he would have another horse. Another horse for his very own.

But Richard was inconsolable. He smiled and thanked my grandpapa, but he said quietly that he did not want another horse, just yet. Not for a while anyway. 'I don't think we could ever replace her,' he said.

The grown-ups shook their heads and agreed with him. And my heart ached for the lovely Scheherazade and for the wonderful ride I had, that once, with her.

But most of all I ached for Richard's loss; that the horse he loved was dead.

Grandpapa posted bills offering a reward for Dench's capture. Injuring an animal is a capital offence, and Dench could have been transported or, more likely, hanged. But no one came forward to betray him, and his family in Acre had not heard from him.

'I'd trust their word!' said Grandpapa scathingly. 'Really, m'dear, the sooner your precious John MacAndrew comes home and sets that village to rights, the happier I'll be. A gentleman can scarcely sleep in his bed o' nights with that murdering crew in Acre.'

Mama nodded, her head down for shame that Acre, our village, should be such a place. And I sensed that she did not want Grandpapa to inveigh against the village with me there, listening. The village where the miller's wife would not turn out her men for a son of Beatrice Lacey's. There was a deep old enmity between Acre and the Laceys, and Mama would not tell me of it.

I could see all the signs. Mama would not visit in the village. She took every opportunity she could to go to church in Chichester, not to our parish church in Acre. Our boots were made in Midhurst, and the Acre cobbler was idle. Our laundry went to Lavington. It all came down to that odd phrase of the blacksmith's – that Beatrice had gone bad.

Richard knew of the tension in the village. And Richard spoke of it openly. 'They're scum, they are,' he told me harshly. 'They're as filthy as pigs in a sty. They don't work for anyone else, they don't even plant their own patches. They're poachers and thieves. When I am squire, I shall clear the land of the lot of them, and plough that dirty village under.'

I had caught my breath at that and shaken my head in mute disagreement, but I knew that Richard's words came from bravado. Richard was afraid. He was only a little eleven-year-old boy and he had cause for fear.

The village children were after him. They knew, as well as the two of us, that the village and the Wideacre family were sworn enemies. And after Dench ran away it got very much worse. They would catcall and jeer at him as he went past, his school-books under his arm. They would sneer at his old coat, at his boots, which were worn and getting too tight for him. And always, when they could think of nothing else to say, they shouted loudly to one another that here was someone calling himself a squire and a Lacey, yet he could not stay on a horse.

Richard walked, fearful as a stable cat through the crowd, and his eyes blazed defiance and hatred. He saw them as a mob and thought that if he challenged one, then they would all attack him. I think he feared too that the adults would come out of their cottages to watch Miss Beatrice's boy being torn apart on the village street and do nothing to help him.

Most of this I guessed. Richard was too proud to tell me. He told me only that he hated to walk through the village; and I saw that if the day was fine – which meant that the children would be out playing in the lane – he would leave early to go up the downland track and around the back of the village so that he could avoid the village street.

He never told Mama. He had a fine sharp courage, my cousin Richard; and he never told Mama that he was afraid. He asked her once what was meant by the phrase 'a mother's boy'. Mama was brushing out her hair before her mirror in her bedroom, and Richard was pulling a silk ribbon through his fingers and watching her. I was sitting in the window-seat looking out, out over the trees of Wideacre where the leaves were whirling away into the wintry sky, but at Richard's question I looked sharply at Mama.

She put down her brush and looked at him, at his pale heart-shaped face and his mop of black hair, at the ribbon in his hand and at the way he was leaning so comfortably at her side. 'Where have you heard that phrase, my dear?' she asked steadily.

Richard shrugged. 'They called it after me in the village today,' he said. 'I paid no heed. I never pay any heed to them.'

Mama put out a gentle hand to touch his face. 'It will get better,' she said gently. 'When your papa comes home, it will be better.'

Richard caught her hand and kissed it, as graceful as a courtier. 'I don't mind him being away,' he said. 'I like it just as we are.'

I said nothing then, I said nothing later. But when he came home one day with his collar torn and face white, I knew it was getting worse.

I don't know why I thought I might be able to help, but I did not fear Acre like the two of them. I was at home on Wideacre and at odds with no part of it, not even the worst village in Sussex. I knew with such certainty that I belonged on the land, and that included Acre. And I had a clear memory of Ned Smith's half-smile, and of Mrs Green giving Richard her most precious phial of laudanum.

I used that phial as my excuse, and told Mama that I should return it to the mill. I would walk to Acre with Richard, go on to the mill and meet him from his lessons after my visit.

I had a little grin from Richard as a reward for that, and a surprised glance from Mama.

'Walking through Acre?' she asked tentatively.

'Why not?' I said boldly. 'I'll just call on Mrs Green and then I'll sit with Dr Pearce's housekeeper until Richard is ready to come home.'

'Very well,' she said. There was a world of reservation behind those level tones. I guessed that she did not want to make me afraid of Acre, and I think she saw also something she did not understand, something she had seen before: the Lacey confidence in the people of Acre. I ran to fetch my coat and bonnet, for Richard was ready to leave.

It was last winter's coat, and I saw Mama frown as she looked at it. It was too short and uncomfortably tight under the arms and across the back. The sleeves ended too high, and there was a little gap between my gloves and the cuff where my wrist showed bony and cold.

'I am sorry, Mama,' I said, making a joke of it. 'I cannot help growing!'

'Well, I wish you would stop!' she said, her face lightening. Then Richard and I were off and Mama waved to us from the parlour window as we walked down the drive and turned left down the lane towards Acre.

As soon as we approached the village, I felt Richard's unease. He was afraid for us both. He transferred his bundle of books to the other arm and felt for my hand. Hand-clasped, we walked steadily down the chalk-dirt track and past the cottage windows, which seemed to eye us as if they did not much like what they saw.

On our left was the cobbler, still sitting idle in his bow-window. Next to him was the carter's cottage with the wagon they had used to take Scheherazade away. He had sold his horses long ago, but he had managed to keep his wagon. He still waited on in Acre for times to get better. There was nowhere else he could go. If he left the parish, neither he nor his family of six scruffy children could claim the poor rate. If he stayed, he had only a cold house, a dead fireplace and a wagon outside the door with nothing to carry and no horse to pull it.

Next to him was the blacksmith's yard, the forge still unlit. For who would want horseshoes in a hurry in Acre where no one owned a horse? As we walked along the lane, I peered at every cottage, wondering that so many people could stay alive at all in such a desolate little village. They could eat the game from the Wideacre woods and the rabbits from the common. But they had no seeds to plant for vegetables, and they must need money for clothing, for tools. I was so absorbed in wondering how people survived with no money – no money at all – that I did not notice we were being followed.

There was a little group of ragged urchins trailing along behind us. Not many – about a dozen of them – but a frightening enough mob for Richard and me. They followed us like a half-starved wolf-pack, and they looked at Richard's books and my shabby coat as though they were unimaginable luxuries.

Richard hardly drew breath until we reached the vicar's front porch. 'Don't go back out, Julia,' he said in an urgent undertone while we waited for the housekeeper to answer the bell. 'Wait here until I have finished my lessons. The children will look at you oddly, and they might say something to you.'

I gave him a little smile to hide the fact that my knees were trembling. 'They're only little children,' I said dismissively, 'and I have to see Mrs Green. I shan't be long. If they are rude, I shall just run. I bet I can run faster than any of them.'

Richard nodded at that. He knew I was as fleet as a courser. The barefoot hungry children would never be able to catch me, not even running in a pack. 'I'd rather you waited,' he said.

'No, I can go,' I said decisively, and the door opened. He did not give me a kiss in front of the housekeeper and the watching children but the hand which still held mine gave me a warm squeeze which mattered very much to me. Just that one gesture, that touch of his palm against mine, gave me the courage to turn and face the children, Richard's tormentors, and walk down the path towards them.

I stopped at the gate and eyed them over it. I was taller than all but the three biggest: two boys and a girl with her hair down her back in a lank plait. All their faces were closed, sullen; but she had her eyes on me. She was examining every stitch of my old dress and my too tight coat as if I were a princess dressed for a ball. I pushed my hands into my pockets and calmly surveyed her. Then, taking my time, I stepped towards the garden gate and opened it, and walked out into the lane.

That surprised them. I think they had thought I would stay in the shelter of the garden and they melted away as I walked through them. But then they fell into step behind me and I led the way down the bridle-path to the common and the new mill with the motley band behind me. When the silence of the wood closed around us, they grew loud and started jeering. Then I heard the older girl's voice start a chant: 'Julia Lacey! Julia Lacey! Hasn't got a carriage! Hasn't got a carriage!' Over and over.

I set my teeth and schooled myself to walk at the same pace while the insulting singsong went on – louder and more fearless. Then the big girl changed it: 'Julia Lacey! Julia Lacey! Hasn't got a horse! Hasn't got a horse!'

At the mention of Scheherazade my temper rose a few more notches, but I walked on with my head up as if I were alone.

She started another chant: 'Julia Lacey! Julia Lacey! Hasn't got a father! Hasn't got a father!'

'He died of fright!' said another voice and there was a ripple of laughter from them; I flinched at the abuse of my papa and the insult to the Laceys.

I was a little afraid. I was afraid, like Richard, that I might be badly hurt in a scrap with them, or that they might surround and bully me. But I knew, as Richard, with all his charm and cleverness, did not, that the children must be faced and fought or we would never be able to walk through Acre. Richard might dream of clearing the land of them, he might plan for a future where every insult was revenged a hundred times over. But I wanted to live in peace on my land with the families who had been here as long as the Laceys. I did not want to clear Acre village, I wanted to set things right. Whether Uncle John came home with a fortune or as poor as when he left, I wanted to be able to walk in Acre, without apologizing. And feel no fear.

I walked on past the mill. At the end of this track there was a great hollow in the ground where they say there was once a grand oak tree uprooted by Beatrice when she turned everywhere into wheatfields like the one behind it which was sprawled all over now with rust-coloured bracken and mauve with heather. But still the odd head of wheat blew spindly-yellow in the wind. I led my tormentors there and at the lip of the hollow where the oak tree had stood I turned and faced them. They fell back like a pack of hungry dogs baiting a badger.

'What's your name?' I said, picking on the girl. She looked at me with sharp black eyes.

'Clary Dench,' she said. She would be Dench's niece, I thought.

'What's yours?' I asked the boy at her side.

'M-M-Matthew Merry,' he said, blinking convulsively as he fought against his stammer.

I had to bite back the urge to giggle. The stammer was such a relief, coming from the mouth of such a frighteningly big boy. It made him seem childlike, no threat to me.

'And yours?' I said sharply to the only other big boy.

'Ted Tyacke,' he said. He looked closely at me, expecting the name to mean something to a Lacey. I had never heard that name before but I felt a shiver down my spine; somehow in the past the Laceys had injured the Tyackes, and hurt them badly. *I* might not know what we had done, but this lout of a boy knew that we were sworn enemies.

'I'm Julia Lacey,' I said as if they had not been making a chant of my name all the way down the track, careful not to give myself the 'Miss' which was my right. 'You've been unkind to my cousin,' I said accusingly. 'You've been bullying my cousin Richard.'

'And he sent you out to do his fighting for him, I s'pose?' the girl sneered. I did not flinch back as she pushed her dirty face close to mine.

'No,' I said steadily, 'he went to his schooling today like he always does, and I came down here to see Mrs Green. But you all followed me down so I ask you what you want.'

'We don't want nothing from the Laceys!' said the boy called Ted Tyacke with a sudden explosion of hatred. 'We don't want kind words from you. We know your sort.' The others nodded, and I could feel their mounting anger, and it made me afraid.

'I've said and done nothing to you,' I protested, and heard my voice sound plaintive. My weakness gave them courage and now they crowded around me, encircled me.

'We know about the Laceys,' said Clary spitefully. 'We all know all about you. You rob the poor of reapers' rights. You don't pay your tithes. You set the soldiers on young men. And the Lacey women are witches!' She hissed out the word and I saw all the children, even the smallest, clench their hands in the sign against witchcraft, the little thumbs held tight between the middle finger and forefinger to make the sign of a cross.

'That's none of it true,' I said steadily. 'I am not a witch, and neither is Richard. You are talking nonsense. You've got no cause against us, and if you say you have, then you are liars.'

Clary sprang forward at that and gave me a push which sent

me reeling back. I lost my footing on the slope of the hollow and tumbled down into the bottom. The little children hooted with delight and Clary came scrambling down after me, her dirty face alight with malice.

I bunched myself up like a coiled spring, and leaped on her as soon as she was beside me. With the impetus of my jump from the ground I knocked her down and we rolled over and over, hitting and scratching. I felt her claw-like fingers at my mouth and tasted blood. Then I got hold of the rope of the plait of hair and pulled as hard as I could. She gave a shriek of pain and instinctively leaned back towards the pull. In a minute I had scrambled atop her, and I sat heavily on her bony little chest and felt, for the first time, a rush of pity at how thin and light she was.

'D'you give up?' I demanded tersely, using the words Richard so often said to me when he won in our half-playful, half-painful rompings.

'Aye,' she said. She spoke without a trace of a sneer, and I got up at once and put out a hand to pull her to her feet. She took it, without thinking, and then stood up, surprised to find herself handfast with me, apparently shaking on a bargain.

'So you won't tease Richard any more,' I said, going directly to my one objective. She smiled a slow grudging smile that showed a couple of blackened teeth.

'All right,' she said slowly, the easy Sussex drawl reminding me of Dench and of his kindness to me. 'We'll leave him be.'

We dropped hands then, awkwardly, as if we had forgotten how we had come to be standing as close as friends. But she saw my mouth and said, 'You're bleeding' in an indifferent voice. And I was careful to match her tone and say, 'Am I?' as if I did not care at all.

'Come to the Fenny,' she offered, and all of us walked deeper into the wood to the bank of the River Fenny for a drink and a splash of cold water on our hurts. And this time I walked neither alone in the front, nor encircled, but side by side with different children who came up to me and told me their names. I realized that I had not only won Richard's safety, I had found some friends.

There were three Smith children: Henry, a stocky eight-year-old, his sister Jilly, and their little brother, who came with them, trotting to keep up with the pace of the older children. He was four. They called him Little 'Un. He had not been expected to live and had been christened Henry like his brother. But his survival, thus far, meant there were two Henrys in the house, so the little boy had lost his name.

It did not matter, Clary told me, her voice dry. They did not expect him to survive the next winter. He coughed blood all the time like his mother had done. She had died after his birth and they had delayed her funeral a week so he could be put in her coffin and they could bury two for the cost of one. But Little 'Un had clung on.

I stared at him. His skin was as pale as skimmed milk, a bluish pallor. When he felt my eyes on him, he gave me a smile of such sweetness that it was like a little candle in a dark corner.

'You can call me Little 'Un,' he said, his breath rapid and light.

'You can call me Julia,' I said, looking at his thin face and huge eyes with a sense of hopelessness so intense that it felt like pain.

'I'm Jane Carter,' said another girl, pushing forward. 'And this is my sister Em'ly. We've got another sister, but she's at home with Baby. And we've got two brothers. And one of them is simple.'

I nodded, trying to take in the rush of information.

'They're out snaring rabbits,' she said defiantly. I noticed the quick exchange of looks among the others to see how I would react to the news of poaching.

'I hope they're lucky,' I said and I told the truth. 'With six of you to feed you'll need the meat.'

Jane nodded at the self-evident fact. 'We poach pheasants too,' she said. 'And hare, and grouse.'

It was an open challenge.

'Good,' I said. 'I wish you luck with it.'

They nodded at that, as though I had passed some crucial test, and two cobbler's children, fair-headed twins, came either side of me and put their little cold hands in mine.

Clary and I glanced at the sun coming higher over the woods, and started on a jog-trot for home without a word exchanged between us. She set a quick pace for a scrawny girl, and the other children trailed away behind us; only Matthew Merry and Ted Tyacke kept up. I tried to control my breath so she would not hear me pant. But then I could tell by the way she was slackening that she was tiring too.

The track to Acre ran uphill. It was stony and bad going for a child with holes in her boots like mine, but worse for barefoot children like the three of them. I pounded on determinedly, my tight coat squeezing me mercilessly across my chest and under my arms. When I reached the top, I was panting for breath, but I got there first.

'W-W-Well done,' said Matthew, his stammer worse with no breath left in his skinny frame to say the words. 'You're a f-f-fast runner.'

'My cousin Richard is faster than me,' I said, dropping to the ground while we waited for Clary and Ted and then the string of little children.

Matthew spat on the ground like a rude grown-up. 'We d-d-don't care for him,' he said dismissively.

I was about to fire up in defence of Richard, but something told me he might be better served by me keeping my peace. 'He's nice,' I said, keeping my voice light. 'He's my best friend.'

Matthew nodded, unimpressed. 'We don't have best friends in Acre any more,' he said.

'Why not?' I asked.

Clary slumped down beside me, and Ted beside her. She lay on her back on the damp ground and squinted up at the bright sky with the sharp winter sun blazing coldly down on us.

'They die,' she said coolly. 'Last winter my best friend Rachel died. She had got ill.'

'And my friend Michael,' offered Ted.

'And my friend, I've f-f-forgotten her name,' Matthew said.

'Sally,' Clary volunteered.

I sat in silence, taking this in.

'Sally died away from Acre,' Clary said with a hint of extra resentment. 'The parish overseer took all the children he could get from their parents to work in the workshops. That's why we're the oldest in the village.'

I nodded. 'I heard about it,' I said. 'I couldn't understand what had happened. Who took the children?'

Ted looked at me as if I were ignorant indeed. 'In the north,' he said, his voice hard. 'Even further away than London. They need children to work there in great barns, with great engines. They order paupers from all the parishes in the country and the parish overseer takes the children whose parents are on poor relief. They took all the big children they could the last time they came. None of them have come back, but we heard that Sal died. She was always sickly.'

I hesitated. I had nearly said again, 'I am sorry.' But the stealing of Acre's children was too great a grief for an easily spoken apology.

'Th-Th-They didn't take me!' Matthew said with pride.

Clary smiled at him, as tender as a mother. 'They thought he was simple,' she said to me with a smile. 'He gets worse when he is frightened and they asked him questions in loud voices and he lost his speech altogether. They thought he was simple and they left him here.'

'To b-b-be with you,' Matthew said with a look of utter adoration at his muddy little heroine.

'Aye,' she said with quiet pride. 'I look after him, and I look after all the little 'uns.'

'You're like a squire then,' I said with a smile.

Ted spat on the ground, as rude as Matthew. 'No squire we've ever had,' he said. 'No Lacey has ever cared for the village. Squires don't look after people.'

I shook my head, puzzled. 'What d'you mean?' I said. 'Acre

was well cared for when the Laceys had their wealth. When my papa was alive, and Beatrice. It's only since they died, and since the fire, that things have been bad on the land.'

There was a hiss, like a wind blowing before a storm, at my mention of the name Beatrice, and I saw all the grimy hands clench suddenly into an odd fist with the thumb between the second and third finger. I caught Clary's hand.

'Why are you doing that?' I asked.

She looked at me, her dark eyes puzzled. 'Don't *you* know?' she demanded.

'Know what?' I said. 'No, I don't know.'

'Not about the Lacey magic? And about Beatrice?' She said the name oddly, as if she were whispering the name of a spell, not the name of my long-dead aunt.

'What magic?' I said, scoffing, but then I looked around the circle of intent young faces and I felt myself shiver as though a cold breeze had blown down my spine.

'Beatrice was a witch,' Clary said very softly. 'She knew how to make the land grow, she knew how to make the weather fair. She could call up storms. She could fell trees by casting a spell on them. She took a young man to husband every spring, and every autumn she destroyed him.'

'That's not so . . .' I stammered. The singsong tone was weaving a spell of its own around me.

'It *was* so,' Clary insisted. 'One of the men she took from the village was John Tyacke.'

'My uncle,' Ted supplemented.

'Where's *he* now?' Clary continued. 'Gone!'

'Or Sam Frosterly, or Ned Hunter! Ask for them in Acre and see what they tell you! Beatrice took them. Took them all.'

I said nothing. I was too bemused to speak.

'But one she took, the first one she took when she was a girl, was from the Old People too,' Clary said. 'His mother was Meg, a gypsy woman, and his father was one of the old gods. No one ever saw him in human shape. She took him, but she could not destroy him. He went into the dark world, into the silence, and he waited until she knew for sure he was coming. And then he came against her.'

'How?' I said. My mouth was dry. I knew this was a fairy story made up by ignorant people on long dark nights, but I had to hear the ending.

'He came in his rightful shape, half-man, half-horse,' Clary's voice was a low mesmerizing whisper. 'And at every hoofprint there was a circle of fire. He rode up the wooden stairs of the great hall, of Wideacre Hall, and everywhere he went the flames took hold. He threw her across his shoulders and rode away with her to the dark world where they both live. And the house burned down behind them. And the fields never grew again.'

The children were utterly silent, though they knew the story well. I stared blankly at Clary, my head whirling with the picture of a black horse and a man riding away with Beatrice to the dark world where she would live with him for ever.

'Is that the end of the story?' I asked.

Clary shook her head. 'They left an heir,' she said. 'A child who will have their magic. A child who will be able to make things grow by setting foot to the earth, hand to the ploughshare. The favoured child.'

'And who is it?' I asked. I had truly forgotten I had any part in this story. Clary smiled, a wise old smile.

'We have to wait and see,' she said. 'All of us in Acre are waiting for the sign. It could be you, or it could be your cousin Richard. He is her son. But you have the looks of her, and you're a Lacey. And Ned Smith said the horse knew you were her.'

I shook my head. The air was cold, and I noticed for the first time that the ground was damp and I was chilled. 'All that is nonsense,' I said stoutly.

I expected a childish squabble with Clary, but she smiled at me with her eyelashes veiling her eyes. 'You know it is not,' she said. And she said no more.

I got to my feet. 'I must go,' I said.

'Home to dinner?' asked Clary, accepting a return to the prosaic world.

'Yes,' I said, thinking of the two or three dishes for the main course and then the pudding, and then the cheese.

'W-W-What are you having?' Matthew asked with longing.

'Nothing much,' I said resolutely.

'Do you have tea?' Little 'Un asked. There was real longing in his voice.

'Yes,' I said, not understanding. 'Don't you?'

'No,' he said. 'We just gets water.'

'D'you have meat?' one of the Carter girls asked me.

'Yes,' I said, and I felt ashamed that I should have been eating so well while less than two miles down our own lane they had been going hungry. I had known that Acre was poor, but I had not understood that they had been hungry for years. I had not understood that these children would never have felt a full belly, that since infancy they had hungered and thought of little else but food. And while I had my dreams of gardens and horse-riding, of balls and parties and gowns, all they dreamed of in reveries, and even in their sleep, was food.

I turned and walked towards Acre, and I heard them scramble to their feet and come after me. Clary caught me up and we walked side by side into Acre like old friends.

'Goodbye,' I said as we reached the dirty little lane which is Acre's main street.

Clary halted. 'He has apples in his garden, Dr Pearce,' she said.

I nodded. 'I know,' I said.

Clary looked at me speculatively. 'Still on the tree,' she said. 'He hasn't picked them all.'

I nodded again. They were apples on old trees, part blighted and not very good eating.

Little 'Un came up and slipped a thin hand in mine. 'I can just see them,' he said in his breathy voice. 'I'd love 'em.'

I looked at Clary.

'If we bunked you up . . .' she started. 'Over the side wall into the garden. You could throw them over to us, and then go round to the front and go in the front door, like usual.'

'Why don't you go?' I asked.

''Cause if they catch me stealing, I could be hanged,' she said with brutal frankness. 'If they catch you, it's not even stealing when gentry does the taking.'

I hesitated.

'She won't do it,' Ted said. The dislike towards me, towards all squires, made his young voice hard. 'She came out to make it all right for her cousin, not to be with us.'

'I will do it,' I said, rising to the challenge.

'Go over the wall and steal the parson's apples?' he sneered.

'Yes,' I said. All at once we all got the giggles. Even Ted's harsh young face crumpled at the thought of setting me to stealing. We skittered around to the vicar's high back wall, the little children sluggish with merriment, and Ted Tyacke and Matthew Merry linked hands together, and Clary helped me up to stand on them. They staggered at my weight and Clary said, 'Go on! Throw her!'

I snorted with laughter at that, and grabbed the top of the wall as the two lads staggered with my weight and with the giggles.

'One . . . two . . . three . . . and up!' counted Clary, and the insecure footing underneath my boots suddenly heaved me upwards and against the top of the wall. It was topped with sharp flints, and I heard a seam rip. I looked down into the garden, swung my legs over and was readying myself to slide down and jump when I froze.

There was Dr Pearce, almost immediately below me, looking upward, his face a mask of surprise. 'Miss Lacey?' he said as if he could not believe his eyes. 'Miss Lacey? What on earth are you doing?'

I could think of no answer; I turned around to check that Ted and Matthew were still there. 'Catch me!' I squealed like a stuck pig and just toppled backwards off the wall towards them.

We went down in a tumbled heap on to the hard ground with the two of them taking the weight of my fall. They jumped up, but I was laughing so much I could not move.

'What was it? What was it?' Clary asked, smiling already at my helpless gales.

'It was Dr Pearce!' I said. 'Right below me. He looked up . . . and he said . . . "Miss Lacey. What on earth are you doing?"'

Clary gave a great wail of laughter and fell into Matthew's arms. Ted put out a hand and pulled me to my feet, his brown round face contorted. The smaller children dropped down where they stood and howled with irrepressible mirth.

'I've got to go,' I said, wiping my streaming eyes. 'I've got to go. I've got to go in the front garden gate and up the path.'

That set us off again even worse than before, and we staggered like a band of drunkards around to the lane.

'Don't come with me,' I begged. 'I must stop laughing.'

Clary nodded, still chuckling. 'Come down to Acre again soon,' she said. Her dirty face was streaked with the tears she had shed, and she still held her sides. 'We could really use you in the gang. Great thief you are, Julia Lacey.'

I nodded, still unable to speak, and then turned towards the vicar's front gate. Half-way up the path to the pretty house I stopped and drew in a deep breath. I did not know Dr Pearce well, and I did not think I would face anything worse than a scolding. But I did not want to disgrace myself utterly by bursting out laughing on the doorstep.

A hoot from behind me told me that Clary was watching, but I did not look around. I tapped on the door and the vicar's housekeeper, Miss Green, opened it. She dipped a curtsy and held it wide, and I stepped into the hall, back into the world where I belonged.

Dr Pearce came out of the library with Richard and nodded to me as if it were the first time he had seen me that morning.

'Hello, Miss Lacey,' he said pleasantly. 'Come to walk home with your cousin? We are just finished.'

For a moment I gaped at him, then I took my cue. Dr Pearce was not a man to seek difficulties. If he could turn a blind eye to them, then he would do so. He really did not want to know what I was doing sitting on his high garden wall with my coat torn and my face muddy and the naughty children of Acre catcalling encouragement from the lane below.

I curtsied demurely. 'Yes, Dr Pearce,' I said. I held Richard's books while he pulled on his coat and hat, and we went back outside and home for dinner.

The children had gone, vanished like idle fox-cubs at the sound of a strange footstep. The weather had changed from the sunny morning. There were thick clouds piled all over the sky. Richard and I started at a jog-trot for home, speeded by a warning scud of rain on our backs.

'Did you see Mrs Green?' Richard asked breathlessly.

'No,' I said. I was having trouble keeping up for I was tired from my run with the village children and bruised from the fight with Clary and the fall from Dr Pearce's wall.

'Why not?' Richard demanded. His blue eyes were bright. As soon as I had stepped over the vicar's threshold, he had seen the scratch on my face and my tangled hair. He knew something had happened, but he would not ask me directly.

'Tell you later,' I puffed. I had no breath for a long explanation and I wanted time to think about exactly what I would tell Richard. I had a feeling, which I could not have explained, but which I thought was right, that I did not want to tell Richard the strange stories they had invented in the village about his mama. They might distress him. And I was sure, though I could not have said why, that I did not want to tell him of this newly woven fable of a favoured child, the one who was the true heir.

Richard heard the hesitation in my voice and skidded to a sudden stop and grabbed me by the arm so I swung around to face him. The rain stung my right cheek, but we were a little sheltered by the trees which overhung on the Wideacre side of Acre lane. In the field behind me the wind whistled and the rain sliced down on the self-seeded wheat and brambles.

'Tell me now,' he said.

I heard the warning note in his voice and I stood, uncomplaining, in the rain and told him of the walk to the wood and the fight with Clary and the truce we seemed to have made. I told him every single word spoken except Clary's story about Beatrice. Richard's stillness warned me that I had better sound thorough; and I was. I also omitted the taunt that I fought his battles for him. I did not tell him that Matthew had spat at the mention of his name. And I said nothing about scrumping the apples.

Richard heard me out, although the rain was making his hair curly with the damp so that he looked more like a fallen cherub than ever. 'Well done, Julia!' he said warmly when I had finished. 'You are a brave girl. I am glad that you are not afraid of Acre any more. You were quite right to tackle the children. Now you will not be afraid to come with me when I go to have my lessons.'

I glowed under his approval.

'I never minded them,' he said carelessly, 'but I am glad you have got over your fear.'

He let my arm go and turned to walk on. I hesitated only for a moment. One part of me wanted to correct him, the anxious proud voice in me which wanted to say, 'But wait, Richard, *you* were afraid. I tackled the children for *you*.' Then I thought of my grandmama's warning that a lady's place is second place, and I smiled a little secret smile, kept my peace and strode alongside him. Then the storm came down on our heads and we broke into a run and splashed up the drive in the milky puddles and dived in the back door, calling for towels and clean clothes. We were greeted by a scolding from Mrs Gough for tracking mud all over her clean kitchen floor.

4

That was the start of a friendship for me – my friendship with Clary Dench – which did so much to reconcile me to my task of becoming a young lady of Quality. Not because Clary knew my world, or cared anything for its arcane restrictions, but because with her I had an escape and a hiding-place from the standards of my mama and from the discipline I had imposed on myself by my determination to be a good daughter and, in the future, a good wife.

With Clary I could be myself. I loved her despite the differences in our lives, despite the fight at our first meeting and our regular quarrels thereafter. We forged an unquestioning friendship, in that we took enormous pleasure in each other's company without ever wondering why we liked each other so much. I just found that it suited me very well to go every morning to the vicarage with Richard, to leave him there for his lessons and then to meet Clary and spend an hour or two of my leisured empty days with her.

We often walked together, past the mill down to the Fenny. Old Mrs Green always had a smile for me now, and sometimes I would beg a twist of tea in a piece of paper from the Dower House larder, and Clary and I would go and sit by the tiny fire in the huge fireplace while Mrs Green made tea and told our fortunes in the tea-leaves. It was all a game – I think she had no real skill. She was copying what the gypsies did when they pitched their wagons on the common land for winter and came around to the houses, selling little wooden toys and whittled flowers, and offering to tell fortunes.

When the weather was good, Clary and I would walk on the

PHILIPPA GREGORY

common, or down to the Fenny. During the long hot summertime we would strip down to our shifts and bathe in the
deeper pools of the river. Neither of us could swim properly, but
if Clary held my chin above water-level with one brown hand
over my mouth to keep the water out, I could kick along for a
few yards before sinking inelegantly in splashes and gales of
laughter.

Clary was better. Within the week she could splash from one
side of the pool to the other, and she even learned to plunge
underwater and swim for half the length before coming up gasping, hair streaming. 'I must have been born with a caul!' she
said. 'I shan't never drown at any rate.'

I was lazing in the shallows, in bright sunlight, but I shivered
as if a cold wind had suddenly blown over me. A shadow came
over the sun as she spoke, and every hair on my body stood up
and pimpled the surface of my skin.

'What is it?' she asked me. 'Your face has gone all pale and
funny.'

'It's nothing,' I said hastily. I had suddenly seen her face
deathly white and her hair washing around it, and water, river
water, oozing from her mouth. 'Ugh!' I said. 'A horrid picture in
my head. Come out, come out of the water, Clary.'

'All right,' she said equably and swam towards me and heaved
herself out on to the bank to dry beside me in the sunshine, our
naked bodies as white and shiny as the breasts of doves.

'Promise me something,' I said, suddenly serious, that picture
of her face, soaked and sodden, still vivid in my mind. 'Promise
me you'll never swim alone.'

She twisted around propped on one elbow. 'Why's that, Julia?'
she asked. 'Why d'you look so odd?' And then, seeing my face,
she said, 'All right! All right! I promise. But why do you look so
strange?'

'I saw . . .' I said, but I was vague and the picture was fading
from my mind. 'I thought I saw something,' I said.

'It's the sight,' she said, portentously. 'I heard my ma talking
to Mrs Green. They were talking about you and Richard. They

say whichever one of you is the true heir is going to have the sight. One of you'll get it as soon as you're grown.'

'That's Richard,' I said definitely. I rolled on my front and picked a grass stem to chew. The pith of the stalk was as sweet as nectar.

'They say in the village that it could be you,' Clary said warningly. 'They say you're the spit of Beatrice as a girl when she used to come riding into the village with her pa. They say you're her all over again. They say that you'll be the one.'

I sat up and pulled my crumpled gown on over my head. 'No,' I said firmly. 'I wouldn't want it if it was offered to me on a plate. Richard is her son. Richard is her heir. Together we will be Laceys on the land again, but Richard will be the squire and I will be his lady. I *want* that, Clary!'

'Aye,' she nodded, and smiled her slow smile. 'Does he kiss you, Julia?'

'No, not really,' I said. 'I suppose it's not like that for Quality, Clary. He's more like a brother to me. Sometimes we're very close, sometimes we quarrel. But it's not like in novels.'

Clary looked sceptical and worldly-wise. 'Wouldn't do for me, then, Quality life,' she said boldly. 'Matthew and me hold hands and kiss often. And we've plighted our troth and carved our names in a tree, and everything. But he's not strong,' she said anxiously. 'I wish there was more money in the village. I'm afraid for him. He coughs so much in winter, his gran thought she'd never rear him.'

'Maybe he'll get work indoors,' I said helpfully. 'You say yourself he's thoughtful and clever. Maybe he'll become a clerk or something and work in Midhurst! Or even Chichester! I'd like to see you in a fine town house, Clary!'

We laughed at that, but Clary tossed her head. 'I'd not leave Wideacre,' she said. 'But my Matthew is clever enough for anything. Even when we were little children, he taught himself to read, and he's always written and read letters for people in the village. *And* he can make rhymes as good as in books.'

I nodded, impressed; and then I turned for her to button up

the back of my gown so that I could arrive at the vicarage to go home with Richard looking at least half presentable.

I had laughed off her belief in the sight and in Beatrice's heir. But the way they looked at me in the village and the story of the old god of Wideacre stayed with me all the time I was growing and trying to be an ordinary girl in the Dower House. All the time in the back of my mind was the thought of Beatrice and the dark god who came for her and the legacy of magic she had left for her special heir, whichever one of us it was.

I tried to shrug off the Acre legend. I always knew it was some fanciful version of the night of the Wideacre fire, all exaggeration and pretence. Mama had scolded me often enough for being scared out of my wits by Richard's ghost stories. I should not be made fearful by some silly village gossip.

But I could not forget it. It haunted me: the story of the man who was one of the old gods, who came for Beatrice. And Beatrice, who was the beautiful cruel goddess-destroyer. I carried that picture of her in my head, despite myself. It was so unlike Mama's version of those days – Beatrice and Harry working the land in harmonious partnership. Half a dozen times I shrugged my shoulders and told myself it was forgotten. But the horse which left flaming hoofprints up the oak stairs rode into my dreams every night.

And then I started dreaming a special dream.

It was like the other – the dream I have of the woman who was me, and the baby who must be taken to the river. But this time the woman was not me. Even in my sleep I knew I was seeing through her eyes and smiling her smile. But I knew she was not me.

I first had the special dream a few nights after Clary had held me spellbound in the woods with her fairytale. But then I dreamed it again, and again. Each time the colours were a little brighter. Each time the sounds were a little clearer – like a scene in mist which is burned off by the morning sun as you watch. Every time my heartbeat went a little faster as the terror and the delight of the dream grew stronger. Then, the night before my sixteenth birthday, I dreamed it as brightly and as vividly as if I were living it.

In the dream I was in an empty house. A large house, a beautiful house, one I had never visited in my waking life. I did not know the house, and yet it was the most familiar, the most beloved, the most precious place in the world. It was a large house, a gracious house, the home of a landowner who lived on fertile lands. I was entranced by the silence of the house, of this house which was my home. I sighed in my delight that it was at last mine, all mine, and my breath was the only thing which stirred in the great echoing hall, the only thing which moved in the still silent rooms.

I walked from room to room like a ghost, like a dream of a ghost. I was as silent as a cat, with a cat's unwinking stare, looking, looking, looking, as if I had to see everything now, every beloved inch of my home, as if I would never be able to see it again. I was printing the picture of it on my mind as if I were about to go into exile, or to fall under an enchantment. And I was imprinting myself on the place, so that this place, my home, would never, never forget me. I belonged here. I should be here for ever.

It was all so still. I made no sound, not even the quietest footfall. The silence held echoes of people who were here – but I could not be quite sure who they were. There were echoes of people who had only just left: loud voices and bitter words and the slam of a distant door. But now the house was empty. It was mine at last.

I touched things, touched like a priestess at a shrine, a worshipper of these smooth sweet things. The carved newel post at the foot of the sweep of the stairs had intricate pictures beneath my caressing fingertips, pictures of a land ripe with fertility, a cow in calf, a sheep's fleecy side, sheaves of wheat. I knew it was my land which was celebrated here in wood smelling of beeswax, and it was warm and silky as if it loved my caress.

Opposite the newel post in the shadows of the wall was a gilt mirror, and I turned from the stairs to face it. But it was not my reflection in the dark glass. It was not my childish round-faced prettiness, my light hair, my grey eyes. It was the face of a stranger, a woman I had never met in my waking life. Yet I knew her face as well as I knew my own; for in the dream that vivid chestnut hair and those slanty green eyes were my features, and her vague half-mad look was mine. I stared at the reflection of the stranger, which was my face, for long unblinking moments, and then I dropped my eyes with a secret sly smile.

Beneath the mirror was a mahogany table. I placed my palm upon it and felt the coolness of the wood warming under my touch. There was a silver bowl on the table, filled with drooping cream roses, heavy headed, looking down at their own reflections in the polished surface. I brushed one flower with the tip of a careless finger and it shed its petals in a swift flurry like a creamy snowdrift. In my head I heard a voice – a voice just like my mama's but in a tone I had never heard from her – saying, 'You are a wrecker, Beatrice.' Her voice was full of disdain.

Further up the hall was a great china bowl of pot-pourri and I stood beside it and dipped my hand in to feel the papery rose petals, the spiky lavender seeds, and bent to smell the sweet dried hay scent. The lighter petals and the dust spilled over the floor as I carelessly took a handful to sniff. It did not matter. Soon nothing would ever matter again.

A storm had been rumbling in the distance and now it was louder, rolling back over the head of the downs and coming close over the woods to this house. I thought of the two children, the little girl and the baby boy, fleeing from this house in a carriage with the rain drumming on the roof and the horses in a panic of fear at the storm. I knew they would be safe. They were on my land, and they were the bone of my bone and they were my blood. They would inherit Wideacre, and one of them would surely learn to hear the heartbeat of the land. One of them would make the magic of the harvest as I once did. One of them would be the favoured child.

The wallpaper was soft underneath my fingertips, rich. The

velvet drapes at the window of the parlour were as silky soft as the fleece of a new-born lamb. The thick glass in the windows was icy cold from the rain pouring down outside. I leaned my forehead against its coolness and smiled.

The house was filled with silence. I could hear the parlour clock tick with a light metallic tick . . . tick . . . tick. In the hall the grandfather clock had a deeper wooden tone, tock . . . tock . . . tock. And I could hear another sound. There was the deep rumble of the storm but that noise did not alarm me. Above that rumble there was another sound, a new sound. I was listening carefully for it, as sharp-eared as a rat in a dark hole.

It was the sound of many feet, bare feet, on the drive, coming to the house. I could hear it before it was more than a distant shuffle, because I was expecting to hear it. I had been waiting for it. I knew this dream; and I knew what happened next. I could not stop it. I could not halt it. There was no escape for me. For what was coming for me was my destiny. What was coming for me was rough justice. What was coming for me was the village I had tried to destroy and the man I had attacked. For I was Beatrice. Beatrice Lacey of Wideacre Hall, with a wild smile on my lips, staring into the storm-drenched darkness. I was Beatrice, waiting in the darkened house. I was Beatrice and I was alone at Wideacre, waiting for the men who were coming from Acre led by a god who was half-man and half-horse, who would ride up the oak stairs, leaving hoofprints of fire, and take me away to the secret world of his own.

I awoke in terror, but with a feeling also of mad elation, as though the world were ending, but ending by my will. The excitement and the fear drained from me as I looked around my room, and my real life – plain ordinary Julia Lacey's life – came back to me. I was no copper-headed witch. I was plain ordinary Julia Lacey in her patched nightgown in her cold room.

I turned and lay on my back and looked up at the ceiling, which was pale yellow in the spring dawn. The dream faded from me, and the richness of the colours and the delight of the textures went with it. It was a dream, it was nothing but a dream. But it left me longing to know the woman who had been Beatrice, longing to know her life and her death. And it left me confused, and somehow dissatisfied with this little house and my quiet pleasures and my bending to Richard's will and to Mama's gentle rule. It left me with a feeling that the woman who was Beatrice would never have tolerated the indoors life which I was teaching myself to enjoy. She would have snapped her fingers at it, insisted on having her own horse and ridden out every day. She would not have let her inheritance go to rack and ruin – she would have borrowed money to plant the fields, to buy stock. And her skill and determination and her magic would have made it work.

I sighed. I knew I was not like that. I was too loving and obedient to my mama to overrule her, or even to challenge what she said. And I was too much Richard's faithful betrothed to think an independent thought. It seemed I had been set in a mould before I had time to make a choice. I was a docile, ordinary young lady and I must take my little enjoyments indoors and with proper decorum.

But then I suddenly remembered what day it was, and I forgot my passing irritation with my life. Today was not a plain ordinary day at all. It was the day of my sixteenth birthday. The dream slid away from me and I jumped out of bed and pattered to the window to see what sort of day it was. I wrapped myself in a shawl and waited for my morning chocolate and for the day to begin.

I expected some changes. But I had expected slight, trivial, delightful changes. I thought that the most exciting things would be Mama coming to my room after breakfast, with her tortoise-shell hairbrushes and a box full of pins, and seating me before my little spotted looking-glass and pinning up my hair. My thick ripple of light-brown hair was to be pinned up for ever. And my skirts were to be longer. I was to be a young lady. In so far as Mama could do it – with no money, and no London season, and no ball – I was Out.

Richard banged at the door. 'Am I allowed to watch?' he called.

'Certainly not,' Mama said, her mouth full of hairpins. 'You may wait in the parlour in awed silence until we are ready.'

'I don't want Julia to look all different,' he said mutinously.

'She is going to look like a lady and not like a hoyden,' Mama said firmly. 'Now, go away, Richard!'

We heard the clatter of his boots as he went downstairs, and I met my mama's eyes in the mirror and smiled.

'I can't do it very well,' she said apologetically. 'You should really have it cut properly. But hairdressers are very dear, I'm afraid. I so wish that you could have had a party and we could have gone to the Assembly Rooms. But there is little point waiting. You are sixteen, and it has to be now, with just me as your dresser and dinner this afternoon as your coming-out ball.'

I nodded, not minding, impressed already with the changes she was making. Mama had swept up my thick mass of hair and was coiling it like a fat snake round and round and pinning it skilfully on my head. On either side of my face she parted the hair and trimmed it shorter, twisting it with her fingers into soft waves. She was intent upon my hair and did not look into the mirror to see the overall effect until she had her pins firmly in place. Then she looked up to see me and the smile faded from her face and she was suddenly pale.

'What is it?' I demanded. I was smiling; I thought myself at the very pinnacle of style.

Mama swallowed. 'It is nothing,' she said. She smiled, but she did not seem happy. 'It is that you are suddenly so grown-up,' she said. She dropped a kiss on the top of my head.

'When I was a girl, hair was worn powdered. But I think it is prettier left in its natural fairness,' she said. 'Especially in the summer when it goes lighter and you are quite fair.' She gathered up her brushes and pins and swept from the room as if she were in a hurry to leave. I watched her abrupt departure, puzzled; but then I looked back at my mirror.

I knew at once whom she had seen.

She had seen Beatrice.

I looked like the face in the dream. The plaits I usually wore had hidden the clear lines of my profile, had blurred the shape of my face. Now, with my hair swept up and the teasing little waves around my face, you could see my high cheek-bones and the odd little slant to my eyes which I had inherited – as clear as a voice calling across a generation – from my aunt. My face was still round, distressingly chubby, I thought. I smiled an experimental smile at myself in the glass. In a few years' time I could count on being pretty. But if I became beautiful, it would be Beatrice's clear loveliness shining through.

Perhaps it should have troubled me, but I was just sixteen and I wanted, more than anything else in the world, to be a pretty girl. If I had inherited the notorious beauty of Beatrice, then my delight in that outweighed my fear of the woman in the dream. I smiled again at my reflection.

I did not look so very much like the woman in the dream, I thought. I did not want to think of the dream today. Today I wanted everything to be joyful and normal and ordinary. I did not want to be a haunted Lacey heir reaching adulthood. I wanted to be Julia, finally old enough to wear her hair up, and with a very good chance of a pair of silver-backed hairbrushes of her very own wrapped in pretty paper by her place at dinner that afternoon.

'Julia! Aren't you done yet?' Richard called from the foot of the stairs. 'If you don't hurry and come, we won't get to Havering Hall and back again in time for dinner!'

'Coming!' I called back, and I looked once more at myself in the mirror and ran from the room, banging the door behind me and clattering down the uncarpeted stairs.

I had hoped that Richard would fall back on his heels at the change in my appearance. I was young enough and silly enough and vain enough to think that he might think me pretty, perhaps even beautiful. But he just grinned when he saw me. 'Very smart,' he said. 'Very grown-up. I s'pose you're too grown-up now to run through the wood to Havering and we'll have to walk around by the road?'

I grinned back and lost my disappointment in my relief that

nothing had changed between us. 'No,' I said. 'We can go through the woods. But if my hair falls down, you'll have to pin it up before we go in to Grandmama, Richard, for I've not learned how to do it yet.'

'No worse than tying knots, I suppose,' Richard said, and we stepped out of the front door into a spring day of sunlight as bright as peach wine.

Wideacre glowed like a gift for me. It had rained overnight and the buds on the trees and the grassy banks were glittering with raindrops. The hedges were pale green with buds as if someone had thrown a gauze veil over the black twigs and branches. Pale strips of clouds lay on the horizon and the sweet wind of Wideacre blew in my face, saying welcome from the land to a Lacey. To my left the downs reared up, up to the pale sky, streaked with chalk scree and covered in the sweet green colour of chalk-grown grass. And ahead of us, like a wall of tree-trunks, were the thick woods of Wideacre Park.

Without another word Richard and I turned up the drive towards Wideacre Hall and then plunged into the woods following the little track which would take us to Havering.

The Fenny was in spate, flooded with the winter rain and the bubbling little chalk springs from the downs. As we walked beside it, we said nothing, listening to it singing over the stones which glowed golden in the depths. Bits of wood, twigs and last year's brown leaves tumbled over and over in the current. We paused for a moment to toss in some bracken fronds and watch them whirl away down river, past the Greens' idle mill, over the weir, past Acre, southwards to the sea.

The bridge we used was a felled tree. Once there was a path clearly marked across it, for people from Acre used to walk this way and take the short cut over the tree-bridge to Wideacre Hall. But it had been many years since the poor of Acre would seek out a Lacey, and few people went to the hall after it was burned, except Richard and me and the Lacey ghosts. The path was overgrown and I had to pull my gown away from brambles and burrs as we walked. Mama had let down the hem for me, and I saw, as she had warned me, that I might not always relish the change.

'Wait, Richard,' I said impatiently. 'I'm going to hitch it up.'

Richard chuckled and held my coat out of my way as I kilted up my skirt. 'You're a hoyden,' he said, smiling. 'Not a young lady at all.'

'I *am* a young lady,' I said grimly, and my picture of Beatrice was bright in my mind. 'But I cannot always be a perfect young lady on Wideacre.'

I walked easier after that, and we balanced our way across the slippery tree-trunk, holding on to the branches without mishap. Then it was a stroll down a grassy ride to the Havering estate, where Grandmama congratulated me on my new hairstyle and was generous enough to overlook that my newly lengthened gown was very muddy around the hem. We stayed for a dish of tea and then Grandmama ordered the carriage out to take us home.

'We can walk, Lady Havering,' Richard said courteously.

She smiled. 'My granddaughter is a young lady today,' she said. 'I think she should certainly ride home in a carriage.'

So we arrived home in fine style in the shabby carriage with the faded crest on the door, and Mama waved to us from the parlour window and hastened out on to the front step.

'My second carriage visitor today!' she said, and her eyes were shining. 'We have a guest for dinner! You two, upstairs at once and change. I won't have you in my parlour in all your dirt. Hurry now!' And she whisked back into the parlour with a ripple of laughter as if she were a young girl, refusing to respond to our bemused faces, running from our questions.

Richard turned at once for the kitchen. The place was in chaos. The fire was burning fiercely, and Mrs Gough's white cap was askew and she was alarmingly red in the face.

'Who is here?' Richard demanded. 'Mrs Gough, who is the extra place at dinner?'

'Wait and see!' she said tersely, slapping a mound of pastry on the floured table. 'But your ma said to tell you, Miss Julia, to change into your best gown, and you are to put on your Sunday suit, Master Richard!'

'Lord Havering,' I hazarded. Mrs Gough pressed her lips together, rolled out some of the pastry and turned it a quarter of the way around to keep it smooth.

'Lady de Courcey!' Richard guessed.

'Oh, get along, do!' she said with the tolerance in her voice which was always there for Richard. 'Can't you see that I'm rushed off my feet! Go and get dressed, Master Richard! And you, Miss Julia, be a good girl and go into the yard and see if Jem is back yet. He's fetching some fruit and vegetables and some game for me from Midhurst, and I cannot get on without it!'

I nodded and went obediently to the back door, but Richard stood his ground and went on guessing. Jem still had not come, and the rising flush on Mrs Gough's pink cheeks warned even Richard that her temper was about to boil over. We made ourselves scarce, creeping through the green baize door into the hall. A gentleman's hat was on the hall table with tan gloves beside it, good-quality leather. We could hear the murmur of voices in the parlour and suddenly Mama's laugh rang out as clear as a flute. I had never heard her laugh so joyously in all my life before.

Richard would have listened at the door, but Stride came out of the dining-room and shooed us upstairs.

'Who is it, Stride?' I asked in a whisper as I hovered on the stairs.

'The sooner you are dressed for dinner, the sooner you will know,' he said unhelpfully. 'Now, go, Miss Julia!'

I dropped my muddy things on my bedroom floor and drew my new cream silk gown out of the chest. 'New to you,' Mama had said ruefully. It was cut down from an old gown from Mama's half-sister, and the seams showed pale where the colour had faded. But the main silk of the gown was shiny and yellow, bright as the heart of a primrose, and I felt taller and older as soon as the ripple of sweet-smelling silk eased in a flurry over my head. I stood on tiptoe to see as much of it as I could in my little mirror and saw how the colour made my face glow warm and my eyes show hazy and grey. Then Richard banged on my door and I spun around to slip into my best shoes and we went downstairs to see who was the guest for dinner so important that his identity was an exciting secret and Mrs Gough was allowed to buy fruit and game for his meal.

It was John MacAndrew.

I knew it the second the door opened. Not because he was standing, tall but slightly stooping, at the fireplace as close to the hot fire as he could get, needing the heat, but because I saw Mama's face, pink and rosy like a girl's, glowing with a happiness I had never seen before.

'Julia! This is . . .'

'My Uncle John!' I interrupted, and ran into the room with both hands held out to him. He beamed at my welcome and caught both hands in his and drew me to him for a hug. Then he set me back and kissed my forehead like a blessing, and stepped back to see me.

Suddenly the easy smile went cold on his lips and his pale blue eyes lost their warmth. He looked at me as if he were seeing an enemy, not his own niece. He looked over my head to Mama, who had risen from her chair and was watching his face with something like fear in her face.

'What is it, John?' she asked, her voice urgent.

'She reminded me so . . . she reminds me so . . .' he said, searching for words, his eyes fixed on my face. He looked afraid. I stepped awkwardly away from him, towards my mama, and looked to her for prompting.

'No!' she said abruptly, and I jumped at the sharpness in her voice. 'She is nothing like Beatrice!'

At the mention of her name Uncle John breathed out.

'She is not like Beatrice at all,' Mama said again, like some brave rider going for a difficult fence. 'She has quite different hair colour, quite different eyes. Quite different altogether. You have been away too long, John. You have had the picture of Beatrice in your mind for too long. Julia is not in the least like her. She is very much my daughter. She is very like me. She is naughty sometimes, and Wideacre-mad! But all children are naughty at times and it means nothing. Julia is *my* little girl. If you had seen her yesterday – before she put up her hair – you would not have thought her a young lady at all!'

Uncle John shuddered and shook his head to clear his mind. 'Of course,' he said, and he smiled at me, drawing strength from Mama's common sense. 'Of course. It was the way she ran into the parlour, and her voice, her smile, and the set of her head . . . but she will have learned that grace from you, Celia, I know.'

'I am glad you think so,' Mama said. 'For I think her a most mannerless hoyden!'

He smiled at that and I saw the warmth in his eyes which made me glad for Mama. I could see at once that he loved her. And the first picture I had – of a man stooped and tired, yellow-faced and ill – faded before the sparkle in his eyes and the way his mouth made a little secret smile as though he could not help laughing but was trying to stay serious.

'Uncle John,' I said shyly. 'Here is Richard too.'

John turned swiftly towards his son, and I saw his shoulders suddenly straighten, taking on a burden that he had long promised himself. He put out a hand as Richard came into the room, and his voice and his smile were practised. 'Richard,' he said, 'I am very glad to see you', and he put his arm around Richard's shoulders and hugged him hard, and then, still holding him, turned to Mama and laughed. 'Celia, all this while I have been picturing you with little children, and here is Richard nearly as tall as me and Julia up to my shoulder.'

Mama laughed too, and I knew that she had expected that hesitation from Uncle John and was skilfully glossing over it before it could be noticed. 'And the clothes they need! And the shoes!' she exclaimed.

'I see I shall need all my rubies and diamonds,' Uncle John beamed.

'Do you have rubies and diamonds, sir?' Richard asked quickly.

'Minefuls of 'em!' Uncle John replied promptly.

Mama beamed at him. 'We shall spend them all,' she promised. 'But do sit down now, John, and rest before Stride serves dinner. And tell us your news. You can unpack your elephants later!'

The dinner was the best that Mrs Gough could rush together and was served on the Havering china with the crest; and we used the best crystal glasses. Lady Havering had spared no trouble when Jem had been sent out again after his return from Midhurst to tell her that Dr MacAndrew was home. She had even packed a cold bottle of champagne, and we drank it with the pudding and toasted all our futures.

'We must talk, Celia,' said Uncle John when Mama rang for Stride to come and clear the plates.

'We can talk later,' she offered with a loving concerned glance at his pale face.

John summoned a smile. 'No,' he said. 'I *am* tired, and I don't mind admitting it. I had dose after dose of fever in India, and it has left me weaker than I should be. But there are things I want us to decide as a family, and I want us to decide quickly. Let's go into the parlour and have a council of war.'

'Who are we making war on, Uncle John?' I asked him with a smile as we crossed the hall to the parlour. The fire had burned down in the grate and Mama rang for fresh logs as we settled ourselves around the parlour table.

'I think we are making war on the past,' Uncle John said seriously. 'The old bad ways of thinking, and the old bad ways of doing things. I want us to remake Wideacre, and that would be a victory indeed.

'I have been a lucky man in India,' Uncle John said by way of introduction. 'I was able to do a service to one of the independent Indian princes.' He paused and smiled wryly. 'The villages under my supervision escaped an epidemic which was very serious for the rest of the country. The combination of luck and cleanliness was credited to me and he has awarded me a very large grant of land. It is good land for growing tea and spices. In addition to that there is a small mine, which is profitable now and could be expanded.'

Richard raised his head. 'A mine?' he asked. 'Mining what?'

'Opals,' said Uncle John. He smiled, but his tone was ironic. 'It seems I am to have another chance at being a wealthy man,' he said. 'I lost my last fortune on Wideacre. I shall take better care of this one!'

'Opals,' said Richard softly. He licked his lips as if they were something sweet to eat.

'I have come home to help,' Uncle John said firmly. 'I have come home to set the land right, and the people right. Wideacre is notorious. Acre men are blacklisted locally and cannot find work. The local farmers will not have fire-raisers on their land. That is a heavy legacy for a village to carry. It is Beatrice's legacy,' John said quietly. 'Poverty in Acre, hatred between village and gentry, a village notorious for violence. And a wicked inheritance for the children.'

'Uncle John,' I interrupted, but when he turned his severe face towards me, I could say little except, 'I don't understand.'

He glanced at my mama. 'You have told them nothing?' he asked.

'As we agreed,' she said steadily. 'We agreed they should not be burdened with such a past while they were young. I have told them nothing but that there was a fire and the Laceys and Acre were ruined, even though at times they pressed me for more information. I think they are ready to know the outlines of the story now.' I fancied she emphasized the word 'outlines'.

John nodded. 'Very well, then. You will have heard that the estate was farmed well by Julia's papa, the squire, and his sister, Beatrice. But that was not so. They wrung the land dry to meet mortgages to pay to change the entail so that the two of you could inherit jointly. Both Celia and I opposed them. We opposed both the changing of the entail and the planting of nothing but wheat.

'The countryside was very poor, and there were starving mobs.

One night a mob came to Wideacre Hall. We had received advance warning, and Celia and I took you children away to Havering Hall. But Beatrice decided to stay. She died in the fire. Julia's papa died of an attack of apoplexy. He always had a weak heart. It is a family weakness.'

Richard and I exchanged one long bemused look.

'Oh,' Richard said blankly. 'My mama was left all alone at the hall with the mob coming?'

'Yes,' Uncle John replied levelly. 'It was her choice, and we had not lived as husband and wife for some time. It was not my duty to make her leave, nor to stay and protect her. I considered my duty to be to protect the two of you. Beatrice elected to stay behind. She could have come in the carriage if she wished.'

There was a bowl of pale primroses on the table, and I was staring at them. Staring at them but hardly seeing them. They were wilting over the rim of the silver bowl and they reminded me of another silver bowl and the heavy heads of cream roses looking down at their reflections and my mama's voice saying so bitterly, 'You are a wrecker, Beatrice.'

They had left her in hatred. I knew it. I did not know why. But I remembered the silence of the dream and the sense of peace I had felt to know that at last they had all gone and the house was empty. That all the work and the lying and the cheating were over. And I remembered Beatrice looking down the drive, waiting for the mob.

'Did they have a leader?' I asked suddenly, thinking of the old god who was half-man, half-horse.

'No one was ever taken,' John said steadily.

'Where did they all come from?' Richard asked.

'No one ever knew,' John said again in the same level tone.

I looked up from the flowers and saw his pale-blue eyes upon me. I knew he was keeping back the truth from us. Beatrice knew the mob. I thought she even knew the man they now called a god in Acre. But I had a strong sense of grown-up secrets and long-ago fears, and I knew nothing for certain.

'What does this mean?' I asked. 'What does this all mean for us?'

'It means I want to set the estate to rights,' John said. 'It is time for a new chance for the estate. A new life for all of us. I have some detailed ideas about new crops – fruit and vegetables which we might sell in Chichester or London. And I want us to try to share the profits with the village. That will bring them back to work, and draw them into the new century which is coming.

'I have been following the events in France,' John said, and his eyes were bright with enthusiasm. 'I truly believe that there is a new age coming, a time when people will work together and share the wealth. A time of science and progress and a brushing away of old restrictions and superstitions. The new age is truly coming, and I want Wideacre to be part of it!'

We were all silent, a little overwhelmed by Uncle John's fervour, and also by the prospect of a changed Wideacre.

'Julia will have a proper season,' my mama said slowly. John nodded.

'And the hall can be rebuilt,' Richard said.

'Rebuilt, and the parkland refenced, and the estate growing and fertile again,' John confirmed.

'And no more poverty in the village,' I said, thinking of the children and the parish overseer due for another visit to take paupers away to the mills in the north.

'That is my first priority,' Uncle John said.

There was a silence while we absorbed the fact that all our dreams might be a reality.

'I am counting on all of you,' Uncle John said. 'I shall find a manager to run the farmland. But I shall need all your advice and support. This is your inheritance we are setting to rights, Richard, Julia.' He nodded gravely to each of us in turn. 'I shall need your help.'

'Shall I not go to university, sir?' Richard asked eagerly.

John smiled, his eyes suddenly warm. 'You most certainly shall,' he said firmly. 'The time for squires who know nothing but their crops is long gone. You shall go to Oxford, and Julia shall go to Bath for the season and to London also. There will be time enough during the summer months for you to work on the land.'

'Good,' said Richard.

Uncle John looked at me. 'Does that suit you, Miss Julia?' he said with an affectionate, jesting tone.

I beamed at him. 'Yes,' I said. 'Yes, indeed. Ever since I first made friends in the village I have been longing for the day when it would be possible to put it right. I am very, very happy.'

Uncle John exchanged a long look with my mama. 'Then we are all content,' he said. 'And *now* I shall unpack my bags and see if I have remembered to bring you all anything from my travels!'

Uncle John set himself out to please us at supper. We were all still strange with him. Mama was anxious and loving, and I was shy, showing my country-bred awkwardness; but Richard was as relaxed and as charming as only he knew how to be. Uncle John sat at the head of the table in Richard's seat and smiled on us like the father of a fine family. He had unpacked his presents and had some wonderful yards of silk and muslin for Mama and me, as well as a slim velveteen box for Mama.

He pushed it towards her when Stride had cleared the plates, and he smiled mysteriously when she asked, 'What is it, John?'

She opened the catch and drew out a necklace. It was exquisite. They were matched pearls, hatched from oysters in the warm waters of oceans thousands of miles from Wideacre, each one a perfect, smooth sphere.

'But they're pink!' exclaimed Mama as she held them up to the candlelight.

'Pink pearls,' Uncle John said with satisfaction. 'I know pearls are your favourites, Celia, and I could not resist them. There are matching ear-rings too.'

'Wherever did you find them?' she exclaimed. 'Oh! India, I suppose.'

'And the devil's own job I had getting them!' John said, his face quite serious. 'Pearl-diving every Sunday after church in a shark-infested sea is no joke, Celia, I can tell you.'

Mama gave a gurgle of laughter, sounding as delighted as a courted girl at his nonsense, and put the necklace around her neck. I waited as she fumbled with the catch in case Uncle John would put them on her. But he was deliberately holding back from playing the part of her lover before our bright curious gazes.

'They're wonderful,' she said with pleasure. 'Must I save them for best?'

'No!' John said. 'You shall have finer things for "best", Celia, I promise you. This is just a home-coming present, for everyday wear.'

She smiled down the table at him, her eyes very warm. 'I shall wear them every day then,' she said. 'And when they do not match my gown, I shall still keep them on. And nothing you buy me in future could be finer for me than the present you brought home when you were safe home at last.'

John was silent as their eyes met and held.

'I believe that pearl-fishing is very cruel to the natives,' Richard observed.

Uncle John glanced at him. 'In general it is,' he said. 'It happens that these pearls grow in relatively shallow waters and the divers work for a man who trains them well and cares for their health. I would not have bought them otherwise.'

There was a little silence. Richard, ousted from his old place at the head of the table, looked at the tablecloth as if the pattern were new to him.

'Uncle John,' I said tentatively, 'what is that package?'

'What is that package indeed!' Uncle John said, recalled to business with a start. 'As if you did not know, little Miss Lacey, that it has your name on the front!' He pushed it across to me and I unwrapped it. It was a fine box of watercolours, and Uncle John smiled at my thanks and then gave a rueful chuckle when Mama said he might have saved his money, for all I could ever be prevailed upon to draw was field plans and landscapes.

'Richard is the artist of the household,' Mama said gently. 'He has a great interest in fine buildings and classic sculpture.'

'Is he?' John said, smiling approvingly at his son.

'But perhaps such a lovely box of colours and a palette will encourage you, Julia,' Mama said, prompting me.

'It shall,' I promised. 'And you are a very dear uncle to bring me such a lovely gift.' I rose from my chair and went to him and gave him a kiss on his tired, lined forehead, which was both a kiss of thanks and a half-apology for not being the indoors pretty-miss niece he had imagined.

'What has Uncle John given you, Richard?' I asked, for Richard's parcel stood in the corner of the room, a pole as high as his chest with a fascinating knobby bit at the foot. Richard tore at the wrapping and out came some sort of mallets – a pair of them – and half a dozen hard heavy balls. He glanced at his father in bewilderment and hefted the mallet in his hands.

'Polo sticks and balls,' said Uncle John. 'Ever seen it played, Richard?'

Richard shook his head.

'It's a wonderful game for a good horseman, and an exciting game for a poor one! We can hire a couple of horses until we find a decent hunter for you, and I will have a knock with you.'

I think no one but I would have noticed Richard's sudden pallor. John's eyes were bright as he explained to Richard how the game was played, and the speed and the danger, while Stride brought in the fruit and sweetmeats and port. Uncle John and Richard passed the decanter civilly, one to another, and Mama smiled to see the two of them learning to be friends.

We left them still talking horses and withdrew to the parlour. Mama went straight to the mirror over the fireplace and smoothed her hair with a little smile at her own reflection. I watched her in silence. It was the first trace of vanity I had ever seen in her, and I smiled. In the reflected image, lit by the best beeswax candles sent from the Havering store, the picture was a kind one. Her delight in Uncle John's return had smoothed the lines off her forehead and around her eyes like a warm iron on cream silk. Her brown eyes were velvety with happiness, the grey in her fair hair was all that betrayed her age. And her widow's cap was pinned so far back on her head that it was just a scrap of lace on her chignon. She saw my eyes on her and coloured up, and turned from the mirror with a smile.

'I am so glad they can at least talk horses,' she said. 'I was afraid that they would have nothing in common. It matters so much that they should be friends.'

I nodded and tucked myself up on the window-seat, drawing the curtains to one side so I could see the drive, eerie in the silver light of the moon, bordered by the shadowy woods. A wind was moving in the upper branches like a sigh for a life which had all gone wrong.

Inside the house the candlelight was warm, yellow. Mama moved a candelabra closer to light her sewing. But outside in the darkness and the moonlight, the land remembered. And it called to me.

I fell into a dreamy reverie, sitting there, my face to the cool glass and my eyes staring out into the shadows. I knew that Uncle John had told us only half of the story. I felt certain that the woman in the dream was Beatrice at the hall. And she had *known* – I had dreamed her certainty – that the mob was led by a man she knew. They were coming from Acre, and she had earned their anger.

I knew also that they hated her in Acre no more. They had forgotten the frozen seasons when her shadow had meant death and the young men had feared her. They remembered now the smiling girl who had brought them hayfields and wheatfields thicker and taller than had ever grown before. And staring out into the cold moonlit garden I longed to be a girl like that. With my back to the little parlour and Mama bending over her stitchery, I longed with all my heart to be someone who could make the land grow and could bring Acre back to life. I suppose for the first time that evening I faced the fact that I wanted to be the favoured child.

I sat so still, and in such a dream, that I jumped when the parlour door opened and the two of them came in. Richard saw the night and the moonlight in my face and he raised an eyebrow at me as if he were listening for the wind. But he could hear nothing. It was a night for talking about horses and for travellers' tales from Uncle John, and for reminiscences of the time when the land was easy and good. It was very late before we went to bed. But when I was in bed, I did not dream of the hall and the rioters coming through the darkness. I dreamed of new gowns and ballrooms, like any young girl who has just become a young lady.

5

Living with Uncle John was not all delight, as Richard and I discovered over the next few days. He ordered us each into the parlour and took us through a galloping examination to test our abilities and our learning to date. I was foolish enough to boast that I had learned Latin and Greek over Richard's shoulder, and had two pages to translate for my pains. I had been confident about my French accent, but John rattled away at me and I could catch only one word in twenty and only managed to stammer a reply. Poor Richard fared even worse and came out of the parlour red-faced and seething. He muttered something about people coming back from India and throwing their weight around like nabobs – and flung himself out. I took myself into the dining-room with Richard's school-books and my pride much humbled.

That evening Uncle John announced that he had to go to London to see his papa, the senior director of the MacAndrew Shipping Company. 'I am to serve as the company consultant on our Indian affairs,' he explained. 'But while I am there – consulting away – I shall make a final choice of the best man to be our manager here on Wideacre.' He nodded to my mama. 'Can I bring you anything back from London, Celia? Some patterns for gowns perhaps?'

Mama glanced down at her well-worn dark dress. 'I badly need some new gowns,' she admitted. 'And Julia has never had a new dress in her life, poor child! But I do not trust you to choose our fashions, John!'

'I should bring you back scarlet saris,' John said at once. 'They're what the Indian ladies wear. Quite ravishing the two of you would look, I assure you.'

'Possibly,' Mama said, laughing, 'but I would rather Julia made her Bath début in something a little more conventional. I have written to my old sempstress at Chichester to run us both up a couple of gowns to keep us going until I can consult her properly. Bring nothing back but your dear self. And don't work too hard.'

Uncle John was ready to leave as we rose from the breakfast table the next morning. 'I cannot say how long I will be,' he said, shrugging himself into his greatcoat. 'But while I am away, you will all be busy enough. Richard – I want you to work harder at your studies. You will have no chance at Oxford unless you can show them a higher standard than I have seen thus far.

'I do not blame Dr Pearce; there is no one to blame but you, Richard,' Uncle John said, opening the door and taking Richard's arm as he walked down the garden path in the pale spring sunshine. 'You have not sufficiently applied yourself. If you hope to make your own way in the world, landed squire or no, you must learn to concentrate. I cannot say I am pleased with your progress. Why, Julia's Latin is as good as your own, and she is only learning by proxy!'

Richard, sunny-tempered Richard, smiled his angelic smile at his papa and said, 'I am sorry, sir. I dare say I should have worked harder. My cousin puts me to shame, I know. She has always been quick-witted.'

His words were a reprieve for me, for I had feared he would be offended by the comparison. Uncle John smiled at Richard's generosity as he got in the coach and waved goodbye to us all and left for London.

But Richard's sunny humour lasted only until the coach was out of sight. As soon as it had gone, he announced he was going to do some studying in the parlour. At once I turned back to go into the house with him.

'Not with you,' he said roughly. 'You will chatter and distract me. Go and sit with your mama. You heard what Papa said, he wants me to work harder. I will never get on if you are always wanting to talk to me or for me to come out for a walk with you.'

'Richard!' I said amazed. 'I was only coming to help you with your work.'

'I don't need your help,' he said untruthfully. 'A fine pickle I should be in if I depended on your understanding. Go and sit in the parlour with your mama, Julia. I am working hard to please my papa.'

I went without another word, but I thought him unjust. And I knew that it would take him twice as long without me to look up the words for him. I said nothing to Mama about that low-voiced exchange, but after I had finished some darning for her, I asked if I might go to the kitchen and make some of Richard's favourite bon-bons as a reward for him for his sudden application to his studies. At dinner I had a little dish of creams for him, and then I had his thanks in one of his sunny smiles and a careless hug outside the door of my room at bed-time. I went to bed warmed by that smile and happy to be restored to his good graces. And I felt I had learned once again that a lady's way is to return hard words with a smile, until everything is at peace again. It always works. Provided you can smile for long enough.

We heard nothing from John for three long days, but on Friday morning, looming out of a miserable unseasonal mist, his carriage came quietly up the drive. Mama and I dropped our sewing to the floor in the parlour and tumbled out down the garden path to greet him. Uncle John swung down from the carriage and caught my mama up to him for a great hug and a smacking kiss which could have been heard on the coast.

'Celia!' he said, and they beamed at each other as if nothing more needed saying.

Uncle John gave me a smile and a quick wink over my mama's head. 'And Miss Julia too!' he said with pleasure. 'But let's get in! You two will freeze out here in this beastly weather. It has been foggy all morning. I stopped at Petersfield last night – simply could not see my way further forward! Otherwise I should have been with you yesterday!'

Mama ushered him into the parlour and rang the bell for more logs for the fire and hot coffee. Uncle John held his thin hands to the blaze and shivered a little.

'I thought I was home for summer!' he complained. 'This is as damp as an Indian monsoon.'

'Julia, go and fetch your uncle's quilted jacket,' Mama asked me. 'And perhaps a glass of brandy, John?'

I ran to his bedroom at the top of the house for his jacket, then to the kitchen to tell Stride about the brandy and when I came back, Mama had him settled in a chair drawn up to the blaze and the colour was back in his cheeks.

'Where's Richard?' he asked as Mama poured coffee and Stride heaped more logs on the fire.

'At his lessons,' Mama said. 'He has been studying like a scholarship boy ever since you left! Do remember to praise him, John. He took your reproof to heart.'

'Shall I go and fetch him?' I asked. 'Sometimes he stays late, but I know he would want to come home if he knew Uncle John was back.'

'Yes,' said John. 'Do! For I have some rough drawings for the rebuilding of the hall with me and I can hardly wait to show them to you all. And that's not all!' he said, turning to my mama. 'We have an estate manager! I dropped him off at the village before coming here. You may meet him as you walk through, Julia. His name is Mr Megson, Ralph Megson.'

There was a noise in my head like a crystal glass splitting, and then I heard a sweet high humming, which seemed to come from the very trees of Wideacre Park as they leaned towards the house. The mist seemed to be singing to me, the hills hidden in the greyness seemed to be calling. I shook my head to clear my ears, but I could still hear the sound. A sweet high singing like a thousand leaves budding.

'That's very quick!' said my mama, impressed. 'However have you managed so well?'

'Skill and efficiency,' Uncle John said promptly; and Mama laughed. 'Pure luck, actually,' he confessed. 'I had placed an advertisement and I had two replies, but the bad reputation of Wideacre is still very much alive, I am afraid, and no suitable agent seemed likely to appear. I had just decided on the one who seemed the least likely to cause difficulties when a message was sent up to my room that another man had come for the job.

'In he came,' Uncle John said, smiling, 'and proceeded to interview *me* as to my plans for Wideacre. When I had passed what seemed to be a series of tests by assuring him that I was not looking for a swift sale and profit and that, on the contrary, I was interested in farming it as a model estate with a profit-sharing scheme, he was gracious enough to tell me he would take the post. When I said that I was not sure if he was the man for me, he gave a little chuckle and said, "Dr MacAndrew, I am the *only* man for you."'

'How odd!' said Mama, diverted. 'Whatever did he mean?'

'It emerged that he is of old Acre stock, though he left the village when he was a lad,' John explained. 'He seems to think he has friends in Acre still and he claims – I must say I believe him – that he can talk the village round to working for the Laceys again. But he prides himself on being a man of some principles, and that was why I suffered the inquisition. He would not get them back to work if there were any chance of us becoming absentee landlords, or selling the estate to a profiteer.'

Mama nodded, but she hesitated. 'When did he leave?' she asked diffidently.

Uncle John heard the uneasiness in her voice and smiled. 'I asked him that, my dear,' he said gently. 'He is about our age, and he left when he was but a lad. He was gone before the old squire was killed in his riding accident. He was not working in Acre when Beatrice was running the estate. He was far away when the riot took place.

'Besides,' he added, 'he's certainly a radical, but not a hell-raiser by any means. He has strong ideas against property and against landlords, but they are nothing more than sensible people have been thinking for some time. He's not a firebrand. He's travelled. He's a man of experience. I get the feeling he is anxious to come home to his roots and live in a prosperous village. We have much in common.'

'Where will he live?' I asked, visualizing Acre in my mind.

'Is there a family called the Tyackes?' John asked.

'Yes!' I replied.

'He asked most particularly after their cottage,' Uncle John said. 'I think, when he was a lad, it may have been the best cottage in the village, and he has had his heart on it all these years. Julia, do you know them? Would they move?'

I nodded. 'There's only Ted Tyacke and his mother now,' I said. 'The cottage is too big for them. Ted's father was hurt in an accident, felling trees, and he died last year. Since then they've been struggling. If we could offer them a smaller property – perhaps that little cottage by the church which is empty – and a little present of some money, they'd be glad enough to go, I think.'

Uncle John nodded, and he looked at me, somehow measuring me. 'Whose cottage is it by the church?' he asked as if he were testing Richard in Greek grammar.

'It *was* the Lewes family's,' I said. 'But a year ago they went back to Petworth where his brother has a shop.'

'All the Acre history,' John said to Mama, raising his eyebrows.

'Julia knows the village better than all of us,' she confirmed.

'Well, if you see Mr Megson, you may tell him what you have told me about the Tyackes,' John said. 'And if he can arrange it to everyone's satisfaction, he may have their cottage.'

'May I go now, Mama?' I asked.

'Yes,' she said. 'But wear your cloak with the hood up against the mist, my dear. Who would believe we were in spring with this weather!'

I fetched my hat and my winter coat and went outside into the greyness. It had seemed dark and forbidding from the parlour window, but to walk in the mist was a strange pleasure. I could not hear my footsteps, they were so muffled by the fog. The beech leaves which had been so rustling and noisy only yesterday were now damp and silent. In the distance I could just hear the Fenny as it slithered over grey stones, but the loudest sound in the sheltered overhung lane was the steady drip, drip, drip as the beech trees collected mist on their clinging fresh leaves and distilled it into drops which fell with cold explosions on the hood of my cloak. I could not see the old fields on either side of the track. I could only sense the grey space of them and see the mist rolling off their damp sides to coil through the roots of the hawthorn hedge. I could not see the outline of the downs at all. There was not even a trace of the darker forehead of the land against the sky. It was all a universal greyness like a pale blanket held up before my eyes. There was nothing in the whole world but me, and the dripping trees, and the paler sticky streak of the chalk lane leading me towards Acre, taking me, so confidently and surely, to where I wanted to go on my homeland.

The walk was like a little excursion into dreamland, into the loneliness which everyone dreads. A world in which you are the only living thing and a cry would not be heard. But it was not a fearful walk for me. I am never afraid alone on Wideacre. However much of a silly girl I sometimes seem to my mama, however much I irritate Richard, when I am alone on Wideacre I am sure-footed.

It is not a place for words, and I am so clumsy with words. It is a place for sensing whether or not the land is easy. And self-seeded and running wild though Wideacre is, it is an easy land for the Laceys. When I am alone on Wideacre, I am a Lacey through and through.

I was almost sorry when the mist thinned, broken up by the little shanties at the start of the village. Then a shape came at me out of the fog and made me gasp with fright.

''Sme,' said Clary Dench. Her speech was muffled by a great square of oatmeal cake which she was cramming into her mouth. 'Hello, Julia.' Her eyes were shining with excitement over her fist. ''Ve you come to see him?' she demanded. 'He's gone to Midhurst to buy some things at the market.'

'See who?' I asked, but I had already guessed the answer.

'Ralph,' she said. 'Ralph's back, and he brought a great box of food with him, but he says we can't eat it all at once or we'll be sick. He gave everyone oatmeal cakes, and then he went to Midhurst to buy milk and bacon and cheese, and ale, and all sorts. We're going to have a party when the food is ready. My pa says it's all going to be different now Ralph's back.'

'He came home with Uncle John,' I volunteered. 'He's going to be the Wideacre estate manager. But who is he, Clary? Has he been gone long?'

Clary's eyes were alight with mischief. 'Don't you know who he is? Nor what he did?' she demanded. 'Oh! Oh!' and she gave a little wriggle of pure delight. 'Julia! There's no use looking at me like that, I can't tell you. You'll have to ask him yourself.'

'Was it something in the old days?' I asked intuitively. 'Did he know Beatrice and Harry? Did he work here before?'

Clary snorted on a laugh and crammed the last morsel of oatcake in. 'Can't tell you,' she said.

I curbed my impatience as Clary tucked her cold hand into my pocket and fell into pace beside me. 'Where has he been all this time?' I asked. 'Uncle John said he was an Acre man.'

'He's been a smuggler,' she said in an awed undertone. 'And he's led a bread riot. He lived with the gypsies for years, and he can do magic and tell fortunes. He used to send money to the village when times started getting hard. And it was him . . .' she broke off and bit her lip. 'I can't tell you any more,' she said again. 'You'll have to ask him yourself.'

'I will, then,' I said. 'I am sick to death of all these mysteries.'

We had reached the vicarage gate and Clary stood on the bottom rung as I swung it open.

'Wait for me,' I invited. 'And you can walk home with me and Richard.'

'Nay,' she said with the slow drawl which is the voice of Acre insolence. 'Richard has no time for a village girl. I'll see you when you next come to Acre.'

I nodded. I could not defend Richard against a charge of arrogance. I had tried to make him friends with the Acre village children when we had all been young together. But Richard had prickled up and become lordly; and they had become surly and rude, and then riotous and cheeky. It was odd to me that Richard's manners – so flawless in my grandmama's drawing-room, and so popular even in the kitchen of the Dower House, should desert him so utterly when he was faced with Clary or Ted or any of the Acre children. I think he did not care enough for them to try to charm them. All he expected from them was a minimum of civility, and all he offered them was one of his calculating looks as if he were wondering what they might do for him.

'Anyway,' Clary said conclusively, 'I want to help get Ralph Megson's party ready.'

She nodded towards the church and I saw the porch door open and men coming out carrying the trestle-table which is stored there. Then I saw, for the first time ever, smoking chimneys in Acre. The women had lit the fires and were getting ready to cook food and boil water; and for once there was food for the pot and fuel for the fire.

I lingered and Clary grinned at me. 'Go on,' she said, and gave me a push towards the chilly gentility of the vicar's house. 'You're gentry! Go away!'

I made a face at her to express my disappointment at missing the bustle of preparation, and to register my protest at being called gentry. Then I went up the path to the vicar's front door.

It opened at my knock and the housekeeper let me in. Richard was still at his studies and I waited in the parlour and drank coffee and ate sweet biscuits until he should be ready. It seemed so odd: to be here in the warm with a little fire in the grate and some arrowroot biscuits on the table when only yards from the garden gate there were families who had been hungry for years. I thought I understood why Dr Pearce's hair was so very white and why he seldom smiled. Every death in the village he noted in the parish register. Every little child's coffin was lowered into the open grave at his feet. And there were more mothers with naked grief in their faces than there were answers in his theology.

In the Dower House we were at a small remove from Acre; but here in the heart of the village the cruelty of the Laceys – the cruelty of a nation divided into the wealthy and the weak – was inescapable.

The parlour door opened and Richard came in, tightening a strap around his books. 'Julia!' he said, pleased. 'I didn't expect to see you here.'

'I thought I'd walk to meet you,' I said. 'Uncle John has come home, and I knew you would want to know. He's brought some drawings for Wideacre Hall with him, and a new manager for the estate!'

'Did you see the man?' Richard asked. 'What's he like?'

'He didn't come to the house; Uncle John dropped him off in Acre,' I said. 'He lived here some years ago. I met Clary Dench on my way in, and she says they're all set to have a party to welcome him home. He has gone to Midhurst to buy some food, and he has given oatcakes to all the young people. Everyone seems to like him.'

'I should think they would if he's handing out free food,' said Richard disdainfully. 'That's not the way to manage Acre! I hope my papa has not chosen the wrong man for the work.'

'We may see him,' I said. 'Clary said he went into Midhurst as soon as he arrived. He may be back by now.'

Richard nodded and held open the gate for me. We turned out on to Acre's only street, the chalk-mud lane I had tracked through the fog this morning, keeping our eyes open for signs of the stranger.

We need not have been alert. You could tell a difference had come over Acre by one glance down the little street. It had been a deserted lane flanked with blank-windowed hovels, but now it was a village alive with bustle and excitement. I thought of the kiss of the prince in the fairytale of Sleeping Beauty and decided Ralph Megson must be a magician that Acre should come alive again at his touch.

They had set up the trestle-table outside Mrs Merry's cottage and the carter's wagon was beside it. He had a horse between the shafts again, and his swarthy face was set in hard lines to restrain a grin of delight. Men and women were gathered around, unloading and laying the table. It was the first time in years that Acre had worked for a common aim, and I suddenly saw the familiar individuals anew: as a skilled working unit. It was the first time I had ever heard laughter in Acre other than the bitter ring of savage humour at another misfortune.

Cottage doors were banging as people ran into their homes to bring out a pair of knives or a wooden platter. A travelling trunk, which I guessed belonged to Ralph Megson, had been tossed down in Mrs Merry's unplanted vegetable patch and gaped open, a hessian bag of tea and one of sugar, a great round cheese and a massive haunch of ham on the top. It was an open invitation to thievery, but I somehow knew that Acre was a village of thieves no more. Mrs Merry's cottage chimney blew a plume of smoke at the sky like a flying flag to say, 'Ralph Megson is come home' to the billowing roof of clouds which had watched over Acre's ruin. And amid it all, sending children scurrying for spring flowers and buds to decorate the table, hammering the carter on the back, hugging Mrs Merry and – I gaped – actually snatching up sad-faced Mrs Green for a great smacking kiss, amid it all was the new estate manager like a dark god dropped out of a stormy sky to set Acre to rights.

He was a man of about forty years of age, his hair black, but greying at the temples, cropped short with just a little plait at the back like sailors wear. He looked like a sailor – no, truly, he looked like a pirate. His skin was as brown as a gypsy's, and the pale lines around his eyes suggested he had been watching in bright sunlight for many years.

His clothes were plain but well made in brown homespun; and his linen was as fine as a gentleman's, with a very plain low cravat at his throat. He stood on the cart, legs planted firmly astride, and he was like a maypole with people dancing around him.

I had a humming in my head sweet and clear and getting louder all the time. I could not take my eyes from him.

'Good God,' said Richard beside me. We stood still, in an Acre we had never known. A buzzing purposeful community, busy as a hive, joyful as a May Day fair.

The new manager stretched out a hand to one of the men on the ground and hauled him up on to the cart beside him to help hand down the food he had bought in Midhurst. As he moved, I saw for the first time why he was standing astride so still. He was a cripple. He had virtually no legs. They had been cut off at the knees and his breeches were cut short and tucked into two wooden legs. Now I understood why his shoulders were so broad and his chest so strong. He had spent many years supporting himself with crutches to keep himself steady on the unsafe peg-legs. As soon as I saw his awkwardness with the legs and the way he staggered when the cart moved, I could hear nothing in my head but the singing noise, and see nothing but him. Nothing but him at all. I forgot all my speculation about who he was and what he meant to Wideacre and I said in a voice of utter pity, and I said aloud, which was worse, 'Oh, Ralph!'

He spun around at my voice, his face suddenly white under the tan colour of his skin. He stared and stared at me and, as his eyes met mine, I heard the sweet singing grow louder until the noise of Acre and even Richard's sharp voice quite blotted out and I was in the dream itself, and I was Beatrice in waking life. Beatrice was coming and coming with every note of the singing and with every hazy moment until the crowd between us melted away and I could see nothing and know nothing, not even Richard. All I saw was Ralph, and I saw him with Beatrice's loving, beloved eyes.

'Oh, Ralph,' I said again, in her voice which was now my voice.

An odd, almost rueful smile was on his face as he looked at me and heard me speak his name like an old familiar lover. He grasped the side of the cart and got down nimbly, well accustomed to the clumsiness of his wooden legs. Someone handed him his crutches and he tucked one under each arm and came towards me. The crowd made way for him as if he were a Stuart prince back from exile over the water; and they watched the two of us as if we were making magic in some secret ritual.

He was pale around his black eyes, and his nostrils were flared as if he were smelling the air for smoke. He looked wary. He looked at me as if I were his destiny and he had to screw up his courage to come through the crowd and face me.

'Who are you?' he said, staring and staring at my face under the unfashionable bonnet overshadowed by the hood.

His voice broke the spell for me, and I was suddenly aware of the bright curious glances of the crowd, and Richard, scandalized, at my side.

'I am Julia Lacey, Miss Julia Lacey,' I said. The words were commonplace, my voice was my own, a schoolgirl's voice, prim. It was not the languorous passionate voice which had said, 'Oh, Ralph!' to him on greeting. He dipped his head as he recognized the change in my tone.

'A Lacey?' he said, apparently trying to recollect something.

'I am the daughter of the late Sir Harry Lacey of Wideacre Hall,' I said formally. 'This is my cousin, Richard MacAndrew.'

Mr Megson nodded, having placed us in his mind. 'Harry's daughter,' he said and looked at me, half incredulous. 'Who would have thought that pudding could have bred so fair? But you're a Lacey, right enough. And as like . . .' he broke off before he said a name. I knew he was thinking of Beatrice, and I was aware that he had the discretion to leave his sentence unfinished.

He turned instead to Richard. 'So you're Beatrice's lad,' he said. I felt Richard stiffen and I put a gentle hand on his sleeve. I could feel the warmth of his arm through the cloth and he seemed to me too hot. I did not want Richard in a temper. I did not want him to fly up into the boughs with Mr Megson. No one knew better than Richard how to charm with one smile. But he could also turn a potential friend into an enemy with one of his challenges. Richard was a proud boy, irked by our poverty and ready to fight for his honour. I admired that bright pride in him, but I felt anxious, just this once, that he might try to demand respect from Ralph Megson. Mr Megson did not seem to me to be a man who would be easily rebuked.

'Richard,' I said softly. 'This is Mr Megson. Uncle John's new manager, you know.'

Richard nodded. 'I am Dr MacAndrew's son,' he said to Ralph. 'Your employer is my papa.'

One dark eyebrow was cocked at once at Richard's tone. Ralph nodded. 'You don't take after the Laceys,' he said. 'They're mostly fair.'

Richard said nothing. I could tell he was taking Ralph's measure. 'How do you know the Laceys?' Richard demanded abruptly. 'And how come you're so fêted in Acre?'

Ralph smiled, but did not seem to think Richard's question worth answering. 'You'll excuse me,' he said politely. 'I've a dinner to prepare.' And he turned his back on us as if Richard were of no importance at all, and took a helping hand to haul himself back on the cart. He took a tray of fine white bread rolls from the man on the cart and handed them to the carter's wife with a gentle word to her. 'Mind that, Margaret,' he said and his voice was kind. 'It's heavy.'

Richard gave a quick exclamation and pushed past one of the Green sons and jumped up on the cart. 'Now, see here, fellow,' he said, his voice a furious whisper. Few people could have heard him, but no one could have missed the tension on the cart. All the activity up and down the lane stopped at once and all the faces turned to look. Richard had moved too fast for me to stop him and I could not call him back.

'See here,' he said furiously. 'This is *my* land, and *my* village, and if you try and come between me and the land you'll be sorry. I'm the heir to Wideacre and I shall be the squire here when I'm of age. When I ask a question from one of my workers, I expect an answer. I expect an answer and I expect a handle to my name. Is that clear, Megson?'

Ralph had not stopped working, and he swung around with a sack of oatmeal in his arms. He buffeted into Richard and the blow pushed Richard backwards off the cart to sprawl on the ground. I started forward, but Sonny Green stayed me with an arm barring my way. Ralph swung himself down off the cart and grabbed Richard's elbow and pulled him to his feet like a child. Richard's face was scarlet with rage, and he stammered with temper and could get no words out.

'Eh, I'm sorry, lad,' Ralph said carelessly. 'I didn't know you were up on the cart behind me.' He kept Richard's hand and pulled him a little closer so that he spoke for his ears alone. 'You may be the heir,' he said softly, 'but you'll never be squire until you can be loved in Acre. And you'll make no way here until you show respect.'

Richard was blank with an expression I could not read. I ducked under Sonny Green's arm to get to him.

'Richard, let's go,' I said urgently, but he did not hear me. His inky-blue eyes were fixed on Ralph Megson's face with a hot intensity.

'You insulted me!' he exclaimed.

Ralph's face was dark for an instant, but then it cleared. 'Nay, lad,' he said kindly. 'You got what was coming to you. You're fratched now, but think it over, you'll see you were in the wrong.' He turned his back on Richard as if the heir to Wideacre were nothing more than an impertinent schoolboy, and he reached his hands up to the men on the cart for them to haul him up again.

Richard started forward and I grabbed his arm and held him back. He was incoherent with anger. 'I will kill him . . .' he started.

'Richard, everyone is looking at you!' I hissed.

It worked.

Richard shook me off, but he did not rush at the cart. He looked around at the bright curious faces and he took a deep breath, then he took my arm in a protective gesture and nodded dismissively at Ralph's back, and at the crowd around the cart. We swept through them like a play-acting king and queen in a travelling theatre; and they parted to let us through. Richard looked straight before him, blinded by his rage, but I glanced to left and to right with a half-smile of apology.

I saw Clary Dench openly grin at me, and I realized how ridiculous we seemed. If I had been less wary of Richard and his anger, I should have laughed out loud. We proceeded like dukes in ermine until the bend in the road hid us and Richard dropped my hand at once.

I expected him to rage, but he was quiet. 'Richard, I am sure he meant no harm . . .' I started.

Richard's look at me was icy. 'He threw me in the road!' he said softly. 'I'll never forget that.'

'He just bumped you by accident,' I said. 'And he got down at once to help you up.'

Richard looked at me blackly, and he turned for home at a fast pace. I followed in his wake at a trot.

'He did say sorry,' I offered. Richard hardly heard me.

'He insulted me,' I heard him say in an undertone. 'He'll be sorry.'

'He is Uncle John's new manager,' I said warningly. 'Uncle John needs him to run Wideacre. If he is the right man for the job, then we all need him to run Wideacre for us. We saw today that he can make Acre work as one, and he might be the only man who can save Wideacre.'

'I don't care,' said Richard. 'This is more important than any manager for the estate. He insulted me before all of Acre. He should be punished.'

I pulled up short at that. 'Nothing is more important than Wideacre,' I said. 'There is nothing more important than getting Acre working.'

Richard paused in his long strides to stand still and look at me. The mist swirled around us so that we were as ghostly as the trees leaning over our heads. I shivered from the cold and the damp. Richard's eyes had a radiance about them.

'He insulted me,' Richard said. 'He insulted me before all Acre. I won't stand for that. He must apologize to me for that. He has challenged me, and I must win.'

'Richard,' I said uneasily, 'it was not as bad as that! It was not as serious as that!'

'It is a matter of honour. You would not understand that, for you are a girl. But my papa and I know that it is vital that the gentry retain their control over the mob. I shall tell him at once.'

While I hesitated, thinking about whether Acre was a 'mob', thinking about whether Mr Megson was part of a 'mob', Richard turned for the lights of home, banged open the front gate and bounded up the four steps to the garden path. The door was open and he pushed it and was gone. I followed more slowly. I had done all I could to prevent him telling Uncle John, and had earned a scolding for my pains. I gritted my teeth on a spurt of temper. I trusted my judgement with the people of Acre. I trusted my judgement with Mr Megson. I did not think Richard had been insulted. I thought he was behaving like a fool. I thought he had acted like a fool. And I did not see that his precious honour was concerned in the least.

But then I checked myself. My grandmama had warned me, my mama had shown me: the duty of a proper woman is to keep her own counsel. And there are many things which men understand and women do not. If Richard thought his honour was involved, it was not my part to challenge him and argue with him. I paused for a few moments in the chill mist and breathed the damp air deeply until my own temper was still again. If I wanted to be a proper lady of Quality – and I did – then I would have to curb my independent judgement. If I wanted to be a true wife to Richard – and I wanted that more than anything in the world – then I would have to learn to support his thoughts and actions whatever my private opinions.

While I stood hesitating at the garden gate, I realized my hand was cold. I had dropped my left glove in Acre. My hand had been tucked under Richard's arm and warmed by his grip and I had not noticed when I had lost it. They were my only pair of gloves – tan leather – once belonging to one of Mama's stepsisters and scarcely worn. Lady Havering had found them and given them to me, and I dared not lose one. I turned on my heel and started the weary walk back to Acre.

I had trudged less than a few yards when I heard a call behind me and my heart leaped, for I thought it might be Richard. But instead, there was Uncle John. He had thrown a riding coat over his shoulders and the great capes swung as he strode down the drive after me. I stopped to wait for him.

'I have to go back to Acre. I dropped my glove,' I explained.

'I'm going to Acre too,' he said. 'Richard tells me he had some words with Mr Megson.'

I nodded. 'Yes,' I said shortly.

'Were you there?' Uncle John asked, surprised. 'It sounded like some sort of brawl. What were you doing amid it all, Julia?'

'It was nothing,' I said. Uncle John seemed to have quite misunderstood Richard. Richard could not have said that there was a brawl, when all there had been was a few sharp words from him and an accident which hurt no one. 'Richard asked Mr Megson a question, and Mr Megson didn't answer. Richard jumped up on the cart and then Mr Megson bumped into him with a sack of meal. Richard fell off the cart and Mr Megson helped him up. That was all.'

John paused and looked at me. 'Is this right, Julia?' he asked. 'Was that really all there was to it?'

'Yes,' I said. I was holding to my decision to keep my private thoughts to myself. 'Mr Megson was a bit disrespectful, and Richard was upset. But it was nothing serious.'

John was visibly relieved. 'Well, thank the Lord for that,' he said. 'Young Richard made me think that I had hired a prize-fighting Jacobin. Ralph Megson is the very man for me, but I should have no place for him on the estate if he could not be civil.'

'He is not uncivil,' I said, thinking of his gentle voice to Margaret Carter. 'He and Richard misunderstood each other. That was all.'

John nodded. 'Well, now I've come this far I'll walk on with you,' he said agreeably. 'I gave Mr Megson some money on account to alleviate some of the worst hardship in the village at once. I told him to assess people's needs and spend it carefully. Is he doing some kind of food distribution?'

I could not help myself. I laughed out loud. 'No!' I said. 'They're having a party.'

We rounded the bend and John could see the table nearly ready for dinner and the people bringing stools and round logs of wood from the cottages to serve as chairs.

Then I froze, because the Dench cottage door opened and a man came out. He was upon us before I could give a warning cry. He did not even see us. He had a great saucepan of boiling soup in his hands and his eyes were on the steaming liquid and not where he was going.

It was the outlaw John Dench. It was Clary's uncle, the wounder of Richard's horse Scheherazade, the Havering groom who had trusted me to ride her. I knew him the second I saw him. But I did not know what to do.

'Look out, man!' Uncle John said abruptly, and Dench stopped and looked up from the saucepan in sudden surprise.

He recognized me at once and he took in the fine quality of Uncle John's clothes and knew he was before the gentry. He shot a look from right to left as if thinking of dropping the saucepan, soup and all, and making a run for it, a dash to the common before the hue and cry was raised. But then he looked at us again and saw that I was alone with Uncle John. His eyes were that of a hunted animal and the colour drained from his face so that he looked grey and dirty.

'Who are you?' Uncle John demanded.

Uncle John had heard the story of Scheherazade, in Mama's letters, and from his son. He would remember the name of the guilty man, would demand his arrest and take him to Chichester for trial at the next quarter sessions. Dench's eyes flew to my face, and the whole street was silent; every man, woman and child in Acre seemed to be holding their breaths and waiting for the answer. Dench opened his mouth to speak, but he said nothing.

'This is Dan Tayler,' I said. My voice was as clear as a bell, confident. 'Dan used to live here, but he now works on an estate at . . . at . . . at . . . Petersfield.'

Clary was suddenly at his side and she gave her uncle a little push. 'They're waiting for the soup,' she said. She gave me an unsmiling straight glance.

'And this is Clary Dench,' I said unwavering. 'And this is Sonny Green, and Mr and Mrs Miller Green, and Ned Smith with Henry, Jilly, and that is Little 'Un. This is Matthew Merry, and over there is his grandmother, Mrs Merry, and beside her is Mrs Tyacke, and that is her son, Ted. That is Peter the cobbler and his wife, Sairey, and those are their twins. You know George the carter, and those are his girls, Jane and Emily.'

I named them all. Uncle John nodded and smiled and the women curtsied to him and the men pulled their forelocks. Many of the names were familiar to him, but he smiled at the people who had come to Acre in recent years, or young men who had been little children when he left.

I glanced around. Dench had disappeared.

Ralph came forward. 'Would you like to share the dinner, Dr MacAndrew?' he asked politely. 'You and Miss Lacey would be most welcome.'

'We'll not interrupt you,' Uncle John said equally civil. 'We came only for Miss Julia's glove. She dropped it somewhere here.'

One of the little Dench children darted under the table and came out with the glove like a trophy, and brought it to me.

'Thank you, Sally,' I said smiling.

John nodded to Ralph. 'I see you're settling in,' he said. 'I knew you would be glad to be home, but I never guessed you would be greeted as a returning hero.'

Ralph smiled. 'Acre people never forget their friends,' he said, and I heard a message to me in that. 'We've long memories in this part of the world.'

'I'm glad,' Uncle John said. 'It will be easier to set the estate to rights if they feel they are working for someone they trust.' He hesitated. 'I expected you to organize the distribution of food, not to set in train a village revel.'

Ralph Megson threw back his dark head and laughed. 'I know

you did, Dr MacAndrew,' he said jovially. 'But there are some things you must leave to me. I'll not tell you how to doctor, don't you tell me how to bring Acre alive again. It is not money they want. It is not even food. They have been hungering all this time for a little joy in their lives – you'd know that feeling yourself, I dare say. Setting the village to rights is a lifetime's work which we can start as soon as we have properly understood the problems. Giving them a bit of hope is something which can begin at once.'

Uncle John hesitated, but then he looked at the village street alive with chatter and laughter. 'It's not what I had planned,' he said slowly, 'but I can see you may be in the right.'

Ralph Megson nodded. 'You can trust me,' he said simply. 'I am serving Acre's interests, not yours. But while your wishes and Acre's run in harness, you can trust me.'

Uncle John nodded, and a smile went between the two of them. 'We'll leave you now,' Uncle John said. 'Perhaps you'll come to the Dower House after your dinner?'

Ralph nodded and Uncle John turned to leave. He stopped for a word with Miller Green, and Ralph said to me in an undertone, 'That was well done, Miss Julia. Well done indeed.'

I shot a quick glance at his face and caught a warm smile that made me drop my gaze to my boots, white with drying chalk mud. I should not have told a lie and I should not have been praised for it. So I said nothing and he stood beside me in a silence which was not awkward, but was somehow delightful. I would have stood beside that man, even in silence, all day.

'Mr Megson,' I said tentatively.

'Yes, Miss Julia,' he said, his voice amused.

'Why are you a hero to Acre, Mr Megson?' I risked a quick glance up at his face and found his dark eyes dancing with mischief.

'Why,' he said, 'I would have thought that you would have known. Knowing everyone in Acre as you do – and they say you have the sight as well! Do you not know without my telling you, Miss Julia?'

I shook my head, a wary eye on Uncle John, who was still deep in conversation.

'I would have thought you would have known at once,' he said sweetly. 'I was told you had the sight.'

I shook my head again.

'Whose voice was it when you first saw me?' he demanded abruptly.

My eyes flew to his face and I shook my head. 'I don't know,' I said. His eyes narrowed as he noted the lie I was telling, and I flushed scarlet that he should catch me in a deceit. 'I am sorry, I *do* know,' I amended lamely. 'But it sounds so silly . . . and I did not want to say.'

He gave a crack of laughter which made Uncle John turn and smile at the two of us. Ralph's broad shoulders were shaking and his eyes danced. 'No reason in the world why you should answer my question, and no reason why you should tell me the truth if you do not choose to,' he said fairly. 'But I'll answer yours for free and for nothing.'

He looked at me closely, taking my measure, and then he beamed at me as if he were telling me the lightest most inconsequential secret. 'I was here the night of the fire,' he said confidingly. 'I led them up to the hall, to burn it down, and to murder Beatrice. I'm Ralph Megson, her lover from the old days, and her killer. In those days they called me the Culler.'

My eyes flew to his face and I gasped aloud, but Ralph Megson's confident easy smile never wavered. He turned away from me as if he had told me only the slightest of trivialities and then he went towards the head of the table where they were waiting for him to take his place.

I stood where he had left me, in stunned silence. Uncle John had to speak to me twice and touch my elbow before I came out of my shock and was able to smile absently at him and start to walk home.

Mr Megson watched me go. I could see his glance in our direction, and his casual, friendly wave to Uncle John. But I knew his eyes were on me. And that rueful almost apologetic smile was for me, and me alone. In the mist, with the weak sun trying to break through, I shuddered as if it were full night and I was caught in the cold rain of a thunderstorm.

I knew that smile. I had seen it before. He smiled like that in the dream, though I had never seen his face. And I knew that the next time I dreamed it I would look up over the great horse's shoulder and see Ralph Megson bending down to scoop me up to him and to knife me under the ribs as carefully and as tenderly as he might perform an act of love. And, though the girl in the bed in the grip of the nightmare would be screaming with fright, I knew that the woman in the dream was not afraid. I knew she would see Ralph's smile as he came for her and she would be smiling too.

6

'So what is he like?' asked Mama with polite interest. Stride was setting the decanter of port before Uncle John, but Mama and I were lingering with the informality of a happy family, with ratafia to drink and comfits to eat. 'Your new manager,' she said, 'what is he like? Is he going to be of any use to you?'

Uncle John was at the head of the table and he poured himself a glass of the tawny-coloured port. 'I do indeed think so,' he said. 'In a London hotel room he was impressive, but in the Acre street he was magnificent! I think you will like him, Celia. He's very much his own man. I would trust him entirely with money and with responsibility.'

Mama smiled. 'Good,' she said, 'for I am counting on having all three of you at home a good deal. If we have a proper manager on the land, then you, John, can concentrate on getting well and I can take Julia to Bath with a clear conscience.'

'He was rude to me,' Richard said abruptly. His head was turned away from his papa towards the foot of the table, to my mama, who always attended to his needs. 'He knocked me with a sack of meal off the cart and into the road before all Acre.'

Mama gasped and looked to John.

'Forget it,' John advised briefly. He raised his glass and looked at Richard over the rim. Richard turned at once to my mama again. 'In front of all of Acre,' he said.

My mama opened her mouth to say something, but she hesitated.

John leaned forward. 'Forget it,' he said, his voice stronger. 'You and Mr Megson had some difference. No one in Acre even noticed. I have been down there and I asked specifically if there was any trouble. No one even saw.'

I had to dip my head down to look at my hands clasped on my lap at that. No one *ever* saw anything in Acre which looked like trouble.

'Ralph Megson is a man of the world and his judgement is good,' Uncle John said gently. 'He will not refer to whatever took place. I advise you to forget it, Richard. You will need to be on good terms with him.'

Richard shot a swift burning look at his father, then he turned his shoulder towards him and addressed my mama. 'I don't like him,' he said. 'He insulted me and he should not work here if he cannot be civil.'

Mama looked at Richard and her face was infinitely tender. 'I know you are thinking of us,' she said gently. Then her gaze slid away from his young cross face to Uncle John, calm at the head of the table. 'Richard has had responsibilities beyond his years,' she said, speaking to him directly. 'He is only thinking of what would be the best for us.'

John nodded. 'It is a good sign that Richard is so responsible,' he said kindly, 'but I shall be the judge of this.'

Mama nodded and smiled at Richard. He gave her one long level look, and I knew that he felt betrayed. Mama, who had relied so much on him, now had the man she loved at her side, and she would prefer his advice. She sipped at her glass. 'Does he know enough about farming?' she asked. 'What is his background?'

'He was a tenant farmer in Kent and was bought out by an improving landlord at a considerable loss to himself,' Uncle John said. He answered her as if the matter of Richard's opinion was of small moment. 'Losing his land like that would have made a lesser man bitter. It made him think about the rights of the landlord, and the rights of the tenants and workers. He's a radical, of course, but I don't mind that at all! I'm glad to have a manager who thinks of the good of the people, rather than simply the profits of the estate. And I don't think a grasping man would last long in Acre anyway!'

'No,' Mama said. 'As long as they will do as they're bid . . .'

Uncle John smiled down the table at me. 'They were falling over themselves to please him when we left,' he said. 'If he remains that popular I should think they'll plough up their kitchen gardens for Lacey wheat at his request. He seemed an absolute hero, didn't he, Julia?'

'Yes,' I agreed, and I said no more.

'Odd I never heard of him,' Mama said. 'He must have left Acre many years ago, for I never met him. I wonder how he can be so popular since he left when he was just a lad.'

I shifted uneasily in my chair and Richard came out of his brown study and shot a swift hard look at me. The very question I had feared had been raised on this first afternoon of Mr Megson's return home. I had his life in my hands. All I had to do was to repeat what he had told me and he would be taken to Chichester and hanged. It would hardly matter that the fire had taken place fourteen years ago. Ralph Megson was a fire-raiser roaming free on Wideacre, and only I knew it. It should be me who gave the warning.

He had told me a secret which would hang him, and many of the villagers as well. And he had told it me in utter freedom and in jest and daring, and he had known, he *must* have known, that it would place me in the position I was in now: I had to choose between the claims of my family, my Quality family, and the preferences of Acre.

Before the whole village he had told me that he was an arsonist and a murderer, and I had not cried out against him then. I had not rushed to Uncle John and told him. I had not taken Uncle John to one side before we reached home and told him the appalling news. Mr Megson's warm smile, his dazzling defiance of the law and the outside world and his matchless confidence had won me into complete complicity. Now I had to decide whether to lie outright to my mama or to betray Mr Megson, a stranger and a murderer.

I never lied to my mama.

I had hoped I never would lie to my mama.

I had hoped there would never be a single thing I could not tell her.

'I've heard he left when he was quite young,' I said. 'The reason that he is so popular is that he used to send money back to people in the village during the bad years. Prize money,' I said, improvising wildly. 'From when he was at sea.'

Richard looked at me, his face impassive. He knew from my paleness, and from the way the tablecloth twitched before me as I pleated and twisted it under the cover of the table, that I was lying. And lying not at all well. And he knew I was lying to protect Mr Megson. Mr Megson – whom Richard had named as his enemy.

'How very creditable,' said Mama lightly. She took her shawl from the back of her chair and draped it around her shoulders.

'Yes, and most unlikely,' Uncle John said.

I had risen, and I whirled around to face him, my face suddenly white. 'What do you mean?' I demanded, and I knew my eyes were blazing.

'My dear Julia,' Uncle John said in faint surprise, 'I mean only that I suspect that it is a respectable version of the man's life history. I should imagine that an early apprenticeship with smugglers would be more like it. And the favours he could do Acre as a local smuggler would certainly be worth remembering.' He smiled at my scared face. 'No need to look so shocked,' he said gently. 'It makes little odds. Smuggling will always take place while we have absurd excise laws, and if he can command a gang of smugglers, he can certainly organize a ploughing team, I should think!'

'Oh!' I said. 'I was only repeating what I heard in the village. But if he *was* a smuggler and now he has stopped smuggling, there could be nothing against him, could there?'

Uncle John held the door open for Mama and me. 'I don't think the law gives much credit to people who retire from a life of crime to a life of comfort,' he said with a smile. 'But there is obviously no one who would betray him in Acre. And I do not hold it against him. What I will do is have a quiet word with Lord Havering and one or two other Justices of the Peace locally, and see if there is anyone of Mr Megson's description wanted. I don't mind having a retired smuggler on my land, but I *would* object to an ex-privateer or a retired highwayman.'

'Good gracious, yes!' said Mama, settling herself in her chair in the parlour. 'Why can Acre never be normal! Surely John, you could have found a manager who was not a criminal? Even if he is a retired one?'

'A poacher turned gamekeeper is the best man to guard the game,' Uncle John quoted with a smile. 'Acre has always been an eccentric sort of village, my dear. I fear it will continue that way. And when it is set to rights, it may be that some of its finer sons come home again. There was an exile back today, wasn't there, Julia? The man who had come all the way from Petersfield for the dinner.'

The guilty look on my face was as clear as a bell to Richard. I knew it as soon as our eyes met. But I was sitting at Mama's feet at the fireside and I could not hide my face.

'Who from Petersfield?' he asked, seeming to care very little.

'I don't recall the name,' Uncle John said. But then he remembered. 'Tayler, Dan Tayler, was it not, Julia?'

'Yes,' I said, monosyllabic, my eyes on the fire.

'Who is he?' Richard asked blankly.

'Don't you know?' Uncle John asked. 'I should have thought you two knew Acre inside out. Julia seems quite expert. Who is he, Julia?'

'He is . . . he is . . .' I could improvise nothing with Uncle John's guileless pale eyes on me and Richard's gaze darkening with suspicion.

'There is no Tayler family in the village,' Richard said.

'There is!' I said quickly. 'In the shanties, the cottagers.' I knew Richard knew nothing of the families who lived on the outer limits of Acre, scraping a living off the common land. No one could ever say with certainty who was there. Only the gypsies who lived further out on the common were more wild.

'Never heard of them,' Richard said stubbornly. 'Who is this man, anyway?'

Mama's eyes were on me, and Uncle John's. Richard was sharp and alert. I had told one lie and then another, and now I was being forced into a whole string of untruths. If they discovered the identity of the man who had nearly bumped into us with his saucepan, Richard would never forgive me for a lie and that would be bad enough; but Dench would be taken.

I might brave Richard's anger, or even Mama's mystified disapproval. But if I let slip Dench's name, Uncle John would order his coachman (a London man with no local loyalties) down to Acre to arrest Dench. And at the next quarter sessions he would be tried and hanged. I could not let that happen.

The lie I had already told that day to protect Mr Megson had been weak enough. I leaned my head back against my mama's knees to draw some strength from the feel of her satin gown on the back of my bare neck. Richard saw my fatigue and pressed me for answers.

'Where did you meet a cottager, Julia?' he asked. His tone was concerned and his eyes went to Mama, as if to remind her that I should not be let free to wander in the most notorious village in Sussex. 'Did he approach you when you were walking after having left me at the vicarage? Is he a friend of that common little village girl you keep going to see? Why did you never tell us?'

'I met him when I was walking with Clary, and Matthew Merry and some of the other Acre young people,' I said. Uncle John held his hands to the fire and nodded, but Richard could smell a lie like a hound smells blood from a fresh wound and was hot on my trail.

'When was this?' he demanded. 'You never told me. And why were the Acre children talking to one of the cottagers?'

'Oh, I don't know! I don't remember!' I said in sudden impatience and in real fear that they would get the truth out of me. I had to get myself out of the room. I jumped up from my seat at Mama's feet and took a hasty few steps towards the door.

'What is he doing now, this mysterious cottager?' Richard harried me. 'And how did he get to Acre so quickly?'

'Can't we just forget all about him!' I exclaimed with as near a tone of petulance as I could manage when my heart was in my mouth to hide Dench's identity from Mama and Uncle John. My courage nearly failed me when I saw Mama's astonished face and then caught her look at John, as if she were ashamed that I should be so rude in front of him. But I was trapped and I could see no way to go but forward.

'Honestly, Richard! You and Mama treat me as if I were a child! I won't be cross-questioned! I met the man in Acre, where I know many people. Mama! Please excuse me!' I said and I whirled towards the door.

Stride was coming in with the tea-tray in his hand and he stood on the threshold and gaped to see me striding from the room in temper. He hesitated, not knowing whether to put down his burden to hold the door for me or to let me push past him in defiance of good manners.

'Miss Julia!' he said in a reproachful undertone. I flashed an angry glance at him and saw his friendly face full of concern.

I grabbed for the door-knob and swirled out of the room and shut the door behind me.

Then I stood still as still and leaned my head back against the closed parlour door, and stared blankly at nothing. I had never in all my life spoken thus to my mama and I felt I had hurt myself in complaining of her to her very face. And the angry tone which had come to my lips was one she had never heard before from me! And the claim that she gave me no freedom which was nonsense! And the rudeness before Uncle John! I sighed.

I did not stand there on purpose to eavesdrop, but I heard the silence in the room. And then I heard Richard say so kindly, so gently, 'Please don't be upset, Mama-Aunt, please don't be offended, sir. Julia is never like this usually. Mama-Aunt will tell you that, and indeed it is true. There never was a sweeter-tempered girl than my cousin. I have never seen her like this before.'

I let out a silent sigh at Richard's loyalty. He was defending me in the next breath after I had raged at him. Then I remembered that I should not be standing there, within earshot, and I moved away from the door.

I could have gone to my room, or gone to sit in the empty dining-room, but I needed to see the sky over Wideacre and needed the wind from the woods to blow away my temper and my confusion. I opened the front door and slipped out into the late afternoon.

Careless of my gown, I sat on the stone steps and welcomed the chill of the damp air. Evenings had been pearl-light this spring, but today had been as dark as winter all day and the afternoon was grey and shady from the fog of the morning and the lowering clouds. I gulped in the damp air and felt it wet as mist against my cheek. Across the drive the woods of Wideacre were hazy with green growth, and invisible birds in the wet paleness were singing and singing with boundless energy, not to be distracted by the cold or the darkness, knowing in their little leaping hearts that it was spring and time for loving and courting and mating.

I sighed. I felt the anger and the confusion drift away from me like blossoms tossed on the floodtide Fenny. It was all right. I had told a lie, a set of lies. But I had done it to protect an Acre man who looked to the Laceys for help. There had been enough arrests and threats in Acre in the past. Neither Richard nor I would add to it. Ralph Megson had returned with the promise of new hope for Acre, and if a little lie, or even a set of little lies, could keep that prospect safe, then I would tell those lies.

I could forgive myself for the lie about Dench, and the secret told to me by Mr Megson I would not consider at all. Like the young girl they expected me to be, I would trust Uncle John's judgement and make no judgement of my own. He thought Mr Megson a fit manager for the estate, and he knew something of his past. He had praised Mr Megson's character and he was prepared to ignore the turbulence in the man's youth. I could not betray Mr Megson, and I would not judge him. I let that lie go too – I let it melt from my mind like frost in the mornings. I took a deep breath of Wideacre air and let it out in a sigh.

I must have appeared a rude ill-bred spoiled little miss; and that before the man my mama most loved and respected in the world. But it was a small enough thing for a Lacey to do for Acre. I would apologize to my mama, I would apologize to Uncle John and I might be able to tell the truth to Richard. I thought Richard might understand. And if he was not angry with me, then I could face anything.

And thus I sat, while the rooks cawed hoarsely and tumbled home to their straggly nests, swaying at the very tops of the trees. Thus I sat and let the peace of Wideacre wash over me, until I was a Lacey on Wideacre again, knowing my home.

The door behind me opened with a click and Richard came out. He nearly stumbled over me, not seeing me in the gloom.

'Oh, there you are,' he said abruptly. 'You'll have to face them and apologize sooner or later, you know.'

'I know,' I said comfortably. I smiled up at him. 'Wasn't I a shrew?' I said ruefully. 'But I didn't know what to do.'

'I knew you were trying to tell some plumper, but I couldn't think what you were saying,' Richard said. He dropped down to sit on the step beside me and his shoulder brushed mine. I leaned slightly towards it and felt warmed with the comfort of his presence.

'Who on earth is the mysterious Dan Tayler?' he said. 'You were trying to lead Mama all around the house on that taradiddle, Julia. But anyone who knows you could have seen you were fibbing. What were you trying to hide?'

'Oh Richard,' I said. 'I know, it's no good trying to lie to you. And I wouldn't want to lie to Mama either, or Uncle John. But I was afraid to tell them!'

Richard took my hand in his warm clasp. 'Afraid to tell them what?' he asked mystified. 'What great secret have you, little Julia?'

'It was Dench!' I said in a rush. 'John Dench, the Havering groom. He had obviously been hiding in Acre or near by all this time, perhaps Midhurst. And when they had the party, of course he came to it. We nearly bumped into him in the village street! It was quite awful. I didn't know what Uncle John would do, but I could not have borne it if he had ordered Dench's arrest.'

Richard put his arm around my shoulder and I laid my head into the warm crook of his neck and sniffed at his warmth like a little sensual animal.

'But Grandpapa Havering put out a reward for Dench's arrest,' Richard said softly. 'You are a little criminal yourself, Julia, to help hide him.'

I nodded. Richard's gentle hand came up from my shoulder and caressed my cheek. I nearly purred like a stroked kitten.

'I know,' I said, 'I cannot explain it, Richard. I just thought how kind he had been to you when he was teaching you to ride, and how anxious he was for you on that awful day when you had your accident. And I know Clary Dench now, and he is her uncle and she loves him so much, you know, Richard. I just couldn't have named him to Uncle John and watched them take him away.'

'So you lied,' Richard said. His voice was still gentle.

'Yes,' I said, and I was no longer melting with his touch. I could hear an edge of anxiety in my voice. 'It was all such a long time ago,' I said, but I was less confident. 'It was years ago. I could not have borne for the new start for Acre and Mr Megson's first day here to be spoiled by an old, old score.'

'You deliberately told my papa a false name. And then you lied to Mama-Aunt and to me?' Richard's voice was as smooth as silk.

'Yes,' I said again. 'But I knew you would understand, Richard. I was sure you would understand. I was not lying to you, for see, I have told you as soon as I could. This is the first moment we have been together and I have told you at once. I was not lying to you, Richard.'

'No,' he said judicially. 'You have told me the truth as soon as you could. But you have not told me something that I find very strange.'

'What is that Richard?' I asked. My voice was as thin as a child's. 'I will tell you anything, Richard. You know I never keep secrets from you.'

Richard's hand on my shoulder was no longer a caress. He was holding me to his side so there was no chance that I could get away. His voice was as soft and as gentle as ever. But I felt like a foolish rabbit hopping towards a snare.

'Had you forgotten, Julia, why Grandpapa Havering wanted Dench arrested? Had you forgotten what he had done to my horse?'

'Oh, no, Richard!' I cried. 'How could I forget? I cried every night for a week for poor Scheherazade, and for you and your disappointment. You know how upset I was. Of course I had not forgotten!' I broke off and paused, for it was the wrong answer and I knew it as soon as it had left my lips. 'At least,' I said, correcting myself, 'I have not forgotten; but I did not remember it quite at the time. All I could really think of was poor Clary who loves her uncle so, and poor Dench who must have been living so poorly and so badly in hiding somewhere. And the village was so happy and alive that I could not bear to be the one who spoiled all that. And everyone was listening, Richard, and looking. You know how they do in Acre. I could not bear to be a Lacey breaking hearts in Acre again, Richard! I really could not have named him to Uncle John!'

Richard's grip on my shoulder was so hard that it hurt. His fingers were digging into the soft flesh of my upper arm like four blunt knives. But he said nothing.

'Richard,' I said. 'You are hurting me, you are holding me too tight.'

'Yes,' he said, and there was a smile in his voice, but it was not a nice smile. It was too dark for me to see his eyes, but I knew they were black with rage. I had been wrong to lie and then I had been wrong to try to explain the lie to Richard. I had the old familiar sensation of the ground slipping away from under my feet, and I knew that there was no way of saving myself from Richard's torrent of anger.

'You deserve that I should hurt you,' he said. 'You have hidden the man who injured my horse, injured my horse so badly that she had to be killed. You saw him in Acre, and you lied to my papa so that he should be safe. I know why you did that, Miss Lacey of Wideacre. You did it so that you could queen it around Acre as the favourite of the village. You said yourself that everyone was looking at you and listening. You wanted them to think you were so nice, so sweet, such a little princess that you thought nothing of me and of the fact that John Dench killed my horse out of spite and hatred towards me!'

'No, Richard!' I said aghast. 'No! That is not right! That is not how it was!'

'You want to be the favourite in Acre,' he said. His grip on my shoulder was like iron. 'You think that if you can be little precious Miss Lacey of Wideacre, then the village will see you as the squire and they will all forget about me, me and my rights. That is what you are thinking of! I know it!'

'No, Richard! No!' I said.

'You are trying to steal Wideacre from me!' he accused.

'No! Never! Never, Richard! I never could or would. When anyone asks me, I tell them that you are to be squire. That you are the favoured child!'

'The what?' he asked momentarily diverted.

'It's nothing, nothing,' I said hastily. 'Just a legend, a silly legend from the village.' He stared at me and waited. I had to go on. 'It is a legend they have,' I said. 'They believe that one of us is Beatrice's true heir, with her gift of the sight, and the gift to make the land grow. They are wondering which of us it is. I always say it is you.'

Richard suddenly released me with such a violent shove that I fell backwards on the stone step. My head hit the door with a thud and for a moment I could see nothing and hear nothing but the ringing in my ears from the blow.

'Richard!' I said shocked.

'It *is* me!' he hissed in absolute passion. 'It *is* me! And yet I have been stuck in Dr Pearce's study while you have been free to roam all around and make friends with people and make them think you are the natural heir. You would never even have told me if it had not slipped out like this! You are a cheat, Julia. You are an encroacher! This is my land, and I am Beatrice's son. I shall be the heir.'

I could say nothing. I was shattered that he should treat me so, dizzy from the blow. My fingers stroking through my tumbled hair found a swelling lump. My eyes were blurred with tears at the hurt, and the tears were spilling down my cheeks, but my voice was choked and I could say nothing in my defence. Richard was wrong, quite wrong. But he had the advantage of rage and the high ground of an accusation. And I looked very bad. Shielding Dench was exactly the sort of thing which would make me beloved in Acre, and I *had* kept the legend of the favoured child to myself.

'I am sorry, Richard . . .' I started.

But it was no good. He spun on his heel and left me sitting like a peasant woman weeping on the doorstep. He opened the front door and went inside without another word to me. My hand was flat on the doorstep and as he shut the door it crushed the first joint of my middle finger with a sudden sharp agony which made me cry out in pain. I caught the finger in my other hand and squeezed it as tight as I could in an effort to stop the pain, and wept like a hurt child. He had not meant to do it, I knew he had not meant to do it; he had simply shut the door quickly. But the pain of the bruised flesh and the nail – which already wore a white half-moon of a scar across it – made me weep with self-pity.

I did not sit there, sobbing on the doorstep, for very long. It seemed like a long time indeed, but I knew it was not. I wobbled my finger-nail cautiously, but it did not come away as I had feared it might.

My tears stopped, and the thudding of my heart from fright gradually stilled, and the pain in my head from the blow and the tremble all over at Richard's rage faded little by little as I sat on the stone steps in the darkening garden. The stone was cold – I could feel it through my silk gown – but still I sat on, waiting until the tears had dried on my cheeks and until my hands were steady, and trying to find, from deep inside myself, some source of peace and calm again. Richard was my betrothed, and my own grandmama had warned me that he would not always be a loving boy. I had promised myself to him and he had a right – he even had a legal right – to use me as he would. A bump on the head and an accidental injury to my hand was not unreasonable. So I sat still and quiet and worked to persuade myself that I was not insulted, that I was not injured, that I was not abused. And if I wanted to marry Richard – and I *did* want to marry Richard – then I would have to learn to take the rough parts of his temper with the smooth. It was his right.

I sat there, getting colder and calmer as the little pale sickle moon came up behind a bank of clouds and shone on me with a veiled light. I heard a clatter of horse's hooves and then the garden gate opened and Mr Megson came up the path with his rolling stride, balancing without crutches on the flagged path. He stopped short at seeing me, hair tumbling down, red-eyed and wet-cheeked, sitting on the doorstep of my own home like a beggar-girl.

'What's this?' he said softly. He glanced up at the parlour window where the candlelight spilled out. 'Locked out? Or sulking? Miss Julia?'

I was silent for a minute and then I gave a watery chuckle that was almost a sob. 'Sulking, I suppose,' I said. 'For I'm not locked out.'

Mr Megson nodded, and put out one hand to steady himself on the doorknob and the other to pull me to my feet. I gave him the hurt hand and pulled back with a little cry of pain at his touch on my finger.

'I shut my hand in the door,' I explained. I gave him my other hand and he helped me to my feet and put a hand under my elbow when I staggered.

'Dizzy?' he asked.

'I bumped my head on the step,' I told him, and put my hand to the back of my head to feel the swelling. It was a little bigger and very tender to the touch.

'When you sulk, you do it properly!' Mr Megson said, a ripple of amusement in his voice. 'Were you banging your head in a rage?'

'Of course not!' I said stung. 'It was an accident.'

'And your finger?' he asked.

'That *was* an accident,' I said, unconsciously betraying myself.

'How did you bang your head?' he asked.

I flushed to the roots of my hair. 'It was an accident, as I've said.' Richard was my husband-to-be. It was my duty to protect his reputation and my pride. If he had beaten me, I should never have told anyone.

'Is Richard at home?' Ralph asked.

'No,' I said at once. 'It was an accident.' And then I put out my hand to the cold stone of the doorpost to steady myself. 'I beg your pardon,' I said, clinging to my manners, though the dusky woods were wavering before my eyes and I was afraid of what Mr Megson might be thinking of me, might be thinking of Richard. 'I beg your pardon,' I said again. 'I misunderstood you. Yes, Richard is home, and Mama and Uncle John. May I take you in?'

Mr Megson nodded. He did not bow like a gentleman, but he offered me his arm with a grace which a gentleman might envy. I took it with a little smile and we went into the house.

Stride was in the hall. 'Miss Julia!' he said reprovingly. 'Miss Julia, I don't know what possessed you. And what have you done to yourself now?'

I smiled wanly at his anxious face. 'I don't feel very well, Stride,' I said. 'I shall go to bed. Please apologize for me to Mama and Uncle John, for I shan't come down again this evening. And please tell Uncle John that Mr Megson is here to see him.'

Stride nodded and took Mr Megson towards the library. I went wearily up the stairs to my room.

I slid my clothes off and left them in a heap on the foot of the bed. The thin linen pillow was cool under my cheek, and when I swept my hair off my neck the bruise was eased by the touch of the chill cloth. I lay on my back, nursing my hurt finger, waiting for the throbbing in my head to cease, and waiting for the pain in my heart to ease. I felt very alone, and very sad.

And then I slept.

The dream started at once, I think.

I knew, I knew it was the dream. But some real days have seemed less real than that dream.

I was gazing blank-eyed into a fire burning in a hearth I had never seen in waking life, in a room I had never visited. It was evening, late, late evening, and the sky was dark with a storm. There was thunder, and the sharp crack of lightning, but I had no fear, no fear at all. It was as though I had died and was a ghost and had nothing to fear any more.

As I gazed at the flames of the fire, I heard a noise above the sound of the storm. I heard a window creak. The light from the stormy cloud-chased sky was blocked and the room went utterly black, for someone was climbing through the window into my room. I turned my head languidly, but I did not call for help. I opened my mouth, but did not scream. I froze, waiting, sprawled before the fire for what was coming to me.

He came silently to me and he pushed the chair from behind my shoulders so that I lay flat on the floor. I trembled as if his very touch were an icy wind, but I did not move. Only my eyes blinked and gazed in a gleam of moonlight.

He kissed my collar-bone, this dark familiar stranger in the dream. He opened my gown and kissed one breast, the nipple as hard as a blackberry, and then he kissed the other. In the dream I made a moan of soft longing, and in waking life the girl in the bed, a virgin, stirred and cried and struggled against a knowledge she did not yet want.

In the dream the woman's skilful hands went flat against his chest and smoothed down his belly till she felt his hardness; but he brushed her hand away and opened the front of her gown and slid his face, the stubble scratching her soft skin, down over her warm belly to take her in his mouth.

The woman in the dream arched her back and gasped, the girl in the waking life tossed her head on the pillows and called out – she was calling for her mama, she was calling for her cousin. She was entranced by the dream and yet full of fear. She struggled with her sleep and the blankets slid askew to the floor. The thud as they fell from the bed detached her from her sleep and she sat upright in bed, the dream fading from her mind. She said one word into the darkened silent room.

'Ralph!' she said.

It was Beatrice's voice.

I turned over and went to sleep at once, and I dreamed no more. But in the morning I stared at the ceiling and walls of my room as if it were a strange place for me to wake. I had thought, I don't know why, that I should have opened my eyes and seen a great carved wooden canopy above me. I could scarcely recognize my bedroom, though I had seen that ceiling every morning of my girlhood. I hardly knew my room, I hardly knew myself.

I thought I had been dreaming in the night; but I could not remember what I had dreamed, except that I had not been afraid. For some reason the dream, the familiar terror-filled dream, had altered, and there was some delight in it. But I could not remember what it was. I saw my pillow on the floor and the disorder of my bed, and knew I must have been tossing and turning in the grip of the dream, but I could remember no fear. And I thought, but I could not understand it, that there had been no fear because I had met the man they called the Culler; I had looked in his face, and I knew him to be a man with the kindest of eyes and the warmest of smiles.

I knew that whatever he had done, he had done it with love.

I leaned out of the bed and picked up my pillow and tucked it behind me. There was a tap on my door and the kitchenmaid came in with my morning cup of chocolate. I drank it, looking at the sky out of my window.

The mist had blown away in ribbons of cloud like streamers across the blue sky and the sun was ripping through them with a warm yellow light. At last Uncle John might have a taste of his beloved English summer, I thought with satisfaction, and then I gave a little grimace of dismay, because I had forgotten.

I was in disgrace with him for my rudeness. I had been rude to Mama, and Richard was angry with me. All my pleasure – in the tops of the trees tossing, and the cloud-riven sky and the wind blowing – disappeared as fast as the morning mist. I got out of bed and cautiously felt my head for the bruise. It was about the size of a wood-pigeon's egg; it felt perfectly round, and the touch of my fingers on it made me wince. I had to steel myself to brush my hair and pile the mass of pale-brown ringlets up on my head. Then I threw on a wrapper and went to my bedroom door and listened.

It was early. They were working in the kitchen, but Mama's morning chocolate had not yet been brought to her room. I slipped softly down the stairs and through the green baize door to the kitchen. I could hear Mrs Gough's voice as she thumped dough for the breakfast rolls on the floured table.

'I always said she was wilful,' she said, her voice raised so that Stride, polishing cutlery and setting the trays, could hear her. 'She was so close to her mama, I think she's jealous now the master's come home.'

I realized with a sudden start that they were talking about me.

'But the lad is the bonniest one,' she said, her voice warm. 'It will be a fine thing when he is squire and the hall rebuilt and the good days come again.'

'He's no Lacey,' Stride said briefly. 'The hall is Miss Julia's home.'

I reached a hand behind me and banged the door so they could hear it in the kitchen. I had not meant to listen and I did not want to hear more. I clattered down the passage and Mrs Gough gave me a brief 'Good morning' with no suspicion that I had heard.

'I'd like to take Mama's tray to her room,' I said.

Stride gave me a quick smile. 'That's right,' he said. 'She won't be angry. She was not angry last night.'

Mrs Gough tutted under her breath and turned to the stove where the milk was warming. She dipped a finger into the pan and then poured it into the chocolate jug. Stride ran a quick glance over the tray and then nodded to me to take it. He came and held the door for me and watched my slow progress up the stairs, and my careful balancing of the tray in one hand as I knocked on Mama's door.

She was awake sitting up in bed with her wrapper around her shoulders, looking out of the window at the fresh leaves on the trees which pressed so close and at the blue sky above them.

'Julia!' she said with pleasure. Then her face grew more reserved as she remembered that I was still in disgrace.

'Good morning, Mama,' I said, putting the tray by her bedside and bending over to kiss her. 'I have come to say I am sorry.'

At once her arms were around me in a hug. 'Oh, my darling!' she said. 'You know that it is all right.'

And that was all the apology she needed; that was all I had to say.

I sat at the bottom of her bed as she sipped her chocolate.

'Is there anything troubling you?' she asked. 'Is there anything you want to tell me?'

The impulse to tell the truth was too strong for me, and the whole story of my seeing Dench, of my instinctive lie and of Richard's anger – poured out. I knew Dench would be safely in hiding again, and I needed to explain myself to my mama.

Three things I did not tell her. Not a word about Mr Megson passed my lips. I let his laughing confession drop from my mind as if it had never been said. I was never going to think of it again if I could keep myself from thinking.

I did not tell her that Richard had accused me of trying to make myself beloved in Acre. That accusation seemed so dreadful that I could not bear to tell anyone. I did not want to remember it myself.

And I did not tell her that Richard had hurt me. She would never know of that from me.

But I was right to tell her about Dench. She nodded her

understanding and spoke only of the aspect which she knew would distress me most. 'Is Richard very angry with you?' she asked.

'Yes,' I said. I said nothing more.

Mama sighed. 'I know that will make you very sad, Julia,' she said consolingly. 'But I do think that your ups and downs with Richard are a result of living so very close together.'

I nodded. But I had nothing to say.

'That will get better,' she said certainly. 'Now we have to set the land to rights, Richard will have an occupation, he will be more out on the land. There will be a very great deal for you and me to do as well. Then you will have your first season at Bath. We'll go there in the autumn and be back home in time for Christmas!' She paused and looked at me. 'Don't look so woe-begone, little duckling! Richard's crossness will blow over, he is never angry for long. And you must learn to mind less when he is in a temper with you.'

I smiled and did not disagree, for I had heard Richard's footsteps on the stairs and I felt my heart lift at the thought that I could go to him and deal with him directly and fairly. And we should be friends again. I left Mama to dress and went confidently downstairs to find him.

He had his books out before him at the parlour table, and he glanced up without a smile as I slid in the door; he did not seem pleased at being interrupted. When I saw his frown, I knew I was not forgiven yet.

I went quietly to the table to stand by his elbow. But I said nothing. I waited for him to speak. I was hoping, against all probability, that he would give me one of his sweet rueful smiles, or even speak civilly to me so that I would know that even if I was not forgiven, the heat of his anger had cooled.

'You can stand there all day, Julia,' he said softly. 'And you will not get a word from me.'

His tone was like a slap in my face.

'You are wrong when you think I want Wideacre all to myself,' I said, trying to keep my voice steady. 'I don't mind which one of us has it. And I have always hoped that we would share it, because we would be married and live here together.'

Despite myself, at the mention of our marriage plans, my voice quavered, and I could feel the tears starting to come to my eyes. 'Whether you want to marry me or not, I know that you would be squire,' I said.

He looked at me sternly.

'I know you are Beatrice's son,' I said, my voice low. 'I know you have her gifts. I know you are the favoured child.'

'I do have,' he said swiftly. 'I do have her gifts. I am the true heir and all Acre can see it.'

'Yes,' I said. I waited, but he said nothing more.'I'm sorry about Dench,' I offered. 'I know I did wrong not to tell your papa who it was. But I did not do it to try to be first in Acre, you know, Richard.'

'Very well,' he said magisterially. 'I believe you, Julia.' He managed to make it sound by the tone of his voice that I was not believable, and that he did not believe me. But he was generously overlooking a fault. I bowed my head. 'I am working,' he said. 'My papa and I are agreed that I should use the time before breakfast for quiet study.'

I nodded, looking at his books. He was parsing a passage from Dr Johnson. I could tell, reading Richard's large script at an angle, that he had made a mistake. But I did not think he would welcome my help. 'I will go out for a walk,' I said.

He made no reply, so I went in silence from the room up to my bedroom and dressed in a plain gown and threw a shawl over my head and around my shoulders as a concession to the cool morning and to convention. Then I went out of the front door and stood on the doorstep in a daze.

I did not know where to go. I did not know what I wanted. The brief exchange with Richard had left me feeling that the struggle to be a proper wife, to be a properly behaved lady, might cost me more than I was able to pay. I seemed to have to bite my tongue against angry words over and over again. For the first time in my life I thought of my mama's solitude with no pity. However much she mourned my papa, she could sit in peace with her feet up on her own fender in the evening. She could order the meals she preferred, she could suit herself in her plans for her life. She did not have to watch her words, and apologize for her mistakes, and guard her thoughts, and consider every word and every action in the light of a man's prejudices. I shook my head. I supposed I was being very foolish. I supposed this was the wildness in me which Mama had tried to train away. Now I was paying the price for not being an indoors girl. Now I had to learn from Richard what was expected of a young lady, of a young bride. And Richard was an impatient master.

But then I took in a great gulp of the morning air and felt my spirits, as mercurial as a morning lark, lift at the very sight of the head of the downs, and the streaky sky above them. The smell of the morning air, warm with the promise of summer, and the sight of the leaves, so fresh and green and washed after the rain, set my heart singing and my pulse beating. I could almost hear Wideacre growing around me – a sweet humming noise – as gentle as a standing harp vibrating with a draught of air on the strings.

I did not know where to go for my walk. I wanted to be prompt for breakfast to earn a smile from Mama, and to seek my return to Uncle John's favour. So I wanted a walk which would give me time to rid my feet of the fidgets, and to give me some time on the heart of the land to feel the wind blowing my resentment away and to hear the water running.

In my head was the low sweet humming which told me that Wideacre magic was all around me, and the dream of Beatrice was very close. I drifted down the garden path to the drive, drifted as if there were some magic thread pulling me in the direction I should walk. The garden gate did not squeak when I opened it as it usually did; a bramble caught at my dress but it did not tear. I walked like a ghost and the air did not stir at my passing.

I could hear the clear humming in my head that I heard when the dream was there, and I knew my eyes were hazy and fey.

There was a ghost walking on Wideacre, and she and I were one this wind-blown morning. She and I were walking on the sweet land with the cool wind blowing. And my footsteps were as light as a goddess's.

I turned right up the drive and walked up towards the ruin of the hall. The sunlight was dappled on my face from the overhanging trees of the drive, and the hawthorn hedge on my right was coming into flower and smelling sweet. A few bees bumbled among the flowers, and their noise and the noise in my head were as loud as a hundred voices singing low. In my mind there was nothing.

Nothing.

Nothing.

Nothing but this gentle whisper of sound which seemed to be drawing me onwards. It was the only clear sweet thing on a day when there were too many people and too many things I had to do. There was only one clear voice in the babble of the world and that was the voice of Wideacre which had called me from the house and was calling me to the hall.

There was a great chestnut tree at the bend of the drive, and a squirrel had nipped a spray of the fresh finger-shaped leaves and dropped it down. I bent and picked it up and waved it before my face like a fan. The air it wafted to my face smelled sweet with flowers blooming, and a hint of rain at the back of the wind warned me that the storm of the night had not gone but simply turned around, and we would have more rain before the end of the morning.

The stones of the Wideacre drive crunched beneath my boots and I remembered how in the dream there was the sound of the hundreds of feet on the drive when they walked barefoot up to the hall, lit by torches, lit by lightning, with Ralph Megson riding high at their head.

I was half in the dream, half out of it. The air was so sweet it was like the cool rooms in the dream when the woman prowls around the empty hall. I glanced up at the clearing sky, half expecting to feel raindrops on my upturned face as Beatrice had done when she went out into the storm to meet him.

It was not raining yet. Today was a different day. It was not the dream. It was just me, walking aimlessly up to the hall before I settled down to a morning's work for my mama, or looked at the plans of the hall with Uncle John. Why I should be walking up here risking a wetting I did not really know. Why I should feel I was being pulled, I did not know. Why I should have this singing humming noise in my head and this ache which felt almost like heartache under my ribs, I did not know.

So, knowing nothing, I walked on. I walked like a sleep-walker, tranced and unknowing, walked up the drive and turned to my left into the rose garden where the weeds grew as high as the rose trees and all you could see of the roses was the fresh crimson-leaved growth and the first tiny buds with little splits of colour: scarlet, and white and cream and pink, half hidden among the green of self-seeded ash trees and elder bushes and tall pink campion. I paused and broke off one of the wands of campion and looked at the flowers, as sweetly shaped as shells, each one a perfect structure. Then I raised my eyes from the bloom and walked up the steps to the broken-down white wooden summer-house.

He was there.

At my step on the path he came to the doorway and stood there waiting for me. I raised my eyes to his dark face and smiled in such welcome and such joy to see him. The ache beneath my ribs eased at once at the sight of him. The singing in my head was cut off in silence as if someone had laid a gentle hand on the strings of the lonely harp. The sun came out, suddenly strong, and smiled in my eyes with rays of gold which made the garden suddenly too bright and hazy. I went lightly up the treacherous steps, as lightly as a ghost, a dancing ghost. He opened his arms to me and held me close to him and I lifted my face for his kiss.

His mouth was very hard on mine and I leaned back, away from the weight of him, but my hands came up behind his head and held him to me. The plume of campion fell from my fingers, to the floor, unnoticed, and I leaned back until I was against the door-frame and Ralph was pressed against me and I could feel the length of his warm body, as sweet and as firm as a young lad's.

He scooped me up into his arms, lifted me as if we were familiar lovers and then he laid me down gently on the floor of the summer-house as if it were a bed for a princess. He lay beside me and I pulled his face down to me so I could kiss his mouth, and his closed smooth eyelids, and his warm smooth forehead, and the little crest of dark hair at the hairline. I rubbed his cropped head with my palms in wordless ecstasy of pleasure at the strangeness of him, and at my love for him, and at the madness of this day.

Then I felt him unbuttoning my gown at the back with clumsy hurrying fingers, and I raised my shoulders off the dirty floor to make the task easier for him and watched his face grow grave with concentration as he meticulously undid each tiny button, and then took two great handfuls of material at the hem and stripped it off me, pulled it over my head. I raised my hips to free it from under me, and then lifted my arms so that it would slide over my head, and lay, naked except for my linen shift, on the floor of the summer-house beside him.

He rolled upon me like a wave breaking and kissed my throat, one hand cupping my breast, and then lowered his head to kiss my breast. He pushed up my shift to kiss my warm belly and then kissed between my legs so that I was sprawled, paralysed and astounded with pleasure. I cried out at that; I said, 'Ralph!' and he looked up at me, his dark eyes darker than ever with his desire.

'My love,' he said softly, as though I had no other name. And then he dipped his head and licked me with his hard pointy tongue until I clenched his cropped hair in my hands and breathed out little soft cries of pleasure.

He reared up from me with a smile, a mocking rueful smile which suggested we were both fools to be thus infatuated. And he pulled his shirt over his head, and pulled his boots off and pulled his breeches down. He was naked underneath, and I drew breath in simple, shameless lust. Then he fell upon me as if he could stand delay no longer, and I felt his warm naked body and the soft hairs of his chest and his broad throat against my forehead as he lay on me and I tucked my face into his shoulder and breathed out my desire against his sweet-smelling skin.

'Ralph,' I said again, and the world, the world of Wideacre, seemed to echo to his name. The summer-house was full of him, so was the garden with the weeds growing, the house which had been burned to the ground by him and the village which worshipped him.

'Ralph,' I said again, and then he entered me and it was like the stab of the knife in the dream and when I looked up, I could see him smiling as he smiled in the dream. And when he looked down with eyes so dark and so loving, he could see that I was smiling too.

'Miss Lacey,' he said gently, and he kissed my eyelids and the hollows of my temples and the delicate skin beneath my eyes, and he licked one tear from the corner of my eye, and then he moved in me.

He was gentle, as if he were afraid of hurting me. And indeed there were little times when he did hurt me. But each sharp pain was such pleasure, and each dizzying moment was such delight that I clung to him and arched my back to greet his body with mine, like a chevalier's lady welcoming her lost lord home. Then the pleasure grew more intense and his movements were faster and faster until there was just a blur of pleasure in my mind and I had no knowledge of where I was or who I was or what I was doing. There was just Ralph.

We lay in silence.

After a few moments he sat up and reached for his jacket and my shawl and pulled them over us like a blanket, for the breeze which had blown me up the steps and into his arms was getting stronger.

Ralph leaned on one arm and held me as if I were some precious rare object which had been entrusted to his care. My head leaned against his shoulder, my face to his neck, and I could smell with every indrawn breath the clean animal smell of his skin and a deeper sweeter smell like musk.

I existed nowhere but here. There was no time but this second.

There was no sensation but that of the warm well-touched delighted body. All I could see was his profile as he looked away from me out of the open door. All I could feel was his warmth where he had lain on me, and the soreness where he had been, and the strange peace which seemed to go from the centre of my body up to my head and behind my eyes so all I wanted to do was go to sleep in his arms and wake when he wakened me. I closed my eyes and half dozed, his arm around my bare shoulders, his coat covering me, rough and smelling of heather and wood-smoke.

'Here's the rain,' Ralph said softly. 'I thought those clouds were building up.'

I opened my eyes. Through the ruined walls of the house we could see the rain coming like a great wall of water across the common. The wind preceded the rain, beating the light birches down, and their leaves turned over like my hand smoothing the top of Ralph's cropped head. We felt the coldness of it when it reached the summer-house, and the roof creaked as the draught got in underneath it. Then the rain followed in shafts of silver with drops as long as stair-rods lancing down at the ground.

The storm hammered on the roof like hands on a drum and the summer-house creaked like a barge at sea. We were swept in a curtain of water, at once utterly shielded, utterly private.

'Come on,' said Ralph. 'You'll take cold.'

He tossed my dress to me and pulled on his own shirt. I dressed myself by guess and then I turned back to him. He was sitting with his back to the wall of the summer-house and his legs spread wide.

'Would you like to sit with me for a while?' he invited gently.

I went to him in a little rush and sat beside him, leaning back against him, his arm carelessly holding me. We watched the rain in silence.

We sat for long minutes. The clouds over the common were massed very thick and very dark now, almost violet. But as we watched, the wind which had blown the storm towards us blew it onwards over the hall, over the summer-house, towards Acre and onwards to the sea where the rain could fall on the churning waves, sweet water on salt. The wind tore little gaps in the cloud-cover and then there were patches of blue sky. The hammering on the roof eased and grew softer, and the rain no longer blurred our view, so we could see the dripping garden. The leaves were shiny, brilliant with wetness, and when the sun came out the raindrops on every leaf sparkled like precious stones. There was a wonderful smell on the air of Wideacre: new-washed soaking wetness, drying and growing. In the distance I could hear the Fenny bubbling a little louder, as all the drainage ditches and little streams poured into it, adding to the flow.

My hair had tumbled down and I took one thick ringlet and absently curled it around my finger. Then I paused. The humming in my head was very loud. The lock of hair around my index finger was as red as a fox. As red as a vixen. It was Beatrice's red hair.

And the hall was not ruined, there was no smell of old smoke. The rose garden was perfect, blushing with new roses. The stones of the terrace were smooth and even. The hall was a yellow pearl, with dark curtains at the windows, a great wooden door hospitably open, the wind blowing a plume of smoke away from the chimneys.

I stared, and I blinked. I put my hands to the floor in bewilderment and terror. I had a feeling like falling, as if the very ground beneath my feet had opened up and I was tumbling downwards into a madness where I could dream the dream in real life, where Beatrice could enter my head at any moment, where I could no longer tell the difference between the dream and reality.

The floor was solid, of well-laid new pale planks. The windows were whole, of sparkling clean glass, the white trellis work freshly painted.

Staring disbelievingly out of the door, I turned back to say, 'Ralph! Help me! Whether I am Beatrice or Julia, I know you would not hurt me. Help me! For I am lost and I don't know who I am!'

There was no one there.

There was a pile of dust and leaves in the corner and they stirred as the wind blew through the broken panes. I was fully dressed, leaning against the ramshackle door-frame. I put my hand to my head and pulled at one of my ringlets. It was fair.

I gave a great shuddering sigh and looked out at the wet garden. It was the familiar wilderness of my childhood, the overgrown sprawling rose garden, with the suckers thrusting up, and smoke-stained walls, and the tumbling masonry. I was Julia.

My knees buckled beneath me and I put my face into my hands.

I felt I had to think. I had to understand what was happening to me. I thought of the blow to my head on the stone doorstep, which seemed to have happened years ago – but it was just last night. Perhaps that had injured my mind? But then I thought of the dream, and of the humming noise when I first saw Ralph in the village street. And my body – more certain and more confident than my puzzled worried head – felt as sleek and as comfortable as a well-stroked cat's. I knew I should have been afraid or worried. But I could not feel that there was anything very badly wrong.

And I could not help but feel glad.

I had seen the hall in its prime. I had seen the beauty of the garden and the warmth of the walls. I had seen the terrace whole, I had seen the chimneys smoking as fires were lit in morning-rooms and the kitchen fire was lit ready for cooking.

And I had lain with Ralph as I knew Beatrice had done. And I had been beloved. And he had called me – in a little loving parody of respect – Miss Lacey. That was her name.

And it was also mine.

That was her lover, and her land and her home.

And also mine.

I glanced up at the sun; it was time I went home for breakfast. I got to my feet and went lightly, easily down the steps to the rose garden. The buds themselves were starting to smell sweet in the wetness, and the weeds glowed green. I felt as if nothing could touch me. Nothing could threaten me. I was Beatrice's heir, and there were times when I was Beatrice herself. I might be going home to try to lead the life of a good girl – of Mama's indoor girl – but I had a secret strength inside me which came from Beatrice, my aunt, my other self. I knew I was on my way to loving the land, to understanding the land, as Beatrice had done. And I should work on it with her lover, whom I knew and loved as she had once done, long ago.

I walked home in a daze and I did not think. The breeze which had blown me up the drive to the hall had died down and caressed my face with a damp sweet breath. I smelled the wet earth and the good things growing, and my warm young body floated up the drive as if I were still dreaming. I had no thoughts. There could be no thoughts. It was easy. There were no thoughts which could encompass what had happened. I felt I just had to flow with this madness, with this joy, like a trout on the floodtide of the Fenny. And hope that what I felt was right. And the best thing was not to think at all.

7

I ran up the steps to the front door in a rush and found the door on the latch and the hall deserted. I peeped into the dining-room and saw the table set. I was not late. I had not missed breakfast. The parlour door was firmly shut, and I guessed Richard was still hard at work.

The hem of my dress was muddy from walking in the lane, and the back all dusty. I hurried to my room to change it. One of the new gowns Mama had ordered from the Chichester sempstress had arrived, and I took it from its box.

It was a wonderful colour, the palest green, almost silver, the colour of new corn before it grows tall and strong. In my haste, tumbling into fresh petticoats and the new gown, I glimpsed myself in the mirror and it made me pause.

It was an old mirror, speckled and shadowy, but the reflection of myself that it showed me – my shift cut square across my growing breasts, the line of my cheek-bones, the shadow of my hair tumbling down over my shoulders, the tilt of my head and the haziness of my eyes, which gleamed like grey slates in rain – drew me across the room to look at myself more closely. The reflected eyes gazed back into mine. If only I could learn who I was by staring. Mama had been right to scold me for not wearing a hat every day – I had a speckle of freckles across my nose like the pinpricks of colour you see on a hen's egg. My skin was hen's-egg cream, and as smooth. My face seemed to have lost, in this one morning, my rounded girlish prettiness, and become finer, clearer.

I gazed at myself as though I had never seen myself before.

'I have taken Beatrice's lover,' I said in an awestruck whisper.

'She has possessed me utterly. I went up the drive to her home and met her lover in the very place where she met him. And we lay together as if I were her. I was full of the longing that she felt for him, and I could not bear the longing until she possessed me and I did what she used to do.'

My eyes dropped from the mirror and I turned away. I had to hide this secret joy, and I had to hide this secret strength. This morning I had to make my peace with the two men who ruled this household – Uncle John and Richard – and I would not be able to do it with that sated look in my eyes and that secret smile on my lips.

The gong for breakfast sounded and I shook my head, clearing it of magic, and turned and ran downstairs, pushing one final pin into the ringlets on the top of my head as I ran.

The newly drawn plans for the hall had arrived, and we hurried breakfast so that we might look at them before Richard went down the lane to his lessons in Acre. The architect had drawn a fascinating house, very much in the modern style, a fine plain building with a delightful rounded tower at one corner and a square frontage with the familiar great doorway and high clear windows. It was three storeys high.

'A palace!' Mama said.

'The old hall was as big,' Uncle John reminded her. 'You have been living in Lilliput-land for so long you have forgotten how to live in a proper-sized house.'

'Gracious,' I said, awed. 'It does look very fine, Uncle John.'

'We shall be very fine to match it,' he said firmly. 'How will you like to be Miss Lacey of Wideacre Hall, Julia?'

'Very much,' I said. Then I remembered what Richard wanted of me. 'But more than anything I am looking forward to seeing Richard as squire in a proper hall.'

'And speaking of fresh starts and new plans,' Uncle John said, smiling, 'I think it is time the pair of you started learning to ride in earnest. It is Chichester horse fair today, and I am going with the hope of buying a useful hunter for myself, and I have a mind to buy a horse each for you. If I can find something suitable.'

I did not say a word, I could not speak. I realized my hands were clasped under my chin and I had half risen from my seat, but I said nothing.

Richard was oddly silent too.

'I will assume that silence betokens consent,' Uncle John said teasingly.

'Oh, yes!' I said longingly. 'Oh, yes! Oh, yes! Oh, yes!'

Uncle John laughed, his eyes on Mama. 'They really are delightful, Celia,' he said, speaking over our heads as if we were very small children. 'They truly are delightfully unspoiled, I agree. But Wideacre or no, they must go to town and university and have a little polish rubbed on them.'

'Dreadful!' Mama said. 'Julia, you put me utterly to the blush! Stop saying, "Oh, yes" like that and say, "Thank you," as though you had a ha'p'orth of wit. And, Richard, it's not like you to have nothing to say for yourself.'

Richard cleared his throat. 'Thank you, sir,' he said politely. I think only I could hear the lack of enthusiasm in his voice, and I had a twinge of remorse and sympathy for Richard. I guessed he was thinking of Scheherazade.

'Thank you, Uncle John,' I said softly. 'Mama is right and I have no manners at all. I was just so . . . so . . . so . . .'

Uncle John smiled at Mama as I ran out of words.

'Boarding-school?' he suggested.

'Bedlam!' Mama replied. 'Julia, if you have nothing to say, you can go and fetch some writing-paper and ink for me, instead of kneeling there on the floor with your mouth open. Richard, it must be time for you to go to Dr Pearce.'

Richard bowed to her and bid us a general farewell and then took one last lingering look at the exquisite drawing, like a hungry man looking at a meal which might be taken from him. 'Yes,' he said unwillingly, and went to the door.

I waited for a smile from him, but I had none. He went from the house with his head down and not even a glance towards me, though I stood in the hall as he shrugged on his greatcoat and was at the front door when he went out. He went without a look at me. He went without a word to me, though he knew I was waiting patiently for either. I stood at the parlour window and watched him stride down the drive, watched in case he relented and waved to me, but he did not. Mama saw my stillness and my eyes upon his vanishing figure when she came into the parlour.

'Will you write some letters for me, my dear?' she said invitingly.

'Yes, I will,' I said without hesitation.

She looked at me closely. 'Is Richard still angry with you about John Dench?' she asked softly.

I did not have tears in my eyes. I did not feel an ache in my heart. I did not feel the sense of dread which I learned in childhood when I thought of Richard's rage. I gave a little impatient grimace. 'He's in the sullens,' I said, unimpressed. 'He'll get out of them.'

And ignoring Mama's look of surprise, I sat up at the table, collected some notepaper, dipped the pen in the standish and set to writing to her dictation as if I had never cried for Richard's approval in my life.

Uncle John was lucky at the horse sales; but Richard and I were not.

'I could see nothing which would suit either of you,' he said. 'I *am* sorry to disappoint you, and I am disappointed too. I had promised myself the pleasure of coming home in the carriage with three horses trotting behind me. I found this grand old hunter for me, but nothing suitable for the two of you.'

'What was the problem, sir?' Richard asked courteously.

We were sitting down to a late dinner, and Uncle John smiled down the table at Richard as he carved a plump goose into wafer-thin slices and Stride passed them around.

'Bad breeding,' he said briefly. 'I wanted something steady and sound for both of you, but something with a bit of breeding so that you could have more fun when you were used to riding. I'd have looked for something fairly lively for you, Richard, don't fret! And something slow and steady for Julia. But there was nothing except some broken-winded hunters who would never get out of a trot without gasping like a landed fish.'

Richard laughed heartily. I watched him closely. He was out of his ill humour with me, and he seemed relaxed, even pleased. I could not understand it. I was trying very hard not to seem sulky, but I was so disappointed at Uncle John's bad luck at the horse fair that I could have wept.

'Perhaps you have saved your money, sir,' Richard said. 'I was thinking that, as I am going to Oxford, you would have bought a horse for me for nothing. I could not ride one there, I suppose?'

'No,' Uncle John agreed, carving the last slices of goose and sitting down to his own place. Stride served him with crunchy roasted potatoes, some succulent carrots from the Havering kitchen garden and roasted parsnip. Uncle John waved away the gravy, but took a liberal helping of Mrs Gough's smooth lemon sauce. 'But I had thought, Richard, to keep your horse here for you to use in the holidays. That is no great burden on the stables, you know.'

Richard smiled sweetly. 'You're kind to me, sir!' he said. 'But since you have had such trouble in finding a suitable horse at this fair, I do beg you not to trouble yourself any further. I have walked around Wideacre all my life, and am well able to continue to do so in the meantime. I am sure Julia feels the same.'

I opened my mouth to disagree, but a sharp blue look from Richard silenced me.

'At any rate, there is no need for a horse this summer,' Richard said smoothly. 'I know Julia's grandmama does not approve of ladies riding in summertime, and I am happy to go horseless to keep my cousin company.'

Mama smiled. 'That is sweet of you, Richard!' she said approvingly, and Uncle John nodded. 'And he is quite right,' she said to John. 'It is not really the season to start to learn to ride. If there are no good horses available, perhaps the two of them can wait until the Christmas holidays.'

Uncle John shrugged. 'As you wish,' he said. 'I should have liked to have produced two horses for the pair of you without further ado, but there is certainly nothing suitable in the neighbourhood for sale at the moment. I shall keep my eyes open for you both, you may be sure. If we cannot find suitable riding horses, then you will have to drive around and I shall get a cob or something to pull the gig.'

I bit my lip and looked down. I seemed forever to be getting so close to having a horse and then being disappointed.

Mama saw my downcast face and smiled sweetly at me. 'Never mind, Julia,' she said. 'We will order you a riding habit when we are next in Chichester and then at least when we find the right horse, you will be ready to ride at once.'

'Thank you, Mama,' I said, trying to sound pleased. And I turned my attention to the roast goose as if I had been fasting all day.

'I met Lord Havering in Chichester and told him some of my ideas about the revival of the estate,' Uncle John said. 'He was kind enough to call them radical poppycock!'

'You did not quarrel?' Mama asked with an anxious frown.

'Most certainly not,' John said. 'It takes two to make a quarrel, and his lordship made sure I did not have a word to say. I told him some of the ideas I had and he was torn between laughter at my naïvety and rage at my revolutionary opinions.'

'*Are* you a revolutionary, Uncle John?' I said, regarding him with some awe.

'Compared to your grandpapa, I am a veritable traitor to the State!' Uncle John said cheerfully. 'But in all seriousness, Julia, I am just one of very many men who think that the world would be better run if the nation were not divided into a vast army of workers – something like six million people – who have no land, and a tiny minority – some four hundred families – who between them own it all.'

'What would you do?' I asked. 'What would you do to change things?'

'If I were made king tomorrow,' Uncle John said, smiling, 'I would pass a statute which would give everyone equal shares in the land, and order them to work in communities and farm the land all together. Everyone would have his own house and his own patch of private land, his own little garden and his own animals – see, Celia, I am *not* against private property, whatever your step-papa says! – But everyone would work together on land which was held in common. Like the old village fields when the elders of the village decided what was planted and how it was to be done.'

'Hurrah for John's kingdom!' I said, and Uncle John laughed at my bright face.

'I have a convert,' he said to Mama. 'There is no need for you to look so grave, Celia. I have a convert and the future is on my side.'

'What will you do before you become king of England?' she asked. 'How will you explain to Acre that the golden age has come around again?'

'I shall consult my adviser,' he said solemnly and turned to me. 'Prime Minister, Miss Julia: how shall we persuade Acre that they must all work together and take a share in the profits?'

I thought for a moment. 'Is it a serious plan, Uncle John?' I asked. 'Do you really want Acre to share in the profits of the estate?'

'I'm tempted,' he admitted. 'I spent many hours in India reading and thinking about what went wrong on Acre. It seemed to me then that the only way to run an estate justly is if everyone has a say in how it is to be run and a slice of the profits.' He paused and looked at my intent face and Mama's doubtful one. Richard was listening with his habitual courtesy.

'How would it be if every cottager – tenant or labourer – in Acre was invited to buy a share in the profits of the estate?' John asked. 'They work the first year and the profits are put into a central fund. Out of the fund come the costs of running the estate, and the new equipment and seeds and animals needed, and the share which is to be paid to each worker. But the rest of the fund is their own savings.'

'And what about us?' Richard asked. It was the first time he had spoken, and his voice sounded sharp. 'We're Laceys of

Wideacre,' he said. 'Where do we figure in this scheme? What do we benefit?'

'We take our share of the profits,' Uncle John replied. 'We consider the money invested in Wideacre as our share of work, and we take out a share every year which would be the same as if we had invested money in speculation.'

'We share the profits of our land with Acre?' Richard asked. The question itself sounded as if he were just trying to understand, but something in his voice made the nape of my neck feel cold and prickly. 'Won't that make them think they have rights over our land? And won't they argue for a greater share than they have earned?'

Uncle John nodded. 'Perhaps,' he said. 'But you would be the judge of their rights.'

Stride came forward to clear the table. He took the plates and refilled the wineglasses before Mama and John. No one was looking at Richard except me. He had gone quite white and his eyes were as black as a midnight sky, without a gleam of starlight or moonlight. He was trembling with rage as he sat at the table, and I dropped my gaze to the embroidered napkin on my lap, afraid that Richard would shout his claim to Wideacre and disgrace himself by an outburst of the temper he usually kept so well in check.

I should have known him better. By the time Stride came back with the puddings, a wonderful cream confection with meringue and apple sauce on top, and a plain jam tart, Richard was smiling and calm.

'It's a most exciting idea, sir,' he said politely. I think no one but me could have heard the passion which was hidden beneath the calm tone. 'Do you think you can take it beyond the stage of an idea?'

Stride served Mama and then me, and Uncle John accepted a plate with the jam tart from him and added Havering cream with a generous hand.

'It depends,' he said. 'It depends on many factors. The people would have to like the idea. They suffered badly at the hands of

Lacey innovators once, and they're not likely to want to repeat the experience. Mr Megson assures me that they will not go to work for us unless they have some belief in the future and some trust in us.' He paused and smiled down the table at Richard and me. 'It depends on you two,' he said gently. 'It is your inheritance. It will be your decision whether this land is run in the old way which brought so much wealth and so much grief in one lifetime, or whether you would want to try a new way.'

I glanced at Richard; his smile was untroubled, his face clear. 'I agree with you, sir,' he said. 'I can think of no better way to run the estate than to share the profits of the land with the people who work on it.'

Uncle John nodded and looked at me. 'Julia?' he asked.

'Yes,' I said. I did not sound as enthusiastic as Richard. But I could not readily explain how the thought of feeling no guilt in Acre – none at all – of being free of the cruelty of the Laceys and the cruelty of the whole class of gentry was like a hard cleansing wind after rain. 'Yes,' I said.

'Early days for any decision,' Uncle John said gently. 'But I should like the two of you to go and see Mr Megson and tell him of your support for these ideas, and discuss with him his thoughts on them. It's a good way for him to get to know the two of you, and a good way for you to learn the obstacles you will face in Acre. He's a hard man to persuade – he's not susceptible to sweetening! But he's as straight as a die. I'd like the two of you to tell him of this talk of ours and see what he thinks the chances are for a plan like that.'

'I'd be pleased to go,' Richard said, claiming the right of the boy and the squire-to-be to work for the estate.

'And Julia will go too,' Uncle John said, reminding him.

'Yes,' I said. 'I should like to go.'

'No reason why you should not go down to Acre this evening,' Mama said, determinedly brave with us, her two children, going to the village she still disliked. 'You could take the gig, and the carriage horse,' she said.

Uncle John smiled. 'Indeed, yes!' he said. 'Mr Megson will

doubtless give you tea and you can come home before it is dark if you would like it.'

I glanced at Richard. I had been in disgrace with him all day and I was not disposed to force my company on him if he was still angry with me. But the threat to his inheritance had driven all other injuries from his mind.

I ran to fetch my hat, and Richard went to the stable to tell Jem that we wanted the horse and the new gig. The sun was round and pink above a bank of rosy clouds as we trotted down the lane to Acre and I saw, with relief, that Richard was at ease on the seat of the gig, handling the reins well, unafraid.

'I hope Megson is in,' Richard said.

'I'll wager he's expecting us,' I said shrewdly. 'I should think that Uncle John and he have spent some time with their heads together about the two of us as heirs to the estate.'

Richard glanced at me in surprise. 'I suppose they might have done,' he said. 'Megson setting himself up as some kind of judge!' He paused. 'I don't have to remind you not to put yourself forward in Acre,' he said. It was not a question.

'No, I remember,' I said steadily.

He gave me a swift sideways glance but said nothing, and then we sat in silence as the gig bowled down the street of Acre. The Dench children were playing in the patch of earth outside the cottage; Clary was sitting on the bench watching them in the evening sunlight, with a bowl of potatoes on her knees and a bucket of water to wash them.

I waved and Richard obligingly brought the gig to a halt. Clary came down the garden path with her long stride.

'Good day,' she said to the two of us. And with a smile to me she said, 'Carriage folk at last, Julia?'

'I'm so grand I can hardly trouble myself to speak to you,' I said, grinning at her.

She laughed. 'It's a fine gig, Master Richard,' she said with a smile to him.

Richard nodded but made no reply. He looked at her under lowered brows, his eyes a bright blue. 'Maybe I'll give you a ride in it one day,' he said, making an effort. He was looking at her, but he lacked his easy smile. He looked at her as if she were something he might decide to buy in a market.

'Thank you,' Clary said easily, and stepped back from the side of the gig. 'Are you going to see Ralph Megson?' she asked me.

'Yes,' I said. 'Is he settled in the Tyackes' cottage?'

'Aye,' she said. 'And Becky Miles is keeping house and cleaning for him. He's expecting you.'

I nodded, and Richard clicked to the horse and we drove on down the lane to the cottage which was set back from the street down a little track on the left-hand side.

Richard looped the reins over the garden gate and the horse dipped its head. There was no hedge to crop. All the leaves had been taken for animal feed years ago, and then the bare sticks themselves used for firewood. Like every other garden in Acre, the earth was bare. First all the vegetables had been lifted and eaten, and then the surviving scrawny hens had picked the garden clean. Now there was nothing but grey dust and, when it rained, a mire of mud.

We walked up the flagstone path and I shivered at the thought of seeing Ralph, a tension so strong it was almost dread. When I raised my hand to knock, I saw it was trembling. I could hear the kettle singing on the stove, and its note was not higher or sweeter than the noise in my head now I was so close to Ralph. The door was opened to us not by Ralph Megson, but by Becky Miles, who seemed to have installed herself as cook, parlourmaid and kitchenmaid.

I looked at her sharply. She was a big lumpy downland girl with masses of fair hair and big dim blue eyes. The poverty of her family was held to be sufficient excuse for the fact that she wore dresses with bodices cut so low that you could see the top of her plump breasts and hems so high that you could see her ankles. I had always quite liked her. She had been one of the children who trailed around after Clary. I liked her cheery nature and the way she threw back her head to laugh. And I liked her sweet voice, which would rise in a clear soprano in carols at

Christmastide. But today, for some reason, she seemed to me too large, too bright, too overpowering in the little room, and I wondered that Ralph Megson did not feel crowded by her and send her away.

He did not look crowded. He looked very much at home. The Tyackes' cottage was the best in Acre, but it had only two rooms downstairs and three poky little bedrooms upstairs. The main downstairs room was the brick-floored one which served as kitchen and dining- and living-room. The front door opened directly into it, and winter and summer it was hot and stifling with the fire in the grate for the cooking.

Ralph owned a great round table, which was in the middle of the room, rocky on the uneven floor, and a high-backed settle, which had its back to the door. The master chair – a wheel-backed carver – was at the head of the table with its back to the fire, and beneath the table were three stools for guests. Through a doorway to the left was the parlour, used for the most solemn occasions. Only if there were a funeral or a wedding in the house would the neighbours get over the threshold into that room. And then in Acre – where poverty was a way of life and people had forgotten the time when they had furniture – they would find the room swept clean and as empty as a Wideacre wheat barn. The parlour table and chairs had been sold for pennies when the family was hungry, and they had never risen from the grip of poverty and been able to buy more.

Seeing Ralph Megson here reminded me that he was not Quality. He was one of the tenants. He lived in a cottage which was no more than five rooms. But I realized that he was wealthy in Acre terms. He had a proper chair, a proper table. He had china to eat from, not wooden plates and bowls. He had linen – there was a good plain tablecloth laid ready – he had a servant, if one could honour sluttish Becky Miles with that title.

He was not gentry, living here and served thus, but I had been quick to note that Uncle John always referred to him as Mr Megson. Although he could never be Quality, he had a certain air which made you question the whole idea of 'sorts' of people.

He rose to his feet when we came in and greeted us confidently as equals. He waved us towards the stools on either side of the table and took the chair again without a thought that perhaps it should have been offered to me. And he nodded to Becky to serve the tea as if she (who had never seen a tablecloth in her life, at my guess) might know what she was doing.

She did tolerably well. I tried not to watch her, but when she opened little cupboards or pulled out a drawer of cutlery, I could not help my eyes sliding towards her, partly to see what she was doing and partly to see what things he had. Pure curiosity, and I hoped he would not see it; but Becky made a clatter behind me and I glanced over my shoulder and he saw me look. He gave me a little smile – he knew very well that I was inspecting his goods, and his eyes were tolerant.

I settled on my stool then with a little silent sigh. He might be on company behaviour, and so was I, but there was an understanding between us which was a current flowing under the stream of talk. I had some silly, superstitious fear that he might know that I dreamed of him – that I dreamed of desiring him, and loving him, and holding him. The mere thought of him knowing that dream made me colour so red that the blush hurt my cheeks and made my eyes water. I kept my head facing down and felt myself burn with embarrassment.

I felt his eyes upon me and I flashed a quick look at him.

He knew something. He sensed something, like a keen bright-eyed animal. But the smile he gave me was easy. I did not think he guessed my thoughts. But I remembered that he had been very much in love with Beatrice, and I felt, with his eyes upon me, that he was tender to me. So I straightened my back, waited for my blush to die down and found the courage to smile and meet his eyes.

There are some things which need no words, and Ralph knew that better than I. So I sipped my tea and did not flinch when Becky clattered the kettle close to me behind my back, and I passed Richard some lardy cake as though I had not a care in the world.

We talked firstly about the plans Uncle John had for the land, and Ralph made us describe them in detail.

'The idea is that everyone in the village should share in the profits of the land, not draw a wage as such,' Richard explained, his tone neutral. 'The profits are paid into a common fund which buys new seeds and equipment. We landlords draw a wage which represents interest on the money invested in the land. And the remainder of the fund is divided according to the amount of work each individual has done.'

'The idea is to establish some sort of communality?' asked Ralph. I knew he knew the answer, and I stayed silent, watching his face, watching him test Richard, judge him. Richard's eyes were as limpid as a pool. You would have thought him a most ardent land reformer.

Richard nodded. 'So that the difference between masters and men is erased,' he said. 'We are all working together. Success or failure, we all share in the profits.'

Ralph nodded. 'It's a good plan,' he said. He looked at Richard carefully. 'A generous one,' he said. 'What do the landowners gain from it, d'you think, Master Richard?'

'Very little,' Richard said frankly. 'It's my papa's idea, to set Acre to rights. To repay for the bad things which happened in the past. It benefits the village. It helps the poor.' He paused, glanced at Ralph's dark face, tested the air: 'Perhaps the best way is the old way, with the Laceys as squires owning the land, paying fair wages and supplying suitable charity in cases of especial need.'

Ralph nodded. 'Is that the way you'd prefer?' he asked.

Richard glanced at him, his eyes bright with calculation. 'I want to make sure Acre is a good place for everyone,' he said. 'Whatever way we decide to do it, I want to ensure that the village is set to rights. At least in the old way, everyone knew where they were.'

Ralph nodded as if he had learned something. 'And you, Miss Julia?' he asked.

'I agree with Richard,' I said steadily, holding to my promise.

Ralph smiled at me, a little intimate smile which suggested he knew I was lying and that in my heart I wanted the village to own its land outright. One of the logs shifted in the hearth and a little plume of ash and smoke went up. There was a moment of utter peace, his eyes upon me and me smiling at him.

Richard moved irritably, and the spell was broken. 'What shall I tell my papa?' he said. 'He asked us to discuss the scheme with you. May I tell him you prefer the old ways?'

Ralph pushed back his chair from the table and stamped on his wooden legs to the door to throw it open and look out, up the little back track to Acre. 'Look, you,' he said, leaning on the doorpost and looking out. 'This is a fine scheme, and a generous one from any landowner, even a bankrupt one. I respect that. But you are asking for someone to give up the way he has lived for the past fourteen years, wild, and without a master. Starving in winter maybe, but eating game and fish and fowl all summer. And free to work as he pleases, or poach as he pleases, or fish as he pleases every day of the year. You are asking a man like that to settle down into a routine of working.

'And for what? You are not even offering a decent wage. You are offering the promise of a share in the profits on crops which are not yet in the ground. If the profits are small, you yourselves tell me that first out of the fund is the needs of the land, second is your share, and last are the workers. If there are no profits at all – well, you have the option to sell the land. And sell it now as a going concern with a village eager for work. But if there are no profits, then the people of Acre starve for another winter.

'You landlords risk nothing – you have a derelict estate you cannot work or sell. If the village was to go for this scheme, you would have them back at work at no cost to you, and if they fail to work hard enough to make the profits your scheme needs, they are the ones who suffer. Landlords never suffer. They write the laws, they invent the rules. They make the world, and then they expect people to be grateful for small mercies!'

Ralph leaned back against the doorpost and smiled at us both as though we were rather charming brigands. 'You offer no guarantees,' he said. 'Acre is guaranteed to you. Everyone here is so poor that there is nowhere they can go, and no freedom they can take. But you can suit yourselves. You can play at being radical for a few years, or you can sell the estate tomorrow at a profit, to the first buyer who comes your way, rack-renter, corn-forestaller, whatever. There are no controls over the gentry,' he said and paused. 'There never are,' he added.

Richard and I sat in stunned silence. In everything Uncle John had said since his return from India, we had never seen the scheme like this. Ralph Megson, who was not of the Quality, saw the objections in a flash. And he had seen it as another ruse by the masters against the men, concealed, this time, in some persuasive egalitarian fair-share scheme, profiteering wrapped up prettily. I dropped my eyes to the tablecloth and coloured up to my ears with shame at my foolishness in not spotting such an obvious argument against the idea, and in my shame at being seen by Ralph Megson as one of the gentry who take what they have not earned and use what they have not made.

He left the door open and the evening sunlight streamed on to the brick floor and turned the dust into little stars floating in infinity. He trod heavily back to the table and the stars swirled at his passing. As he went behind me, the back of his hand just brushed the nape of my neck, and I knew it was a touch which meant forgiveness.

'Tell Dr MacAndrew I'll think on it,' Ralph said, surprisingly. 'It's a bold scheme and if there were such a thing as a landlord one could trust, it would be a good one. It needs some guarantees from the two of you, or you will never persuade Acre to do it; and you'd not have my support. But if the two of you are committed to the idea, it might work.'

'If you advise that the land is best worked in the old ways, with the squire owning everything and good wages paid, I think my papa would take your advice,' Richard said quickly.

Ralph looked hard at him. 'Do you now?' he asked. And he said no more.

'We must go,' I said after a little pause. 'Thank you for our tea, Mr Megson.'

'You're welcome,' he said pleasantly. 'Both of you must come and see me again.' He nodded at Richard. 'If you're interested in hawking, my goshawk will be sent down from London in the next few days. I'd be happy to take you out with me.'

'Thank you, I will!' Richard said, and for the first time that afternoon his smile to Ralph was genuine – not the calculating charm he had donned since Mama and Uncle John had joined in backing Mr Megson against his accusation.

Ralph walked with us to the gate and helped me up the step into the gig while Richard loosed the horse. I put out my hand to him.

'Good day, Miss Julia,' he said with the mocking courtesy I had dreamed of this morning. Then he bent his proud greying head and kissed my hand. At the touch of his lips on my fingers I shivered like a birch tree in a breeze. He stepped back into his patch of garden and waved farewell to us.

8

The news we brought of Ralph Megson's reaction made Uncle John look anxious at supper and sent him into the library to look at the provisional leases he had drawn up. The next day he ordered the carriage for Chichester to see the Wideacre lawyers to ask them what they thought about a contract which would bind both the workers and the squires.

He paused as he came down the steps. I was in the front garden, the very picture of a demure young lady in a high-waisted white gown and a sun-bonnet to shield my face. But my fingers were suspiciously muddy, and when Uncle John came down the path, I was not quick enough to tuck the little spade out of sight.

'Gardening, Julia?' Uncle John said. He sounded appropriately scandalized, but there was an undercurrent of laughter in his voice. 'Julia! My niece Julia! What are we going to do with you! What does your mama say about you gardening?'

'She tries not to know,' I said, shamefaced. 'Uncle John, I know it is not proper, but someone had to do it. And Stride is too old, and all Jem's plants died. And there was no one else. And you know how Mama loves flowers,' I said, striking the very note which would persuade him.

'Mama and I agreed that I might do it providing that no one of the Quality sees me. And *that* is all right, Uncle John, because no one ever comes down the drive in a carriage in the morning. And I never do it in the afternoon.'

Uncle John tried to look severe, but he cracked into a laugh of irrepressible merriment. 'Miss Julia! You are having a clandestine affair with Nature!' he said. 'But how do you know anything at all about gardening?'

'I just know,' I said vaguely. 'I knew of Mama's favourite flowers from Wideacre Hall, and when I was very little, I collected the seed pods to give her. I planted them in little pots in my bedroom and when they grew, I planted them here so Mama should have her favourite flowers around her, so she should not be homesick for the hall, and the gardens.'

Uncle John nodded, his face understanding. 'That was well done indeed,' he said. 'But who told you where the plants should go? Whether they like light or shade?'

I shrugged. I could not have explained. 'I suppose I looked where they were growing and doing well in the old garden,' I said, trying to remember. 'But also, when I have a little bulb or a handful of seeds in my hand, I can somehow feel where they want to go. Whether they like the soil moist or dry.' I broke off. 'It makes no sense when I speak of it,' I said. 'But I seem to have been born knowing how to grow things.'

Uncle John looked at me hard, and the laughter was gone from his eyes. 'Do they always grow for you?' he asked suddenly. 'No diseased plants, no sudden disappointments? No seedlings all shrivelled when you thought they were doing well?'

'No,' I said, surprised. 'But the earth is so good here, Uncle John. And the weather just right. And I am only planting things which are accustomed to Wideacre, which have already done well here.' I took a few steps towards him and put out a rather grubby hand. 'Why do you look like that?' I asked shyly. 'I can stop gardening now you are home. Now you are home, you can hire a gardener. I should miss it, but if you dislike it so much, I can stop doing it.'

Uncle John shook his head, as if to clear a whirl of thoughts. 'No,' he said. 'It is I who am in the wrong. I was a little shocked to find you resembling your Aunt Beatrice in this skill with the land. That was a talent she had. By the time she was dead, they had made it into some fairytale black art in the village, but that need not concern you. All it ever was, which you have inherited, was a very valuable skill. And it strikes me that if you are a good gardener, you might make a good farmer. We will need all the skills we can to teach Acre how to make the land yield again. Would you work on the land, Julia? If your mama agreed?'

I gasped. 'Uncle John, I should *love* to farm!' I exclaimed. 'You mean help getting the hayfields back to hay and planting wheat? Uncle John! I should *love* it!'

Uncle John smiled at my bright face and patted my cheek. 'Lacey girls!' he said with much love. 'Land-crazed, all of them. But I shall do my best to make sure that this one does not go wrong. If your mama permits, I shall be glad to see you taking this talent of yours to the fields and getting them growing. And in return, you will remember that people matter more than crops; the village of Acre matters more than the wealth of Wideacre.'

I nodded, only partly understanding what he meant.

'But we will get nowhere unless I can get an agreement past my stiff-necked farm manager,' Uncle John said dourly, and went towards the garden gate. 'Anyone would think that he was employing me and giving me orders instead of vice versa. What he will not understand is that I am no more free than the workers of Acre. I have to find some way to convince the lawyers that I am not cheating you and Richard of your inheritance. And, indeed, I *am* cheating you! You would make more money if we simply got Acre working and sold it as a going concern.'

I opened the gate for him and stood by it as he went through towards the waiting carriage, with Jem standing by the steps. I heard the sense in Uncle John's words and my own Quality-trained mind responded at once to the idea of high profits for the landlords. But the dream of Ralph had put me in tune with the land. Since yesterday morning in the summer-house I had seemed to feel the air on my cheek like a caress, the sun on my face more warm; the grass on the Dower House lawn was softer, greener than any summer grass before. The great lush forest that was Wideacre woods took my breath away, and the circles of downs beyond were ripe mountains.

Ralph's words in the living-room of the cottage which was the best cottage in Acre and yet still a hovel compared with the Dower House had taught me, in a sudden bolt of shame, that we

were rich because Acre was poor. And however kindly inten-
tioned we were, or however we planned to make the division of
profits more fair, none the less we belonged to the wider world,
and we could live as we pleased. We were rich and free in a way
that the villagers never would be. And we did not invite them to
tea.

'It is not just ownership of the land,' I said tentatively to
Uncle John. 'It is power. We can make all the promises we like,
and yet, if we wish, we can walk away from Acre tomorrow, and
sell to the first comer. They know that.'

Uncle John grinned wryly. 'You are as bad as Acre,' he said.
'They think that the gentry are incapable of sharing their rights.
They will not believe a gift when they see it. And so they argue
and want guarantees when you and I and Richard and your
mama want nothing more than to make the land right again.'

He smiled at me, the swift grin of a man who knows his own
mind, and I felt myself smile back. I liked Uncle John, and I
knew why my mama loved him. He had no feeling for the land;
he was an utter outsider on Wideacre. But he was a man of such
honour that he would never leave a debt unpaid. He felt he owed
a debt to Acre, and he would work until it was clear. He was a
man without deceit, a man one could trust.

'No one doubts you, Uncle John,' I said. 'They only doubt the
world you live in.' He smiled at that. 'Have a pleasant day,' I
said, almost as a blessing, 'and do not get too tired.'

Uncle John threw me a mock salute and climbed into the
carriage. Jem folded up the steps, shut the door and climbed on
to the driving box. He twirled his whip in a salute to me and set
the bays going. They were fresh and happy to be out in the
spring sunshine and they leaped forward; the carriage was gone
in a swirl of white dust.

I glanced back at the house, but there was no one waving from
the windows. Mama had some patterns for brocades for curtains,
and the morning's post had brought her details of houses for sale
in Bath. She had taken them to the parlour to read, and she was
not looking out of the window, not even to wave farewell to

Uncle John. Richard had long since gone to his lessons with Dr Pearce.

No one was watching me.

I was alone.

I laid my basket of seedlings down in the shade of a flowering currant bush. An early bee buzzed hopefully around the scarlet buds, looking for pollen and nectar, and the sound reminded me of high summer. There was not a muscle in my body which was not pliable and soft. My skin felt like warm cream, melting in the sunlight. I wandered down to the garden gate without a thought in my head. I wanted to be in a place where I could lie down in the shade and daydream.

I went up the drive as I had done before. But this time I did not want to go to the hall. I half thought the dream might be waiting for me there, but there was no singing which called me onwards in that direction. I wanted to see the Fenny. I wanted to lie beside the river and hear it burble over the stones. I wanted to see it flow and watch the sunshine dance in dappled brilliance on the water. I wanted to lie in shifting sun and shadow and dream of the young man who had held me.

I turned down the little path which leads from the drive to our childhood fishing pool, secret and dark amid the tall trees of the wood. It was a tight fit now that the early summer growth was sprouting, and a bramble caught at my gown as I pushed through. But once I was inside the deep wood I could move easily.

The wood-pigeons in the trees above my head cooed of love and mating and the thrushes in the lower branches warbled a long lovely liquid song which went on and on, like someone playing on a flute without a tune or pattern. The brown leaf-mould soft under my feet was starred with wood anemones in a carpet of white, and at the base of each broad grey tree-trunk there was a mass of spiky green leaves, promising a rich crop of bluebells later in the month. The land, supposedly wrecked and derelict, was thick with life. The woods, which had not been clipped or pruned or cropped in fourteen years, were rich with growth. I touched a beech tree and felt the bark warm under my palm. Then I followed the little path to the pool, to Richard's pool, to my pool, where no one else ever came.

Ralph was there.

Of course he was there.

Without my knowing it, my feet had brought me here to be with him. Without an idea in my head, I had been seeking him ever since I had left the garden. Ralph was here.

He was seated on the ground, leaning back against a great fir tree which stretched even higher than the others, like a great tall pillar up to the blue sky, beyond the thick criss-crossing branches which were the roof of the wood, the ceiling of this private shadowy world. He was wearing a felt hat, pulled down to shade his eyes, like a common man. I stood silently, watching him, thinking that he might be asleep. He had laid aside his wooden legs and his body looked oddly short, stopping thus at the knees, as if in some jest he had buried himself in the leaves.

I realized, with a shock, that he was no younger than Uncle John, whom I had sent on his way with an anxious reminder not to get too tired. But John was worn with longing and duty, and Ralph – for all the pain he had suffered and the danger he had run – had never gone against his own inclination once in his life.

He tipped back his hat and his eyes were open. 'Miss Julia,' he said sleepily. 'I give you good day.'

'Mr Megson,' I said, equally formal, but my voice shook and gave me away.

He looked up at me with a smile, his eyes warm. 'Do sit down,' he said, as courteous as he would have been in a drawing-room. 'The ground is not damp.'

I gathered my pale skirts under me and sat beside him, within reach, but not too close. I had a feeling that he measured the distance I had chosen with eyes of some experience.

'I am here poaching,' Ralph said. 'Would you like to watch me tickle for trout? Was there anyone to teach you when you and Richard were little?'

'No,' I said. 'No one. There was only Mama, and the servants, of course.'

'There was a whole village of poachers down the lane who could have shown you,' Ralph said. 'But, of course, they would not count.'

'We hardly ever went there when we were small,' I said, half apologetic. 'It was only when I made friends with Clary that I started to know the people in Acre at all. It is still unusual for Mama to go to the village, except for church on Sunday.'

'Because of the fire?' Ralph asked as if it were an historical event of no great interest.

'Yes,' I said. 'She was afraid of the village after that.'

He nodded, his face non-committal. 'No need,' he said. 'Everyone in Acre respected your mama. They knew what she tried to do for them. The firing of the hall was to break the power of the Laceys – Beatrice and Harry – no attack upon your mama or your Uncle John.'

'Perhaps it was a little hard for her to make the distinction,' I said waspishly. 'That night left her a widow with a bankrupt estate and two children to rear alone. If Acre did not mean to harm her, then it botched the job pretty thoroughly.'

Ralph beamed down at me, not at all put out by my suddenly sharp tone. 'Oh, the gentry!' he said, amused. 'The Quality voice!'

Then he swung around and shuffled to the side of the pool. I was ready to retract everything I had said, but Ralph had forgotten it already.

'The way to do it is to make the trout think that your hand is part of the water,' he said as he leaned over the lip of the pool. 'They have very sensitive skins, and I think they can smell the water too. So one of the first tricks is to make your hands clean and cold. Before you even start to feel for him, you leave your hand in the water for a while.'

Ralph stripped off his jacket and spread it out for me to lie on. Then he rolled up his sleeves and washed his hands carefully in the water of the pool, and rubbed a little mud from the side into his palms. I pushed my lacy cuffs up above my elbows and copied him exactly, and then we lay, faces staring into the pool, hands in the water, for silent minutes.

The ripples from our touching the water cleared and steadied, and I found I was gazing at the reflection of us, side by side. The dark water was kind to Ralph, and he did not look old enough to be my father. It hid the dark lines drawn by pain on either side of his mouth and the deep parallel furrows between his eyebrows. In the shifting sunlight which filtered through the budding leaves over our heads he looked not old and not young, but timeless; as ageless as one of the trees around us, as the earth they were rooted in.

I thought of the legend about the Culler in the village, that he was one of the dark gods of the earth who had taken Beatrice away to the heart of the land, and I gave a little shudder and felt suddenly icy down my spine as I realized I was alone in the darkest part of the Wideacre woods with a killer.

Ralph turned his head at the almost imperceptible movement and gave me a long unsmiling stare. 'Look at yourself,' he said in a whisper, as if he knew what I had been thinking.

I turned my gaze back to the waters and saw my own face. I knew at once why John had turned pale to see me and why Ralph had stared at me that day in the village.

I had never seen Beatrice's picture, nor heard a description of her, other than that her hair was chestnut red and her eyes hazel, almost green. But I had seen her face in the mirror of the dream and I had seen her smile in my mirror. Robbed of colour by the darkness of the pool, so my light hair and grey eyes were all one shadowy tone, I knew I was as like to her as a daughter. My eyes were not set at such a slant as Beatrice's and my chin was not as determined as the one of the woman who had ruled this land. But seeing my reflection in that pool, alongside the reflection of her lover, no one could have said whether it was her or me.

'You have no call to fear me,' Ralph said, speaking to my reflection in the water, his face gentle. 'I am not likely to forget that she is dead. I am not likely to forget that you are quite another lovely girl – however much you resemble her. And I am not a man to be haunted by ghosts.'

We were silent for a few minutes.

'Hands cold?' he asked. I nodded. 'Now, without making a ripple, without disturbing the water, you move your hands under the bank. Make your hand straight, like the fish itself.' Ralph drew his hands in towards the bank and spread out his arms, questing with blind fingertips under the water. 'I have one,' he said with quiet satisfaction. 'Do you stay still now.'

I froze obediently and saw Ralph's face darken with concentration.

'You stroke his belly,' he said, the words hardly louder than a breath. 'You softly, softly run a finger down his belly. He likes that, it makes him all sleepy, all dreamy, all unawares. Then, when you feel him growing heavier and come into your hand, you snatch him with two fingers under his gills and flick him out!'

As he spoke, Ralph suddenly twitched and flung on to the bank between us a silver, slithering, gasping fish. I flinched back in instinctive fright and Ralph laughed aloud at my face. He took a stone from the bank and knocked the trout on the head, impartially, accurately, and then the thing was still except for a little twitch along the spine.

'It's still alive,' I said uneasily.

'Nay,' Ralph said gently. 'It is twitching from habit. It's dead right enough.'

I regarded the smooth speckled scales with awe.

'Next time you will do it,' Ralph promised. 'I should have let you try your luck with this one. But it is so long since I last poached that I could not resist the temptation when I felt him hiding under the bank like that.'

I smiled and nodded; but I understood not at all.

'Would you like to try your luck again?' Ralph invited. 'Or should you be home?'

'I have to be home at three for dinner,' I said.

Ralph rolled on his back and squinted up at the sun through the criss-crossing branches. 'You've half an hour,' he said with certainty.

'Uncle John will be late anyway,' I said idly. 'He went to

Chichester to see the lawyers again. He really does want to turn over the farmland to Acre, you know.'

'Aye,' said Ralph. 'I know he does. It's what the future holds that worries me.'

'I thought you would be pleased,' I said shyly. 'I thought you would see this as a great chance for Acre. Not just to get free of the poverty, but to be free of the power of the squires for ever.'

Ralph gave me a quick little smile. 'But it doesn't work like that, does it?' he said gently. 'Acre is not an island. Acre men and women have to leave the village to earn wages, and have to come home again. I can't see anyone persuading them that their wages should be paid into a common fund! So the brightest and the best of the young people will try to leave the village and work outside where they earn good rates and keep all their money. Then there's the gentry . . .' He paused.

'They're not all bad,' I said.

He smiled at me again. 'Nay,' he said. 'Even the worst of them can be likeable enough rogues. But they have the power. If Acre was successful, they'd use that power against the village, I've no doubt of that. They'd find a statute on the books which said it was illegal. Or if they had no law, they'd pass one in a hurry. You cannot defeat the whole country by making one little place right.'

'It could be a start,' I said earnestly. I rolled around and lay on my front, hands under my chin so that our heads were close. 'If it worked here, perhaps people would try it elsewhere.'

'Aye,' Ralph said. 'And even if it worked for a short time, it would be good to say we tried it, and good to know why it failed. If the gentry came against it, that would be a lesson worth show-ing to the people who come after us with their own hopes and their ideas.' He sighed heavily. 'I'm torn,' he said frankly. 'I know in my heart it won't work. It depends for its success on the whim of the squire. Unless the land was bought outright by the village and owned in law by them, then it depends on the will of the squire to keep going. So the power of the Laceys over Acre is unbroken. And I could trust no single person with that much power. It is as natural to abuse power as it is to breathe. That is true for every man and every woman. And if you are reared to having power, and in a class which is used to it, and in a country which permits you – nay! encourages you – to abuse the power you have, you're corrupt! You cannot help it.'

'Do you think *I* am corrupted?' I asked in a small voice.

Ralph had been staring up at the branches above us, and he turned his head to look at me with a smile. 'Of course,' he said gently, stating an obvious fact. 'I'm not abusing you. But you come from the Quality and you are used to controlling everyone who is poorer than yourself. Put you in the hall, with a child to think of, and perhaps a couple of bad harvests and money getting tight, and I think you would do what anyone would do – you'd look to how you could make more money. And then you'd see Acre, and the people taking a share of the profits that you consider your own from the land you have claimed as your own for generations. I don't think you're evil, but I don't think you're a saint either. John has high ideas about what people can and cannot do. But I'd not trust even him if he lost his fortune and was poor and anxious.'

'Will you not do it, then?' I asked.

I was so sorry – sorry for Uncle John who had such high hopes of what we could do in Acre, and sorry for Acre that it should not be a place where the tradition of cruelty to the poor could be pushed back, even if it was in just this one little place. And very anxious for myself, for if Ralph Megson would not manage Wideacre, then I thought that John and Mama would insist that it must be sold.

Ralph sat up and gave a little laugh with no humour in it. 'I'll do it,' he said. 'I destroyed the power of the Laceys over the land and I have a duty to try and make something better. I always knew that it was easier to pull down than to build, and this is going to teach me that lesson in the hardest way.

'I'll do it if I can. And if I fail, if *we* fail, then I shall have the great pleasure of being able to say that I was right!'

I sat up and threw an arm around his shoulders and hugged

him in my delight. 'Oh, yes!' I said. 'But it will not fail! You think all the squires are bad, but Richard would keep to a bargain with Acre, and John will be there, and you know I would! And you will be here to make it work, and it will be good!'

Ralph smiled at my enthusiasm and slid an arm around my waist to hold me to him, but his face was still set. 'Nothing else I can do,' he said, 'but I'm just leading them out into the dark again.'

A kingfisher, like a spark of blue, arrowed up the little rill which goes to the Fenny from this pool and dived into a hole in the bank. We were still and it did not notice us for a moment, but sat on the edge of the hole, looking at us with dark bright eyes. Then it dipped its head and launched off down the little stream again, so close to the water that you could see the reflection, turquoise on the surface of the stream.

Ralph's eyes were on it and he stayed still so as not to disturb it. I was frozen too, but not for the benefit of a river bird. Ralph's hand was warm on the thin muslin at my waist. My arm was still around his shoulders. Our sides were touching. I had embraced him in a moment of quick thoughtless delight, but now I found myself close to him, held by him. And with the dream, and the pleasure of the dream in my mind, I could not bring myself to move away, though I knew I must.

Ralph dropped his hand, shook himself and glanced up at the sky. 'You'd best go,' he said. 'You don't want them to start wondering about you. Would you like the trout?'

'You caught it,' I said fairly, 'you keep it.'

'I caught it in a Lacey pool, on Lacey land, under a Lacey sky,' Ralph said, 'but I'm glad to have poached my dinner. Thank you.'

He wrapped it carefully in a couple of dock leaves and stuffed it in his jacket pocket as I rose to my feet. My knees were shaking, but I did not want him to know that. My face burned again. He was a man old enough to be my father, and a working man. And I had thrown my arm around him, and then not had the sense to immediately withdraw.

I stood to one side as he swung himself over to his wooden

legs. He pulled down the breeches and smoothed them carefully over the angry skin of the stumps of his legs, and then he eased them into the wooden peg-legs. He grimaced, and there were small drops of sweat on his forehead by the time he had them on.

'Are they very painful?' I asked. From the glimpse I had, it looked as if they had been cauterized with boiling tar. Old wounds, but still red with the daily chafing of the wooden legs.

'They're the devil,' Ralph said coolly. 'But I am lucky to have survived at all.'

I wanted to ask him how the accident had happened, but some prickle down my spine warned me to keep silent. And I simply stood and watched as he put his back to a tree-trunk and pushed against it until he was upright. It was not easy, and the lines in his face deepened when he had done.

'You can bring me my horse,' he said, and it was a concession to me rather than a request for help.

I untied the mare he had hired from the Midhurst stables, and brought her over to him and then stood, awkward, at her head. I could not see how he would get into the saddle. She was not high – even I could have vaulted up – but I had sound legs, and ankles and knees to spring from. I held her head and waited.

Ralph grasped the pommel and the crupper of the saddle and hauled himself up the horse until he was level with the saddle and half-way across it. He reared up, taking his weight on his hands, and swung one leg over. Then he smiled sweetly down at me as I stood at his horse's head.

'You're easy with horses,' he said, noting the casual way I stood beside her. 'They tell me in the village you ride like Beatrice.'

I shrugged, my face rueful at another similarity between me and the Wideacre witch.

'I'm surprised you have no horse of your own,' he said.

'Uncle John went to buy us horses,' I said. 'One for Richard and a horse of my own for me.' I could not hide the longing in my voice. 'But there was nothing suitable at the Chichester fair, and so now it is all put off.'

Ralph made a funny face, like you might make at a crying

baby. 'I'll see what I can do,' he said; and that half-promise from Ralph was worth more than a contract written in blood from another man. 'Thank you for my trout, Miss Lacey,' he said, teasing me with my name.

I went closer to the horse's shoulder, pretending I wanted to pat her neck. In truth I wanted to be near him. He caught my hand as it stroked her shoulder and bent low. He kissed it, with a kiss as gentle as the brush of a little bird's wing. 'Good day,' he said and his voice was warm, almost tender. 'Good day.'

He turned his horse's head and was gone. The dappled shadow of the woods hid him at once. I could hear the chink of the bridle, but he was swiftly hidden, following the old path I thought was known only to Richard and me. I stood, dazed, by the pool, watching the flicker of light and shade on the brown surface; and then I brushed down my dress with meticulous care, retied my bonnet and headed for home.

But I was not happy. Ralph might be at peace, with his hands cold from the river and a fresh trout in his pocket. But Ralph was a simple man, blessedly simple. He was content to have been Beatrice's lover, and her murderer, and to have my eyes upon him; he could smile at my measured closeness. When I was with him, I could feel only delight. But when he rode away and left me alone I was uneasy.

The old anxiety of the dream was coming back to me. The sweet humming of Wideacre now seemed more like a warning. I could not live in both worlds. I could not be the daughter my mama wanted and the tranced, passionate, careless girl of the Wideacre woods. I could not be both Quality and a girl who would throw her arm around a working man's shoulders. I could not be freely myself and also be an indoor girl. I went home scowling against the bright sunlight. The thread of longing which had drawn me out into the woods like a golden skein pulled by a skilled spinner was now broken and crumpled. And it did not seem like gold, it seemed as if it were gilt. Muddy gilt, tangled; and all wrong.

*

Uncle John came home from Chichester after dinner, smiling but wan. 'I think I have a compromise solution,' he said.

'Not now,' Mama said firmly. 'Now you must rest.'

He laughed a little at her authoritative tone, but went wearily enough to the stairs. 'I should like to see Mr Megson in the library before supper,' he said to Richard, who stood in the hall with me and watched him slowly mounting the stairs, his knuckles white on the stair-rail.

'Richard may go and tell him,' Mama said. 'But tell Mr Megson not to be later than nine, and explain that John may not talk all evening, Richard.'

'Make sure he knows that I am an utter baby who has to be tucked up in bed by eleven o'clock!' Uncle John said with a sidelong gleam at Mama. 'And say that if he is in any doubts about me, he is to call in Dr Celia!'

Mama chuckled at that, but her grip on Uncle John's arm never wavered, and she led him upstairs without another word from him.

Richard watched them go, and his expression was sour. 'Do you want to come too?' he asked.

I shook my head. The wildness, the dreaminess, was gone from me. I wanted to be the girl behind the tea-urn at tea-time, the young lady of the house stitching in the parlour. The seedlings I had left so carelessly in the garden when I had run off were wilted, but might recover left in the cool and steeped with water. I wanted to sit in the front parlour and chat with Mama. I had a sudden distaste for the brightness of the sun outside the window, for the waves of sweet-smelling greenness and the summer heat. 'No,' I said. 'Mama wants me at home. I'll stay in.'

Richard shot me a swift searching glance. 'Not like you,' he said, 'not like you not to want to come down to Acre with me.'

'No,' I said languidly. I was so tired I did not even care for the hint of complaint in Richard's voice. He surely could not imagine himself neglected. And if he did, I should make it up to him another day. I simply could not face the walk down the dusty lane to Acre in the bright sunlight, and I did not want to see Ralph in that cramped little cottage with Becky Miles waiting on us, and Richard watching me.

'I shall stay indoors this afternoon,' I said again. The front parlour seemed like a refuge and I hoped the company of my mama would keep me safe from Beatrice and from the dreamy bliss I had known when I was Beatrice lying in Ralph's arms.

'All right,' said Richard. 'If you've developed a sudden liking for embroidery, I shan't dissuade you. I'll take tea with him if he asks me. I wonder if his goshawk has come yet.'

'No, it hasn't,' I said, and could have bitten my tongue off with irritation at the slip. I knew, without being told, that Ralph would never have been out tickling for trout if his goshawk had just arrived, bumped and angry from the London stage.

'How do you know?' Richard demanded. He looked at me closely, and under his narrow scrutiny I felt my colour rise.

'Mrs Gough told me,' I said, grasping for the nearest lie. 'She slept in Acre last night, with her sister. She said the London stage was delayed yesterday, so it can't have come.'

Richard nodded as if he believed me, but there was a shadow in his blue eyes which warned me that he doubted what I had said. He chose not to pursue it then. 'Tell Mama-Aunt I shall be back for supper,' he said.

I nodded. He bent his head to kiss me on the lips at parting, but I turned my face away and his mouth touched my cheek instead. He drew back and looked at me curiously, but said nothing. He turned to the front door and I let him go.

I went to the window-seat in the parlour and watched him jog down the drive, his gait less coltish now he had grown broader and his legs seemed less long. Then the parlour door opened and Mama came in.

'Oh, good!' she exclaimed, seeing me waiting for her. 'I wanted you to help me choose a new brocade for the seats and the curtains in the dining-room.'

I crossed the room to her and hugged her tight. 'You know I have no eye for colour,' I said, 'but I shall agree with you. I want to work indoors this afternoon, Mama,' I said, 'and I wish you would find me something to do indoors tomorrow as well. The sun hurt my eyes in the garden this morning, and I feel weary.'

Her soft brown eyes examined my face carefully. 'I had thought you were not yourself,' she said gently, 'when you were so irritable at dinner. What is the matter, my dear?'

'It's . . .' I started and then stopped. Then I spoke in a rush. 'It is since I put up my hair and Uncle John came home, and I reminded him of Beatrice, Mama. Everyone in the village, and even Mrs Gough and Stride, look at me as if they half expect to see her. It makes me feel so odd. And she was not even a very nice woman, was she?'

'No!' Mama said instantly. 'She was many things, but she was never that. There is much about her that I feel I should tell you, my dear. But not while we are here on Wideacre. Not while there are so many people around us who are still so haunted here. While we live here, I just want you to remember that you are Beatrice's kin, but you are my daughter. Any resemblance between you and her is because you have the Lacey pride, and the Lacey tilt to your head. All else is fancy and the fault of this tiny little world where no one goes anywhere but Chichester, and there are long nights to make up nonsense and frighten each other half to death with ghost stories.

'You are *my* child,' she said firmly, as if that were the key to keep me safe. 'Whatever your breeding, I reared you for my own. I am not haunted by Beatrice or Wideacre, and you need not be either. Anyway,' she said, reliably prosaic, 'you are just a girl growing up, my dear, and they are the moodiest people in the world. My half-sister was a thousand times worse than you at your age. She once threw a plate at a footman! My mama had her whipped. You will have to learn to curb your temper and your tongue, whatever your feelings. Everything else is just fancy.'

I shifted along the window-seat and laid my head on her shoulder, and she put a protective arm around me. I closed my eyes and sniffed the sweet flower water she wore on her hair and silks, and we sat in the sunshine in the bow-window for a long, long time, until the sun started dropping behind the higher trees of the park, and I no longer ached for Ralph, Beatrice's young lover, Ralph, nor shied away in fear from the thought of him.

After tea in the parlour, when Uncle John did not join us, nor Richard return home, Mama ordered Stride to lay up a little tray with a scone and some jam and cream, a couple of macaroons and a pot of fresh-brewed Indian tea – the way Uncle John liked it, strong and black with neither cream nor lemon nor sugar – and carried it herself into the library. She closed the door behind her, but I heard his soft words of welcome to her and his exclamation at the pretty tray, and then her voice explaining something to him, asking something of him. I guessed that she was talking about me and took care to close the parlour door so I should not be tempted to eavesdrop. I took my seat in the parlour, the tea-urn still hissing softly before me, and I longed to be the girl my mama thought she had, a good daughter whose only wildness was due to her being reared with a boy cousin in rural isolation, and whose only moodiness was due to her becoming, slowly and awkwardly, a woman.

I did not open my eyes, even when the tea things were cleared. It was not Stride waiting in the parlour, but Jenny Hodgett from the lodge gate, who had been trained at Havering Hall and was now back to work on Wideacre. Her parents had kept the gate at the hall for my papa and for his papa before him. When the hall was burned down and the squire died, no one thought to evict them. So they stayed on, keepers of an open gate, guardians of a deserted drive. She cleared the things as softly as she could and took the urn from the table without disturbing me. I heard the door close behind her and then I think I dozed, for when I opened my eyes again my mama was there, and she had been in the library with Uncle John for some time.

'Tired, my dear?' she asked gently.

'A little,' I acknowledged, smiling to take the invalidish tone out of the words.

Mama nodded and went to her usual seat at the hearth, where the grate was now filled with a little pot of pale peonies I had dug up in the garden of Wideacre Hall and brought on in the warmth of the room.

'I have been speaking to your uncle about his plans for us all,' she said. 'And I have some ideas of my own too!'

'Were the Chichester solicitors helpful?' I asked politely. 'Can he offer some guarantees for Acre?'

'Yes,' Mama said. 'The Wideacre heir and Acre village have to be equally bound by a legal contract, and they will both contribute to a savings scheme. Both can withdraw, but Acre keeps the fund. And if Acre is sold within five years, then a proportion of the profit is to be paid to Acre as compensation.'

I nodded. 'Is Uncle John going to ask Mr . . . Megson what he thinks?' I asked. I hesitated over his name, and it sounded odd in my voice.

'Of course,' said Mama. 'John thinks that Mr Megson is the key to winning Acre to the plan. It will only work if all of us, Mr Megson, Richard, you and I are prepared to work very hard until the village is put to rights again, she said. 'John wants me to take responsibility for the health and education of the village children and babies. He wants Richard to supervise the rebuilding of the hall, and he wants the two of you to assist Mr Megson on the land.'

I said nothing, but looked at her wide-eyed. She gave me a little smile. 'I know what you're thinking,' she said wryly. 'You are thinking that you have never seen me involved with Acre. That I was afraid of the village and did not like you going there. That was once true, but it all must change. Everything must change on Wideacre if this experiment is to work.

'And I was not always afraid of Acre,' she said honestly. 'There was a season, two seasons, when I was very much involved in the lives of the village people. Now I have something to offer them, something more than mere sympathy. I want to go back into the village and set things to rights, as I should have done earlier if we had had the money to do it.'

I looked at her with new respect. This was a side to Mama that I had not seen before when I had thought of her as the frightened widow in the Dower House, dependent on her step-papa's charity for her food and on her brother-in-law's gifts for her money. Something of that must have shown in my eyes, for she gave a little chuckle of amusement.

'I am well aware, Julia, that you think that no one knows the land but you and Richard! But I do assure you that I am not entirely incompetent!'

'Not at all, Mama!' I said hastily and untruthfully. 'But what does Uncle John want me to do? And when do I start?'

'You may as well start at once,' Mama said calmly. 'And so may I. Mr Megson is coming this evening, and if he agrees to the new proposals, then I shall go down to the village tomorrow and speak to Dr Pearce about opening the village school again. You and Richard and Mr Megson will have to decide about priorities on the land. I suppose you'll start ploughing and sowing?'

'Too late this season,' I said. 'But if Uncle John plans to use turnips, and also wants to try some new crops of fruit, we could get them in ready for them to be productive next year.'

Mama looked at me shrewdly. She had supervised my education, taught me my letters and the names of the birds and flowers. She had seen me learn Latin and Greek at Richard's shoulder. She knew full well that no one had ever taught me the times when the land should be readied and crops sown, and that I had never seen a ploughing team on Wideacre. 'How do you know?' she asked softly.

I met her wary look with absolute honesty. 'I don't know,' I said truthfully. 'I just do.'

She nodded as if it confirmed something she had already heard from John. 'It would be possible to make a great deal of fuss about that,' she said levelly, 'and about the slight resemblance you bear to your Aunt Beatrice in your looks. But it is *essential*, Julia, that you do not concern yourself with it. Your Uncle John believes that you have inherited the Lacey ability to farm. All well and good. But do not start worrying that you are therefore like your Aunt Beatrice. You are *my* daughter, and as such you can be a farmer, just as I shall have to be a village schoolteacher for this next year. We are all going to have to work for the good of Wideacre.'

I beamed at her. I had a wonderful sense of home-coming, of growth, of at last seeing my way before me. And if I could feel unafraid of the dream and unafraid of Beatrice, and work and live on Wideacre then I should have an enviable life indeed.

9

It was as well that I welcomed the work like a sheepdog come late to training, for that day of idleness in garden, wood and parlour was the last lazy day I had. From that evening – when Uncle John and Ralph Megson shook hands over the deal which was to share the profits between masters and men – none of us ever had an empty hour again.

Richard's life changed the least, for Uncle John insisted that his education be kept up, and every morning he still went to Dr Pearce.

'You may want to go to university,' Uncle John had said firmly when Richard remonstrated with him, 'and, in any case, no youth under my guardianship is going to be a dunce.'

So every morning Richard jogged off down the lane to Acre with his books and was not home until dinner-time. Sometimes he was late. The old antipathy between him and my friends the village children seemed to have gone. Richard basked in the glory of being the young squire-to-be. The village girls blushed scarlet when he strode down the lane and bobbed curtsies with their faces tilted downwards, but their eyes smiling up. Muddy-faced friends of my childhood were now young women preening themselves in their new dresses, and always with some business which kept them outside the vicarage gate when Richard was due to arrive or at the time when he left.

Whenever Richard drove the gig to Midhurst, there was always a couple of girls with pressing business in the village that day. And whenever he went to Chichester, he always brought back a handful of ribbons as presents for them. The village lads liked him too. The old sour resentments had been blown away from

Acre as if Ralph's coming were a spring wind. And though Richard was a demigod to the girls, the boys were not jealous. Richard was unobtainable and he seemed uninterested. I fancied that it was because he loved me, because he considered himself betrothed, but Uncle John was perhaps nearer the mark when he told my mama that Richard was too young for village girls.

'He is not arrogant in the village?' Mama asked.

Uncle John shook his head, but turned to me for confirmation.

'Oh, no,' I said. 'He is trying very hard to be liked. Besides, he can do no wrong, for he is Uncle John's son!'

It was true. To the village which had become accustomed to four deaths for every child safely raised, Dr MacAndrew was a heaven-sent angel. Uncle John held a free doctor's surgery in the village every week, when the thin-faced women brought their crying babies to see him and Uncle John stripped off the lice-ridden clothes and probed the skinny bodies, which looked as they twisted themselves up in pain from hunger and from years of bad nourishment.

'Will 'e live?' whispered Margery Sharp to Uncle John while I waited for his orders one morning in the sunlit vestry of the church where he had set up an impromptu consulting room.

'Aye,' Uncle John said kindly.

Her hard eyes filled with tears as though John himself had taught her how to cry. 'I thought he would die,' she said bleakly. 'All the others did.'

'How many?' John asked gently, flexing the little hands and feet. The baby was tiny, about eight months old, and skinny, with his ribs showing. His flesh was speckled with the scars of old flea-bites and bug-bites, spotted with a rash. He smelled. He was fouled with old excrement and urine. Uncle John handled him as if his skin were silk, his hands full of love.

'Four,' she said. 'No, five!'

I said nothing, but I flinched a little, amazed that a woman could be brought so low as to forget how many babies she had buried.

'The last one only lived a day,' she explained. 'I never had time to name her, nor nothing.'

'No christening?' John asked, knowing what that would mean to a superstitious village woman.

She nodded. 'Dr Pearce done it,' she said. 'Dr Pearce done it for me, because he knew I couldn't have borne to see her in hell. He christened her although she was dead. Now, there's another good man.'

'A good man indeed,' John agreed. 'Now, Mistress Sharp, I'll tell you what you must do. You must get this little lad here into some clean clothes. Go to the school room and see Lady Lacey. She'll give you what you need. He's not to have swaddling clothes, and he's not to be wrapped too tight.'

She raised her head to protest, and I saw Uncle John's weary smile.

'I know you like to swaddle them,' he said kindly, 'and I know it stills their crying. But that is because when they are swaddled really tight, they cannot get breath to cry. It's like being bound too tight would be for us. You've done well to keep this child alive, Mistress Sharp. Let's not take any chances with the little lad now.'

She nodded at that, responding to the affection in his voice.

'He's to be washed,' said Uncle John. She gave a gasp of protest, but Uncle John ignored her and carried on. 'He's to be washed every time he soils himself,' he said firmly. 'Washed and put into a clean clout. And he's to be taken out into the sunshine all this summer. Have one of the village children watch him.'

Margery Sharp nodded, her eyes wide at this string of ridiculous instructions.

'Have the big child carry the little one outside,' Uncle John said. 'If he stays indoors all the time, he won't eat. The fresh air will give him an appetite and help him to sleep at night and stay awake during the day.'

'But washing . . .' the woman protested.

'Miss Julia here is organizing a fuel store for the whole village so you can always have a fire,' Uncle John said steadily. 'You can keep a kettle by the hearth so you can have warm water to wash him. When he has soiled his clout, you can wash it out and dry it by the fire. Then you'll have a clean one to put on him next time.'

'He'd need changing time after time all day!' Mrs Sharp protested.

'I know,' John said kindly. 'I've cared for a baby too, you know. But if you keep them clean, they don't get sores and they cry less, and they don't get ill. I *promise* you it will work, Margery. Will you try it?'

Still she hesitated, her face full of doubt.

John's tone became warmer and more charming. 'Will you try it for *me*, Margery?' he asked, his voice very low.

She blushed scarlet and shot an embarrassed look at me. 'Oh, Doctor!' she said, and I saw that beneath the defeated, exhausted woman there had once been a flighty amorous village girl. 'All right, then,' she said unwillingly. 'If you're sure it will work. But if he gets ill from all that washing, I'll stop it, mind!'

'Agreed,' said John, and bundled the little child into his rags again. 'Now, you go over to the village school, and Lady Lacey will find some clothes for him, and some clouts, and a towel as well. And she'll show you how to wash him all over, I'll be bound. You know what her ladyship is like with babies!'

The woman found a smile from some remembered happiness and looked Uncle John full in the face. 'It's good to have you back, sir,' she said, and then she bundled up her son, her only little survivor from a family of six, and took him away.

'Uncle John, you flirt!' I exclaimed.

The face he turned to me was alight with mischief. 'Just trying to teach Acre to raise healthy children,' he protested.

'Outrageous,' I accused. 'You put on a soft voice and your accent got as broad as if you had just come down from the Highlands with a kilt still on! I shall tell Mama of you! You should be ashamed!'

Uncle John laughed aloud. 'Don't tell Celia,' he begged. 'She'll have me publicly named as a charlatan! I promise you, Julia, it's all part of my teaching technique!'

We laughed together, and then there was a tap at the door and another woman with a wan child held by the hand.

'Here is Mrs Miles and her son Peter,' I said to John. 'Is Peter not well, Mrs Miles?'

'He can't keep his food in his belly,' she said, talking past me to John. 'All this new food which you and Mr Megson have bought, and I can't get him to eat it, then when he does it comes straight up again. 'Tis not the worms, not the bloody flux, 'tis not the gripes . . .'

'I must go,' I said, shamefaced but hopelessly queasy at this list.

'Chicken-hearted,' Uncle John said in an undertone. 'I'd rather be a flirt than a coward any day.'

'You are,' I said, and made my way towards the door.

'One moment, Mrs Miles,' John said with a smile to her. 'Julia, if you're on your way to find Mr Megson, he's setting them to hedging and ditching on Three Gate Meadow. Will you tell him that the apple trees will be delivered this afternoon? He'll need a gang to plant them out as soon as the ground is ready.'

'It's ready now,' I confirmed. 'The ploughing team finished yesterday. I'll check it for stones and waterlogging and if it's clear, they can go in at once.'

'Good.' John nodded and turned his attention to whey-faced little Peter, who was explaining in a whiny voice that he could fancy nothing but sweetmeats now that the good times had come.

Outside the sun was bright in the churchyard. The fleet of fresh graves from the winter's deaths was greened over with new grass, and the work Uncle John was doing in the vestry was a promise that there would not again be deaths like that, nor another merciless winter. I strode out through the graveyard, past the imposing gates of the Lacey vault and under the lich-gate to where I had left the new pony, Rusty, grazing on the corner outside the church wall which, for some reason, they called Miss Beatrice's Corner. There were two mounds there, like misplaced graves, and Rusty was eating some old flowers which had been left on one of them. I gathered my smart new driving dress in one hand to hold it clear and hauled myself up into the gig.

Our new carriage was waiting outside the old tithe barn which Mama had commandeered for a village school. As I turned the gig, I could hear the children's excited voices and Mama's orders clear above the noise. I could hardly believe my ears. In all my childhood I think she had raised her voice to me once. Now I heard her yell, 'That is enough! John Smith, Sally Cooper, you twins! Stop fighting and sit down at once.'

There was a sudden hush at that, and then a scrabbling noise as a dozen untamed children rushed for a place on the bench and seated themselves to look at her.

'That's better,' my mama said calmly. 'Now, who can tell me what this is? Hands up, don't shout out!'

I waited no longer. I had a very clear picture of what she was doing inside the old barn with her little class seated on the benches before her. She would teach them to wash and brush their hair. She would teach them how to sew, how to light a lamp without burning themselves, how to prepare a meal.

'Children want to learn,' Uncle John had said to her. 'They must have toys to encourage them to read and write. They must be helped to question things all the time. Then they will teach themselves. All the philosophers agree . . .'

'Philosophers indeed!' Mama had interrupted. 'This is a village school for village children. When your philosophers control the country, they may tell me what a working child should learn. Until then I shall teach them how to feed themselves and how to keep themselves clean, and get them ready for their work!'

'Tory!' said John, using his worst term of abuse.

'Jacobin!' Mama had retorted; and she was running her school in her own way.

I turned the gig left down the track past the squatters' cottages, towards the land which had once been all common land. A waste, it was now. Beatrice had cleared the common land of its wealth of trees and scrub and bracken, and with the sweet natural growth had gone the wild animals: the game birds, the hares, the rabbits and the deer. Once Beatrice was gone, the common had regained its own, and the only trace left of her was the odd head of wheat, spindly on the wind.

Now I was another Lacey girl, coming to change the face of the land, and I whispered a brief promise to myself that this time the changes should last for longer than a season and should be for the best.

Even as a derelict wheatfield, this great common field had been lovely. But I had ordered them to fence it and plough it, and in three days there were no smooth sweet slopes greening with bracken and hazy with heather buds, but a morass of mud in wriggly lines from the blades of the plough. I drove the gig up to the very foot of the field and looked up at it.

I heard a singing in my head.

'It is good,' I said fervently. I think I spoke aloud.

It was as if the earth itself were speaking to me, as if Wideacre could tell me that the land was good and that the plans were good, and that if the common was no longer breathtakingly lovely in this one single field, then it was none the less good earth in good heart, and it would grow a crop which would feed Acre.

The wind blew down the gentle slopes towards me. Beatrice had literally moved mountains to make this field. She had infilled valleys and uprooted a great oak tree. The work had been done badly. I could see the line of the valleys and even the faintest trace of a footpath going across the field. And the hollow where the oak tree had once stood had been the scene of my long-ago fight with Clary.

I smiled. It was not just Beatrice who had a history here. All the Lacey landowners had left their marks here, and I would leave mine. This field would be remembered by Acre as the one which Beatrice had clawed out of common land and wrested from the people. But they would also remember it as the field where Julia Lacey had planted apples. And next summer that gamble might pay.

I backed the pony carefully and turned the gig, and trotted

home through Acre. The carriage was gone from outside the tithe barn, so Mama was before me, and I guessed she would have taken Richard and John with her. I had only one errand to do before my dinner and I set the pony into a brisk trot past the gates to the Wideacre drive and along to Three Gate Meadow.

Ralph was sitting on the bank under the hedge with the working men, but he raised his head when he heard the sound of the gig. The men were taking their dinner break and they stayed seated and kept on eating, contenting themselves with a courteous wave in my direction. I waved back, got down into the road and looped the reins over the gate.

'Good day, Miss Lacey,' Ralph said, coming to the gate and smiling at me across the top.

'Good day, Mr Megson,' I said. 'Uncle John asked me to tell you that the apple trees are arriving this afternoon. I have checked the common-land field and it looks dry and fairly clear of stones. I think we can plant without further ploughing or drainage work.'

Ralph frowned. 'I've no workers free this afternoon,' he said, 'and tomorrow I have to go to Petersfield and buy some sheep for the new flock. There will be enough men to do the planting tomorrow, but I can't be here. It's new work to them; I'd not like to leave them without help. Not that I know much. I was going to do it from your uncle's farming book!'

'If it's only a question of following a book, I can do it,' I said. 'I don't know much about farming, but I can read!'

Ralph smiled. 'You *do* know about farming, though, don't you, Julia?' he said gently. 'How else can you tell that the field is ready for planting?'

'That's true,' I said, not wanting to discuss the point. 'What time shall I come to work?'

'They can be in the field at seven,' Ralph said. 'They'll stop for their breakfast at ten. Then stop again for dinner at one. They'll need a break at four, and they can go home at sunset. You're not like to be finished before.'

'I know it,' I said with feeling. 'It's a huge field. I should think we should be prepared for two days of planting.'

'Yes, Squire!' said Ralph, and pulled his forelock to me.

'Don't call me that,' I said steadily, 'not even in jest. Richard will be the squire. We are joint heirs, but he is the boy.'

'But you inherit jointly,' Ralph said. 'I should think you would insist on your rights.'

I thought of my grandmama's warning that a woman's way is not to insist, and I shook my head in denial, but I said nothing.

Ralph smiled. 'Then you're no Lacey at all!' he said, his voice warm with amusement. 'Any Lacey would ride roughshod over anyone in the world to keep a hold on the land they own, and to gain more. And Beatrice was the worst of all of them. She stopped at nothing to get control of the land. And there you are – a legitimate Lacey heir – talking of sharing your land as if the Fenny were not in your blood and the Wideacre earth not in your bones!'

'I am not Beatrice!' I said in sudden impatience. 'I have been raised by my mama, and I take her advice. A woman's part is to give – not to grab. Besides, if I am generous and fair with Richard, he will . . .' I broke off before I said too much.

'Sits the wind in that quarter?' Ralph said softly, almost to himself. He walked stiffly along the gate, swung it open and came out to meet me in the lane.

'Land and loving,' he said, making it sound like a proverb, 'that's what the Laceys want. And Lacey women want it most of all. Beatrice chose the land. I think you are choosing love.'

I scanned his dark face, his kind eyes with the pale lines streaked around them.

'Is it worth it?' he asked gently. 'Is his love worth the sweetest land in the whole of England?'

'Oh, yes,' I said with confidence. I had loved Richard from childhood. I had promised to love him for ever.

Ralph nodded. 'You've made your choice, then,' he said gently. 'For love. For love, and the indoor life, and being a young lady.' He gave an abrupt laugh. 'Beatrice 'ud take her hand to your backside if she were alive!'

'I *have* to be a young lady!' I protested. 'I have no choice. I was born a young lady. That is my part in life. That is what I am.'

'Nay,' he said reassuringly. 'You're no bread-and-butter miss. You've been mewed up like a young hawk all your life and it's made you weak and foolish, so you fancy yourself in love with that young puppy and make a virtue out of letting him bully you. Such a little fool that you cannot even see what you want. You should be out on the land making it grow. You're Beatrice's heir. Of course your life will be quiet and empty if you live it in a little parlour thinking of nothing but being a young lady and loving your cousin!'

He smiled at me like a dark prophet telling some simple truth which I had always known but never before heard in words. Suddenly the Dower House seemed a strange forcing-house for turning a wild free little girl into a young lady who could be shouted at, abused, and who would pride herself that she could return love for pain. I scowled with concentration, trying to think what this view of myself meant.

'What should I do, then?' I asked.

'Grow up,' Ralph said, unsympathetically. 'Work it out for yourself, Julia. You've got a brain not entirely addled by a lady-like education: use it. You've got a heart which can feel the land, a voice which can talk clearly to people and ears that can listen. So grow up.'

I gave him a level look in reply to his bracing tone. But he was unrepentant. He gave me a mischievous grin and a gentle push towards the gig.

'Run along, Miss Julia,' he said. 'I'm always vexed when I am hungry. Remember never to interrupt a working man at his dinner break. Go home – and don't think too much! And don't promise anything to anyone until you've had a chance to find out what you really want.' He untied the reins for me and gave me his hand to help me into the gig.

'I am sorry to have vexed you, Mr Megson,' I said in my smallest voice, keeping my eyes down. 'I did not mean to make you angry.'

'Nay!' he exclaimed, instantly concerned, but then he caught a glimpse of my smile and realized I was mocking him. 'Go home, Julia Lacey, go home!' he said crossly. 'Go and tease someone who has the leisure and the wit for it. I am a simple man, and I am hungry.'

I clicked to the pony, still laughing, and waved at him, and trotted off back home down the lane.

But I was very far from laughter the next morning when Jenny brought me my morning chocolate at half past five with the news that it was raining in a light penetrating drizzle and looked set to stay bad all day.

'Oh, no!' I said, rolling over and burying my face in my pillows.

"'Tis cold too,' she said with the cheeriness of someone who is up and dressed to someone who will soon have to be.

I sat up and looked out of the window. It was a miserable day, foggy and grey, with the raindrops dripping off the leaves of the trees of Wideacre Park.

'Too wet to set the apple trees,' I said.

'Is it?' she asked, looking out of the window.

'No,' I said crossly. 'It's perfectly all right. Jenny, do light me a fire. I cannot get up into winter weather without one.'

She gave me a nod and went down to the kitchen for some kindling and little logs. I watched her lay the fire while I sipped my morning chocolate and only when the chill was off the room could I find the courage to jump out of bed and dress myself.

I had yet another new driving dress, thanks to Mama, who had guessed that I would wear the first one thin in the first months of my outdoors work. She had ordered the Chichester dressmaker to make me two extra dresses to the same pattern and measurements; today I chose the thicker one of pale-grey wool with a matching hat. The grey took up the colour of my eyes and made them seem large and luminous in my pale face. It was cut well; a bit tight, in truth, for I had been eating like a hunter in training in the past few weeks. It made me seem tall and slim and elegant.

Jenny looked up from sweeping the hearth.

'Oh, Miss Julia, you look lovely!' she said. 'That colour do suit you!'

'It's to be hoped anyone can see me at all!' I said, glaring out of the window at the greyness outside. 'I shall blend in with that beastly fog and they will drive the tree cart over me.'

She laughed at my ill humour and went down to the kitchen. Stride was not yet up, nor Mrs Gough, but she had left me a saddle-bag packed with my breakfast. 'We didn't know if you'd eat your breakfast in the field or come home,' Jenny said. 'Beatrice always had her breakfast in the field, so Mrs Gough left that out for you if you wanted to stay.' There was a momentary pause as both Jenny and I realized the casual comparison. But she went on, 'And Mrs Gough said to ask you if you want your dinner sent down?'

'If I'm not back by two, could you send something down for me?' I asked. 'But I dare say I'll be back. It's not the weather for a picnic.'

I nodded farewell to her and went out by the back door. The great cedar tree in the garden had its high head in the clouds; its dark trunk was streaked with wetness. There was a steady patter of rain on the leaves. I bent down and touched the ground. The grass was soaked, but it had not been raining for that long. The trees could go in. The ground would be wet and difficult to work, but I was not afraid that the roots would get waterlogged. I knew the trees would take. I knew it as well as I knew my own name, or the outline of the downs beyond the mist.

Jem was in the stables and the pony was in the gig.

'Thank you,' I said. I had been unwilling to get up, but Jem was even worse. He had his greatcoat on, and I caught a glimpse of very dirty flannels underneath. He was not even dressed.

'If Uncle John saw you like that, he'd turn you off,' I observed.

Jem nodded. 'I overslept,' he said. 'I thought you'd rather have your pony harnessed on time by me like this than brought to you by me in livery half an hour from now.'

'I'd rather have it on time *and* you in your livery,' I said.

He gave me his hand up to the gig and I gave him a smile. That was one of my first experiments in giving a reprimand, and I was not sure if I had done it right. 'I hope you are not offended, Jem?' I asked.

His dirty face creased into a smile. 'You're in the right,' he said grudgingly. 'Don't get above yourself; you'll do.'

'Thank you,' I said, and that little bit of extra confidence carried me through the day, even when the tree cart overturned and we had to lift the saplings out of the mud of the lane without breaking their springy branches; even when they put a row of trees too close to another, leaving no room for the pickers and weeders to get through, and we had to dig them out and do it all again; even when they vanished away to Acre early for their dinner break and were late back.

'It won't do!' I said crossly to Ted Tyacke. 'I took an hour for my dinner, and I had to go all the way back to the Dower House. If this is a partnership between the Laceys and Acre, then I should not be overseer and timekeeper here. You should be here on time because you want to be.'

And Ted, the friend of my girlhood, nodded and put out a dirty hand to help me down from the gig. 'You're right,' he said. 'I think we all find it hard to believe we are all working for the same end.'

After that exchange – in the muddy field with the pile of saplings behind us and half the field planted in unpromising spindly rows – the work went faster. They were learning their skills, even as I was; and when I had precisely worked out how many trees to a row, how many rows to the field, and then ended up with one extra sapling, they laughed so hard at my puzzled face that Ted had tear-stains down his grimy cheeks.

'Oh, take the stupid thing!' I said in impatience. 'I've worked it out wrong, and now there's no room for it! Plant it on the village green and the children can have the apples off it. Perhaps it will keep them out of this orchard!'

'N-N-Nothing will keep them out of this orchard!' Matthew

Merry told me, his brown eyes twinkling. 'They're b-b-brigands. Don't you remember how we were?'

'Yes,' I said, 'and look at us now!'

Clary came over to stand with us at the gate and we looked back at the field. Ralph had been wrong. I had been wrong. We had planted it in the day and, although it was dusk and time to trudge wearily home, we had done what we had promised ourselves. Indeed, we had done better.

'I'm tired,' she said.

I looked at her with quick sympathy. Her mother had just given birth to another baby and Clary had been walking with it all night, keeping it quiet so that her mother could sleep.

'I'll drive you,' I said; and she and Matthew and Ted walked with me to the gig.

'We'll follow,' Ted said. 'We'd overbalance the gig and the pony couldn't manage the weight. We'll see you tomorrow, Julia.'

I nodded and smiled, too tired myself for extra words. But Matthew touched Clary's hand as she gripped the side of the gig and hauled herself wearily up.

'I'll come around tonight,' he said, 'about nine o'clock. I'll walk the baby tonight when she wakes.'

Clary nodded and leaned forward to pat his cheek with her hand. Then I slapped the reins on the pony's rump and he set off up the muddy track for Acre. The rain had stopped, but the clouds were still low and it was very dark and quiet under the trees.

'Matthew helps you with the baby?' I queried.

'Aye,' she said shortly. 'He'd do the cooking as well if I let him. But he gets enough teasing about nursemaiding for my family without that as well.'

'That's kind of him,' I said. 'But he always loved you.'

'Yes,' she said. 'We're betrothed now, you know, Julia. Properly. And we've spoken to Ralph Megson about a cottage. He says we can have that empty one on the green.'

I gave her hand a squeeze. 'I'm glad,' I said. 'I always liked

Matthew. And I've always liked the way he treated you. But how will your mother manage without you?'

Clary gave a little sigh, her head half turned from me so she could look out into the woods with the trees going past us, ghostly slow.

'I'll take the two older children to live with me, and Alice is going into service at Midhurst. So that'll only leave Ma with Joe and the new baby.'

I nodded. Clary had mothered her brothers and sisters for so long that I could not have imagined her leaving them. Hearing her talk like that made me feel more than simple pleasure at a friend's happiness. I felt as I did when I saw the saplings going in, or when I saw the ditches newly dug or a ploughshare going into fallow ground. That Acre was coming right. Coming right for the land and for the people.

'What about you?' asked Clary abruptly. 'Is it to be Richard for you?'

I nodded. 'It's a secret,' I warned her.

'Pretty well known for a secret, then,' she said with a smile. 'Everyone in Acre has known you two would be married ever since you were born.'

'They may know it in Acre,' I said drily, 'but if it gets back to Mama or Uncle John, I should be in trouble.'

Clary shot a sideways glance at me. 'Are they *still* against it?' she asked. 'Even now that there is money?'

'Yes,' I said. 'They've not changed on that.'

'Maybe your ma thinks you could do better,' Clary suggested tentatively.

'There could hardly be a better match for the estate,' I protested, but Clary shook her head.

'Not for the estate, Julia,' she said. 'For you. Someone who would come to you fresh, who would love you, who would see you for yourself and not as part of his childhood and his fortune.' Her voice was so low I could scarcely hear her. 'Someone who would treat you tender,' she said softly.

We had reached her cottage gate and I checked the pony and sat very still in the twilight.

'We can't all have a Matthew,' I said at length. 'I love Richard and I don't complain.'

'I know,' she said. And we were both silent.

'Drat,' she said in a quite different voice looking at the dark silhouette of her cottage. 'The fire's gone out again.'

'I'll come in and help,' I offered.

'Nay,' she said kindly. 'You've done a full day's work too. I reckon you were working harder than any of us. You were up and down those rows twenty times measuring the distance.'

'And then I got it wrong!' I said.

Clary laughed. 'That was the funniest thing I ever did see,' she said. 'I thought Ted was going to choke.'

'Yes,' I said. 'Well, at least Acre's got an apple tree out of it. Are you sure you don't want me to come in?'

'No,' she said. 'The sooner I start, the sooner I'll get done.' She got down from the gig, stiff with tiredness as if she were an old lady and not a lass of seventeen. 'Eh,' she said ruefully, 'I shan't be dancing tonight!'

'Me neither,' I agreed, and she turned up the path to her little cottage as I waved my whip at her in farewell and headed the pony for home.

10

'Julia! Julia! *Julia*! I say! Are you deaf!' It was Uncle John's voice, shouting up the stairs.

I jumped from my bed and pattered across the floor to open the door. 'What is it?' I called down.

'A surprise,' he said. 'Come down at once!'

I threw off my wrapper and pulled on my oldest gown, a muslin sprig, which had once been pink but was now pale as a lily with much washing. In obedience to Uncle John's haste, I did not wait to dress my hair, but tied a ribbon around my head and let it tumble down my back as if I were still a little girl. Then I pulled on my sandals and scampered downstairs.

The front door was wide open and Uncle John was on the doorstep.

Beyond him was Ralph.

Ralph was mounted high on a black horse, a new black horse, and I caught my breath at the sight of it. It was so like the horse in the dream when he rode up to the hall. I put my hand out to the door to steady myself and looked half fearfully up at Ralph. His face was smiling, warm. He knew what I was thinking and his smile said as clear as words, 'Don't be silly, Julia.'

I nodded, and then took in something else. Ralph was leading another horse. A mare. Her coat was so pale that it seemed almost silver. Her eyes were deep, deep liquid black. Her mane and tail were as white as the surf on a winter sea, tumbling over.

'Look at this!' Uncle John said, delighted. 'I told Mr Megson I was looking for a horse for you, and see what he has found us!'

Ralph Megson smiled at me. 'She's a lady's horse,' he said. 'She's being sold by a farmer over by Rogate, whose daughter is giving up riding. He paid a handsome price for her and he's asking an outrageous one. But I thought you should try her paces. I've seen her ridden and she's a sweet goer indeed. I called in there yesterday, after the sheep auction.'

'Wonderful looking,' Uncle John said enthusiastically. 'I had a grey once, Mr Megson, an Arab. That was a marvellous horse.'

Ralph nodded. 'They still talk of it in the village,' he said courteously. 'Sea Fern you called him, wasn't it?'

John smiled. 'Fancy anyone remembering!' he exclaimed. 'Yes, he was Sea Fern, and as clean and bright a coat as this beauty.'

I hardly heard either of them. I had floated down the steps in a complete daze. Over my head Uncle John and Ralph exchanged amused glances, and then John was beside me, saying gently, 'I dare say you'd like to try her at once, Julia?'

I nodded. The smooth grey head came down and nuzzled at my fingers, the lustrous eyes gazed at me. I went to her side and Uncle John threw me up in the saddle, as careless as I of my walking dress. I hooked one leg around the pommel and tried to pull my skirts down with little success. It was only the second time in my life I had ridden, and the first time in a lady's saddle.

'Take her out,' Uncle John said to Mr Megson. 'You'd like to try her, Julia?'

'Yes,' I breathed, quite speechless with delight at the feeling of the horse so warm and quiet beneath me.

Ralph nodded and leaned over towards me to give me the reins. He showed me how to hold them – like driving – and they felt easy and natural between my bare fingers. Then he turned his horse's head and my sweet grey mare fell into pace beside Ralph's rangy black hunter as if she were a grey satin ribbon with a broad black shadow.

'This is good,' Ralph said abruptly as we went slowly down the lane. 'It is good to be riding down this track with you beside me.'

I said nothing. I scarcely heard him. I was completely absorbed in the rhythm of the horse's pace and of the odd, and not very steady, feeling of riding side-saddle. 'I'd rather ride astride,' I said. 'I feel so uneven.'

'I should think you would!' he said, chuckling. 'But I can imagine your mama's face if you asked her for breeches. And your Grandmama Havering's!'

I laughed too at that, and returned with a bump to the real world. I had heard such a sweet singing in my head as soon as I saw the mare. I had been in a dream.

'Beatrice rode as well as any man, and she rode side-saddle,' Ralph said consolingly. 'I think ladies would be safer astride indeed, but the world we live in cares more for ladies' looks and less for what they can do.'

I considered that and nodded.

'Let's trot,' Ralph said, and we did. I had some ungraceful lunges at the saddle to keep my balance, but then I found the rhythm and I could ride steady.

'What is she called?' I asked when Ralph had drawn rein and we were walking again.

'Peggy,' Ralph said. 'I dare say that is not fancy enough for you!'

'No,' I said, 'but isn't it bad luck to change a horse's name?'

Ralph gave a little laugh. 'If you ride like Beatrice, you'll have no need of luck with horses,' he said. 'You'll make your own luck.'

'Can I name her, then?' I asked.

'If you like her enough to keep her,' he said, teasing me.

I thought for a moment. 'What was Uncle John's grey called?' I asked.

'Sea Fern,' Ralph replied.

'I'll call her Sea Mist,' I said. 'Her mane and tail are as white as breakers.'

'Misty for when you're calling her?' Ralph suggested.

'Yes,' I said, smiling. So my horse was named, and we rode on in companionable silence. We went a little way down the drive and then we turned the horses for home.

'Like to canter?' he asked obligingly. When I nodded, he took the lead and let his horse slide into an easy steady-paced canter. I grabbed at the pommel for fear of falling, and the moment Sea Mist lunged forward I felt she was taking a high jump. Ralph glanced over his shoulder and laughed at my determined face and kept the pace steady. We thundered down the drive, and the shadows and light flickered over me, and I forgot about being nervous and anxious not to fall and look a fool; I bent down low over her mane and urged her on faster, and gave a great whoop of delight that made Ralph ahead of me laugh and let his horse go faster.

'Good!' Ralph said, pulling his big black stallion up outside the gate. 'But remember, even if you think you are falling, hang on to the saddle or the mane. Don't damage her mouth. She's got a mouth like satin, that horse. I wouldn't have brought her for you if I didn't trust you to have light hands.'

I nodded.

'What of Richard?' Ralph said casually. 'Does he want a horse?'

'I think not,' I said. 'He didn't want John to have the expense while he is busy studying. And when he wants to ride, he likes John's horse, Prince, for hacking around the estate.'

'What sort of a lad is he? What sort of a squire will he make?' Ralph asked lightly.

'He cares very much about being a Lacey,' I said, choosing my words with care. I had a feeling, and rightly, that the question was very serious and the answer had better be accurate. 'He would do anything for us to stay on the estate.'

Ralph nodded. 'What about his temper?' he asked.

'It's good,' I said. 'He is very seldom angry. Never with Mama, and never in public.'

'Doesn't sound much like temper to me,' Ralph said. 'Sounds more like spite. What sets it off?'

I frowned, puzzled. I had never tried to understand Richard's moments of black-eyed rage. I had merely accepted them, like the occasional storm in an otherwise sunny summer. 'When he is crossed . . .' I said slowly, hunting for ideas. And then I checked. 'No!' I said. 'It is when he is afraid he is not first with someone.'

'Likes to be the favourite, does he?' Ralph asked.

The word struck a chord in my mind. 'He likes to be the favoured child,' I said. My eyes met Ralph's look and we both heard the resonance in the words as deep as a bell tolling. 'He says he is the favoured child,' I repeated.

Ralph was still for a moment. 'Oh, that village and its superstition!' he said, exasperated. 'And even the Quality as bad as the worst of them!' He shook his head to clear his mind of nonsense as old as fairytales. 'Would you trust him to keep his word?' he asked. 'If he was first on Wideacre? If he was the favoured child indeed?'

'Yes,' I said. I trusted Richard from a lifetime of watching him and loving him.

'I'm not blind,' Ralph said brusquely. 'I can see perfectly well that Richard cares little for this profit-sharing scheme. But if he is tied into it by John, and held to it by you, would he break it wilfully? Or would he feel honour bound?'

I was certain. 'If he gives his word, he will keep it,' I said.

Ralph looked sceptical, but he nodded and swung down from the saddle, and then took my reins.

The front door opened and Richard came out. At once I froze. The childhood memory of my ride on Scheherazade was still vivid in my mind, even after all these years, and I had an immediate rush of guilt that he should see me on horseback at all.

I kicked my feet out of the stirrups and slid down to the ground without waiting for Ralph to help me. I wanted to be at a distance from the horse, the lovely horse, in case the sight of her upset Richard, angered him. Despite my confidence that Richard did not want a horse, I was not sure how he would respond to the sight of me on one.

'Richard!' I said smiling nervously. 'Look at this lovely horse Mr Megson has brought over from Rogate.'

I peeped up at Richard's face, but to my relief he was smiling, and there was no shadow in his face.

'A most beautiful animal,' he said, courteously nodding to Ralph. 'For sale, is she?'

'Aye,' said Ralph laconically. 'She and Miss Julia suit well enough.'

'Julia is a natural rider, I think,' Richard said generously.

'She's a Lacey,' Ralph said as if that explained it all. 'I'll take the mare around to your stable, Miss Julia,' he said to me. 'She's on loan to you for a couple of days, and then you can decide if you'll suit. If you don't want her, I can take her back when I'm next over that way. But if you like her, I've told your uncle the price they are asking for her.'

'Expensive, is she?' Richard asked.

Ralph looked down at him and his face was expressionless. 'Miss Julia needs a good horse,' he said levelly. 'Since she's part heir to Wideacre, she needs to ride out on the land to see what is doing. And she needs a good animal in her position.'

Richard blinked. 'Of course,' he said. 'There should be nothing but the best for Miss Julia.' There was an edge to his voice which warned me that he was not best pleased, but when he turned to me, he was smiling. He took my arm and led me towards the garden gate, bowing me in with a pretty little play of courtesy. I hesitated and looked back at Ralph with a smile.

'Thank you, Ralph,' I said. And only he would have known how deep those thanks were felt.

'Don't get so grand on your lovely horse that you forget me!' Richard said, walking up the path with me. 'You looked quite the young lady. Don't forget that you will always be little cousin to me!'

We went into the house together and we were alone in the hall. It was shadowy, lit only by the fanlight over the front door. Richard's face in the dusk seemed leaner, strange. I could feel my heartbeat speeding and I felt breathless, as if Richard were not my dear familiar cousin, but someone exciting and unknown to me. I did not feel familiar and easy. I felt a great ripple of something – certainly not pain, but not quite pleasure – and my knees felt weak.

Richard came closer to me and put his arm around my waist. 'You look pale, Julia,' he said. 'I hope the ride did not tire you?'

'No,' I said softly. 'No, I am not tired at all.'

'Why,' he said, his voice very low, 'how slight you are, Julia! You must have lost some weight – or I have grown heavier! You have grown taller, but you are no plumper at all. See, I can almost span your waist with my hands.' He stood before me and put his hands either side of my body. Through my muslin gown I could feel the warmth of his palms and the tightness of his grip.

'Nowhere near!' I said breathlessly. His face was very near mine and he still had his hands on my back. I could not resist glancing up at him and raising my face to him.

I could feel his breath against my cheek. His eyes were very dark, but not with anger. We stood for a moment, quite transfixed in that shadowy hall, not daring to move forward and quite unable to move back.

Then I heard Mama's laugh from the parlour and we both jumped apart as guiltily as though we had been doing something wrong.

'I had better go,' I muttered, and I went to the stairs to change from my crumpled gown. It was nearly time for breakfast, and Mama would not thank me for coming to the table straight from horseback.

'Julia,' Richard said, and stopped me as I had my foot on the first step.

My hand was on the banister and I made no move as he came towards the foot of the stairs, but I could feel my head going swimmy with apprehension and delight.

He came no closer to me, but stood on the far side of the stair-rail. Then he dropped his dark head and kissed my hand, where it rested. He looked at me, his blue eyes quite inscrutable. And then he turned on his heel and went into the library and left me in the dark lovely hall all alone.

I put the back of my hand to my cheek where he had kissed it, and pressed it to my face. Then I went slowly, slowly, up to my bedroom. I felt I needed to be alone to think very, very carefully about something. But when I was upstairs with the door shut behind me, I could think of nothing. I had no thought in my head. All I could be sure of was two very different feelings – feelings which pulled me two ways. One was the sensual longing which I had come to think of as Beatrice's; I knew that feeling was desire, and it suited me to think of it as Beatrice's desire, and to think myself a little haunted by her in that dark hall. The other feeling was a great unease. I had lived with Richard so close for so long that I loved him as my brother, I thought of him as my brother. And although we had talked and talked about our future marriage and our ownership of the land, I had never thought that he would court me. I had never thought that he would naturally, one day, touch me. That touch of his hands on my waist, and the warmth of his breath on the back of my hand, filled me with desire, but made me shiver as if there were something wrong.

Something very badly wrong.

The unease held with me through breakfast, fuelled by a secret look from Richard when I entered the room. Uncle John and Mama were laughing together over a letter she had received and neither of them noticed my awkwardness.

'What are your plans for today, my dear?' John asked Mama as she poured coffee for all of us.

'Today I become a sempstress, or milliner,' she said with a merry smile. 'The girls have begged to learn how to trim a gown with ribbons and how to trim a hat, so I am packing a box with scraps of material to teach them. The Acre poor-box must be the most frivolous in the country! I dread that Dr Pearce will see it!'

'The parish accounts don't bear inspection either,' John replied. 'Mr Megson's idea of urgent need is to give the girls dowries so they can marry when they wish. I live in daily dread of your step-papa coming home and finding me amid all this joyful improvidence.'

'It's not improvident,' I said, defending Ralph at once. 'It's sound sense. If the girls can marry in Acre, then they do not have to go away into service. We keep families together and there are more reliable people to work the land.'

'I know,' John said, smiling across the table at me. 'I do know that, Julia. And I know that if this estate cannot make young people happy, then we have all been wasting our time.'

Mama nodded. 'I have to go soon,' she said. 'I want to have my materials laid ready for the girls to start. What are you doing today, Julia?'

I glanced at John. 'Taking some of the day as a holiday, if I may?' I said. 'I want to try Misty's paces up on the downs and see the new sheep Mr Megson has bought. And I shall look at some pamphlets on fruit farming first; there are some horrible diseases the trees can get, and I really don't understand enough about them.'

'Can't you doctor Julia's trees, sir?' Richard asked his father. 'Dose them, feed them up?'

'One ought to be able to do so, certainly,' John said, 'but today I am off into Acre. If you need a prescription for your apple trees, Julia, you must let me know.'

We rose from the table and I followed Mama out into the hall. The front door stood open to the warm air. The mist and rain had cleared and Wideacre was new washed, well watered, alive with growth. I blinked at the brightness of the fresh leaves of the trees of the park.

'How green it is today,' I said.

Mama nodded, packing balls of wool into her reticule. 'A good day today at last,' she said. 'But please be careful on your new horse. Only as far as the sheep field on the downs, and promise me you won't try to canter,' she cautioned. 'Richard can ride home with you for dinner.'

I promised and then kissed her farewell and watched her down the garden path and into the carriage where it waited by the gate. Then I told Richard I should be at the barn at two, and watched him trot slowly up the drive on Prince, whose rolling stride seemed to eat up yards without effort. Then I put my feet up on a footstool and drew up the table with pamphlets and set to reading.

No! Not pamphlets! Alas for my good resolutions! Among the pamphlets were Mama's novels from the Chichester circulating library. I just glanced at the title page to see if it was of any interest, and the next thing I knew Stride had tapped on the door to bring me my coffee and it was after one o'clock!

'Oh, no!' I exlaimed. 'I promised Richard I should be on the downs at two. Stride, ask Jem to saddle Misty for me at once, will you? I shall be there as soon as I am changed.'

I carried my cup upstairs with me, and drank it as I pulled on my new riding habit. Mama had held to her promise to buy me a habit against the time when I would have a horse, and this was the first time I had been able to wear it. It was a deep cream colour, almost yellow, the colour of the mildest of butter sauces. It went over my head in a ripple of stiff velvet, and I smoothed it down over the curves of my breasts and the swell of my hips with a purr of pleasure at the feel of it, and the smell of it, and the look of it. It had a pretty little hat to match, with a feather dyed to the same colour, and at John's insistence Mama had bought me riding boots with little yellow tassels, which I thought were the last word in elegance. I could have preened for hours before the little spotted mirror, but I remembered that Richard would be waiting for me and – almost more important – that Misty would be ready in the stable yard.

The sheen on her coat was so bright it made her look white instead of dappled. Jem had washed her tail and her mane as soon as Ralph Megson had left her in our loose box, and she looked like a unicorn out of a fairy story, not a horse at all. He grinned at my face and held out his cupped hand for my foot to toss me up into the saddle.

'Take 'er slowly, mind,' he said seriously, and I was reminded of his uncle, John Dench, who had given me my first ride. 'Don't canter her at all this first day,' he said. 'You takes your time with her, Miss Julia. We want you coming home on top of her, not on a hurdle.'

I nodded, only half hearing him, sweeping the white locks of her mane over to the right of her shining neck. 'I'll be careful,' I promised, and I turned her lovely head for the drive. I saw her ears prick; I felt her mince lightly across the paving stones of the yard and sensed the spring come into her step as she reached the drive.

The branches over my head glowed green in the sunlight; the fresh new leaves were vibrant with growth. In the hedges on either side of the driveway were patches of cream from dogroses, and the banks were dancing with Lady's smock. Deeper in the woods the ground was hazy with a mist of late bluebells and sharp with the smell of wild garlic. Above the canopy of the summertime leaves the skies were criss-crossed with frantic parent birds, and the wood was alive with the insistent calls of courting wood-pigeons. Above their dreamy call I heard the flutelike two-tone lilt of the cuckoo, calling for a mate away up on the downs.

At the lodge gates Jenny's sister and her two small children were planting potatoes in their garden. They waved as I rode by, and the two little girls, Nell and Molly, came running down to their garden gate.

'Oh, Miss Julia! What a lovely horse!' they called, their faces peeping through the splintery bars.

They were through the gate at once, at my smile, and stood in the driveway, twisting their ragged short dresses in their dirty hands.

'I cannot give you a ride today,' I said, answering the unspoken question. 'I am not nearly safe enough yet on this horse. She is new to me and I have to learn how to ride before I take anyone else up! But as soon as I feel safe enough, I shall come down and have each of you up in front of me.'

The children beamed and I waved at them and turned Misty left down the lane towards Acre. I did not go into the village itself but turned up the bridle-track which runs past the field which used to be farmed jointly by the village. Ralph Megson had insisted that the little strips of land – one for each cottage – be restored at once, so that the men and their wives could start growing their own food again and planting at once. But it had been my advice that one of the new fields enclosed by Beatrice would be better. It had only been sown the once, and left to fallow the rest of the time. It was nearer the village, and nearer the Fenny – an advantage if someone chose to plant a crop which needed watering.

'And it was common land enclosed by Beatrice and now restored by you to the village as farmland,' Ralph Megson had said sharply. 'Miss Julia, I would hate to have you as an enemy. That is a clever move.'

I had smiled then. 'Mr Megson, I hope you never will have me as an enemy,' I had said smugly. 'While my interests, and yours, and Acre's all run the same way, there could be no cause for disagreement, let alone enmity!'

And Ralph had thrown back his grey head and laughed. 'No cause at all!' he said, chuckling. 'And total unity between masters and managers and men for ever.'

'Well, amen to that!' John had said, looking from one to another of us.

'Amen?' Ralph had said, still smiling. 'More like alleluia! Because the kingdom of heaven has come at once! Here as well as in France!'

We had laughed at that, but they had agreed that the field by the bridle-way should be planted with clover this year to put some strength back into the soil. Later we might use it for wheat or for vegetables, or even fruit.

You could still see the indentations in the grass where the division between one strip and another had been dug; and the older men of the village could still point to a nettle-strewn corner of the field and say, 'That was once mine, and I grew carrots and parsnips and potatoes there.' Although there were no deeds, and no entails, they could trace back the ownership of one strip or another for more than two centuries, naming not just the owners but the crops they planted.

Sea Mist put her ears forward at the sight of the smooth grassy track curving up the hill, and I forgot my promise to Mama and my promise to Jem as she altered her stride and broke into a smooth canter, which was an easier pace for me than her trot. I leaned towards her undulating neck to put my weight further forward and urged her faster and faster until we were thundering up the slope in a mud-slinging, wind-whistling gallop and the only noise was the drumming of her hooves and the rushing of the air and my calling, 'Go on! Go on!' to her as she went faster and faster and faster as if we were riding a race.

She checked of her own accord at the entrance to the field where the path narrowed; it was as well, for I had not thought how I would stop her if she had chosen to run off with me. But she was a lovely horse, a truly sweet-mannered mare, and I believe the thought of taking off up the path to the top of the downs was less in her head than it was in mine. I felt only too ready to play truant and ride away for the day, but I had promised Richard, and my conscience pricked me when I saw Prince tied outside the new barn. I took Misty over beside him and slid from the saddle, hitched her to one of the struts and went to the open doorway.

My eyes were dazzled by the bright sunlight, and for a moment I could not see what was happening inside. And then I blinked again, for I could not *believe* what was happening inside.

Richard was pressed flat against the wall at the far end of the barn. His hat had fallen off and in the gloom he appeared as white as a ghost; his eyes, huge in his pale face, were black with terror.

The sheep were around him in a great semicircle, standing shoulder to shoulder in a big wedge of a flock, impenetrable. I looked wildly around the barn for the shepherd, for his dog, for I had never seen sheep go so close, except when driven or perhaps protecting a ewe with a new-born lamb from some danger. But there was no one there except Richard and this arch of sheep some twenty feet away from him, packed as tight as if they were in a cart.

And they were getting closer to him.

As I watched, incredulous, the tup, a heavy-shouldered animal, stamped his cloven hoof down once, twice, and dropped his head. In a half-visible surge they moved forwards, their fleeces pressed a little tighter, their mad yellow eyes a little brighter and their white rounded faces with the dark slits of noses a little closer, just a little closer, to where Richard was backed up to the wall of the barn.

They were mobbing him, in the way that an angry upset flock will mob a little dog. But these sheep were mobbing a human.

For a moment I felt the terror which had pinned Richard to the back wall. That deep primeval terror of something one does not understand, something which is against nature or, at the least, against everything one has ever seen and known before. If I had been a superstitious woman, I should have thought them possessed by the devil, and when the ram stamped his pointy little hoof – as he did again – I should have fled in fright.

As it was I sniffed in abruptly – as if the very air of Wideacre could give me courage – and said, 'No!' – as if you could command sheep as you would a dog. 'No!' I said, and Richard's head snapped around towards the door and he squinted against the bright square of it and me standing in the doorway.

'Julia!' he said, and his voice was a hoarse whisper of utter terror. 'Julia! Get help! The sheep have gone mad!'

'No!' I said again, and I took a fistful of my riding habit in my hand to give me courage and walked straight towards them in my new boots with the yellow tassels.

They parted as I came. Of course they did. Sheep always do. They flurried out of the way and left my way clear right through the flock to Richard. The tup lowered his head at me and presented his horns, but I heard my voice say, 'No!' and he backed away on his dainty cloven hooves to the other side of the barn.

Richard did not move until I was beside him, and then he reached out his arms and clung to me as though he were drowning and going under for the third time.

I held him tight and we walked together, Richard half stumbling, towards the doorway. As he swung a leg over the hurdle, the tup and a couple of the ewes beside him came a little closer, their blank yellow eyes fixed on Richard. I said, 'Shoo!' like a farmgirl to her hens, and they stopped. I glanced around the barn. Richard had not fed them. There was a bucket of meal left beside the door. I picked it up and poured it into their trough and they went to it eagerly enough and paid me no more mind. I pushed through them towards the door and slid the hurdle aside so I could get out.

Richard was sitting outside in the sunlight, his eyes shut, his face turned up to the light and the heat. I went and sat down beside him on the springy turf of the downs, saying nothing. I did not know what had taken place in that dark barn.

But what I had seen was impossible.

'They came for me,' Richard said very low. 'I went in to feed them and water them, and they made a ring around me. I put the buckets of feed down, thinking they were going for the pails, but they were not. They came for me.'

'Where's the shepherd?' I asked.

'He sent his child up to say he was ill,' Richard said, shaking his head, for he could not believe what had happened. 'I said it didn't matter. I knew I could feed them and water them on my own. I was going to give them some hay too. But as soon as I was inside the barn, over the hurdle, they made a ring around me, and they started coming towards me. I stepped backwards, and still they kept coming. I went backwards and backwards and backwards, and still there were more of them between me and the door. And then I was back against the wall and they started coming closer.' He gave a shudder and put his head down on to his knees. 'Sheep don't *do* that,' he said.

I said nothing. I put an arm around Richard's shoulder, and my fingers slipped under the collar of his jacket. His linen shirt underneath was damp with sweat. He had been terrified. In a sudden moment of clear memory I had a picture of Richard in the stable yard the day he first saw Scheherazade, and remembered how she had shied and put her ears back when Richard had come close to her.

'It doesn't matter,' I said softly. There was nothing I could say. The scene in that darkened barn had been a nightmare, one of those insane nightmares where the most normal objects become infinitely menacing.

'No,' Richard said as if he wanted to forget as quickly as he could those moments of abject fear. 'It doesn't matter at all.'

'Would you like to go home?' I asked. I glanced at the sun and reckoned it was nearing half past two.

'In a minute,' Richard said. 'What should we do about the sheep?'

'I'll open the doors and let them out into the field,' I said, getting to my feet. 'I'll check them as they come out and Giles Shepherd can look at them properly when he is well again.'

'I'll close the gate for you,' Richard said. He went to fetch the horses and I saw him glance back nervously at me. I stayed still so that he would know that I would not release the sheep until I saw he was through the gate with it closed safe behind him. Prince stood rock-steady while Richard untied his reins, but Sea Mist threw up her head and sidled. He led the two horses through the gate and then closed it behind him. Only when he had swung into the saddle and nodded towards me did I move towards the barn.

In the gloom inside I saw the whiteness of the faces which turned to me. For a moment I felt a flash of the terror which had made it possible for them to herd Richard, the terror which every animal feels at being trapped or outnumbered.

'No,' I said again; and behind my own certainty was a line of power and knowledge which I knew came from the Laceys. I threw my head up like proud, red-headed Beatrice herself with her natural arrogance. 'Certainly not,' I said to the flock firmly, and dragged back the hurdle just wide enough to let one through at a time.

They dithered, but the sight of the downland turf was too much for them, and the old tup dipped his head and went quickly past me. Then the others scuttered after him until there was only one foolish one left, too afraid to go forward and nervous at being on her own. I opened the hurdle wide and shied an old turnip at her bobbing rump as she dashed past me. I was glad I hit her. I had been scared too.

'All done,' I said cheerfully to Richard as I climbed over the gate. He led Sea Mist up alongside so I could step from the gate into the stirrup.

'I hate sheep,' Richard said lightly. 'I shall tell my papa that I will never make a shepherd and that I don't propose to try. I shall tell him I won't supervise that flock. I'd rather concentrate on building the hall anyway. And there's enough work to do there, Lord knows!'

'Is there?' I said, and we turned the horses and our minds away from the barn and the flock of sheep. 'How near are you to finding the stone the architect wants to use?'

'I think it will have to be Bath stone,' Richard said. 'The stone they can quarry here is much too soft, he thinks. I was hoping we could get some a little closer to home because of the cost of transport. Indeed, I am sure we can. But the design of the house does call for that yellow sandstone.'

'I love the colour when it's new,' I said. 'Can he use much of the old stone of the hall?'

'That's the other problem,' Richard said. 'I am trying to persuade him to follow the outlines of the hall as much as possible to save labour, so we don't have to dig new cellars and foundations, and to reuse the stones and incorporate the walls which are still standing. But, of course, he wants to start from scratch.'

I nodded, and when the track broadened I brought Sea Mist up beside Prince and let Richard talk about the hall all the way home. We never mentioned the flock left on the lower slopes of the downs. Richard took a few moments alone with his papa before dinner to tell him that he would not work with livestock.

Uncle John – a town-bred man, and the son of a line of traders – did not think it odd. The sheep and the little herd of dairy cows became my responsibility from that day onwards. Someone had to do the work. Mama had her school, Uncle John had the health of the village and the business side of the estate, Ralph Megson supervised everything on the land, Richard took charge of the hall and I was out every day looking at the animals, and the fields, and the crops. I was busy, and weary . . . and very much a Lacey on her land.

Richard did not deal with livestock.

Richard did not deal with the land and the crops.

Richard did not deal with the tenants, and the copy-holders, and the cottagers and the labourers and the intricate details of land ownership and land sharing on Wideacre.

Richard's great love, his great project, was his work on the hall. And Mama and I, and even Uncle John, had to accept that he knew more and more about the rebuilding of our home every day. Only Richard had the love – almost a passion – to pursue the right colour of stone through twenty quarries until he found one he thought fit.

'It is darker than the usual sandstone,' he explained to Uncle John and Ralph Megson and me in the library one morning when we had gathered to take a decision about planting soft-fruit crops. 'It will blend with the old stone of the hall. The architect wanted it all new, and the builder too. But I am sure that I am doing the right thing in choosing this stone, even though it is so far to transport it. We will need half as much by using the old stone. And I like the idea of the hall being rebuilt from the ruins.' Ralph Megson cocked an eyebrow at that, but kept his head bent low over the plans of the hall spread before us on the table. 'I cannot spare many men,' he said briefly. 'They have not the skills. They could only do day labouring for you.'

Richard nodded. 'I have spoken to the architect and we think it best to bring in experienced building labourers,' he said. 'They can be housed in Midhurst and come out daily in a wagon. D'you think that will cause any unrest in Acre?'

Ralph puffed out his cheeks and looked hard at John. 'These men are on wages, I take it? No profit-sharing scheme for them?'

Uncle John met Ralph's ironic gaze steadily. 'I do not need to argue the fall of the Bastille here,' he said. 'They are on fair rates. After all, we are bringing in a ploughing and sowing gang this autumn to sow the wheat. They will be on day wages too. I see no reason why Acre should object.'

'As long as we make a profit which is better than day wages, no,' Ralph said.

'Well, that is my intention,' Uncle John said. 'Mr Megson, will you oblige me by looking at this map . . .' and he covered up Richard's plan of the hall with a map of the fields of Wideacre coloured in different shades to denote the different crops. Richard and I exchanged a rueful smile. No one cared for the hall as much as Richard. 'My intention is to have a thoroughly balanced farming estate,' Uncle John said. 'Whatever weather the climate produces should suit one crop. I should like us to grow a wide variety.'

'All fruit needs sunshine,' Ralph observed, looking at the swaths of fields coloured green to show fruit crops.

'Yes, indeed,' Uncle John replied. 'But it can tolerate rain, and they are developing strains of fruit which are more and more hardy. There is a great market out there in the growing towns. I want Wideacre fruit to go to Chichester, to Portsmouth, even to London.'

Ralph nodded. 'I think you see the future aright,' he said briefly. 'There will be more and more people in the cities and they will need to be fed. But if there is any chance of a war against France, the price of bread will go sky-high. Wheat is a good crop in wartime.'

Uncle John nodded. 'What of Acre?' he said. 'How would they feel about a large corn crop?'

There was a silence in the sunny room. You could almost smell the smoke of old riots.

Then Ralph smiled. 'Why not?' he said wryly. 'No one in Acre was ever against a reasonable profit. No one in Acre was ever against the export of food. No bread riot ever took place except with hungry people seeing their food sent away.'

'You make riots sound reasonable,' Richard said. His voice was level, encouraging. 'Have you had personal experience of such affrays?'

'I've seen bread riots,' Ralph said. The slight sideways smile he shot at me told me well enough that he had never been a neutral observer. 'I've never seen one that was not, in its own way, orderly.'

'An orderly riot?' Uncle John queried. But John had been raised in Edinburgh and had lived the past fourteen years in India.

'Yes,' Ralph said simply, 'it's generally the women anyway, so it is not as if it was fighting men or trouble-makers. I saw one in Portsmouth, where they surrounded a bread shop where the baker was selling light-weight loaves for the full price. They took the door off the front of the shop and sat on the baker while someone called for a Justice of the Peace. He looked at the weights the baker had been using. They were underweight, for he had shaved them off. The magistrate reweighed every loaf in the shop and sold them to the women at the proper price. Then they got off the baker's fat belly and left him. He was unhurt, and his shop was not damaged, except that the door was off the frame, and he had cash in his cash-box.'

Uncle John was puzzled, but Richard and I were smiling. 'The Justice of the Peace agreed with the rioters?' John asked incredulously.

Ralph shrugged and smiled. 'He believed in the old ways too. No one likes a cheating tradesman, no one likes bread-hoarders. And the women were pleasant respectable women, but, oh, my, they were angry! I'd have given them half the shop if they had so much as looked at me!'

'They did look at you, though, didn't they, Mr Megson?' I asked slyly. 'What were you doing there?'

'I was doing nothing,' Ralph Megson said innocently. 'I was just standing there, holding the door . . . and the chisel . . . and the hammer.'

Uncle John, Richard and I laughed out loud, and Ralph chuckled too.

'Those days are over,' Ralph Megson said, sounding regretful. 'The days when the poor people could insist on a fair price in the local market. It took me some time to see it, but I know it now. That's why I've no objection to Wideacre sowing corn and selling it at a profit. The only way the poor of England are going to be fed is if there is enough food in all the markets, and food being moved around the country. The poor can no longer depend on their local produce, and they cannot control the movement of grain.'

Uncle John nodded. 'With our profit-sharing scheme, we should sell surplus corn in London,' he said. 'Everyone would do better with the profits from a London sale than with cheap-priced corn in the Midhurst market.'

Ralph nodded. 'You'd always need to keep enough back to feed Acre,' he said, 'but you could grow that on half a dozen fields, and Wideacre has the capacity for scores of fields.'

'It's not just Acre that should be fed,' I said. 'When our corn goes into Midhurst, it is bought by the poor from all around the area. The sensible thing would be to agree with other landowners that we should all supply the local market at a reasonable price, and then make what profits were possible with the surplus.'

'A selling ring to benefit the poor!' Ralph said with a chuckle in the back of his voice. 'Miss Julia, you should be on the barricades. I have heard of selling rings to obtain the best price, but you are talking of one to make a fair price! A ring of producers to benefit the consumers! It would be a great novelty.'

'And it might even work,' Uncle John said thoughtfully. 'You were not here, Mr Megson, when Julia's papa, the squire, started his agricultural experiments and Beatrice ran the estate. During the good years Wideacre held sway in the whole county. Wideacre was much respected then and its example followed. If we could show that the estate was feeding the poor neighbours and all the workers *and* making a good commercial profit, there are many who would follow suit.'

'And Wideacre showed that the other way, of chasing profit, did not work at all,' I said.

Ralph smiled at my enthusiasm. 'Aye,' he said. 'You are in the right, Miss Julia.'

'I agree!' Richard said surprisingly. The two men turned to look at him, but he was smiling at me. 'The prosperity of Acre does not depend solely on profits,' he said. 'The prosperity of any estate depends on its good relationship with neighbours. Let us sow large acres of corn and sell it at a fair price locally, and make what profits we can with the surplus. That's fair.'

'Done!' said Uncle John as if we had shaken on a deal. 'But I am still having a couple of fields for raspberries and strawberries.'

'Aye,' said Ralph dourly. 'I know you are. And you may worry about how we will harvest them when they ripen at haymaking time.'

'I shall harvest them!' Richard said grandly. 'For I will do anything rather than farm sheep!'

We all laughed at that, and Richard's terror in that shadowy barn was hidden from everyone and half forgotten by me. It was generally known instead that young Master Richard could not be bothered with the stock. The stock was to be handled by Mr Megson or Miss Julia, and for this autumn Ralph would hire plough-boys and sowing gangs with their own gear and horses to plant Wideacre with wheat again.

II

No one expected Wideacre to show a profit that first season, but we had cut a good crop of hay – 'Half flowers,' Ralph said crossly – and that meant we could feed the sheep and the cows more cheaply through the winter. None of the fruit yielded that first year, of course, but we got the raspberry canes planted in straight smooth rows in the lower fields alongside the drive to Wideacre Hall. We planted the strawberries in a new field alongside the Fenny where we thought they would catch the sun and be sheltered from the wind which blows off the downs. My apple trees had taken and were growing straight and tall. They were spaced right too, which I thought something of a small miracle, so I took Ted Tyacke's ironic congratulations at face value – and as no more than my due.

Richard was much away in the autumn, preparing for his entry to the University of Oxford after Christmas. Uncle John took him up to Oxford and left him there, coming back by London to advise the MacAndrew Company about the likely changes in India which would come from the French wars, so Mama and I had a few weeks alone together on the land, working like skivvies all day and meeting only at dinner.

Mama's schoolchildren had progressed from their practical training and were starting to learn their letters; the parlour was littered every evening with brightly coloured paints and card which Mama used to cut out letter shapes.

I was working: in Acre, ordering repairs to cottages too long neglected; on the downs overseeing the planting of hedges and the building of fences to control the sheep; on the common, watching the coppices for the cutting and letting them collect firewood; and, mostly, in the fields. Wherever I was, crossing my fingers behind my back for luck as I made a decision, Ralph Megson was there too.

I could not have said what he was to me. Sometimes he was like a father, sometimes he was like a lover, sometimes he was like a teacher. All the time he was a friend. And as the days went past, and the November days got shorter and colder and more and more miserable for outdoors work, we became less like pupil and teacher and more like partners.

He met me on the bridge over the Fenny one day at the start of December. I had stopped Misty to watch the river swirling under the stone arches, and Ralph had strolled up the lane from Acre.

'You look warm,' he said.

I nodded. I had a new riding habit, as purple as a plum, made from thick wool. I had it buttoned tight around my neck, for the day was damp and there was the smell of slushy snow on the air.

'Sheep all right?' Ralph asked. He knew I had been up to check them that morning.

'Yes,' I said. 'But I think Giles Shepherd is getting too old. He is ill again and his son Jimmy is too small to take over. Besides, Mama wants him in school.'

Ralph nodded. 'I know,' he said briefly. 'There's no one else who knows about sheep in the village. We'll have to think about maybes hiring a shepherd for a season or two after Christmas. He could work with a couple of the village lads and teach them how it's done.'

'Mama would know which boys,' I said. 'But Jimmy does love the sheep. He'd be an obvious choice. His best friend is Simon. Perhaps they could work on the sheep together.'

Ralph nodded then clutched at my arm. 'Look!' he said. 'Grilse! Coming upstream!'

I bent over and stared at the water. Very slowly, as if very weary, a female salmon was swimming heavily in the water. She had made the long journey up river from the sea, leaping over the dams for mill ponds, beating her way up against the current. She was heavy with eggs, and all the little salmon which hatched from the eggs would leave the Fenny, returning when they were grown.

'I love salmon,' Ralph said emphatically. 'Miss Julia, you must excuse me for the day. I shall follow her, and when she has spawned I shall net her. And you will forgive me.'

'I will indeed,' I said, smiling at the absorbed face. 'And you may send a couple of salmon steaks up to the Dower House and Mrs Gough will cook them for your dinner if you will dine with us.'

'Aye,' Ralph said absently. 'Honoured.' And he put two fingers in his mouth and let out a piercing whistle.

At once two of the little boys of Acre came running to him, and Ralph told them to watch the salmon and follow her wherever she went without molesting her, while he fetched his horse. Without another word to me he went as fast as his rolling stride could carry him, back to his cottage for his horse and his net.

Later that day three plump salmon steaks were carried to the back door by Little 'Un, who presented Mr Megson's compliments in a bashful whisper. That night for dinner we had salmon pie with a pale brown crust of pastry on top and a creamy white sauce inside.

'Will we have a Christmas party this year?' Mr Megson asked Mama. 'I could set one in train in the village. You'd be cramped here.'

'I'd like us to do something here at the Dower House,' she said. 'You organize a party in the village for Christmas; but we will have at least the children here later, perhaps at Twelfth Night. I must write and ask Dr MacAndrew what he would wish.'

'Does he know when he is coming home?' Ralph Megson asked, passing Mama a bowl of crystallized fruits.

'Not yet,' she replied. 'The business of the MacAndrew Company is complex, and no one knows as much about India as John. Do you need him here?'

'Not at all,' he said, smiling at me. 'He left behind a very competent deputy.'

Mama smiled. 'I believe so,' she said. 'I cannot get a word of sense out of her unless it concerns something which grows on Wideacre or eats a Wideacre crop. I don't believe she has opened a book or played a tune in months.'

I nodded my head. It was true.

'She's a Lacey,' Ralph said softly. 'She takes after her papa.'

'After Harry?' My mother's eyes were suddenly sharp on Ralph's face. 'Do you think she resembles Harry?'

Ralph Megson nodded. I think only I would have known he was lying, and I knew why. He was trying to protect Mama and me from the whispers of the village which were growing into a chorus – the whispers which said that I was not just as like to Beatrice as two peas in a pod, but that I *was* Beatrice, that Beatrice the golden girl had come back to them to make the village good and the land grow again.

'They talk in the village of her being a Lacey girl like Beatrice,' he said, 'but to my mind it is her father she resembles the most. And they tell me that when he inherited, at much the same age as Miss Julia, he was Wideacre-mad for many seasons.'

The tension around Mama's brown eyes softened as if Ralph had given her a draught of poppies. 'Indeed, yes,' she said. 'Harry was out on the land almost every day the summer before we were married. D'you know, Mr Megson, I had almost forgot! Everyone remembers Beatrice running the estate, but for a couple of years it was all Harry.'

Stride brought in the port, and Mama and I rose to leave Mr Megson with the decanter, but he stayed us with a gesture.

'Please don't leave me in solitary state,' he said. 'I am a working man, Lady Lacey, and I never drink port. May we have a glass of ratafia together – before I have to go home?'

So Ralph Megson, a labouring man, sat in our dining-room and laughed with me, and smiled at my mama, and went home under a clear sky with a cold wintry moon to light his way.

He took with him a secret, the open secret which everyone knew, which they whispered in Acre: every day I grew more and more like Beatrice, the last Lacey girl on the land. Every day I resembled her more closely, every day they heard her clear voice giving orders, they heard her laughter when someone joked with me. Out of respect to Mama and to me, no one spoke of it directly. But the whole village knew – in their credulous be-nighted imaginations – that Beatrice had come back to them.

That I was her.

I could not learn to laugh at it.

Often and often I heard the singing in my ears which meant that Beatrice was coming to me, and I would give an order, or answer a question, and have that strange dreamy sensation of having been in that field, waited by that gate before. And then the old man or old woman to whom I was talking would nod and smile at me and say softly, 'Welcome, child, welcome,' and I knew that they had been there with Beatrice, and that I had just spoken her words.

It made me shiver; even in the brightest wintry sunshine it would make me shiver when they looked at me and spoke to me thus. But I would shake my head, like a puppy coming out of a river, and say, 'No! No! It is me! Julia Lacey! Don't think of anyone else.'

And they would smile at me with their eyes bright with know-ledge, with no sense at all that what they thought they saw, what they thought they knew, was quite impossible.

Christmas was quiet by old Wideacre standards, but Uncle John was home from London, and Richard home from Oxford, and that made Mama happy, and me happy. So Ralph held a Christ-mas party in the village and Mama planned a Twelfth Night party for her schoolchildren in the stable yard of the Dower House.

The old fiddle-player of Acre had died long since, and we feared there would be no dancing. But on Boxing Day Richard came in and said that Jem had told him the gypsies on the common would play in return for their supper and a shilling, so the children of Acre could have their little dance after all.

All we had to worry about on the eve of Twelfth Night was

that the starry sky would stay clear for a sunny day so that the children could eat and dance and romp in the yard.

We need not have worried. Uncle John's greeting to Mama in the morning when she came downstairs was a joyous, 'Good morning! The sun is smiling on the righteous and you have a wonderful day for your party!'

We breakfasted late, for Mama and I went down to the kitchen to prepare and bake tray after tray of sweetmeats for the party. Just as Stride was clearing away the plates, we heard the scrape of a violin and the sharp clear whistle of a wooden flute and we ran to the window to see the gypsies playing an introductory jig for us, just for us, on the front lawn of the house.

'Oh! They're very good!' cried Mama, her feet tapping, and then she laughed aloud as Richard caught her around the waist and galloped her round the breakfast table, the china rattling and Mama's silk skirts sweeping perilously close to the coffee-pots.

'Not in here!' she cried, breaking away. 'Richard! You are a gypsy yourself! If you must dance, take Julia outside and dance on the lawn. There is not room in here to shuffle a minuet, let alone one of your gallops!'

Richard laughed and we opened the front door and tumbled out to dance on the lawn to gypsy music while Mrs Gough, Jenny, Stride and Jem laid the tables in the stable yard and the children from Acre lined up along the garden wall to wave and smile at us.

They came in quick enough when I called them to the stable yard and cleared the table so that not a crumb was left. I saw that they did not grab at the food as if they were starving, and they did not tuck food into the waistbands of their clothes for hungry mouths at home. The immediate provision in Acre had been the start of a long plan of putting money and food into the village, and there was no starvation in this part of the downs any more. John nodded at Mama and I saw her smile in return as they both recognized that Acre was coming right at last.

It was well the sun shone that day, for that was the last we saw of it for some time. We had constant snow and ice, but worst of all was the freezing fog which rolled up from the Fenny every night and morning and chilled the little house until the very sandstone walls seemed to hold the coldness and to ooze icy water like cold sweat. We had fires in every room and Mama marvelled that we had managed before with only one fire in the parlour and fires lit in the bedrooms only in the mornings.

The last weeks of January were no better, with gales which blew the fog away but set the house creaking like a ship at sea. In the nights we could hear slates clattering off the roof into the stable yard. The ground was frozen hard and there was no plough-ing or planting possible until the freeze broke. The men did not even dig ditches. The only work they could do was cutting the hedgerows back, and that was a task which took some time.

So I had many hours sitting indoors and gazing blankly out of the Dower House windows at the freezing fog in the lane, and many evenings watching the firelight in the parlour. It seemed that whenever I was still and alone, whenever I had ears to listen, Beatrice was there.

And then one night I had a dream.

It started with that strange sweet singing which came in my ears sleeping or waking, warning me that Beatrice was near. I think I turned in my bed then, for I remember staring blankly at the ceiling of my room with wide-open eyes and seeing from the grey light of the ceiling that it was a cold dawn, and hearing the wind moan around the chimney-pots. It moaned like the ghost of someone just died, ill loved and locked out. I pulled the covers around my ears and buried my face deeper in the pillow to shut out the eerie calling.

And then I slept.

At once I dreamed I was in Acre, not the Acre of Beatrice's day, with the front gardens bright with flowers, but Acre as it is now: walls newly lime-washed, roofs mended, and the front gar-dens a frigid mess of new-turned earth and dung ready for plant-ing seeds. I was standing on the little patch of ground they called Miss Beatrice's Corner, outside Acre church. The vicarage was in front of me, the tall spire of the church behind. And the wind was blowing through my hair and tearing at my gown in utter silence, in deathly quiet, though the rain was sheeting down upon me, around me, and when I turned my face up to the thick sky, I felt it was raining through me. But I was not cold. I did not even feel wet.

I was afraid then, for I knew it was not an ordinary dream. And I knew I had to do something, but I did not know what it was.

I turned around to look at the church, and as I did so there was a deep heart-stopping roar of thunder, as if the very clouds were bumping together right overhead, and a crack like the spheres breaking as a shard of lightning came down and rammed a cross-bow bolt into the church spire.

It split it – as a good archer can split a wand. I watched in silence as the spire peeled apart like a shredded bough and leaned perilously outward. And fell – still in the dreamy absolute silence – towards the cottages. The pretty little cottage where Ted Tyacke and his mother lived, the Brewers' one next door and the third cottage in the row, which belonged to the Clay family – all of them came under the grotesque shadow of the falling spire.

I opened my mouth to scream for them, to warn them; but no sound came. The tower fell upon them like the finger of a cruel god and crushed the houses into dust.

I stood in the rain, the silent rain, and watched.

At once the fire bloomed out of the ruins like some mad weed, too fast in the growing. It shot great fat greedy flames into the rain and hissed against the water like a nest of snakes. It leaped down the ruins, feeding on the thatch of the cottages and the light wood of the inside walls and floorboards. And I waited in silence, for I knew I could say nothing and do nothing as it ran riot down the thatched roofs of the row of cottages.

People tumbled screaming out into the street in the pouring rain, one of the Carter children with her nightgown afire. I saw them jump on her to try to smother the flames and I saw her mouth open to scream, but I could hear nothing. Her father tried to plunge back into the burning house, for one of the children was left behind, and I saw his face, as naked as an anguished animal's, when they held him back.

The fire took long effective strides down the street, and every house it touched bloomed red. Acre was wrecked.

I woke then, shuddering with a cold sweat, and with my bed-clothes on the floor. It was early, it was too early to rise. It was only just dawn. It had been the noise of the high wind which had given me the dream, the high wind and the sound of the rain on my window-pane. A fearful dream. A most frightful dream.

I shivered as if I had really been out there in the storm, and leaned out of my bed and heaved my blankets back on to the bed. I burrowed down in them like a chilled and frightened child.

I dozed at once.

At once I was standing on the corner of grass outside the churchyard and I was in the dream again. I looked around again and saw the lightning split the spire in two. I heard the great boom of thunder, and saw the spire toppling sideways to crash down on to the Tyackes' cottage, and I cried out for Ted and his mother, and my voice made no sound in the silent storm.

I could feel myself tossing in my bed to be free of the dream, and I could feel it holding me like a torturer in a merciless grip; and I had to watch it, all over again: the fire, the burning child, the end of Acre.

Then it stopped, and I felt my half-waking body shudder and sob, and turn over once again for sleep.

And then it started again.

I was outside the churchyard on the patch of ground they called Miss Beatrice's Corner.

I dreamed that dream over and over again like a trapped ferret which runs up and down its cage on a treadmill which no one but it can see.

'Miss Julia?' said Jenny, standing by my bedside with my hot chocolate in her hand. 'Are you ill?'

I gaped up at her.

'Oh, Jenny, I'm so glad you woke me!' I exclaimed. 'I have

had such a nightmare you wouldn't believe! And I dreamed it over and over!'

I sat up in bed and pushed the hair from my forehead. It was lank and damp as if I had been tossing on my pillow and sweating all night.

'Did you dream true?' she asked. She turned her back to me and went to tend the fire. 'If you dream over and over, 'tis said to be a message,' she threw over her shoulder. 'Was there a message, Miss Julia?'

Her hand was on the coal-scuttle, and I saw her fingers. They were clasped in the age-old sign against witchcraft: thumb between the first and second finger, to make the one-handed sign of the cross to ward off the devil and his sisters. The sign, her words, the dream, all came together and I lost my wits indeed.

'Yes,' I said. And it was not my voice which spoke. 'I must dress and go to Acre,' I said, and my tongue felt heavy in my mouth.

She shot one frightened look at me, but I did not mind her. 'It's raining . . .' she said weakly.

'It will be worse than rain if I do not go,' I said, and I slid out of bed and did not feel the floorboards cold and hard beneath my bare feet. She held out my linen to me and I did not feel it chill against my skin. I let her pull my laces tight and I did not breathe in against the constriction. She held out my riding habit to me in silence and I wordlessly stepped into it. Then she dipped a curtsy and whirled from the room while I twisted my hair into a knot and pinned my hat.

She would tell Jem I needed Misty, I knew. And sure enough, when I walked hazy-eyed into the stable yard, he was holding her reins and waiting for me.

'Jenny's a fool,' he said abruptly. 'What are you doing up this early without notice to your ma?'

I looked at him without seeing him. 'I have to go to Acre,' I said. 'There is danger for them in the village.'

Jem scowled in anger. 'I don't believe in none of that,' he said truculently. 'What are you doing in the village, Miss Julia?'

'I'll see Ralph,' I said.

At once Jem looked relieved and put his hand out to throw me up into the saddle. 'Aye,' he said. 'Ralph Megson'll know what's best.'

Misty stood as still as a statue, her coat darkening with the drenching rain. I felt a trickle of water dripping from my hat and going down my back but I did not shiver. I clicked to her and she went smooth-paced out of the stable yard into the mire of the drive. It was heavy going, but she managed a canter out of the drive and down the lane towards Acre. And all the time, though my body moved with the horse, my mind was enmeshed in the dream. All I could see was the spire splitting like an axed stake.

Ralph was awake and out of his bed. I could see his silhouette before the firelight in the front room. He turned his head at the sound of the hoofbeats, came to his front door and opened it to look out.

'Julia!' he said in surprise. 'What's the matter?'

I stayed on horseback looking down on him, and I knew that I had the face of a madwoman. A face without expression, a face blank with fear at a horror which no one but me could see.

'We have to clear the cottages on the north side of the lane,' I said. It was hard to speak. I could scarce move my tongue or my lips. 'The church spire is going to be struck by lightning and it will fall on the Tyackes' cottage, and on the Brewers' and the Clays'. Then there will be a fire. It will wipe out Acre,' I said, my voice very low. 'We have to clear them out of those three cottages and then we have to make a fire-break.'

Ralph stared at me. He opened his mouth to speak, and then he stopped. He strode out into the rain and glared at me, trying to read my mind in my face. 'Julia?' he asked.

'It is true,' I said. 'I have dreamed it over and over all night. I *know* it is true, Ralph. And if you will not help me, then I will order them out on my own.'

'Wait,' he said, and turned back into his house, leaving me like a wet marble statue on a wet marble horse in the rain.

I meant to wait. Who in Acre ever disobeyed an order of

Ralph's? But as soon as his back was turned on me, I touched my heel against Misty's side and rode back up the lane towards the church.

I did not dare stand where I had stood in the dream. I feared that would make the thunder bellow and the lightning come down upon us. I could not remember from the dream what time of day it had been. I did not know how long we had to save Acre, to keep the Carter girl from burning, to keep the dreadful weight of the broken spire off the fragile roof above Ted and his mother, but I knew we did not have long.

The sky had been grey in the dream and I could not tell if it was a stormy dawn or stormy noontide; but the little girl had been in her nightshift, and the Carters were early risers.

I slid from the saddle and tied Misty to the vicarage gate – the south side of the street – and then I ran up the front path to Ted Tyacke's cottage, hammered on his door and stepped back so he could see me.

'Julia! What is it?'

'Come down, Ted,' was all I said. And I waited for my old playmate in the rain by his cottage door.

He had pulled on his breeches and a jerkin but was still barefoot. 'Come in,' he said, and took my hand to draw me into the cottage out of the rain. I shied back like a frightened horse and took one scared look over my shoulder at the church spire beside the cottage.

'No!' I said.

He saw the fright on my face and that scared him. It made him listen to me as I told him I had dreamed I saw his home crushed and Acre fired. Then he turned his head and called to his mother, and went indoors and pulled on his boots. 'I believe you,' he said briefly. 'We'll get our things out into the lane. Go and wake the others.'

I turned back to the lane and Ralph Megson was there, waiting beside my horse, his dark face inscrutable, his greying hair spiky with the wet. 'What now?' he asked as though he had nothing to say in the matter.

'We must wake the village,' I said. 'The first three cottages will be wrecked, but if we pull down the next two – the Smiths' and the Coopers' – then that can be a fire-break. We can fight the fire there.'

Ralph nodded.

'Will you ring the church bell?' he inquired.

'Oh, yes!' I said. I had not thought of it before. 'Yes!' But then I stopped dead at the thought of going into the church with the storm coming nearer. And as I hesitated, there was a dull rumble of thunder at the head of the downs and the sky darkened.

I gave a little sob. 'I don't dare,' I said.

Ralph folded his arms. 'Your dream,' he said coldly. 'Your sight. If you think you have seen aright, then you must do it.' And he turned his back on me to loosen Misty's girth as if I were paying a social call to Acre and as if there were not a thunderstorm at our heels and the rain pouring down on our heads.

'Ralph . . .' I said. It was the first time I had ever deliberately used his first name.

He turned, and his smile was as old as the land. 'If you are the favoured child, then you are in the right,' he said softly. 'Prove yourself, Julia.'

I gasped and whirled on my heel and ran up the couple of steps to the lich-gate and flung it open. I was inside the church porch before I had time to think of it, before I had time to be afraid; and I had the furry bell-pull in my hand before I took breath. I dropped my weight on it and gritted my teeth when there was no sound. The wheel-mounted bell had moved, but not enough for the clapper to strike. I took my feet off the ground and swung like a playing child, and then I heard the deep loud tolling of the bell and tugged it down and dropped my weight on it for half a dozen times before I left off and went back outside.

The sky had darkened even in that short time and its ominous yellowy tinge made the faces of the people in the lane look white. They had gathered around Ralph, but I saw him nod towards me and I knew he had refused them an explanation. I came down the church path and paused at the head of the steps where they could see me.

'I had a dream,' I said awkwardly. I could hear my voice was thin, girlish, without authority. I sounded silly; it needed only one laugh, only one quick jest and they would go back to their houses cursing the vanity of a girl who would drag them out of warm beds into the rain because she had a nightmare.

'Listen to me!' I said desperately. 'I dreamed there was a storm and the church was struck and the spire fell down that way.' I made a chopping gesture with my hand towards Ted's cottage. 'It crushed the three cottages, and then they caught fire. The fire spread down the row.'

I paused. Ned Smith, his face blurred with sleep, rubbed his hands across his face. 'Are you saying you dreamed true?' he demanded.

'Yes,' I said, 'I am sure.'

'We must pull down two cottages, the two after the Clays',' I said. 'That's the Coopers' cottage ... and yours, Ned Smith.'

His face darkened, and there was a murmur from the crowd. 'Pull down my cottage for a fire-break for a fire which has not happened?' he demanded.

I looked around for Ralph. He was at the back of the crowd beside my horse. He was not going to help me. Ted was there, and Matthew Merry; Clary was running up the lane, her skirts held high out of the mud, her legs bare. But none of them could help me; not even those three, my best friends, could help me. I feared I could not do it on my own. I waited for a moment. There was nothing I could say.

And then, like the answer to a prayer, I heard the high sweet singing over the noise of the wind and the rain and the rumble of thunder ringing on the downs.

'Yes,' I said, and there was something in my voice which would not be contradicted. 'Yes. I *know* it is necessary. I would not order it if I did not know.'

There was a sigh, like the wind before a rainstorm, which ran through all the older ones when they heard me speak thus. And I knew it was because they recognized my voice. Her voice.

'I am Beatrice's heir,' I said, calling on her name recklessly, regardless of what it would cost me come the time I wanted to be an indoor girl again. 'I am the favoured child. I have the sight. Pull down the houses.'

They moved then, they moved as if we were all in a dream, as if we were all as mad as one another, and they went into the cottages which were to be pulled down, and into the cottages which would be crushed, and carried out the furniture and stacked it in the street. They made a chain of people and passed the bedding and dry goods hand to hand into the Smiths' loose boxes; and then Ned Smith took his bill hook and his axe and started ripping the thatch off his house and throwing it down in the street, and the other men climbed up with hatchets to hack the rafters out.

The vicarage door opened, and I saw Dr Pearce, his face white, his wig askew, tying the cord of his dressing-gown as he ran down the garden path to the gate where my horse was tied.

'Are you mad?' he demanded. 'Have you all gone quite mad? Julia! What are you . . .' His hand was on the latch and he would have come out into the lane, but Ralph put a hand down on the top of the gate and held it shut. 'Away, Vicar,' he said softly. 'This is not for you.'

They had wavered at the sound of Dr Pearce's voice. The voice of the real world, the world where seeings could not happen, that voice called to them from a well-kept garden. But Acre had been steeped in madness and magic for years, and they carried on, wrecking their own houses, tearing a great gap in the village street.

'What are they doing?' Dr Pearce demanded of Ralph. 'What do they think they are doing?'

'Get you inside, Vicar,' Ralph said gently, 'and watch.'

Dr Pearce looked blankly at Ralph, and then at me. I tried to smile at him, to find some words to say, but I knew my face was tranced, mad. 'Go!' I said to him. And it was not me speaking. 'Don't stop us. We have little time.'

Dr Pearce looked again at Ralph barring his gate, as moveable as a block of granite in a chalk landscape, and then he turned and went back into his house. I saw the curtains of his study flutter and I knew he was watching.

The storm was growing nearer, and I was starting to feel afraid. The thunder was louder and the sky had grown darker just in the short time since I had been on the church steps. They were working fast now. The Smiths' cottage was down – just the walls left standing – and the dry floorboards and the tinder-box rafters were piled higgledy-piggledy in the yard of the forge. The next-door cottage, belonging to the Coopers, was half down. At least the roof was off, and then I heard a dull rumble of thunder and a crack of lightning so loud that I thought it directly overhead.

'It is here!' I called to Ralph, and I was utterly afraid.

And Ralph – that creature of madness and bad weather – smiled at me as I knew he had smiled at Beatrice when he and the storm had come for her. 'Well, they are ready,' he said, and he might have been speaking of a field fit for sowing.

I stepped down from the lich-gate and was going towards him, afraid of being too close to the church, when a sudden rumble of thunder, infinitely menacing, made me lose my footing and stagger to one side. I was on the patch of grass they called Miss Beatrice's Corner and the rain was sheeting down on me like a river off a water-wheel. The thunder was right overhead in a bang like a thousand cannon, and I spun around and saw the lightning come down, an angel's arrow, and split the church spire like a cleaver through a carrot. I screamed then, but in the storm and the thunder I made no noise, and, deafened by the thunder, in a silence as deep as the dream, I saw the spire topple and fall on to the three empty cottages and the cloud of dust grow from the rubble.

It was not dust, it was smoke, heavy dull-red smoke, and then bright flames leaped and stretched out, seeking to swallow all of Acre. Misty threw up her head and shrieked in her terror, and Ralph had tight hold of her reins. I wanted to go to her, but I found I was on my knees in the soaking grass, trembling with fright and waiting for the horror of the burning child and the wreck of the village.

The chain was handing buckets down the line towards the fire. They had thought of that – I had not. And they were soaking the ruins of the Smiths' cottage and the Coopers' cottage so that the greedy flames had nowhere to go but up into the grey sky, into the rain, and they grew more and more smoky and I choked in the smoke when the wind spun the clouds of grey around, and then I got to my feet and stumbled through the rain and the smoke towards Ralph. He spoke to me, but my head was full of the noise of the thunder, and my eyes were blinded by the lightning, and I heard nothing, nothing at all. I just put out my hands to him, and my knees buckled beneath me, and I went down before he was near enough to catch me.

'I don't understand exactly what you are saying, Mr Megson.' The voice was my mama's, and it was the anxiety in her tone which pulled me from my sleep. I opened my eyes and leaned up on one elbow. I was not in my bedroom at home. I blinked at the pretty patterned wallpaper and the pale curtains at the window. The air smelled of smoke.

'She came to my cottage and said she had a dream.' Ralph was patient, reassuring. I had heard him use that tone with frightened animals, I had seen him still them with his voice.

I looked around the room. It was the guest bedroom at the vicarage; I was lying on top of the counterpane, covered with a thick wool shawl, still dressed in my damp riding habit. Through the thin walls I could hear Mama as clearly as if we were in the same room.

'It is not unusual,' Ralph said gently. 'She is a very sensitive and perceptive young woman.'

'Are you saying she had some kind of premonition of the lightning strike?' That was Uncle John's voice. He had himself under tight control, but I knew he hated talk of anything outside an ordered universe. He was a logical man, my Uncle John.

Ralph knew that too. 'Why not?' he asked easily. 'Everyone knows that animals can sense a storm coming. Many a farmer will tell you of horses or stock breaking out of a stable before a storm and the stable catching fire. Miss Julia seems to have a gift to sense danger for Acre. That is special, but it is not unheard of.'

There was silence from downstairs. I sat up in bed and put my hand to my head. I felt light-headed and dizzy, but filled with the most enormous elation. The Carter child had not been burned. The baby had not been left inside a blazing cottage. Ted Tyacke and his mother had not been buried under tons of rubble. Acre was safe.

'It is the illness of that family.' Uncle John sounded appalled. 'Julia has the unbalanced nature of the Laceys. I have feared it, I have seen it coming. They bred too close and it has come out in her.'

'No!' I heard Mama exclaim. 'She is *my* daughter. She is not bred badly. She has been overwrought and distressed. She has been worked too hard. It is our fault for not taking better care of her, John. It is not her fault, nor the fault of her family.'

'She looked strange . . .' Dr Pearce said, his voice very low. 'For a moment I mistook her, I thought it was . . .'

'No!' my mama interrupted sharply. 'Julia has been overworked. It is my fault, it is our fault. It has made her look pale and she has got thinner.'

'Lady Lacey is right,' came Ralph's reassuring rumble. 'And she is a special girl with special gifts. She sensed the thunder coming and she did the right thing. It is nothing more than ships' captains do at sea every day.'

I sat up in my bed and called out, 'Mama!'

At once the parlour door opened and I heard her run up the stairs. She came breathlessly into my room. 'Oh, my darling!' she said. 'Awake at last! You were just like the Sleeping Beauty up here. But John insisted you should be left until you were ready to wake. What a fright you have given us all!' Her smile was forced. 'Do you have any pain? Do you feel all right now?' she asked.

'I am quite well,' I said, and it was true. 'Just . . .' I stretched like a lazy cat. 'Just . . . oh, Mama! . . . so weary!'

'We'll have you home at once,' she said. 'The carriage is at the door. John and I came down as soon as Jem had the sense to tell us where you had gone. We'll have you home at once and out of those wet things and into a warm bed, and you shall sleep all day if you need to.'

I rose to my feet and she steadied me with an arm around my waist. I was full-grown now, and our faces were on a level. It made me feel as if I were her equal, no longer a child. I looked at her shrewdly and saw the strain in her face. 'It was nothing wrong, Mama,' I said softly. 'It was just a dream which came over and over. It did not feel bad, it did not feel frightening. I just knew the storm was coming.'

Her eyes flickered away from my face. She did not want to look at me. 'No, my darling,' she lied with her loving courage. 'No one thinks there is anything wrong at all. You cleared Acre and saved many lives, which is a great blessing for all of us. We'll talk about it more when you are rested, but now I want you to come home.'

I was too tired to insist and I leaned a little on her and let her help me downstairs. Dr Pearce was at the foot of the stairs, still in his dressing-gown, but with a smile for me which was strained and wary.

Uncle John stepped forward and gave me a hug and put his hand on my forehead to feel if I had a fever. 'I am glad you slept,' he said. 'We'll soon have you home, and you must rest some more. That little mind of yours has been under too much strain.'

I was about to deny that, but I said nothing, for Ralph Megson came in from the garden, his face alight to see me. Like me, he was still wet from the rainstorm, and he – alone of all of them – was beaming at me with unreserved joy. 'Julia,' he said, and his voice was full of love.

'Ralph,' I replied, and gave him both my hands as if we were lovers.

He tucked one hand under his arm against his wet fustian jacket, and put an arm around my waist and led me to the door. Miss Green, the vicar's housekeeper, opened it and I saw it was still raining, a light end-of-storm shower which would soon pass.

Before the vicarage was the wreckage of what had once been the three little cottages, and the roofless ruins of the Smiths' and

Coopers' homes. The cottage where my friend Ted Tyacke had slept last night was a smouldering ruin, the smoke drifting into the lane.

At the gateway, around the carriage, was every man, woman and child belonging to Acre, and as the door opened and Ralph led me out, they cheered me in a great deafening wall of sound, so loud that I actually flinched; and Ralph laughed and tightened his grip around my waist.

'Unharness the horses and we'll pull her home!' shouted someone, and there was a rush to turn John's smart carriage into a triumphal chariot.

'Nay!' Ralph hallooed as he might order a ploughing team. 'Julia is weary and she should be home at once in her bed. We'll honour her another time, not today. She's just a little lass and she's wet and cold and tired.'

I smiled at Ralph protecting me – whom he had sent riding up to the downs to check on the sheep in every sort of bad weather – and he glanced down and smiled back. Then he handed me up the carriage steps, and stepped back and gave his hand to my mama. Uncle John climbed in after us, and Jem put the steps in and shut the door.

They did not cheer then, but each one of them called my name and smiled and waved, and the tears stung under my eyelids at my tiredness, and at my sense of wordless love for all of them, for the village, for the estate. And then slowly – with the wheels sticking badly in the mud – we went home.

'Misty,' I said as Jem lifted me from the carriage. He carried me up the front steps and all the way up to my bedroom, with my mama following behind and Mrs Gough and Stride making up the procession with a hot posset and hot water to wash, and a hot brick for the bed.

'Ralph Megson'll care for her,' Jem said briefly. 'I'll walk down when I've stabled the carriage horses and bring her back.'

I nodded and said no more as I let my mama undress me like a baby and tuck me up into my own bed; then I fell asleep.

*

At once I had a dream, the oldest dream.

It must have come from the storm, from the rain and the storm, but it was not like the dream of the woman waiting for the Culler. Nor was it the dream of the church spire. It was a strange dream, one I knew as if I had dreamed it every night of my life. And it was full of the most anguished pain and sense of loss.

I was hurt, hurt physically, but also heartbroken with a pain. I felt I had lost everything – everyone who was most dear to me, every possession I had ever prized. My bare feet were sore from walking far on stony cold ground, and they were wet with mud, Wideacre mud, and blood from a hundred cuts from the sharp chalk and flint stones. I was cold and dressed only in my night-gown and my cloak, which dragged wet around my ankles. I was stumbling in midnight darkness through the woods near our house towards the river, the River Fenny, and I could hear the roar of its winter-deep waters, louder even than the howling and tossing of the wind in the treetops. It was too dark for me to see my way and I nearly fell in the blackness, stubbing my toes on the stones, gasping with fright when I stumbled, dazzled rather than helped by the shattering blasts of lightning.

I could have walked easier but for my burden. The only warm dry part about me was the little bundle of a new-born baby which I was holding tight to my heart under my cape. I knew that this baby was my responsibility. She was mine. She belonged to me; and yet I must destroy her. I must take her down to the river and hold that tiny body under the turbulent waters. Then I could let her go, and the little body in the white shawl would be rolled over and over by the rushing flood away from my empty hands. I must let her go.

The roaring noise of water got louder as I struggled down the muddy footpath, and then I caught my breath with fear when I saw the river – broader than it had ever been before, buffeting the trunks of the trees high on the banks, for it had burst out of its course. The fallen tree across the river which served as a bridge was gone, hidden by boiling depths of rushing water. I gave a little cry, which I could not even hear above the noise of the storm, for I did not know how I was to get the baby into the river. And she must be drowned. I had to drown her. It was my duty as a Lacey.

It was too much for me, this fresh obstacle on top of my tears and the pain in my heart and the pain in my feet, and I started to struggle to wake. I could not see how to get this warm soft sleeping baby to the cold dashing river water, and yet I had to do it. I was stumbling forward, sobbing, towards the river, which was boiling like a cauldron in hell. But at the same time a part of my mind knew it was a dream. I struggled to be free of it, but it held me. I was imprisoned in the dream, even though I knew also that I was tossing in my bed in my little room and crying like a baby for my mama to come and wake me. But the dream held me, although I fought against it. I knew I was dreaming true. I knew that I saw now what I would one day be: an anguished woman holding a baby warm and safe in her heart, with an utter determination to drown her like an inbred puppy in the cold waters of the river which rushed from the slopes of the downs and through Wideacre and away.

I awoke to daylight and a blue sky with ribbons of clouds tearing northward from the sea winds. The dream of the darkness and despair should have faded before the bright sunlight. But it did not. It stayed with me, a hard lump of prescience and foreboding. I looked wan and low in spirits, and Mama insisted that I stay in bed all that day, and the next, as though I were in the grip of some strange unknown malady. I took her hand and kissed it as she smoothed my forehead. It was as if someone had told me, for the first time in my life, that everyone had to die one day. For the first time in my life I realized that my mama would not always be at my side when I needed her.

She patted my cheek. 'Don't worry,' she said. 'You have been overworked and overtired, and your brain has become feverish. You shall rest and you will soon be well again.'

I felt tears starting to roll down my cheeks. I was as weak as if I were mortally ill. 'Such a dreadful dream . . .' I said. But she would not hear it.

'No more dreams, my darling,' she said gently, and bent and kissed my forehead with her cool lips. 'I do not want to hear about them, and you must forget them as you wake. Dreams are meaningless. They are nothing. Go to sleep now for me, and sleep without dreaming. I shall sit here and do my sewing, and if you have a bad dream I shall wake you.'

She took a little wineglass from my bedside table and gave it to me. 'John left this for you,' she said. 'It will help you to sleep without dreaming. So drink it all up and rest, my darling.'

I took it, obedient as an invalid and drank it up and lay back on my pillows. Through a golden sleepy glow I saw my mama pull a chair over to the window and take up her sewing. She sat beside me, a guardian of my peace, and I watched her until my eyelids closed and I slept.

Mama sat with me all the time as I slept and woke and dozed again. I did not dream. John's medicine lifted me into a daze of sleepiness. But I did not dream.

On the second day my grandmama, Lady Havering, drove over from Havering Hall for a dish of tea, and stumped heavily up the uncarpeted stairs to my little room to regard me with jaundiced eyes through her lorgnette.

'You seem to be blooming on it,' she remarked acidly. 'Eccentricity always did become the Laceys.'

'I am not eccentric, Grandmama,' I said politely. 'At least, I do not mean to be.'

She smiled at that and gave me a gentle pat on the cheek. 'No, my dear,' she said. 'That would be quite unbearable.'

With that she went downstairs to what was a full family conference, with her and Uncle John and Mama – and even Richard, come home from Oxford on the stage-coach that morning.

'You're to go to Bath,' Richard said smugly. He had come upstairs with my dish of tea and a slice of apricot bread from the tea-tray. 'They've been talking it over since dinner and they've decided that you are going to go to Bath with your mama as soon as you are well enough. Your mama says that you are highly strung and need a rest. Papa says that there is bad blood in the

Laceys and it is coming out in you. Your grandmama says that the Laceys were always a wild lot, and that the best thing they can do is get you married to someone normal at once. So you're to leave.'

I clattered my dish of tea on the tray and put out both hands to Richard in alarm. 'Not for ever!' I exclaimed. 'Not for ever, Richard!'

'No,' he said, 'just for a couple of months. Your mama wants you to take the waters, and my papa wants you to see a doctor who is a friend of his, and your grandmama wants you affianced. They think a couple of months in Bath should do all that.'

I looked at him carefully. He was smiling, but it was a tight mean smile. He was angry with me and trying not to show it.

'And you,' I asked breathlessly, 'what did you say?'

'I said nothing,' he said. 'There was little I needed to say. I have my own opinions as to what you were doing, and I shall keep them.'

'I shan't go,' I said.

'It's quite decided,' Richard said blithely. 'You'll go with your mama, and the two of you will stay at some dreary lodging-house. I should think it's fearfully slow. You're to leave as soon as they confirm the booking of the rooms and as soon as my papa has ordered horses for the journey. You'll see this friend of his, a specialist. They trained together at Edinburgh, but since that time this doctor has specialized in particular complaints.' His look at me was radiant. 'Don't you want to know what complaints those are?' he asked.

I hesitated. Some streak of self-preservation in my head warned me that I did *not* want to know what they were. But I felt as weary and defeated as if that dream had been a promise of my future. 'What?' I said.

'Insanity in young ladies,' Richard said sweetly. 'He specializes in young ladies who have gone off their heads. And *he* is the one you are to see in Bath. For they all think you are mad. They think you are off your clever little head.'

My plate clattered to the floor as I reached out for his hand.

'No, Richard,' I choked. 'I will not go. They are wrong, you know they are wrong.'

He twisted away from my grasp. 'That's not all,' he said. 'Until you leave, you are not to go into Acre at all.'

I gaped at him. 'Am I in disgrace?' I asked. 'Are they angry with me for what happened in Acre?'

'They *say* they are afraid for you,' Richard said smugly. 'It's to be given out that you are unwell. But they all believe that you are going mad.'

I put one hand on the wooden headboard of my bed, and the other hand to my cheek to steady myself. 'This is nonsense,' I said weakly. 'I have always had dreams. This was just a dream like the others. It was a seeing. Everyone knows about seeings.'

'Dirty old gypsies have seeings,' Richard said cruelly. 'Young ladies do not. Unless they are going mad. You have always tried to resemble my mama, Beatrice; they all say that in the end she went mad. Now they are saying it is a family madness. That you are going mad too.'

The room swam around me. 'No, Richard,' I said steadily. 'It is not like that. You know it is not like that.'

'I *don't* know,' Richard said swiftly. 'I used to think I knew you, but ever since my papa came home, you have been trying to be his favourite. Ralph Megson arrived in the village and you have tried to make yourself first with him, and first with Acre. Just because you are friends with those stupid little peasants, you are queening it around the whole time trying to play the squire. I get sent to my lessons, but you roam around as you please. Then as soon as I have to leave for Oxford, you are down there all the time, making up to Megson and pretending to work the land as if you were *my* mama come again. Now you see what comes of it! Much good it has done you! You plotted to make it seem as if you are the favoured child and now no one believes you; they just think you are crazy.'

'I am not!' I said, suddenly angry, fighting through the soporific haze of the drug and through my sense of fatigue and defeat. I threw back the bedcovers and started to rise. 'I have the sight,'

I said defiantly. 'And it meant I was able to save the village from the falling spire and from the fire. I did not plan to do it. I did not plot. I was drawn down there and I could not help myself. It *was* Beatrice. It *was* a seeing.'

He put hard hands on my shoulders and pinned me, seated, to the bed. 'There are no such things,' he hissed, his face black with fury. 'There are no such things as seeings. Beatrice is dead, and what you just said proves that we are all right and you are mad. You are going mad, Julia, and we will have to put you in a madhouse; and you will never live in the new Wideacre Hall, and you will never be the favoured child in Acre.'

I put up my hands to hold his wrists and silence him. But nothing would stop him.

'You are going mad, and they will send you to Bath, and your mama will take you to see a doctor, and he will know at once that all these dreams and these seeings and these singings in your head are because you are mad, and getting madder every day.'

I screamed.

I took my hands from holding him and punched him hard, punched at his body and screamed at him.

At once he thrust me face down into the pillow and held me there, half stifled, with all his force while I writhed and struggled and tried to push myself up. When I lay limp, he relaxed his grip and turned my face around towards him.

'Better be quiet,' he said, and his whisper was infinitely sweet. 'If they hear you screaming, or think that you are getting violent, it would make it so much worse.' He smiled at me, untroubled, his face alight with joy. 'You look mad,' he said sweetly. 'And you were screaming just then, quite out of control. You were violent with me, you attacked me, and now you are crying. Anyone who saw you would be certain that you have to be put in a madhouse. Better stay quiet, Julia.' He stroked my hair from my hot forehead in a terrifying parody of care. 'There, there,' he said.

I shuddered under his touch.

He lifted my bare feet from the floor and tucked them under

the bed covers again and smoothed the sheet under my chin. 'Lie still,' he whispered softly, his mouth very close to my ear. 'Lie still. Your grandmama is still downstairs, and you would not want her to hear you screaming, would you? Little pet of the family.'

I lay frozen. I did not even move when he kissed me softly on the cheek, gently, as if he loved me. Then he turned his back on me and trod light-footed to the door and shut it behind him.

I lay where he had left me, staring blankly at the ceiling, my cheeks wet with cooling tears, with the start of a secret panic building inside me.

It was like a nightmare, the next few days. Every sweet smile of my mama's, every time Uncle John looked at me and asked how I was feeling was a confirmation of what Richard had said: they thought I was going mad. I knew my face was strained and my eyes wary. I tried so hard to act normally, to seem like an ordinary girl, but every day my behaviour grew odder and odder.

The weather tormented me, for the wind and the rain had blown away into half a dozen cold sharp days with a frost in the morning and a bright red sun in the afternoon. Misty in her stable ate oats and grew restless, and yet they would not let me ride. I hardly dared glance out of the window for fear that Mama should see some wildness in my face which would appear abnormal. I was afraid even to sit on a stool at her feet and gaze into the log fire in case Uncle John should say gently, 'What are you thinking, Julia?'

His eyes were on me all the time and when I looked idly into the flames, he watched my rapt face. I was under observation.

Misty was restless in the loose box of the Dower House, for Ralph had brought her back the very next day, loaded with little presents from the children of Acre. They had made me chains of little paper flowers, they had made me a bouquet of twigs with tiny buds as a promise of spring and they had collected farthings and walked to Midhurst to buy me a box of sweetmeats. But Ralph had not been allowed to see me. They had told him, they had told all the callers from Acre, that I was resting and would be leaving for Bath within the week.

My place on the land was taken by Richard.

Every day he ordered Prince out of the stables and rode to Acre to consult with Ralph on what should be done that day. And Ralph – easygoing, imperturbable – accepted the change as our wishes, as my wishes. He knew that Richard had no eye for the cows and did not like to work with the sheep, but January is a slack time of the year and there was little to do on the land. The urgent work was to shore up the west wall of the church to make the roof waterproof and then to rebuild the five wrecked cottages as soon as possible.

Richard knew the builders, knew them better than anyone. Richard had done the round of the local quarries and knew exactly the cost of stone at each one and when they could deliver. Richard could draw a plan himself or adapt one from out of his own library of building books. Richard was the one they needed in Acre in that month, with little farming work to do, but with an urgent need for someone to plan and supervise the repair of the church and the rebuilding of the cottages.

Richard set them to work to rethatch and reroof the Smiths' and the Coopers' homes, and he was out in the lane of Acre every day, watching them replace the rafters and lay the thatch. In the afternoon when the light started to fail, he would take them down to the Bush and treat them to great mugs of ale at his own expense.

He did not forget the women or children either. When Little 'Un was ill, Richard called out the carriage to take him up to the Dower House to see Uncle John and brought him home again, wrapped up warm around the throat and dosed with laudanum against the pain. He always had a handful of ribbons in his pocket for the pretty girls of Acre. He acted like a beloved young squire and showed no preference. Clary was still the leader of the young people of the village, and he always saved the broadest, reddest ribbon for her. Only Ted Tyacke stood out against Richard's charm. Only Ted refused to drink with him, failed to pull a forelock to him. 'He's surly,' Richard said at dinner, his smile newly confident, 'but he doesn't matter. I can manage the village without the blessing of Ted Tyacke.'

It was as if I had died on that night of the church spire falling. Died, and my place taken by Richard. Died and been forgotten.

Mama and Uncle John ordered Stride to deny me at the front door to visitors. In the kitchen they told village callers that I was unwell and resting. If you wanted a decision on the land, you went to Ralph Megson. If you wanted a decision on buildings, or a favour, you went to Richard. It was as if I were not there, as if I had already gone to Bath and would never return.

Mama knew that I was unhappy, but she did not ask me for an explanation, and I was as wary of opening my heart to her as a suspected criminal. The worst thing for me was how they watched me, but also I could not rid myself of that bleak memory of the dream. It was as if I had looked into an enchanted mirror and seen my face, haggard with suffering, lined with age, as if I had been cursed with a glimpse of the future which held no restored Acre, no rebuilt hall, just loneliness and pain and fear, and an unwanted baby which had to be murdered.

If I could have rested, if they could have let me alone, I might have recovered my spirits, I might have looked less strange. But they watched me all the time, with anxious loving eyes. And neither my mama nor Uncle John could conceal their impatience to get me away, off the land, away from my home, exiled. I watched the post-bag and I knew that Uncle John had written to his friend the doctor. The reply came on the same day as the confirmation that the rooms booked by Mama were available.

'We can leave tomorrow,' Mama said to Uncle John over the coffee-pot at breakfast-time.

'And Dr Phillips will see you at your convenience,' he said.

Both of them were studiously avoiding looking at me. I kept my eyes on my plate. I was afraid to say anything. The room was full of fearful silences.

'I'll be off!' Richard said brightly. We all looked up at him as he pushed back his chair and went towards the door, pausing only to kiss Mama on the top of her lace cap as he went past her. 'The Smiths and the Coopers should be able to move back in today, and I can start work in earnest on the other three cottages,' he said cheerfully. 'You *do* agree, don't you, sir, that I need not go back to university until I have seen this work through, and the cottages up again?'

Uncle John nodded approvingly at Richard. 'Yes, indeed,' he said. 'No one else could have drawn up the plans and ordered the goods so quickly. Acre is in your debt. No one could take over now.'

Richard smiled sweetly. 'I'm glad to help!' he said. 'But I don't think we should let Julia home from Bath until she promises not to pull down any more of Acre. I agree there are times when I could quite cheerfully raze it to the ground, but *not* in the middle of a thunderstorm in the middle of January!'

The three of them laughed, but only Richard seemed to relish the joke. I could feel my face stiffen in a blank, insincere smile. I knew I looked odd, smiling like that with my eyes filling with tears. Richard was the only one who did not seem to notice. He blew a kiss to me and swung to the door, then he checked with an eye on me. 'May we have dinner late tonight?' he asked. 'I won't be finished before nightfall.'

Mama smiled at his enthusiasm. 'Of course,' she said. 'If you are so busy, we can dine later if that suits you, Richard.'

'Part business, part pleasure!' he said provocatively, watching me to see how I took it. 'Getting Acre to work is costing me a fortune in ribbons!'

I kept my eyes down and said nothing while John and Mama bantered with Richard about flirting with the village girls. I knew he had said that to distress me, and it did distress me. They had taken him to their hearts very thoroughly in Acre. Then he said goodbye again and we heard his boots clatter across the wooden floor and then the front door slam.

There was an awkward silence.

'Can you be ready to leave tomorrow, Julia?' Mama asked me gently. 'There is no need to pack very many dresses. I want to buy you some new costumes in Bath.'

I nodded. There was nothing I could say but yes. I took myself out of the room before they wondered aloud at the contrast between my bright healthy cousin and myself.

He was in the ascendant. He was the support of Mama and even of Uncle John, who relied upon him to carry messages to and from Acre. He was employed by Ralph Megson to do some of the tasks I had done. He was indispensable in the rebuilding of the cottages, and he was increasingly popular in the village. In those cold sharp days he was like a ploughing team testing a new harness. He kept trying a little more, he kept stretching his strength.

There was more and more he could do on the land. John's gentle old hunter was glad of a little ambling exercise, and Richard gained praise from Uncle John for not despising him. In truth, Richard had never looked so happy with a horse as he was on that easy-tempered animal who looked showy and was bred well, but was so near retirement as to be as safe and as comfortable as an armchair.

I had become nothing to Richard. He had the land, he had Acre, he had some village flirtation.

I had become nothing to Acre. I had worked for them and saved them. And now they were ready to rebuild and turn their faces to the future. They would forget me in weeks.

I had become – not nothing, no, I did not imagine that – but I had become a source of worry and unease to my mama and to Uncle John. I was not a favoured child. I was a very troublesome one.

I went into the parlour with my cheeks burning and my eyes bright, and when Uncle John and Mama came in, I caught a glance between the two of them brimful of worry and concern. They thought I was moody, or volatile, or hysterical. Indeed, I felt that I was all three.

I went as close to my mama as I could go, as though her mere presence could keep me safe from the appearance of madness, and from the feelings of madness itself, the panic that I was losing everything and my dread of being that barefoot woman of my dream. I pulled up a footstool and sat at her feet and helped her unpick the hems of gowns which we were taking to Bath to be remodelled. I unstitched like a careful sempstress, detaching the antique lace which would be used to trim new gowns. I took it to the kitchen and washed it and rinsed it with meticulous care, and then patted it with a soft linen cloth and spread it out to dry.

Richard was out at work all day and did not come home until dinner-time. They had ordered dinner to be late to suit his convenience. I was beyond impatience or jealousy or anger. Richard was the squire. He would do as he pleased.

He came home late, as he had said he would, and threw down his cape over the banister and ran up to his room to dress. I could smell the frosty air in the folds of the wool and it called me, as clear as a voice calling my name. I threw on a shawl and went out of the front door and around to the back garden where I could see the dark shadow of the downs, black against a blue-black sky.

The grass was crunchy with the frost, and the sky was an arch of darkness with sharp stars. A shadow went across the sky and I heard an owl call a long clear hunting note. The great cedar tree stood like a splay-fingered giant against the starlit sky. A figure moved out from the shadow and came near to me.

It was Clary Dench. 'Julia?' she said. 'It's me.'

'Oh, Clary!' I said. 'I am so pleased to see you! How did you know I needed you so badly?'

'I was to see Richard,' she said, 'after work, in the woods. But I was late and he was gone. I thought it would be a message from you for me. So I came on up here.'

'*You* were meeting Richard?' I asked incredulously. 'Meeting Richard after dark in the woods?'

Clary gave an unladylike whoop of laughter. 'Don't be a fool, Julia,' she begged me. 'What d'you think I am? Some daft village slut chasing after the boy squire? He asked me to meet him and I thought it was a message from you. Why else?'

I nodded slowly. It was another thread of Richard's skein of teasing and misreading which was winding around me and colouring my world.

'Oh,' I said. 'Oh, but Clary, it's good to see you!'

I put an arm around her waist and hugged her and felt the familiar warmth of her plump body and the familiar tickle of her long hair against my cheek. We turned and walked across the lawn together, and stopped at the foot of the cedar tree. I rubbed my hand against the bark, feeling the flaky contours, smelling the sweet spicy scent of it.

'I'm glad you're here, because I have to say goodbye to you,' I said. I put my hands out to her. 'I've not been allowed down to Acre since the night of the storm, Clary. They say that I am ill, and in truth they are half-way to making me believe that I am. They are sending me to Bath tomorrow, and I dare say I won't be allowed down to say farewell to my friends. Tell them in the village that I thought of all of them, and that I sent them my love.'

She held my hands between two cold palms. 'Going?' she said blankly. 'Going from here? What for, Julia? Are you going for long?'

I tried to laugh and say, 'Oh! Of course not!'

I tried to smile and say, 'Oh! I shall have such fun in Bath!'

But instead I found I had sobbed aloud, and flung myself into Clary's arms and said piteously, 'Oh, Clary! Clary! Just because of the dream and because of the night of the thunderstorm, they think that I am going mad and they are taking me away from here and I don't know what will happen!'

And I wept for the first time since Richard had warned me that I must not seem odd, and felt the fear and the anxiety ease from me as Clary patted my back, and dried my face on her thin shawl, and then pulled me over to the swing – ghostly on its frozen ropes – and sat me down.

'What is wrong?' she asked gently. 'You are not in the least mad, but I have never seen you so unhappy. You look odd too.'

'How odd?' I asked afraid.

'Older,' she said, fumbling for words. 'Sad. As if you knew something awful. What's happening, Julia?'

I had a lie, a lie for my dear Clary ready on my tongue, and I was poised, one toe on the ground, to set the pendulum swinging so that I could lie, and swing backwards and forwards like a clock telling the wrong time. But I did not launch myself. I kept my toe on the ground and then I slowly eased the swing down into the upright position again. I did not want to lie to her. Whatever might be going wrong, there were some things in my life which went back a long way, which I wanted to keep safe.

'It's Beatrice,' I said slowly. In the still garden, drained of colour, Clary and I faced each other, the horror of what I had said smiling at us both. She shivered, although her shawl was wrapped tight around her; and I knew that same chill inside me.

'It is Beatrice and her magic,' I said in a whisper.

Clary's eyes were dark with fear and I could feel the hairs on the nape of my own neck prickle like a threatened dog's.

'Are you seeing her?' she asked, her voice soft.

'No,' I said in an undertone. 'It is worse than that. I feel as if I am becoming her.'

There was an utter silence between the two of us. The little wind blew the smell of the cold downs to us, but underneath there was the scent of fear, sharp as sage.

'Was it when Ralph Megson arrived?' she asked.

'Yes,' I said. 'He heard her then in my voice. I think he even saw her likeness then in my face.'

She nodded and put out a hand to tighten her shawl around her. With a prickle of fear up my spine I saw that her hand was clenched in the old sign against witchcraft, the thumb between the forefinger and the third finger to make the cross. I leaned forward and put my hand over hers, imploring, accusing. 'Clary, you make that sign to *me*?'

She flexed her fingers and dipped her head, and in the starlight her face grew dark as she blushed. 'Oh! Lord love you, no!' she said. She turned away from me and went to the trunk of the cedar tree and rested her head against the trunk as if to clear the whirl in her mind by the touch of the bark. 'No,' she said, turning back to me and leaning against the tree-trunk. 'I did not make that sign to *you*. But I did make it to something I saw. I saw something in your eyes, Julia. It had me scared, I admit it.'

'You see her in my eyes,' I said blankly.

She looked at me with the eyes of a friendship which went back to the time when we were just little children playing in the woods. 'Yes, I suppose so,' she said. 'It's nothing more than they've been saying in the village all this year. That you are the favoured child. That you are her heir.'

'It doesn't feel much like being favoured,' I said resentfully. 'I have had a dream, oh, Clary, such a nightmare!' She said nothing. 'Not a nightmare like one of my dreams of Beatrice,' I said. 'Just a feeling of being utterly alone. So terribly, terribly alone and with no one to love me, and no one to love at all. No one to love except a little tiny baby in a white shawl, and knowing I have to drown her.'

Clary gasped, her face white in the moonlight, then she came towards the swing and knelt on the frozen grass at my feet and put her hands on mine. 'I will always love you,' she said in the deep sweet drawl of Acre. 'I will always be here.'

For a moment I was warmed by the affection in her voice, but even as I started to smile, I heard a noise, like an icy wind blowing from far, far away. 'No, you won't,' I said, and we heard the desolate certainty in my voice.

For a moment Clary's eyes questioned me, but she was a village girl and wise. She shrugged her shoulders and gave me a gleam of her defiant urchin smile. 'Well, at least I shan't have to put up with the sight of you lording it as squire, then,' she said.

It was a weak joke, and our smiles were faint. We were still and silent in the garden a long while.

'What will you do? Can you refuse to go?' she asked.

'I shall have to go,' I said sullenly. 'I shall have to go and not know when they will let me come back.'

I tried to smile, but I could manage only a sad little grimace. The wind was icy, blowing down from the stars, but I had a throbbing headache so heavy over my eyes that I could hardly see the garden. I seemed to be well on the way to losing every thing I had ever wanted: Richard, Wideacre and my girl-hood. All stolen from me by the lost dead witch of Wideacre. And nothing given to me in their place but a handful of superstitions and a wildness which I could not control.

'I shall have to do as they all want,' I said. 'Mama, Uncle John and Richard. I have to go to Bath.' I wiped away a couple of tears from my cheek with the back of my hand, gave Clary a watery smile and a kiss; and went towards the house.

She stayed me with a gentle touch on my arm. 'What if you do have her gifts?' she asked, her loving courage for me nerving her to speak of Beatrice. 'What if you have? Can't they just see that it does not matter? The old people in Acre have said it of you ever since you were a little girl. They always said you were Beatrice come back to set things right. Can't it just be a secret? A secret for the Laceys and Acre?'

'No,' I said wearily. 'The world is changing, Clary. There is no room for such secrets any more. More and more people come into the village to work, more and more Acre folk work away. Everyone in the outside world is set against seeings and dreams and the things that we know happen. But they have no explanation for it; and so they will not hear of it.'

Clary made a face. 'They think they are so wise,' she said scathingly. 'Men like your Uncle John – good men, who do a good job – but they have to know everything in words.' She broke off. 'I'll go home now, before the clouds come up. But I'll stop at Ralph Megson's cottage and tell him you're to be sent away in the morning. Your precious cousin told no one of it. None of us knew.'

I nodded my thanks for that and put my cheek against hers in a hug. I felt her quiver as I touched her and I knew that she was afraid that the coldness of my cheek was not just the chill of the night air, but the embrace of a ghost. I stepped back from her and tried to smile normally, but I knew my eyes were hazy and fey.

'Don't be afraid, Clary,' I said. 'I am still the little girl who rolled in the mud with you. I may have it all wrong. They may be right that I have no sight at all but just a fever on the brain.'

She nodded, and gave me a pat on the cheek with one grimy hand, then she drew her shawl around her and slid from the garden.

I looked for Ralph Megson that evening, for he knew our time for the tea-tray, and I had thought he might have ridden under the frost-hazed moon to see us. I stayed up an extra half-hour after supper, waiting to see if he would come, and I went to bed and wept in absolute silence into my pillow that he should have failed me and I should have to leave without seeing him.

I should have trusted him. In the morning when Jenny brought me my cup of chocolate, she told me that Mr Megson was in the stable yard, come to bid me safe journey. I threw a wrapper on, and my riding jacket atop for good measure, and went down. The sun was as bright as midsummer, but the ground was hard as rock. It was a brilliant still day, with a sky as blue as ice and Ralph Megson high on his black hunter in the stable yard, smiling down on me.

I walked up to the horse's neck and stroked him, looking up at Ralph.

'Have you been ill?' he asked softly.

'No,' I said. 'I was not allowed out. They were afraid to let me.'

'No need,' he said gently, and I felt the tension and the pain of the last few days start to let me go, like cords slipping away from around my neck and shoulders.

'I have to go to Bath,' I said abruptly. It sounded like a sentence of doom. Ralph glanced at me, his eyes warm, full of sympathy. 'They will take me to see a doctor,' I said. 'They think that I am unbalanced because of the dreams, and because of the night of the storm!'

Ralph made a little grimace. 'Aye,' he said, 'I suppose they would.' He said nothing for a moment. 'No doctor of any sense will meddle with you, Julia,' he said gently. 'Anyone can see you are a bright and lovely young woman. Any doctor with half a mind would see that you have special gifts, special powers, and you should be glad of them. You should let them flow through you like a river through the arches of a bridge.'

'I cannot,' I said urgently. 'I am to be a young lady. I cannot be as fey as some half-mad gypsy. I am not the village midwife. I am not a teller of fortunes. All of the seeing and dreaming will have to go. I have to move in society. I have to be the wife of a squire!'

Ralph pursed his mouth as if he were about to spit; but then he remembered where he was and thought better of it. 'I beg your pardon,' he said with exaggerated courtesy. 'For a moment I forgot that you had such a glorious future ahead of you. A young lady in society indeed! Well, that is worth a few sacrifices, I should say!' He looked down at my wan face, and the harsh humour left his eyes. 'You are Quality born and bred,' he said more gently. 'If you want to run from the wildness that is in you, if you want to knock it out of yourself, then you may be able to do that. You *may* be able to turn yourself into a bread-and-butter Bath miss. I should think not. But I could be wrong. If anywhere could do it, then Bath can!'

The tone of disgust in his voice was too much for me. I giggled. 'Have you ever been to Bath?' I asked smiling.

'Aye,' Ralph said. 'They didn't make me into a proper young lady either! But they'd have a better chance with you.' He captured my hand where it was patting his horse's neck and held it in a comforting clasp. 'Follow your heart,' he said gently. 'I think this land is the place for you, and I think you are Beatrice's heir. But John and your mama want different things for you. It is you who will have to live the life you choose – none of us. Try the taste of Bath – see how it suits you. Then come home to us if you like Wideacre best.'

I nodded. Ralph's wisdom was as simple as grass growing.

'I am afraid of this doctor,' I confessed.

Ralph's gentle touch turned into a handclasp as if we were shaking on a deal. 'While I am alive, no one will coerce you,' he said briefly. 'That is a promise.'

I looked up at him and I had a sudden sharp ringing sound in my head. 'There will come a time when you will not be able to help me,' I said certainly, in a voice which was not my own. 'There will come a time when I will not be able to help you.'

I fell silent and Ralph said nothing, waiting patiently in case there was more. 'That will be a dark hour for the two of us,' he said. 'But it is not here now. Don't be afraid of the future, little Julia. Take your present life and live it.' He was about to turn his horse away when he checked and put his hand in his pocket. 'I brought a present for you,' he said casually. He lifted the pocket flap and brought out something hidden in his broad clenched hand. I reached up for it.

It was a little wooden carved owl, warm from the warmth of his body, carved in a pale wood; hard and smooth-polished.

'Ralph,' I said, entranced. 'Did you make it yourself? For me?'

'Aye,' he said. 'I'm a gypsy's lad, remember? I was up at the camp the other day, and I borrowed their tools for a while. You should be grateful I didn't bring you a bag of clothes-pegs too.'

I giggled at that. But as my fingers closed around the little wooden owl, I felt a long shudder sway me, a calling from the past, from Beatrice. 'You gave her an owl,' I said with certainty.

Ralph's glance at me was sharp. 'If you were mad, you could not know that,' he said. 'No one knew of it but her and me. No one could have told you. I gave her an owl for love of her, on her birthday the year we were lovers, and she called it "Canny" for wisdom. I sent her a little china owl in hatred one year to frighten her when we were enemies, after she had lost all her wisdom and skill. And now I give a little wooden owl to you, her heir, with my love. To remind you to keep your wisdom as well as you can.'

'I will,' I said with all my heart. 'Thank you, Ralph. You are so . . .' I groped for the word. 'You are so *sweet* to me.'

Ralph looked utterly thunderstruck. 'I must be nearing my dotage,' he said in disgust. 'A beddable wench like you finds me *sweet*? Good God!' And he turned his horse's head at once and waved farewell to me, still muttering.

'Goodbye, Ralph!' I called after him, happy as only he could make me. 'I'll be home for ploughing!'

I don't know if he heard me. His horse's hooves were loud on the frost-hard ground, but he left me with a smile on my face, an escape from my fear . . . and a little wooden owl safe in the palm of my hand.

I went back to the house to pack and dress for the journey. The gong went for breakfast and Mama ate her meal with a list and a pencil by her plate, there was so much to remember.

We were late leaving, the boxes had to be finally corded up and tied on the back of the chaise. Mama forgot a novel she wanted and I had to run back in to fetch it, and she had a hundred things to tell Stride before she was ready to put both hands out of the window to John and say, 'Goodbye, God bless you, and don't work too hard.'

He kissed both her hands and then stepped up to the window and kissed her on the lips. 'God speed, Celia,' he said gently. 'Don't buy a queen's wardrobe, and come home soon.'

Richard was on my side of the carriage. 'I hope you will get better,' he said, his voice light and insincere.

I nodded.

'If you are unwell and you stay in Bath, they will accept me as the squire in Acre, won't they?' he asked. 'They believe you have the sight, but they know that I am the favoured child?'

I did not have the energy to defend myself. 'They will come to like you more and more,' I said wearily, 'and anyway, they will come to think that the sight means nothing.'

I looked at him, scanning his face for a hint of kindliness towards me, for the love I had trusted all my childhood and girlhood. Richard, stone-faced Richard, smiled again his complacent smile and stepped back from the carriage window. 'I shall make Acre mine while you are gone,' he said. 'I have been waiting for my time. The hall will be how I have planned it, and Acre will come to my hand. I do indeed hope you soon feel well, Julia, but I dare say you will be there for months. Goodbye.'

'We are joint heirs,' I said in a sharp undertone. 'The land will always be partly mine.'

Richard smiled, a smile like midsummer skies. 'I shan't regard it,' he said sweetly. 'And you don't know the law, my clever little cousin. If they commit you to an asylum, you are disinherited at once. Did you not know that, my dear? If you go on with your seeings and your dreamings, you will lose everything.'

I could feel my eyes widen until I was blind with terror. 'No,' I said under my breath, but already Richard's face was wavering in a haze. The carriage moved forward before I could call out a denial, a denial of everything he said. All I could do was to lean forward and see Richard, my stunningly handsome cousin Richard, with his dark curls and his bright blue eyes, standing arms akimbo in the lane as if he owned every inch of the land outright.

→ 13 ←

The journey from Wideacre to Bath took two days of hard travelling. If I had not been sick to my very heart and missing my home from the moment we left the estate, I should have enjoyed it: the bustle of the coaching inns when we changed the horses, the steep wide slopes of the great plain around Salisbury, the rocking motion of the carriage which lulled me to sleep and then woke me again with a jolt, and Mama, fresh in a new bonnet, stepping into coffee-rooms and dining-rooms as if she had been a lady of means every day of her life.

The best part of the journey was across the humped back of southern England. It was good country, not unlike our downland scenery. Lower, of course; for whoever could build a carriage road over the top of my high and lovely downs? But rolling, and sweet and green, with that special springy grass which grows when the roots are in pale earth on a bedrock of chalk. The streams were clear and sweet too, with the clarity of water flowing cleanly off chalk. My mouth watered to taste them and I had a sudden pang of longing for a glass of Wideacre water.

They farmed sheep there in great flocks, and for much of the way the road was unfenced; the white-faced sheep had learned to scurry out of the way of the stage-coach when the guard blew on his horn. Even here the mania for wheat was gripping the farmers, and I saw many fields which had been newly cut from the free long sheep-runs and fenced and ploughed, ready for spring sowing.

I liked the drive and watching the scenery. I liked listening to Jem spinning yarns about us to the ostlers in the coaching inns. And I enjoyed listening to Mama promising me the treats I should have in Bath.

But it was no good, and I could not make it good. I felt I was in disgrace. I felt I was on trial. When Mama glanced anxiously at me when I woke from a half-dreaming sleep, my head against the soft squabs of the coach, I flushed for fear that I might have spoken aloud, for fear that she might have seen my eyelids flutter in my sleep, for fear that she thought that I had been dreaming again.

We shared a bedchamber for the night we stopped on the road in a coaching inn just before Salisbury. I woke in the night with Mama's hand gentle on my shoulder and her face grave under her nightcap.

'What is it?' I said, still bemused from sleep and from a dream I had had of being a little girl again on Wideacre, playing with a lad as dark-haired as Richard and with a smile as roguish.

'You were dreaming,' she said low. 'And you spoke in your sleep. You said, "Ralph."'

I raised myself up on one arm and stretched out a hand to her. 'It does not matter, Mama,' I said earnestly. 'I was thinking of the apple trees, of something I had to say to Mr Megson. That was all.'

She nodded. 'I am sorry to have woken you, then,' she said tentatively. 'John said . . .' she hesitated. 'John said that perhaps it would be better if you did not sleep and have your . . . your dreams, for a little while. He thinks they overtax your imagination.'

I nodded; I kept my eyes down. 'It does not matter, Mama,' I said again, and I knew I sounded surly.

'No,' she said softly. She went to her travelling bag and brought out the little bottle of medicine which I had come both to love and to dread. 'Perhaps you should take some of this,' she said.

I sighed, resigned, rubbing the sleep from my eyes. I swallowed the medicine to please her and waited for the familiar dreamy sense of unreality to overtake me. They were robbing me of my dreams, of my very being. They were dissolving the strange unpredictable part of me in the golden syrup so I lost my clear bright dream-given wisdom, and learned instead of a dozy un-reality.

'G'night,' I said, the drug clogging my speech. Mama kissed me on the forehead as I lay down, and crossed back to her own bed and slipped between the covers.

'Goodnight again,' she said sweetly; and then, under her breath so I could hardly hear her, she added, 'God bless you and keep you safe.'

She had booked us some lodgings in Gay Street, Bath. 'It was just being built when my mama married Lord Havering and we came to Havering Hall,' she told me as we rattled along the last few miles on the high road over the hills towards the city. 'I dare say I shall be completely lost. We used to live near to the baths for my own papa to take the water and to bathe. Even when I was a little girl, the whole place was changing almost every day, it seemed. Since then they have built street after street.'

'Yes,' I said. I was looking from the carriage window down the hill. The broad river, a little faster and deeper than usual from the winter rains, was spilling over its banks into the water-meadows. The willow trees stood in water, their sparse branches reflected and the grey sky above them. The Fenny would be in flood too, I thought.

'Richard would love to see the buildings,' Mama said. 'We must ask him and John to come and visit us, at least for a few days, as soon as we are settled and you have seen Dr Phillips.'

'Yes,' I said again.

'And the shops are certain to be wonderful,' Mama said. She was leaning forward on her seat to look ahead down the road. Even in my drug-given stupidity, I could not help but smile at her eagerness. The carriage brakes went on as we turned down a steep hill and Mama gasped at the view. The city was a sea of gold like some new Jerusalem set down on a plain of sunshine. The abbey in the middle dominated the town, with its tall tower reaching up to touch the very floor of heaven; and gathered all around it like square pats of dairy butter were the houses in the lemon-rind paleness of the Bath stone.

We rattled over the bridge and at once Jem on the box checked the horses and brought them to a nervous walk. The streets were impossibly crowded, and I did not see how we should find our way through at all. Everywhere there were sedan chairs, Bath chairs, swaying perilously as sweating brawny chairmen trotted like mad pedlars, one in front, one behind. Many of the chairs had the curtains drawn, but in one or two I caught a glimpse of blankets and towels and a pale white face, and in another a red-faced dandy snoring. There were street-sellers shouting and link-boys and crossing-sweepers jostling at the roadside. There were pedlars spreading their packs out on the pavements, and a tooth-drawer with a stool and a bloodstained apron. And in the door-ways were beggars with bitter ingratiating smiles and scabby hands held out, and little children on their knees flushed rosy red with some disease of the skin.

'This is just the outskirts,' Mama said excusingly. 'Every city has its poorer quarters, Julia. Even Chichester.'

'I know,' I said, and I leaned back inside the carriage, for there were two drunk men reeling across the cobbled road to-wards us, and I did not want them to see me and start calling names.

The wagon ahead of us, which had been blocking the road, started up, so Jem could move the horses forward. I heard him yell, 'Thank 'ee gents' to a couple of chairmen who had been giving him directions for our street, and I smiled to hear the Sussex drawl raised loud above the noise of the city.

'Gracious,' said Mama. 'I had forgotten how noisy it was!'

I nodded, and she stared from her window and I from mine, like a pair of milkmaids seeing a city for the first time.

The noise and the confusion on the roads eased a little as we turned away from the centre of the town, but we went no faster. The carriage creaked against the hill.

'This is a fearful slope for horses,' I said to Mama. She had her guidebook out on her lap.

'Hardly anyone uses a carriage,' she said. 'I think this is Gay Street. We must find number twelve.'

The carriage-wheels slid and bumped on the cobbles, and I heard Jem curse the horses, and then we came to a standstill and the postboy came around and opened the door and set the steps down.

'Thank you,' Mama said and smiled at him and waited while he ran up the steps to the house and banged on the knocker. The door opened at once and our landlady, Mrs Gibson, was there to greet us. She swept Mama a deep curtsy and bobbed to me, exclaimed over the length of our journey and the coldness of the day and swept us into the parlour, where the table was laid for tea and the kettle just set to boil.

We had taken only one parlour, a dining-room and two bed-rooms in the house. Mama had the large bedroom at the front of the house, but I thought I had done better with the smaller room which looked out over some gardens down the valley. 'At least I can see some trees when I wake in the morning,' I said. But I said it softly so that Mama should not hear.

Jem would have lodgings at the stables where the carriage was to be kept. There was no room for him in the house. Mama had not even brought Jenny Hodgett to wait on her. Instead we would have Mrs Gibson's maid. Her name was Meg and she brought us two letters for Mama into the parlour while we were having our tea, with an air so gracious and condescending that I nearly rose to my feet to curtsy to her.

Mama smiled at me when the door closed behind her. 'Town polish, Julia,' she said. 'We have just been patronized by a maid-servant. We must certainly go to the dressmaker's tomorrow!'

I smiled back, but my eyes were on Mama's letters. One bore a heavy red seal and I thought it would be from the doctor Uncle John wished me to see.

I was right.

'Dr Phillips will call this evening,' Mama said. 'Good. That will give us time to unpack at least.' She glanced across at me. 'Cheer up, my darling,' she said. 'He is certain to be pleasant, for John knew him at university and liked him. And he may take one look at you and say – as I think – that no one should work as hard on the land as you have been doing. And he will say that it is all my fault, and that to make it up to you I must take you to a great many balls and parties and not home until midsummer!'

I managed a smile. 'I'll unpack for you, Mama,' I said. 'What dress will you wear this evening?'

She told me she would wear her pink brocade and I set it out for her, and asked Meg if she would be so good, if it was no trouble, if she would not object, could she please press the petticoat which was creased, and then I dressed myself in a new cream velvet gown, which reminded me of my riding habit left hanging up in the cupboard at home. I went down to sit in the parlour and wait for the doctor who was going to cure me of feeling at home in my place, who was going to stop me sleeping as I have always slept, who was going to make me into a proper young lady at last.

He was not as bad as I had feared, but I disliked him on sight. He was a tall rounded man with a pink baby-face under a bulky white wig, soft white hands that fluttered as he spoke, bulbous blue eyes, and behind them a sharpness. He talked to Mama; but he was watching me. He had heard from John about the dream, and he had been told about the night the church spire fell.

'Wationalism,' he said to Mama; and I had to turn my head aside and bite my lip not to laugh. 'Weason. In the old days we could fear magic and spells and possession. But now we know the mind has its own wules and weasons. If we learn them – and we can map them like a new countwy – if we learn them, then we can be as we want to be.' He turned and smiled at me. 'Would you like to keep your dweams, Miss Lacey? Or would you like to be an ordinary young lady?'

I hesitated. I felt I should be betraying Wideacre, and the Lacey inheritance, and my very self if I answered him as they wanted me to do. 'I do not want to grieve my mama and my friends,' I said slowly. 'But I cannot want to grow strange to the land which is my family home. And the dreams have been a part of me for as long as I can remember. I cannot think how I could be myself and *not* sometimes dream.'

He nodded. 'You will cling to them for a while,' he said. 'The mind has little twicks and habits. But I shall fwee you fwom them.'

He turned back to Mama and brought out a little diary and noted times and days that I should go to his house and see him. Mama was to be with me, but he would sit and talk to me and I should tell him all my dreams and my seeings, and in time – perhaps in quite a short time – we should see why these aberrations had come upon me.

I sat very still and listened to this stranger planning with my mama to change me. And the confusion and unhappiness which had been inside me throughout the long journey, and the hurried leave-taking, slid away from me as I knew that the doctor was wrong, and Mama was wrong, and Uncle John was wrong, and Richard was wrong. They were all wrong, and the dreams and the seeings were right.

And there was nothing wrong with me.

I felt my shoulders go back and my head come up, and I smiled at the doctor and promised to be prompt at his house in the morning; and as I smiled I sensed all the familiar strength – the strength which I sometimes named as Lacey strength, Beatrice strength – come back to me, and I looked him in his pale-blue eyes and thought to myself: you and I are enemies while you try to change me, for I will not change.

But I made him a pretty curtsy, and then I kissed Mama on the cheek like a dutiful daughter, and I went up the stairs to bed as if I were indeed an invalid, as if I did indeed need to be made well.

Dr Phillips's house was one of the great palaces of Bath in Royal Crescent, so we walked up the hill from our lodgings. I gasped at the top, and it was not from the steepness of the hill: the crescent was magnificent. It was a sweep of gold looking out over a frosty-grey garden, as regular as a platoon of marching soldiers, as graceful as the drape of a golden curtain.

Mama knocked at the door, and it was opened by a footman,

very grave in a dark-green livery, who stood back to admit us into the sombre hall. I had not liked the look of Dr Phillips; and in his own house, with the smell of his new leather chairs and the scent of his shop-bought pot-pourri, I could not help feeling uneasy.

'Mama,' I said as softly as a child, and she took her hand from her muff and held mine as if I were an infant at the tooth-drawer.

The footman held the door open and we were about to go in when a young lady, around my age, came down the stairs. Her eyes were red, perhaps from crying, and she was as pale and as thin as a wraith. I paused and looked at her; I stared. She stopped on the stairs and I saw her look me over, inspect, price and date the Chichester bonnet with the old feather in it, the pelisse and the gown. Then her eyes came to my face and she gave me a little rueful smile as if we were both in some scrape together.

She came down the rest of the stairs and dipped a little curtsy to Mama and waited while the footman fetched her cape. 'My brother is collecting me,' she said to him. 'I will wait in the library.' The footman opened a door on the opposite side of the hall from the parlour, and I recollected my manners and followed Mama into the parlour. I glanced behind me and she was looking at me. She smiled at me again, that odd enigmatic smile, as if we had been naughty children and would have to take a brief punishment, well worth the petty sin. I smiled back, and then the door closed on her.

'Did you see her gown?' Mama asked at once. 'Mechlin-lace trimming all over! And the cut of it! So slim for a walking gown. I saw that was how they were wearing them this season in the magazine, but I never dreamed it could look so elegant!'

'Yes,' I said. 'Did you think she had been crying?'

Mama went to the window. 'Yes,' she said with a little hesitation. 'But Dr Phillips only deals with nervous disorders. She might well be distressed because she was unwell.'

I thought of that rueful smile. 'Perhaps she disagrees with the diagnosis,' I said.

'Perhaps,' Mama said equably. 'Oh, my! What fine horses!'

I went to her side and we peeped from the window, as furtive as a pair of Acre gossips. It was a smart phaeton with bright-yellow wheels, pulled by a pair of glossy chestnut horses, their coats gleaming, almost red. A gentleman was driving, and he pulled up outside the house and glanced towards the door. He was wearing a tricorne hat, tipped slightly back, and curly brown hair tied in a neat bow behind. He might have been handsome – I could not think of his looks because I was struck by the niceness of his face. He looked like a man you could trust with anything. He looked like a man incapable of a lie, or of meanness, or of an unkind word. He had a broad smiling face and brown eyes. He held the reins well, and he whistled towards the doorway, as cheeky as a stable lad.

The door opened and the young lady came out.

'Come on, Marianne!' he said cheerfully. 'I swear I cannot hold them! I'll take you out to Coombe Down and back again in time for dinner. Mama said we may! But come quick!'

And she picked up her skirts and clambered up into the phaeton and sat beside him, and I saw his arm go around her waist and he gave her a hard hug and a quick glance to see if she was upset.

I rather wished I had a brother to collect me from my visit to the doctor and to watch my face and to whirl me away behind a pair of the best horses I had ever seen. But then the door opened and Mama and I went upstairs to Dr Phillips.

He had left the large room very free of furniture. There was a fire in the grate and a comfortable chair before it, an embroidered fire-screen, an ormolu clock, a harpsichord in the corner and a heavy desk with writing-paper and an inkstand. He gestured Mama to a seat by the window beside a little table with magazines and a couple of novels. He directed me to a seat at the fireside and took a chair beside me, sitting at an angle so I could not see his face but he could watch me. I slid my hand into my reticule so that I could hold the little wooden owl, Ralph's owl, tightly. And I waited for him to speak.

'Tell me about the dweams,' he said gently; and his inability to pronounce his r's seemed no longer amusing but infinitely threatening. 'When do you first wemember dweaming?'

I was unwilling to speak, uneasy. But there was nothing I could do *but* answer him, and I had a resentful feeling that I would have to go on and on explaining until he knew what he thought he needed to know. And I had a little fear that he might be right – that he might be able to make me into a girl who cared most for clothes and dances and could not hear the beat of the land.

I told him of the dream of being alone in the old hall at Wideacre. I told him it all: the sense of peace, the quietness of the empty house, knowing that the men were coming from Acre, and fearing their coming and yet wanting it; of the thunderstorm and the man on the black horse, and seeing lightning flash bright on the blade of a knife . . .

'And then?' he asked softly.

I told him that was all I dreamed; but he asked for other dreams. So I told him how I sometimes dreamed that I was a little girl running wild on Wideacre. And I said that sometimes, without warning, I would see the land through her eyes, even though I was awake.

'And who is the girl?' he asked as if it were the most natural question in the world.

'She is Beatrice,' I answered stupidly, and I heard Mama's sharp indrawn breath from the window-seat. The doctor spoke smoothly over the top of the gasp so that I should keep talking, keep talking, talking my most private truths out and out and out into the pretty room far away from my home.

'And now we will stop,' he said gently, and I glanced up at the clock and saw an hour had gone by; it was midday, and the logs had burned low in the grate.

My head ached.

'The same time tomorrow,' he said to Mama. 'We have made gweat pwogwess today.'

She nodded and went towards the door. I followed her as

though I were walking in a dream – a new dream – one where I had talked out everything I knew and was left an ordinary girl indeed. The shell of what I had been.

'Now what?' Mama said with forced brightness as we found ourselves on the pavement outside the doctor's house with a chill wind blowing and a smell of snow in the air. 'We should go to the Assembly Rooms and see what the programme of events is for the week. And we must go to the Pump Room and taste the water and put our names in the book. And perhaps you would like to go to a bakery for a coffee – oh! and Julia! Bath buns! We must have some Bath buns!'

'Please may I go home?' I asked miserably. 'I am sorry, Mama, but I have a pitiful headache. Please may I go home?'

She took my arm at once and we walked back down Gay Street to our lodgings. My mama's step beside me was lighter than my own. I thought then, as I wearily went up to the front door and up the stairs to my bedroom, that if this was how it felt to become well, I had rather a thousand times remain ill.

Mama left me to sleep until dinner-time, but after we had eaten and my headache was quite gone, she insisted that we go out at once to shop, to see the sights and to put our names down in the Visitors' Book so as to announce to the polite world that we had arrived.

'I wish we knew someone,' I said as we went into the Pump Room and hesitated in the doorway with three dozen strangers looking at us.

'We will,' Mama said cheerfully. 'Bath is the most sociable place in the world. It always has been. We will have dozens of friends before the end of the week.'

'There's that girl!' I said suddenly. 'The girl we saw at the doctor's!'

She was sitting at a table, drinking a glass of the waters, among a group of young people. I looked for the brown-eyed man, but he was not with her. There were two other girls, one standing behind her chair and laughing with a young man, and one sitting beside her looking at plates in a fashion magazine. Two young men were looking over her shoulder and laughing at something. In the bright candlelight of the public room, with her friends around her, she seemed to look more frail and vulnerable than ever. As if she felt my eyes on her, she looked up, and recognized me. She rose from her seat and walked over towards us, shrugging her shawl on her shoulders. She dropped a curtsy to Mama and said, 'How do you do? I am Marianne Fortescue. I think I saw you at Dr Phillips's, did I not?'

'Yes, indeed,' Mama said. 'I am Lady Lacey and this is my daughter, Julia.'

'I have not seen you there before,' Miss Fortescue said. She had a soft languid way of speaking, as though she were extremely tired. 'I go to the doctor every morning now.'

'I have to go every morning too,' I said. 'While we are staying in Bath, that is. We will go home in April.'

She nodded. 'Where is your home?' she asked.

'Sussex,' I said. There was no singing in my head. I could have been saying an ordinary name. 'A place called Wideacre, near Chichester,' I said.

She nodded. 'We live in Clifton, near Bristol,' she said, 'so I drive over every day. My brother brought me today in his phaeton. I was quite sure he would overturn us. And I quite froze on the journey.'

'Will you drive home this evening?' Mama asked.

'Oh, no,' Miss Fortescue said. 'There is a concert tonight which my brother especially wanted to hear. We stay tonight at my aunt's house. Do you go to it?'

'Yes,' said Mama, much to my surprise. 'Perhaps we shall see you there.'

'Oh, good,' said Miss Fortescue and curtsied once more to us and walked back to her group of friends.

'Concert, Mama?' I asked.

She shot me a quick mischievous look. 'You wanted friends in Bath, Julia,' she said frankly. 'You are on the way to having them. Miss Fortescue's shawl alone would have cost two hundred pounds. I think her a perfectly suitable acquaintance for you!'

'Very vulgar,' I said. 'I am surprised at you, Mama.'

'Town polish,' she said witheringly. 'You would not understand, my Sussex milkmaid. Now we must put our names in the book and buy you a new gown for tonight.'

Mama designed that evening as my formal introduction to Bath; and she showed me that I was indeed a Sussex milkmaid, for I did not know that it could be done so smoothly. Marianne Fortescue was there with her brother, whose name was James, and the two girls who had been with her in the Pump Room – her sister Charlotte and her cousin Emily. She was in the party of Emily's mama, Mrs Densham, who lived in Bath and who remembered my Grandmama Havering from all those years ago. Somehow we joined their party, and I sat on the concert bench between Marianne and Emily; we went into supper with them and drank tea with them at Mrs Densham's house when the concert finished early.

Marianne ate nothing at the supper table; later she only drank a dish of tea and did not touch the little cakes or the savoury pastry. I saw her brother's eyes on her, and then I saw him scowl at Emily when she said softly, 'Marianne, please eat a little cake at least.'

He interrupted them at once and complained that his tea was cold and had been standing too long. Between Emily's protestations that the pot was fresh and had been properly heated too, whatever he might say, the moment when Marianne had blushed and then suddenly paled passed unnoticed by anyone except me.

'I expect we shall meet at the doctor's tomorrow,' Marianne said to me as we stood at the head of the stairs waiting for my mama to say goodbye to Mrs Densham. 'You will forgive me if I don't speak to you then. I never feel very well after I have been with him, though I know he is an excellent man. I know he is doing me good.'

'Quack,' said James Fortescue so suddenly that I jumped. 'Quack! Quack! Quack!'

Marianne laughed aloud, the first time I had heard her laugh all evening, and she flushed pink and her eyes sparkled. 'Don't, James!' she said. 'And you should not say so! Miss Lacey will think you so rude!'

'Quack! Quack!' said James Fortescue, unrepentant and smiling at me. 'Miss Lacey can make her own mind up. Just because he lives in a big house and has some of the smartest girls in Bath trailing in to cry on his sofa does not make him any less of a quack than if he was selling flour as medicine in Cheap Street!'

Marianne shot an apologetic look at me. 'My brother has a prejudice against him,' she said. 'Everyone I know speaks very highly of him . . .'

'A pwejudice,' James said outrageously. 'A pwejudice indeed!'

'Why do you see him?' I asked shyly.

Marianne glanced downwards. 'I find it very hard to eat,' she said as if she were confessing some secret vice. 'It sounds very silly. I *am* very silly to have such a difficulty. Mama and Papa have become so concerned that they have sent me to a number of physicians.'

James Fortescue grimaced. 'I believe in none of this,' he said frankly to me. 'I like to take her, and I like to collect her, because everyone else thinks it an act of high tragedy that she started off eating little, and has gone on to eating less, and will no doubt eat more when she is hungry.'

Marianne smiled at me, that odd smile of complicity. 'Things never seem that simple when other people talk at you, do they?' she asked. 'What about you?'

I flushed scarlet. 'I have dreams,' I said awkwardly. 'Sometimes nightmares. And I had one dream which was . . .' I broke off and looked around the brightly lit stairs, the chandelier sparkling above the stairwell, the bright silk wallpaper and the rich carpet. I could not tell this world about a world where thunder crashed and a church spire fell and I stood on the lichgate steps like some old warning prophet. 'I have disturbing dreams,' I said lamely.

James took my hand and raised it to his lips very gently. It was a courteous kiss to bid me goodnight, but he kept my hand for a moment longer than I expected, and he smiled at me with his brown eyes crinkled. 'I have bad dreams too,' he said. 'Especially when I have eaten toasted cheese for supper.'

Marianne and I both laughed, then Mama was at my side and it was time for me to go. But I knew I liked James Fortescue, and I smiled all the way home at the thought of telling Dr Phillips that I dreamed because I ate toasted cheese late at night.

14

I truly was a Sussex milkmaid, for it took me several days to realize that I had been adopted by the best society that Bath had to offer this season.

That first day set the pattern for my days in Bath. In the morning I would go to the doctor and sit in his soft armchair by the flickering fire and tell him about Wideacre and about the dreams. I tried to hold tight to what I was saying, to keep as much as I could from him. There was so much I did not want him to know: the lightning glinting on the blade of the knife and Ralph's face in the thunderstorm when Beatrice went out in the rain to meet him; the dream I had of love-making in the summer-house with Ralph and the knowledge I had that no young lady should have of that delight, the secrets of Acre, the way animals feared Richard, that night of dark unsayable pleasure before the fire; and the dream that had come over and over again of the falling spire and me standing under the lich-gate calling the people to pull down the cottages to make the village safe.

I did everything I could to lie to Dr Phillips and to lock the Wideacre secrets safely away in a corner of my mind. But he was clever, and the room was too hot, and the firelight flickered as I watched it, and day after day he drew more and more from me until I felt robbed and betrayed, and I knew I was losing my Wideacre self. It was being sucked from me and I was becoming an empty, pretty shell.

'Now, tell me,' he would say insinuatingly. And something inside me would flinch as if a snail had crawled on to my hair as I lay in the grass. 'Tell me about this woman, your Aunt ... Beatrice, is it? Tell me why you think you are like her.'

And I would start haltingly to tell him, trying all the time to tell him as little as possible. 'I look like her, I suppose,' I ventured. 'And everyone in the village says I look like her.'

'Have you seen her picture?' Dr Phillips asked.

'No,' I said slowly. I shifted in my chair. The cushions were very deep and soft, the firelight flickered on my face.

'Then how do you know you look like her?' he asked. Whenever he asked a question like that, his voice took on a slightly querulous note of surprise. He was inviting contradiction.

'Because . . .' I broke off. 'They all say I do,' I said.

'I don't think so!' he said sweetly. He almost sung the words. 'I don't think that is why. Have you dweamed her, Julia? You can tell me, you know.'

'I have not seen her in dreams,' I temporized. But he was quick to hear the note of deception.

'But you have dweams with her in them?' he asked.

I sighed. There was a strange perfume about the room, as if the windows were never opened, as if all the air had been burned away by the flickering flames, as if I should never be free, like some poor Persephone, underground, for ever.

'Yes, I have dreams with her in them,' I said wearily.

'And yet you say you do not see her?' His voice was very soft, very sweet.

'Only in a mirror,' I said.

'In a mirror' he repeated as if that were a little bon-bon to be savoured. 'How do you see her in a mirror? Are you beside her?' He did not wait for me to reply. 'Beside her? In fwont of her? Behind her?'

'I am her!' I broke in, suddenly impatient. 'I dream that I am her!'

I expected him to be shocked. Instead he put his pudgy fingers together like a little tower over his rounded waistcoat and said softly, 'Vewy good, and I think that is enough for today.'

It was like that every time. At the very point when I thought I had said something so startling that it would break the spell of the room, shake his poise, release me, then it was always time for me to go. The next day when I went again, he would start from where we had left off. And somehow, in the interval, the shock had gone from what I said. It had become *his* information. My dream had become his dream. I was, each day, diminished by the loss of my dreams and my secrets.

There was nowhere I could be renewed. Every morning the dreams I spoke of seemed more and more remote. The sight seemed less likely, a mistake, or a lucky guess. Soon Dr Phillips was not just listening to me, he was telling me that I must have misunderstood, that things could not happen the way I had thought, that Beatrice could not walk Wideacre and see through my eyes, that the land had no heartbeat.

Bath itself eroded the bedrock of my certainties. Ralph Megson was right when he said that if one was to choose anywhere to forget the land, then Bath would be a good place. I sighed for the smell of Wideacre air as I walked in the parks and gardens. Bath was so paved and cobbled and tiled that I never saw a scrap of pure earth all the time I was there. I never saw a leaf that had not been trimmed into some fashionable shape. I never saw a flower which had grown of its own free will. Even the river, flowing through the town, was walled in and channelled and guided under the pretty bridge and over the stone-built weir.

As for the hot springs, I thought them simply disgusting. Not just disgusting to drink, which Mama insisted we did – three glasses every day! – but I found the very idea of hot water coming out of the ground quite repellent. It was hot enough to bathe in! Every time we passed the bath-houses and smelled the steam coming out and the hot metallic odour of the water, I longed for the downs at Wideacre, where all along the spring line the water comes out from the chalk as cold as ice and tasting of clean rain.

I longed for Wideacre then, when I smelled the baths. I longed for Wideacre when I awoke in the morning and looked out of my window and saw row on row of stone-tiled roofs, stretching, it seemed, for ever and ever. I longed for Wideacre at night when I could not get to sleep. The rattle of the coach-wheels on the cobbles seemed to be sounding inside my head, and my bedroom grew bright and then black as the dipping light of a link-boy went past, instead of being lit by the cool beam of a Wideacre moon. I longed for Wideacre at meal-times when I thought the bread looked grey and the milk tasted strange, and we did not know where either had come from, whose cows had given the milk, whose wheat had made the flour.

I longed for Wideacre most of all when I walked in the park and all there was to see was a frozen patch of ice with sulky ducks around it begging for bread, and nowhere to walk but meandering little paths which ran round and round in circles instead of going the quickest straight route as we do in the country. But in the country we walked because we wanted to get somewhere, not because we wanted to waste time. In Bath wasting time was all people ever did. Every day I spent there was full of minutes and hours when my only occupation was spreading out little tasks to fill up the emptiness. Then I would walk in the park and look at the toes of my new half-boots – which would not have survived one minute in the mire of Acre lane – and wonder what on earth I was supposed to do with myself to fit myself for the life they wanted me to lead. I did not know how I could bear to change that much.

One day I was so deep in such hopeless rebellion that I did not hear at first when someone called my name.

'Julia!' the voice said again, and I looked up and saw Mary Gillespie.

'You were far away!' she said teasingly. 'Were you dreaming of James Fortescue? Elizabeth will hardly speak to you this morning. You danced twice with him last night, you know!'

I laughed and smiled at Elizabeth, who looked not in the least piqued. She was a large fair girl, very placid and sweet-natured, and she bore her sister's teasing with the equanimity of the eldest.

'It is true!' I said promptly. 'I can think of nothing but him.'

'But really,' Mary said and drew my arm through hers, 'you must like him, Julia. He is absolutely the catch of the season.' She caught Elizabeth's scowl and tossed her brown ringlets.

'Well, I know it is vulgar, but he is! And he has simply heaps of money, and his papa would let him marry a church mouse as long as she had a good name and title to an estate – and Julia has both!'

I made a little grimace. 'Not much of an estate,' I said. 'If you could see it, you would not speak of it like that. No house at all but a ruin, and only crops planted this season!' I stopped, because just describing Wideacre like that brought a lump to my throat. I was very, very homesick. 'And I have only a right to half of it,' I finished gruffly.

'Yes, but do you like him?' Mary persisted, wanting to hear of love when my heart was aching for two hundred acres of mixed arable and woodland, common and downs.

'Oh, no,' I said absently, thinking of the smell of the wind that comes down the hillsides through Acre on cold days like this one.

'Then it's the cousin at home!' Mary proclaimed triumphantly to her sister across me. 'I knew it was all along! You've come to Bath to have your season and then you'll go home and be married as soon as you are of age, and live in the lovely new house and we will all come to visit you when we have married our lords.'

I could not laugh at Mary as I usually did. 'No, it is not my cousin,' I said with a sigh which I kept to myself. I had had no word from Richard since I had come to Bath, not so much as a scrawl at the end of a letter from John. But I heard of him. He was becoming beloved in the village. He was working alongside Ralph. In the days of fine weather he was pressing on with the rebuilding of the hall; in days of bad weather he was in the new barn where the men were sharpening ploughshares. Richard was charming them in Acre, just as he could charm Mrs Gough, and Lady Havering, and Mama, and me. Every time I read that Richard had been helpful with one job or another I felt my heart sink a little lower, for I knew that while I was being taught to do without Wideacre, Wideacre was learning to do without me.

'Well, then, you are certain to like James Fortescue enough in time,' Mary said, pressing my arm for emphasis. 'All the girls in

Bath are wild about him. Elizabeth is not the only one who wants to push you in the Avon.'

We all three laughed at that but what she said was half true. And others had noticed that James Fortescue had danced with me twice. His papa and mama came to stay with Mrs Densham one weekend, and Mama and I were invited to dine with them. They wanted to see the girl who was the best friend of their daughter, Marianne, and a potential bride for their youngest son. And Mama wanted to inspect them.

They were all well pleased. I knew his family liked me; his mama kissed me on the cheek at meeting and at parting, and her warmth suggested she had heard many kind things about me. My mama measured their wealth and their sharp city-trader manners with a keen eye and smiled. The Fortescues were a family of Bristol merchants, great traders. They were not long-established landowners like us Laceys of Wideacre; but they had a position which many would envy. His papa was an alderman – well thought of in Bristol and his mama was related to the Kent family.

I came home from the dinner with something of a rueful smile. I knew I had been looked over and found satisfactory as much as if I had been a brood-mare. I also knew that Mama had been assessing them. I had learned some town gloss in Bath – I could not escape it, watching the workings of the Bath marriage market. We might all pretend we were here for the waters, or here to buy some fashionable clothes, or to meet acquaintances; but the season was all about courtship and marriage, as obvious a task of pairing as choosing stock. Mary's vulgarity was nothing worse than a recognition that she, and her sister, and even I, were in Bath to see and to be seen, to choose and to be chosen, to like and to be liked. My delicate mama trod a very narrow road when she tried to ignore the vulgarity of arranging her daughter's marriage to one of the most wealthy young men in society that season.

She would not have forced me. She had the right to do so, and there were many parents who would order their daughters to marry the man that had been chosen for them. But my mama had never been that sort of a mother. She would not even have tried to persuade me if she had seen my mind set against this or that young man. But she would not have been human if she had not been flattered that her daughter should be dancing often with James Fortescue. She would not have been a good mother if she had not made sure that James Fortescue's family knew that I was part heir to an estate which had once been great, and which would be great again.

In the meantime there were many new friends – not just the Fortescues. For, once I was in their party, I seemed to meet more and more young people, until our gilt mirror over the mantelpiece was rimmed with invitation cards, and the bowl at the foot of the stairs was filled with calling cards. Early every morning, before my visit to Dr Phillips, James Fortescue would drive his high-slung phaeton to our door and ask the landlady if Miss Lacey would care to come for a drive with him that day.

Miss Lacey almost always *did*.

He was good company, and he let me hold the reins, and when he saw how I handled his horses, he promised himself the pleasure of teaching me to drive a pair in earnest.

'You have good hands,' he said, and I laughed, remembering the last time I had heard that. He wanted to know all about it, and I found I was telling him about Dench and about the wild ride into Acre, and about Richard's rescue. He hooted with laughter when I told him I had been riding astride with my gown all pulled up, and I had to make him swear to tell no one.

'It sounds a wonderful estate, your Wideacre,' he said wistfully. 'I can understand my papa's longing for a country home for himself, and a home for me. Your mama says that you could own it entire if you bought out your cousin.'

'Yes,' I said, and an awkward silence fell between the two of us as we both realized that my mama and his papa had been match-making.

He chuckled. 'Don't look so grave, Miss Lacey,' he said. 'My papa can perfectly well afford to buy his own estate. I need not marry to oblige him, and you need not think of obliging the two of us.'

I gave an irresistible ripple of laughter. It was quite improper to talk like this, but it felt so very much easier than pretending, for the sake of convention, that neither of us knew all of Bath had been planning our marriage for weeks.

'I could always give you the estate outright,' I said outrageously.

'Yes!' he said at once. 'Please, I beg of you. Anything rather than having to act out this impossible part that I have to sustain. I have to pretend all the time that I like you, and I have to take you for drives, and ask you to dance. And next I suppose I shall have to send you flowers!'

'And I have to accept,' I said mournfully. 'It's terrible being such an obedient daughter!'

'You could always elope with a footman,' he suggested helpfully, 'but you don't have one, do you? What about the butler?'

I laughed aloud at that and forgot I was driving; I dropped my hands on the reins so that his horses lengthened their stride, and I had to lean back and put just an extra touch on the reins to steady them.

'I am sorry,' I said, 'but you should see our butler! He is a dear, but he is old enough to be my grandpapa!'

'Then it may have to be me,' he said apologetically. 'I like it no better than you, my dear Miss Lacey; but we shall have to reconcile ourselves.'

The laughter caught in my throat at his words, which seemed still to be part of our indiscreet jest and yet also seemed a little warmer. I shot a sideways glance at him and he was looking at me, his brown eyes intent and smiling.

'It is just a joke,' I said quickly. 'One that I should not be making. I have no intention of marrying for many years.'

'I knew it!' he said with such energy that he made me jump; but then I saw he was smiling still. 'A jilt! And one so young too!'

I could not help but laugh at that, though I knew full well I should not; and I was still smiling when he took the reins as we drew up outside the door. He leaned over to give me a hand as I clambered down, but refused my invitation to come in.

'I shall have to see you at the ball tonight, I suppose,' he said gloomily, 'and I suppose I shall have to dance with you.'

I turned at the front door and swept him a most dignified curtsy. 'Not at all,' I said helpfully. 'Though thank you for asking. I regret I have every dance taken.'

He looked twice at me then, and I saw the confident smile on his face slightly shaken at the thought that we might not dance together. But then he coiled up his long carriage whip and pointed it at me. 'Miss Lacey,' he said firmly, 'if you have not saved the dance before and after supper for me, and if I do not take you into supper, then I shall tell Marianne and all our acquaintance that you are a gazetted flirt. And I shall speak nothing but the truth.'

And I, conscious for the first time in my life of being pretty, conscious for the first time in my life of being desired, looked up at him, seated on the high carriage, and laughed in his face. 'Wait and see,' I said, and flicked around on my heel and went indoors without another word.

I did not like him just for those drives in the cold wintry sunshine. I was not yet entirely an ordinary girl who would have her head turned by a posy of flowers or the fact that he was recognized as being the most desirable young man in Bath. I had called out a ploughing team, so I was far from thinking that the most important thing in the world was the whiteness of a man's gloves and the number of dance-steps he could perform. More than anything else I liked James Fortescue because of how he was with his sister Marianne. Against the opinion of all the family and the family doctor, he maintained that there was nothing in the least wrong with her. His impossibly rude imitation of a duck quacking every time someone mentioned Dr Phillips, did not only bring a smile to Marianne's face, it also made me feel more cheerful about the long draining hours which I spent in that close room.

'What does he do with you?' James Fortescue asked me as we sat at a table in a coffee-house waiting for Marianne to join us from taking the waters.

'He talks at me,' I said gloomily. 'To start with I was talking all the time. He wanted to know everything I thought. Bit by bit, the more I told him, the more the feelings slipped away from me, until now I hardly know what to think. I know I miss my home more than I thought possible to bear; but the special feeling I had – a sense of being somehow magic there – has almost gone from me.'

'How do you mean? Magic?' James asked gently. I glanced up at him quickly, but he was not laughing at me. He was not patronizing me in the way which sent my hackles on the rise when Dr Phillips spoke to me. This was a young man, my own age, with a good deal more experience of the world than I had. But he trusted his own counsel, and I thought I could in turn trust him.

'There's a long tradition,' I said awkwardly. 'A belief that my family is somehow special on the land, that the Lacey heir can make the land grow, can make it especially fertile. And I feel that. I believe when I put my face to the ground, I can almost hear a heart beating at the very centre of the earth – as if it were a living thing and it loved me.'

Someone dropped a spoon and it clattered against a plate near me. I jumped and looked around me. I was not on Wideacre, I was many miles from my home. I was suddenly aware of the dozens of people in the coffee-house, of the hundreds of people in the town, and of my own arrogance and folly in claiming to be special. I shot a nervous look at James Fortescue. He was watching me, and in his face I could see nothing but quiet attentiveness.

'Or at least, I did,' I said. 'I was very sure of it. But since I have told Dr Phillips, and had to explain it over and over, I am not so sure. I expect it was all nonsense.'

James Fortescue huffed in temper and caught one of my restless hands. 'That is *exactly* what I don't like about this Dr Phillips,' he said. 'It is the same thing for Marianne. When she started going to see him, she certainly did have trouble in eating proper food at proper times. I had some ideas about why that should be.

'You have a small family and perhaps you live peacefully together,' he said diffidently. 'It is not the same everywhere. My papa and my mama have differences of opinion, and there are five of us generally sitting down to dinner together. When there is a disagreement, there is an argument which is often long and loud. You will know by now how sensitive Marianne is; she simply cannot tolerate raised voices. By refusing to eat, she was excused dinner with the family. I was certain that was the start of the difficulty, and at one time she thought so herself. But since she has been seeing Dr Phillips, she does not know herself what the matter might be. He has taken all her certainty from her and has nothing to put in its place but a vague sense that it is her fault and that she is somehow in the wrong.'

I nodded. I had already had some idea of this from Marianne herself. James would not have spoken of it if he had not known I was in her confidence.

'I cannot imagine how she could blame herself,' I said hesitantly.

'I can,' he said, 'and you should be able to imagine it. When you came to Bath, I dare say you thought it perfectly all right that you should feel so special about your home. Now you think that feeling somehow wrong, and you are even in danger of losing it altogether!'

'Oh no!' I said. 'I was already unhappy about what Wideacre meant to me . . .' I broke off and looked at him.

'Why?' he asked, as gentle as a sister.

I hesitated, and then I found I could tell him. I did not tell him the version which Dr Phillips had persuaded me was the truth: that I had been awakened by the storm and calculated the danger of the spire falling on the village, that I had made a lucky guess. I told him that I believed I had been given a premonition, and that I had acted on it. I finished the story of that strange night in a rush and I kept my eyes down. It sounded so bizarre. But then I felt the brush of his fingertips on the back of my gloved hand and I looked up.

'I could not do that,' he said gently. 'But I should be a fool indeed if I said that anything I could not do was beyond the ability of anyone else. Perhaps you have a special gift. Perhaps you should cherish that gift and use it, rather than trying to knock it out of yourself.'

I was about to reply – searching for words to thank him for that brief sentence which had suddenly returned to me a share of my lost confidence in Wideacre, in myself as an heir to Wideacre – when Marianne and Emily and Mary and Elizabeth came to the table in a flurry of bandboxes and news, and the moment when I could have thanked him was gone.

But I did not forget it. Although my days were now a whirl of outings, shopping, dances and conversations, each night before I slept I used to lie for a few minutes and think about the day. It seemed to me that I was gaining a new sort of assertiveness, that even while Dr Phillips stole from me my bright faith in myself as the squire of Wideacre and the favoured child of a magic tradition, Bath was teaching me the assurance of a pretty girl who could give an answer – pertly enough, maybe – and who could hold her head up and deal with her peers as equals. And as the acknowledged favourite of the most eligible young man in Bath that season, I had a confidence I would never have learned at home. I had James to thank for that too.

— 15 —

I had not been lying to James Fortescue when I told him that all the dances for the evening were taken. But he was right to be confident of me – I had saved the dance before supper so that he might take me from the bright crowded ballroom into the supper-room and sit down with me on a bench with half a dozen of the young people whom I now called my friends.

Mama had been playing cards and she came up behind me when I was at supper and dropped a hand on my shoulder to prevent me rising. 'You stay,' she said softly. 'I don't want you to leave early, but I have to go home. This beastly cold I took the other day outside the milliner's has made me too hot to enjoy playing any more. It has so destroyed my judgement that I am likely to game away John's fortune unless I leave.'

'How will you get home?' I asked.

'I'll take a chair,' Mama said equably, 'and I'll send out one of Mrs Gibson's men to bring a chair to fetch you home.'

'Excuse me, Lady Lacey,' James interrupted, rising to his feet, 'but I beg you will not take such trouble. I will undertake to bring Miss Lacey safe home to you. And if you will allow me, I will go and make sure there is a chair waiting for you at the doorway now.'

Mama smiled. 'Thank you, Mr Fortescue,' she said. 'I should have known that you would be so kind. I shall expect Julia home at eleven, when the ball closes.'

James gave her his arm and took her through the crowds of the supper-room to the bright hall beyond.

'Lucky you!' Mary Gillespie said under her breath. 'I'd push my mama downstairs and break her leg if I thought James Fortescue would take me home.'

'Mary!' I exclaimed, and collapsed into giggles. 'Anyway, it's not true. You'd lock her in the cellar as well to be on the safe side.'

We were still laughing when James came back and he looked at the two of us suspiciously. 'It's true!' he said. 'My heart is set on Julia's mama. She really is so fetching, Julia. She must have been stunning when she was young. Did she ever have a London season?'

'I think so,' I said. 'But I believe she was shy and retiring and did not enjoy it.'

James nodded.

'Like me,' I added, keeping my face straight.

'Very like,' James said, equally grave. 'I was saying to Marianne the other day that you would be quite pleasing if she could prevail upon you to put yourself forward a little more.'

'You! . . .' I started, but the quartet began playing in the other room.

'Is this the last dance I can have with you this evening?' he asked.

I flickered my dance programme before him with a smug beam. 'It is,' I said. 'But there is no need to stay until the end of the ball. I dare say one of my other partners will escort me home if I ask.'

'You are a baggage,' he said feelingly. 'Come and let me tread on your toes, Julia Lacey; and I hope I disable you for the rest of the evening.'

I laughed and went to dance with him, and then with George Gillespie, and with Sir Clive, and Major Peterson, and all the other new friends, until the quartet played the last dance and the clock struck eleven. The players started packing up their instruments, though Sir Peter Laverock went and begged them to play one more dance so that he could dance with me.

'I am so sorry,' James Fortescue said to him, sounding not at all sorry, 'but I have promised Lady Lacey that I would see Miss Lacey home at eleven o'clock, and we must leave now.'

Sir Peter took one look at James Fortescue, and one look at my smiling face. 'Well, really, James,' he said. 'I can't like the thought of you walking all alone back from Gay Street. I'll come with you both to see Miss Lacey safe home, and then walk with you.'

'Very kind,' said James. 'But I couldn't ask it of you.'

'I insist,' said Sir Peter, teasingly. 'What do you say, Miss Lacey?'

James Fortescue offered me his arm with an air of absolute neutral courtesy, then he slid his hand on top of mine and pinched my fingers hard.

'I will not trouble you, Sir Peter,' I said politely, 'and I'll bid you good night and hope to see you tomorrow.' Then, as we turned away, I said softly to James Fortescue, 'And if I weren't a lady, I'd kick you on the ankles!'

He laughed aloud at that and swept me to the entrance of the rooms. 'Would you like a sedan chair?' he asked. 'Or can you brave the frosts and walk?'

I sniffed at the air. It was icy cold with a promise of snow behind it. I knew it lacked something, some scent I needed, and I turned my face up to the cloudless ink-black sky for some hint of it. I was missing the smell of my home, the faint scent of cold beech leaves, the hint of icy grass. I was far away from Wideacre tonight.

'Let's walk,' I said, and we stepped out into the stars and I pulled the scarlet-lined hood of my new cape up over my head.

I had one hand tucked inside the furry recesses of my muff, and James Fortescue had the other under his arm, warm against his cloak. It was a brilliant night, as bright as only a winter night can be. The stars were as thick as meadow flowers across a purple-black sky, and the moon had that hazy halo which always means frost. Our footsteps clattered on the paving stones and we walked uphill from the Assembly Rooms with an easy, even pace, close together to get through the throng of dancers coming out and calling goodnight to each other. The chairmen shouted for people crossing the road to make way for them, and a linkboy ran up to us with a torch in his hand and said to James, 'Light your way, sir?'

'Starlight is enough tonight,' James said gently, and he reached inside his cape seeking a coin.

I was looking at the lad's feet. He had shoes, but they were gone at the soles, tied on with rags. Above the ragged tongue of leather his bare ankles were blue with cold, scarred with old flea-bites. His breeches stopped between knee and calf – a dirty pair of rags which had once been velvet. His jacket was a man's coat folded over and over at the cuffs so that his skinny wrists showed and his hands were free. He was one of the scum of Bath that float on the rising tide of wealth in the city. He was one of the many that survive on a little luck, a little thieving and a little beggary. I had seen poverty in Acre, but country poverty is nothing compared to the degradation that the poor suffered in this most elegant of towns. One might throw a penny into an outstretched bowl at the market, or give to a special collection in church, but it was possible to spend all one's days among the wealthy and the beautiful and to see no hardship at all. The city councillors kept it well hidden, fearing to shock their wealthy patrons. And we – the ones with the money and the leisure and the Christian compassion – we liked the streets to be clean and clear of paupers.

'Here you are,' James said kindly and the little lad looked up at him and smiled. He must have been about fourteen, but he was so slight and so thin that he looked younger. But there was something about his face which struck me, that square forehead and the deep-set eyes.

As I stared at him, the singing noise of Wideacre fell upon me like a waterfall and drowned out the street sounds and the street sights. All I could see was his pale peaked face and all I could hear was a voice saying, 'Take him home! Take him home!' in a tone of such longing and grief that you would have thought it was his mother calling for him.

'I am going to take you home,' I said, making it sound like the most simple thing in the world. 'I am going to take you home.'

His sharp face turned up towards me, yellowy pale in the light from the torch. 'To Acre?' he asked.

And then I knew him for one of the lost children of Acre who had been taken for the mills in the north and never returned. 'Yes,' I said, and I smiled at him, though I could have wept. 'Yes,' I said again. 'I am Julia Lacey. It is all coming right in Acre now, and there will be work for you if you will let me send you home. I am Clary Dench's friend, and Matthew Merry's, and Ted Tyacke's. They are all working for wages in Acre now, and Ralph Megson has come home and is managing the estate.'

He thrust his torch at James and grabbed both my hands in his bare dirty grip. 'Is that right?' he said urgently. 'Are they working in the village again? Can I really get home? Won't they send me back here if I go home?'

'No,' I said firmly. 'I am part heir to the estate. I am Julia Lacey, and what I say is done in Wideacre. There will be work for you, and I shall pay for your journey home. I shall write ahead and tell them that you are coming, and there will be a place for you to live and a job for you to do. I can promise you that, and I *do* promise it.'

He shook both my hands at once then as if we might suddenly dance together in the cold streets of night-time Bath. 'I can hardly believe it!' he said, and he was grinning and shaking my hands, and tossing his head as if to try to wake from a dream of good luck. 'I can't believe I should meet you like this!'

'How did you recognize him?' James asked quietly.

I turned towards him. I had quite forgotten he was there. He had thrust the torch in a bracket on the railings and was leaning against them, watching the two of us. 'I don't know. I just guessed, I suppose,' I said with the lie I had learned from Dr Phillips who had taught me to disbelieve my own senses. Then I hesitated. I had trusted James Fortescue with the truth about my dreams and my seeings. 'No, that's not true,' I said simply. 'It was the sight. I knew I had to take him home; but I did not know why. I did not know who he was. But now I come to look at him, he *does* look Sussex-bred to me.'

'I'm Jimmy Dart,' he said. 'My ma was in service at Havering Hall and when she got big with me, they sent her away. She stayed in Acre and worked for Wideacre. But when I was five or six, she run off, and they took me on the parish. They put me in the workhouse. When Mr Blithe came around for paupers, they sent me and the others. We worked for him in his mill. Cruel work that was. Then he could get no more cotton and he shut the mill and we all had to leave. They wouldn't take us on the parish, because we hadn't been born and bred there, and they wouldn't take us back on Wideacre. Julie heard that paupers could get into Bath, but we had no money for the journey. It was winter an' all. Cold, and we had no shoes. We walked. A long walk, and little Sally died on the way. Just curled up in a field and wouldn't walk no more. We stayed with her till she was cold and stiff and then we left her. Didn't know what else we could do. Julie cried then. She said it was the last time she ever would cry. Then we got to Bath, and I had a fight with a boy and won it, so I got his torch.'

'He gave it to you?' I asked.

'I killed him,' Jimmy said, off-handedly. 'In the fight. I choked him. It wasn't much, he was only a little boy. But I got his torch, so I could start earning us money. I've done it for a long time now.'

I put a hand out to steady myself on the railings. 'You killed him?' I asked faintly.

'Yes,' he said. 'We got the place where he used to sleep as well after that. We stay there now.'

I said nothing. Jimmy looked me over in the silence, taking in the handsome pelisse with the rich gold fringe and the fur muff.

'You couldn't give me a penny, could you?' he asked. 'Then I could buy some gin for Julie. She'd like that. It's better than bread for us if we can buy gin.'

I was about to say no, that I could not bear them to buy gin, that they should have food and clothing and a passage to Wideacre, but that they must not drink gin, never drink again. But James Fortescue stepped forward and put a hand under my elbow. 'Yes, you shall have some money at once,' he said gently. 'Is this Julie from Wideacre too?'

'Oh, aye,' Jimmy said, watching the movement of James's hand in his pocket, and watching him bring out a shilling glinting as bright as a knife in the moonlight. 'We stayed together, us Wideacre paupers. Not little Sal who died, and not George who threw himself in the river last winter when he was drunk, but the rest of us live down by the Fish Quay.'

James handed over the shilling. 'Would the rest of them like to go home?' he asked. 'To Wideacre, if it could be arranged?'

A smile spread over Jimmy's face like the sun rising over the downs. 'Oh, aye,' he said, 'I reckon they would.'

'I'll come and see you all,' I said with sudden decision. Whatever they had done, however they now lived, they were Acre children who should have been raised on Acre. The little girl who had died in the field and the youth who had jumped into the river were in cold water and hard earth far from their homes. And that was the fault of the Laceys. The Laceys, and the squires, and the world which works the way we like it, with very many poor people, and very few rich. 'I'll come and see you, and I'll write to Acre tonight,' I promised.

'You'll never find it on your own,' Jimmy said. 'I'll meet you down at the Fish Quay in the morning if you like.' He nodded at James. 'You'd best come with her,' he said. 'Some of them are rough.'

'I'll be there,' James said grimly. 'We'll come at about nine o'clock.'

Jimmy nodded, and picked up his torch. 'I can go straight home now,' he said, stowing the coins carefully inside the ragged jacket and turning to leave. Then he paused. 'You will come, won't you?' he said, suddenly doubting.

I put a hand on his shoulder, I could feel the sharp shoulder and collar-bone through the thin jacket. 'I promise,' I said. 'You could always come to me. We are lodging with Mrs Gibson at number twelve Gay Street. You can always find me there. But I shall come to you tomorrow morning.'

He nodded at that. 'Till tomorrow, then,' he said, and turned on his heel and melted into the shadows of the elegant streets of

Bath, for the very poor – if they are not working – are better in-visible.

James took my hand and we walked on in silence. 'I'll call for you at a quarter to nine,' he said as we reached the doorstep of the lodging-house. I glanced up. Mama's bedroom shutters were lined with light; she was waiting up for me.

'Thank you,' I said, 'but I could go alone. Jem Dench would go with me.'

James shook his head with a smile, but did not trouble to reply. 'You knew at once, didn't you?' he asked. 'I saw your eyes go all hazy, and you smiled as if someone was calling your name, and then you said, "I'm going to take you home." You knew him at once, didn't you?'

'Yes,' I said simply.

'It's a great gift,' he said. 'You are a lucky woman.' He paused then as a thought struck him. 'Why don't you cancel your appointment with Phillips tomorrow?' he suggested. 'You may find you need to spend some time with the Wideacre children.'

'I shall,' I said. I hesitated. 'I hope he will not mind,' I said. 'And then there's Mama . . .'

James stepped back a little and looked at me with his head on one side. He was smiling. 'I should perhaps not suggest this,' he said mischievously, 'but until you know more about the situation, do you think it would be very wrong simply to play truant? If your mama is unwell tomorrow, she will not go with you to Dr Phillips. You could tell her afterwards that you had not gone, and explain why.'

'Mr Fortescue!' I exclaimed. 'That would be deceitful and dis-honest.'

'Yes,' he confessed at once.

'And very convenient,' I acknowledged. 'I shall decide what best to do in the morning. But whether I explain to Mama or not, I shall be ready for you at quarter to nine.'

He bowed and smiled to hear that note of decision in my voice. I put out both hands to him in sudden gratitude for the way he had been with Jimmy and the way he seemed to understand. 'Goodnight, James,' I said.

'Goodnight, Julia,' he replied.

And then sleepy-faced Meg let me in the front door and I crept upstairs to my bedroom. After writing to Ralph, I tumbled into bed and slept as well as if I were home.

In the morning the Fish Quay was noisy and crowded with women buying for the lodging-houses and restaurants of Bath and occasional eccentric gentlemen, choosing their own catch, who eyed James and me with surprise. It was impossibly busy, with people bidding and shouting, and calling their wares, fishermen crashing great crates down on to the cobbles and fishwives shoving their baskets around and tying muslin squares over the top. But at least it was light there, and it only smelled of old and rotting fish.

The streets beyond it, where Jimmy led us, stank of fish, and vomit, and excrement. The lane was wet with slurry, and little streams of filth formed pools in the gutters where rubbish blocked their path. There was no pavement, there was no paving. The lane was a mud track, heaped with muck and refuse thrown from the windows of the overarching houses on each side. It was as dark as twilight, since the buildings stood so close, and not a breath of wind came down it. As we walked along, me with my skirts bunched in one hand to try to hold the hems clear of the muck, James with one hand firmly under my elbow, we could hear from each house, from each blocked doorway and unglazed uncurtained window, the crying of little babies and the moaning of old and ill men and women, and the ceaseless quarrels of those with breath and energy to be moved to anger rather than silent despair.

Jimmy glanced at James's dark face. 'The best we can afford,' he said defensively. James nodded; he was not surprised.

We had only gone a little way before they started following us. At first people looked at us from doorways and from the windows, but then they fell in behind us, a murmuring crowd who looked like they might heckle or stone or rob us. The grip on my arm tightened and James and Jimmy exchanged a look.

'Nearly there,' Jimmy said anxiously. 'I oughtn't to have asked you.'

I wanted to say that my place was there. If Wideacre children were living here, then I should know how they were living. But the smell of the street made me keep my mouth shut, and I did not feel brave and determined. I felt sick and I wished very much that I had not come.

'Here,' Jimmy said suddenly, and turned abruptly to the side.

It was not a doorway at all, but a basement window. Someone had built a little plank bridge down to it, but that was scarcely needed now; so much rubbish and dirt had been dropped from the street that if you had a strong stomach and stout boots, you could have walked from the lane to the window-sill.

'Mind you don't slip,' James said, and walked ahead of me and put a hand out to me when he was half-way along the plank. We tumbled together into the room and I heard something scurry away at the noise we made. I blinked in the darkness, and then, as my eyes grew accustomed, I could see there were four people in the room.

A girl, about my age, lay sprawled on the floor, an old pelisse under her, a dirty greatcoat over her, a tin mug at her side. Her hair, which might have been copper if it had been washed, was half pinned, half tumbled down. Her eyes were heavy with dark paint around them and crusty with sleep. She was as thin as if she were starving and her cheeks were bright as bright with rouge.

'This is Julie,' Jimmy said, and anyone could have heard the love and pride in his voice.

'Hello,' I said quietly. 'I am Julia Lacey.' As I said it, I realized that we had the same name. She was probably a year younger than me and she had been called after me, in the tradition of Wideacre. She raised herself on her elbow and looked at James Fortescue and then at me without a change of expression. 'Aye,' she said, 'Jimmy told us you'd come. I didn't believe it.' She reached for the tin mug and took a gulp from it.

'This is Nat,' Jimmy said.

A boy as black as an African slave got to his feet and came towards us. He was a little taller than Jimmy, but about the same age, I thought. In the darkness of the room I could scarce make out his features; all I could see were his shining eyes, bright blue, looking odd in that blackened face.

'He's a sweeper's lad,' Jimmy said. 'He can't talk because of the soot in his throat. He lost his voice – last winter, it was, wasn't it, Nat?' The boy nodded vigorously. A cloud of soot rose from his mop of hair. 'But he's getting too big,' Jimmy said. 'He can't get up the chimney, whatever he does. Pretty soon he'll have no work. Won't even be able to beg without a voice.'

Nat nodded again, and then turned to a heap of paper on the floor. They were old newspapers, and I thought for a moment that he was going to show us some item of news. But he burrowed among them, and I realized they were his bedding. He came out with some small object cupped in his blackened palm and proffered it to me.

'It's his flint,' Jimmy said in explanation. 'When they took him from Acre, his ma gave him a flint off the common to remember his home by. D'you know flints like that? Flints like that on the common?'

I held the sharp little stone in my hand and closed my palm on it to keep the tears out of my eyes and out of my voice. 'Yes, I do,' I said. It was white on the outside, like a shell, and dark crimson and shiny inside, a hard little keepsake to carry for years. I gave it carefully back to him. 'What is his family?' I asked.

'He's the son of Tom Brewer,' Jimmy said. 'His pa used to work in the Midhurst breweries until they laid him off because of him living in Acre. Are they still there?'

I glanced at Nat. He looked indifferent, as if he had learned long ago that his family had surrendered him to the greater strength of the legal authorities and that he should surrender to them.

'They are,' I said. I remembered the cottage under the falling spire. 'They have a new cottage in Acre,' I said. 'It is being built now. And at home you have two little sisters and a new brother.'

The sooty head nodded, suggesting the news was of interest, but not of vital importance.

A movement in the corner of the room caught my eye.

'That's Rosie Dench,' said Jimmy. 'She's sick again.'

I went cautiously towards the heap on the floor, and then I stopped by her. At her head, on a sheet of startling whiteness in that grime-encrusted room, was an exquisite pair of gloves covered in embroidery, with a great full-blown pink rose coiling around the wrist and around the fingers of the glove. The work was some of the finest I had ever seen.

'What's this?' I asked. 'It's beautiful.'

'It's my work,' she said hoarsely. She raised her head a little from the cloth under her head. Her face was very pale and her lips red from the sores around them. 'When the light is a little brighter, I'll do some more. I gets paid for them; they sell them in Mrs Williams's millinery shop. They pays me well for them too 'cause I make 'em up as I sew. I don't need a pattern drawed for me.' She stopped to cough and she turned her head away from the spotless cloth and the exquisite glove. She coughed into a corner of the rags that were covering her, and in the gloom I could see that her spittle was dark.

'I know that shop,' I said. I had thought it too dear, and Mama and I had gone elsewhere for gloves. They had been selling them at five pounds a pair. 'You could buy a month's work from a ploughing team for that,' I had protested. Mama had laughed at the comparison, but we had bought our gloves in a cheaper shop.

'Five shillin's, they pays me!' she said with pride. 'Five whole shillin's. And if the light is good, I can do a pair in three weeks' working.'

I said nothing. I said absolutely nothing. I looked from the exquisite glove to the white face of the Acre girl, and suddenly the embroidered rose did not look beautiful any more. It looked like a parasite growing over the glove, feeding on her pallor and hunger and ill health.

'Are you one of the Acre Dench family?' I asked softly. 'Clary Dench is one of my best friends.'

'Aye,' she said, 'Clary is my half-sister. Her and me have the same pa, but he never married my ma. When she died, I used to live with Clary's ma, in the cottage at the end of the lane. But when Mr Blithe came, they had to let me go with him. There were too many of us to keep fed. I don't blame them for it. Besides, he'd have had the law on them. The parish overseer said all the children he wanted had to go.'

'I've come to take you home,' I said. 'Acre is different now. They're getting it back to work. Ralph Megson has come home and he is managing it for my uncle, John MacAndrew. We will make a profit on the crops next year and Acre will have a share of the profit – not just wages, but fair shares. I wrote to Ralph Megson last night to tell him I had met Jimmy. May I write today and tell him that you will come home?'

She glanced sideways at the gloves. 'I'd have to finish them first,' she said. 'But then I'd go.'

'Finish them!' I exclaimed. 'I'll take them back to the shop for you myself. Why should you finish them when you are so ill and so poorly paid?'

'I owe,' she said.

I stared at her blankly.

'They pays me a pair behind,' she said. 'And I had to borrow from them to buy my own silks and needles. Aye, and pins. If I don't finish the work and take it back, they'd have me for stealing the goods.'

I was speechless. I looked around for James.

'I think we can make that all right,' he said gently. 'If you would like Miss Lacey and me to take the gloves back to the shop for you as they are, we could discharge your debt.'

I was about to protest, but James shot me a quick frown which warned me to be silent.

'If it can be done,' she said hesitantly.

'Yes, it can,' James said firmly. 'And if the shop owner – Mrs Williams, is it? – is disappointed at losing such a good worker, well, it matters little, for you will never work for her again. You will be in Wideacre with your friends.'

She nodded her head, and dropped back. She had been pale when we started talking, but she was deathly white now.

'I will write, then,' I said, looking around and speaking to them all. 'But while we are waiting for a reply, we must find somewhere for you to live where you will all be more comfortable. And Rosie should see a doctor.'

Jimmy and Nat were looking at me with hard sharp looks, wondering if I would keep my word.

'May I make some arrangements for a lodging-house?' I asked.

They nodded, wordless.

'I will go and see what I can do, and then I will come back. Will you still be in this afternoon?' I asked.

'Nat will be at work,' Jimmy said, 'but Rosie and Julie and me will be here. Julie and me work at nights.'

'I will be back before dinner,' I promised. 'I brought you some money to buy your breakfasts.' I had put half a crown in the pocket of my jacket and I put my hand in. The pocket was empty.

James shook his head resignedly. 'I didn't see a thing,' he said. 'It was quickly done, whoever did it.' He patted the inner jacket of his coat. 'I brought half a crown in case you had no money with you, Julia.' He handed it to Jimmy. 'Bread,' he said. 'And milk, especially for Rosie. No gin this morning.'

Jimmy grinned; Nat's eyes were fixed on the coin.

'We'll be back this afternoon,' I said. I picked up the gloves, wrapped them in the clean cloth, and turned for the half-window and the rickety plank.

The smell of the street was almost sweet after the fetid darkness of the tiny room. The crowd which had followed us had dispersed. James and I exchanged one look and then set off down the mire of the lane to where his phaeton and groom and horses were waiting at the fish market.

'Where first?' James asked as he helped me into my seat and

his groom swung up behind us. 'A good lodging-house, or Mrs Williams's hat-and-glove shop?'

'Lodgings first,' I said. 'I'd like it to be somewhere near here, so it is not too strange for them.'

'We passed a little inn on this road,' James said. 'It looked all right, and it should only be for a few nights.'

He turned the phaeton in a sharp curve and drove us back to it.

'Will you hold the reins while I ask if they have rooms?' he said, and he passed the reins to me and went inside.

The sun came out, and it was warm on the box of the phaeton. I looked down at my gloved hands. They were trembling. I was trembling with anger. I was angry at the poverty of that miserable room and at the knowledge that there were rooms like that in every house down that filthy lane, and many and many filthy lanes in this pretty city. I was angry that every exquisite shawl, every embroidered glove had been made by young girls losing their eyesight bent over their work in dirty rooms.

James came out smiling. 'That's done,' he said; but then he paused at the black expression on my face. 'What is it?' he asked. 'You look like a thundercloud.'

'It's the children,' I said. 'Acre's children. I am so angry at how they have been treated that I can scarcely speak.'

James nodded. 'If you had not recognized Jimmy Dart, he would have been a linkboy all his life, unless someone bigger than him fought him for his torch. And that poor little foursome would have been there for ever.' He paused. 'Just as well for them that you have the sight,' he said, and clicked to the horses and we moved off.

Mrs Williams's shop was in Milsom Street. James pulled up outside the elegant façade with the white and gold swinging sign and waited for me to dismount from the carriage.

'You're coming in to speak to her?' I asked.

'I thought you would do it,' he said. I could see some private smile behind his eyes, but his face was serious.

I remembered Mrs Williams from when Mama and I had

been in her shop. She was an imposing woman, tall, with iron-grey hair and a sharp hard face. When we had decided not to buy her gloves, she had raised one eyebrow as if at some private derogatory thought, and gestured to the serving lady to pack the boxes away. There was always a lady customer or two in the shop taking tea or coffee; there was always a lady in the fitting rooms with a couple of sempstresses taking measurements. And there was a light muslin curtain across the doorway to the work-shop at the back where the girls would stop talking and listen when a customer came in.

My heart sank. 'Please do it, James,' I said. 'I'll come in with you, but I cannot speak to her. I could not stand it if she made a scene.'

'All right,' he said equably and nodded to his groom to go to the horses' heads.

The silver bell over the door tinkled as we went in, and one of the serving ladies came forward with a shallow smile which widened when she recognized James.

'Mr Fortescue!' she exclaimed. 'How delightful! And Miss . . . Miss Lacey! I shall call Mrs Williams; she would want to serve you herself.' She twitched back the muslin curtain to the workshop and called sharply to one of the girls. 'Clarinda! Fetch Mrs Williams, please. Tell her that Mr Fortescue and Miss Lacey are here.'

She left the curtain open and I knew the sewing girls were all staring at me. I had on my oldest pelisse over my plainest gown, for I had not wanted to look too fine visiting Jimmy. Now I flushed scarlet at looking so shabby in this opulent blue-carpeted shop. I knew without glancing down that the hem of my gown was wet and muddy, and I feared very much that the smell of the dirty lane behind the Fish Quay was hanging about me.

A lady I did not know was sitting in the corner of the shop on one of the gilt and white chairs with her daughter. She raised her lorgnette and inspected me, from the top of my plainest bonnet down to my filthy boots, and then she leaned towards her daughter and whispered something behind her gloved hand, and they both laughed.

Mrs Williams came in through a side door, wreathed in smiles. 'Mr Fortescue! What a pleasure. How is Mrs Fortescue? And your sisters? Please give them my compliments.'

James bowed.

'And Miss Lacey!' she said, glancing at me and managing to take in the muddy footprints I had left on the thick blue carpet. 'How nice to see you again. What can I do for you today?'

I hesitated and glanced towards James. His eyes were on me. I felt a sense of utter relief that it would be his voice which would carry to the girls sewing in the back room, and his words which would be carried to every drawing-room in Bath by the elegant lady who had laughed at my muddy petticoat. All I had to do was to stand a little behind him and nod my assent as he returned the gloves.

'Miss Lacey has some business with you,' he said politely. He turned to me and put his hand in the small of my back and gave me a hard little shove forward. Then he stepped back and left me facing Mrs Williams, who raised her eyebrows as the smile slowly left her face.

The serving lady returned to the little desk which served as a counter, and another came from the fitting rooms with the elegant lady's other daughter, looking very fine in a walking dress. The seated lady raised a hand to her daughter to warn her to be silent. The whole shop waited to hear what my business might be.

'I have come to return these,' I said baldly in a small voice, and I thrust the package of half-finished work towards her.

Mrs Williams gave a puzzled frown and handed it to her assistant; the task of unwrapping it was clearly too menial for her.

The woman opened the parcel and held up a glove for her to see. Mrs Williams looked at me, her face blank, and waited for an explanation.

'I am sorry,' I said, 'but the girl who was doing the sewing is ill and should not work any more. I have brought the gloves back.'

'How very kind,' said Mrs Williams, icy.

'She comes from the village on my estate,' I said, my voice trembling a little. I could feel that the girls in the workroom had laid down their work and gathered in the doorway to stare at me with unfriendly bright eyes. 'I am making arrangements for her to go home to the country. She will not be able to work for you again.'

Mrs Williams inclined her head. 'Unfortunately, she is in debt to these premises,' she said, as smooth as silk. 'Unfortunately, I had trusted her with some valuable work which I had to return to be redone. I insist on the highest of standards because my customers are of the highest of the Quality. Unfortunately, I cannot release her from her contract with me until she has repaid her debt.'

'How much?' I said.

Mrs Williams sighed as if I were causing a great deal of trouble, and the young lady in the walking dress giggled aloud. Her mama glanced at her and put up a hand to hide her own smile.

'Mrs Foster?' Mrs Williams asked languidly.

The serving lady reached into a great drawer in the desk and drew out a ledger. With deliberate slowness she turned over one page and then another. 'The name of the young person?' she asked me.

'Rosie Dench,' I said.

Mrs Williams looked at the seated lady and her two daughters. 'My dear Lady Querry, I do apologize for this. I generally see applicants for work at the tradesmen's entrance, and by appointment only. Miss Lacey has chosen to come in at the customers' door, during shop hours. I would hate to delay you for this rather complicated inquiry. Is there anything else I can do for you?'

'We should like to see some shawls,' said Lady Querry. Mrs Williams nodded to the other serving lady and she brought out a box of fine embroidered shawls. I knew that Lady Querry and her daughters were merely delaying their departure to see my discomfort. I looked around for James. He had taken a seat by the door and was waiting for me, arms folded. He looked as if he had nothing to do with me at all. I shot him a look which was a clear plea for him to help me, but he just smiled politely at me as if we had agreed that he would simply drive me to the shop for my own private business.

'Dench owes sixty-four shillings,' Mrs Foster said languidly. 'And if she is returning these gloves as spoiled, that will be, I suppose, eight pounds and four shillings.'

'Spoiled!' I exclaimed. 'They are beautifully sewn, and all but finished!'

'Unfinished work is called "spoiled",' Mrs Foster said, not raising her eyes from the ledger. 'It is very hard, Miss Lacey, to persuade flighty young girls to complete work they have undertaken. We have to have a system of fines to encourage them in habits of self-discipline and responsibility. I hope you are certain that you are doing the right thing in encouraging Dench to throw up her work in this way.'

I gasped, and looked around for James. He was watching his horses out of the window. Lady Querry's daughters were smothering their giggles, bending low over the box of shawls.

'I hardly think this is the time or the place,' Mrs Williams said grandly. 'Tone matters so much to me. I really cannot be dunned in my own premises, Miss Lacey! Forgive me, but may I ask you to send Dench around to the tradesmen's entrance with the money for her debt, or with the finished gloves? She is late with them already.'

There was a ripple of laughter from the sewing girls in the back room.

'Was there anything you wished to purchase, Miss Lacey?' Mrs Williams asked smoothly.

When I said nothing, for I was speechless with rage and frozen with shame at the way I was being treated, she nodded at Mrs Foster, who shut the ledger and glided past me with her nose in the air and opened the door for me to leave.

I could feel my face burning. Lady Querry and her two daughters had abandoned all pretence of looking at shawls and were openly staring at me. James had risen to his feet, ready to leave with me without saying a word. I took two steps, and then I spun around on my heel.

'No!' I said fiercely, and as I spoke I felt my anger leap up in me, and I knew I had shed the discipline of being a pretty Bath miss. I was *not* a pretty young girl. I was the heir to the Laceys, I was a Lacey of Wideacre. And this arrogant woman had been ill-treating one of *my* people.

'That is *not* how I do business,' I said. 'I have come to return these gloves to you, which I do not doubt you will get some other poor girl to finish and sell at a usurious price. And I have taken the trouble to come and see you to tell you that Rosie Dench will work for you no more. And if I had the power, *no* young girl would work for you again. You pay rates which barely keep a worker alive, and then you make them buy their materials from you, and fine them, and keep them in debt so they can work nowhere else. Rosie Dench is coughing blood in a dirty room, trying to sew gloves for you in half-darkness. So don't tell me that tone is so important to you. You are no better than a madame in a bagnio!'

Lady Querry half screamed at the insult and Mrs Williams strode around from the desk to the door.

'You had better go!' she hissed.

'I *am* going,' I said. 'And I am not coming back, and neither is Rosie Dench. And if I hear one word from you about calling Rosie a thief or about this ridiculous debt, I shall tell everyone that you are no better than a slave-driver. I shall tell them how Rosie was when I found her. And I shall tell them that you pay her five shillings for her most beautiful work, and how you sell the gloves for five pounds. And I will go on doing it until I have cost you far more than eight pounds and four shillings in lost custom. I shall go on doing it until you are ruined.'

I rounded on Lady Querry as she sat, mouth agape, drinking in every word. 'And when you repeat this to all your friends, your ladyship,' I said scathingly, 'remember to tell them that their gloves and their stockings and their shawls are embroidered in filthy rooms by girls with consumption, and smallpox, and fevers. That the shifts which you buy to wear next to your skin have been touched, every inch of them, by girls with sores on their hands. That they are sold to you at a price which would make all those girls well, and well fed if they saw even half of it.'

I spun round then and marched to the carriage and climbed up on to the seat, still trembling with rage and my head still ringing with things I wanted to say. In my fury I saw James sweep a low bow to Lady Querry and even to Mrs Williams.

'Good day, ladies,' I heard him say pleasantly, and then he strolled out to the phaeton, and climbed on to the box and took up the reins.

I said nothing until he had turned left into George Street.

'How could you just sit there?' I said through my teeth. 'You said you would speak to her, and you left it all to me. I felt an utter fool and they were all laughing at me and you did nothing, nothing! And then you said, "Good day" to them when we left. "Good day, ladies." Ladies! How *could* you?'

James waited for a sedan chair to get out of the way before turning up the hill to Gay Street. 'I wanted to see how you would do,' he said. 'I wanted to see how you would stand up to her.'

'What?' I shrieked.

'I wanted to see how you are when you are being a squire,' he said. He pulled the horse to a standstill and got down from the seat and came around to my side to help me down. I scrambled down on my own and pushed past him. If I could have knocked him down and walked over him, I would have done so. He seemed to me entirely part of the unfeeling Quality world who laughed like Lady Querry. I would never, *never* forgive him for saying, 'Good day, ladies.'

I stormed up the steps and found I could scarcely see the door knocker for the tears of anger in my eyes. James reached over my shoulder and tapped at the door for me.

'I wanted to ask you something,' he said as we waited for Meg to come to the door.

I shot him one angry look which should have warned him that

nothing he could say would draw a civil response from me ever again.

'Will you marry me, Julia?' he asked.

I could not believe my ears. 'What did you say?' I demanded.

'I asked you to marry me,' he repeated. I could hear from inside the house someone coming down the stairs to open the front door. I was still boiling with anger towards Lady Querry, towards Mrs Williams and her beastly shop and shopgirls and the whole unjust unequal cruelty of the Quality world. But more than anything else I was in a blind rage with James Fortescue, who had promised he would speak to Mrs Williams and then left me all alone to look a fool in front of the most fashionable modiste and the biggest gossip in Bath.

Meg opened the door, dipped a curtsy and held it for me.

I turned to face James and put out my hand to him. I was still trembling with anger and my hand shook. He took it and carried it to his lips. I could feel the warmth of his kiss through the glove. I could tell by his eyes that he was smiling.

'Don't be cross,' he said, oblivious of Meg, blind to the people on the street who were watching us with curiosity. 'Don't be cross. I love you much too much to want to make you cross for long. I wanted to see how you would handle old Williams. And I wanted you to know that you could do it. Because you will have to handle Dr Phillips, and perhaps your uncle and your cousin. But I will promise to help you with them. And on that occasion I will *not* leave you all on your own. Will you marry me, Julia?'

I felt the anger flow away from me as if I had no temper at all, and I forgot that Meg was watching, and the people on the street. I put my other hand up to his face and cupped it around his cheek.

'Yes,' I said simply. 'Yes, I will.'

— ◆ 16 ◆ —

'Your mama is in her bedroom,' Meg said. 'She asked after you and thought you had gone to the doctor's on your own.'

'I'll go on up,' I said, moving towards the stairs.

'She'll have heard the carriage,' Meg said in warning. I turned back to look at her. She was smiling, certain she had caught me in some clandestine courtship.

'Thank you, Meg,' I said pointedly. 'That will be all.'

I waited until she had curtsied and gone to the kitchen stairs before I went to knock on Mama's door.

She was obviously unwell. I don't think I ever saw her ill more than twice in all my childhood. Although she was so slight-looking, she was strong, and she seemed incapable of taking fevers or colds, having nursed Richard and me through every sort of childhood ailment.

But now she was lying in bed, very pale, with her forehead and hands very hot and dry. She was moving restlessly on her pillow, seeking a cool spot to lay her head.

'Lie still, Mama,' I said, going to the bell-pull. 'I'll order a cold drink for you, and some warm water to sponge your forehead with. And I'll have them fetch a doctor to see you.'

'Oh, it's you,' she said in relief. 'What a long time you have been with Dr Phillips today!'

I should have told her then that I had played truant that morning, but she seemed so wan and ill that I let the omission slip into a lie. I raised her up and turned the pillows and took one of the blankets off the bed, and then I went to the door to ask Meg for the things I needed and to send the footman out to the best doctor in Bath.

341

He came at once and felt Mama's forehead and looked at her eyes and asked her how she felt. Then he smiled and said very soothingly that it was nothing more than a putrid sore throat, and that she would feel very ill indeed for a week or so, and then perfectly well. He gave her some laudanum and left a small bottle for the pain and to help her sleep, and he recommended lemon tea with a dash of brandy in it.

As soon as he had gone, I scribbled a note to James to ask him to come back and see me, if it was convenient, and one to Mrs Densham to make our excuses from her card party and dinner that afternoon.

James walked back with the footman and learned from him that my mama was ill. 'Leave it to me,' he said comfortably. 'I'll go to Jimmy Dart and the rest of them and get them moved into the inn. I'll give them some money to be going along with, and I'll have the landlady of the inn fetch a doctor for Rosie. You stay here and look after your mama, and I'll drop in on my way home to tell you how I have done.'

'Oh, thank you, James,' I said, and put out my hand to him. 'I knew you would. You are kind to interest yourself in them.'

He smiled. 'I am interested in them,' he conceded. 'But I think I am more interested in you, Julia Lacey. Is your mama too ill for you to speak to her about us? I should like to speak to her as soon as possible.'

'To ask for permission to propose?' I asked, teasing. 'You seem to have left it a little late for that!'

He drew me to him with an arm around my waist and turned my face up to him with his cupped hand under my chin. 'Oh, my darling, you are very, very silly,' he said softly. 'I asked permission of your mama a week ago! I told my parents that I should propose to you whenever your mama had heard from Wideacre and given her consent. She told me last night as I took her to her chair that as far as she and your Uncle John were concerned, you might take or leave me as you wished.'

'Oh!' I said blankly. 'She never said anything to me.'

'Well, they all have this maggot in their heads, don't they?'

said James easily. 'They all want to know whether you can be an ordinary young lady or not. And they all think that unless you live elsewhere, you will be plagued with dreams and seeings and hobgoblins. I think they thought you would turn me down.'

'I should hate to leave Wideacre altogether,' I said, suddenly afraid that James might want me to live in his home town of Bristol.

'I don't see why you should leave it at all,' James said. He sat down on a sofa by the fire and drew me down to sit beside him. 'I have a substantial inheritance, which comes to me on my marriage. Why don't we buy your cousin out of his share of the hall and live there? I could fancy being a country squire if Acre is as you describe it now!'

'We couldn't!' I said, remembering Richard's passion for the hall, and remembering with some discomfort the old childhood promise that we would marry and live there together.

'If your cousin cares little for the stock and for farming, then I don't see why we should not offer him a good price for his half,' James said reasonably. 'Or you could sell your share of the hall to him. We could build our own house, and farm your share of the land from there.'

I looked at him suspiciously. 'You have been planning this!' I accused. He drew me a little closer to him until it was most easy and comfortable to rest against him, and look up and smile into his warm brown eyes.

'Of course I have!' he said. 'You didn't think that I was going to take my lovely squire Julia and shut her up in a Bristol town house, did you? Of course I want you to have Wideacre. And I shall buy it for you.'

'And the dreams and the seeings and the hobgoblins?' I asked softly.

'If you are mad, my darling, then I am moving into Bedlam at once,' he said firmly and drew my face towards his and punctuated his sentence with small gentle kisses on my cheeks, my eyelids and my nose. 'For you [kiss] are the sweetest [kiss] and the wisest [kiss] and the bravest [kiss] and the cleverest [kiss] and the angriest [kiss, kiss] young woman I have ever had the pleasure of kissing while her mama is too ill to chaperon us!'

I leaped to my feet at that, gasped, blushed and then laughed. 'Oh, that is dreadful!' I said. 'And I am dreadful to be sitting here with you. And you, James Fortescue, are no gentleman at all!'

'I know,' he said mournfully. 'Trade, my dear. Only the first generation out of the counting-house and still smelling of shop!'

'You do indeed,' I said firmly. 'Now go and run my errands for me, and don't come and see me again without one of your sisters to sit with us.'

'I should think they would bless me for that,' James said as I pushed him out of the room to find Meg industriously polishing the table in the hall.

'I shall shout through the keyhole that I have the children from Acre safe,' James said. 'Or sing it up to your window. Anything rather than be alone with you again. Will you come to dinner tonight?'

'No,' I said while Meg dawdled over handing James his cape, hat and gloves. 'I have written to your aunt. I shall stay at home with Mama.'

'I'll go back home to Clifton then,' James said. 'I want to have a word with my papa. He'll want to know his son has joined the minor gentry.'

'Minor!' I said in mock outrage.

'A very little estate,' James said dampeningly, 'and scarcely a dowry at all, I understand.'

I gleamed at him. 'Not bad for a tradesman's son,' I said.

'Not bad at all,' he said with satisfaction. 'Thank you, Meg,' he said as he took his hat from her, and then he stepped forward and kissed me on the lips and was out of the door and down the steps before I could say a word.

'Congratulations, Miss,' Meg said, reverently shutting the door behind him. 'Cook will be so surprised.'

And she was away down to the kitchen quarters before I could ask her not to tell them in the kitchen, because I had not even told my own mama yet, nor my uncle. Nor had I written to my cousin.

I should have written to Uncle John and Richard that very day, but Mama awoke from her sleep so hot and so feverish that I sat with her all the afternoon and barely had time to dash off a note to Ralph Megson telling him that I would send the Acre pauper children home to Wideacre as soon as I had confirmation from him.

I waited for his reply; and I nursed my mama. I did not leave her bedroom for more than a few minutes for my meals, or for a little rest in the afternoon when Marianne or Mrs Densham came to sit with my mama. James called every day with flowers for Mama or wonderful out-of-season fruit. She did not seem to be getting worse, so I did not write to Uncle John to bid him come to us; but as the doctor had predicted, she was very ill indeed.

I learned to love James very well during those days. Every day he came with a posy for me as well as for Mama; and his family did his bidding and offered every help they could to make Mama's illness and my nursing easier. He was a very comfortable person. He was easy to be with, he had no moods, no storms of introspection. James was as blessedly open and as contented as a well-loved child. He cared for me well. He teased me and laughed at me; but when I was tired, he would ask Marianne to play the pianoforte for us so that we could sit side by side on the sofa in silence. In those gentle afternoons he would draw my head down to rest on his shoulder, and on one occasion I slept.

'You snored,' he said provokingly as he was leaving.

'I never did!' I protested. 'I never snore!'

His eyes crinkled in his familiar loving smile. 'Well, I'll soon know, won't I?' he asked in a voice as soft and as warm as a caress. 'When you and I sleep together in the same bed, every night of our lives.'

My cheeks warmed with a blush at that, but I held his gaze. 'I should like that,' I said honestly.

James sighed very softly and bent and kissed me gently and was gone.

Every time he came he brought me a little gift, a bunch of flowers or a single unseasonal daisy from his garden at Bristol. One day he brought me a hoop and a stick.

'I thought we should take some exercise,' he said innocently. And despite my protestations, he took me out to the park and we bowled the hoop down the paths, weak with laughter, while the old Bath tabbies looked at us askance.

Every time he left he kissed me. He kissed, with meticulous care, the fingertips of both hands, then the two thumbs, and then finally, as light as the brush of a feather, he kissed me on the mouth.

Every time except once, when Marianne had forgotten her reticule and he came back inside to fetch it. I had gone to the drawing-room window to wave goodbye, and when the door opened, I spun around in surprise. He crossed the room in a few swift strides and caught me into his arms without saying a word. He held me so hard that I could scarcely breathe and he covered my face with kisses and then buried his face into the warmth of my neck and sniffed at my skin hungrily.

'My God, Julia,' he said breathlessly. He pulled back a little. 'I am sorry,' he said awkwardly. 'Did I startle you?'

I smiled at him as an equal. I knew he was apologizing for this sudden eruption of passion into our temperate life. He was anxious in case I was a true Bath miss, full of fluster and girlish fears.

I beamed at him. 'Startle me again,' I recommended.

We collapsed with giggles at that.

'Strumpet,' James said with deep satisfaction, and he cupped his hand under my chin and turned my face up to him. I gazed into his brown eyes without a flicker of unease. If he had wanted, he could have taken me, then and there, on the deep carpet in the afternoon sunshine.

'Julia Lacey,' he said slowly. 'I want you to know that it is only the chaperon system which stands between you and total dishonour.'

'You love me dishonourably?' I asked, a little smile lurking at the back of my voice.

'Deeply dishonourably,' he assured me, and he bent his brown head down and his mouth sought mine.

We stood, locked in each other's arms, for long minutes. I was pressing closer and closer to him so that I could feel him down the length of my body; as he tasted my mouth, he groaned very softly.

There was a tap on the door behind us. We moved apart as slowly as if we were swimming underwater. I looked at James. His eyes were dark with desire, his hair rumpled. I put my hand to my head and tried to pin a straying ringlet. Neither of us was able to say, 'Come in.'

The door opened with commendable caution, and Marianne put her head around it.

'My reticule,' she said conversationally to the carpet midway between James and me, 'was in the hall, where it has been all along. I have now collected it. I am now ready to leave. However, if it is your wish that I should chaperon the two of you from beyond your front door, I should be very glad to have a rug and a cushion on the step, and perhaps a candle at nightfall.'

James laughed and took his sister's hand. 'Forgive us,' he said. 'We treat you shamefully. Let me take you home now.' He turned to me with a smile. 'Until tomorrow, Julia Lacey,' he said. Then he walked out of the drawing-room and was gone.

I sank down into the window-seat and leaned my head against the shutter and did not know whether to laugh or to weep in my delight at being so well loved. So well loved at last.

Mama remained ill, and she was especially restless in the early hours of the morning. James wanted me to hire a night nurse and undertook to find me one, but four interviews convinced him that there was no one in Bath he would trust.

'Besides, the doctor is confident that her illness is reaching a crisis and then she will be better,' I said to him. 'I am sure it is the fault of the horrid damp city. If she were on Wideacre, she would be well again.'

He nodded. The dry weather had broken and the days I had spent indoors had been damp, foggy and cold.

'It has been miserable,' he said. 'Thank God we got little Rosie Dench out of that cellar before this bad weather started. I don't think she would have survived.'

James went every day to visit the Acre four. He said they were settling into their new quarters fairly well. Nat was gradually getting a little paler as the years of soot wore off under his enthusiastic scrubbing. Jimmy Dart was fattening up daily, and Rosie was coughing still, but looking better, and could get up and sit in the parlour downstairs most days. Only Julie seemed unable to settle.

'They do understand why I have not been to see them, don't they?' I asked.

James nodded. 'I made sure they did,' he said reassuringly. 'And they know we are just waiting for the reply from Acre to say that all is ready for them to leave.'

That reply came the next day, in Ralph's untutored script.

Send them home, he wrote. *Everyone here wants them back. And everyone here blesses you for finding them.*

Come back with them. Come back in time for the sowing. You should be here then.

I showed the letter to James.

'Not a man for lengthy speeches, is he?' James said, smiling.

'And he's not vague,' I said, pointing to the paragraph which started, 'Come back with them.' 'That sounds very like an order to me,' I said.

James nodded. 'The best servants are our masters,' he said lightly. 'My papa has a chief clerk who runs the business all on his own. If he ever knew how valuable he was, he could indent for twice the salary. Your Mr Megson sounds like that.'

I laughed. 'Mr Megson knows exactly how much he is worth,' I said ruefully. 'The only reason he does not charge a king's ransom is because he wants to work on Wideacre, and work for the good of the village. It was he who developed the profit-sharing scheme and persuaded the village. My Uncle John says that he would go further if he could.'

'How?' James asked.

'Oh, I don't know,' I said idly. We were taking tea together in the parlour, and Marianne was nobly sitting at the window and alternately looking at the passers-by and at a newspaper. Under the cover of the tea-table James took my hand.

'I think he would like the village to have common rights to all the land,' I said. 'He would have them own the land outright and farm it in common, in the old way.'

James looked extraordinarily interested. 'He's not the only one in the country to be thinking of such ideas,' he said. 'Could such a scheme work?'

'It might,' I said cautiously, 'if the land was handed over to the people in good heart, and they had enough funds to buy equipment and stock and enough cash to pay wages until the profits could be shared. Under those circumstances it would work. But of course those circumstances never come about. No landlord would hand over good land. No one would gift the sort of amounts of money one needs to launch such a massive estate.'

James looked at me, half serious. 'I tell you what, Julia Lacey,' he said. I paid a great deal of attention. Whenever James called me Julia Lacey, I listened well. It was generally something very loving, or something very shocking, or – best of all – both. 'I tell you what,' he said again. '*I* have those sorts of funds, and if you tell me that you and I and then our children would have a good life in Acre if the village owned its own land, then I would be prepared to offer that sort of capital. We could build our own house and have our own share in the village, and yet not be the sort of squires and the sort of masters who bring about the poverty which we saw in Fish Quay Lane.'

I hesitated. 'No,' I said. 'It is your inheritance, not mine. Before you decide how it is spent or where you wish to live, you must see Wideacre and the village. I cannot imagine being happy living all my life anywhere else. But you and I must agree such things together. It would be as unjust to you if we were all our days at Wideacre as it would be unjust to me if you took me to Bristol and I could never see my home again.'

James held his free hand out across the tea-urn in a parody of a street trader. 'Done,' he said. 'And remember what I have offered. My papa calls me a radical and a Jacobin, but I have no use for such labels. What I do care about is trying to follow the French lead in an especial English way. To make a new society here, as they are trying to do there. I want to do so with you, for I think I loved you the most when I saw you in the best fashion shop in Bath telling the proprietor she was worse than a madame in a bagnio. I have been a rebel all my life and I want to find a way to make that rebellion a comfortable way to live – something for the future rather than just a reaction against the way things are.'

'Yes!' I said, and my heart leaped to think of trying to build a life in Acre where there were no masters and squires but just James and me and our children, and Clary Dench and Matthew Merry and their children, and all the other village children living as neighbours.

'If you two are holding hands above the tea-urn as well as below it, then I cannot help but feel that my presence here is somewhat superfluous,' Marianne observed drily.

We released each other and laughed like a pair of guilty children.

'Never that,' James said, and crossed to the window to kiss her cheek. 'At your least you are always ornamental. Tell us what Dr Phillips said today,' he commanded, sitting beside her and taking the newspaper from her. 'Julia has to see him for the first time in days tomorrow and she is going to tell him that she will discontinue her visits. They need her back at home and since she has survived perfectly well without seeing him, I am trying to convince her that she is as sane as anyone in the world, and a good deal saner than anyone I have ever known before.'

Marianne shot me a shy smile. 'Except for your liking for my brother, I would agree,' she said. Then her face grew graver. 'Dr Phillips is working very hard to help me eat properly,' she said.

'Even if I find it sometimes very wearying, I cannot deny that he is very painstaking. I cannot help but wish that sometimes everyone would just leave the whole thing alone. If I was on a desert island, I am sure that I would be hungry and eat. It is just that everywhere I go, people press food on me, and when I refuse, they look at me and argue with me. Since I have been to Dr Phillips, and Mama has told people about it, everything has got worse.'

'When we are married, and living in earthly paradise in the heart of Sussex, you shall come and stay with us and you shall eat nothing!' James promised. 'Nothing at all for days at a time until you feel you could fancy a little something. And no one will look at you, and no one will question you.'

Marianne sighed. 'I look forward to being your first guest. But you are a little forward, James. The engagement has not even been announced, and I don't think Julia has even told her mama.'

'I cannot,' I said. 'She has been so ill and so tired, I did not want to trouble her. She would at once start planning parties and wedding gowns. I want her to be entirely well before she starts such a campaign.'

'In the meantime, you must chaperon us,' James said. 'Do you have time tomorrow to go with Julia to Dr Phillips? We are to dispatch the Acre paupers in the afternoon, and Julia thought of seeing Dr Phillips first thing.'

Marianne agreed to escort me, and then go with me down to the inn to see that the four lost Acre children were ready to go home.

'Would you like me to visit the doctor with you?' James whispered softly to me as we said goodbye in the drawing-room while Marianne slowly tied on her bonnet before the mirror in the hall.

I hesitated. I was tempted to say yes and call on the help I knew he would give me. But I had been tempered in the fire of the most fashionable modiste in Bath, and I thought I could defend myself against Dr Phillips.

'No,' I said. 'There will be much to arrange tomorrow. I shall meet you at the Fish Quay Inn; and I shall be a free woman then, for I shall have told Dr Phillips I shall visit him no longer. I should tell him on my own, face to face. It is only fair, for he has spent a deal of time with me, doing the best that he could. I am a little apprehensive, but it will be no worse than Mrs Williams's shop. Nothing could be worse than that.'

'And I was so much help there!' James exclaimed. He took both my hands and took one to his lips and turned the other around to cup his face. 'Keep me in your mind until tomorrow,' he said. 'For I cannot sleep at nights for thinking about you.'

Then he kissed me on my lips and strode out to the hall, swept up Marianne and was gone with a little smile for me.

'I shall see you tomorrow at the doctor's,' Marianne called. 'Don't be late!'

I nodded and I was not late, for it was nine o'clock when I slammed the front door and started to run up the hill; I was still there ahead of Marianne. The solemn footman showed us into Dr Phillips's bleak parlour like two twin flies for a plump spider at exactly five minutes after nine o'clock.

Marianne went to the seat by the window where my mama usually sat, and Dr Phillips waved me towards the comfortable seat before the fire. But I remained standing with one hand on the back of the armchair where I had poured out my dreams and nearly lost them altogether.

'I have come to thank you and to bid you farewell,' I said. 'My mama has been unwell and as soon as she is well enough to travel, I shall want to take her home. They need me at home on the estate.'

Dr Phillips went behind his heavy wooden desk and leaned back in his chair, watching me over his folded hands. 'I think that would be unwise,' he said gently. 'Unweasonable. Have you consulted your mama? No? Have you witten to your uncle? No?' He smiled gently at me. 'These things are genewally better done by pawents or guardians,' he said. 'When you first came to me, you were suffewing from a number of delusions. I am pleased to say that we have made inwoads. I think you have had no dweams since you came to me? And no experience of the singing in your head? And no hallucinations?' He nodded to himself. 'I think we have been making gweat pwogwess. I shall expect you to come again when your mama is well enough to bwing you, unless I hear to the contwawy fwom her or fwom your uncle.'

'No,' I said steadily. This was worse than the millinery shop, for I had no tide of anger to sweep me into certainty. 'No,' I said. 'This is a decision I may take for myself. I will not be coming back to see you again. I shall tell you why,' I said. My hands were trembling and I thrust them into my muff so he should not see. 'You have indeed stopped my dreams, and I think in time you could have stopped the seeings altogether. But if you succeeded in that, I would no longer be Julia Lacey. I should be someone else. I do not know if I want that. I suspect that you have given no thought to that at all. You saw what you thought was a silly girl having delusions. But I believe that I am a special private person with special private experiences – with a gift, if you like – and I should resist being robbed of that as strongly as I should resist being robbed of my money.'

'Has something happened?' he asked acutely.

'Yes,' I said honestly. 'Out of all the linkboys in Bath I recognized one as an Acre child, one who was taken from Acre ten years ago, one I had never seen before. I heard a voice in my head saying, "Take him home." And I am going to take him home.'

Dr Phillips never moved, but his eyes were suddenly sharper. 'Are you saying this is a pwoven experience of what is called second sight?' he asked.

I shrugged with a little laugh. 'I don't know!' I said. 'I don't care what it is called. It is as natural to me as seeing the colour of the sky, or hearing music when it is played. I will not have my sight and my hearing taken from me because other people do not have a name for it.'

He nodded, and rose to his feet. 'Vewy well,' he said. 'But let me give you one word of warning. What you think of as second sight can be a guide in certain times and places. But you cannot be a seer and also a young Bath lady. Most of the time you would do well to be guided by convention and manners.'

I nodded. 'Thank you,' I said.

Marianne stepped forward beside me. 'I too am saying good-bye,' she said softly. I saw her face was white and strained but her teeth were gritted. 'I thank you for the work you have done for me,' she said, 'but I want time to consider my own position without forever having to explain myself.'

Dr Phillips sat plump down on his chair again and looked at both of us. 'My entire system depends upon the patient talking the twouble out of their minds,' he said. 'And I have a pwoven success wate.'

'I have no trouble in my mind,' Marianne said steadily. 'My trouble is in my home where my mama is unhappy and my papa ill-treats her. The only time we ever see Papa is at mealtimes, and I am so distressed that I cannot eat. My papa pays your fees, Dr Phillips, and you have never wanted to hear this simple explanation from me. I understand that you will not hear it, but there is no reason in the world why I should go on pretending that all this is my fault, and that I can somehow be cured from the consequence of my parents' bad marriage. I cannot eat at home because I am miserable there. I am miserable because my papa is unfaithful to my mama, and because they choose the family dinner table as a place for their disagreements. I will not sit in your armchair and talk and weep and blame myself any longer.'

'Yes,' I said softly. I felt more like shouting, 'Hurrah!' and throwing my bonnet in the air.

Dr Phillips got to his feet again and looked at us unpleasantly. 'If this is the new wadical woman, then I cannot say I am im-pwessed,' he said. 'You may tell your mamas that I will submit my final bill and that I, not you, terminated our discussions. I find you both unsympathetic.'

I bit back a retort, and curtsied in silence instead. Then Marianne and I got ourselves to the door and out into the damp street and around the corner into Gay Street before we whooped and laughed and congratulated ourselves, tumbled into a pair of sedan chairs and set off for the Fish Quay Inn.

They were in a delightful flurry of packing. All their new possessions, which James had provided, could have gone in one small bandbox; but the joy of private ownership was upon them and each had a separate box. Nat was now flesh-coloured all over his face, except for odd-looking sooty traces around his eyes, and he was very smart in a new suit. Rosie Dench was pale and thin still, but the sores around her mouth were healing and she did not cough at all. Jimmy Dart bustled around them both, as spry as a Bath sparrow in a brown homespun suit. I could not have recognized them for the sorry little crew in that dirty room. But I could not see Julie.

'She won't come,' Jimmy said, his face losing all its light at once. 'She won't come with us. She's in her room. She won't even come down for her dinner before the journey. She says she's staying in Bath. She only just told us.'

I looked around for James. 'It's as well,' he said softly. 'She could hardly ply her trade in Acre. And she could not do without drink.'

'Trade?' I said blankly. 'I did not realize she worked. What trade?'

James made a little grimace. 'Leave it, Julia,' he said. 'I'll explain later. She does not wish to leave Bath, that's all.'

'No,' I said. 'She's an Acre child. It is my duty to know what is happening.' Ignoring him, I turned into the inn and ran up the stairs to the bedroom she shared with Rosie.

She was lying on the bed, fully dressed, with her face to the wall. The lattice window was shut, but you could still hear the noise outside of coaches coming and going and passengers calling orders about their bags.

'Julie?' I asked hesitantly.

She turned around to see me and her eyes were as red as her rouged cheeks. She had been crying. 'Oh, it's you,' she said.

'Go to Acre with the others,' I said intently. 'You can go down now and take the coach with them this afternoon. Go home, Julie.'

She sat up and leaned back against the wall; her eyes were hard as Wideacre flints. 'I can't,' she said blankly.

'Why not?' I asked. 'Is there some trouble here?'

'No.' She said it like a sigh.

'What is it, then?' I demanded. 'Why won't you go home?'

There was a tap on the door behind me and James came quietly into the room.

'Ask him!' she said, wearied. 'Ask him! Don't ask me! You are the little miss perfect Julia Lacey! You are the one who will marry the man with the fortune. Don't ask me to explain it to you. Ask your fiancé. Ask him what men of his type do, and what they pay. Ask him where he goes and how much it costs him.'

I turned to James. 'What is all this about?' I asked. I had not an idea what Julie was saying.

James's face was grave. 'Can you not put this behind you, leave it and forget it, and start again in Acre?' he asked her.

Julie's face was bright with bitterness. 'It's my trade,' she said harshly. 'Will the little princess here let me practise my trade in Acre? Will there be customers for me there?'

'What *is* your trade, Julie?' I demanded. I was all at sea with her sharpness and her especial malice towards me. There was also some private knowledge between James and her which disturbed me.

'Little fool,' she said. And then she nodded at James. 'You tell her.'

I turned to James; his eyes were sombre. 'She's a prostitute,' he said baldly. 'A whore.'

'That's what I am,' Julie said to me. 'I am a street-trader, I sell my body to men. I did it when we were working at the mill so that the little children could have bread. I did it first when I was eleven. It hurt, and I hated to do it. I have done it since, and I have learned to endure it. Sometimes I like it. It is the only way I know of getting money to buy bread and gin. If I had not sold my body – oh! again and again! – all the way down the weary road from Manchester to here, then the children would have starved and I would have lost them all, as well as little Sally. Now you can take them home, and keep them safe. But I cannot come home. Acre is no longer a home for me. I need gin to drink and men to pay to take their pleasure on me. I am lost, Julia Lacey. And though I carry your name, I might as well be a slave in the sugar islands for the gulf there is between us.'

My head was thudding.

'I did not know,' I said to Julie, but I knew it was no excuse. 'I did not know such things happened to a girl as young as you.'

She gave a harsh laugh. 'They happen!' she exclaimed. 'Oh, yes, they happen. It is whores like me who make it possible for you to keep your precious virginity until it is sold in marriage. How old is this man of yours? Is he a virgin? Silly fool, Julia Lacey! He has lain with whores. He will have been with whores like me. And it is because he has been with them that he can dance with you and walk with you and kiss your hand and wait for a wedding night that may be years away. Isn't that so?'

I looked blankly at James. 'You have been with women?' I asked, my voice very thin. I sounded like the silly child they thought me.

'Yes,' he said. 'It is true, and I do not deny it. I am twenty-four and I have lain with women. All whores. I never hurt them, I always give them more money than they ask of me. I am a man with desires. What would you have me do?'

I hesitated.

The whore who had been bought and sold like meat at Smithfield looked from one to another of us with hard eyes. And I saw that the man that I loved was one of the gentry – as I am – who take their pleasures or satisfy their needs, but never, never pay in full.

'I don't know,' I said.

A coach horn outside the window blew loudly to warn the passengers that the stage was going. It reminded me of the immediate issue of the journey home this afternoon.

'Go to Acre,' I said to Julie.

She lay down and turned her face to the wall again. 'Nay,' she said, and her voice had something of the Sussex drawl of our home. 'I'm lost. Let them go, and you give them a job and somewhere to live. But it is too late for me. The Laceys ruined me, and the mill ruined me, and the cheap gin and no work ruined me. I am lost. I won't see you again.'

I stepped forward hesitantly and put my hand on her shoulder. She shrugged it off as if I were a beggar.

'If I could be melted with a touch, I should be drowned in tears by now,' she said harshly. 'Get out of my room, Julia Lacey, and take your man with you. Or leave him here. I only charge a shilling during the day.'

I opened my reticule and took out all the money I had – three guineas – and laid them on the pillow beside her tumbled copper hair. Then without looking at James I walked past him and down to the inn parlour.

It was not easy to smile and say farewell to the children and promise them that the hired coach would come for them at two o'clock prompt that afternoon, and that I would see them in a few weeks at Acre. I think I deceived them with my smiles. But not Marianne.

'What's the matter?' she said in an undertone as we left the parlour and walked across the wet cobbles.

'Nothing,' I said. 'Julie won't go home and it upset me. I must get back to Mama. I'll take a chair.'

I moved towards the waiting chairmen, but James was at my elbow.

'Julia . . .' he said hesitantly.

I waited in silence.

'I hope you don't think too badly of me,' he said awkwardly. 'It is true that men do go with such women, me among them. You've seen well enough how everything in our world goes to the highest bidder. It's true for this too. Everything in this world is for sale. Even little girls.' His eyes scanned my face. 'You are disappointed in me,' he said evenly.

'Yes, I am!' I said in a sudden rush of words. 'I thought that you were different. I thought that you were not one of those who take and ill-treat the poor. There is no fair price for a woman's body. There is no fair price for her ruin. You have helped to ruin girls. None of them will ever be able to go home – just like Julie. None of them will be able to marry – like her. I did not know how such things happened. I would not have dreamed that you would be part of it.'

James smiled a wry smile. 'I am no hero, Julia,' he said gently. 'I am an ordinary man, very ordinary, I dare say. You must not think too highly of me – or of anyone. I am no better than times allow.'

'Well, you should be,' I said fiercely. 'I did not think you were a hero, but I did think you were special, very special. And now . . .' I stopped. My voice was failing as my throat grew tighter with tears. 'Everything is spoiled,' I said like a little child.

James put his arm around my waist and guided me towards the waiting chair. 'Don't say that,' he said gently. 'I do not believe you mean it, but it cuts me to the quick. I cannot tease you out of words like that, Julia. Don't say such final things unless you mean them indeed.'

'I don't know,' I said. 'I don't know what to think. I shall go home now and I shall write you a note this afternoon.'

He bowed as formally to me as if we had been strangers, and then he turned to Marianne and guided her to his phaeton. She was chattering and laughing and I saw him make an effort to smile and guessed she was telling him that she was no longer visiting Dr Phillips. She waved as they went past my chair, but James just looked at me. He looked at me as if I were a ship sailing out of harbour and away from him.

I drew the curtains on the window of the chair and put my head in my hands. I did not cry. I just sighed out my disappointment and my love and my longing into my gloved hands and wondered that the world we gentry had made to suit ourselves should sometimes give us so little joy.

➤ 17 ➤

I had asked for time to think; but then there was no time at all. When the chair brought me back to Gay Street, our own travelling coach was outside with the boot opened, and Mama's trunks were being carried out. Inside the house, on the hall table, was Uncle John's Malacca cane and grey round hat, and in Mama's bedroom, sitting on her bed, was Uncle John himself.

Mama was upright in bed, her wrapper on, her hair in a plait down her back, looking a thousand times better than when I had left her that morning.

Uncle John had received two letters from me, one telling him that Mama was a little unwell and that I had called the doctor, and then another telling him that she was as yet no better.

'Of course I had to come,' he said reasonably. 'Do you two have any idea of the cost of a Bath physician? Celia, it is essential that you come home where I can treat you for free.'

Mama chuckled ruefully, her voice a croaky shadow of its usual ripple. 'We cannot go,' she said. 'Julia is in the middle of her season, and she has appointments with Dr Phillips.'

John looked across the room at me. 'I think she should stay,' he said. 'Could you stay with these friends of yours so that you can continue seeing Dr Phillips?'

I rose from the chair at Mama's bedside and went over to the window and twisted the cord for the curtains in my hand. 'I have finished with Dr Phillips,' I said. I shot a quick glance back at my mama. 'I told him so this morning.'

John stood up very tall at the mantelpiece, looking down at the logs burning in the grate. His face was in profile to me; I could not read it.

'How is that?' he asked softly. 'Your mama wrote to me that he was doing you so much good.'

I shook my head. 'He was not,' I said positively. 'He could show me that there was no favoured sense in what I see and hear – no sense at all. But he could not prove that it does not happen.'

Uncle John nodded. 'He could not prove that you do not experience it,' he said fairly. 'But, Julia, if you know that such a thing *cannot* happen, you have to accept that it is a delusion if you think it does happen.'

'It is *my* mind!' I said in a sudden spurt of defiance. 'If I see things and hear things, I don't see why I should permit anyone else to tell me different!'

John's face was grim. 'You must not resist this, Julia,' he said severely. 'Your mama and I are agreed that if you cannot be cured of these delusions during this visit, then it would be better for you not to return to Wideacre but to stay in Dr Phillips's house on your own, until you can improve your understanding.'

I gasped and looked at my mama for help. She was sitting forward, her face as white as the lace trim on her sheets, but she met my eyes. 'No, John,' she said, her voice thin. 'I know I said that on Wideacre, the day after the storm when I thought Julia quite overset. But I have seen her in Bath and seen her with people her own age now. She has told me how she found the missing children of Acre, and we saw how she cleared the cottages which would have been crushed or fired. I trust her. And I believe in her too. If she thinks Dr Phillips is doing her no good, then she need not see him.'

'You feared that she inherited the Lacey oddness,' John said in a low voice. 'You feared Beatrice.'

There was a sudden stillness in the room, as if the mere mention of her name would conjure her up, the witch of Wideacre, even to a Bath lodging-house.

'Julia is *my* daughter, raised by me,' Mama said steadily. The white colour of her face had changed and now she was ashen. 'She is to come home with us.'

'But your friend Miss Fortescue goes to him as well, does she not?' John turned to me. 'You can see that he is doing her good.'

'He was not doing her good,' I said. 'And she has left him too. He made her feel that she was in the wrong. He made me feel I was wrong. He could cure me of the dreams and of the sight, but he could only do it by destroying me, changing me from my very self.'

John was about to reply, but my mama raised herself a little in her bed. 'I've never gone against your advice, John,' she said, 'but I do so now. I am sorry.'

In two strides John was across the room and at her bedside, his arm around her shoulders to lower her back to her pillows. 'It is I who should be sorry,' he said. 'I am quite wrong to tire you out with talking. I know well enough what it is to be sent away from one's home with an accusation of madness. Forgive me, Celia. She is your daughter indeed and you have the final word on her upbringing.' He looked over at me. 'And you forgive me, Julia,' he said. 'I was only trying to do the best for you. Do you wish to come home with us? Or stay perhaps with your Bath friends?'

'I'll come home,' I answered. I did not want to be thrust into the Denshams' cheerful, noisy household, and I was uncertain about James now.

'Well, we'll leave it at that, then,' Uncle John said pacifically. 'Let us get your mama safe home and see how things are when you are there.'

He put the disagreement behind him and smiled at me. 'I cannot deny that I shall be glad enough to have you to help on the estate. Richard went back to university three weeks ago, and Mr Megson needs another pair of eyes on the land. I do not know enough about it. If you are happy and well, Julia, then that is all your mama and I ever wanted. No one wanted to make you into anything different.'

I nodded. 'That night when the spire fell,' I began. Uncle John stiffened and looked at me. 'It was a true seeing,' I said. 'I have the sight.'

He shrugged his shoulders with a little smile. 'Very well,' he said. 'I suppose I have to accept it. Until there is a more reasonable explanation.'

'And you have to accept me,' I pressed. 'Whether I look like Beatrice or whether I seem to have the sight, or whether I am just an ordinary girl or no.'

John nodded. 'Yes,' he said simply, 'I will.'

And it was on that easy basis that I went home to Wideacre.

Uncle John had not run his papa's company in India for nothing. The news that I wished to travel in convoy with a hired carriage of Acre paupers he took as the most reasonable thing in the world. Apart from reminding me to send a message down to them to delay their departure until we called for them, he left my arrangements for the hire of their carriage as they were. He had had Mama's boxes packed and loaded, and Meg was packing mine when I got to my bedroom. He wanted us to start at once and dine and sleep that night in Salisbury. The next night we would stop at Winchester, and the third night would see us home.

I checked that Meg had remembered my laces, which were with the washerwoman, and then went down to the parlour to write my note to James. There was very little to say, for I still did not know my own mind. In the end I just dashed off a line to say that my Uncle John had come to take Mama and me home, and that I would write to him during the journey, or from home. If I could have thought of some reason for us to stay another day, so that I might have spoken to him again, I would have done so. But Uncle John came into the parlour while I was writing my note and said that he could not be easy about Mama's health; he wanted her safe back at Wideacre with her own things around her, and servants who would nurse her, and himself to watch over her.

I could hardly argue with that, so I nodded in agreement and sent the footman around to the Denshams' house with the note for James.

I should have known him better. As I came down the front steps to the carriage, my arm around my mama's waist to help her walk, James was at the carriage door talking to Uncle John. He turned when he saw me and, as soon as we saw Mama was safe inside with a rug around her, he put a peremptory hand under my elbow and drew me to one side.

'Forgive me for coming without an invitation,' he said. The tension in his voice made him sound formal.

I nodded, my eyes wide, waiting for what would follow.

'She is right,' he said awkwardly. 'All men have desires, women too. A girl brought up to be a lady is not permitted to satisfy those desires. I think we both know that they are none the less there.'

I made a little contradictory gesture with my hand. 'Not like that!' I said.

James caught the hand and held it firmly. 'I won't say that it is different for men,' he said, 'but I will say that the world makes it easy for men if they desire a woman.'

My face was shut; I looked away from him. 'I cannot bear to think how she has been treated,' I said. 'I cannot understand how anyone could justify treating another human being – and her such a young girl – in such a way.'

He nodded, his head bowed. 'I've been much at fault,' he said. 'Forgive me if I insist on trying to explain myself to you. It is nothing like the emotion I feel for you. I have been taught – I think many men are taught – to treat it like an appetite which has to be satisfied, to deal with lust as they would deal with hunger.'

I tried to pull my hand away, but James held it firmly. 'Hear me out,' he said urgently. 'I think now that is wrong. I shall try to be more like a woman – if that makes any sense at all. I shall make my heart and my desires follow the one course. I shall not love one thing and lust for another. If you will forgive me this one time, this one discovery, it will be the last.'

I looked at him hard, though my eyes were filled with tears. 'And if you had found that I had been unchaste, would you have thus easily forgiven me?' I asked bitterly. 'If I told you that I had made a mistake but I would not do it again?'

James hesitated, his innate honesty warring with the temptation to lie and win the argument. He smiled ruefully. 'I hope I would have the good sense to realize that it is not your past but your future which concerns me,' he said. 'I am sure I would find the thought of you being with another man almost unbearable. I am sure I would try to understand. Will you try to understand me?'

I paused. The old sad wisdom from Wideacre spoke silently to me, and I knew, whatever the outcome of this conversation, that my idle laughing loving days with James were over. 'Yes,' I said. But I knew this promise would make no difference. Our courting time was over.

His face lightened at once. He bent his head and kissed my gloved hands and then pulled down the glove so that he could kiss the warm skin at the inside of my wrists where the pulse beat a little faster at his touch. 'I thank you,' he said. 'I will not forget this.'

We stood still, without speaking, for a few moments. James's hands were trembling. He gave a little laugh. 'I could fall at your feet and weep,' he said. 'I have been in such terror that you would cast me off.'

I smiled, but my eyes were still sad. I was so sure that I would not see him again.

'I will see if something can be done for Julie,' he said. 'When you are gone, I will ask my Aunt Densham to see if she can be helped. She is young yet, there could be a future for her.' I nodded. 'You take care of the children you have safe,' he said. 'Write to me as soon as you get home, and be very sure to send for me if you need me at all. If you need me for anything.'

I was about to nod again and say yes. I was about to say, loverlike, that he should send for me if he needed me, that nothing should ever keep us apart. But I paused. The light around me grew grey, James's voice seemed to come from a long way away, and I felt a sudden pang of such loneliness, as if I were all alone in the world, as if no one cared for me, or ever would care for me again. I was utterly certain that James would not come for me, could not come for me, however great my need.

'What is it?' he asked, his voice very low. 'Do you see something, Julia?'

I blinked. 'No,' I said. The clear impression I had was fading, going from me like a lantern on the back of a jolting wagon. Nothing I could see for sure.

'You will send for me if you need me?' he repeated.

'Yes,' I said, but I knew I would not be able to send.

'And you know that I will come.'

'Yes,' I said again. But I knew he would not come.

John called from the coach. 'Excuse me, Julia, excuse me, Mr Fortescue, but we must leave.'

We turned and went back to the coach. James handed me in without another word. 'I won't say goodbye,' he said to me through the window. 'I shall say God bless you until I see you again.'

I smiled at him, smiled as though I were not close to tears. And I waited until the coach had moved off and I could see him no more before I said, very sadly, very softly, 'Goodbye, James, goodbye, my darling. Goodbye.'

We had an easy journey that afternoon. The children were in the hired carriage waiting for us outside the door of the Fish Quay Inn and we did not even stop to greet them. I waved from the window and they waved back – three beaming faces – and their coach fell in behind ours and we took the road east. It was comfortable travelling with my Uncle John. The carriage was warm, with wraps and blankets, and Mama and I had hot bricks under our feet. When we stopped to change horses, we were served with hot drinks in the carriage, and on the two overnight halts we had a private parlour with a bright fire burning, and even Mama laughed to see the children's faces at the size of their dinners and the comfort of their rooms.

On the last morning, while Uncle John settled the bill, I went outside to order the carriage for the final leg of the journey. Jem Dench was very full of his own importance, cussing the ostlers and complaining of the looks of the pair. I glanced at them, but they seemed all right to me. The sun was overhead in a clear blue sky, but there were wisps of cloud on the horizon in that palest sparkling white which meant snow.

Above the noise of the stable yard and the clatter of wheels as another coach came in, I could hear a singing so high that it seemed sweeter and higher than the cry of bats, as if it were the music of the spheres which no one believes in any more, and so cannot hear. It sounded like a noise the snow-clouds might make on the eastward horizon where my home lay. It sounded like a noise which sunbeams might make as they slid down to warm me in the dirty little yard. I dug my hands deeper in my fur muff and leaned back against the inn's door. Wideacre was calling me.

A lady in the coach looked at me curiously with the attentive stare I had met in Bath. I had filled out since I had left Wideacre. I had grown a little, and the Bath pastries had put some weight on me. I was as tall as Mama now. I wore heels as high as hers, and I had learned the knack of walking on them too! More than that, I had learned some poise and elegance from my long weeks in the town, and that sense which Mama called 'the Lacey arrogance' had put a tilt to my head and a way of walking as though I owned the land for a hundred miles in all directions, wherever I happened to be.

I gave a polite smile to the lady, and called to Jem that we were ready to go. He drew the carriage up beside me, and Mama and John came out into the yard.

'Wonderful weather,' Mama said as the coach rolled out of the yard and on to the high road again, followed by the hired carriage.

'It may snow tomorrow,' I said. 'Or it may be snowing on Wideacre even now.'

It had frozen overnight and the ground was good and hard. Jem suggested going over the hills on the little tracks to Petersfield, and we took a chance that the roads would not be soft and the going difficult. We were right to gamble. The frost had made the mud firm, and we were rewarded for our daring by a drive through the sweetest countryside in England: the Hampshire–Sussex border. Best in Sussex, of course.

The beech hedges around the larger houses had kept their leaves and were bay-coloured or violet. The grass beneath them was white with frost, and until the sun melted it, every little twig which leaned over the road from the bordering trees was a little stick of ice: white perfection. The streams were not flooding but were small and pretty under the stone bridges of the roads; and it was warm enough for the children to play out on the village greens. This was the wider landscape in which my home was set, and I knew from the size of the streams, from the ice in the shadows and from the set of the wind how things would be at home. The land would be dry, crunchy with frost, but not frozen hard. The Fenny would be full but not flooded, and there would be little corners of the common and little hollows on the downs where it would still be warm enough to sit and put your face up to the winter sunshine.

We dropped down the steep hill into Midhurst, the brakes hard on and the wheels slipping, Jem whispering curses on the driving box. Then we rattled through the little town; the inns leaned in so far that the whip in the stock tapped on the walls as we went past. It was market day and the streets were full of people; the stalls were unpacked and wares were being sold in the square. I glanced at the price of wheat and saw it low – a sure sign of good stocks still with the merchants, and the likelihood of getting through the rest of the winter. There was the usual crowd of labourers looking for work, and some of the faces were pinched and pale with hunger. In one corner of the square there was a group of beggars, in filthy rags, blue with cold. Lying face down by some steps was a working man, dead drunk. I could see the holes in his boots as the carriage drove past.

Then we were clear of the village and trotting up the steep hill on the road towards Chichester. I felt my heart beating a little faster and I leaned forward in my seat and looked out of the window as if I could absorb through the very skin of my face all of Wideacre which I had missed for so long. The singing in my head was like a tolling bell calling me home, and the carriage could not go fast enough for me as we swept around the left-hand bend down the track towards Acre. It was only a short distance, and now I was in no hurry, for the trees on one side of the road were Wideacre trees, and the fields on the other side were Wideacre fields; and I was home.

Uncle John smiled at me. 'You look like someone who has run a race and come in first,' he said. 'Anyone would think you have been pulling the carriage yourself, you look so relieved to be here.'

'I am,' I said with feeling. 'It is so good to be home.'

We swirled in at the lodge gates and I bent forward and waved to the Hodgett children who were leaping at the roadside, then we pulled up outside the Dower House, and I caught my breath in my joy at my home-coming.

'Now,' said Uncle John, 'I have a surprise and a half for you, Celia! See how hard we bachelors have worked to tidy the house for your return!'

Mama gasped. There was indeed a transformation. Ever since Uncle John had brought his fortune home, she had been buying little things to make the house more comfortable for us all. But Uncle John had worked a miracle. The old furniture of the house, which had been ours on permanent loan from Havering Hall, was all gone, and the little scraps of rugs which had been an attempt to make the house less echoey and cold had been thrown away. In their place were gleaming new rugs of fresh wool, and standing on them were beautifully crafted pieces of deep-brown teak and mahogany furniture.

'It's an enchantment!' Mama exclaimed. Uncle John flung open the door to the parlour and showed us the room remade, the walls a clear, pale blue, the cornice newly plastered and gleaming white. A deep white carpet was spread on the shining floorboards and a brand-new round table and four chairs were standing against the wall. Mama's favourite chair was in its usual place, but unrecognizable; it had been re-covered with a pale-blue velvet which matched the other chair seats, the window-seat covers and curtains.

'Do you like it?' Uncle John demanded, his eyes on Mama's awestruck face. 'It was the devil's own job deciding on the colours. We nearly lost our nerve altogether and thought of writing to you to ask. But I wanted you to have a surprise.'

Mama was speechless. She could only nod.

'But see the library!' Uncle John said, as enthusiastic as a boy, and swept her from the room. All my childhood the library had stood empty. We had no volumes to fill the shelves, only the few reading primers and children's books and Mama's novels from the Chichester Book Society.

Now all that was changed. The walls glowed with the red of tooled morocco leather. There was a new great polished table in the centre of the room and a heavy chair behind it. A pair of easy chairs was on either side of the fireplace and matching little tables were within easy reach.

'This is *my* room,' Uncle John said with pride. 'But you may look at my books if you knock before entering and stay very quiet while you are in here.'

'I shall do my poor best,' Mama said faintly. 'But, John, you must have spent a fortune! And all this while Julia and I have been buying dress after dress in Bath, and renting lodgings, and giving parties, and I don't know what else!'

'I knew it was a mistake to let you go alone,' Uncle John said gloomily, and then, seeing that Mama was genuinely concerned, he gave her a quick hug and said cheerfully, 'My dear, there is plenty of money, and even if there was only a competence, you should still have a house in the town and one in the country.'

Mama smiled and sat on one of the new chairs.

'Enough of this!' Uncle John said. 'I prescribe a warm bed for this invalid and a rest until dinner, which you shall have served in your room. Upstairs with you.'

'I'll come with you, Mama,' I said. 'But then I will take the children down to Acre.'

'Of course!' Uncle John said. 'You will be wanting to change into another gown, I dare say. You may have been in that one for – oh! all morning!'

'Yes, indeed,' I said solemnly. 'And tomorrow I shall have to order some more. This one is going out of fashion even as I stand here!'

Uncle John laughed, and then I saw my mama into her bed,

where she looked glad enough to be, and went up to my room, up to the room of my girlhood and childhood where I had hidden when Richard had been angry with me and where I had dreamed my dreams and wept when I feared I was going mad.

It looked out over the back garden, over the paddock and orchard, towards the common with the high horizon of the downs beyond. The twilight was falling and the sun had gone, leaving only strip upon strip of rose, jasmine and violet clouds to show the west. An icy-cold star was low in the sky, sparkling like a snow-flake.

I swung the window open and leaned my elbows on the sill to look out. The downs were as dense as the wool of a black lamb against the shadowy sky. I could dimly see the streak of white which was the chalk on the forehead of Acre hill, pointing down to the village. The air was scentless and cold. I could feel the night-time frost coming. In the distance an early owl hooted twice.

If ever I should have felt Beatrice, it would have been then. I waited in utter stillness and silence for her coming. I waited, getting chilled in my new sleek gown, and I dared her to come. I breathed a half-silent sigh and waited for the shiver that meant she was passing near me, or for the hum in my mind which meant she was coming, or for the slide into unreasoning mindless joy which meant I had become her.

Nothing.

Nothing happened.

No shiver shook me, no humming sounded in me, no daydream overtook me. I was not ridden by hobgoblins. I was at peace. Alone, gazing at Beatrice's sky over Beatrice's land and lit by a small sliver of a rising moon, I was at peace with myself and with the ghost of her. She did not come for me wilfully. I was not haunted by an unquiet spirit. I heard her voice when I needed it. I had her strength when I could not manage alone. She was there to help me. I closed the window and turned for the door.

Bath had not done the job they had hoped: Mama had wanted me to become wholly her daughter; Uncle John had wanted me to be cured of my Lacey traits; and Richard had wanted me to be an indoor girl, off the land. They had all thought that I was haunted, possessed.

Bath had not cured me of that. Bath had taught me that it was no illness, that Beatrice's voice in my head was a gift not a terror, that I could live on Beatrice's land and be proud to be her heir, be determined to avoid her mistakes and be here to set things right. And Bath had taught me that I was a young girl of courage and looks who could give and receive love as an equal. I had set aside my foreboding about James on the journey and told my mama that I loved him and would marry him. And she and Uncle John had been pleased and proud. There was nothing to stand in the way of my happiness. There was no reason for me to fear.

I took Ralph's little wooden owl from my reticule and put it on my bedside table. Ralph's owl, Beatrice's owl, my owl. I would keep it by my bed, this symbol from Beatrice and Ralph, which was also mine.

I glanced around my room to ensure it was impeccably neat, and then I slipped down the stairs, taking the little steps enforced by my slim-cut skirt.

The children were in the kitchen finishing bowls of tea and plates of bread and butter.

'They're ready for you in Acre,' Mrs Gough told them as I came into the kitchen. 'They've a cottage opposite the church, beside the vicarage, ready for you.'

Their faces were bright around the table.

'Would you like to leave now?' I asked.

Their stools clattered on the stone-flagged floor as they pushed them back.

'Thank you for the tea, ma'am,' said Rosie Dench to Mrs Gough with an eye on the others. Nat and Jimmy knuckled their foreheads for thanks, and snatched up their caps and backed out of the kitchen as if they were not sorry to leave. They followed me out of the front door as I pulled on a cape, and out into the carriage.

'This is the drive to the old Wideacre Hall,' I said. 'You may remember it. Here are the lodge gates. To the right the lane goes to the London and Chichester Road, but we turn left for Acre.'

They gazed wide-eyed out of the windows at the newly turned fields, hard with frost now, and the spindly sticks of fruit trees.

'And this is Acre,' I said. 'On your left there, Rosie, that's the Dench cottage, which you will remember . . .' Then there was a sudden crash of noise, a great drum-roll and skirl of mad pipes; it sounded like a thousand Highlanders were coming.

'What on earth . . .' I started.

The carriage stopped with a jolt and Ralph's bright beaming face was at the window opening the door.

'Welcome!' he said. 'Welcome home, children, and welcome, Julia, for bringing them.'

The children tumbled out before the steps were down, and Ralph put out a hand to help me jump after them. All of Acre village had turned out to greet the children, and there was a great bonfire stacked for lighting on the village green, with a trestle-table laid with food near by. There were two pipers, their cheeks blown out like clowns, to pipe the children home, and Matthew Merry was giving them the beat on a drum.

'Ralph!' I said, laughing but near to tears. 'Oh, Ralph! I feel as if I have been away all my life as well!'

Before the eyes of all of Acre Ralph pulled me towards him, put his arms around me and hugged the breath out of me, saying very softly in my ear, 'Julia Lacey, you are a darling girl and I am gladder to see you than I had thought possible.'

'Mr Megson! Miss Lacey!' came a voice over the noise of the pipes and the drum, and Ralph let me go, without the least hurry, and Dr Pearce stood before us. 'Really, Miss Lacey,' he said reprovingly. But then he could not help but smile too. 'Oh, Julia! This is very well done!' he said, and he took both my hands in his and drew me to him for a kiss on both cheeks.

I looked past him at the village people welcoming their children. Rosie was surrounded by Clary and all the Dench family. The little ones were especially fascinated, fingering the new dress and cloak of their half-sister; and Clary's pale mother was there, the baby on her hip, hugging Rosie and crying to have her safe home again.

The Brewer family was hugging Nat and exclaiming at the dark stripes still marking his skin. Only little Jimmy was alone. He had been a pauper in the village, one of the first taken. Ralph left my side and put an arm around his shoulder.

'I'm Ralph Megson,' I heard him say gently. 'I badly need a young lad to work with me. A quick lad, one that's no fool. D'you think we'd suit?'

'Oh, aye,' Jimmy said, beaming up at Ralph's face. 'Oh, aye, Mr Megson, sir. I'm the very lad for you, sir.'

Ralph nodded, and clapped the boy gently on the shoulder. 'Let's eat!' he called out loud.

The pipes and drum stopped as short as if they had been silenced by a curtain falling, and Matthew cast aside his drum and came over to me.

'W-W-Well done, Julia!' he said, and he hugged me and kissed me until Ted Tyacke appeared from nowhere and swept me into his arms in a great hug which knocked my bonnet sideways.

Everyone moved towards the table and seated themselves on stools and looked expectantly towards Dr Pearce's gate. Clary came out carrying a flaming torch and beckoned to Jimmy Dart.

'Light the bonfire,' she said with a smile. 'You've no kin here now, but every one of us is your family. We built this for you, for the three of you, to welcome you home to a warm fire and good food. May Acre always be warm and hospitable to the three of you.'

Jimmy stepped forward, his sharp little face serious, and took the torch carefully from Clary and walked towards the great heap of wood. It was coated with pitch, and at the touch of the flames it flared up with a great whoosh so that Jimmy jumped back and flung the torch on to it.

Clary turned to me and put a hand around my waist. 'Safe home?' she asked.

Our walk together in the moonlit garden when I had been so

afraid of leaving Wideacre and yet too afraid to stay seemed like a lifetime ago.

'Safe home,' I confirmed. 'Is all well with you, Clary?'

Her smile was the contented smile of a woman who is well loved and who knows it. 'Aye,' she said. 'Come and sit down, and tell me all about Bath.'

And in the gathering dusk of a cold winter light we made merry on the village green of Acre. They celebrated because they had their children home. And I celebrated because I was safe home myself, because I was loved by a good man, because I was loved by a whole village of people and because I was a Lacey on her land again.

My mama was not fully well for two more weeks, and the weather was cold and hard until the middle of March, so she was well content to stay indoors beside a warm fire.

I was well content too, for although I rode out in all the daylight hours and came home chilled to the bone and very often wet through, I had the joy of seeing the colour come back to her cheeks, and for myself there was the delight at being back on my land.

Even my lingering anxiety about my parting with James was removed early in the month when I came home to find Uncle John and Mama toasting crumpets at the parlour fire and smiling at some secret.

'Don't tease her,' Mama said after I had demanded to know the joke. 'Tell her about your visitor today.'

'Oh, yes,' Uncle John said. He smiled at my interested expression and went over to the parlour window and stood behind Mama's chair in the window embrasure. 'Guess who came to see me today?'

'The Mayor of London!' I said promptly.

'No,' Uncle John said. 'More important.'

'Thomas Paine,' I said.

'No,' Uncle John said. 'But just as radical.'

'Someone I know?' I asked.

PHILIPPA GREGORY

'Someone you know well,' he said. 'An intimate acquaintance.'

I flushed a little and I could hear my heart thudding. 'Anyone from Bath?' I asked as casually as I could.

'Yes,' Uncle John said.

'Was it Marianne Fortescue?' I asked with a weak attempt at deception.

'Pshaw!' said Uncle John. 'Don't be missish, Julia.'

'Was it James?' I asked.

Mama laughed and clapped her hands.

'Yes,' Uncle John said. 'He came in his curricle and pair and he would not stay for dinner. He was running an errand for his papa in London; and for some reason he did not explain to me, the quickest way to London from Bristol is now via Chichester.'

I was hot up to my ears. 'What did he say?' I asked. 'How did he look? Why did you not send for me? Did he see much of Wideacre? Did he say if he liked it?'

Uncle John struck the answers off his fingers. 'One: he said that he wanted to marry you and that he loves you and that he wants the legal business for the marriage to start at once. Two: he looked well enough to me.'

'He looked sorry that you were not here,' Mama said. 'He really loves you, Julia.'

I nodded and dropped my eyes down to look at my hands in my lap.

'Three,' Uncle John said pedantically: 'I did not send for you because he could stop for only an hour, and no one had the least clue where you might be. Four: he saw a little of Wideacre because he drove me into Acre. He met Ralph Megson and saw the village. He asked after the children from Bath, but they were all out working, except Rosie Dench, and she fell on his neck and blessed him as her saviour. And five, and one of the most interesting things, I think: he told me that if you were serious about developing the profit-sharing scheme, he was prepared to put his money into it, and that if the two of you were to be married, that he would want to have his country home on Wideacre.'

'Oh,' I said blankly.

Mama held out her arms to me, and I slid to my knees before her and hugged her tight. 'Oh, my darling, I'm so very glad,' she said softly. 'You are a lucky girl indeed.'

'Yes,' I said. 'Oh, yes.'

Mama smoothed my hair. 'There, there,' she said vaguely. 'When did he say he will come back?'

'He has to stay in London for two days,' Uncle John said. 'Then he has to take ship for Belgium. His father's trade is expanding into Europe, and James has to make something of a tour. I promised that you might receive his letters, but he says he cannot give you an address to reply to. He does say he will be back in this country in eight or nine weeks. Between then and now his papa's lawyers and mine will draw up your marriage contracts and you can be married whenever you wish.'

I sat bolt upright at once. 'As soon as possible,' I said.

'Not so missish?' Mama said, smiling to Uncle John.

'No,' he replied.

'You will need at least two months to get your clothes ready, and then there is also the house to be built,' Mama said. 'Even if you want a quiet wedding out of this house, there will still be a very great deal to be done. Unless you would want to be married in Bath, Julia? Or in Bristol?'

'Here,' I said without a moment's doubt. 'Here in our parish church with a party on the green afterwards. Here, where we are going to live and be happy for always.'

I smiled as I spoke, but that odd shiver was cold down my spine. Everything was going to be all right. James would come back from Belgium, would come straight to me here on Wideacre. We would find a good site to build our house – I had half a dozen in mind already! – and we would marry. There was no obstacle, for both families were contented with the match. More than that, it was an ideal match! Bristol money and Sussex land. In James I knew I was giving the village a master who would spend all his time and money on furthering the schemes which Ralph and I had already planned so far into the future. There was nothing to give me unease in this.

And yet I feared in my heart that it would never happen.

18

'I am writing a letter to Richard,' Mama said to me that evening. 'You'll want to write him a note to go in it?'

'Yes,' I said. Indeed it was time.

I had written regularly to Richard from Bath, but he had never replied. His work on the hall and in the village was sufficient excuse.

Then, when the rebuilding of the Acre cottages was well under way, he had gone back to university. I knew he would have heard from Uncle John that I had made many friends in Bath, and that he would have heard of James Fortescue. But I did not know whether he would have guessed how far matters had gone between us.

I was in love, and I felt careless. I was happy and I could not believe that anyone could begrudge me such happiness. Richard's open enmity towards me before I left for Bath seemed part of the past when I had been so frightened and so distressed because the whole world seemed to be conspiring against me. I could forgive him his greed about the estate. We were both grown now, and I was engaged to marry the best man I had ever known. I felt able to be generous with Richard. So I wrote him a light-hearted note which said with certainty that I knew he would be happy to hear the news that I was engaged to marry James Fortescue. And – best news of all, as far as I was concerned – that James had seen and liked Wideacre and wanted us to live on the estate.

I said little more about him. I wanted Richard and James to be friends. I had enough sense – even in my dizzy mood of courtship – to remember that Richard never liked to be anything but first.

I thought that if they had a chance to meet without prejudgement on either side, they might be friends. In any case, I could not write at length, for Ralph Megson was waiting for me down at Three Gate Meadow where we had wild garlic growing in the very field we were ploughing for corn.

Ever since my return from Bath, I had been out on the land from morning till dinner-time, checking the crops, checking the animals, organizing hedging teams, ditching teams and bands of women to weed and clear the fields. The roads were too muddy for anything but horseback, and Uncle John wanted to stay in-doors to watch over Mama's convalescence. The work of the estate was left almost entirely to me – and to Ralph Megson.

He taught me. He taught me like a man handing over the reins of a most valuable carriage and pair to a novice. He never once met me in the lane, or at a barn, or just leaning on the bridge and watching the Fenny flow below me, without telling me something about the land, about the northerly movement of the birds, or about the weather we might expect.

I was in training as an apprentice squire, and Ralph was a stringent master. He took me for long punishing rides all around the estate, teaching me the name of every field, showing me every sort of fungus or disease in the woods, naming the weeds which seemed to be shooting up even as we watched and arguing with me, constantly arguing, about who should own the land and the rights they had on it.

We argued about poachers, we argued about gleaners, we argued about payment in kind, about house servants, about the rights of tenants. Every imposition a landlord legally makes on his workers to gain a little extra from them, Ralph opposed. He would have resisted every claim of a landlord, until in impatience one day I accused him of not being our farm manager at all, but owing all his loyalty to the village.

'Oh, yes,' he said, quite unperturbed. 'I am working for the good of Acre. I care nothing for the benefit of the Laceys.'

I gaped at him. We were riding around the back of the corn-fields on the common, checking that they had been properly fenced, for the common was overrun with deer that not even the appetite of Acre could keep down.

'We pay your wages,' I retorted. I should have been more sensible than to use such an argument with Ralph – it was simply giving him the victory.

'Don't be silly, Miss Julia,' he said gently. 'There aren't wages minted that could buy my loyalty against my own people. You know that.'

'But why did you agree to work for my Uncle John?' I demanded. 'He employed you as the Lacey manager.'

'And I work as the Lacey manager,' Ralph said. 'The Laceys' future depends on giving the land to the people who live on it and work it.'

We turned our horses away from the field and trotted down the broad sweep of sand which cuts across the common. It was overgrown with bracken, and heather was encroaching on the edges.

'This must be cut back,' Ralph said, indicating the dead-looking heather clumps and the brown bracken. 'It will soon be spreading over, and if you have a heather fire, it will blaze out of control. I'll have a couple of men out on it before the end of the week.'

I nodded. 'Don't turn the talk, Mr Megson,' I said. 'You know that Uncle John's plan was profit-sharing. There was never any suggestion that there should be outright gifts from the estate. You cannot imagine that my uncle is going to give the Wideacre estate to Acre village.'

Ralph smiled his dark slow smile. 'Hardly,' he said. 'He's a good man, but he was born to wealth and he knows the value of his land. He won't be giving anything away.'

'What are your hopes, then?' I demanded.

'I think *you* will give it,' said Ralph as if it were the simplest thing in the world.

He turned his horse's head down the track towards the park and set it at a canter towards the little jump over the newly repaired wall. I gaped at him and nearly lost my balance as Misty followed his lead and popped over the wall without a touch of command from me.

'I will?' I asked, coming up alongside him. 'Why should you think that I would give Wideacre away? After all you have said about Lacey women loving the land!'

'Aye,' said Ralph calmly, and then he chuckled to see my rising colour. 'Don't be so vexed, Miss Julia,' he said comfortably. 'I thought you were no true Lacey when I saw you trying to throw away your share of the estate and make yourself into something you are not. But the ideas I have for you and Wideacre are not the worries of a young girl. They are the way that I think the whole country will have to go if it is to avoid cruelty and great sorrow.'

We turned the horses for home down the bridle-way under the great smooth beech branches, their hooves squelching in the mire.

'Now, look,' he said, suddenly serious, 'we live in a cruel world. You saw the poverty in Acre, you don't need me to tell you of the harshness of this world. That whole village could have died of starvation and no one would have cared. There were numberless unnecessary deaths – young babies and old people, dying in cold weather, dying of little ailments because their bodies were too frail to take the burden of illness. You know that. You saw it.'

I nodded. I had seen it in Acre. It was true.

'It is not just Acre,' Ralph said, his voice low. 'There are whole parts of this country where the same thing is happening. Sometimes it is an accident – a crop fails and there is no food, an incompetent squire and no charity. Sometimes it is worse. There are places north of the border where the landlords have decided they want their estates cleared of people – and they have done just that.'

'Cleared?' I asked, challenging that odd, ambiguous word.

'They want sheep-runs,' Ralph said. 'Or deer for game. Or, nearer to Wideacre, they want a pretty view from the parlour windows. If there is a village in the way, they simply pull it down, or burn it.'

'And the villagers?' I asked.

'Some of them leave when they are asked,' Ralph said. 'They became vagrants then, for no parish will take them in. Some of them refuse to go and try to take the great landlords to court.' He smiled mirthlessly. 'That's a painful process,' he said. 'The law is drafted by landlords, the courts are ordered by landlords and the judges are landlords. It's likely they'd hand down a judgement against themselves.'

I said nothing. I had heard Grandpapa Havering crowing at sentencing a man to death for stealing to feed his starving family. I knew what Ralph meant. And I had seen some of the consequences of the way we chose to live in the streets behind the Fish Quay.

'Some of them refuse to go altogether,' he said. 'I've heard of people dying in their homes, burned alive when the villages are fired. And of ugly pitched battles between starving people and armed bailiffs. It happens, Julia. It is the power of the landlord. That is why I wanted guarantees from you and Richard.'

'I would never let it happen on Wideacre!' I said fiercely.

'You're not perfect,' Ralph said simply. 'Your young man, James Fortescue, might suddenly want to try his hand at modern farming, or picturesque landscaping. Or you might find yourself short of money and decide to sell off in packages, or break your agreements with Acre and make them work for day wages again. You cannot tell what you would do when you have the power to do as you please.'

I waited. Ralph was leading me somewhere, and I could not yet see where he was taking me.

'You must rid yourself of the power,' he said solemnly. 'You must not be satisfied with John's scheme of sharing the profits, and perhaps the tenants becoming wealthy enough to buy long leases. That would take years and years and years, and perhaps be unworkable at the last. It only needs a change of heart by one Lacey, and then the whole thing is lost. I want to see changes made at once. I want to see it done in my lifetime. I want you to be the Lacey who does it. You will return the land to Acre, and everyone in the village will have a right to decide what crops are grown and what plans are made. No one will take a wage, they will all share in the profit. And your only fortune will be the share you take in the profits. The whole of the estate will be given back to the people who had it before the Laceys, to run as they know how, for their own security.'

I looked at Ralph blankly. 'Is that what you want me to do?' I asked incredulously.

Ralph beamed at me. 'Aye,' he said. 'Mad scheme, ain't it?'

And he clicked his horse into a trot, as though he had not a care in the world, and slumped in his saddle as he does since he cannot rise to the pace because of his legs. I cantered behind him and caught him up.

'It would never work,' I said.

Ralph grinned at me.

'They would farm the land out,' I said. 'They would forget to rest it. They would plant only vegetable crops for themselves. They would not have the capital to buy good seed-corn, to buy new animals for stock.'

'Aye,' said Ralph. 'You'd have to put up the capital to make it work.'

'Why should I?' I demanded. 'Why should anyone choose to chance their money for a scheme which might not even work?'

Ralph wheeled his horse around suddenly so that it blocked my path. He looked down on me from its high back and his face was very dark and very stern. 'Because there are things which matter more than two per cent on Consols,' he said. 'Because you have been a privileged person in a country where there are people going hungry and you know there can be no peace for you. Because you know that to be one of the lucky ones when there is poverty all around is not to be lucky at all. It is to be miserable without even seeing your own misery. For it leaves you with a choice either to rejoice that you are doing well, when you know there are others who are doing badly, most badly, or to harden your heart. There are those who learn to harden their hearts so well that they can actually forget what has happened. They teach themselves to believe that they are rich through their own cleverness, or as a just reward for their virtues. They force themselves to think that the poor are thus because they are stupid, and deserve their poverty. And when that has happened, you have a country divided into two. And both sides are most ugly.'

I gasped. I could not keep up with Ralph. I had heard the complacency in the voices of the wealthy, I had heard the desperation in the voices of the poor. I wanted to belong to neither. 'It would never work,' I said uncertainly.

Ralph gave a little 'Pfui!' of disdain and turned his horse for home again. It was growing darker with the speed of a spring evening and the wood-pigeons were cooing lovingly, longingly. The rooks were flying late, crossing the grey sky with beakfuls of twigs. The blackbird sang as clear as a flute.

'It would never work,' I said again.

'It's not working now, is it?' Ralph said lightly, as if the statement hardly merited an answer. 'Thousands dying of want in the countryside, hundreds dying of dirt and drink and hunger in the towns. You can hardly call that "working", can you?'

We came on to the drive while I was still puzzling for a reply, and minutes later we had reined in at the garden gate of the Dower House. Ralph would not come in but sat on his horse while Jem came out into the lane and helped me down.

'You are not . . . angry, Mr Megson?' I asked tentatively, watching the darkness of his face under his tricorne hat.

At once his face cleared and he smiled at me. 'Lord love you for a fool, Julia Lacey,' he said easily. 'So full of your own importance that you think you are responsible for the Norman Conquest and for the abuse of the lords of the land ever since. Nay, I'm not angry, Miss Vanity. And if I was, it would not be with you.' He paused and scrutinized me, his head on one side. '*And* furthermore, if I was, you would be quite able to tell me to keep my ill humour to myself, wouldn't you?'

I hesitated at that. I had gone to Bath as a girl who was used to watching Richard's face for the warning signs of his displeasure.

But I had come back a woman with confidence in herself and in her gifts. I looked at Ralph and I smiled at him and narrowed my eyes. 'I think I could,' I said.

'You surely could,' Ralph said, and grinned at me in his democratic, disrespectful fashion. Then he leaned down low and pulled me to his horse's side, and before the parlour window of the Dower House he gave me a kiss on the cheeks as if I were a serving maid to be kissed in the lane. Then he straightened up, tipped his hat to me and trotted off down the drive.

I took one horror-struck survey of the Dower House windows, to check that Mama had indeed *not* seen, made one fearful scowling face at Jem to wipe the grin from his face at my discomfort, then I picked up the trailing hem of my riding habit and ran indoors with a ripple of laughter caught inside me at Ralph Megson's impertinence.

I was so very busy that spring that if I had wanted to mope around, missing James, I would not have been able to do so. Uncle John and the Chichester lawyers had drawn up a set of contracts between the workers, the tenant farmers and the Wideacre estate. But I wanted to be there when they signed the contracts. It should be clear to them that I was giving my word as they were giving theirs. I spent many hours in the library with John, making sure that I understood the agreements we were making, the length of the individual leases, the proportion of the wages which were to be paid into the common fund, the time for repayment of loans for seed and equipment to tenant farmers and the interest we decided to charge. Often it was I who checked the lease through and exclaimed, 'But, Uncle John! In addition to his debt to us, this tenant has to pay the poor rate and tithes. He has too costly a burden; we must make the debt run longer or he will not make enough to keep himself and a family in the first few years!' Then John would recheck the figures and nod and say, 'You are right, Julia. But it cuts back Wideacre profits.'

Uncle John and Ralph and I also had long planning sessions in the library with the maps of Wideacre spread before us. Ralph understood the land and could say what crops would grow and what would not take to the chalky Sussex earth. But John had read much about modern agricultural experiments and had lived on Wideacre during its prime and could speak about crops. I stayed quiet, but I kept my eyes and ears open, and I learned all I could during those friendly, easy talks.

Ralph and I were the ones out on the land, up on the downs checking the sheep, through the village checking for hardship as the cold weather grew damp and the frosts melted and became slushy and chill, riding around the lanes checking the hedges and the ditches. Sheep-proof and flood-proof, we wanted the land to be, and everything in readiness for the ploughing.

All the equipment had to be bought new. What had been left after the ruin of the Laceys after the last harvest had been sold or bartered for pitiful amounts of food during the years of Acre's poverty. We had to buy new ploughs, new work-horses, new seed. A whole generation of young men had to be trained to drive a horse and follow a plough, for they had never seen it done by their fathers, and they had never been plough-boys themselves.

'It can't be done!' John would sometimes say to me when I came home tired out from a day's riding and with a list of things which had to be ready before the spring weather came and set the land in its cycle of growth. 'It cannot be done this year!'

But, from somewhere, I had a great fund of confidence. I would smile at John not like a sixteen-year-old green girl but like someone far older and far wiser, and I would say, 'It can be done, Uncle John. Mr Megson thinks so too, and I am sure it will be all right. Acre is working all the daylight hours to be ready in time for sowing. It *can* be done. And you, and I, and Mr Megson, and Acre are doing it.'

As if the planning and the preparation for sowing were not enough, the flock of sheep Uncle John had bought were not hardy and took against the lower fields that we thought would suit them. We lost two or three lambs, and even a ewe, which was more serious. After that Ralph said that, cost what it may, the animals would have to lamb under cover.

The barn they had used in autumn was too small for the whole flock, and it was too far for the shepherd to go every day. All the old barns had been pulled down years ago, the wood taken for firewood and the stones for building. So we had to have the flock in the Dower House stable block, with beams thrown across the yard and a loose thatch over the top. The smell was appalling – and the noise they made! Mama said that she would never again read poems about the life of a shepherdess with any pleasure.

'Hey Nonny No,' John said at dinner, and grinned at her.

We were not like Quality, that spring.

'We are pioneers,' Mama said; and I loved her for understanding that working Wideacre in this way felt less like farming an estate in the heart of England and more like building a new country, a fresh country where one might forget the mistakes of the past and try to make something new and clean.

'Squire Julia,' Clary Dench called me ironically when I met her in Acre lane. She had taken her father's dinner to him and was coming home with a jug and a plate under her arm. He had been working on the ditches and Clary too was speckled with the sandy mud.

'You'd better curtsy,' I said dourly. I looked little smarter than she did. I was wearing my cream riding habit, but it had lost its early style and was now creased and crumpled with a darn on the skirt where I had taken a tumble and ripped it. I was on foot, leading two plough-horses down to the village to be shod and for the plough-boys to practise driving a team. Clary and I both walked awkwardly, with the glutinous mud sticking to our boots. Her boots were older, the soles patched and re-patched. But when we were both muddy up to our eyebrows, one could tell little difference between the young lady of Quality and the village girl.

Clary laughed. 'You look a sight!' she said.

'I know,' I said ruefully. 'I can hardly remember Bath now, and it's not been that long.'

She nodded. 'Remember the time when the village was bad?' she asked. 'It's not an easy life now, no one could say it was. But at least we can see where we're going. This spring is going to bring the sowing, and then there'll be haymaking and harvest-time. There will be a proper harvest home. All the old parties and fair-days will come back. My ma and pa can't talk of nothing else but the sowing and the maying.'

'Maying!' I said, stopping the horses with difficulty. People like to think of the great plough-horses as gentle giants, but I had led these two down from the Dower House stables and I could attest that they were hulking idiots without a listening ear between them, and without a brain in their heads.

'Woah! you two,' I said crossly. 'What happens at the maying, Clary?'

'It's the Whitsun festival,' she said, 'when all the sowing is done and the early spring work is over. It's a celebration of the spring. All the young men and women, all the lads and maids go up on to the downs before it is light, before dawn. They cut branches of the hawthorn tree and they dress them with ribbons, and they see the sunrise and welcome the spring in.'

'Oh, yes,' I said. It sounded rather tame. 'Is that all, Clary?'

She gave me a sideways smiling glance. We had both grown up from the little girls who fought in the woods. 'Well,' she said, 'it's no accident that there's a lot of marriages six months after that day. There's a lot of courting that goes on while the sun is coming up, you know, Julia. And there are no elders there, and no one thinks the worse of anyone who slips away up on the downs. No one watches and no one counts, because it is the maying, you see.'

I smiled a little. 'Oh,' I said. I was a child compared to Clary, who had helped at childbirth and had wept already over a still-born babe which would have been another sister for her. Clary and all the Acre children knew all about lust and birthing and dying, while Richard and I in the Dower House were naïve beginners. But I had been in James's arms, and felt his mouth on mine, and longed for his touch again. And I had Beatrice's know-ledge and Beatrice's desires in my head. So I gave Clary a little smile and said, 'Oh,' which acknowledged that I was not squire, nor Miss Julia, but a maid like her with love to give and a longing to receive it.

'Would you come out with us?' she asked invitingly. 'There'd be no harm. Many lasses just come out to watch the sunrise, and to cut the branches and take the spring home to their families.'

'I should like that,' I said.

'I'll tell 'em you'll come out with us,' said Clary. 'Maybe they'll make you the Queen of the May. And you tell your ma and your Uncle John that the village will take a week for the festival. At least some days.'

'I will,' I said. 'But what happens?'

'It's the festival of misrule,' Clary said. I turned the horses' heads and she took one of the reins to help me lead them towards the forge. 'Everyone dresses up in costume and there is a feast. The farmers with money give some when the band come around and demand a fee. The people who have no money give food for the feast. The Wideacre people go over to Havering, or to Single-ton, or to Ambersham, and wherever they go, there is a party and dancing and free drink and free food. Then next year we have the other villages back to us. It's been so long since Acre could dance that this year it is to be our turn.'

'And who is the Queen of the May?' I asked.

'She's queen of the feast,' said Clary. 'She wears a crown of hawthorn blossoms and she brings in the spring, and she sets the plough going, and the dancers dancing. And if I tell 'em all that you are coming, it will likely be you!'

I beamed. 'Tell them I'll come, then, Clary, for it sounds such fun. And I'll tell Mama and Uncle John that there will be a holi-day.'

Clary nodded and led the horse into Ned Smith's yard, then waved goodbye to me and went home to her own cottage. I stayed only to see the plough-boys were waiting to take the horses when they had been shod and trudged home alone up the lane. I would be late for dinner again, but during those days of readying the land for the plough I was hardly ever on time.

*

We did not sow until quite late, the ground was so hard from the frost, and then so wet. But Ralph and John and I had to pick a day. 'Let it be Miss Julia's birthday, for luck!' Ralph said. So we told the village when it would begin, and then crossed our fingers for luck that the village which had been away from the plough-share and away from sowing for so long would remember how the work went, and would forget about the anger of the year they sowed pain and reaped a riot.

The wind had warmed overnight and the sun was shining. All the wisps of cloud and the lumpy sleet thunderheads had been torn aside and rushed over the head of the downs in a hurrying breeze which smelled of salt from the sea. Chased off like a scattered flock, they went, and when I looked out of my bedroom window in the morning, the sky was a clear opalescent blue, innocent of shadow, and the sun a warm spring yellow.

'A happy birthday to you, and it is a good drying day,' said Mrs Gough in the kitchen as I went in to beg a last cup of coffee on my way to the stable. She was thinking of linen and I was thinking of land, but our satisfaction was mutual.

'Yes,' I said. 'We're sowing today. I must be off.'

Her head came up from her work; she was patting the breakfast rolls into shape. 'I'll send Jem down with your breakfast to the field if you wish,' she said with unusual kindness. 'I dare say you won't want to come back once the work has started.'

'Thank you, Mrs Gough,' I said, surprised.

She gave me one of her rare smiles. 'I hear all around you're working hard on the land, Miss Julia. They do say you're as good as Miss Beatrice was when she was a girl. I don't hold with women owning land, but I know you're getting it in good heart for Master Richard.'

I could have argued with that. I could have said that I was getting it in good heart for a dowry for James. Or I could have said that I was getting it in good heart to hand back to the people who worked it. But in truth, in those days, I was working in the same way that a sheepdog gathers the flock: I could not be myself and do anything else. It was as natural for me to farm the land as it was for me to breathe. So I held my tongue and just smiled at Mrs Gough and slipped out of the back door.

All at once the sight and smell of Wideacre tumbled over me like a spring flood over a waterfall. Before me the cedar tree showed the tiniest hint of lime green about its lower branches, and the rising sap oozed at the cut in its trunk where we had lopped a dangerous branch. I could hear a thrush singing, and from behind the house came the insistent coo of a wood-pigeon, trying out his voice after the season of silence. Behind the cedar tree was the paddock and the buds on the apple tree were as small as rice grains but scarlet with promise. Beyond the paddock the earth of the old meadow turned cornfield was white with frost, but away from the lee of the hedges I could see the weeds growing green, and beyond it and to my left was the common, rolling as sweet and free as wind-fetched breakers on an empty sea, yellow-brown with last year's bracken and just a promise of green in the sleepy valleys.

To my right, southwards, were the high smooth folds of the downs, like green-velvet shoulders shrugging off the uneven borders of our fields, and I knew, although I could not see them, that the flock with the new lambs would be out on the fresh grass today. I stepped out into the garden and gulped in the scents, the sounds, the warmth of Wideacre on a sweet spring morning, and I felt my shoulders drop, and my lips smile, and my face turn blindly, like a winter mole, to the sunlight.

Minutes I stood there, half dazed and then – above the birdsong, above the pulse that was my own heart beating (though it sounded like a heart in the very land itself) – I heard a high sweet humming as if the waking earth were calling to me to come out and plough and sow and make it grow.

Ralph was already down at the field. We were starting with Three Gate Meadow, and then we would split the sowers into teams and ride among them to check the supply of seed-corn, the strength of the new ploughs and the ability of lads who had never ploughed a furrow before and men who had last ploughed fifteen years ago. I turned my mare towards Acre and Three

Gate Meadow, with no one to break the daze upon me which came from the sudden sunshine and the promise of the day and the magic of Wideacre which was part of my blood and bone.

I slid from my mare's back and tied her to the gate. The sowers were in the field, and their great bags filled with seed-corn bulged before them like the fat bellies of pregnant women. They had chosen Jimmy Dart – the lost son of Acre – to take the plough for the first wobbly furrow for luck. As I walked through the gate, I saw the plough coming towards me, his slight city-starved body hanging on to the handles for dear life, his weight too light to keep it straight.

'Speed the plough!' I called, and everyone waiting around the field turned and smiled at me and called, 'Speed the plough!' in return.

Clary was by the gate, a great bag of seed-corn over her shoulder and she gestured to me to take it from her. 'Happy birthday, Julia!' she said sweetly. 'I've been waiting for you. You sow the first seeds. Everyone 'ud like it. It'd be good luck. Take a handful of seeds and just scatter them out in a big sweep.'

I half staggered under the weight of the bag and waited until the first furrow had been cut. The great horses bent their necks to pull the plough, knowing the work better than Jimmy. I stepped into the furrow behind him and dug deep into the bag that was weighing me down. The seeds stuck, moist and pale, to my hands and I threw them in a great flinging sweep out to the very boundaries of Wideacre so the whole green world should grow at my bidding and there should never be hunger on my land again.

Again and again I cast the seed in generous prodigal fistfuls, up to the sky as if I wanted the greedy wheeling seagulls to share in the bounty of the land so that there should be no crying – not even the crying of gulls on this day. In my head was a great sweet singing as the seed flew out in acres of silver and fell on the deep thick mud. I felt so strong, and so magical, that I half expected it to sprout as it fell.

I hardly heard the sound of hooves in the lane, I was so

absorbed with keeping my balance on the heavy new-turned earth, and with the fascination of the damp sticky seed-bag and the sight of the flung seed. But then I heard someone call my name, and I looked around to the gate. There at the entrance to the field, sliding from his horse, with his black hair all curly and windblown and his eyes bright, was Richard.

I walked towards him in a dream, my hands still full of seed. He seemed to be the centre of the world whose heartbeat I had heard in my head this morning, his feet planted as surely as a rooted tree in the safe earth of Wideacre, his head warmed by the Wideacre sun.

The bedraggled muddy hem of my riding habit flapped around me as I staggered across the furrows, and the mud of Wideacre was caked on my boots. Richard reached out a soft white hand to me and drew me towards him, without saying a word. With the eyes of all of Acre upon us and with the plough-boys stopped to watch, I turned my face up to Richard like a common girl and let him kiss me long and passionately under the spring sky.

His arms held me tight to him and I was enveloped by his driving cape, which swirled around us. Sheltered by it, half hidden by it, I put my hands inside his cape and around his hard hot back, and clung to him as though I were drowning in the river. His head came down harder and I opened my lips under his and tasted his mouth on mine.

As if that taste had been poison, I suddenly leaped backward, struggling out of the folds of his cape, shrugging off his grip. Heedless of what he would think I put the muddy back of my hand to my mouth and rubbed hard, wiping away the taste of Richard's tongue.

'Don't, Richard!' I exclaimed and there was no magic between us, and no mindless delight left in me at all.

Richard's face was as black as thunder. 'I got your note . . .' he started.

But then there was a warning call from Clary at the gate. 'Look out, Julia, 'tis your ma!'

I stumbled back another pace and looked guiltily down the

lane. Uncle John's curricle was turning from the drive into Acre lane and coming towards us, but I guessed they would have seen nothing more than Richard and I exchanging a hug of greeting. I coloured scarlet in a great wave of shame. I could not raise my eyes from the ground. I could not look around the field for fear of someone beaming at me, or winking at Richard. Even if my mama had not seen, it was not fear of her disapproval which made me recoil from Richard. I had jumped back from his embrace because his touch – which I had once loved so well – seemed suddenly heavy with evil.

I did not look at him. What he was thinking, I could not imagine. And when I thought of James, and of myself as his promised bride, I felt hot and kept my eyes down.

Not Richard. He always had a way of sailing through scrapes and he turned from me and strode up to the curricle. 'Mama-Aunt!' he said with delight, and leaped up to the step to give her a hearty kiss. 'And Papa!' he said, and stretched across my mama to shake John's hand. 'You will think me undutiful,' he said, 'but as I rode towards home I saw some people coming this way and they told me it was the first sowing day. I would not have missed it for the world. And here in the middle of the field was Julia, casting corn away as if she were feeding seagulls.'

Uncle John laughed. 'We came to see the ceremonial ploughing, but I see we are too late.' He nodded at Ralph, who came to the gate to greet them. 'Good day, Mr Megson. Here is Richard home on a surprise visit for Julia's birthday and to see your sowing.'

Ralph nodded to Mama and to Richard. I knew him well enough by now to know he could be trusted never to breathe a word that I had fled into Richard's arms as if we were acknowledged lovers. No one in Acre would ever betray me on purpose. Only Ralph knew that I was affianced to another man and Richard should be no closer than arm's length, but Ralph of all people would not care for that. I moved towards the plough and scowled at Ralph to warn him against teasing me. I might as well tell the sun to stop shining.

'Hussy,' he said in a provocative whisper, and I flamed scarlet again and frowned at him.

No one now would expect me to take my breakfast in the field with the sowers and the plough-boys but I was stubborn. 'You go on home, Richard,' I said pleasantly. 'You will have things you wish to unpack. Have breakfast with Mama and Uncle John. I will be home as soon as ever I can, but I have promised to do a full day's work here. If you want to come out again, I shall either be here or in Oak Tree Meadow. I cannot leave the ploughing now it has just started, there is too much for one person to watch alone. Mr Megson cannot be left with the work like that.'

Uncle John nodded his approval, but I saw the shadow cross Richard's face. 'I know everything comes second to the Wideacre crop,' he said.

'It is not that,' I said softly. 'It is just that I promised to work here today and I cannot break my promise.'

'Well, come home as soon as you are done,' Mama said tactfully, 'and do be home in time for an early dinner, Julia. Mrs Gough is planning something special for you.'

'I will, I will,' I said, smiling.

Richard came close to help me up into the saddle. 'I shall be waiting for you,' he said softly. 'You are mine.'

I knew it was wrong.

I knew he was wrong to say it and I should contradict him at once. I should remind him that the childhood betrothal had not been a serious wish of his for many years now. It was me who had clung to that game long after it should have been outgrown. The last time we had been together he had not behaved anything like a lover.

I let it go for now. The shock of seeing him at the gate when the world seemed so lush and fresh and fertile, when I had seeds still clinging to my hands like some spring goddess, had been too much for my thin veneer of town gloss. If he had wanted to lie with me in the furrow then and there, I would have done so. I was as amorous as this morning's wood-pigeon, as naturally fertile as the new-turned soil. I was a Lacey woman on Wideacre, and Lacey women care for nothing more than love and the land. This morning, with Richard waiting for me at the side of a newly ploughed field, I could not resist.

But we would not always meet at a field gate. As I rode home, I knew there would be words between Richard and me and that when we spoke, I should use the wisdom I had learned in these last few months. I should use that wisdom to defend myself against him. I was not the child who had left for Bath, left her home to be run by someone else, frightened of herself and of the land, and ready to give the land away as carelessly as a shanty cottage. I was not the child who feared her own nature, who feared male authority, who feared everything.

I had stood against the most fashionable doctor in Bath and shrugged aside his influence as if he were an outgrown toy. I had raised my voice in the best modiste's shop in Bath and felt my cheeks blaze with anger. I had looked into the eyes of the man I loved and learned that he was just an ordinary man, with ordinary failings; and loved him just the same. I was no longer Richard's plaything for the bidding or the breaking. I might have been in a dream of pleasure with seeds in my hands this morning, but this afternoon I would be my own self.

I cantered home in an easy stride with the dusk falling around me and a clear sky above me promising good weather for a working day tomorrow. Behind me were two fields, nearly ploughed and sown, under the sickle moon, and around me were acres of land waiting for the plough under the cold skies.

I tossed the reins of my mare to Jem and made my way indoors and up to my bedroom. Stride was crossing the hall as I went upstairs. 'You've not long before dinner, Miss Julia,' he said warningly.

I gave him a grimace and put my hands together in a mock prayer. 'Stride, have a little pity,' I said. 'I have been in the fields since early morning. If you want to eat Wideacre bread again, you must treat the sowers well. Please delay dinner for me for half an hour so I can soak in a bath and get the stiffness out of my body. I feel like an old lady.'

It was another measure of the way things had changed that Stride did not scold me as he would a naughty child late for dinner. Instead he looked at the grandfather clock at the foot of the stairs and said, 'Very well, Miss Julia, I will tell Lady Lacey and Dr MacAndrew that dinner will be delayed.'

So I had a bath so hot that my skin turned as pink as a river trout, and I came downstairs with my face damp from the sweat at the heat of it, smelling expensively of best Bath soap and toilet waters and dressed in a silk gown of pale blue.

Richard saw my newly acquired confidence. He saw it in the way I joked with Uncle John, and in the way I nodded to Stride. He saw how I had changed towards my mama – no less loving and tender than in the childhood days, but we now talked as equals. Bath had put a veneer of fashion on me. Bath had curled my hair and taught me how to dress and how to dance, and how to make small talk. Conquering my fear of Beatrice and my fear of the sight had turned me into a woman who could make decisions, who could give and take orders, who could make a promise and keep it and who would never, never be bullied by imaginary fears.

Or so I thought that evening.

It was my evening. There were hot-house flowers at my place and a basket full of prettily wrapped presents from as far away as James's hotel in Belgium, and as near as Jimmy Dart's cottage. But it was also Richard's evening. We all wanted to know how he found university life and whether he had made many friends. We wanted to know about his lodgings, and about his tutors, and whether he liked his studies. Richard laid himself out to be entertaining and had us laughing and laughing with tales of the older students in his college.

'They sound fearfully wild,' Mama said anxiously. 'I hope that is not your set, Richard.'

'Nonsense, Mama-Aunt!' Richard said cheerfully. 'They are the greatest of fellows, but they won't have a thing to do with me. Students who have just arrived in town are just about the last entrants on the great chain of being, I assure you! They have no time for me at all!'

He laughed heartily at that, but I knew my cousin Richard, and I knew that a state of affairs in which he was not highly regarded would not strike him as amusing at all. It was odd indeed that at the very time when I had been finding my feet on the land, discovering I was a young woman with desires of my own and finding a serious job to do, Richard had become the youngest and least important young man in a town where young men were not taken seriously.

I looked at him with judging eyes. He would always be my darling cousin, and today the earth and the sky and the humming in my head had been too much for me and I had gone to him and he had held me and he could have taken me, as if I knew nothing of the indoor Quality life at all; but when I was back in my senses, I could see him clearly. I think I saw him that evening for the first time . . . and I saw a young man whom I would not trust with a ploughing team.

I laughed out loud at that thought and Mama asked me what had amused me, and I had to invent some taradiddle to divert the attention away from me. For now Richard was home from Oxford and I had been out on the fields all day, it was obvious, as it had been obvious at the start to Acre, to Ralph Megson and to Uncle John, that I was the one who had inherited the Lacey love of the land, and Richard would never love it and care for it and work it as I did.

19

Mama had held Acre, and all of us in the Dower House, to strict observance of the sabbath, and even in the middle of ploughing she could not be moved from it. To my surprise Ralph Megson agreed with her, and when I had said, 'Lose a ploughing day?' he had given me one of his sideways glances and asked, 'And you would add up all the Sundays worked and give the village a week's holiday every month and a half would you?'

The carriage took us to church in the morning and back for breakfast, but Mama agreed that provided we stayed inside the boundaries of the estate, we might ride in the afternoon.

'I have to leave tomorrow first thing,' Richard said, 'so will you come out at once, Julia?'

'Indeed I will,' I said, 'but I shall have to change.'

'Be quick, then!' he said in his familiar peremptory tone of command.

I fled up to my bedroom. I had a choice of three riding habits now: my original one in cream, now sadly shabby, and the two newer ones, one in a soft grey with a grey tweeded jacket, which matched my eyes and which I thought fearfully smart, and the other a deep purple. When I had first worn the grey one downstairs, John had drawn in his breath with a little hiss and his eyes had met Mama's in a look I could not fathom.

'It is just that she always wore her riding dress,' Mama had said, 'and she had a grey one that she wore in second mourning after their father died.'

John had nodded, and I knew they were speaking of Beatrice. 'The resemblance is so striking . . .' he started.

'Not at all,' Mama had interrupted in a forceful voice without her usual courtesy. 'It is just the dress.'

'But is it a nice dress?' I had demanded, impatient with the past, free from superstition. 'Don't you think it a lovely dress, Uncle John?'

'I think you a very vain Bath miss,' he had said fondly, 'fishing for compliments like a hussy. Indeed, it is a very nice dress, and you are a very nice niece, and you have a nice horse. Matched greys, the two of you! Now, go and preen elsewhere, Squire Julia. I have work to do!'

'I am working too!' I had said, stung. 'I am going down to Acre to see if they have gravel and sand ready to put down on the lane if it becomes too boggy.'

'Squire Julia indeed,' John had said, smiling. 'Go and do your work, then, and call in at the hall on your way back. I want to know if they are able to carry on with their work. The foreman yesterday was saying that if the wind got up too high, they would have to stop.'

I had nodded and gone, unperturbed that my resemblance to Beatrice could still make John catch his breath. He and I had agreed that we had to live with the ghost of Beatrice, and we were both increasingly easy with our understanding.

Richard had not seen the riding habit on that day, for he had been away. I could not help wondering if he would think it was pretty too.

He did.

I could tell from the way he looked at me. He was waiting for me at the foot of the stairs, and I walked down towards him with the velvet skirts shushing on every step. His eyes narrowed as he watched me, and he lifted my hand from the banister and kissed it, watching my face.

'You are lovely, Julia,' he said softly. 'I can hardly believe it, because I grew up knowing you all my life, but without my noticing, you have grown into the loveliest girl.'

I flushed scarlet up to the roots of my hair and looked at him. I could think of nothing to say. This was a Richard I did not know. I felt oddly uncomfortable. I was used to Richard as my brother, as my friend, as my tormentor and trusted companion, but words of love from him made me uneasy.

'Thank you,' I said like a fool, and I gave him an apologetic smile. 'I feel so silly, Richard,' I said. 'I can't think what to say when you speak to me like that.'

He frowned at that and went before me towards the kitchen door to go out of the house the back way, but Mrs Gough stayed him with a loving hand on his sleeve and made him eat a fresh-baked roll and drink a cup of coffee before he went out into the cold air. 'For you're all skin and bone from that lodging-house food of yours,' she said anxiously. 'I doubt you are fed as well there as you are at home.'

Richard was charming, and ate what she wanted and praised last night's dinner and begged for his favourite dish this afternoon. I watched him with a smile. He was always so very persuasive. He could charm his way into any position, into anyone's heart.

Mrs Gough was wrong, though. He was not all skin and bone. He did look a little taller, and I thought he had grown. He was still a head taller than me, but he had filled out and become broader. He would never be weighty – he would always have that lean, supple look – but he had lost his coltish awkwardness and was no longer a gangling youth.

I turned my eyes down to my own cup of coffee. I could not look at Richard critically and assess the changes in his appearance. He was dazzling. Even at his youngest and most awkward stage, he had had looks which anyone might envy, with eyelashes as long as a girl's, a complexion as clear and as vital as a healthy child's, and a rangy leanness.

He had caught my eyes on him and he half raised an eyebrow in a silent question. I tried to smile but found that I was almost trembling. Richard nodded, as if he knew something that I did not, and his smile at me was very, very confident.

'We must go, Mother Gough!' he said firmly. 'I want to ride all around before dinner.'

'Aye, it's a fine estate they're making for you,' she said, opening the door for us.

'Just half for me,' Richard corrected her gently.

'Ah, nonsense,' said Mrs Gough roundly, with a smile for me but with her eyes on his face. 'The hall and land like this need a handsome young squire to run them on his own. You'd want Master Richard to be master here, wouldn't you, Miss Julia?'

I tried to find some light reply, but I found I was blushing furiously and could not put a sentence together. I stammered something, and got myself out of the kitchen and into the cold garden and towards the stables before Mrs Gough could be even more indiscreet.

Jem had my mare ready for me, but had not known Richard would be riding.

'How's this?' Richard asked. 'Do you ride every day, Julia?'

'Yes,' I said. Richard tossed me up into the saddle. 'We have been so busy on the land and Uncle John is not well enough to be out all day. Mr Megson cannot be everywhere at once.'

'You *are* busy,' Richard said, and his tone was not approving. I felt uneasy and shifted slightly in the saddle.

'There has been a lot to do,' I said defensively.

'And I can see you do it all,' Richard said. The words sounded like praise, but I knew Richard was not pleased. 'What a wonderful little miss squire you are, Julia. Acre must adore you.'

'Stuff,' I said awkwardly. 'It is just work, Richard, as Beatrice used to do.'

He would have said more, but Prince came out of the stable with his head thrown up and Jem clinging on to the reins. 'He's rather fresh,' Richard said, and he sounded almost apprehensive.

'He's not been ridden very often,' I said. 'Jem has taken him out, but John has been too tired to ride much in the cold weather.'

Richard nodded. 'Hold him still, can't you?' he said abruptly to Jem as the animal shifted when he was trying to mount. Jem nodded, but shot a disrespectful wink at me which I pretended not to see.

Once Richard was in the saddle, he seemed more confident, though he was a little pale. 'I shouldn't think he's been out of his stable for a sennight,' he complained. 'Really, Julia, if you are squiring it around the estate so much, you might ensure that the horses are properly exercised.'

'I'm sorry,' I said neutrally. I knew Prince would settle down soon. He was too well mannered to let his enthusiasm for being out overcome his normal steadiness. 'Mr Megson stables one of his horses here,' I offered. 'If you don't like Prince, you could try him.'

'I'll ride our horse,' Richard snapped, and he let Prince start forward and brushed past me to trot down the drive.

'Prince is all right,' Jem said reassuringly. 'He's got no vices. If he bolts, he'll only come home. All Master Richard has to do is to hold on tight and stay on top. I suppose he can do that, Miss Julia.'

'Thank you, Jem,' I said repressively, and I trotted out into the sunlit drive after Richard.

I had hoped we would go towards Acre, because I wanted to see what they were planting in the common strips, but Richard turned to the right before we got to the village and led the way up towards the downs.

'I thought we would ride along the top of the downs and then drop down to the common,' he said over his shoulder.

'Yes,' I agreed. I could at least check the sheep as we rode past the flock. They were out on the high downs at last, and I wanted to see if the lambs were looking well enough and standing up to their first days out.

'Why do you not know what to say when I tell you how much I admire you?' Richard asked abruptly as the two horses breasted the rise of the track and came out at the top of the downs, blowing hard.

I coloured again. 'I suppose because we have known each other for so long . . .' I said awkwardly, 'and been friends for so long, Richard. It just seems so strange to hear you speak to me like that.'

'But your Bath friends, James Fortescue and the others, no doubt pay you compliments, don't they?' Richard continued. 'Does it sound odd to you from them?'

'Not from them,' I said honestly. The horses fell into an easy walk side by side, along the old drovers' way that runs along the top of the downs. Looking to my left, I could see Acre and the Wideacre woods, the London road and half of Sussex, and Hampshire as well. Looking southwards, I could see the gleam of the sea and the thousand little mud islands of Chichester harbour.

'Is that because you prefer them to me?' Richard suddenly demanded. I jumped and switched my eyes from the view to Richard. He was breathing fast; his colour came and went in his cheeks, and his eyes were blazing blue. 'Tell me, Julia,' he said urgently. 'I have to know! You wrote me a letter which I could not begin to understand. That is why I came straight home to see you. I believed us to be betrothed. You have given me your word; and then you write to me as if it were a little piece of gossip and tell me that you are affianced to someone else!'

'Richard! No!' I said. I stopped my horse and put my hand out to him. He jumped down from Prince and lifted me down from the saddle. When my feet touched the frosty grass he did not release me, but kept hold of me in a tight grip, looking down at my face.

'Tell me, then,' he said huskily, 'tell me that you have not changed towards me, even though your clothes have changed, and you are so grown-up and confident. Remember how it was when I came to the field just yesterday? Tell me that you still love me.'

'Of course I do,' I said simply. 'I always have done. From as far back as I can remember I have always loved you, Richard. How can you doubt that?'

'You love me as a cousin, I know,' he said tightly, 'but you have promised me more than that, Julia. I love you as a lover, I think you know that. We both know what it means. I am asking you, do you love me too?'

It was not true.

There was a lie, somewhere.

I was not a fool. I had been a fool over Richard many, many times. I had loved him without encouragement and without return. I had always thought there would be a time when he would take me in his arms and say he loved me, and our love would have changed, grown into adult love. Now that time had come.

But it had come too late.

'I do love you,' I said slowly, 'but I am not sure what that love means for us both.'

'You have promised to marry me,' Richard pressed. 'When I am done at Oxford and we are of age, you will marry me, as we always planned.'

'Richard . . .' I said helplessly. His hands on my waist were closed in a hard grip, hardly a caress at all. I was trying to think of words to explain to him that he was my dearest brother and friend, but that the feeling of being *in* love was quite different, that he should not mistake his feelings for me.

He drew me a little closer to him and his hand slid around my back. I felt my mouth grow dry with apprehension. He put a hand under my chin and turned my face up to him.

He had always done as he wished with me. I had never said no to Richard, I had never even run away from his anger. How could I now learn to pull away from his touch?

'Richard . . .' I said softly.

His hand smoothed my back and I could feel his warm body pressing against mine. One hand stroked my face, my cheek, my neck. But my body did not respond to him. It did not melt to his touch. Instead I heard a buzzing in my head like an angry bee and I could feel the hair on the nape of my neck standing up like the hackles on a frightened dog. For the first time in our lives, when Richard touched me, I drew away. I could not help but draw away. He made my skin crawl.

Richard's face came down lower and he kissed me lightly on the lips.

I held myself still. Nothing would be gained by pulling away, and anyway I had my back against Misty and could step backwards no further. But when his lips were pressed harder on my passive mouth, I could not help but shudder.

He misunderstood that shiver. He broke from the kiss and smiled down at me. 'You are hot for me,' he said confidently. 'You love me and you want me.'

'No,' I said instantly. 'I am sorry, Richard, but that is not how it is.'

'You are wanton,' Richard said coolly. 'You have always been mine. You would come to me at any time, night or day, if I so much as snapped my fingers. But then you go away to Bath and think you have found another master, another lover. But I have come to claim you back. And here and now I *do* take you back.'

'No, Richard,' I said steadily. I was breathing fast, but there was a very sharp awareness in my mind that what Richard was saying was not true.

'You are a whore and a wanton,' Richard said pleasantly. 'You would go with any man who flattered your monstrous vanity. You played the little squire all around Bath and made a show of yourself with finding the paupers and bringing them home. Now you have some cheap tradesman's son sniffing around you and I am supposed to believe this is love! It is vanity and lust, Julia. You are my betrothed, and I will take care to keep you.'

I wrenched myself from him and turned my head into Misty's silver-grey shoulder. The clean smell of her warmth steadied me.

'None of that is true,' I said quietly. My temper was rising, but I had endured Dr Phillips's stripping away of my most private hopes and fears, and I no longer rose to the slightest bait. 'None of that is true,' I said again. 'I am in love with James Fortescue. I went to Bath a free woman. We did play at being engaged when we were children, but neither your papa nor my mama ever encouraged that. Since we have been grown, I have never felt that you loved me in that way. I love you as if you were my brother and I will continue to do so, provided you treat me well. There is no other relationship between us.'

'Julia!' Richard cried. His tone was so anguished that I turned back to look at him. His mouth was working, but his eyes were sharp. 'You are breaking my heart!' he exclaimed. 'I have loved you all my life. I have refused invitations to balls and dinners in Oxford because I considered myself a betrothed man. Now you tell me this means nothing to you! Have you forgotten how much we loved each other in childhood, before all of Acre started to come between us? Before Mr Megson came back, before you started going out of the house instead of waiting at home for me.'

It just did not sound right. I pulled back so that I could scan his face. 'What is the matter with you?' I asked softly.

'Nothing,' he said quickly. He said it too quickly, I heard it.

'You do not have to love me,' I said slowly. I spoke almost sadly. 'You know that I love you and that I shall love you for always, as my dearest friend, as my brother. No one could take that love away from us. No one could replace you in my heart. There is no need for you to pretend you feel desire for me when you do not.'

There was an invitation there if Richard had been the person to hear it, and understand it. But he was not.

It was odd, for I had believed that it was women who were the romantic ones, who cling to lies and pretty mannered courtesies. I would have given every florist's bloom in the world to have known what was in Richard's heart on that bright day on the top of the downs. But he would not tell me.

'I know I do not have to love you,' he said gently. 'But I can tell you, I can tell you freely, that I do love you with all my heart and soul.'

He bent his dark head and kissed me again, and I felt such pity for him if he was telling the truth and such confusion about what I should do to help him that I let him kiss me. His breathing was coming faster and he was murmuring my name over and over as his lips went up and down the line of my neck from my collarbone to my ear.

I wrenched my face away from him, and I put both my hands against his shoulders and tried to push him off me. Then I saw his face, quite empty of emotion, not warm and loving nor hot with passion, but with an absolute coldness behind his eyes as he looked at me and measured me.

'Is it the truth that you no longer want me?' he asked. His voice was like ice.

I pulled my stock up around my throat and smoothed my jacket down. My hat had come off altogether and I pinned it back on as best I could. I felt rumpled and foolish. 'Yes,' I said. 'I am sorry. I am betrothed to another man and I love him as a lover. I love you as a brother and that is all.'

'Then you are faithless and you have broken my heart!' he cried out and spun around to Prince and vaulted up into the saddle.

'Richard!' I said. But he wheeled Prince around so close that the flick of his tail stung me in the face. Richard, high on his back, was scowling. He jerked Prince to face back along the way we had come and then dug his heels in hard and used his whip too. Prince threw up his head and thundered away from us. Misty sidled, anxious, and I grabbed her reins.

I did not hurry to follow. I let him go. I waited on the downs and I wept for the pain I had caused him, and that I should have been so stupid as to think that Richard could readily accept another in his place. I had never known before how much he loved me. I wept for my folly, and for the loss of that love.

I led Misty over to a hummock which I could use as a mounting-block to help me into the high saddle, and I wiped my eyes on the back of my glove and sniffed miserably. Then I turned her head for home and went slowly down the bridle-track to the foot of the downs. And there he was.

He was waiting for me, with Prince held on a short rein, standing very still at the side of the path. He was waiting for me with his sweetest smile.

'Julia, I beg your pardon,' he said handsomely, and put his hand out to shake mine.

I was swept with a flood of relief that we were no longer quarrelling. 'Oh! Richard!' I said, lost for words.

'To tell the truth, I am jealous,' he said frankly, 'but I make a very poor Othello. All this time I thought of you as a little girl, and you have been growing into a strong and beautiful woman. I only hope your James is worthy of you! But I promise you I will dance at your wedding with a glad pair of heels. And I promise you that you will never hear me reproach you again!'

I dropped Misty's reins and held Richard's hand in both of mine. 'Oh, Richard,' I said, 'I do thank you. I am sure I have been thoughtless and selfish in not explaining earlier to you what was happening. It was all so sudden . . .'

'Tell me!' he said invitingly, and we turned our horses downhill at an easy pace. I rode with the companion of my childhood and the best friend of my girlhood and told him about falling in love, and how good a man I had chosen. Richard smiled and asked me about the family and our days in Bath; he pledged himself to love them all for me.

Misty jinked at a rag fluttering in the hedgerow as we slid downhill on the wet mud.

'She's fresh,' I said, gentling her. 'She missed her gallop on the downs.'

'Oh, let's forget the downs!' Richard said. 'I behaved like a fool, and like a surly ill-natured fool at that. Let's take them home by the common and have a good gallop.'

'Oh, yes!' I said and we turned to our right at the village lane and trotted around the back of the village, past the squatters, up to the crest of the common where the fire-break had been cut back. It made a grand track of white soft sand, as broad as a river. Sea Mist's ears went forward.

'A race?' I called to Richard. I could tell he was confident on Prince. Richard nodded. We reined in the horses and they sidled and blew out, knowing what was coming.

'One, two, three, go!' I yelled, the wind whipping my words from me as the horses leaped forward.

Prince was away first, but Sea Mist drew level and I was beside Richard. We glanced sideways at each other through the flurry of wind and the tossing manes and the sand thrown up. There was a thundering noise of hooves and Prince pulled ahead, and my face was showered in sand and grit as he came past. Sea Mist liked it no more than I, and she instinctively slowed as we chased Prince and Richard round a slight curve and then up a steep hill. The gradient told on the older horse and Prince's gallop became a canter and then was more and more laboured, while Sea Mist took the deep shifting sand and the steepness of the hill in her stride. We passed Richard at a canter. I was leaning forward and clinging like a louse to Misty's mane. Then I pulled her up on the pinnacle of the hill and waited for Richard and Prince to come alongside.

Richard's blue eyes were blazing with pleasure, his face spotted with mud. 'That was grand!' he said. 'I would have won but for the hill.'

'He's a lovely old horse,' I said, leaning over to pat Prince on his sweat-streaked neck. 'He must have been a fine hunter when he was young.'

'You ride so well,' Richard said generously. 'It must be true, what they say, that you are a natural rider.'

'It's in our blood,' I said. 'We're both of Lacey stock.'

Richard smiled at that. 'You and me,' he said with quiet satisfaction, 'you and me.'

'I've got sand in my eyes,' I said, blinking and rubbing them with the back of my glove. 'Is my face all muddy?'

'Yes,' said Richard with brotherly unconcern, 'and your hair is all falling down.'

'Hold my reins,' I said and handed them to him and pulled my gloves off and felt at the back of my head for hairpins. I pinned up the stray curls and took my reins back from Richard, and we sat in silence, resting the horses and getting our own breath back.

Below us were the growing walls of the new Wideacre Hall, to the left was the little golden box of the Dower House. Further along the valley again was Acre village, although we could only see the church spire and glimpse some of the cottages hidden by the trees of the parkland. Straggling out from the village, along the edge of the common, were the squatters' huts, half roofed with moss and bracken, little wooden shelters built by people who lived on the very edge of society, always near starvation and always in danger of losing what little rights they had over grazing and cutting turf and firewood, always ill, always accused of thievery or poaching.

In the bad years on Acre the estate had become known as land where there was no squire. New people had come to squat on a corner of the common land and now there was almost a little village – a little community beside Acre – scattered along the margin of the common.

Beyond them again was a neat circle of painted carts and tents, picturesque at this distance, where the gypsies had come for the autumn and winter. They came every year, trusting to a tradition which said Wideacre once belonged to gypsies, back in the earliest years. No one could prove it or deny it, and whether it was true or not hardly mattered. They affected to believe it, and no one would challenge a gypsy man, who would fight to the death over a matter of pride, or a gypsy woman, who could cast a spell on you if she wished.

They claimed they had been camping here, in a little circle of carts and tents, three families living as one, since the time of the Romans. At any rate, Wideacre accepted them as another element in a natural order which sent foot-rot to the sheep in winter and flukes in summer. In the old days the women in Acre would complain that they lost washing off the line, and when there had been vegetable patches, a few turnips or sweet carrots would disappear from the plots. But no one could stop them coming or going as they wished.

Every winter they made their camp in the same place, in the same small circle with a fire in the middle. People said that if they came early, it was a sure sign of a hard winter, that they could tell the seasons as well as the bushes in the hedgerows or the animals. This winter they had come late, and for reasons of their own they had stayed on.

We turned the horses and headed for a track which ran alongside a little woodland. We rode in silence, in quiet companionship. The horses made little noise, their hooves muffled by the sandy soil which was still soggy from the rain. Then Sea Mist threw up her head as a rabbit burst from the wood and scuttered across the path ahead of us. There was a stream of ringing bells, and a goshawk shot out of the wood on the rabbit's tail, its wings open to break its speed as the taloned feet came forward and it dived on to the rabbit's neck. The rabbit screamed like a child and bucked, but then dropped still – a quick clean kill. The goshawk settled its wings with a satisfied shrug and looked around. It looked straight at us, frozen in surprise, and then its deep marigold-coloured eyes stared back without fear.

'Is it Ralph Megson's?' Richard asked me softly.

I nodded without speaking. The goshawk's gaze was holding my own. Then there was a rustling in the undergrowth and a black dog came out. Black as mourning velvet, it was, a lurcher, and it shot out of the undergrowth, nose to the ground, until it saw the goshawk and her kill. It dropped then, splendidly trained, into lying position, front paws out, head up, like a couchant lion on a crest.

Then we heard a soft rustle and Ralph came out of the shadow of the trees, one crutch to steady himself tucked under his arm. He nodded at the two of us but said nothing, and we kept silent also. His eyes were on his hawk. He walked towards her without speaking, pulling something out of a little bag he had at his side. It was a strip of meat, and he held it in his gloved hand and flapped it at her temptingly. She glanced from him to the skull of the rabbit, undecided, and then she opened her wings and half hopped, half flew to his proffered fist. She bent her lovely head and pulled at the meat, straining against it as she gripped with her yellow claws.

Ralph pulled a leash from his belt and fastened it to the jesses on her legs and then looped it carefully into his palm. He nodded at the dog and it scooted forward, picked up the rabbit and brought it to him. Ralph tossed it into his bag and patted the dog's head and gave it a scrap of meat too. Only then did he turn and smile at us, his hawk balancing on his fist, her cream and grey speckled breast feathers still sleek and smooth with excitement.

'Good day, Miss Julia, Master Richard,' he said, smiling at the two of us.

'Preserving the sabbath and the game at once, Mr Megson!' I said, delighted to have caught him out.

He smiled his slow warm smile. 'I'm a godless man indeed,' he said. 'But I do have to eat, Miss Lacey!'

'Good day,' Richard interrupted stiffly, but then he forgot his dignity. 'That was a wonderful kill! We saw it! It was right in front of us! I've never seen a hawk kill so close before! Right under our noses!'

'Aye, she's a beauty,' said Ralph proudly. 'Three years I've had her, and I've yet to see her miss.'

'What's the biggest thing she's ever taken?' Richard asked.

'She's had a couple of hare,' Ralph said, 'and she can take a pheasant too. She'll take grouse without trouble, and duck. A family could eat like royalty on what she'd bring them.'

'I don't suppose she'd let anyone else hold her . . .' Richard said insinuatingly.

Ralph laughed at him. 'Yes, you can hold her,' he said easily. 'You'll have to come off your horse, though – she doesn't like being held on horseback. It's her only fault, and a great nuisance for me. I can keep up with her on short flights, but I'm very tired by the end of the day, looking for game with her and putting it up.'

Richard was off Prince in a flash, and Ralph put his hand out to hold the reins. He took a spare gauntlet out of the bag and Richard pulled it on.

'Ever handled a hawk before?' he asked softly. Richard shook his head. 'Well, you take her from behind,' he said. 'Just rest your hand a little above mine, where you think her ankles would be.' Richard put his hand out, and the hawk stepped back on to his fist as naturally as she had gone to Ralph.

'Faithless,' Ralph said with satisfaction. He handed the leash to Richard and showed him how to loop it into his hand. 'It feels right like that, and you can't drop it by accident,' he said. 'You always hold a hawk's leash like that.'

Richard nodded, his face bright with concentration.

I noticed that the fluffy feathers of her breast had gone smooth so that she looked lean, discontented. Her orange eyes were sharp. She made me feel somehow uneasy, and there was a hum in my head like half a dozen people whispering a warning all at once.

'Want to walk her?' Ralph offered. Richard nodded again. 'Just take her down the track a little way,' Ralph advised. 'Get the feel of her on your hand.'

Richard moved off delicately, trying to walk smoothly on the rutted sand.

'No need to be too careful!' Ralph called after him. 'She's used to my limping, and she'll find you as smooth as a yacht in calm seas.'

Richard walked a little faster, and we could see the hawk bobbing to keep her balance.

Ralph smoothed Sea Mist's neck and glanced up at me. 'No trouble at home, after the sowing?' he asked.

I shook my head. 'No,' I said.

'Is he staying long?' he asked, nodding his head to where Richard was turning and walking back to us.

'No,' I said, 'he's leaving tomorrow.'

'We are ploughing the common field tomorrow,' Ralph said laconically.

'I'll be there,' I said steadily.

Richard came up to us, and I could tell, without knowing how, that the hawk was afraid. I felt a pricking in my thumbs, in the thumbs of both hands, as sharp as darning needles. The sensation was so acute and so sudden that I exclaimed and looked down at my riding gloves to see if I had gorse thorns stuck in the leather. Then I looked back at the hawk and saw her breast feathers tight. She was skinny with fright.

As soon as she saw Ralph, she opened her wings and flung herself towards him. Richard had the leash tight and it jerked on her legs, catching her in mid-flight. In a second she was upside-down, spinning around on the leash, her wings flailing wildly in a panic to get herself upright again.

'Steady,' Ralph said quickly; he thrust Prince's reins at me and took two rolling strides towards Richard.

Richard's face was murderous. He jerked at the hawk as if she were a doll on a piece of string, not a living creature at all. 'Back to me!' he shouted, and he snatched his hand up so she bounced helplessly at the end of the leash.

Prince threw his head up and Misty pulled away, her ears flat against her head. I nearly lost my seat trying to hold the two restive horses.

'Steady!' Ralph shouted in a tone I had never heard him use before. He grabbed Richard's arm and held it still, then he put his other hand under the twisting flailing bird and cradled her breast. Richard still had the leash tight in his hand so Ralph lifted her gently, as gently as if he were holding a fledgling, back to Richard's glove.

The second her feet were on it she bated again, directly towards Ralph, as in a panic to be with him and away from Richard. Ralph instinctively put his hands out to catch her and released Richard's arm. Richard jerked hard on the leash, as he would have pulled a dog to heel, and we all heard a horrid crack, crack, like two twigs breaking.

Misty reared up as if the ground had opened beneath her front hooves, and I tumbled from her back with a spinning thud which knocked the breath out of me. I ducked my head down and bunched up small in instinctive fright while she reared over me and wheeled away, then slowed and dipped her head to some fresh heather a few yards away. I had kept my hold on Prince's reins, and he stood steady, though his eyes showed white.

Ralph snatched the leash from Richard's fist and looped it quickly around his own. Then he caught his bird, pinning her two wings to her side so she could flutter no more. He held her head into his jacket with one broad hand while he searched in his gamebag with the other. He brought out a little hood, intricately worked and made of exquisite soft leather, with a little crest of hen's feathers on the top. He hooded her smoothly, pulling the hood tight with his teeth and hand on the leather thongs. Then he pulled out something like a stocking from the bottom of the bag and pulled it over her head so her wings were held to her side; he laid her in the bag, on top of the rabbit she had killed when she had been a proud free hawk and not a trussed bird.

Only then, when she was safely hooded and muffled and lying soft in his bag, did he turn to look at me and ask, 'All right, lass?'

I nodded and got to my feet. We both stared at Richard who stood, guilty, in front of us.

Ralph eyed him warily. 'What ails you?' he asked very low.

Something in the way he said that made me cold.

He was not asking Richard in the way a man with a beloved hawk just injured would speak. He was not shouting in hot anger. He was not even icy with rage. He asked Richard in a voice which put Richard at a distance so that Ralph could inspect him. He spoke as if Richard had some secret dangerous ailment which could infect us all. He stared at him as if he would see into his very soul.

Richard was scarlet to his hairline. 'I don't know,' he said awkwardly. 'She flew off my wrist and I did not know what to do. I did not know what I was doing.'

There was a desert of silence.

'I *am* sorry, Mr Megson,' Richard said. His voice had gathered strength and I saw him shoot a sideways glance at Ralph. 'I would not have frightened your hawk for the world. I hope she is not hurt?'

'You know full well that both her legs are broken,' Ralph said evenly. 'You heard them snap when you jerked on the leash. Why did you pull her like that?'

'I did not!' Richard said, blustering. 'That is not so! She simply flew out and I held the leash to keep her safe!'

'You did not,' said Ralph, and his voice was like ice. 'You jerked her back in a rage.'

He hesitated, and he looked at Richard thoughtfully. 'Many

people have held her and she has never bated before,' he said to himself. There was a long silence while Ralph thought something through. 'Animals don't like you, do they?' he said.

Richard said nothing. I reached out a hand to touch Prince's thick neck, as if to reassure myself that the real world was still there. The voices in my head had grown in strength like a dozen, twenty people murmuring at me to be warned, to listen, to take care, to know real danger when I saw it. I felt hazed, almost snow-blinded. There was a buzzing in my head as if Beatrice were very near to me, somehow trying to summon me, a hard insistent calling. I should be listening to something, I should have ears to hear her message. The balls of both my thumbs were as sore as if they were bleeding from a hundred tiny pin-pricks.

I was distressed for the hawk and afraid of Ralph's anger, and concerned for Richard.

Ralph turned abruptly to me. 'You have the sight, Julia,' he challenged me. 'You should know. What do you see when you look at Richard?'

I turned my eyes to my cousin and he looked at me with his clear blue stare. The noise in my head was too loud for me to think of anything. I saw Richard, my beloved Richard, my co-heir and the playmate of my childhood. And I saw as well some awful danger and fear and horror.

'I can see nothing. Nothing,' I said desperately. 'I can hear nothing and see nothing. I do not have the sight as you think. I cannot see.' I turned my head from Ralph and spoke to Richard. 'I want to go home,' I said, as pettish as a schoolgirl.

Ralph limped over to where Sea Mist restlessly cropped the heather. As she saw him coming, she wheeled around and put her hindquarters to him as if she thought of kicking – Misty, who had never shown an ounce of spite in all the time we had known her.

'Give over,' Ralph said gruffly, and walked towards her and took her reins to lead her back to me. He threw me up into the saddle and said not a word more, not to Richard, not to me. We rode away in silence. He let us leave without a word. We left him standing before that little coppice with his gamebag on his back and his black dog lying at his feet. As we left him, I felt his eyes on my back and I felt him brooding, brooding, over the two of us, and watching us all the way home.

20

We rode home in silence, Richard and I. The accord we had formed after the quarrel on the downs had been broken by the odd, disturbing incident with Ralph's goshawk. Mama and Uncle John were laughing at some private joke over dinner and did not notice that Richard and I were awkward and quiet. When it was my bedtime, I gave Richard my hand and said my farewells then; he would have left for the early stage-coach in the morning before I was awake.

Richard kissed my hand, and then drew me to him and kissed my cheek. 'All all right?' he asked in the phrase from our childhood.

'All all right,' I confirmed.

But we both knew that it was not.

Scheherazade had feared him. The sheep had mobbed him. And now Ralph's goshawk had been afraid of him.

I expected Ralph to speak to me about Richard as soon as I rode into the common field on Monday morning – a grey damp Monday morning with no joy or magic to it that day – but he just tipped his hat to me and said not a word.

'How is your hawk?' I asked him when we stopped for breakfast.

He was sitting on horseback beside me, and the plough-boys and the sowing girls were standing in the squelchy mud to eat their breakfasts. He sank his teeth into a crust of bread and chewed slowly before he answered me.

'I wrung her neck,' he said, his voice even. 'Her legs would not have mended strong enough to kill again, and I don't keep pets. She was a working bird; I'd not have liked her to grow fat and idle.'

The shock showed on my face, but I did not offer Ralph Megson a sympathetic word.

'Her nerve had gone,' he said briefly. The words sounded very ominous. 'She had never bated from the hand before in her life, not since I waked her – sat up all night with her – and trained her to the glove three years ago. But she didn't like Richard, did she? Something about him scared her. Scared her so badly she broke her legs trying to get away from him.'

I said nothing. I sat on my horse like a grey statue against a grey sky. In my head was that deep low murmur as if a hive of sleepy bees were stirring, swarming.

'You say you cannot hear it, or see it,' Ralph said thoughtfully. He was staring out into the darkness, but he swung around in the saddle and scanned my face. 'God lack! You're a fool, Julia Lacey,' he said abruptly. 'I thought you'd learned to use the sight, but you only use it when it suits you. *Listen* to your voices. *See* with your eyes.'

I put out a hand to him, but he shrugged me off, and his horse, always sensitive to his movements, shifted to one side.

'I've no patience with you!' he said abruptly. 'Beatrice would have taken her riding crop to you!' He clicked to his horse and went to check the binding on the ploughshares, which was sound, and the state of the horses, which was good, and the straightness of the furrows, which was adequate. Then he called them back to work a couple of minutes before they were due, which was un-heard of.

I watched them for half an hour after the breakfast rest and then I trotted over to Ralph and asked him if he had any errands for me. When he scowled and said, no, I said that I would come back to the field in an hour or so, but that I wanted to exercise Sea Mist on the common.

He nodded curtly. I was not forgiven, and every working day over the next few weeks there was a reserve between us because Ralph thought me wilfully stupid, and I was offended. If it had been in the middle of harvesting, we should both have been out of the sullens in a day because we would have been too busy for resentments, but the urgency of the early weeks of the spring was over. The ploughing was done, and the men and women could sow without being watched. The sheep on the downs had broken down some of the fences, and they had to be repaired, but that was swiftly done. The lambs were weaned and out on the grass and caused no trouble. The Fenny was flooded with melt-water and with water from some days of rain, and I went out daily to check that the banks were holding, for some of Beatrice's cornfields had been dangerously close to the river edge and I was regretting that we had followed her lead.

Uncle John had bought half a dozen cows and a bull and we had turned them out on the lower fields by the Fenny. He was a great red animal with a strong ring in his nose. I was afraid of him at first and inspected the animals through the gate. But as I grew accustomed to them, and they to me, I would ride Misty right into their field to see that they were all sound.

I was starting to find myself with time on my hands. My work checking the land would take me all the morning, but in the afternoon there was little for me to do. It was a warm spring. I could feel the sun warming the land like my own skin. Everything on Wideacre was pairing, courting that spring. Everywhere I went I could hear birds calling and calling for a mate, or pairs of birds playing tender silly courtship games, feeding each other, feathers fluffed out and mouths agape, or nest-building together in a frenzy of displaced desire. When I walked down to the Home Farm, I saw the great shire stallion in the field tossing his mane as thick as sea spume and hollering for a mare.

On the downs the lambs were growing strong and the ewes were surrounded by dozens of young. In the field by the river the bull grazed with his herd, his favourite cow always at his shoulder, their heads rubbing together when they walked. They would freeze for minutes at a time while he licked their faces with his massive rubbery tongue as if there were love between them as well as an insistent need to couple.

I missed James more than I could have believed possible. I walked alone under trees full of birds singing love-songs, under a sky criss-crossed with nest-building flights, watched the red deer nuzzling together in the twilit evenings; at night I could not sleep, for I fancied even the owls were calling to each other of their passion and their desire under an enlarging moon.

After I had finished my farming work in the morning, I was free for the afternoons. Mama and Uncle John took out the gig for little drives together and I put on my coolest muslins with a light shawl and walked and walked in the deep greening woods and daydreamed of how my life would be when James came home and we were married. Above me, in the great trees of Wideacre, the birds mated and nested and then brooded under the safe canopy of the opening leaves. Wideacre swelled with life like the fat buds on the trees. Everything was courting, mating, birthing that spring, and I was full of longing for my own lover as I wandered alone in the woods with my straw hat on my fair head, my muslin pale among the green shadows, my feet awash in the bluebells.

Richard was due home before May Day and wrote that he would be in on the early-morning stage-coach. I had Misty saddled and rode up the lane towards the stop leading Prince to meet him.

The stage-coach sets down passengers for Acre at the corner where the lane meets the Chichester–London road, and I sat there on Misty's back in the spring sunshine, waiting for it. It had been warm and dry the previous week, and the deep rutted tracks of the lane were dried out at last from the winter mud. I turned my face up to the sunshine and felt its warmth on my closed eyelids. Prince dropped his head to the fresh leaves of the hedge and cropped them, his bit jingling as he munched. In the distance I could hear the creaky rumble of the stage-coach and the chink of the harness. The road was hilly, and I could see the hats and shoulders of the roof-passengers rising and falling as the coach breasted the hills and sank into the hollows of the road. The horses were labouring as they came into sight towards the Acre corner, and when the guard saw me waiting, he blew his horn and shouted a ribald comment about a lucky passenger being met at Acre corner.

The coachman pulled his horses up and tipped his whip to me. I smiled and nodded and watched as they let down the steps and Richard came out of the coach, rubbing his eyes and yawning. They passed down his box and Richard humped it over towards me.

I bent down for his kiss and hugged him around the shoulders. Some wag on the roof of the stage-coach cheered, but many of the passengers were Midhurst people and knew me by sight and nudged him into silence.

'What about my box?' Richard asked. 'It weighs a ton.'

'Oxford fashions?' I teased him.

'Holiday reading,' he said with a grimace. 'My Greek is still supposed to be a disgrace. I'm bid to work with Dr Pearce through this holiday.'

'You can leave it here,' I said. Richard pushed it into the hedge behind the stage-coach. The Acre carter could collect it for us later in the day. 'I thought you'd like a ride.'

'Yes,' he said. 'I've been cooped up in that coach for half a lifetime.'

He swung into the saddle and we turned the horses' heads for home. Richard made me laugh with sketches of his fellow passengers – the farmer's wife who would insist on carrying a basket with a live hen in it on her lap, the country wench who giggled every time she caught Richard's eye.

'And how's everything here?' he asked. 'Papa and Mama-Aunt all right? You?'

'Yes,' I said, nodding. 'Everything is just the same. Mama is quite well again now, though she still gets a little tired. She and Uncle John have a ritual drive out for her health every afternoon in the gig like a pair of tenant farmers.'

'Heard from Mr Fortescue?' Richard asked with careful nonchalance.

I kept my eyes on the greening hedge. 'Yes,' I said. I could not keep the tenderness from my voice. 'He writes to me every week and I reply when I have an address for him. He is back in Belgium at the moment, but he has been travelling around. His father is importing lace and James is responsible for finding reliable suppliers.'

'Any date for the wedding?' Richard asked lightly.

'Not yet,' I said. 'His papa's lawyers and Uncle John's man are drawing up the marriage contract to arrange the dowry and an allowance for me. We can hardly plan until we know when he will come home.'

Richard nodded. 'It could be some time, then,' he said.

'Yes,' I said. I could not keep the longing out of my voice. 'It sometimes seems like years and years. It should be this summer. We can announce our betrothal when he comes home.'

'And the hall?' Richard said. 'The builders are working well? Are the roofbeams in place?'

'Yes,' I said reassuringly. 'You would be the first to hear if anything had gone amiss. It is all working well. And the crop is just about showing in some fields already!'

'And what are they doing here?' Richard asked, pulling up Prince at a gateway. It was one of the new fruit fields where Uncle John had insisted that we should try raspberries. They looked a sorrowful little crop, row upon row of spindly canes with the tiniest green buds showing on each one. Down each narrow gangway between the rows were Acre women weeding, a rough piece of cloth beside each of them piled high with the bolting weeds of this damp warm spring. The lovely sun-warmed hollow was as sunny as in midsummer. I looked along the line of bent backs for Clary, but I could not see her. A cloud came over the sun and I shivered in the sudden chill. Richard and I pulled up at the gate and Ralph trotted over.

'Good day,' he said to us both and then spoke directly to me. 'I started them weeding while the men finish the sowing today,' he said with a note of pride in his voice. 'They've never sown quicker, I don't think.' He tipped his hat carelessly to Richard. 'Good morning,' he said coolly.

There was an awkward silence. Ralph's dislike of Richard was almost tangible on the warm air. Richard flushed and I spoke quickly to mask the silence. 'Then let's hope it grows at record speed too,' I said. 'The village always used to take a holiday after the sowing was done, did it not?'

'Aye,' Ralph said. 'I've reminded Dr MacAndrew that they'll want to keep the maying in the old way. They tell me they'd like you to be the Queen of the May if you'd go out on the hills to bring the spring in with them tomorrow at dawn.'

'I will!' I said. 'Clary spoke to me about it.' Then I paused as my training as a Bath young lady struck me, and I glanced at Ralph and asked him, 'It *is* all right, isn't it, Ralph? I mean, it's not fearfully improper or anything?'

Ralph's face looked as if he had bitten on a lemon rind. 'Don't ask me!' he said curtly. 'You know I know nothing about it. Ask your mama about these things, and take her advice.'

'She does not know the traditions of Acre,' I challenged him. 'You're the one who knows Acre. I'm asking you if it is all right for me to go.'

Ralph looked at me, wearied of the whole question. 'I should not pass on an invitation if I did not think it was all right,' he said carefully. 'You will come to no harm out on the downs at daybreak with all the young people of Acre village. You will pass your time until the sun comes up in picking hawthorn branches and tying ribbons to them. Then they will crown you with a circlet of flowers, mount you on a white horse, if they can find one – perhaps you would lend them your mare – and then you will ride down to Acre and bring in the spring. For three days after – for Dr MacAndrew does not think we can afford a week of idleness, and neither do I – you can be the queen of any revels they devise, or not, as you wish. There is nothing proper or improper about it – as far as I can see. But don't ask me about ladylike behaviour, Miss Julia, for I am but a poor working man.' This last was said with an absolutely grave face and with a tone so ironic that I wondered Richard could not hear the insult behind it.

'Tell them to come for me before daybreak, then,' I said. 'And tell them they can take my mare from the stables as soon as I have done with her today.'

Ralph nodded. 'And you, Master Richard, will you be going up to the top of the downs to welcome the spring?' he asked.

Richard nodded. 'I shall go,' he said. 'All that you describe sounds very pleasant, but I'm sure Lady Lacey would feel happier if I was there with Miss Julia.'

Ralph nodded, his eyes on the ground. He would not even look at Richard, and he had no friendly smile for me with Richard by my side. 'I am sure,' he said, and then he wheeled his horse around and trotted back into the field as if he had wasted too much time already.

Richard was wrong about Mama. She had no reservations about my bringing in the spring with Acre at all.

'Oh, heavens, Richard,' she said. 'If I wanted Julia to behave like a proper young lady, I should have to kidnap her and lock her up in Bath! She has been riding out on the land unaccompanied ever since you went off to Oxford. John insists she will take no hurt, and I trust to her own common sense – and the fact that she is so well loved.'

Richard nodded. 'It still seems most unconventional to me,' he said. We were taking tea after dinner, and Richard stood with his back to the fire, a dish of tea in his hand. I saw Mama and Uncle John exchange a smiling glance to see Richard so masterful at the fireplace.

'It is unconventional,' Uncle John agreed. 'But James Fortescue has no objection, and Wideacre has a tradition of eccentric women. At the moment Julia is the key to Acre and I have to use her. No one but Julia and Mr Megson carry any weight with Acre folk, and while we are dragging them back to work, it has to be Julia and Mr Megson in the traces.'

Richard gave a little bow. 'I am sure your judgement could not be wrong, sir,' he said. 'But all the same, I shall be glad to escort Julia to this daybreak merrymaking.'

'For tuppence I'd come too!' Uncle John said. 'I love these traditions. When I was a lad in Edinburgh, it was an Easter custom to roll hard-boiled eggs down Arthur's Seat – a great hill on the outskirts of the town. You would roll it, without touching it with your hands, all the way down to the bottom and then crack it and eat it.'

'Really!' said Mama, instantly diverted. 'Did all your family go? Your brothers and sisters too?'

'Oh, aye,' said Uncle John. 'All of Edinburgh went. And the egg tasted better then, at dawn on Easter morning, than at any other time.'

'I believe this expedition is just for the young men and women,' Richard said quickly. 'The girls wear white and the young men wear white favours.'

I could tell by Mama's absorbed expression that she was trying to remember if I had a white gown and a white wrap against the chill. And I was right. When I went upstairs to bed that night, I found she had laid out her own white cashmere shawl on the bed for my use, with a bunch of white ribbons for Richard's cockade and to tie around my branch when I brought the spring home.

I woke early and heard voices in the back garden outside my window. I jumped out of bed and pattered across the wooden floor. My feet were icy, and it was still dark. There were a couple of torches and, around them, perhaps ten or twelve of the young people from Acre, giggling and trying to start up a song. I pulled on my white gown and tied the white ribbon around my waist, without the help of a maid, for Jenny Hodgett was out with the merrymakers herself. Then I tossed the wrap over my shoulders and went up to tap on the door of Richard's little garret bedroom.

He was ready, pulling on his boots, and I pinned the favour of white ribbons to his hat. Then we crept downstairs as quietly as we could so as not to wake the sleeping house. The kitchen was silent, lit by a warm red glow from the embers of the kitchen fire. A cat was sleeping in the fireplace, dusty from the ashes. Richard shot the iron bolts on the back door and we went out into the cold and the darkness.

The cedar tree was pitch black against the sky, the yellow

torches no brighter than candles in the darkness. The moon was a slim white sickle and the stars shone like little pinpricks of silver in the purple blackness of the sky. Someone from the back of the crowd hummed a note and they sang a song like one of the ploughing chants, a three- or four-note song, refined by centuries of singing. It was sung only once a year, sung only now, in the blue-black hour before dawn on the first morning of spring, and always sung for the Queen of the May, to call her to her duties as the girl who brings the spring to the land.

Richard closed the door behind us and I stood still on the doorstep in my pale dress and let the chant sweep over me. The air was as cold as spring water, but Mama's wrap was warm and I held it tight around me. I felt magical, as though the great tree and the stars and the song and I were all part of some timeless powerful pattern which drew a continuous line down through the centuries and would go through me to the Laceys who came after me. Underneath the chant I could hear a drumbeat, a deep and solemn sound, and I knew there was no drum but my own thudding heart and the sound of the land itself.

The song finished and I gave a deep sigh; I looked at the bright faces of the young people from Acre who were ready to call me their friend and had wanted me to be the girl who brought in the spring.

Then we turned without speaking and I led the way out of the garden under the ghostly arch into the silent stable yard and out of the Dower House grounds, along the drive towards the footpath to the downs. I glanced up at the dark bulk of the house as we went past. Mama's window was dark, and Uncle John's. Everyone in the whole world was asleep except the young people in all the downland villages who would be walking quietly through the Sussex lanes and climbing up the dark grassy shoulders of the downs to see the sun rise pale over the land.

Richard walked beside me and I glanced at him and smiled. He took my chilled hand and slipped it in the pocket of his jacket and held it, and we walked hand-clasped in the centre of the crowd along the pale road towards Acre.

When we turned right up the bridle-way to the downs, there was room for no more than two abreast, and the others fell into line behind us, two by two, some girls walking side by side and some lads with each other, but mostly Acre was in pairs. The spring had been calling to them as insistently as it had been calling to me, and the young people of Acre were impatient to be courting.

We climbed up the little path, and my boots slid on the mud and I was glad of Richard's firm grip. He did not say a word to me and I felt more and more dreamlike as we walked together under the great beech trees of the coppice with courting couples behind us and nothing but the sleeping land around us.

It was a long walk, for I was accustomed to ride, and I was surprised how breathless and slow I was in getting to the top. At the very head of the footpath was a fence to keep the sheep in, breached by a kissing gate. Richard stood back to let me go first and as I closed the gate to let myself out the other side, he put his hands on top of mine to hold me still, with the gate between us. I looked up wonderingly into his face and he bent his dark head slowly down to me. My lips parted and his mouth came down and gently, gently, kissed me, as soft as a moth to a candle-flame.

I stepped back with a little gasp, but behind Richard were the Acre young people and they were all smiles. I looked among them for Clary's dear face and I saw her beam at me and wink, inviting me to romp in a hollow with Richard and deny my loyalty to James and my training as an indoor child. I frowned at her, for she should know well enough by now that Richard would never touch me in that way. But she smiled on, unrepentant.

Matthew was near her, but walking at arm's length, and when she came through the gate, he did not take the opportunity to kiss her as the following couples did.

'What's the matter with you two?' I asked as she came to where I waited on a little bank of downland turf, watching the others come through the gate.

Clary gave a grimace. 'We're at daggers drawn,' she said. 'He's a fool. Everything's spoiled.'

'Why, what's happened?' I asked.

'It's those silly rhymes he's always been writing,' she said impatiently. 'I never paid them no mind. But he showed them to some publisher in Chichester and the damned man has printed them and is selling them and all.'

'But, Clary, that's wonderful . . .' I started.

Clary rounded on me, her eyes flashing. 'Wonderful it is not!' she said, crudely mimicking my word. 'The man took his poems and printed them all pretty in his little book. And d'you know what they've called it? They've called it *Cuckoos Calling: The Poems of a Sussex Simpleton*.'

I gaped. 'A what?' I asked. I could not believe I had heard aright.

'Yes,' Clary said viciously. '"A Sussex Simpleton". And they've told him he has a fine untutored voice and that he is in touch with the beauty of nature because he is an idiot! So that's why I am not as proud as Punch for him. Just when everyone was forgetting that the parish guardians ever called him simple in the first place!' She ended on a little sob.

'How did they ever think it?' I demanded bewildered.

'His gran told them,' Clary said, dashing at her eyes with the hem of her gown. 'The silly old fool told them his entire life-history when they came out to Acre in their fine carriage to tell him they liked his poems and ask if he had any more. She told them that he had been left behind when the parish roundsman took the other children because they thought he was simple. She told them that he stammered and that he could not speak right when he was a lad. So they are calling him the dumb nightingale. And the newspaper called him the idiot songster . . .' She broke off and openly wept with her apron up to her face.

'They can be stopped . . .' I said. 'We can stop them publishing the book. We can stop them talking about him like that in the newspaper. They won't speak of him like that when we explain . . .'

'He won't!' Clary said sharply. 'I never thought he was a fool until the day I saw him smile at a newspaper which had called him an inspired natural for all the world to see – and him glad about it. They've paid him twelve guineas already, and that's just to buy him paper and pens. They're going to pay him more. He is set to be a rich young man. And he thinks he'll go to Chichester and then to London. He thinks he'll be taken around to the great poets and writers and they will like him. And he'll never come back to Acre at all!'

'Clary!' I said aghast.

'I hate him!' she said with sudden energy. 'You'd have thought he'd never walked all night for me with one of the babbies. You'd have thought he'd forgotten what the real world is like. He thinks he'll take me with him. He told the gentlemen that he's betrothed to a girl from his village, and they asked him if I was presentable.' Clary broke off. 'Presentable!' she said scathingly. But then her anger fell away from her as rapidly as water off a water-wheel. 'Julia, I tell you true, I think he's broke my heart,' she ended.

I put my hands out to her and she moved to me and laid her head on my shoulder. 'Oh, poor Clary,' I said to her, as tenderly as her mother. 'Don't cry, Clary, darling, I've never seen you cry. It'll come out right. Matthew could never love anyone but you. There could never be anyone for you but Matthew. This has just turned his head for a little while. But look – he's up here on the downs with us today. He's not that different. He'll maybe stay a little while in London, but he'll come home again. He'd always come home to you.'

Clary pulled away from me and rubbed her red eyes. 'I'll not have him!' she declared. 'I'll not have a man who will let people call him an idiot and think himself clever. I've not told him so yet, but I will tell him that I won't marry him; and I'll tell him why and all. He's shamed me. He's shamed himself. I'll tell him that and I'll break our betrothal.'

I put my hands out to her in a helpless gesture, half trying to hold her. I pitied Matthew and I feared for their happiness. But in the back of my mind was a voice as deep as a tolling bell which warned me to hold Clary, to keep her beside me, to keep her near me, as if some mortal danger threatened her.

But she would not stay. She tore away from my embrace and rubbed her eyes again. 'I'm a fool to have come,' she said bitterly. 'I thought it would be like the old days when my ma and pa came up here when the land was good and they were courting. I thought we would make friends – him and me – up here when the sun came up. But he brought his silly little pen and his paper and he told me he would write a poem about it. And now I have lost my temper, and cried, and told you. I had thought to keep it all a secret. I'll go home,' she said briskly. 'There's nothing to keep me here.'

'Clary, don't go,' I said urgently. I felt I should never see her again if I let her go. 'Stay with me. Richard and I were just going to walk around and pick hawthorn. Stay with us, Clary, dearest. Don't go.'

She slipped from my hands even though I was clinging to her.

'Nay,' she said sadly. 'I'm away. I'll see you this afternoon, at the dancing?'

'Promise you'll be there,' I said urgently. The tolling noise inside my head was louder. I felt I needed Clary to swear she would be there, without fail.

'Where else should I be?' she said wearily. 'I'm not likely to write a sonnet on my walk home. I'll be there, Julia,' she said as she gently unlaced my fingers from the corner of her shawl. 'Do you have a pleasant time maying now; I'll see you this afternoon, and I shall tell Matthew I will not stand for it, and break the betrothal as soon as they have brought the spring home.'

'Clary . . .' I said, making one more effort to keep her by me. 'Don't go, Clary. I have the sight. I am sure there is some danger.'

She smiled at me, an old wise smile, a smile as wise as a woman who has no foresight except the knowledge that all women are born to grieve. 'Never mind,' she said sadly. 'I have had the worst pain these past few days I am ever likely to have. If he had killed me with his own hands, it would not have been worse than to see him taken away from me and from Acre for such a trumpery cause. But the worst of it is over now. I fought against the men from Chichester, and they have won. All I have to do now is to tell him I will see him no more. That I love him no more. And then the worst will be over. Let me go now, Julia,' she said sweetly. 'There's no trouble you, or your sight, can save me from. There is just me, and my anger, and Matthew's folly. And the sorrow we make out of that is our own concern.'

She left me then. She turned away from me and made her way back through the kissing gate where Matthew had not kissed her, and down the track to Acre, to her little cottage, to think about the love she had known, and the promises she had made, and the future she had planned with the lad who no longer knew where his heart lay.

I stood as cold as a marble statue in the darkness, and then someone called to me in a friendly voice, 'You must find a hawthorn bush and pick a branch, Miss Julia! We all gather at the head of the chalky streak when the sun comes up!'

It was Jimmy Dart, with his arm around Rosie. She was flushed from the walk but scarcely out of breath. I could not have recognized in her the pale girl who coughed over her work in the dirty cellar. She laid her head on Jimmy's shoulder; the love between them was as strong and as warm as the night breeze blowing.

'Are you robbing Ralph Megson of his apprentice?' I accused her in mock severity. She and Jimmy exchanged a glance and laughed.

'It's from his being a linkboy,' she explained. 'He can't stop himself crossing the road.'

I laughed too. Ralph's cottage was on the other side of Acre lane from the little cottage where Rosie lived, and Jimmy crossing from one side of the lane to the other was a regular sight.

'We're betrothed,' Rosie said shyly. 'We'll marry when we're sixteen. Mr Megson has promised us a cottage of our own.'

I nodded, smiling. Ralph had mentioned it to me, and I had written the news to James. 'No more glove-making,' I said with satisfaction.

Rosie looked sly. 'Just one last pair,' she said. 'I've started them already, but I don't know when they'll be needed.' She gleamed at me. 'Your wedding-day gloves, Miss Julia! For the day you marry Mr Fortescue. I'm making you special Wideacre gloves, with a sheaf of wheat on them!'

'Oh, Rosie!' I said in delight. 'Thank you! But you know the engagement has not been announced yet. Mr Fortescue and I are not betrothed.'

Jimmy laughed aloud at that. 'Not formally engaged!' he exclaimed. 'Why the first time I ever met you, he wouldn't have a light because he wanted to walk you home from the Pump Room in the dark!'

'Come on,' Richard interrupted suddenly. 'Come on, Julia!' His arm slid round my waist and his face was so close to me that I could feel the warmth of his breath on my hair. 'Come on, my springtime lady, and let us search for your hawthorn bush,' he said softly, drawing me away from the others. We walked slowly to the right along the hilltop, seeking the darker shadow of a hawthorn bush.

Richard was wearing his driving cape and as we walked arm in arm, he swung the side of it around me in a gesture which both warmed and claimed me for his own. I felt light-headed and sure-footed, walking on my land in the darkness.

We startled a ewe and her lamb, and they jumped up before us with a complaining bleat and scurried off into the darkness. The patch of grass where they had been lying was warmed and smelled of fleece. Richard tossed his cape down and I sat on a corner, then he wrapped the rest around me.

I was tense, remembering the last time we were on the downs together when he had kissed me without invitation and touched me against my will. But he held true to his word, and his arm around my shoulders was friendly, brotherly, nothing more.

We sat in silence for a time while the morning skies grew pearly; all around us the grass seemed at first grey, then it slowly grew green as the colour seeped into it with the morning warmth.

'I love you, little Julia,' Richard said softly, his voice tender. 'I wish you would forget your city friends and come back to me, come back to me and to Wideacre.'

I looked at his hazy smiling eyes and saw my old love, the love of my childhood and girlhood.

'It's too late,' I said, half regretfully. 'You will understand when you fall in love, Richard. You will understand then.'

His smile in the brightening light was rueful. 'I think I will never love anyone but you,' he said sweetly. Then he said no more.

The sky was growing brighter now, and the first tentative notes of birdsong were growing louder, with more birds waking and singing too. All about us couples were rising up and out of the hollows, brushing off their clothes and smiling at each other, sly-eyed with stolen pleasures.

Everyone was making their way towards the head of the downs where the hills looked down into Acre. There was an outcrop of chalk there which could be seen from anywhere on Wideacre, like a white stripe up the forehead of the downs. They called it Chalky Streak, and when Richard and I were little children and had lost our sense of direction, we could always find our way home by putting Chalky Streak directly before us and walking towards it. Now the young people from Acre and Richard and I stood at the top of it and waited for the sun to rise.

We faced the east, and the rising sun turned our faces rosy with its pink light. They sang the song again. I had learned the chanting little tune now and I could sing it with them. I was happy there, in the sunlight, with Richard holding my hand and the young people of Acre around me. But my heart was heavy, thinking of Clary, and when I looked around for Matthew, I saw that he was gone too. I shuddered. Some shadow touched me.

We finished our song with a little ripple of half-embarrassed laughter, and then turned towards the gate to walk back down the footpath to Acre. They had brought Misty for me, and Richard cupped his hands for me and tossed me up into the saddle. She was a carnival horse, with a wreath of hawthorn around her neck. They gave me a flower crown and a peeled wand to carry in my right hand and told me to lead them down the track to Acre. Misty tossed her head – disliking the flowers around her neck – and I had my usual trouble with riding side-saddle in a walking dress. I pulled my skirt down as well as I could. Ted Tyacke gave me a cheeky wink at seeing my ankles, but I could not play the Bath miss at dawn on the top of the downs.

They sang as we came down the track, and together we brought the spring home to Acre and the springtime jokes with us. In the old tradition the young people went around the village with their branches and played little tricks on the villagers. A spinster who loved a boy who did not care for her knew her secret was a public joke when she opened the door and found a stripped wand of willow on the step. A husband who was ruled by his wife was left a branch and a hen's feather to take in to her when he prepared the breakfast that morning. A father whose discipline of his son seemed too stern to the crowd had an ash twig pinned to his door, and a wife who smiled too easily at the young men of Acre had the dubious compliment of a hawthorn branch with red ribbons left at her gate.

On Clary's doorstep they put one half of a flowering branch of hawthorn, and the matching half was pinned to Matthew's door. The most popular couple in Acre was blessed with the crowd's goodwill. Only I felt uneasy and saw them as funeral flowers, not good-luck charms at all. Only I knew that this very day the betrothal which had started in the bad days of Acre would be ended just when things were coming right.

21

Mama was sitting up in bed, drinking her morning chocolate, when I tapped at her door after changing into my riding habit and brushing the hawthorn petals from my hair.

'Good morning!' she said as I came in. 'The Queen of the May herself! Do you have magical powers this morning, my dear? Could you give me eternal youth and beauty, please?'

I laughed. 'I think you have it already, Mama,' I said, sitting on the foot of her bed. 'You have looked quite unfairly pretty ever since Uncle John came home.'

Mama smiled. 'That is from being happy,' she said lightly. 'But how are you? Are you tired after your dawn chorusing?'

I stretched. 'No,' I said. 'Feeling lazy, but not tired, though it is a longer walk than I thought. I always ride up that hill; I've never walked it before.'

'You could have a rest before breakfast,' Mama offered. 'Or perhaps you should go back to bed and I will wake you at noon.'

I got up from the bed and went across to her window-seat. 'Don't tempt me,' I said. 'If the village is merrymaking, it is my job to check the animals. I shall go up to the downs after breakfast and see the sheep, and then down to the Fenny fields to see that the cows are well.'

Mama nodded and threw back the bed covers and slipped out of bed. 'You put me to shame,' she said. 'I had thought we would all take a holiday!'

The garden gate banged.

'Who is that?' she asked, pulling on a wrapper and coming over to the window to stand beside me.

'Jem is just back from the London stage with letters,' I said, going towards the door. 'Maybe there's something from James!'

I sped down the stairs and nearly collided with Jenny Hodgett taking the letters from Jem at the front door. 'Any for me?' I asked.

Jenny turned, smiling. 'Yes, Miss Julia,' she said. 'From your young man, by the looks of it.'

I took it. It had James's familiar sloping writing on the envelope, but it had been franked for him. It had been posted in England.

'Jenny!' I exclaimed. 'This was posted in England. James is home!'

She beamed back at me and I clutched the letter in both hands. 'I'll read it in the stables,' I said, suddenly wanting to be alone and uninterrupted. 'I'll be in for breakfast, tell Mama.' I slipped out of the front door and down the garden path and through the side gate to the stable yard.

Jem had gone back to his room above the tack room and the stables were deserted. Misty was in her loose box where I had put her, still with her saddle and bridle on, her wreath of blossoms on a hook outside her stable. I opened her door and slipped into her stable, and sat down on an upturned bucket. She nuzzled the top of my head gently and I smelled her oaty breath as she sniffed at me. The letter crackled as I slit the envelope and spread it on my knee, leaning towards the half-door of the stable to catch the light.

It was brief.

Dearest heart,

This letter precedes me by no more than six days. I returned to England this afternoon. I shall be with my papa's lawyers tomorrow, and as soon as I have travelled to Bristol and reported to my papa, I shall pack my bags and be with you the day after that – May 6. If you can squeeze me into your little house, I shall come to dinner and stay the night. Or, if you cannot, I shall sleep in the flower-bed beneath your window; but if I cannot see you at once, I shall go utterly and totally insane.

The contracts for our marriage are finally done – I shall sign the deeds tomorrow. The settlement my papa is to make on us will build us a house even grander than your own Wideacre Hall. I shall bring some plans with me when I come and we can set to work building at once.

As far as I am concerned, we can be married tomorrow, if that suits you? Or perhaps you require longer to prepare a trousseau? I would not wish you to think me impatient. Next week will be soon enough.

My darling, I kiss your hands, your feet, the ground beneath your feet, and the rocks beneath the ground.

In all seriousness, all the business preparation for the marriage is done, and it remains only for you to name the day when you will make me wholly happy . . . and half squire of Wideacre!

Make it soon.

Yours for ever,

James

I reached a hand up and stroked Misty's flank without being aware of the warmth of her smooth coat beneath my fingers. James was coming home at last, and there was no hitch, no difficulty. He might joke about being ready to marry tomorrow, but I knew James. If he told me, even in jest, that he was ready to marry, then he was. And, God knew, I was ready to be his wife.

I got to my feet, thinking to go into the house and tell Mama that James was home and to ask Mrs Gough for the best dinner she could devise for the day he was to arrive – but then I paused. I wanted to be somewhere quiet and alone for a little while longer. The happiness I had in this gentle sunlit morning was too much to mislay amid a hustle of menus and gowns and preparations. I tightened Misty's girth and led her out of the stable to the mounting-block. I folded the letter and tucked it neatly into the little pocket of my riding jacket. Then I rode Misty out of the stable yard and turned her right up the drive towards Wideacre Hall.

I rode carelessly, on a loose rein, dreaming of how it would be when James came to me, whether I could go and wait for him at the Acre corner, and if he would drive himself or come in a post-chaise, whether he would smile to see me patient at the corner, or whether I would look foolish, like a village girl waiting for her swain. I passed all my dresses in rapid review, thinking which would suit me the best and wondering if I had any new gowns he had not seen in Bath which he might like. And I thought about the menu for his dinner, and what were his favourite cuts of meat and what puddings he cared for. I smiled as I rode, at peace in a little golden reverie of joy, because James was coming home.

The builders had taken the May holiday, so the garden and the new hall were deserted. I rode past the terrace towards the rose garden. I wanted to sit in the sunshine and dream a little more before I went home to tell Mama that we must start to prepare for my wedding day. I hitched Misty to the trellis on the old summer-house and went inside. It was sheltered here, warm. The birds were singing in the woods around the garden, and the summer-house smelled pleasantly of dry leaves and crumbling timber. I sat on the floor, careless of my cream riding habit, and leaned my head back against the wooden wall. With James's open letter in my hand, I closed my eyes and dozed, still smiling, still dreaming of the day when he would be with me.

It seemed, at first, part of that dream – a kiss, as light as a butterfly's wing, as soft as a feather on my cheek. I smiled and stirred, not opening my eyes. It seemed part of the dream of James, part of that previous dream in the summer-house when I had been a girl, when I had been Beatrice. I felt as tranced, as dreamy as I had then, and I relaxed, as contented as a sleeping child on the dusty floor of the summer-house, and felt my face covered with kisses. The weight of him came on me gently, warm. As feckless as Beatrice herself, I put my arms around his neck and welcomed his touch. He kissed me on the mouth and I opened my lips in pleasure.

The touch of his tongue in my mouth was like ice.

My eyes flew open, I jerked my head away.

It was Richard.

At once I struggled to be up and away from him, but he did not let me up. His weight, which I had welcomed, was suddenly a weapon. He was pinning me down, and I was not able to struggle against him to throw him off.

'Richard!' I said in anger. 'Let me up! Let me up this minute!'

He said nothing in answer, he would not even meet my eyes. Instead he reached down and fumbled with my skirts and petticoats, ignoring my ineffectual pushes against his chest.

I gasped. Richard had pulled my skirt up to my waist. I had a sudden recollection of the goshawk bating away in a frenzy of terror. I struggled to get my left hand free and I slapped his face as hard as I could.

He shook his head like a bullock stung by a horse-fly and grabbed for that hand. His weight pinned my other arm between his body and mine. I wriggled, but I was helpless.

'Richard!' I said more loudly, sharply. There was a hard note of panic in my voice. I heard it, and Richard heard it too. He looked at me then for the first time. His eyes were blank, a glazed blue, bright as glass, expressionless. Then he pushed one hard knee between my legs and parted them, bruising the flesh.

I screamed.

I screamed without thinking if there could be anyone in earshot. I screamed out of terror, without thought of managing Richard or of dealing with him. I screamed in the same mindless fright as that of the goshawk who had launched herself blindly into the air, forgetting she was held fast.

At once, as if my scream were a signal, he twisted the wrist he was holding so tightly that the skin burned with pain and, though I opened my mouth to scream again, all I could do was gasp in horror as I heard the slight click of a small bone breaking, and felt my whole arm, my whole body, burn with pain. Richard dropped my hand and put his palm over my mouth instead.

'If you struggle, I shall break the other wrist,' he said softly, almost conversationally. 'If you scream, I will strangle you. I will strangle you until you lose consciousness, Julia, and then I will do what I have to do, and then I may tighten my hands a little more. Do you understand?'

His face was so close to mine. I could feel his breath on my cheek. He was not panting, he was breathing evenly, steadily; he might have been taking a gentle stroll.

'Richard . . .' I said in a frightened whisper, 'don't do this, Richard, please. Why are you doing this?'

His smile was darker and his eyes more navy blue than I had ever seen them. 'You were going to bring in a rival squire,' he said. His voice was a thread of hatred. 'You were going to build a bigger house than Wideacre Hall. I read it in his letter. While you slept there, beside *my* house on *my* land, you were dreaming of bringing in a rival squire and claiming half of our land.'

I opened my mouth to disagree, my mind scrambling like a trapped animal for some way out.

'You are my betrothed,' Richard said. 'I was a fool to let you leave Wideacre and a fool to try to win you back kindly. Now I am going to claim you for my own.'

His words, and their meaning, sank in.

'Richard, no!' I said. I could feel my throat tightening with terror. This nightmare in the summer-house was too like the bullying of our childhood. I could feel myself slipping from courage, from the strong abilities of my womanhood, into the panic-stricken victim that I had really been when we were children.

'It will hurt,' he said with unconcealed pleasure. 'I think you will be afraid, Julia.'

'No!' I screamed, but my throat had clamped tight and no cry came out. I croaked silently, and Richard guessed that I was now too afraid to make a sound, and his eyes sparkled in utter delight.

He put one hand down and loosened his breeches and pulled them down. Then, with one hand holding my wrist, the other back over my mouth, forcing my head back on the dusty floor, he reared away from me, and with one hating, savage thrust he pushed into me, and my scream of pain was choked on his hard hand and my sobs retched in the depth of my throat.

It was like a nightmare, like the worst of nightmares, and it did not stop. While my hurting body registered the pain, I tried to find some courage from somewhere to say, 'Well, it is done.' But it was not done. Richard pushed into the blood and the hurt flesh again and again and again. He seemed to take delight in paining me so badly that I was screaming for help inside my head and hot tears were spilling down my face.

He gave a great shudder at the pinnacle of the very worst of it and then he collapsed and dropped his weight upon me as if I were nothing more to him than a bale of straw.

I lay spreadeagled on the dusty floor, where once I had dreamed of passion, with the tears pouring down my cheeks in a morass of pain and misery. I could feel I was bleeding, I could feel a bruise forming on my thigh where he had knelt upon me; but I could not comprehend the pain inside me.

He rolled off me and then was suddenly alert, looking out of the open doorway. He jumped to his feet, without a word to me, and, hitching his breeches, ran down the steps into the rose garden as if all the fiends of hell were after him. He ran from me as if he had murdered me indeed and he was leaving a sprawled body. I lay still, as he had left me, and I stared at the white roof and at the little hole in the timbers where the blue sky showed through, and I felt a little trickle of blood between my legs.

My belly seemed to have gone into some sort of regular spasms of pain, for every now and then it eased, but then there was a great wave which came over me and made me gasp and bite the back of my uninjured hand so as not to cry out. My broken wrist was throbbing, and I could see it was bruised black and swelling.

I lay on the dusty floor with my pretty cream riding habit pulled up to my waist and my hair tumbled down and spread in the dust, and I knew myself to be so broken and destroyed that it would have been better for me if Richard had completed his threat and strangled me while I lay there.

I don't know how long it was before I sat up. I did not think, I did not think at all about what had happened, or what I could do. All I could think of was an urgent, passionate need to be home. I wanted to be in my bedroom with the door locked. I wanted to be in my bed with the covers up over my head. I sat up, and then I took hold of the doorjamb and heaved myself to my feet. I staggered, but I did not fall. I seemed to have stopped bleeding. My dress was unmarked. I held tight to the door and took one shallow step at a time into the rose garden.

Misty was gone. I shut my eyes and then opened them again in the hopes that I was mistaken, that she was where I had left her. But she had pulled her reins free and taken herself off home.

I sobbed at that, the first sound I had made since I had said, 'Richard, no!' in a voice which would not have halted a mouse. Misty was gone and I could not see how I could ever get home. All I wanted, all I wanted in the whole world, was to be home and asleep.

My head was swimming, and my knees buckled and I collapsed on to the step of the summer-house. I rested my head in the crook of my elbow and let the spring sunshine warm my back. I did not think I would ever feel warm inside again. I stayed like that, quite still, for what seemed like a lifetime of numb misery.

Then I heard, in the woods, voices calling my name, over and over again, and a little silence between the calling while they listened for me. I heard hoofbeats on the drive, and Jem's voice, harsh with anxiety calling, 'Miss Julia! Miss Julia!'

'I'm here!' I said in a pathetic little voice. 'Here, Jem! At the summer-house!' I got to my feet and went down the drive to meet him.

He was riding Prince, and I saw the horse suddenly leap forward when Jem caught sight of me. He was beside me in an instant.

'Did you take a fall?' he said. 'Sea Mist came home with a broken rein and her saddle too loose. I guessed you'd come off her.'

I nodded, too weary to speak and too full of pain and confusion to say the unsayable, to accuse.

And anyway, I felt that it was me who was in the wrong.

'Could you ride?' he asked me, 'or shall I go home and send for the carriage?'

I nodded dumbly towards Prince. 'I want to go home,' I said pitifully. Jem lifted me up on to Prince's back, and then vaulted up behind me. His arms were around me, holding me safe and steady, but for a moment's madness I was suddenly afraid of him, of Jem, whom I had known all my life and who had come out calling and looking for me.

I bit my bottom lip to keep myself from crying out. I knew I had nothing to fear from Jem.

I had not smiled and walked with him. I had not kissed him before all Acre. And I had not promised that we should be married. All these things I had done with Richard, and then I had lied to him about my plans. I had never told him about the plan to live on Wideacre with James. I had never lied outright indeed; but I had kept silent.

And when he had first kissed me in the summer-house, I had smiled.

And when I had first felt his weight upon me, I had put my arms around his neck and opened my mouth for the taste of his tongue.

'I'm going to be sick,' I said abruptly to Jem, and turned my head away from him as I retched over Prince's shoulder.

Nothing came but a mouthful of bile with the acid taste of fear.

Jem turned Prince's head for home and took us down the drive at a steady walk. 'Your ma stayed at home in case you were found, or walked home,' Jem said gently. 'Everyone else is out looking. I'll sound the gong when we get in so they know. And someone will pull the school bell to tell 'em you're safe found.'

I nodded. Prince was walking on the soft turf in the centre of the drive. Even that smooth walk jolted my broken wrist and my clenched stomach almost more than I could bear. But the Dower House was in sight, and I gritted my teeth and kept silent.

The front-garden gate was open, and Jem rode Prince right up the path to the door and shouted, 'Holloa!' through the open doorway.

I could see a figure coming out from the front hall, and I could feel myself longing for my mama's safe touch.

But it was not my mama. It was Richard. My mama was behind him, but it was Richard who was first out down the steps and who reached up to lift me down from the horse, and who carried me in his arms like a little child come safe home to him.

'Julia! Thank God!' he said. 'I'll take her, Jem. There. Gently with that hand.'

Then Mama was at his side and her cheek was cool against mine. 'Poor darling!' she said gently. 'Did you fall?'

I opened my mouth; Richard's arms around me tightened slightly, imperceptibly. I glanced up at his familiar face, so close to mine. Richard, who had been my dearest love since my earliest childhood. His eyes were shining, he was smiling at me with such warmth, but a little hint of devilry lay at the back of his blue eyes.

'Tell your mama, Julia,' he said, and his voice was warm with laughter. 'Tell us what happened and how you came to hurt your hand like this.'

It was impossible.

I could no more have told her the truth than I could have shouted obscenities at her. I would have been too shamed. Shamed for her, shamed for Richard and shamed for me.

My throat tightened and the tears poured down my face. 'I fell,' I said. My throat was still sore and my voice was croaky. 'I fell from Misty and she ran off.'

Richard turned at once and took me towards the house, Mama holding my sound hand in hers as we went up the stairs to my room. Richard put me gently on the little bed and turned for the door. He paused in the doorway and looked at me, his face alight with amusement, and he closed one eye in a wink as if we shared a most delightful secret. Then he was gone.

I slept until early afternoon when I woke to the noise of my bedroom door opening, and Mama came in with a tray in both hands and her eyes on the level of the milk in the jug.

'Tea,' she said. 'Tea for the invalid. Julia, my darling, I cannot tell you what a fright you gave us all!'

I tried to smile. But I had no smile. And when I sat up in bed, I found my lips were trembling so that I could scarcely speak.

'My wrist hurts,' I said childishly.

Mama looked at it. 'Good gracious,' she said. 'It looks badly bruised, or even broken.' She put down the tray and went straight away out of the room. I heard her footsteps running down the stairs and then I heard her and John come back up together.

He looked at my hand, half clenched against the pain, blue as an iris. 'Broken,' he said across me to my mama. 'You'd best go out, Celia – this is something Julia and I will be better doing alone.'

My mama looked to me. 'Shall I stay?' she asked.

'No,' I said, though I was past caring.

'I'll get my bag,' Uncle John said.

Setting the broken bone in my wrist was a painful business. Brutish. But in some odd way I welcomed the pain. It was clear, forceful. It was one of the few things left in the world which I could be sure of. The pain of a broken wrist. The small square of Wideacre sky seen from my window. And Richard's sly, naughty smile.

'You'll stay abed for dinner,' Mama said, looking at my white face when John allowed her back in the room.

'Yes,' I said feebly.

'Would you like anything now?' she asked.

I drew a breath. I knew I had to tell her. Of course she had to know. 'Mama . . .' I started.

'Richard said he would have his dinner up here with you,'

Mama offered. 'I expect you would like the company, wouldn't you, darling?'

I hesitated. The birdsong outside seemed to go quiet with me.

I could not say it. I could not tell her what he had done to me. I could not tell her how I had lain back and smiled and let it happen. I could not tell them that John's son and the part heir to Wideacre was a rapist.

'Yes,' I whispered. 'Richard can have his dinner up here.'

'Good,' Mama said, businesslike. 'He's out in the stables now, seeing to your horse.'

Something broke in my head at that – through the haze of laudanum and the heaviness of my sin. I sat up in bed, and I spoke across Uncle John to my mama. 'No!' I said. 'Mama, please! Please don't let him touch Misty.'

She shot a bewildered look at John as if this might be some symptom of a blow on the head or high temperature.

'Please!' I said urgently. 'Promise me, Mama! Don't let him touch my horse.'

'No, my darling,' she said gently. 'Not if you do not wish it. I will go down to the stables now and tell him to come away from her, and leave her to Jem if that is what you wish.'

'It is,' I said, and sank back on the pillows.

'Now sleep,' John said authoritatively. 'Sleep until dinner-time. There will be no more pain and there is nothing to worry you, so sleep, Julia.'

I smiled towards him, but I could barely see his face; the room was wavering before my eyes. I think I was asleep before the two of them had left the room.

I slept until dinner.

Richard came upstairs and Jenny Hodgett served our meal and stood discreetly at Richard's elbow throughout.

I ate little, for I was not hungry. And every now and then I would look at Richard and feel my eyes fill with useless, inexplicable tears. I felt that it was my fault. My fault that it had happened. My fault that I had not told at once, the minute I was home, that through my cowardice Richard and Mama, Uncle John and I would all be living a lie. I had not told when I should have told. And now I could say nothing. I could not even stop Richard smiling at me in that familiar, conspiratorial way.

When Jenny brought up a dish of tea for me, she had a message from Uncle John: if I felt well enough, Mr Megson was downstairs and would speak with me. Richard left the room and Jenny helped me from my bed and into my wrapper. I knew it must be something important for Ralph to come to the house at this time of night, and I paused before my mirror to push my hair back and tie it with a ribbon. I knew that I would not be able to tell Ralph either. I wondered if he would know without being told that I had lost my honesty, that I was a liar.

Ralph and Uncle John were downstairs in the library. He smiled at me and asked after my accident, and apologized for calling me downstairs when I was unwell. I nodded. Ralph and I had always been mercifully brief with each other.

'Clary Dench is missing,' he said shortly. 'I'm trying to discover when she was last seen and if she had plans to go away for the holiday.'

I took a deep breath. I could scarcely understand what he was saying. 'I saw her on the downs, at the maying,' I said. 'She said she was going home, and she left early. She was planning no holiday away from Acre.'

Ralph nodded. 'I can't believe she'd go off without a word to anyone,' he said, half to Uncle John, half to me.

'D'you think some harm has befallen the girl?' Uncle John demanded.

Ralph grimaced and glanced at me in case I could help him. 'It's always hard to tell with wenches,' he said. 'I'll not turn out the village to hunt for her on a fool's errand. It's their first holiday in years and they've been out once today already looking for Miss Julia.'

'Clary's not flighty,' I said. The words I was speaking were echoing coldly as if I were speaking down a well. I knew I had seen true on the downs in the morning. I had tried to keep Clary with me then. I had been afraid to tell her how dark a shadow I saw on her. I seemed to be afraid to tell the truth to anyone. 'She'd have told someone if she was going off. And I don't believe she'd have left her family without a word like that.'

Ralph nodded. The door opened and Richard came in quietly and stood at one end of the long table, at the carver chair, where the head of the household would sit.

'What would you wish?' Ralph asked the air midway between Uncle John and me. He did not even glance at Richard.

'Take two or three men and look around the woods for her,' Uncle John said, his eyes on me.

I nodded. 'Start at the Fenny,' I said. 'Clary always went down to the river when she was sad. And she was very sad today.'

Ralph nodded. 'She had quarrelled with Matthew?'

'Yes,' I said, taciturn.

'I'll have a few out to look for her,' he said. 'But it's a nuisance. I had promised Acre they would have a couple of days free of work. Now I shall have to order some men out when they will want to be dancing.'

'I'll help,' Richard said suddenly. We all turned and looked at him. He was very bright. 'I'll help. There's little I can do to help on the land,' he said pleasantly. 'I'd be glad to save you some trouble, Mr Megson, and help with finding Clary.'

'Thank 'ee,' Ralph said slowly. He was looking at Richard very hard, no smile in his eyes. 'That would be a help. I'll send the men down to you tomorrow morn, as soon as it is light, unless the lass turns up home before then.'

'I'll be ready,' Richard promised.

Ralph turned to me. 'And you, Miss Julia? Will you be resting tomorrow or will you be well enough then to come down and at least watch the dancing?'

I was about to say that I would be well enough to go down to Acre tomorrow, but a pang in my belly made me gasp and my eyes filled with ineffectual tears. 'I'm tired,' I said weakly. 'I'll come down to the village when I feel better, Mr Megson.'

'Aye,' Ralph said generously. 'Don't come before you're well. I'm surprised you fell at all, but then, good riders often fall the hardest. I'm truly sorry it was a fall from a horse I'd chosen for you!'

'It was not her fault,' I said. My lips had grown cold and stiff and I could hardly speak. 'It was all my own fault, Ralph. It was all my fault. I should have known better.'

'Now that's enough,' said Richard kindly. 'I'll fetch your mama to put you to bed.' He turned to Ralph. 'She's still shocked from her fall,' he said.

Ralph stepped backwards one pace and bowed. 'I'm sorry to intrude,' he said awkwardly.

I held my hand out to him. I wanted to say that he was not intruding, that he would never intrude. I wanted to beg him to look for Clary, to tell him of my foreboding for her, to make him see with the sight that something was badly wrong. But it was no good. I could not tell him that truth. I could not tell him that I had not fallen from my horse. I could do no more than look towards Ralph with one long imploring glance – and then the tears welled up in my eyes and rolled down my cheeks.

'I am sorry,' I said in a voice choked with weeping. 'I am so sorry. I cannot seem to stop crying.'

'Bedtime,' John said with kind firmness. Richard came in with Mama and she helped me up the stairs to my bedroom and tucked me up in bed as if I were a little girl again. All the time the tears were rolling down my face and she wiped them with her own cool handkerchief which smelled of lilies, and then tucked it under my pillow and left me with one candle for a light.

I lay on my back and felt the tears roll outwards from the corner of my eyes and down my temples in drying little lanes of desolation. Then I gasped and sat up in my bed as I remembered that my petticoat and shift were stained with blood.

Wearily I got out of bed and went to the chest where I had bundled them, and I pulled them out. The blood was brown – old and inoffensive now. I folded them up and stuffed them on the embers of my bedroom fire. They smouldered and burned as

I tumbled back into bed and slept, and it was doubtless the smoke from the fire that made me dream uneasy dreams about an empty house, and men coming with torches, and a fire which burned down the whole house and left nothing but ruin on the land.

Clary was dead.

I had guessed it. I had seen her in danger ever since I had looked along the lines of the raspberry-cane weeders and shuddered because she was not there.

No one knew who had done it, no one could think who would do such a thing to pretty Clary. But Richard said that they had found Matthew Merry beside the body. He was wet through and they guessed he had gone into the Fenny and pulled her out. She was in the river; she had floated down river to the weir above the new mill, but she had not drowned. They thought she had been strangled first and then thrown in the river. Clary would never drown. We had learned to swim together all those hot summers ago.

It looked bad for Matthew. He would not say how he had found her. He would not say how he had come to be beside the river before the search party was out. He would not say or do anything except cradle her distorted face in his arms and weep and stammer her name over and over.

I cried out when Uncle John told me, his face grim with the news Richard brought back to the Dower House. My mama was by my side at once with more hartshorn and water.

'Drink this, my darling,' she said, and I drank it, obedient as a little child, with my eyes fixed on John's face, seeking the merciful numbness of the drug.

'What can have happened?' I asked, grief and sleep clogging my tongue.

'She was strangled,' he replied bluntly. Mama's hand flew out to stop him, but he shook his head. 'She has to know, Celia,' he said. 'She has to know what is happening in Acre. Richard is talking to the village youths and girls. No one can think what could have happened. She had been quarrelling with her be-trothed. They think in Acre that she meant to jilt him.'

'No,' I said swiftly. 'It could not be Matthew Merry. He has the sweetest temper, and he has loved Clary ever since they were children. He could not have hurt her.'

'The lad who had the fainting fits?' Mama asked. Her eyes went to John's face. 'He used to faint, and when he came to his senses, he had no memory of himself or what he had done,' she said, her voice low.

Uncle John nodded.

'He never did anything bad when he had his fits,' I said suddenly. 'Don't look like that, Uncle John. He just had a weak head and sometimes he used to faint. He was the sweetest boy and he is a dear young man. He could not hurt a fly, let alone Clary! They were quarrelling, yes, but that does not mean he would hurt her. He adored her!'

Uncle John nodded. 'He knew where to find her,' he said quietly, 'and they found him holding her body and weeping. It looks very black against him.'

'No,' I said positively. 'It could not be. He would never hurt Clary. He would kill himself first.' I broke off then, for I was afraid I would start weeping again. No one in the Dower House knew Clary and Matthew well but me. Mama and Uncle John might be kind, but they had not played with the Acre children under the Wideacre trees. They did not know that those two had been plighted lovers since they were little children, that Matthew would have died rather than hurt Clary and that this quarrel must have pained them both.

'Perhaps Lord Havering can make something of it all,' Uncle John said. 'He is the nearest Justice of the Peace. Richard has gone to speak with him.'

I nodded. The truth of what had happened was only now starting to come clear to me. 'And Clary is dead,' I said slowly. 'Would she have been in much pain?'

I saw Mama's quick gesture to John again, but he answered me steadily and told me the truth. 'Only for brief moments,' he said. 'The killer strangled her with his hands. But she would not have been in pain or fear for long, Julia. She would have lost consciousness very swiftly.'

I nodded. I could hear the words, but I could not speak, for a rising wave of nausea was threatening to choke me. I could see in my mind Clary's bright pretty face and the tears in her eyes when she said Matthew had broken her heart and she promised she would meet me at the dancing.

'I can't bear it!' I said on a half-sob. 'On Wideacre!'

Then Uncle John took one arm, and Mama the other, and they helped me up the stairs to my bedroom. He poured me a measure of laudanum and Mama held my hand until my tight grip on her loosened and I started falling into sleep.

'Mama!' I suddenly called out, on the very edge of panic as I slid into sleep. 'Mama!'

For in that second between sleeping and wakefulness I thought that I was Clary running for my life through the woods of Wideacre, and behind me was the man who was coming to kill me. Coming to kill me because I had seen something so dreadful that he had no choice but to kill me. I had seen that decision in his eyes, and I knew that if I did not run faster than I had ever run in my life, he would catch me and throw me down to the ground and put his gentry-soft hands around my throat and tighten them until I could breathe no more. And in the dream I was Clary, running as if the devil himself were on her heels. But I was also myself. And I was as afraid as Clary.

I was *more* afraid, because I knew that when he caught her and she turned around and felt his hands at her throat and saw his face . . . then I would know who he was.

22

Matthew Merry had been the butt of the village since he stammered his first words. In the hard years he had done badly for food, since his only protector was his grandmother, old Mrs Merry. While her word was law with the older village people, she carried little weight with the younger ones who could not remember the time when she had been the most skilled midwife and layer-out in the county.

He was easily frightened. Protected only by his grandma, he had been bullied from babyhood. I think that was why Clary first treated him so sweetly. He made her feel motherly and she shielded him from the others in that hard little wolf-pack which she ruled.

When he found her dead, he lost all his shy cleverness, which she had seen first and which Ralph had encouraged. The confidence he had drawn from the men who praised his poems deserted him at once and he behaved like the idiot they called him. They found him with her sodden body held tight in his arms, rocking at the river's edge, crying her name over and over again. The tears were pouring down his cheeks so much that his face was as wet as dear, dead Clary's.

Richard and Lord Havering's man took him abruptly by an arm on each side and he made no effort to resist. They took him away from where he had found her, just above the weir by the mill-pond, where the body had stuck. He called her name louder as they led him away, but when they took him up in the Havering carriage with the coat of arms in the door, he fell silent and did nothing but weep. They made him sit on the floor, because he was so wet and grimy from the river. He did not object.

Then they questioned him. Where had he been that morning? When had he last seen her? As he was afraid, his stammer got worse. Richard blamed the stammer upon a guilty conscience; and all Matthew could do was to weep and say her name, over and over again. He could say no other word at all.

My grandpapa, Lord Havering, was not unkind, but he was brisk, impatient with the common people, familiar with lies and deceptions and accustomed to liars and criminals from Acre village. Richard had brought him an open-and-shut case, and all he needed to hear was young Matthew's confession. He did not shout at Matthew or offer him clemency if he would own up to his crime. He just mended his quill and looked at Matthew with cold eyes. And Matthew, heartbroken, and with the memory of an angry parting with Clary on his conscience – and knowing full well that Clary would only have been walking alone by the Fenny because she was struggling with their quarrel in her mind – stammered like an idiot and wept in his fright. Finally he flung himself down on the floor and said, 'It is my fault. It is my fault. It is my f-f-fault.'

That was as good as a confession of guilt, and his lordship called his clerk and had it written out fair. Young Matthew, blind and numb with grief, put his name to it, perhaps thinking to end this miserable interrogation so that he could go home and grieve for her in peace.

But they did not let him go. The clerk had two constables with him and they bundled him into their own carriage, a horrid affair with no windows and no door-handles on the inside. They took him to Chichester gaol and they threw him in with the self-confessed murderers and rapists to await sentencing at the quarter sessions.

And Richard rode home under a sickle moon humming the tune Matthew had sung with the others when we had brought the spring to Wideacre only the day before.

I was still asleep and I did not wake until the next morning when a great shout from downstairs woke me. It sounded like Ralph's voice, but I could not believe that Ralph could have raised his voice in my mama's house. I glanced at the window. It was late, nearly ten o'clock. Mama must have given orders that they should leave me asleep. For a moment I could not think why, and then my heart sank as I remembered that Clary was dead, killed by a stranger, and that there had been a murderer in the woods of Wideacre, that my wrist was broken in a fall from my horse and that I had somehow lost my courage – perhaps for horse-riding, perhaps for life – and that I could not stop a little tremor in my hands. I could not stop myself from weeping.

I stretched out for my wrapper at the foot of my bed and gave a little gasp of pain. I moved more cautiously then and dragged it on over my shoulders. I opened my bedroom door and listened. It was Ralph's voice and he was shouting in the library.

'An Acre lass dead, an Acre lad in Chichester gaol for her murder and a worthless confession to hang him! My oath, Dr MacAndrew, you have been damned remiss in this!'

Uncle John's voice was soft; I could not make out the words.

'Why was Julia not there, then?' Ralph demanded. 'If you did not summon me, why was it not done before Julia? She is part heir to Wideacre, equal to Master Richard. Why was Master Richard alone so busy in the matter?'

Ralph was silent while Uncle John answered, but I still could not hear what he said.

'If Miss Julia was half dead with typhus fever, she should *still* have been there!' Ralph bellowed. 'This news has gone like wild-fire around the village and everyone is angry, knowing a mistake has been made. Something like this could wreck the accord between the village and you. Acre has trusted you, and now there is an Acre lad behind bars with a hanging crime over his head.'

'He made a confession.' John's voice was clear now, louder.

'Aye,' Ralph said with sarcasm. 'And who was there? Lord Havering, who comes to the county in the shooting season and when he is short of funds. And Master Richard!'

'What exactly are you saying, Mr Megson?' Uncle John demanded, his tone as icy as Ralph's was hot.

'I'm saying that Acre does not trust the ability of Lord Havering to tell a horse from a haystack,' Ralph said rudely. 'We think he is half blind and half drunk. And I am saying that I do not trust Richard farther than I can pitch him. Why he should want poor Matthew Merry to hang, God alone knows, but everyone in Acre believes that Richard has sent that lad to gaol and will send him to the gallows.'

There was absolute silence in the library. I held my breath to listen.

'I take it you will accept a month's wages in lieu of notice, Mr Megson?' asked Uncle John coldly.

'I will,' said Ralph, and only I could have heard the despair in his voice.

'No,' I said, and I ran across the landing to my mama's room. She was sitting before her mirror, her hair down, with Jenny Hodgett frozen behind her, brush upraised. Mama looked around as I came into the room and nodded at the mute appeal in my face. She tossed the lovely unbound hair carelessly over her shoulders and went past me, downstairs. We went in together. I scarcely glanced at Ralph Megson. I was trembling again and praying inwardly that Mama would take control. I was as much use as a new-born kitten. I could feel the tears under my eyelids. Uncle John was sitting at the table, writing out a draft on his bank account.

'Mr Megson must stay,' Mama said. Uncle John looked up and noticed her morning dress and her hair tumbling down her back. His eyes were very pale and cold.

'He has accused your step-papa of drunkenness and incompetence, and he has accused Richard of perjury,' Uncle John said blankly. 'I assume that he would not wish to work for us any more.'

I glanced at Ralph. His face was impassive.

'Mr Megson,' my mama said softly. 'You will withdraw what you have said, won't you? You will stay? There are so many things in Acre yet to be done. And you promised Acre you would help to do them.'

His eyes met hers for a long measuring moment, and then he nodded.

He was about to say yes.

I know he was about to say yes.

But I had left the library door open behind me; the front door opened and Richard came in and checked as he saw us. He took in the scene and he beamed at Ralph as if he were delighted to see him.

'A problem?' he asked.

'Mr Megson thinks that Matthew Merry is innocent,' John said abruptly. 'Are you sure you put no pressure on him, Richard? It is a hanging matter, as I am sure you realize.'

Richard's smile was as candid as a child's. 'Of course not,' he said. 'Lord Havering was there all the time, and his clerk too. It was all completely legal. It was all conducted with perfect propriety.'

Ralph puffed out with a little hissing noise at Richard's mannered enunciation of 'perfect propriety'. I saw my hands were shaking and I clasped them together to keep them still.

'And have you no doubt at all?' Uncle John demanded. 'Matthew is a young man, ill-educated, and he was taken by surprise. Are you certain he knew what he was signing? Are you positive he knew what he was saying?'

'That is really a question for the examining Justice,' Richard said easily. 'You should ask Lord Havering, sir. It was his examination and deposition. I was just there because I reported the crime to him and told him that I thought there was a case against Matthew Merry if he chose to examine it. I had no other role to play in the matter.'

I said nothing. I was watching Ralph. His eyes were narrowed and he was staring at Richard. 'You're your mother's child, all right,' he said. Uncle John looked at him, and they exchanged a hard level gaze.

'I'd like to stay if I can,' Ralph said abruptly. 'May I have a day to think it over, and also to go into Chichester to see what can be done for Matthew?'

Uncle John nodded. 'I should like you to stay if we can agree, Mr Megson,' he said. 'We'll leave the decision for a day and a night, if you please. We were both heated and I should hate to lose you because of hasty words of mine said in anger.'

Ralph's shoulders slumped, and he gave John one of his slow honest smiles. 'You're a good man,' he said, surprisingly. 'I wish we were all clear of this coil.' One swift hard look at Richard made it clear that he blamed Richard for all that had come about.

I looked from one to the other and I could not tell where my loyalty should lie.

Ralph nodded again. 'There'll be no work done today,' he said, businesslike. 'The carpenter is making her coffin and they're digging her grave. She'll be buried this afternoon at two o'clock, if you wish to attend. Tomorrow they'll go back to work. They don't want to keep the maying feast with the prettiest girl in the village dead and the sweetest lad in the village under wrongful arrest. It has all gone wrong for Acre this year.'

Uncle John said, 'Yes' softly, his head down. That last sentence seemed to toll in my head like the echo of a church bell which sounds on and on long after the ringers have stood still. It seemed I had heard it before. Then I saw John's stricken face and guessed that someone had said it to Beatrice when she wrecked Acre, and that he was afraid that the Laceys were wrecking Acre again.

Ralph swung out of the room without another word and we heard his wooden legs clump across the polished floor of the hall. I went weakly into the chair by the fireplace and sank down, my head in my hands, the tears spilling over, helpless.

My mama went to John. 'Don't look so desperate,' she said. 'It will all come right. We cannot help poor Clary, but you and I can go to Chichester, as well as Mr Megson. If Matthew denies his guilt today, now he has had time to think, then perhaps Richard and Lord Havering may find they were mistaken. Certainly the quarter sessions are not for months yet, so there is plenty of time to set things right if a mistake has been made.'

Uncle John's head came up at that and suddenly I could see how aged and tired he looked. 'Yes,' he said. Then, more strongly, 'Yes, Celia, you are right. Nothing is beyond our control. Events have moved very swiftly, but no final decision has been made. We can perfectly well see Matthew in prison, and if he tells a different story, then we can resolve the problem.'

We all looked towards Richard. One might have thought that he would fire up at this challenge to his judgement, but he was smiling and his eyes were the clearest of blues. 'Of course,' he said, 'whatever you wish.'

Something in his voice made me put my head in my hands and weep and weep.

Mama and John never spoke to Matthew. As they were getting in the carriage to go to Chichester to see him, a message came over from Havering Hall. The prison authorities had sent to Lord Havering to tell him that his prisoner, Matthew Merry, had been found hanged in his cell that morning. He had hanged himself with his belt. They had cut him down as they brought him slops in the morning, but he was already cold.

A bad business, Lord Havering wrote in his aristocratic, illegible scrawl, *but saving the cost of the hangman, for the wretch was undoubtedly guilty.*

John, Mama and I sat in silence, and I had a feeling – a bad feeling, and the first time I had known it – that things were going wrong, seriously wrong, and I could not hold them or control them.

'Does this point to his guilt?' Uncle John asked himself softly, and then he said, 'No', without waiting for a word from me. 'This is bad news for Acre,' he said more clearly. But I could see it cost him an effort to speak so calmly. As for me, I had my good hand clenched to stop it shaking.

'How should we tell them?' he asked.

Mama took a breath. 'I will, if you wish,' she said. 'I was planning to go to Clary's funeral. I could speak to them afterwards. But I shall go down now, and tell Mrs Merry.'

Uncle John nodded. 'I'll come with you,' he said.

So instead of driving to Chichester to see if young Matthew

could be shown to be innocent and bailed, they drove to Acre to find his grandmama and tell her that the only child left to her was dead. A shameful death, and by his own hand.

That was the end of the May holiday and the end of the plans to dance on the green and feast and drink and make merry. The next day everyone was back to work and, although there was much to be done and the lambs were growing and the cows in calf, there was little joy for anyone in Acre.

There was little joy in the Dower House. Uncle John had grown quiet and thoughtful and spent the next few days alone in the library, reading and writing. Mama returned to the school-room in the village, but more out of a sense of duty than en-thusiasm. She had appointed a Midhurst girl as a temporary teacher while we had been in Bath, and she spoke to John about giving the woman a cottage in Acre and handing the school over to her entirely. It was a sensible decision, but it gave us all the feeling that a gulf was opening between Acre and the Laceys.

Only Richard was contented. He took Prince out on errands for Mama and for John, and he checked the stock, the cows and sheep, from the far side of their gates without mishap.

And I? I was in a frenzy of anxiety. I was waiting for James. When Clary's funeral was over, I stopped Jimmy Dart at the gate of the church and asked him to seek out James at his father's offices in London. I had a gold coin inside my glove and I gave him it for the coach fare.

'Tell him not to come to the Dower House,' I said quietly. Richard was helping Mama into the carriage and had his back to me. 'Tell him I want to see him privately. I will meet him in Midhurst, in the private room at the Spread Eagle Inn. Tell him I will be there, on Tuesday, at ten o'clock.'

'Spread Eagle, Tuesday, ten o'clock,' said Jimmy promptly. 'I won't fail you, Miss Julia. And neither will Mr James, I'll be bound.'

I looked at him quickly, and blinked away the haze of sudden tears. 'Do you think so, Jimmy?' I asked.

Jimmy looked surprised. 'Why, yes, Miss Julia,' he said. 'Anyone could see!'

I glanced again towards the carriage. Richard was waiting for me, smiling his bright secretive smile. 'I must go,' I said quickly. 'You'll catch the early stage?'

'I'll be in London by noon,' Jimmy promised. 'And I'll find him wherever he is.'

I gave him a little smile and then turned for the carriage.

Then I waited. I waited, and worried.

James had thought that his own unchastity was wrong. Wrong, but forgivable. I was gambling all that I had on one thought, that he loved me enough to forgive me one terrible error, just as I had loved him enough to forgive him. But it was a big gamble. It was everything I wanted.

I was no angel! The thought of saying nothing at all and marrying him as if I were an untouched bride went through my mind. But truly, I think it went through my mind only once. During those waiting days I knew for certain that I only wanted to marry James with honesty and honour between us.

But I did not know how much I dared to tell him. I picked it over, like a woman picking lice out of old rags. I could tell him I had been forced. But I must also tell him that I lay on my back and smiled. I scorched with shame at that memory, and I knew I could never tell him of it. Or anyone. I could tell him it was rape, but he would want to know if I knew the criminal. But I could not tell him it was Richard. I was as fixed on that point as I had been the very afternoon when the lie of a fall from a horse was first told. But if I told him of the rape and said I did not know the man, I should have to invent a whole string of tales about how and where it happened. And why I had not told my mama.

I seemed to have no solutions, no solutions at all, just more and more problems until I started the round again of thinking that I could certainly tell him I had been forced.

On Monday night I did not sleep. At midnight I wrapped my blanket around me and sat in my window-seat and watched the moon travel across a cloudless silvery sky. The circular nagging worry went around and around in my head until I leaned back against my shutter and closed my eyes against the glare of the moon and the drumming of my fear that I would lose James, that I did not know how to hold him. I did not know the words which would make him forgive me. He was the only man I had ever loved, would ever love. And I did not know where to begin to keep his love.

I slept then, cramped on the window-seat, my head against the shutter. I awoke at dawn, chilly and stiff for my pains. I could not sleep again, but put on my grey riding habit in the half-light and washed my face in the cold water in my ewer, and sat in my window-seat again and listened to the birds starting to sing.

At six o'clock I thought I might go down to the stables and saddle Misty. I wanted to avoid my mama and Uncle John this morning. Most of all I wanted to escape the notice of Richard. I was in real fear of meeting Richard this morning, and I was longing for James.

I was awkward, saddling Misty with one hand. But she whinnied when I gave her a carrot from my pocket, and that summoned Jem in his dirty flannels from the stables.

'You can't ride one-handed,' he said, scandalized.

'You know Misty is as gentle as anything. I can manage her, if you would just get the saddle on for me, Jem.'

'And where d'you think you're going?' he demanded truculently.

I looked at him, irresolute, and then my lower lip trembled and I told him the truth. 'I have to meet James Fortescue,' I said baldly. 'We may have to call off the wedding. I have to go and see him this morning, Jem. Please help me.'

His brown face at once creased into tenderness. 'Your fine young man, Miss Julia?' he asked tenderly. 'I'll drive you there in the carriage, of course.'

'No,' I said quickly. 'No. I don't want Mama or Uncle John to know. Nor Richard. Not anyone. Just get Misty ready for me and tell them I wanted an early ride, and that I could handle her. *Please*, Jem.'

He paused. 'Take her carefully, then,' he said. 'I can't think how you came to fall the last time.'

'I misjudged a jump,' I said. 'She didn't throw me. Please put the saddle on her, Jem. I am so afraid of being late.'

He took it from the stable door and swung it on her back, and then slid her bridle on. He led her into the yard and put both hands on my waist to lift me up into the saddle.

'Go easy now,' he said again. 'What time do you have to be in Midhurst?'

'At ten,' I said.

Jem looked at me incredulously. 'Miss Julia, come down and get some breakfast. You don't need to leave for three hours yet!'

I smiled ruefully. I think it was the first time I had smiled all week since May morning. 'I can't eat!' I said. 'And I couldn't sleep either. I thought I'd ride over the common for a while and then down to Midhurst that way.'

Jem smiled at me. 'Good luck, then, Miss Julia. A man would be a fool to let a maid like you go, and your Mr Fortescue knows it. Good luck. I'll tell them you're riding and won't be back till noon.'

I gathered the reins in my one good hand, and Misty moved delicately out of the yard, loud on the cobbles, but silent on the grass outside the bedroom windows. Then I trotted her up the drive and turned right to go to the common to ride away the hours before I needed to turn her head towards Midhurst.

I was still too early, even after riding in a great sweep from our common land over to Ambersham. I was still too early by half an hour. But I was thirsty now, so I handed her to the ostler and went in by the stable door.

They knew us in Midhurst and greeted me by name. I said that I was meeting a friend from London and that I should like coffee in their private parlour while I waited. The landlord showed me in and lit the fire in the grate, though the room was warm. I sat in the window-seat and sipped from my cup.

It was a pretty room, overlooking a little patch of garden at the back which was bright with Maytime flowers. I would rather have been in the taproom, which had a view over the stable yard. But, though I could not see James's arrival, I knew he would be here soon. I waited.

The clock ticked on the mantelpiece. It seemed to be very slow. I checked it against my own little watch, which John had bought me, a tiny copy of his own on a chain like his. The clock was slow, by a couple of minutes. I put a finger under the minute-hand and pushed it up a little. Then I thought of advancing the time by half an hour and pretending to be angry with James for being late. But then, with a great swoop of apprehension, I remembered that we might not be on jesting terms. I went back to my seat and sat down, and waited.

I heard the clatter of the stage from the yard; the ten o'clock coach had arrived from Chichester. I knew at once it could not be James. The noise of the stage with the passengers bawling for drinks and food was unmistakable. I checked the clock and my watch. The stage was a little early, for it was not ten o'clock yet. James could come within the next three or four minutes and still be on time.

I wished I had brought a book, or something to distract me from the slow movements of the hands of the clock. It seemed to time my thoughts as they went around to its rhythm. Tick . . . I shall tell him I am dishonoured. Tock . . . I shall tell him I was unwilling. Tick . . . I shall refuse to name the man. Tock . . . that will make him very angry. Tick . . . if he is angry, he may not believe I was unwilling. Tock . . . I was not completely unwilling, not at first. Tick . . . no! I was unwilling as soon as I knew it was Richard. Tock . . . I must remember not to say Richard's name. Tick . . . whatever happens, I must not say Richard's name.

There were footsteps outside the door and I leaped to my feet, the colour rushing into my face. It was Mr Jeffries, the landlord. Not James. Not James at all.

'Just come for the coffee-tray, Miss Lacey,' he said. 'Coming post, your friend, is she?'

I stammered a reply.

'Late anyway,' Mr Jeffries said cheerfully. 'I expect you are sorry to be indoors on a day like this, and it's a busy time on Wideacre, I hear.'

'Yes,' I said. 'Mr Jeffries, would you bring another pot of coffee, please? And two cups this time. My friend will be here at any moment, I am sure.'

I waited for the coffee. I waited for James. There was a creeper growing up outside the window and it tapped on the glass softly, as soft as a kitten patting a ball of wool; but in the silence of each moment I could hear it. The sunshine was streaming through the window and little motes of dust danced in the beam. The carpet was faded around the window, where the sunshine of countless summers had bleached it. It was worn thin in a little track from the door to the table where landlord and serving wench had walked. I felt I had been in the little room all my life. I felt I would have to stay there for ever.

The clock on the mantelpiece chimed a quarter chime. James was late.

In all our time in Bath he had never been late to see me. He was always there whenever I arrived. He told me once that he often waited for as long as an hour for me. I thought he must have found the roads harder going than he had expected. Or perhaps a horse had gone lame. But then I heard the door from the stable yard bang and my heart leaped. Footsteps came down the corridor and I stood unsteadily and walked towards the table waiting.

The footsteps walked past the room. It was not James.

The coffee came, and I sat beside the cooling pot and watched a blackbird on the patch of grass, making little runs and then freezing in silence, head cocked, listening to sounds which no one but he could hear.

The chime of the half-hour sounded very loud. The coffee was luke-warm. I drank a cup. I would order a fresh pot when James came.

When James came.

I knew he would come. I knew it was not possible that he should not come, just as in my deepest heart I knew that if he came and I told him frankly and truly what had happened to me, he would forgive me. I trusted him, I trusted my love for him, and his for me.

The clock ticked. The blackbird sprang forward, tugged a worm out and carried it triumphantly away in his beak.

The clock chimed the full three-quarters of the tune. It was quarter to eleven. I bet with myself that he would be with me in five minutes. But at ten minutes to eleven he still had not come. I bet myself a hundred guineas that he would dash into the parlour at five minutes to eleven, covered with dust and full of apologies. But he did not.

The clock struck the full chimes, jangly, tedious, loud. Mr Jeffries put his head around the door.

'There's a gentleman here . . .' he began.

'James!' I said certainly and got to my feet.

'Says that the road from London is clear, and he has passed no post-chaise in the last twenty miles,' Mr Jeffries went on. 'Maybe your friend is not coming, Miss Lacey.'

'I'll wait another half-hour,' I said. I could feel the blood draining from my face so fast that I thought I might faint. I sat down on the seat again and leaned my head against the window-pane. The glass was cold. In one pane someone had tried to cut their name with a diamond. It looked like Stephen something, and last year's date.

It was twenty minutes past eleven.

At half past eleven Mr Jeffries came in to ask me if I would like to leave a message with him, and he would promise to deliver it, to save me the further inconvenience of waiting. I said I would wait until noon.

The clock ticked. The blackbird came back.

I said to myself that it was not possible, that James would not just not come. He would never simply fail to meet me. I had asked him to meet me here and he had agreed. He must have had an accident on the road and, instead of sitting here doubting him, I should be sending out people to search the road for him and bring him home safe to Wideacre. But in my heart I knew he had not had an accident. He was not coming.

It was half past twelve before I knew with certainty. Even then I might have seen his post-chaise with delight, not surprise. But at half past twelve, two and a half hours late for our appointment, I told myself he was not coming and I might as well go home.

I rose from the window-seat like an old woman, stiff and tired. He was not coming. He had known I was waiting for him and yet he had not come to me. What I should say to him now was a problem for the future. He was not coming today, though I had asked him to come and see me.

My arm was aching and I did not know if I would manage Misty on the ride home. I was as weary as if I had been riding around on the downs all the day. Misty would be fresh from her rest in the stables, and I would have trouble mounting her with only one hand.

I pinned on my hat and went out into the yard.

Richard was there.

He was sitting in Uncle John's gig with the steadiest of the driving horses between the shafts, and Misty hitched with a halter to the back. He was stretched out in the driver's seat with his smart boots crossed before him on the splashboard. The smoke from his cigar circled in the still air above his head. He turned when he heard the door shut behind me and got down, slowly taking his tricorne hat off and smiling his secretive smile.

'What a long time you have been, my dear,' he said kindly. 'As I had some business to do myself in the inn, I thought I would wait for you. Your mama was concerned at you riding. She will be glad that we met and I could drive you home. Where shall we tell her we met?'

He took me by the waist and lifted me up into the gig before I could say a word, and then he flapped the reins on the horse's back, tossed a coin to the ostler and drove us out of the yard.

I said nothing for a moment. Just seeing Richard there was a shock. But then I found my voice. 'What are you doing here?' I asked.

'Business,' Richard said as if he had business in a Midhurst inn every day of the week. 'I had to see a man.' He gave one of his sly giggles. 'I had to deliver some letters to a gentleman,' he said, 'so I thought I would wait and drive you home. I thought you might be tired, coming out so early and with your hand still sore.'

'I am,' I said briefly. Indeed I was. I was so tired and disappointed I could have wept. All night, all week I had been readying myself to beg James to love me despite everything, and trying to prepare myself for his refusal. But nothing could have been worse than not seeing him.

Richard threw me a sideways glance which was as warm and as sympathetic as if he had known and cared for my despair. 'Why don't you take your hat off and let the wind blow in your face?' he suggested kindly. 'You're looking so pale, little Julia.'

I did as he bid me and held the hat in my lap as we climbed the short hill out of Midhurst. Misty shied at a blowing piece of paper and her hooves clattered on the stones.

'Better have a rest when you get home,' Richard said sweetly. 'You have shadows under your eyes, my darling. You look tired out.'

I tipped my head back so the sun fell on my face and made rosy patterns on my closed eyelids. 'I am tired, for I could not sleep last night,' I said.

'You should have woken me,' he said, making it seem the most reasonable thing in the world. 'You know I would not want you to be wakeful on your own. It is horrible being the only person awake in a house, isn't it? Poor Julia. Did you feel very lonely?'

I did not answer him. I looked down at my wrist and at Uncle John's meticulous strapping, and at the blue bruise which showed above the bandage. I thought of the man he was and the playmate he had been. I thought of his warm friendly tones now, and of his demented hiss of a voice in the summer-house. And I felt so much that I wanted to be safe from his anger, safe from his hatred. No one could keep me safe from Richard, not Mama, not Uncle John, not even Ralph. And now James was gone. I had loved and feared Richard for all my childhood and girlhood.

Now that James was gone, the brief period when I hardly noticed Richard at all seemed an interruption of the normal feelings: my base, cowardly, fearful affection.

'You should not have hurt me,' I said.

It was the only protest I ever made.

Richard chuckled and made no reply at all.

I was bundled into my bed on my return. Mama exclaimed at my paleness and wanted to know what wildness had got into me to make me ride out all day, only days after a bad fall. I submitted without protest. I had nothing to say. I stayed in bed for the afternoon, but after dinner I walked for a little in the front garden to see the flowers. The primroses were as mild a yellow as little butter-pats all along the path, and the pansies were as dark as velvet. I heard hoofbeats, but I did not run to the gate thinking of James. I knew that James would never come. It was Ralph.

He pulled his horse up at the garden wall and I went down the path towards him. He touched his hat to me, but his face was unsmiling. 'I've come to tell you that I've given orders to bring Matthew Merry's body home from Chichester gaol to be buried here. They've released the body at last.'

I nodded, as formal as he. 'Can he be buried in the churchyard?' I asked.

'Nay, he's a suicide,' Ralph said. 'It will have to be Miss Beatrice's Corner for him.'

'What d'you mean?' I asked swiftly. The corner of grass by the church gate was called Miss Beatrice's Corner, but no one had ever told me why, of all the land which my aunt had made her own, that little patch had been named for her.

'It's the corner of the ground nearest to the graveyard, on t'other side of the church wall,' Ralph said. 'When Miss Beatrice ruled here, there were two suicides. They buried them there in unsanctified ground but as close to the church as they could get. They called it Miss Beatrice's Corner in a tribute to the last Lacey squire who brought death to the village. Now there will be another grave there. It's a new generation of Laceys and Acre is still dying for them.'

I gasped and the ready tears came to my eyes. I looked up at Ralph. High on his black horse, he was an inexorable judge, but there was something more than anger in his face. There was also despair.

'I am so sorry,' I said feebly. I could feel my eyes filling with tears and I was afraid they would start rolling down my cheeks.

'Come out on the land, Julia,' Ralph said urgently. 'It's going wrong, but you could catch it, even now, if you came out on the land with your sight and your skills. I can hold Acre together, but I cannot hold them to this trial of sharing with the squires if you and your family stay inside your great house and behave as if you think the village too lowly for you.'

'It's not that,' I said instantly.

'What is it, then?' he demanded. 'Why are you not in Acre these past few days? Why does Richard do all the work that you used to do? We would all rather work with you. No one likes Richard, and everyone blames him for what happened to Matthew. Ted Tyacke will not even speak to him.'

'It was not his fault Matthew died,' I said.

'Matthew died by his own hand, I know,' Ralph said steadily, 'but no one in the village thinks he killed Clary. There are two Acre deaths and no murderer taken, and they all believe that you know who the murderer is.' Ralph's black look at me was intent. 'They all swear that you can see him with the sight.'

'I can't,' I said rapidly. I could feel my heart fluttering with anxiety.

'They all say you would be sure to be able to see her killer,' Ralph said, 'as a Lacey girl with the sight, as her best friend. They all swear that if you looked with the sight, then you would see him, whoever he is. Then we could have him taken up, and hanged, and Clary and Matthew would be avenged and would sleep quiet in their graves. And you would be restored to the village.'

'I can't, Ralph,' I said piteously. 'I have a dream when I think he is coming nearer, but I dare not see his face.'

Ralph's horse shifted impatiently as his grip on the reins tightened. 'For God's sake, Julia,' he said roughly. 'This is not a question of what you wish or what you dare. All our work here is falling apart and you must save it. Go into your dream, take the courage you inherited from Beatrice. Look Death in the face and come back and tell me his name and I will do the rest. Then you'll be the squire in very truth. Then Acre can grow and trust again.'

'I *can't*,' I said, my voice wavering higher. 'I've told you already. I cannot do it! They may say I can, but they are wrong. I cannot do it, Ralph. You should not ask it of me.'

'Then you are a coward and a traitor to Acre,' he said harshly, 'and I am ashamed of you.'

His horse wheeled on its hind legs as he whirled it around, the reins so tight that its mouth gaped, and then it leaped forward and threw up its head as it felt the whip. It took three wide paces of a canter, then jinked and shied in sudden fright at some weed blowing bright on the top of our garden wall. Ralph jerked it to a standstill and looked back at me, standing alone in my pretty garden.

'You are bad blood, you Laceys!' he shouted. And behind the anger in his voice I heard a bitter despair that he had trusted us and had again been betrayed, and that because of the mistake of his trust Clary was dead, and young Matthew too. 'You are bad cursed blood, and I hate the whole race of you!' he yelled, as angry as a rebellious youth. Then he was gone, round the bend in the track and hidden by the trees.

But I stayed as if I could still see him, staring at the track as if he were still there. I stayed without moving, without making a sound. My heartbeat was thudding in my ears and I was damp with sweat under my gown. I knew it had all gone wrong. It was my fault, and all I could say, over and over, was, 'Oh, I am so sorry. I am so very, very sorry.'

They buried Matthew the next day, and Mrs Merry seemed to become yet older as they stamped the earth down on the little grave. It could have no headstone, but the carpenter made a little board with Matthew's name and age on it, and the date. Dr Pearce said nothing when it appeared at the head of the fresh earth, nor did Uncle John.

We had to go to church past the little mound, and I saw that Mama turned her head and looked out of the other window. I was on that side of the carriage as we drew up at the lich-gate and I could not help but see it.

The wooden board was light; it would be rotted and gone in a few years. The little mound of earth was bare. They might plant it with flowers later, or it might simply grow over with weeds and grass like the two neighbouring unmarked graves.

The three little mounds seemed to accuse me as I stepped from the carriage. They were mute witnesses to the power of the Laceys. We went through the gate and I glanced back at the fresh grave. There were two smooth prints where Mrs Merry had knelt on the earth and pressed it flat, the marks of her knees. I knew then, as I had only thought before, that whatever it cost me in money, I might be better off if I did not own Wideacre. Ralph might be right about the ownership of the land and that it should not be trusted to the Laceys, or to any one family, that a squire on Wideacre could do so much wrong.

Uncle John's face was grim as we went into the church, and there were no smiles for us as we walked up the aisle. The pew where Clary used to sit, supervising her brothers and sisters in a row of diminishing figures, was empty. None of the Dench children had come to church this Sunday. I felt the tears prickle under my eyelids at that empty plain wooden pew, and I glanced at Richard for a little comfort.

He was smiling.

He must have been thinking of something else. He must have been miles away in his thoughts. For as we walked up the aisle of that church, between the villagers who were grieving for a murdered girl and a hanged lad, Richard's blue eyes were dancing with mischief and he was beaming at some private joke.

My hand was on his arm and I pressed it gently.

'Richard,' I said softly, 'what are you thinking of?'

He glanced down at me and the delight was wiped from his face at once. 'You are quite right,' he said. 'Thank you for reminding me,' and he at once looked grave and solemn and sad, and stepped back for me to precede him into the pew. Ralph Megson's stony gaze was on me and I felt party to Richard's deceit, as if I too had been laughing and then donned a mask of gravity.

We did not wait to chat after church and no one stayed Uncle John or me with a friendly hand as we walked back to the carriage. In the last few months a villager, or a tenant, or a worker had often stopped me on the way to the carriage to ask me something, or to complain about one of the hundred little problems which come from farming the land. On this day the churchyard was silent.

We walked past the tenants and labourers with no word spoken, and I saw Mama's head was down and her eyes were on her feet. Uncle John looked weary to death. Only Richard's head was up and his face was calm; Richard's eyes were as clear as his conscience, his merry smile not far away.

Mama shivered when we got into the carriage and she stroked the velvet lapel of her jacket for comfort. 'That was awful,' she said in a low voice to John. 'It was like the old days. John, if this scheme does not work with Acre, do say that we can leave at once. I have spent half my life on this land trying to get things right here, and we seem to face one failure after another. If Acre remains unhappy, do say we can sell up and leave.'

Uncle John's face was haggard. 'Celia, after all the plans . . .' he said despairingly. The carriage moved off. Nobody waved to us from the churchyard. 'I can't believe it is hopeless,' he said. 'This gloom is natural indeed, but it is not as it was with Beatrice. Matthew Merry died most horridly, but no Lacey can be blamed. It is you and I who are so superstitious, Celia. Having seen the village in despair once, we are too quick to think it has all gone wrong again. I'm sure the children are more optimistic.'

Mama and Uncle John looked at Richard and me, hoping we had some answer for them.

Richard's smile was sunny and confident. 'Of course,' he said sweetly. 'Acre is in the sullens because the May feast was spoiled and because they are grieving. But that is no cause for us to blame ourselves. If Clary Dench upset her lover and he strangled her and then hanged himself, that is a nasty little tale, but not one that reflects on us at all.' He smiled at my mama. 'Aunt Celia,' he said coaxingly, 'I know what is amiss. You have not been to Chichester for days and you have spent no money!'

Mama smiled, but I could see it was an effort.

'And what do you think, Julia?' John asked.

I was silent for a moment. The noise of the horses' hooves on the lane and the creak of the carriage-wheels on the sticky mud filled the silence. 'I agree with Richard,' I said in a small voice. I did not want to tell Uncle John that Ralph had begged me to use the sight for Acre and that I had refused him, and refused them. I did not want to tell Uncle John that Ralph had raised his voice to me and cursed me and cursed all the Laceys. I did not want to tell Uncle John that Ralph blamed me for cowardice, that the gloom of Acre was my fault; for I had refused them.

'I agree with Richard,' I said again.

Under the shelter of my pelisse and muff Richard's hand came down and brushed the back of my gloved hand with the tips of his warm fingers. I stole a sideways glance at him and he was smiling down at me, his eyes warm. Imperceptibly he leaned towards me so that our shoulders were touching. As the carriage turned up the drive under the greening trees of Wideacre Park, with the air full of birdsong, I knew that the only person I could please was Richard, that only Richard and I knew the truth. We were partners in deceit once more.

23

I had counted on Richard staying at home for the whole of May. But he had a letter from his tutor to say that a Greek expert was prepared to offer him extra lessons before the summer term started, and he smiled ruefully at Mama at breakfast and said, 'Mama-Aunt, it seems that I shall have to leave you and go back to Oxford. It is a hard apprenticeship my father has put me to.'

'I'm sorry indeed,' Uncle John said with a smile. 'But think of the training for your moral character, Richard! I am sure it will do you nothing but good.'

'I would rather have a weak moral character and the rest of my holiday on Wideacre,' Richard said. 'But my tutor is right. My Greek is shamefully weak, and I did not enjoy looking like a fool in front of the others last term. I suppose I shall have to do as I am bid and go back early.'

I held myself very still, but when Mama and Uncle John had left the breakfast table, I said, 'Oh, Richard, I wish you did not have to go!'

He smiled at me. 'I'll be back soon,' he said. 'This is a short term, only a couple of months, though they may ask me to stay for extra tuition at the end of term too! I shall be back at harvesting, I hope, and able to help you then.'

'It's not the work,' I said. 'It's the way everything is now.' I could not make myself say Clary's name, but I thought of her then as I did all the time. I did not know how I would be able to work on Wideacre without her. I felt as if I had known her all my life, as if she *was* Acre, as if in losing her I had lost my special sense of the village, my special place there.

Richard leaned back in his chair and folded his letter. 'I'm afraid I cannot stay,' he said agreeably. 'My tutor is most insistent, Julia. But if the village is surly and your great friend Ralph Megson is of no use, I really think you should mention it to my papa. The estate can hardly work well without some discipline.'

'No,' I said quickly. 'It's not that, Richard. It's the way everything seems suddenly to have gone wrong for all of us. I think it's as bad for Acre as it is for us.'

Richard made a little grimace. 'They're a surly mob,' he said. 'And your great friend Ralph Megson is as big a villain as any of them. I tell you, Julia, you'll get neither work nor respect out of them until you bring in the parish roundsman, and have them working at parish rates. It's what I'd do. And if they didn't work then, I'd bring in Irish labourers and have the whole crew of them thrown out of their houses and on to the parish,' he said with a smile.

'I know you're joking, Richard,' I said uncertainly. 'But don't. Acre is such a sad village these days.'

Richard shrugged. 'So?' he said. 'They'll get over it. All estates have their ups and downs. If it would mean anything to you, I'll take the occasional Friday off and come home for the weekend. I'll take Saint Monday too!'

'Yes,' I said. 'I should like that. I will be lonely here . . .' Without Clary, I thought. But I did not say it.

'I'll promise it to you, then,' he said pleasantly. And he pushed his chair back and went towards the door. 'Oh, Julia . . .' he said from the doorway, seeming suddenly to think of it, 'you will not hear from Mr Fortescue again.'

'Mr Fortescue?' I said blankly. 'James Fortescue?'

'Yes,' Richard said. 'I have returned the letters he sent you and informed him that the engagement, if you called it that, is at an end.'

'You saw him?' I asked blankly.

'Oh, yes,' said Richard. 'At the start he would not take my word for it and he wanted to pester you himself. But when I told him that we were betrothed and that I was empowered to return his letters, he accepted your apologies. He sent you his best wishes.'

For a moment I said nothing. I could not absorb what Richard was saying. 'James?' I said uncertainly.

'He wrote to you three days ago,' Richard said. 'As I was up early, I took the liberty of opening it for you. I did not want him upsetting you again. It was a brief note, just returning your letters to him, and telling you he is going abroad again. He does travel a lot, doesn't he? I suppose it is for his father's business. They are tradesmen, shopkeepers or something, are they not?'

'He wrote to me?' I asked.

'Yes,' Richard said. 'Oh, but it is too late for you to reply. He had no forwarding address. I suppose he goes scurrying around from shop to shop. He left today. He said he would be away for about six months.'

My mind was whirling. I forgot that James would have been within his rights to set aside our betrothal as soon as I told him of my shame. I could only think of him and our time together in Bath, his easy smile and his warm eyes, his fidelity to the children of Acre, his tenderness to my mama. And that time in the glove shop when he had sat with his arms folded and taught me to be a Lacey squire before the most fashionable modiste in the town.

'James,' I said. It was as though I were summoning a ghost, not just his ghost, but also the ghost of the girl I had been when I rode like Beatrice, when I threw back my head and laughed, when I walked as if all the land around me for twenty miles in any direction was my own.

'It was a pleasant flirtation, I dare say,' Richard said coolly. 'But it is ended now.'

'James,' I said again. Then my wits sharpened and I looked at Richard's open cherubic face. 'You met him,' I accused. 'When he was coming to meet me. You stopped him on the road.'

'Of course,' Richard said. He was smiling as at some amusing secret. 'Of course I did, Julia. I met him with your letters in my pocket. You are such a silly little thing to try and hide them under the loose floorboard in your room. Surely you knew that it was the first place I would look. You have always hidden your treasures there, ever since we were little children. As soon as I saw them there, I knew that they were not really hidden at all. You wanted me to find them. So I took them, and read them, and gave them back to him, as a gentleman would do.'

'You took his letters,' I said. There was an anger building inside me, I could taste the heat of it on my tongue. 'You had no right to take them.'

'No right?' Richard said. 'No right?' He shut the dining-room door with a sharp snap and strode back into the room and grabbed me by the upper arms, pulling me up to my feet. He stared down into my face, his colour rising with his temper.

'You dare tell me I have no right!' he exclaimed. 'When you went to Bath betrothed to me and flirted like a coquette with a shopman! Have you forgotten what you wrote in your ridiculous little journal – oh, yes! I read that too! I knew you wanted me to read it. You wrote it just to make me jealous. You wrote it so that I would know how improperly you had behaved. I read it and it made me sick. You made me feel physically sick, thinking of you holding hands with him, and kissing him and promising him your share of Wideacre and then coming home and kissing me in front of all of Acre in the middle of a ploughing field, like the village slut you are! That I have no right, when I found you in the sunshine and you lay on your back and spread your legs and smiled at me!'

My throat was tightening. 'It wasn't like that,' I said unsteadily.

Richard gave me a shake so my head nodded. 'I have every right,' he said harshly. 'You put his letters there so that I might find them. You wrote the journal for me to read. I know you did, you know you did. You were hoping to make me jealous. You plotted with him against me, to take your share of the estate away from me. But you are such a hot little whore that you could not help yourself. Not in the field at the ploughing, not in the summer-house at the maying. You lay back and smiled. You put your arms around me. You stuck your tongue in my mouth, you dirty little whore. I didn't even know that women kissed like that until you did it. That disgusts me! And then you ran off to Midhurst to meet your other lover to say, "Oh, James, I am sorry. But can we still be married?"' Richard had adopted a falsetto whine. 'What were you going to say? "Oh, James, I didn't mean to do it. I thought I was Beatrice!" or "Oh, James, I was thinking of you!"' He flung me away from him and I stumbled against the table.

'It wasn't like that . . .' I tried to say.

'I am sure you wish it wasn't!' Richard said harshly. 'But you tell one lie after another, Julia. I don't think you even know what the truth is any more.'

'I love him,' I said. I drew a deep breath of the stuffy air of the room, thick with breakfast smells and raw anger. I was shaking; but I clung to the edge of the table, and to that one certainty. 'I love him,' I said again. 'And I did not want to lie with you.'

Richard took a quick stride back to me and grabbed my arm. He marched me towards the door and flung it open. 'You tell them, then,' he hissed. 'You tell your mama and your Uncle John that you are betrothed to him, and that you want them to get him back, to write to his family and get the marriage put on again. If this is the truth and you are prepared to swear it, you tell them it all. You tell them that you lay with me but that you did not want to. You tell them that I forced you.' His voice grew louder. 'Tell them that I am a rapist!' he said.

I shot a frightened glance around the hall, wondering if my mama was in her parlour, where she would be certain to hear. 'Tell your mama I am a rapist!' he said again, his anger making his voice louder and louder. 'Tell my papa! And then send to Grandpapa Havering and tell him! And he will have me taken to court, and I will be hanged like a sheep-stealer. Hanged so that you can satisfy your lust with one man and marry another! If that is the truth, then you tell them. Tell them now. Otherwise we shall always know that you are a liar.'

'No!' I said. 'No, Richard. No, Richard. No.' I put both hands out to him and drew him back into the dining-room. He resisted only slightly. I shut the door behind him and tried to speak, though I was shaking so much I could hardly stand. 'Please don't say such things, Richard,' I begged him. 'You know I would not betray you. You know I would not tell them.'

'You dare not,' he replied instantly. 'You know it is a lie and you don't have the courage to say it aloud.'

'It is not, it is not,' I said. I could feel the tears in my eyes and on my cheeks, but I was not crying.

'You desired me and you lay with me,' Richard said coldly. 'Any denial of that is a lie.'

I bowed my head; my tears were falling so fast they were spotting the silk of my morning gown.

He gave me a shake. 'Isn't it?' he insisted.

'Yes,' I said, utterly defeated.

'You can marry no other man now,' Richard said.

I nodded.

'Don't forget that,' he said softly.

I nodded again.

'James Fortescue is gone,' he said firmly. 'Gone, and you will never see him again. There is no gentleman in the world now who will marry you. I have taken your virginity and you are my whore. You belong to me.'

I said not one word in contradiction. Then he pressed a gentle kiss on the top of my bowed head and let himself out of the room, and went quietly up the stairs to his bedroom to pack his books and clothes for Oxford.

Almost as soon as Richard had gone, I started to feel unwell. We had a spell of fine weather which brought the new hedges on so fast that they were bushy and impenetrable. All the trees in Wideacre Park were sweet-smelling with new leaves. The grass in the paddock was suddenly so bright it hurt my eyes, and Sea Mist danced on the springing verges at the side of the track to Acre as if the fresh grass tickled her hooves. I sat heavily on her, without nerves, but without pleasure. My hand was quite well and I could hold her steady. But I had lost my love of riding. I rode her now as a job of work, to get from one end of the estate to another. And I had to ride her, because I had to work. Uncle John advised it and Mama supported him. They both thought me too pale and too nervous indoors. They both thought that working on the land would help me regain my cheerfulness.

It did not.

We had to weed and weed in the hayfields, trying to clear the thick wicked roots of burdock and dandelion to give the grass a chance to grow, and we had to keep the cornfields clear as well. Acre's return to work happened all in a rush, and I rode out every day to check the progress in the fields, to see the sheep and the fattening lambs and to look at the broadening cows whose bellies were as lumpish and as rounded as the swallows' nests stuck on the narrow beams of the barns.

Clary Dench was not forgotten in Acre. Nothing is ever forgotten in Acre. But with the land growing so green and so strong, the sun so hot and the clean wind blowing across the top of the downs, bringing with it day after day of warm weather, no one could keep a surly face and no one blamed me for failing to seek my friend among the shades with my sight.

Ralph Megson had not forgotten. His manner to me was changed; he retreated behind a wall of formality, which was worse, far worse, than his blazing rages. Though we worked side by side on the land, organizing the teams and checking the livestock and the crops, he never so much as smiled at me. And when I once reached out and touched his hand to show him something, he wordlessly withdrew his hand from under mine. His anger was too deep and too silent for any apology of mine; and I had no voice and no courage to broach a topic with Ralph. I did as he bid me on the land like a cipher. I sat at home with my mama like a girl content to have four walls around her. All my rebelliousness, all my keen Lacey courage seemed to have failed me, incongruously, in a season of wealth and growth and confidence.

We were in the very prime of a Wideacre early summer. The sky was full of birds, and the woods around Wideacre were twittery with their excitement. Of all the springs and summers I had seen on Wideacre, I had never before had one where you could almost see the grass growing as you looked. The men at the hall were working all hours, and they even stayed late as the evenings grew lighter, so the hall seemed to be growing as sweetly and as naturally as everything else on the land.

Mama announced that she would have a garden to match the beautiful new house, and tied on a chip bonnet with determination and set three gardeners to work to weed and prune and tidy the garden and uproot the saplings and the encroaching woodland.

The warmer weather suited Uncle John, and he took to riding down to Acre on Prince, who went gently and sweetly with him. He took his regular clinic for the children, but found fewer and fewer patients.

'I shall write a monograph on preventive medicine,' he said to Mama as they took coffee together in the back garden one morning. 'I really am amazed at the effect of good food on the health of the Acre children. It has cured them not only of hunger-related complaints, but also of diseases which I would have thought came from quite different causes.'

Mama nodded. 'It's surprising how much brighter the babies are when they are carried to full term and born of well-fed mothers,' she said. 'But also, John, there are few villages where they have a resident physician working for nothing!'

'And few where the school dame is a baronet's widow!' John said, smiling back at her, 'and quite the most exquisite relic I have ever seen.'

Mama burst out laughing. 'Not a relic, John! What an absolutely hideous word! It makes me sound about a hundred!'

'Well, I feel very aged and settled,' John said comfortably. 'I think everyone in Acre is going to be extraordinarily healthy and live for one hundred and twenty years. And I shall be the first to make a hundred and fifty.'

'And what is your prescription for longevity?' Mama asked him with a smile. She passed him the plate of Mrs Gough's lightest cheese scones.

'Coffee and scones at noon,' John said. 'A leisurely walk up to the hall at two. A thumping great big dinner at three, and an evening of songs in the parlour from you later on.'

'It shall be as you order, Doctor,' Mama said with mock deference. 'The patient is a most important man, you know.'

'A most blessed one, anyway,' said Uncle John, and he leaned across from his chair to hers and kissed her gently on the cheek.

So it was a good season for everyone on Wideacre that year, except for Ralph, who was sad and silent, and except for me. The dreadful trembling which had shaken me for days after my fall had ceased, and I had even stopped crying without cause. But now I felt sick all the time. Whether I was riding or walking or resting, I felt all the time on the verge of sickness. It was worse in the morning when I could hardly bear to sit up in bed, because I knew the room would revolve before my eyes and I would feel nearly ready to retch. I asked my maid to bring me tea rather than chocolate in the morning, and I ate hardly any breakfast. By noon I could generally count on feeling better, but even as I rode up to the downs or along the drive to the hall, I knew something was wrong with me.

'Still not hungry, darling?' Mama said to me at breakfast when I had turned with a grimace from some medium-rare beef on the sideboard. The heart of it was pinky-red and it repelled me as if I were one of John's Indian brahmins.

'No,' I said. 'I have just lost my appetite these last few days.'

Uncle John's eyes were sharp upon me. 'Any fever?' he said, 'or do you have a headache, Julia?'

'No,' I said, curbing my impatience. 'I'm just not hungry this morning.'

'Perhaps John would have a look at you after breakfast,' Mama said. 'You are so pale since that fall of yours, my dear.'

I gave my lower lip a swift little nip. 'I am quite well,' I said, 'and I should hate to be "looked at", Mama, so please don't fuss.'

Uncle John, with his instinctive tact, said no more. After breakfast, when I was out in the hall tying on my hat and looking at my white face in the mirror, he stopped Mama from coming towards me, and said softly, 'Leave her be, Celia. She cannot be seriously ill and riding every day as she does. If it is a reaction to the fall, it will right itself in a day or so, or she will come to you about it.'

That very day the weather changed and became cloudy and cooler. I was able to say at dinner that an east wind always made me irritable, and in the days that followed I continued to blame the weather. While the apple blossom went from pink to white and then snowed down upon the grass, we had week after week of low cloud and a glaring sky. The sky felt heavy, weighing down on the land. It was not grey, or dark, but bright, so bright I had to squint to look down the lane.

The lane itself blazed white and green; the gypsy's lace on the verges was as thick as whipped cream, and the hawthorn flowers rose above them in clusters of whiteness like snowdrifts on the shiny-green hedges. The air was filled with the heavy scent of the summer flowers and weeds. The new cloverfields were purple with flowers and loud with the noise of addicted bees. On the common the bluebells were as thick as sea mist and on the downs the lower slopes were yellow with cowslips, and the air smelled of honey.

The chestnut trees flowered and then dropped their petals, and still the heavy clouds lay unmoving. The men from Acre stripped down to breeches to weed in the cornfields, but there was no sun, so their bodies stayed oddly white, like chalk men out of the chalk land. Sitting at the parlour window, listening to Mama play the pianoforte, I could not catch even a breath of wind. The sky sat on the hills of the downs like a cloth over a bowl of dough set out to rise. Under the soft lid, in the steamy heat, the grass grew and turned pale. The cream roses in the garden at the hall bloomed like an ominous reminder of the bowl of cream roses in my dream, and down the lane their lesser cousins, the dogroses, spotted the banks and the hedges, all as pale as fever patients against the vivid greenness of the bright patchwork counterpane of the Wideacre fields.

I had said I was perfectly well to Uncle John and Mama, but I had lied. I was not; I felt nauseous and tired. One morning, getting to my feet too swiftly from bending over a map in the library, I had stumbled with dizziness and was afraid I would faint. I was not hungry at mealtimes, but found I was tempted to Mrs Gough's jars of bottled fruits and dried plums in the kitchen. My face was thinner and paler; my eyes, when I looked in the mirror, were hazy and fey. I was headachy and weary too, and for days at a time I made excuses and avoided riding out.

'Come out for a drive,' Mama said invitingly to me one morning. 'It is not half so hot and humid this morning. Take me out in the gig and show me the hayfields. Mr Megson told me that they are nearly ready for cutting.'

I nodded and languidly went for my hat and gloves, but I saw the glance between Mama and Uncle John and his approving nod to her.

Mama was right, the weather had lifted. The feeling of the air being too thick to breathe had gone, and the light on the downs was clear and bright rather than too vivid. I clicked to the horse and we bowled down the road to Acre, the bit jingling with the brisk trot. The shadows of the trees flicked over us and the wind of our brisk passing blew in my face and brought some colour to my cheeks. The hayfield I wanted to see was on the far side of Acre, and as we drove through the village, I twirled my whip in greeting to a couple of women working in their front gardens and waved to Ned Smith who was unloading charcoal in his yard.

A hayfield ready for cutting is a sea of palest green, knee-high, studded and scattered with blazes of colour: the scarlet of poppies, the deep blue of cornflowers, the pastel pinks and mauve and white of Lady's smock, all growing spindly and tall up to the sunlight, pushing their bright faces through the grass. On the borders of the field the banks were bright with flowers: sweet-smelling clumps of cowslips, starry dogroses with their pale-pink faces and mustard-yellow stamens. And breathing over it all was the perfume of the wild bean flowers, sprawling over the haw-thorn hedges and twining up the hazel and elder bushes.

'It'll be ready in three, four days of this weather,' Miller Green said cheerily to me as we drew up alongside the lower meadow, where he leaned on the gate and smoked his pipe. I sniffed discreetly at the blue smoke. Tobacco. Miller Green had been smoking hawthorn leaves when he struggled to survive in a silent mill with no corn to grind. Now there were wages coming in, and he could buy his pinch of tobacco again.

'It looks nearly ready,' I agreed.

'It's the wheat I'm wanting,' he said with longing. 'I've been to the common field every day to see it. It's a good crop, tall and strong, and thick as nettles on a dung heap!'

'Good,' I said. I got down from the gig so I could stand on the lower bar of the gate and scan the field to see if it was indeed near ready for cutting.

'Thanks to you, Miss Julia,' said the old man with a sly smile on his face.

'Nonsense,' I said evenly, but without heat. 'You know that is nonsense, Miller Green. It's a good crop because it was good-quality seed, thickly sown with the weather to suit it. Anything else is old wives' nonsense.'

'Aye,' he said, accepting the reproof without caring, 'but widely believed, Miss Julia. They all say in the village that you have the Lacey knack of making the wheat grow. It's a good crop, and you get the credit.'

I shrugged and turned my gaze back to the rippling sea of green. 'As you will,' I said easily. 'Is Mrs Green well, and your sons?'

'Aye,' he said, satisfied. 'We're all well. All of Acre is well. I can scarce remember such a spring and a summer.'

I nodded in farewell and went back to the gig where my mama sat under her grey silk parasol.

'Is it ready?' she asked. 'It still looks very green to me.'

'Three or four days,' I said. 'I'll just drive down to the common to look at the wheatfield, and then we'll go home.'

'Certainly,' she said, and waved her gloved hand at Miller Green, while I clicked to the horse and we turned down the track that leads to the common field.

The field was like a miracle to me. I was Wideacre bred, but I had never seen a wheatfield growing on Wideacre. Yet here it was before me, and the land and the village restored in one season's work by the combination of Uncle John's money, Ralph's authority, my name and the irresistible magic of the Wideacre soil, which I believed would grow orchids and palm trees if one planted them.

The crop was a foot, even eighteen inches high, the kernels of the wheat, green and sweet and small, encased tightly in the blade like tiny peas in a pod. The field was huge; I could still remember how it had been, with the heather and the bracken encroaching on the margins and straggly weeds and tall armies of purple loosestrife and rose-bay willow-herb growing alongside and starving the self-sown crop. Now the drudgery of the weeding had won us a wide sweep of field, properly fenced and clean at the rims and green as green, with all the shrubs and bracken pulled clear. Beside it was the orchard I had planted on that cold grey day, the trees standing tall, and little green berries of apples showing the crop we would have. The wheatfield was a world of waving smoothness, green speckled with flowers and the bright blaze of poppies and misty-blue cornflowers.

'Oh, it's so lovely,' I exclaimed involuntarily. I handed the reins to Mama in a sort of dream and slid down from the gig and went through the gate to stand amid the wheat in the field in its promise of green. 'It's so lovely,' I said to myself, and lifted my skirts clear of the growing shoots and skirted the field to see the crop from another angle.

In my head I could hear the sweet singing noise which sometimes came to me on Wideacre, or when I was missing it. And the feel of the earth under my shoes was like a guarantee of happiness. In the days since Clary's death and my own confusion I had lost my joy in the land. I had lost my ears to hear the singing, and I had lost my delight in the smell and feel of the place. Now, like a waterfall tumbling full upon me, it was coming back to me. Careless of my gown, I knelt down in the earth and sniffed at the crop as if it were a bouquet of flowers. It had the lightest aroma, like grass, but a little sweeter. Then I picked a stem and looked at the sound seeds which would grow and grow and ripen until we could cut it and thresh it, and grind it and bake bread with it, so that no one in Acre need ever go hungry again.

I put the seed in my mouth and nibbled at it like a ravenous harvest mouse. It was hard, not sweet yet. But when I bit on the stalk, I could taste the sap inside the stem, and I turned back to the gig with it in my mouth.

'Oh, Julia,' Mama sighed with a faint smile. 'Do take that bit of grass out of your mouth. You look like an absolute natural.'

I whipped it out with a little jump. 'I am sorry, Mama, I was in an utter daydream. The field is so wonderful.'

She smiled ruefully. 'When Beatrice was a girl, she was just the same,' she said. 'She loved the land rather like you do, I think. And they used to say all sorts of things about her ability to make the land grow.'

I climbed back into the gig. 'They say it about me too,' I said, rather pleased. 'I know it is nonsense, Mama, but it is a rather nice idea that the land grows well for the Laceys.'

She gave a little sigh. 'Yes,' she said, 'I know you like that thought. I suppose I am not country born and bred, and so the passion for a field is never one that I feel. But your papa loved his land very well too.'

I gave one last lingering look at the common field and turned the gig for home. 'It should be ready for harvesting by August,' I said.

'Oh, good,' Mama said, 'for Richard is hoping to come home in time to see it.' She paused. 'What has gone wrong between you and James, my darling?' she asked tentatively. 'I have been waiting and waiting for you to take me into your confidence. You have not had a letter from James for nearly three weeks, and yet he should have come home to England by now. I did not want to press you, especially with you seeming unwell, but you should tell me.'

My face fell at once, and the easy magic of the land deserted me. Mama saw the change. I searched my mind to find a lie I could offer her, to delay the announcement which I would have to make – that James and I would never marry.

'I cannot say, Mama,' I said softly. 'It is private.' I could feel the familiar easy tears coming and the choking feeling in my throat.

She nodded, her eyes on my face. 'His mama wrote to me,' she said. 'She wrote that James had decided suddenly to go abroad again, and that he had told her that the betrothal would not be made. That the two of you had agreed that you would not suit. That it was a mutually agreed decision.'

I nodded. 'Yes,' I said.

'Yet you are not happy,' she suggested.

'No, Mama,' I said quietly.

She said nothing for a moment and I set the pony to walk forward. We climbed the little slope away from the common field and went slowly down the lane, the sunshine dappling the track ahead of us and the shadows sliding up and over her parasol.

She took a breath, and I saw her hands tighten on the handle of the parasol. 'Julia,' she said firmly, 'I am your mama and it is my duty to know these things. You must tell me why you and James are no longer planning marriage.'

I touched the reins and the pony stopped. I knew I would have to betray James, just as my fear of the sight had made me betray Clary and Matthew and my cowardice had made me betray my duty to the whole of Acre. 'I discovered that he was unchaste,' I said softly. 'He has been with a woman.'

Mama drew in her breath sharply. 'I see,' she said. She put out her hand and touched mine. 'I think you are right,' she said. 'But the world we live in is a hard one, Julia. I believe most young men have a woman friend before they are married. As long as they are true to their wives after marriage, there are few people who think badly of them.'

I knew I would have to betray James's private conversation with me and smirch his character. I could feel the tears gathering behind my eyes. 'It was not one woman friend, Mama,' I said, and my voice was a thread as thin as the rope which hanged Judas. 'He consorts with common women, he visits their houses. I could not be sure he would cease to do so.'

'James Fortescue?' Mama said in utter incredulity. And I loved her so dearly then, for disbelieving me, even though I had to convince her.

'One of the Acre children,' I said awkwardly. 'You never heard about her. She was called Julie – named after me, I suppose. She had become a . . . a fallen woman. She called it street-trading.' I took a little breath. 'She recognized him, Mama. He did not deny it.'

My mama gasped. She was a lady who had lived a sheltered life, a childhood in the best part of Bath, a womanhood on the isolated estate of Wideacre. She had never been to a place like Fish Quay Lane. She had never seen a woman like Julie. And she would never have understood, as I did, that someone can be driven one way by their desires, and another way by their duty. For my mama, duty and desire took one path. For the rest of us true-bred Laceys, life was hopelessly contradictory.

'I see,' she said inadequately. 'I am very sorry, my darling. But do remember that you are young, and there are many young men who you will meet, and one of them you will love. I shall not trouble you now to tell me more, my darling.'

I nodded. 'I would rather not,' I said.

She touched my hand again, and I clicked to the pony and we moved forward.

As soon as we were home, Mama sent me to lie down and rest, and she went herself to find John. He was in the library working, and Mama went in, leaving the door open behind her. With a heaviness in my heart I crept downstairs so that I could listen to their conversation. I was a liar, and now I had become an eaves-dropper too.

John's tone was reasonable. 'I can't agree with you, Celia,' he said firmly. 'This is an excuse of delicacy. All young men seek experience, and the general belief is that they are better husbands for it.'

'This is not "experience",' my mama replied. Her voice was a little higher than usual. She was distressed. 'I do not know exactly what you mean by that, John, nor do I wish to know. Julia tells me that Mr Fortescue has consorted with prostitutes, and that she cannot be certain that this would cease on marriage. That seems to me ample reason for breaking the friendship.'

'Prostitutes?' John's voice was suddenly sharp. 'Are you sure?'

'I am merely telling you what Julia told me,' Mama said with dignity. 'I did not press her on it. Apparently one of the lost Acre children had become a prostitute – the one who refused to come home. She recognized him.'

'This is a good deal more serious,' John said. 'I was thinking of perhaps an older married lady. I would be very anxious indeed if Julia's betrothed used bagnios and suchlike.'

'I fail to see the difference,' Mama said impatiently. I heard her heels click on the polished floorboards. 'It is still unchastity.'

John's voice was warm, and I could tell he was smiling at her. 'Morally, you are right, Celia,' he said. 'But speaking as a doctor.' He paused. 'There is a stew-pot of disease among the street women,' he said. 'Many of them are fatal, none of them curable. If James Fortescue has been with prostitutes, we should thank God that Julia learned of it in time.'

'Oh,' Mama said blankly.

'You would not know,' John said gently. 'And I am content that neither you nor Julia will ever know how those women, and infected men, can suffer. But the diseases are easily caught and easily passed on. If James Fortescue habitually goes with such women, the engagement should certainly be ended.'

Mama was silent for a moment. 'I shall take her away, then,' she said, 'for a few days. She shall come with me to Oxford when I visit Richard.'

Uncle John replied, but I had heard enough. I stole up the stairs in my stockinged feet and listened no more. I rang my bell and asked for water to be set on to boil for a bath. I felt utterly dirty. I could not dine with my beloved mama and my dear Uncle John until I had scrubbed myself all over.

'So I am to lose you two gadabouts again, am I?' Uncle John said in an injured tone later at dinner. 'I can see that I have made a rod for my own back and Julia will be all around the country, leaving me to manage her beastly estate.'

The cheerfulness was a little forced, but I appreciated that neither of them wished to tax me further. I tried to smile, but I was fighting back another attack of sickness, with a large portion of Wideacre trout cooked in cream and wine sauce before me. The flesh was as pink as rose petals, the sauce shiny and yellow as butter with rich Wideacre milk. I could hardly bear to sit at the table with the smell of it, and I knew I could not eat it.

'We shan't be long in Oxford,' Mama said when I did not answer. 'And I should think you would be glad to have the house to yourself for a while. You will be able to dine in the library with your maps all around you, and no one will scold you for smoking cigars and going to bed late.'

'Oh, yes,' Uncle John said with relish. 'I shall have a feast of forbidden luxuries. And when you come home, you will have to launder the curtains and scrub the carpets, the place will be so well seasoned with tobacco.'

I could hardly hear the two of them, and I could scarcely see my unwanted plate before me. The table seemed to be rising and falling like an undulating wave.

'Mama, please excuse me,' I whispered. 'I do not feel well.' I rose to my feet and took myself somehow out of the room and went to the parlour, and I sank down on the hearthrug before the flower-filled grate and tipped my head back against the chair.

I had lied to Mama this dinner-time, and I was going to have to go on lying. I had told her there was nothing wrong with me, and that was not true. There was something wrong with me and anyone but a fool would have guessed it weeks before.

I was with child.

My cousin Richard had got me with child, and I was ruined indeed.

I needed no threats or promises now to bind me to him. I was absolutely ruined unless he married me, and I knew full well that I must go to him and tell him that we must be married at once.

It had taken me weeks to understand the cause of my nausea and dizziness, and even then I had clung to the foolish hope that I was sick because my monthly bleeding was late. When it did not come, and did not come, I started to know. And when everything on Wideacre seemed alive and fruitful, I knew I was fertile also.

Twice I had started to write to Richard, and two pages of hot-pressed notepaper had ended up in the fire. I knew that we were betrothed in his eyes, and since the day he left for Oxford, when he had held me in a hard hurting grip and told me that no gentleman would ever want me now, I had known that there was no love for me in the future. No love, no marriage and no children.

I had faced that sentence. Faced it and thought that I could tolerate it. But now I had to face something worse. I did not want to be Richard's wife. I could not bear the thought of a clandestine marriage which would shame Mama, and shame me; or a marriage with her reluctant consent because she knew I was ruined. But I could see no other way. I had spent weeks trying to pretend that the morning in the summer-house had never happened. But it *had* happened; and the bravest thing I had ever had to do was to look my shame in the face and say, 'I should be better off dead than shamed in this way', and know that I would not die. Instead I would have to marry, and marry fast, or run the risk of showing a belly on me which would be obvious enough in the new slim gowns, and my mama would be within her rights to have me turned from her door and never to see me again.

She would be disgraced by a clandestine match – but such a thing could be hushed up and forgotten within a few years. There would be an early baby, but Wideacre was a tolerant place where the old ways were still known. There were few weddings celebrated in the village church at which the bride did not have a broad belly to carry before her, and a flood of banns were read over the few weeks after the May courting on the downs. I would be clinging to my reputation by the skin of my teeth in the world of the Quality with a secret marriage and an early baby. But among the common people of Wideacre, I would be nothing out of the ordinary.

I straightened up and looked at the fire. I would never see James Fortescue ever again, and I flushed suddenly hot at the thought that somebody would be bound to tell him that pretty Julia Lacey, who was the toast of the season last year in Bath and had been quite his favourite for a while, had dashed into marriage not a moment too soon. He would be glad at the narrowness of his escape when he heard that. He might tell the gossip who whispered my name that he had wellnigh married me himself! And they would shake their heads and wonder that such a pleasant young lady should be such a whore. I put my face in my hands at that and sat without another idea in my head for a little while.

Then I shrugged.

I could not help it.

I had made a mistake, a grievous and awful mistake, and I would have to live with it and take the consequences.

It could have been worse, I tried to tell myself, seeking for some courage inside me and finding little. At least I loved my cousin Richard. I had wanted to marry him when we were children. He had held my heart in his hands since we were children together. I might close my eyes in the blankest of horror that we had to be married in such a disgraceful way, but at the end of the day I would have the two constant loves in my life: Richard and Wideacre.

Mama would be grieved. Mama would be distressed but . . .

I gave up the attempt to pretend that it would be all right. I could find no courage in myself, and I was too honest to pretend that a shameful secret marriage and an early baby was anything but a catastrophe in my life. But a pregnancy without being able to own the father would be immeasurably worse. There was no way that I could tell Mama that I was with child. There was no way that I could tell Uncle John. But if Richard would take my part and tell the lies we would need to tell, I might yet come through. Richard was the only person I could trust with the truth. Richard was the only person I could go to for help. There was only one way before me that I could see and that way led me directly to Richard at Oxford.

24

I hardly saw the town; the great grey colleges which fronted the streets looked more like prisons than palaces of learning to me. Mama was entranced by the style and the history of the place as we rattled to Richard's college over the cobblestones; but I thought the windows too small and the façade of the buildings grim.

I learned later that the beauty of the colleges is hidden inside, that they are often built in a square with lovely secret gardens locked away. If the porter at the gate knows your name, you may walk inside the gateway and on through to a place of utter peace and silence where a cedar tree grows or where a fountain splashes.

From the outside they are forbidding, and all the secret gardens behind the walls did not compensate me for the way they seemed to frown at me as if they were all serious and thoughtful men and before them I was a silly girl who had lost her reputation and was growing big with a bastard child. Women were not welcome at Oxford, not even aunts and cousins, and pregnant mistresses would be utterly despised. It was a man's place, and they kept their libraries, their books, their theatres and their gardens to themselves.

Richard was expecting us and had ordered tea for us in his lodgings, but he was quick to see the urgency in my eyes. I had forgotten his ability to deceive, and his start of surprise when he realized he had left some books at his tutor's house would have convinced an all-seeing archangel. Mama agreed to sit down with a newspaper while Richard and I strolled down the road to fetch his books, and Richard turned to me as soon as we were clear of the house.

'What is the matter?' he said abruptly.

I noticed a certain grimness about his face and felt my heart sink. If Richard no longer wished to marry me, then I was lost indeed. 'I had to see you . . .' I started awkwardly. 'Richard, it is about our being betrothed . . .' My voice trailed off at the sudden darkening of his eyes.

'What about it?' he said, and I had to bite back a rush of panic because I had irritated him.

'Richard,' I said weakly. 'Richard, you must help me, Richard, please!'

'What do you want?' he asked levelly.

We were walking down the road before the stone-faced men's colleges as we talked, but at that I put both hands on his sleeve and tugged him to a standstill. 'Richard,' I said, 'please don't speak to me in that cold voice. I will be ruined unless you will save me. Richard! I am with child!'

He was delighted.

I *know* Richard. I could not mistake that blaze of blue in his eyes any more than I could mistake my own wan horror. I put my hands on his arm and told him I was ruined, and he was as delighted as if I had signed over Wideacre to him, and all of Sussex with it.

His eyelids dropped instantly to shield his expression. 'Julia,' he said gravely, 'you are in very serious trouble.'

'I know it!' I said rapidly. But in some clear small corner of my mind I noted that he had said that it was *I* who was in trouble. He did not say *we* were.

'It would kill your mama,' he said. 'She would have to send you away from home. You would not be able to stay at Wideacre. I think it would break her heart.'

I nodded. Anxiety had made my throat so tight that I could say nothing.

'And you would be dropped entirely from society,' Richard said. 'None of your friends would ever see you again. It is a dreadful prospect. I cannot even think where you might live.' He paused. 'I suppose John might set you up in a little house abroad somewhere,' he said thoughtfully, 'or they might arrange a marriage for you with a tenant farmer or someone who would accept your shame.'

I tried to speak, but I could only make a sound like a little whimper. 'Richard!' I said imploringly.

'Yes?' he answered. He sounded distracted, as if he could ill spare the time for my interruption when he was trying to think what would become of me now that I was ruined.

'We were betrothed,' I said very softly. People walking past on the street turned to look at us, a handsome youth and a pretty girl holding tight to his arm and looking up into his face like a despairing beggar. Richard saw their glances and smoothly moved us on, tucking my cold hand under his elbow.

'We were,' he agreed, 'but I thought you had been betrothed to someone else. The last word you gave me on the matter was that you wished to marry no one, that you wanted us to be brother and sister. I had the impression, Julia, I must say, that you were not enthusiastic about our marriage.'

'I was not,' I said honestly. 'I am not.' It was like a nightmare, it was worse than a nightmare. I could hardly walk down the street, my knees were so weak with horror at this conversation. I could hardly believe Richard was triumphant over me and I was a supplicant being tormented. 'But this alters everything, Richard.'

'Yes,' he said, and not even he could conceal the relish in his voice. 'It does indeed.'

Then, all at once, I had taken my fill. 'Don't tease me, Richard,' I said blankly. 'This is no jest for me. If you will not own the child, if you refuse to marry me, you should tell me clearly. You must tell me now.'

The determination in my voice stopped him, and he looked at me narrowly, measuring my will against his own. 'What would you do?' he asked curiously.

'I should tell Mama,' I said, dredging up courage from the very soles of my shoes. 'I should tell Mama, and I should tell Uncle John. I should tell them that I might be shamed, but I should still be the part heir to Wideacre. We have been talking in the village about sharing out the land and running the estate as a joint venture of villagers and Laceys. If I could not be one of the Quality, if I could not be a lady, then I should give my share of the land outright to Acre. I should give it to them as a gift. I should take one of the better cottages in Acre and live there alone, and raise my child there. I know no one would visit me, and I know I would be ruined. But I still have friends among the poor people of Acre, and many of them were born a few months after a wedding, and some of them out of wedlock. Even if society and all my family close their doors to me, I should still have Wideacre.'

He nodded, slowly, and I could see his eyes flicking along the grey roofs and the pale skyline, as if he were trying to calculate something at speed. He did not know whether to believe me or not. He looked down at me and he saw my set face, and knew that I was determined. He believed that I could do such a thing.

Then I saw his eyes warm and he turned his most lovable smile towards me. 'Oh, my darling Julia,' he said sweetly, 'what a silly girl you are! I have loved you all my life, quite adored you! Of course you will not be shamed in that way. I will marry you. I would never dream of not being your husband. And you will have a son, my son, and he will be the heir, the sole heir to Wideacre!'

I gave a little gasp, and the courage which had been holding me steady and upright while we spoke suddenly deserted me and I felt weepy with relief. 'Yes,' I said.

Richard's smile was sweet as a May morning. 'We must plan,' he said in a businesslike manner. 'When will he be born? At the end of January?'

I paused. I had not thought of the birth of the child at all. All I had thought of was the distress it would cause my mama, and the shock to Uncle John, and the shame for me. But to hear Richard speak so confidently of the boy that would be born, that would be the next squire for Wideacre, made my spirits suddenly rise for the first time since I had conceived. The child would be a

Wideacre baby as Richard and I had been. The child would be raised on Wideacre under the wide sweet skies of my home. And she – for I was certain that the baby was a girl – she would be my little daughter, and I would teach her about the land and how to farm it, and she might be the one to give the land back to the people that worked it.

'Yes,' I said, 'I am nearly two months into my time.'

Richard nodded. 'When does it start to show?' he asked.

I frowned. 'Oh, I so wish Clary was alive!' I said in sudden longing for her common sense and for her wealth of knowledge. 'I am trying to remember from seeing Clary's mother, and the other women. I think it starts showing about the third month. But, Richard, I want to be married at once. I have to be married before it starts to show!'

The note of panic in my voice made Richard smile his cruel teasing smile. 'Yes,' he said gently. 'I am sure you do. I don't think I have ever seen you so afraid of anything, Julia.'

I could not retort. I looked up at him and I knew my mouth was trembling.

'It is all right,' he said, his voice silky with his happiness at seeing me in fear, at hearing me beg. 'I shall make the arrangements. Now, stop looking so scared, Julia, we must go back for tea.'

The arrangements were easier than I had thought possible. Richard was given a few days' leave by his tutor and claimed the right to escort us back to Sussex. Once we were home, Mama and Uncle John were tolerant when Richard asked if we might use the curricle and said he wanted to drive me to the coast. They did not expect us home until late, and they did not know what time we left, for we were away in the morning before they were stirring. We drove in the pale early light down the road to Portsmouth, Richard whistling and singing snatches of songs. I was as quiet as if I were going to my own funeral rather than to my wedding. The motion of the carriage made me queasy and tired, and after we had stopped for breakfast and changed the horses, I laid my head on Richard's shoulder and dozed.

An odd sight we must have looked when we drove into the city. I felt I should have been looking about me at the noise and the bustle and the hurry of people. But I stared around dull-eyed and noticed nothing. I was on my way to my wedding and I felt nothing but dread, and when I glanced sideways at Richard, my heart sank.

The streets narrowed, and the sound of the wheels on the cobbles was deafening. The pavements were very crowded, and people continually stepped out into the road so Richard had to pull up the horses all the time.

We were due at the quayside, where there was a captain greedy enough and careless enough to sell us a licence to say that he had married us when on a voyage outside the limit of coastal waters, where his authority was legal.

Richard was following a hand-drawn map spread out on his knee. His friend Wrigley from Chichester had made it out for him and advised him as to the name of the captain. There were no secrets. One young man, living only a few miles from Wideacre, knew that we were to be married, and no doubt Richard told him why. There were no secrets and there was no escaping my shame.

He turned the curricle into a hotel yard and snapped orders at the ostlers: we would be gone two hours and the horses were to be ready for our return. Then he gave me his arm, casually, as one might pick up a valise, and took me down the road to the quayside.

The harbour was a forest of masts, with sailors, impossibly high, clinging to sails and to rigging and clamouring like an aviary full of swearing parrots. I shadowed Richard and clung to his arm.

'How will we ever find the right ship?' I asked; and I knew with a sudden dread that I was hoping we would *not* find the right ship and that we might go home. Even Mama's heartbreak and my shame was better than this hopeless roaming around in a town I did not know with a man whose true character I was just coming to learn.

'It's there,' Richard said. This expedition, which was weakening me with every step we took, was high adventure to Richard; his eyes were sparkling, he was looking around him with excitement. 'There it is!' he said triumphantly. 'Now to find the captain.'

Richard pushed me ahead of him up a narrow gangplank, and I kept my eyes on my footing and tried not to notice that half a dozen grubby faces had appeared over the side of the ship and were inspecting me and passing comment freely on my gown and my bonnet, and what we might want with their ship.

When we reached the deck, they had vanished, and Richard seemed to be deaf and blind to the discomfort of the situation.

'Hey, there!' he called confidently to one of the sailors who appeared, by his sprawling leisure, to be in charge of the crew who were slopping dirty water around the deck of the ship. 'Where's the captain?'

The man looked up from cleaning his nails with a long murderous knife, and eyed us carefully as if to consider whether or not we merited an answer. Richard put his hand in his coat pocket, and the chink of coins was a password. It struck me that Richard was very rich on this trip. Richard was very assured.

''Ee's drunk again,' the man said gloomily. He inspected us with open contempt. I flushed as he looked me up and down with disdain. He knew we were here for a secret marriage. He knew there was only one reason for a young girl of Quality to come to this dirty ship seeking out a drunken captain. He looked at me as though I were a wanton who might go with any man. I shrank back a little behind Richard's shoulder, pulled my light cloak about my shoulders and turned up the collar to hide my face.

I had a feeling, an idea I could not have put in words, that there was some kind of omen for the future in that disdainful stare. I was to become the property of one man, but any man could look at me as he wished. I was a free woman no longer; and well might I shrink back behind Richard, for he was my protector. I would no longer command respect in my own right.

'We'll see him,' Richard said. He did not notice my embarrassment, or he did not think it sufficiently important to check the
man's insolent gaze. The man shrugged, caring neither way, and
then pointed rudely past us to a door. 'Straight dahn there,' he
said, his accent sounding strange to my ears, which were accustomed to the gentle lilt of the Sussex voice.

Richard started for the companion-way, and I caught him up.
'Richard,' I said, staying him as he was about to descend. 'If he
is drunk, perhaps he cannot . . . Perhaps we should . . . Richard,
wait!' I said.

Richard set his feet either side of the ladder and slid skilfully
down to the bottom. 'Come down,' he commanded me.

I hesitated. The crew on deck had stopped their work and
were openly staring, and the man with the knife was watching
me, expressionless. Even the sailors in the rigging were staring
down at me. I gathered my skirts around me. Gripping the ladder
in my hands, I clambered down till I was at Richard's side.

The stench hit me like a physical blow. It was a smell com-
pounded of vomit from a thousand seasick voyages, of old sweat,
of injury and fear, of gunpowder and filthy clothes, of mouldy
food and gangrene. I gagged and fumbled for my handkerchief
and put it over my mouth, inhaling the smell of clean linen and
eau-de-Cologne.

Richard looked at me, his expression hidden in the shadows of
the ill-lit corridor. 'What is it now?' he demanded impatiently.

'We cannot do it like this, Richard,' I said urgently. 'It is
awful! There must be another way we can do this. We cannot be
married here in this dirty place. It . . . it *smells*, Richard.'

He gave a quick exclamation under his breath and then he
turned towards me and took hold of my arms, just above the
elbows, in a grip so hard that I would have cried out had my fear
of the place not been greater than the hurt.

'Look here,' Richard said savagely, '*you* wanted us to be lovers.
You lay back on the floor and smiled. *You* put your arms around
my neck. *You* said no but meant yes. *You* came home on horseback with Jem and held out your arms to me. If you had been

unwilling, you would have struggled more. There is no such thing as rape, everyone knows that. You were willing, you could have stopped me, but you did not want to stop me. And when Jem found you, you told him that you had fallen from Misty. If you had been raped, you would have said so. You were willing. You were willing because you are a whore. And it is generous – very generous – of me to marry you.'

I gaped at him. His hard grip on my arms was nothing to the pain I felt under my ribs. Every time he said, 'You', the word was like a knife which made a little stab into my heart.

He was telling a partial truth, and in any case I was quite incapable of spotting an unjust accusation now. I had blamed myself from the moment I had realized what was happening on the floor of the summer-house. And a woman is always the one at fault. If I had been a true lady, if I had been truly pure, then Richard would not have done it. I had lost my virginity and that was enough to ruin me in everyone's eyes – and in my own.

'I am prepared to marry you,' Richard said fiercely, 'but it is a favour *I* am doing *you*. I could just as well let you face Mama and John on your own, Julia. And if I told them that it was you that tempted me, you who insisted on us being lovers, I should think the shame would kill your mama.'

The torch in the bracket on the wall jumped and flickered in a draught which swept down the companion-way. In the sudden ripple of light I saw Richard's face. He was smiling in the way he used to smile when he had trapped me in our childhood games. I remembered once he had called me up to a loft in a deserted barn by one of the derelict cornfields. 'There is a barn owl's nest,' he had called. He had insisted that I climb the rickety ladder up to see it. I could not see what he was looking at, though he pointed to a dark hole in the wall close to a beam. Then, while I was straining to see, he had suddenly given me a push which caught me off balance and knocked me into the wall, and had run for the ladder. He was down it in a flash and had thrown it to the floor. When I peered over the edge to the floor twenty feet below, he was smiling. 'I think you are stuck,' he had said then.

'I think you are stuck,' he said now.

I looked at him and I was clear-sighted. I felt a breath of courage pass over me as fresh and as sweet as a wind on Wideacre. In the fetid cramped hold of a rotten ship, I felt my shoulders go back and my chin come up. I was not a silly whore taken in lust, I was a Lacey of Wideacre. I was my papa's daughter and I was the heir and natural successor of Beatrice Lacey, the witch of Wideacre, who had made the land and wrecked the land to pave my way to the hall. After Beatrice, nobody in Sussex would ever think women were weak again. With the example of Beatrice before me – even Beatrice the land-killer, the wrecker – I could find some strength inside my young woman's body and inside my loving, vulnerable mind.

I met Richard's smiling gaze without flinching. 'You are right,' I said levelly. 'I am stuck. So let us go into this nasty little room and see this drunken captain and get ourselves married. And then I shall have to go home, and later I shall have to tell my beloved mama and dear Uncle John. And I shall have to face their grief and disappointment in me. And I shall have to walk through the wreckage of their hopes for me. But I can walk through that wreckage,' I said. 'And it is true that I am still not afraid. Or when I *am* afraid, I do not stay afraid. And my fear does not disable me.'

Richard's smile was wiped off his face and he was looking at me with something like respect. 'Yes,' he said softly, 'I know you are not afraid, Julia. Even when you are scared about something, you always seem to find courage from somewhere to face it. I don't know how you do it.'

'I am a Lacey,' I said grimly, and the very word seemed to bring the air of Wideacre into that close place. 'Now, let's go in, Richard, and get it over with.'

He raised his hand at my command and knocked at the door and went in. So, although he was partly lying when he said I was to blame for the conception of the child, it was certainly I who made the marriage. And I had an odd idea that the marriage would ruin me more than the rape had done.

It was horrid.

Of course it was horrid.

I had dreamed all my childhood, girlhood and womanhood of marrying under the great grey stone arch of Acre's Gothic church, with the sun shining through the stained-glass window, making rainbow blocks of colour on my white gown, and Mama smiling in the Lacey pew behind me.

When I was a girl, I had dreamed that Richard would be there with his hand warm in mine and his kisses on my lips when he had given me the ring. I had seen myself, in my conceited dream, in a flurry of white muslin or figured satin. I even knew the flowers I would have carried: Wideacre flowers, for not all my girlish dreams were obvious conventions culled from the journals. I had thought I would carry the wild flowers of Wideacre in a jumble of a bouquet, with scarlet poppies bright in the middle. I would have worn white moon-daisies and blue cornflowers in my hair.

I dare say I should have looked very foolish, and I am sure my grandmama, Lady Havering, would not have approved. I should hardly have set a mode with a bunch full of weeds in my hands and daisies around my head. So perhaps it hardly mattered that I could not be a beloved bride in the church of my home, surrounded by friends and with the good wishes of a village around me.

But nothing could have been worse than that filthy cabin, and the captain and the mumbled promises read in a croaky voice from his little prayer book. When he looked at me to ask for my response, the stale drink on his breath blew in my face. His cabin smelled of dirty clothes, and there was a plate with rancid chop bones on it tucked under the bunk.

But it was legal, and binding, and when he said, 'I now pronounce thee man and wife', we were as much married as if we had made our promises in a grand society wedding in Chichester Cathedral.

'You may kiss the bride,' he said, leering at Richard.

Richard dipped his lovely dark head down to me and I raised

my face for his kiss. His lips were like ice, and mine were no warmer.

'I thought we had to be married at sea,' I said in a small voice.

'I falsified the ship's log,' said the captain, his rotten teeth showing in his smile. 'If anyone ever asks you, you were here this morning when we were off the Isle of Wight. A marriage for the two of you, and extra sea-time for the young officers in training!' He gave a dirty smile at Richard. 'Thought you'd be in a hurry to get the little lady home,' he said insinuatingly.

I turned away at that while Richard paid him, and I went out into the companion-way and up the ladder, caring little this time for my skirts, and I turned my collar up against the chill and against the sadness of this mess that I was in. We went back down the gangway, walked to the inn, drank a silent cup of coffee in the parlour and then went outside to the curricle.

Richard whistled a tune, in high good humour, and turned the horses north for home. The road off Portsmouth is like a causeway over mud-flats and tidal reaches. The tide was in and it was like a sheet of silver, with boats rocking at anchor and a beautiful schooner coming up on the afternoon tide, sailing low in the water from the weight of her load.

'Home,' Richard said with satisfaction, 'and it's my real home at last. For I'm the squire there now; there is only one squire there and it is me.'

The horses tossed their heads and lengthened their stride, and I said nothing while Richard tightened the reins and the curricle stopped its swaying. My heart was like a lump of weighty ice inside me, and the sickness I felt was no longer from the baby but from the knowledge that I had lost my control over Wideacre and that I had given Acre a master I could not trust. I had given myself a master I could not trust.

Already I had learned the slavish skill of watching my words. I waited until the horses' pace was a controlled smooth canter and then I cleared my throat and said levelly, 'There have been promises made by me in Acre, and contracts signed by me for the two of us. Some things cannot be changed, for they have been promised and we are honour bound to keep those promises.'

Richard smiled at me and his eyes were empty of all guile. You could not look at him and not trust him. 'Of course, Julia,' he said, at his sweetest. 'Of course, my dear cousin. My dear wife, I can now say! I was just thinking that now Wideacre is mine, you need not take responsibility for Wideacre in the way that you have done. Wideacre will be my job now, not yours. And besides,' he went on, and his smile was warm, 'you will be busy indoors, my darling, for in seven months' time there will be work for you which no one but yourself can do.'

I nodded, for that was true enough. But it chilled me when he spoke of Wideacre in that tone.

'I shall always want to work on the land,' I said. 'You will be the squire, but I have been working the land since Uncle John came home. I could not give it up now just because we are married.'

Richard said nothing; he was steering the horses past a cart piled high with newly stitched sails. We were clear of the town and I raised my head and smelled the clean air and felt the smells and the humiliation of that horrid ship blow away from me.

Richard took his eyes from the road and glanced sideways at me and saw the colour coming back into my cheeks.

'Oh!' he said, pretending he had suddenly remembered. 'I've written to James Fortescue.'

'You did what?' I asked.

'I've written to James Fortescue,' Richard said lightly. 'Of course I did, Julia. I wrote and told him that we were to be married today. I had a feeling – I don't know why – that you had neglected to tell him yourself. In any case, a gentleman should inform another gentleman of such an event.'

My mouth was numb, as if Richard had smacked me in the face. 'I had not told him,' I said, half to myself. 'I thought there was no need, after you had informed him our betrothal was over.'

'Well, then,' said Richard agreeably, 'now you won't have to!'

I sat in silence. I could not imagine what James would feel when he opened a letter from Richard telling him that I was married. I could not imagine how he would tell Marianne, or his parents, who had been so kind to me. I could not bear to think how he would feel, or what he would think of me.

'I sent the last of his letters back,' Richard said nonchalantly. 'In with my letter to him, I sent them back too. So there's nothing for you to worry about.'

'His letters?' I exclaimed. 'You said you had returned them over a month ago, when you met him on the road.'

'Some of them then,' Richard acknowledged, 'but I kept some of them back to reread. There were some things he said that I wanted to study more carefully. I've sent them all back now anyway. He *did* write a lot, didn't he?'

My hands were hurting and I realized I had been clinging to the seat of the curricle. My knuckles were white.

'He really did love you,' Richard said, as if it were grounds for congratulation. 'I've never read anything so passionate. When he wrote about watching you in the glove-maker's shop, it sounded like he half worshipped you, and when he praised you for finding that Acre pauper. He really did love you, didn't he, Julia? And now you'll never see him again.'

I took the inside of my cheek between my teeth and bit so hard I could feel the delicate skin swell. The pain of it gave me my voice back. 'Yes,' I said. My voice was hard. 'Yes, he did love me very well. And I loved him. But the fact that you stole his letters to me and read them and returned them is not really important now. Even I know that. This is the last time I shall ever mention his name, and it should be the last time you name him to me, for you do not hurt me, Richard, and you do not make me angry.'

We travelled in silence then, for many miles.

'We'll be home in time for supper,' Richard said. 'Probably before dark.'

'Yes,' I said. I was numb.

'I don't think we should tell them right away. I have to go back to Oxford tomorrow. Let's leave it until I come home.'

'Yes,' I said.

'You probably won't be showing it until then,' Richard said cheerfully. 'And if they do start becoming suspicious, you can always write to me at once and I will come home early.'

'Yes,' I said again.

'You don't seem very happy,' Richard said impatiently. 'It has all come out exactly as we planned when we were children, and you are going around with a face like a wet Friday.'

'I know,' I said. I said nothing more. I felt no need to apologize to Richard for being in the sullens. I felt no obligation to pretend I was happy. I was seventeen years old, and it seemed to me that I had been trapped and ensnared into a prison where my land would be taken from me, and my confidence that I was squire would be taken from me, and my happiness would be taken from me. The fact that I had entered the prison thoughtlessly, turned the key with my mind elsewhere and tossed it out of the window in folly meant that I could blame no one but myself for the mess I had made of my life.

So I turned my head away from Richard and looked at the fields slipping by, and the pretty villages, and the clean streams, and the ripening wheat, and I said nothing at all. I did not weep. I did not cry out. I looked at the landscape and thought I must find from somewhere inside me the courage to go on and on and on until I reached a safe haven and could stop.

But I knew I could not stop for a while.

25

I had been right that sad afternoon in the curricle, driving home. I had been right to think that I had to put my head down like a shire horse dragging a harrow through mud which was too thick. I could almost feel a weight of guilt around my neck and I bowed under it, and leaned against it, and tugged and tugged it with me through every warm summery day.

'Julia, you are getting quite round-shouldered,' Mama said in surprise from the parlour window as she watched me cutting roses in the garden outside. 'Do try to stand up, my dear, and don't look so grim. Is anything wrong?'

'No, Mama,' I said. I obediently straightened my shoulders and raised my chin, but I knew that I would forget and slouch forward again. I had the weight of an illegitimate child in my belly; I had a cart-load of guilt on my shoulders. I could not help but lean against it, like a man walking into a wind blowing against him.

The wind was blowing against me all the last weeks of June and the first weeks of July while I waited for Richard to come home and thought about what would happen when we told them.

Uncle John and my mama conspired to leave me alone. They saw that my health was better. The sickness had passed and I was eating properly again, but they were worried at the lines around my mouth and the scowl I wore on my forehead all the time, like a mark of Cain.

I could not look at my darling mama without wondering how the news would affect her. And I found I was longing for her to be angry with me – really furiously enraged. The thing I dreaded most of all was for her to look at me with stricken eyes and blame herself. I had to push the thought of her distress away from me every day of that summer. If I had thought of Mama breaking her heart for me, I could not have gone on.

And I had to go on.

The wheat was ripening well on Acre and we had to ready the work-teams and the carts for harvesting. Even farms which have been harvesting for years find the preparation and the harvest a struggle, and we were all beginners on Wideacre. It is a struggle against the weather: the wheat has to ripen and then it has to be cut and stored at once. It is not like hay, which can survive a drenching and then dry off. Once wheat is cut, it has to be inside.

It is a struggle of organization: the men and the equipment and the gleaners and the wagons all have to be arranged before you start. It is a struggle of business: you have to decide how much of the crop to sell, the straw and the grain, how much to keep for your own use. You have to decide what price to charge: whether to sell as soon as you have harvested in a poor market or to keep the grain back until there is a shortage and prices are rising. And then you have to decide whether to profiteer on the backs of hungry people and refuse to sell at the proper rates, at the traditional rates, to let the price rise and rise and rise until people are starved.

That decision was an easy one on Wideacre. Never again would Acre people go hungry with a good crop in the field and full barns. But Ralph, Uncle John and I were agreed that a proportion of the crop should be sent out of the county and sold in the London markets for the best price it could command. And Ralph thought we would be in no danger of protest from the poor if they saw we were serving the local market first.

Only once in that warm sun-drenched time while I waited for Richard to come home and tell my mama was I directly challenged. It was Ralph Megson who spoke to me. It *would* be Ralph. I was not forgiven by him, though he was my friend, and always would be my friend. He had seen my face getting bleaker and the rings under my eyes getting as dark as bruises.

I had been in the carriage to Chichester to order a batch of sickles for harvesting. Ned in Acre had no time to make them with all the other work waiting for him outside his forge. I asked Jem to take me down to Acre so that I might leave a note for Ralph to tell him they would be delivered in the next week.

When we got to his cottage, he was sitting on the stone step by his front door, smoking a pipe in the sunshine. He smiled when he saw me and did not rise, but waited for me to come up his garden path and sit beside him.

'Feel that sun,' he said luxuriously. 'The only thing I regret about coming home to Wideacre is that we do not have enough sunshine. I was out by the sugar islands for a time, Julia. It gets so hot there you cannot work out in the heat. I used to stretch out like a baking adder on the common and sleep all the day long in the sunshine.'

I sat primly beside him, and saw him smile and shut his eyes and turn his face up to the light. The sun did not warm me, though my skin grew hot. It felt like the blood which was feeding my little girl was a poison for my own flesh. Every time I smiled, or saw a growing leaf, or a playing child, or laughed at some jest, the poison took a grip on me and made me faint to think that soon, very soon, I should have to tell my mama that I was with child and shamefully married in secret to my cousin.

'What ails you?' Ralph said softly. 'You've been as white as skimmed milk for days and as sour as lemons. It is not like you, Julia.'

'Nothing,' I said through my teeth.

'Not with child, are you?' Ralph asked casually. He had kept his eyes tight shut and his face turned up to the sun so he did not see me flush scarlet. He was keeping his eyes shut so I could talk freely.

'No,' I said.

'*If* you were,' he said as if the matter were of little interest, '*if* you were, there would be no need to go rushing off to marry, nor confess to your mama or Uncle John. There are ways of getting rid of a child before your belly gets fat, if you catch it in time.'

'Are there?' I asked.

'Aye,' Ralph said. 'If it was a little lass who was a friend of mine, I'd take her up near where the gypsies camp on the common, and see an old woman who is wise in these things. I could ride up there this very afternoon if you like, Julia.'

'No,' I said. My voice sounded dreary. 'There is no need.'

Ralph opened his eyes and looked sharply at me. 'I'm glad to hear it,' he said frankly. 'I was certain it was that which was pulling you so.' He shut his eyes again like a blind fortune-teller and leaned his head back against the honey-coloured sandstone of his cottage wall.

'A girl constrained into a betrothal is not bound by it, you know,' he said to no one in particular. 'And a lass who loses her virginity is not bound to marry the man. Even carriage folk. They'll tell you that a young lady who loses her virginity would be better off dead. They'll tell you that every young lady who wears white at the altar is a virgin. But that's not true, you know.'

I said nothing. Ralph still did not look at me.

'So if you've been romping with your cousin up on the downs, you're not bound to him,' he said to the sunlight on his eyelids. 'You could refuse him and marry another man tomorrow and no one would know. Anyone who did know would only be Acre folk, and they'd not think the worse of you for it'. He paused. 'And no husband you brought here would ever hear any gossip from us,' he said.

I got to my feet. Ralph opened his eyes and shaded them with his hand, for I stood against the bright sky. My face was in deep shadow.

'Thank you, Ralph,' I said formally. 'I know what you have been saying, but I have no need of any help which you could give me.'

Ralph made a little dismissive gesture with his hands. 'I am yours to command,' he said ironically. 'Excuse me for not getting up.'

I smiled at that; despite my cold darkness I smiled at his

flowery courtesy and his idleness. I turned on my heel and went out of that humming flowering summery garden and drove up to the Dower House where my mama was singing at the pianoforte, not knowing that in a few days I was going to walk into the peaceful home she and John had so painstakingly made and break her heart.

The wheat was ripe before Richard was due to come home.

I was glad. Even in the depths of my despairing sorrow I could be glad that we might get this first Wideacre crop safely gathered in and threshed and stored before I was forced to let loose the storm on our heads and before Uncle John and I could no longer talk of farming.

The weather had got sultry again, and when I met Ralph down at the mill, he spoke of letting the wheat go another few days so that the storm might pass. 'Funny sky,' he said, squinting up at the thick-bellied white clouds and the sun shining so hot on them, but not breaking through.

'It feels as if there should be a storm,' I said, 'but it was like this at haymaking and the weather never broke properly then.'

'If I was at sea, I should run for a port,' Ralph said. He was looking towards the horizon where there was a yellow tinge to the sky over the top of the downs.

'How long can the wheat wait before we cut it?' I asked.

'It can't,' he said with finality. 'We have to start tomorrow unless the storm actually breaks tonight. We cannot tell how long the sickle gangs will take; the old men are badly out of practice and the young ones have never reaped in a gang before. Some of them have even had to go to their fathers to learn how to use a sickle. We can't waste time waiting for bad weather which may not come. We'll start tomorrow.'

'I'll tell John,' I said and turned to my horse which was tethered in the mill yard.

'Aye,' said Ralph. 'And you'll be down to the common field yourself in the morning, won't you, Julia? Everyone would want you to be there.'

'I wouldn't miss it for a fortune,' I assured him with a smile. 'It's my first harvest too, you know.'

I smiled at him, but my face felt stiff. It was the golden time of the year, but I was in shadow. The wheat was ripening, but I felt like ice. I rode home like one of Richard's childhood lead soldiers on a lead horse. My heart felt like lead too.

We dined early and I went to bed early, with Mama and Uncle John wishing me a good day's harvesting tomorrow and promising to visit me in the field with my dinner in a box.

I fell asleep almost at once. Then I had a dream.

Where it came from, I do not know – perhaps Ralph's reference to the gypsies, perhaps my memory of the gypsy who played for us last Christmas. I dreamed almost at once of a gypsy girl who sat at the front of a cart pulled by an old black horse, a horse as big as a hunter, well bred and ill suited to the work of pulling a tawdry painted cart. It was night and the weather was foul, and we were on some empty waste land, perhaps the common. In my dream she was holding a baby in her arms; the reins for the horse were slack on its back and her man was walking by its head. The pots on the side of the cart, the carved sticks for sale and the withe baskets holding clothes-pegs jiggled as the cart rocked on the uneven surface of the track. She went past me, soundless, and I turned to see her go. The rain scudded into my face and I could scarcely see her for the darkness and the driving rain. She had an old cape or a blanket over her shoulders and pulled up to cover her head, and the silhouette of her back was shapeless. One little lantern bobbed at the side of the cart; and it was going away from me.

Inside me, in a burning pain under my ribs, was a great wrench as I saw the cart go, and I called out something into the wind and knew, with despair, that she would not have heard me. I shrieked it again, but the wind was too loud and the rain too strong. I did not even know myself what it was that I had called.

I cried out in my sleep and the sound woke me. It was morning, it was the morning of my first Wideacre harvest, and the rain and the storm had been in my dream and not in real life. Yet I awoke with a sudden lurch of my stomach which felt like fear. As soon as I awoke I held my breath as if to listen, like a householder alerted in deepest sleep by the creak of a floorboard in a silent house. I lay quiet and listened to the fast thudding of my own heart.

My bedroom ceiling was grey-white, and when I raised myself in bed, I could see the sky still unbroken, with slabs of clouds overlying each other, conspiring to roof us in. Tight as slates they lay along the crest of the downs over the roof of the Dower House; although I knew the bright sun was behind them, I could scarcely believe I should ever feel hot sunlight again.

I gave a sigh as if I were not a young woman but an old lady, wearied with the heat of many summers, and I pulled the covers back and got slowly out of bed as if I were tired and defeated. The wooden floorboards were hard under my feet. The water in my ewer was cold. The sky outside the window was too bright and yet it was white, not blue. I splashed water on my face and felt my skin tighten. I dressed in my old grey riding habit, pulled my hair up on my head in a careless knot, crammed my hat on top and pinned it on. My eyes under the pale brim were dull and weary. Then I went down the stairs to the kitchen where Mrs Gough was up early, whisking eggs in a bowl.

She poured me a cup of coffee and I drank it standing by the back door, looking out over the back garden. I felt it scald my tongue, but it did not warm me. It was heavy with sugar, but did not taste sweet. I gave a little sigh. There are some days when nothing seems right, and this day was one of them. She gave me my breakfast in a kerchief, a pastry, a bread roll with butter and honey, a few slices of meat and a peach from Havering.

I went out to the stable; Jem had overslept and Sea Mist was not ready for me. I heaved her saddle out of the tack room and carried her bridle over my shoulder. I tacked her up on my own and hauled myself on to her high back from the mounting-block with no one to help me, and no friendly smile to wish me good harvesting as I trotted out of the yard and turned right down the drive for a canter over the common before I started the day's work.

The field was lined with people when Sea Mist came trotting

PHILIPPA GREGORY

down the hill from the wild side of the common, Ralph among them at the gate, watching Miller Green hand out sickles from his cart.

'Good morning, Miss Julia,' he said courteously, and I said, 'Good day' to him and to all the people around him who smiled and called to me.

'Miss Julia!' a voice said at my horse's head, and I looked down. It was one of the carter's children, a thin, blue-eyed waif, eight years old.

'There are no biscuits for you, Emily, until you have done a morning's gleaning,' I said with mock severity.

She giggled, showing a gap in her teeth and thrust a grimy fist in her mouth to stop the laughter. 'Nay,' she said, 'but could I have a bit of ribbon off your gown, Miss Julia?'

I followed her eyes. The grey habit was well past its best, and when I had finished ripping out my hems walking through the stubble of this crop, I would order another. When it was new and smart, it had been trimmed with satin ribbon and little bows at the cuffs and around the hem. Despite Mama's coercion and my occasional repairs, some of the bows had gone missing. The one on my right cuff was hanging by a thread.

'Of course,' I said kindly. I imagined the child had seen few pretty things in her childhood in Acre. I tugged at the bow until the thread snapped, and I held it out to her. Her white face lit up and she bobbed me a little curtsy – an unschooled copy of her mama's careful downward sweep – and scurried back to the group of her friends who were gathered in the lee of the fence.

'You supervise this field,' Ralph said to me. 'I want to take a Chichester hay merchant around the stacks. Will you be all right on your own?'

'Yes,' I said. I looked around at the men sharpening their sickles and the women rolling up their sleeves. 'They hardly look unwilling!'

'They can't wait to cut it,' Ralph said with satisfaction. 'Your job is merely to stand by in case they have any problems. Anything you cannot resolve on your own, come to me. I shall be in the meadows by the Acre lane.'

I nodded and moved my horse out into the middle of the field. They knew far better than I what they should be doing. Indeed, it seemed that my function was almost ceremonial. They arranged themselves in a line, each as carefully spaced as drilling guardsmen, and the reaper at the end nearest me looked up at me on top of my horse and said, 'Wish us good harvesting, Miss Julia, and put some Wideacre magic into the wheat.'

I gave him a rueful grin. I might not like my role as the spring goddess, as the Queen of the May, as the local harvest deity, but it seemed I could not escape it.

'Good harvesting,' I called, loud enough for everyone in the field to hear, and I reflected that it mattered very little whether or not I felt foolish and self-conscious if two words from me could please them so much.

As if those words were a magic signal, they gripped the sickles and stepped into the waist-high crop and swung the blades in a great flashing rippling arc which said, 'Swish, swish, swish' into the standing corn, which fell before them like a regiment of Richard's toy soldiers on an unsteady table. The sea of pale, feathery yellow collapsed into islands where the broken stalks piled up and were left behind as the row of reapers went in a long smooth line, wading into the crop, pushing it before them, for ever engulfed, for ever slicing, until they had reached the far end of the field and wiped their blades clean of the green blood of Wideacre.

They took a moment to turn around, straightening their backs and chuckling to each other about the weight of the sickles and the forgotten effort of swinging them. They worked steadily and smoothly, faster, I am sure, than they would ever have worked in the old days when the heaps of pale yellow meant profit for the Laceys but the same small wage for the labourer. Now they knew they would have a share in the wealth and they cut up to the very edge of the field, to the roots of the hedges.

The women and the other men coming behind gathered great armfuls of the crop and bound them roughly into stooks. It was new work for many of them. Acre had not touched corn since they burned down the barns fifteen years ago, and only a few of them had learned the skill as day labourers on neighbouring farms. Many of the stooks were lumpy or sloped to the left or the right, or tied too loose. I thought no one would take offence if I said they should be retied. Indeed, I had a rueful grin from Sally Miles, whose stooks were as slanted as a thatched roof.

The breakfast was almost a party, with the reapers sprawled among the fresh stubble and the women handing out food with hands wet from the stalks. The little children were all around me, and I blessed Mrs Gough for the little packet of sugared almonds I found in the bottom of the saddle-bag.

Then the men finished eating and dropped down to lie on their backs and gazed up at the sky, dozing and dreaming, and the women gathered into little groups to admire a nursing baby, or to make plaits and little baskets from the wheat.

Old Mrs Miles was the centre of one of the groups, showing the young women how to make corn dollies. 'I wish you'd show your granddaughter how to tie stooks,' I said, and was rewarded with a ripple of laughter from the women and a laughing scowl from Sally.

When that field was finished, we moved in a body to Three Gate Meadow, which Beatrice had turned over to corn and which now grew golden again.

And that was the Wideacre harvest.

Every day I rose early. Every day I came home late. Every day we cut field after field of pale shimmery wheat until I could see nothing but golden-green fields in my dreams. Even when I closed my eyes, I had that colour printed on my eyelids; it seemed I had forgotten darkness. Every day I rolled out of bed in the pearly shades of a heavy dawn, and dressed myself and went out in the chill, and found the people of Acre up betimes, and ready to go to work.

So we had a good harvest, fruitful, and quickly gathered, and before I had thought possible, we were up on the fields which fringed the downs and harvesting the last, the very last field of Wideacre. I could pride myself on a crop which would have delighted Beatrice herself.

26

We cut that last field in a rush. The clouds were gathering for one of those fast August storms which sometimes come in such heat that there is no rain, but just the crackle of the lightning over the land and the warning rumble of thunder.

But even if this one field had been drenched, we would still have had a harvest which was the envy of the county. The fields had been well rested in the years when Wideacre had gone to the bad, and no place in England had a better work-force.

'You've reason to be proud,' Uncle John had told Ralph and me in the morning of the last day as the sickles were unloaded from the cart and the reapers fell into line. 'No one in the country has harvested faster than Wideacre this season, and that with raw workers. They'll be talking again of Wideacre as they did in the old days as a place where magic can happen.'

Ralph nodded, not troubling to conceal his satisfaction.

'It proves that it can work our way, the new way,' Uncle John said. 'That's especially important this summer. With the news from France as it is.'

'Bad?' Ralph asked, cocking an eyebrow at him.

'They're going to put the king on trial,' John said briefly. 'My guess is that they'll find him guilty and execute him. It'll be a black day for liberty when that happens for it's the end of the French experiment with freedom.'

Ralph smoothed the blade of a sickle with a careful hand. 'Not the end,' he said confidently. 'They have to be rid of their rulers. There's no permanent future without being rid of them, and that parcel of parasites would never have gone of their own free will. They'd have plotted, they'd have led armies back into France armed by other monarchs and financed by other parasites. It's as I've always thought here: you can make some little improvements with the blessing of the landlords, but if you want to make a change which will last, the whole landlord class has to go.'

'You won't do it with that!' Uncle John said, pointing to the sickle. 'No, Mr Megson, you go too far. If it cannot be done by consent and by reason, then it cannot be done at all. You'll never get the right decision by force.'

Ralph smiled his dark slow smile. 'You plough before you sow,' he said. 'I think the French are just breaking the ground. Here on Wideacre we are not done yet either, not in my lifetime, nor maybe in Miss Julia's neither; but Acre people have learned they can plan and work without a landlord. And one day, perhaps many years from now, we will learn in this country that nothing matters more than the well-being of the poorest, humblest person.'

'I'm a radical, not a revolutionary!' Uncle John protested.

Ralph nodded. 'You are what you can be,' he said as if he were consoling John for some failure of will. 'No landlord could be a revolutionary in his heart. He'd have to have mixed motives. You're the most honourable landlord I've ever known – if that's any comfort to you . . .' He broke off with a smile. 'And I'm the worst bailiff!'

'You grow a good crop,' I said pacifically.

'Aye,' Ralph acknowledged, and then turned to John again. 'You'll come back to see the crop taken in?' he asked. 'And you and Lady Lacey will come down to the mill this evening for the harvest dinner?'

'We'll see the wheat taken in, but we'll not come down to the mill,' Uncle John said. He was on horseback and he leaned forward and brushed Prince's mane over to one side, avoiding Ralph's gaze. 'Lady Lacey wouldn't like to come down to the mill,' he said with difficulty. 'You wouldn't know, Mr Megson. The Wideacre riot really started at the harvest supper. We both have bad memories of it . . .' He paused awkwardly and glanced at Ralph.

He nodded. 'Of course,' he said easily. 'Let it be the young generation, then. The future belongs to them. Miss Julia shall represent you, and there will be few people there who will remember that other harvest home.'

'Master Richard too!' John said. I jumped at his name and John smiled at me. 'I've not had a chance to speak to you, Julia, but I had a letter from Richard this morning. He said he'd be coming on the stage today. He'll certainly be here in time for the harvest supper.'

I felt my face flush and I smiled, but my heart sank. Once Richard was home, I could no longer delay telling John and Mama. Today might be the last day I could work and be respected on the land, and tonight would be the last night for many weary evenings that I would be able to ride home and see my mama's face light up as I came in the room.

The thought of seeing Richard did not make me feel safe either. I feared that today was my last day of freedom, the last day I would be free to work on the land with the people I knew and loved. My husband and master was coming closer and closer to my home, which he would call *his* home, and the land which I had planted would yield for him. The heat of the day felt oppressive and threatening to me, and I gave a little shudder.

'To work, then,' Ralph said, and gave his clear whistle to the reaper team, which fell into line, with the gleaners behind. 'You wait and watch here, Miss Julia. I'll get down to the mill to see all's ready and check the space in the barns.'

Uncle John tipped his hat to us both and called, 'Good harvesting!' to the field and trotted home. I cast a wary eye at the stormy sky, and one at the field, the last field to be cut, the field at the top of the downs.

I should have been proud, I should have been happy, but the baby was growing in my belly, and the only way out I had seen was itself a trap for my undoing. I had known that when this harvest was done, Richard would be home and the trap would be sprung.

All day we worked until the field was shaven like a man's

blond head ready for a wig. All over the field were the little islands of stooks, crooked no longer. Even Sally Miles had learned to tie a straight stook. By the time the dinner break had come there was only a swathe left uncut, the width of two reapers.

I sat in the stubble with them and gave the children their sugared almonds. Mrs Gough had packed me the usual feast, but, although my sickness was gone, I was too apprehensive to eat. I was afraid, but I did not know what I feared. I gave away the dainty little meat pie and I shared the sweet pastries. I drank greedily from the glass-stoppered bottle of lemonade, but it did not ease my throbbing head or cool me.

When we had eaten, we leaned back against the bank and looked at the rest of the field. There was no hurry to cut the last swathe, for I thought the weather would hold, but I was nervous, and for some reason I felt disinclined to call them back to work or to face the fact that the harvest was done, and my girlhood cut down as surely as the corn.

But without my bidding two or three of the men went out into the field and started stacking the stooks.

'They're eager to work,' I said to Sally Miles, who sat near by.

'Nay,' she said with a smiling drawl. 'That's play they're after. There's a game, an old reapers' game. They make a corn dolly atop the heap of the last stooks and throw the sickles at it. The one whose sickle pierces it wins the luck of the harvest.'

I nodded and tried to smile, my eyes half shut against the glare of the white sky.

'The dolly's made in a semblance of the favourite of the harvest,' said Sally. 'Maybe it'll be you, Miss Julia. My grandma makes them. She remembers the skill, but there are others who are learning from her now.'

I glanced over. Old Mrs Miles was tying the last knot on a little corn dolly. I caught a glimpse of the grey ribbon from my riding habit and nodded at the little conspiracy. Then I got to my feet and one of the lads helped me into the saddle. I had heard hoofbeats coming up the track and I wanted to meet Richard away from the bright inquisitive eyes of the harvest field.

I rode a little way down the lane, and then I saw him trotting up towards me, his curly mop of black curls bare to the sun. When he saw me, he broke into a sunny blue-eyed smile. 'Julia!' he said in open-faced delight, and pulled his horse up beside me so he could reach over and take my chin in one careless hand and plant a kiss on my mouth.

I let him kiss me, but I did not respond. 'I have been worried,' I said abruptly.

He patted my shoulder in an absent-minded way. 'Not now,' he said. 'Your mama and my papa are following in the gig. They wanted to see the last of the corn coming in. Mr Megson is coming behind with the wagons.'

I nodded and pinned a smile of greeting on my face as Mama and Uncle John came up the hill. Mama was hanging on to the side of the gig as it jolted up the narrow path, the fringe on her parasol dancing as the gig swayed and rocked.

'All done?' Uncle John demanded jubilantly as soon as they were in earshot. 'All done, Squire Julia?'

'All done, except for the reapers' games,' I said, trying to make my voice as delighted as his.

I could never hide anything from my mama. Her eyes were on my face and I knew she noted that I was pale, and that I had deep circles around my eyes from the strain and the worry of this summer, which seemed to go on and on and never give me a moment to rest.

'Are you feeling unwell?' she asked quietly as the gig went on to the gate and I reined back Sea Mist to ride alongside her.

'Just tired,' I said. 'The heat makes me weary, and the glare off the field hurts my eyes.'

'I shall be glad to have you back in the parlour!' she said lovingly. 'Now Richard is home, he can go out and help Mr Megson. I won't have you fading before my eyes, little Julia. You were the toast of the season last year; I won't be robbed of my social triumph next winter.'

I smiled, but I knew very well that next winter there would be no triumph for either of us, but much ill-hidden shame. Next winter I should be near my time and, instead of chaperoning me at my London début, Mama would see her grandchild, conceived out of wedlock and born too early.

'What are the men doing?' John asked.

I glanced around. They were standing at a distance from the heap of stooks, aiming and carefully tossing their sickles. The little corn dolly was perched at the top and I saw my ribbon flutter in the breeze as one of the sickles whistled past it. Instead of smiling at the compliment, I felt a deep unease and a cold finger of fear down my neck that made me shudder in the hot afternoon sun. The anxiety which had been with me all these months seemed to be building into some sort of a crisis.

'Don't wait if you find it too hot, Mama,' I said suddenly.

I wanted her away from the field, though I could not have said why. I wanted her away from the reapers playing their odd ritual game. I wanted her away from this last fruiting of the Wideacre harvest. I feared her seeing the ripeness of the wheat growing at my bidding and somehow knowing that I too was fertile, that the seed inside me was growing too.

'Go for a little walk down to the beech coppice,' I said invitingly. 'It's so cool down there. Don't wait here. We'll be some time before we pack up.'

'Yes, we could,' she said agreeably and looked to John.

He did not look at her; he was watching the men throwing their sickles. 'Very skilful,' he said to Richard.

In a sudden spasm of impatience I wanted them all away, wanted them clear of the field, my field, before the games ended, before anyone brought the doll closer, before anyone gave her to me. I wanted the little gig and my innocent mama away from this field. I felt ill with the certainty that something, a terrible revealing something, was about to happen.

I searched my mind for some way to persuade John to drive on, but he was intent on the sickles glinting in the glare as they were thrown. I glanced to Richard for help, but he had dismounted and was sitting idly on the top bar of the gate. Though he felt my eyes on him, he did not care enough for me to sense my anxiety. Ralph was coming up the hill; I could hear him swearing at the shire horses pulling the wagons. But he was not close enough to help me.

I could feel my anxiety building up to panic as if I were in a coffin of crystal with a glass lid coming down on me. And even if I screamed aloud for help, no one would hear and no one would know that I needed aid. The fragile shell of the lie which hid me from my mama, and from my Uncle John was about to tumble down about my ears, and no skill of mine would ever mend the shattered pieces. I knew that the truth was coming for me in this bright field. I could not even tell which way the cracks were running, but I could hear the structure of my life creaking and beginning to shift.

There was a shout as Jimmy Dart's sickle caught the doll and he leaped up the pile to pull his sickle down. He ran to me with the doll still impaled on the point of the blade so he did not see what he was bringing me. No one in the field saw what it was, and I took it from the proferred blade with some thought of hiding it. My fingers were wary of the sharp edge, and Jimmy held the blade carefully still for me, beaming with his pride. I gazed at it, uncomprehending.

Then I turned scarlet with shame in a blush so deep that even the field and the sky seemed to look rosy red. But then the heat suddenly left my face and left me icy and white as I faced the truth, a clean honest truth which would smash the shell of lies at last.

The straw dolly had a face made of the head of a stalk of corn, and my pale-grey bow had been tied around her body to signify it was meant to be me. Her little arms were tied stalks, sticking out sideways, and her legs were two seed heads. Her belly was huge, unmistakably swollen, made of seed heads tied tightly together. She was pregnant, she was bursting with the fertility of Wideacre. She was massively, grotesquely made. She was meant to be a pregnant woman. She was meant to be me.

At the look on my face John rapped out my name and held out his hand to me in imperious demand. Scarcely knowing what I was doing, I handed the dolly to him, past my mama, who sat, still as stone, on the seat of the gig while the evil little thing was passed across her, under her blank brown gaze.

'Julia . . .' she said. It sounded like she had never said my name before and was trying out a new word. 'Julia.'

John dropped the doll on the floor of the gig between his feet and put his boot down on its fat middle to hold it still.

'Go home at once,' he said to Richard and me. 'At once.'

He backed and turned the gig in a skilled manoeuvre and whirled Mama away from the field before I could glimpse more than her face, so deathly pale that I feared she might faint and fall from the gig. Her parasol lurched, she was whiter than the grey satin. She slumped against John and did not hold to the rocking gig. She looked like a broken doll herself; and John drove her down the hill as if he were rushing a mortally wounded person home to die in her own bed.

I gathered the reins into one cold fist and clicked to Sea Mist to follow them. Richard dropped from the gate like a sleep-walker and heaved himself into the saddle. He pulled his horse over beside mine and we started, shoulder to shoulder, down the track in an illusion of unity.

Ralph had the wagon for the stooks pulled over to one side. 'What's happened?' he demanded urgently. 'Julia! What's happened in the field?'

'They know,' I said. My lips could scarcely move, they were so cold and numb.

Ralph took in my blank face and Richard's fearful scowl and dropped back.

'Shall I come with you?' he offered.

'No,' I said, and I rode past him without another word. To tell the truth, I did not see him.

In the field the reapers stood, sickles dangling in their hands, left without orders, left without a word. Once again the ground had cracked beneath the Laceys and once again Acre village, and the livelihood of Acre, would go tumbling into the crevasse. I glanced back at Jimmy Dart, his sickle still upraised where he had held it out to me, frozen like a statue, his blue eyes puzzled, his broad young face uncomprehending, a little afraid.

I did not blame him, the Bath linkboy I had brought safely home. I did not blame old Mrs Miles, whom I had saved from a pitiful death in the poor house. Jimmy Dart had played the game in the old way, and won. He had not known what he was bringing to me. I truly believed that old Mrs Miles had made the dolly with her fingers and with old magic – no thought in her mind at all. She liked me, she would not have injured me. The truth of my pregnancy had come out in her craft. And I knew – from the way I shuddered when I first saw the corn dolly – that it was not the first time that the old magic had welled up, like an unstoppable spring, on Lacey land.

Sea Mist jinked at a fledgling blackbird fluttering in the hedge, and I checked her with instinctive skill, but I felt my grip on the reins was weak and I feared I would drop them.

I knew I was going home to face the end of my girlhood and the loss of the love of my mama. But I felt some dread, almost a superstitious fear, as if there might be something still worse to come. I was shocked and I was afraid, but a still greater dread, like a pair of black dogs, stalked and circled me all the way as I rode home and then tossed the reins to Jem in silence in the stable yard. When I walked up the garden path, it seemed to me that they lay like couchant black lions on the lawn.

John was waiting for us in the parlour, standing by the mantelpiece; Mama was seated in her usual chair at the fireside. Out of habit she had a piece of work in her hands, some broderie anglaise; and she held her little silver scissors ready to snip out the pattern. For one moment everything seemed the same as it had always been. This was still my safe home.

Then I saw with horror that Mama was not following the intricate pattern which she had taken days to copy. She was snipping aimlessly, shredding the expensive lawn, she was snipping random spiky little holes in the jagged material. John had not even noticed.

Richard and I came into the room. The silence and that mad

little snip, snip, snipping noise rooted us on the threshold. Richard froze and I took one small step to the parlour table and clung to the back of the chair to steady myself. I felt my knees trembling too helplessly to stand without support. I wanted to run to my mama and throw myself down at her feet, but that detached little snip, snip, snip of the scissors frightened me away from her.

She had her head down, and her eyes were on the fine Irish linen in her hand; she was digging the little silver points into the material with her usual meticulous care, except that the holes were all wrong and she was ruining the work.

I kept my eyes on Uncle John. The only sound was the little snipping noise of the scissors and the nagging nerve-tearing call of the wood-pigeon outside the window in Wideacre wood.

'Are you with child, Julia?' John asked, his voice as sharp as Mama's scissors, empty of emotion. But his face was trembling, his mouth working.

'I don't know,' I said weakly.

'Have you felt nauseous? Has your monthly flow ceased? Are your breasts tender?' John rapped out his questions as though I were a kitchenmaid facing dismissal. I nodded like a jointed doll.

'Mama!' I said quietly, summoning her help.

Her head stayed down over the work as she enlarged some of the holes she had hacked and trimmed the ragged edges.

'Excuse me,' John said with mad politeness, and he crossed the room towards me. I flinched and stepped backwards until I was up against the wall. I gasped in horror when he placed his hand low on my belly and pressed hard.

'Mama!' I cried out.

She never even turned her head to see what he was doing to me. He walked back to the fireplace as if I had not spoken. He took out a fine silk handkerchief from his pocket and under my horrified gaze he wiped his hands as if the touch of my riding gown could soil him.

'I conclude *you* are the father, Richard?' John said, his voice an uninterested monotone.

'Yes, sir,' Richard said. Something in his voice made me turn to look at him. He was not blank with horror like the rest of us. His eyes were blazing blue. He looked utterly delighted. I could not think what was in his mind. He must be half mad, or perhaps he was rising to the challenge of this horror. Mama was bent industriously over her work, while I was where John had left me, backed against the wall, and John now clung to the mantelpiece. But Richard stood astride in the doorway, a smile on his face.

'My God,' said John. He made an odd little retching sound in his throat as though he were going to be sick.

'And we are married!' Richard said defiantly. 'The child, the heir to Wideacre, will be born in wedlock. We were secretly married over a month ago, and you cannot break that. We *will* inherit Wideacre jointly, just as my mama planned!'

John's head jerked up, his pale eyes blazing so brightly they looked almost white. 'Not just *your* mama,' he said, hissing through his teeth. 'My God, you pair of fools! You do not know what you have done!' he said, recapturing that precise monotone which told of a horror kept in check. 'You do not know what you have done. She was not just *your* mama! She gave birth to you *both*. You have seduced and married your sister, Richard!'

No one said a word. It was as if we were a tableau in some theatre of horror. Then I gave a little sobbing scream and slumped on to one of the chairs at the parlour table.

Richard's smile was wiped from his face. 'You're lying,' he said uncertainly.

'No,' John said. 'Beatrice conceived Julia with her lover, and she persuaded Celia to take the baby when they were in France on the wedding tour. Harry Lacey never knew the child was not his. Julia was born in France when he was absent. He came home early. The next time Beatrice conceived, she married me. After you were born, I discovered the truth, Richard, the foul truth that you are both Lacey bastards from the same whore.'

Mama's scissors went snip, snip, snip in the silence. She had not looked up once. She had abandoned the little jagged holes and was slicing along the edge of the cloth in a delicate threadlike fringe.

'Who is my father?' Richard asked, utterly bemused.

I could not take my eyes from my mama's downcast face. She was not my mama. She was *not* my mama.

'Who is my father?' Richard asked again.

John dropped into a chair by the empty fireplace; he seemed too weary to go on much longer. 'Harry Lacey,' he said indifferently. 'Beatrice lay with her brother, Harry, and got you both. You are incestuous bastards, and now the two of you have conceived another.'

Mama's head came up. 'Harry's child?' she demanded. 'Julia is Harry's child? Beatrice's lover was my Harry?'

'Didn't you know it?' John demanded, his voice as hard as a costerman's, of the woman he loved. 'Didn't you always know it in your secret heart? And you feared it and hid it from yourself, and I conspired with you in that lie.'

Mama dipped her head again to her work. 'Yes,' she said very softly. 'I knew there was something evil between them. I tried not to wonder what it meant.' She had dropped the scrap of lawn when she looked up, but she did not cease her work. Absentmindedly she took a handful of the figured silk of her driving dress and started to cut perfectly symmetrical little holes in it. Snip, snip, snip went the scissors, and no 'one thought to stop her.

Richard stared. 'So I am Harry Lacey's son,' he said slowly. 'I am the son of the squire.'

Nobody said anything. John's eyes were on the empty grate. It looked like he was watching flames and glowing embers, but there was nothing there. Mama's head was bent down over her dress. It was a cream silk with small yellow flowers. She was cutting the flowers out of the material with careful accuracy. The scraps fell around her feet as though she were sitting under a cherry tree shedding its petals.

'I am the heir,' Richard suddenly said, his voice strong. 'I am the son of the Laceys. Wideacre is my inheritance.'

'Wideacre!' John shouted. He jumped from his chair, explosive with rage. He crossed the room in two swift strides and took

Richard's lapels and dragged him close. 'You have got your own sister with child, and all you can think of is Wideacre?'

His blazing pale eyes scanned Richard's frightened face and then he pushed him away as if he did not want to touch him.

'You are true Laceys,' he said bitterly. He looked at us with loathing. 'Both of you,' he said. His mouth was twisted as though he had accidentally bitten into something dead and rotting. 'Both of you bred very true. All you care for is this filthy estate, all you chase is your own lusts. You are both Beatrice's true children.'

We said nothing. I did not dare look up from the polished surface of the table. I could see my reflection. I was as white as a ghost and my eyes in that darkened mirror were huge and appalled.

John leaned his arm along the mantelpiece. 'It will have to be annulled,' he said levelly. The passion had gone from his voice and he sounded tired and old. 'It can be the last thing I do for the pair of you. I will go to London and get an annulment on the grounds that you are brother and sister, and I shall put the estate on the market while I am there. Wideacre will be sold, and you two will be separated.'

I did not protest. Indeed, I consented.

The nightmare of the Laceys on Wideacre should end, whatever it cost me, whatever it cost Richard. That morning in the summer-house had been even worse than rape. It had also been a perversion. I wanted the Lacey line to be over for ever. I wanted no Lacey on God's earth again after Richard and me. Most of all, I wanted the fairest part of God's earth to be free of us. I wanted to be punished. I wanted to be exiled. I wanted the pain of losing Wideacre and the pain of losing my name and my home and the father of my child to tear my heart out so I would never forget that there should be no future for the Laceys, so that I should never hope and plan again. I wanted to be gutted like a river trout and cleansed. 'Yes,' I said.

My mama spoke. Her dress was pock-marked with circular holes. 'Yes,' she said.

Richard's blue eyes went from one face to another in the room.

I saw a flicker of hesitation pass across it and then he too nodded.

'Yes,' he said.

'I'll start at once,' John said. 'Celia, you will have to come with me as Julia's guardian.'

Mama nodded.

'Julia, you will go to Havering Hall and stay with your Grandmama Havering,' John said. 'You two are not to see each other until we return. Is that clear?'

We nodded in silence.

'Richard, you will stay here until we get back. We should not be gone more than one night.'

Richard nodded.

John went for the door and my mama followed him.

'Mama!' I said pitifully. She paused and looked at me. Her eyes were hard. I had never seen her face as it was then. She looked through me as if she saw a green-eyed whore and not the child she had raised.

I hesitated. There was no appeal I could make. I saw her clear gaze drop down from my face and she looked at my belly where my child was growing.

'You should change your dress, Mama,' I said gently.

She glanced down at the gown, speckled with holes. 'Yes,' she said, and she left the room.

She did not touch me. She did not say farewell. She was gone before I could say goodbye, or ask for her forgiveness, or ask for her love. And I did not tell her how much I loved her.

Richard brought the news to me at Havering Hall in the evening. He came riding over, and as soon as I saw him, I knew something was wrong, for John had ordered him to stay at home and not to see me.

But John was dead, and Richard could do just as he pleased; my mama was dead too.

Richard brought a letter. It was from a Justice of the Peace at Haslemere. The common outside the little town had been troubled with highwaymen. It seemed that a highwayman had held up the travelling coach and ordered Jem to stand to. And then he had shot them dead.

Jem, Uncle John and my mama.

The next travellers along the road saw the coach pulled in at the roadside, the horses grazing on the verge. Jem was dead on the box and John was lying on the floor inside; it seemed he had been trying to shield my mama with his body. My mama had been shot dead.

The cash in John's travelling box had gone. My mama's rose-pearl ear-rings and her beautiful Indian rose-pearl necklace, which she had worn every day since John gave them to her, were missing.

The magistrate, Mr Pearson, said he was very sorry. He said he had posted notices for information about the killer, and that if we wished to offer a reward, we should contact him. He said he was making arrangements for the bodies to be sent home. He said he commiserated with us in our grief.

'What should we do, sir?' Richard asked Lord Havering, his blue eyes wide. 'What should Julia and I do?'

'You'll stay here, of course,' my grandmama interrupted. 'You will stay here with me until we can sort things out. I shall take care of Julia; she is my granddaughter. And there will always be a home for you here, Richard.'

I said nothing. I could think of nothing. In the distant back of my mind was a great gash of pain and longing for my mama and, increasingly, as I sat in silence, a great need of her help. I could not think how I would manage without her. I could not think where I would live or what would become of me, or of my unborn child.

'Lady Havering,' Richard said firmly. 'I have to tell you and his lordship some news which will be a surprise to both of you.'

I did not know what Richard was about to say. I could hardly hear his words. All I could hear was a little cry of pain, as thin as a thread, in the back of my mind, which said, 'Mama.'

So I sat in silence, and I was passive when Richard walked

over to me and drew me to my feet. He held my hand in one hand, the letter announcing my mama's murder in his other. He tucked my icy right hand under his arm and faced my grand-parents.

'Julia and I are married,' he said. 'We will be making our lives together,'

'Good God!' said Lord Havering. He looked at his wife for prompting and then he looked back at the pair of us. Richard seemed assured and somehow prepared for this scene. I was nothing more than a wan shadow at his side, deprived of speech, deprived of thought. I was calling for Mama inside my head, calling for her in silence.

'Good God!' said Lord Havering again.

'Did your father know of this, Richard?' Lady Havering demanded.

'Yes,' Richard said. 'Lady Havering, it is useless for us to pretend to you. My papa gave his permission, and Julia's mama gave her permission, because Julia is with child. I am the father.'

'Good God!' said Lord Havering once more, and dropped into a chair like a stone.

Lady Havering's face was as pale as crumpled vellum, but her first thought was not for the conventions but for the daughter she had lost.

'Oh! My poor Celia!' she exclaimed. 'That would have been the last straw for her. That must have broken her heart.'

I dropped my head. I felt I had killed Mama myself. She had left the house without a word of love between us and she had gone to her death. I was ready to believe that when her killer shot her, he was completing the injury I had started when she learned I was unchaste. I was so ashamed I could not speak.

'I suppose this alters things,' Richard said with careful cour-tesy.

'It does!' Lord Havering said. 'It does, by God!'

Lady Havering made a slight gesture and his lordship fell silent. 'I'll recognize you,' she said grimly. 'Whatever else Julia is, she is my granddaughter, and I'll do it for Celia's sake. I'll acknowledge you, and we'll announce the marriage in the papers. No one will expect any sort of reception with your parents' funeral taking place in the same week. We can make it appear that you have been married for some time.' She hesitated. I did not look up. 'When's the baby due?' she asked.

'At the end of January,' Richard said.

'We'll say you were married privately in the spring, then,' she said. Her voice was as hard and dispassionate as a general planning a campaign. 'In these circumstances, there is no reason why the two of you should not go home at once.'

'No!' I exclaimed suddenly. 'I don't want to go home!'

Richard's eyes met mine with unmistakable menace in their blue hardness.

'Why not?' demanded my grandmama sharply.

I hesitated. Richard's eyes were on me, but I trusted my grandmama's love for me. 'I don't know,' I said weakly. 'I just don't want to, Grandmama. Please let me stay here with you. I don't want to go home.'

She hesitated, and I knew her long affection was weighing more heavily than her shock and dismay at what I had done. I knew she would keep me with her until I felt strong enough to go home and face Richard and decide what we should do in the wreckage of our lives. I felt I had suddenly found some safe ground under my feet. I knew my grandmama saw the appeal in my eyes, and I knew that I had an ally who was very strong.

'You may stay if you wish,' she said slowly. But then she looked away from me. She looked to Richard. 'But you are a married woman now, Julia. You must do as your husband wishes.'

I gaped at her. I could barely understand her. 'Richard?' I queried. I could not believe that she was referring a decision to my childhood playmate. I could not believe that she would permit him to take a decision about me, in her house.

'You are a married woman, Julia,' she said. It was as if there were a cell door closing. 'You are a married woman. It must be as your husband wishes.'

I looked around.

Lord Havering was nodding. My grandmama's face was strained, but her eyes were steady. Last of all I looked at Richard. His eyes were gleaming in secret triumph.

'I think we should go home, Julia,' he said gently. 'This has been a dreadful shock for us both. I think we should go home and you should have some hartshorn and water and go to bed early. There will be much to arrange tomorrow, and this has been an unbearably distressing day. I think you should come home and rest in your own house.'

I glanced at Grandmama for her help, but her face was impassive. My grandpapa stared sombrely at the carpet between his boots. I looked again at Richard. There was only one way out for me. I could tell them that Richard and I were brother and sister and that the marriage must be annulled. But if I spoke of that, then Grandmama would know that I had lain with my own brother and that the little child, my own little child, was the fruit of a perversion. Worse, she would know that I was not her grandchild at all; that I was the daughter of Beatrice, the witch of Wideacre, and her brother Harry, the fool; that I was no kin.

I could not do it. I could not lose mother and grandmother in one day. I could not tell her she must look on me as a stranger stained with sin. I could not find the words.

'Very well,' I said dutifully. I somehow got to my feet. Lord Havering ordered the Havering carriage and I drove home in it alone, while Richard rode behind.

Stride opened the door to me and I could see he had been weeping.

'Oh, Stride!' I said sadly.

There was time for no other words. Richard came in and ordered Stride to send Jenny Hodgett to take me to bed with a bowl of soup and a glass of port. When I was undressed and in my bed, Richard himself came up with a glass of hartshorn and water and said he would sit with me until I slept.

I dropped back on the pillows and closed my eyes so that I should not see him in my window-seat, blocking my view of the late-evening sky and the sighing tree outside the window. My grief for my mama was so strong that I thought it would choke me to hold in the sobs which gathered in great asphyxiating lumps in my throat.

'Hush, Julia,' Richard said tenderly. 'Hush.'

He came to my bedside and stroked my hair back from my forehead as if I were a little child. I tried to pretend it was my mama's hand, and that none of this nightmare was happening, that I should very soon wake up and find myself safe and beloved again.

Richard spent that night in my room thus. And whether he was there as a brother in mourning, as a husband, or even as a gaoler, I never really knew.

27

In the morning there was business to be done. Richard went down to Acre to tell Ralph Megson what had happened, and to instruct him to announce the deaths in Acre.

While he was out, I went into my mama's room. It was a hot summer morning and someone had half opened the sash window, but the curtains were drawn. Every room in the house would be in shadow for this week. In sudden impatience with the conventions of grief I pulled the curtains back and the sunlight and the warmth spilled into the room, making the rose and blue pattern on the carpet suddenly bright.

I gazed carefully around the room as if I were trying to print it on to my memory, as though I could keep the people I loved by clinging to their objects. I felt somehow my mama was still here. Her ghost, like the faint light smell of lilies which she always wore, seemed to linger. Her hairbrush had a few fair hairs tangled in the bristles; there was water in the ewer beside the basin; her nightgown was folded up at the foot of the bed.

The room looked as if she had just stepped out for a moment. I could even see the dent in the cushions of her stool at her dressing-table. She must have sat there to pin her bonnet before she left with John.

It was a pretty room. When I was a little girl, its only pleasant feature was the view of the tossing green trees of Wideacre Park, and the familiar clear smell of flowers. But since John had come home, the room had been carpeted and furnished with the light white and gold furniture which Mama loved. A crystal bowl of roses stood in the fireplace, her silver-backed mirror, brush and comb stood on the neat dressing-table, reflected in the winged mirror above. I peered superstitiously at the mirror. I could not believe that I would not see her face there. I would never see that beloved face again.

I went across the room and looked out of the window. I shut my eyes and pressed my forehead to the cold glass. The summertime smells of Wideacre wafted in around me and stirred the curtains at my side. Everything was warm and green and growing. I could not believe that among all this life my mama lay still and cold.

I would not believe it. I screwed my eyes up tighter and then turned and opened them to look into the room. I was certain that she would be there, sitting on the little stool before the mirror, or nipping a wilted flower from the vase. I willed her to be there with all my strength. I could not believe that she, who had been there so constantly and so reliably for all my childhood, should suddenly and so unexpectedly be gone.

'Mama!' I whispered into the silence of the room.

There was no reply.

She had gone indeed, and I was alone.

I left her room with the curtains blowing and the window open. I went downstairs to the parlour. I stumbled against the table in the sudden gloom and I crossed the window and threw back the curtains.

The maid had not been in here to clean and tidy. She had drawn the curtains but left the room as it had been when my lie split our world, and killed my childhood, and broke my mama's heart. The chair to which I had clung for support was still askew. The seat where John had wearily dropped was still at the fireside. Around my mama's chair, in a shower of gold, like wedding-day rose petals, were the little flowers she had cut from the front of her gown while she sat with her head down and learned her daughter was a whore.

I dropped on my knees on the hearth rug and started to pick them up, like some lost Ophelia in a travelling theatre. When my hand was full, I held out my silk apron like a country girl and heaped them in it. Every scrap of material I meticulously gathered, until I had them all. Then I took them, as carefully as new-laid pheasant's eggs, held in my apron, up the stairs to my room.

I wrapped them in soft white tissue-paper, and I laid them in my top drawer. Even they smelled very faintly of lilies.

I clung to the chest of drawers and wept as though my heart would break.

Their funerals were to be on Saturday, the fourth day after the harvest when I had reaped the Wideacre corn and Lacey ruin in one sunny afternoon. My Grandmama Havering had arranged that there would be an announcement of our private marriage in the newspapers on the following Monday. Richard thought that Ralph should be told before the newspaper announcement, and I agreed.

I agreed in silence with a nod. I felt weary to my very heart with the quiet wordless mourning for my mama. It was doubtless foolish, but I believed that I would never be happy again. Perhaps I was wrong not to seek comfort from my grandmama, or from our vicar, or even from Richard, but I felt that I should never find comfort. No one would ever again mother me, now that my mama was gone.

So, for the first time in many months, I did not think about Wideacre, nor what Acre might be thinking or doing. When Richard told me that he had ordered Ralph to come to the Dower House that evening, I nodded as though I did not much care.

Ralph came in, stepping carefully across the polished hall as if he did not want to wake a sleeping invalid. But though my mama lay in the house, nothing would waken her again. Her coffin was upstairs in the pretty room which smelled of lilies. The lid was nailed down already; I could not even kiss her goodbye on her cold cheek, for they told me she had been too badly injured.

I tried not to think of that.

'I am sorry, Julia,' Ralph said. He took my hand in his and smiled down at me; his dark eyes were very gentle.

'Thank you,' I said awkwardly.

'She wouldn't have been in pain, you know,' he said softly. 'I have seen men shot at close range. She would have died at once.'

I flashed a look up at him. 'You are sure?' I asked. 'You are not just saying that to make me feel better?'

Ralph shook his head. 'Nay,' he said. 'I'd not lie to you on such a subject. She would not have had a lot of pain. Nor John.'

Richard interrupted us. 'Will you come to the library, Mr Megson? You and I have business to discuss.'

Ralph nodded and stepped back for me to precede them into the room.

'Julia need not trouble herself with this,' Richard said smoothly. 'She can sit in the parlour.'

Ralph was suddenly still, as wary as a hare in bracken. 'Miss Lacey should be present,' he said. 'She is joint heir.'

'Not any longer,' Richard said. He smiled at Ralph and their eyes locked. 'I don't do business in the hall,' Richard said coolly. 'Will you come into the library, Mr Megson?'

'After you, Julia,' Ralph said firmly. Even in the numb haze I noted that he used my Christian name and I heard his appeal to me to stand firm for Acre.

I glanced at Richard. He gave me a quick frown which should have warned me to stay out of this struggle between him and Ralph. But Ralph was my friend, and Acre was my village. However weary I might be, however ill with mourning, they had a call on me.

'I'll come in,' I said, and walked past Richard into the library and sat at the side of the table. Richard took the seat at the head, where Uncle John had always sat, and Ralph sat opposite me, facing the bookcases. The window behind Richard was open; outside a thrush was singing loudly.

'We have some news which may surprise you,' Richard said sweetly. 'Miss Lacey and I are married. We were married privately some months ago. And Miss Lacey' – he broke off and smiled – 'I *should* say, Mrs MacAndrew, is expecting our child.'

Ralph gave me a hard look. 'You are pregnant?' he said baldly.

I nodded.

'And married?' he said.

No one corrected his inversion of Richard's statement. We all knew that Ralph assumed I had married because I was pregnant, and not even Richard had the gall to brazen it out.

'Yes,' I said through sour lips.

Ralph dropped his dark head in his hands for a moment. 'Oh, Julia!' he said sorrowfully. 'I *wish* you had come to me.'

Richard let that indiscretion go. 'As Julia's husband, I am now the squire and the sole owner of Wideacre,' he said. 'I called you in, Mr Megson, to ask you to convey the news to the village. There will be an announcement in the newspapers on Monday. I think since we are in mourning, that there should be no celebrations in Acre.'

Ralph scowled very darkly. 'No, indeed,' he said dourly. 'There will be no celebrations that you have married Miss Lacey and made yourself the new squire.'

Richard nodded, and let that go too. 'I shall inherit the MacAndrew fortune, I do not doubt,' he said, 'and, of course, I have total control over my wife's fortune too. I plan no immediate changes, Mr Megson. You may tell them that in Acre. I am satisfied thus far with how the estate is being run.'

'You've not seen the wills,' Ralph said. 'It may be that there are guardians set over the two of you.'

'I've not seen them,' Richard conceded, 'but I believe that guardianship is invested in either Julia's mama or my papa. There was no provision for them dying together.'

Ralph did not even look shaken. He looked sullen. 'I'll tell the village,' he said ungraciously. 'Was there anything else?'

Richard hesitated. 'The grain,' he said negligently. 'I take it you have made arrangements for its sale?'

Ralph shot a swift look at me. 'Yes,' he said. 'We are reserving a portion of it for sale locally. Another portion goes to Midhurst market, and the remainder of the crop to the London market later in the year.'

'I think not,' Richard said. His voice was like silk and his blue eyes were shining. 'I think we should send the whole crop out of the county, to the London market. That is where the profits are. Wideacre has to be farmed as a profitable business, you understand, Mr Megson.'

Ralph measured him with a dark level look. 'Yes, I think I understand,' he said. 'I won't speak of this further tonight. But I am afraid you can do nothing about the wheat. The agreements have already been made.'

Their eyes locked, like a pair of stags in battle. Richard was the master of Wideacre and Ralph was his agent. But Ralph would always be stronger, and it was Richard who looked away. 'We'll see,' he said sulkily. 'But do as I order, and tell Acre, Mr Megson.'

'Of course,' Ralph said. He waited for a moment, and when Richard said nothing more, he pushed back his chair and went to the door. Richard lounged in the carver chair and watched him go, but I rose and went across the hall with him.

He said nothing.

I had expected a word from him, a word of blame, of disappointment, of condemnation of me as another Lacey woman who had been a fool and had betrayed the land. But I had nothing from him except a hard black look which was somehow full of pity. Then his hand was on the door and he was gone.

He had left. He had left me alone, alone with Richard.

I went slowly back to the library, twisting a fringe on my shawl. Richard had pushed his chair back from the table and tipped it on its back legs, balancing his weight with his booted feet against the table's edge.

'Megson all right?' he demanded.

'Yes,' I said. I went to the window. The sun was going down behind the trees, out of sight. It had tinged the sky above the wood into cream and grey and rose. I leaned my aching head against the cool thick glass of the window and stood in silence.

'I shall ride up to the hall tomorrow and see how the work is going,' Richard said, 'and on Monday I shall ask the foreman how quickly it could be completed if we doubled the workers. We shall move in there as soon as possible.'

'Richard . . .' I said. I turned towards him so I could see if he really was as calm and confident as he seemed. 'Richard, we must talk. You cannot truly think that we can live together at the hall!'

His face was as untroubled as a good child's. 'Why not?' he demanded.

I spread my hands out in a vague gesture and then brought them up to cradle my cheeks. 'Richard!' I said. 'What John told us about our true parents alters everything.'

Richard was blank. 'Why?' he asked.

I leaned back against the window. It seemed to me that the world had gone mad all around me and that I had to hold on to my little corner of it or be engulfed.

'We are brother and sister!' I said as if he needed me to tell him. 'Our marriage is invalid. And our child . . .' I broke off. I could not say the word 'incest' and think of my poor little baby, so safe inside me, but so endangered by the madness of this outside world. 'We will have to get the marriage annulled as John and Mama were going to do,' I said. 'Then we will have to live apart. I shall have to bear the shame of the baby somehow. I suppose you will have to live in London or somewhere.'

Richard was as calm as the summer sky. He looked at me with tolerant sympathy, as distant from my confusion and pain as the early-evening stars. 'Oh, no,' he said sweetly, 'it's not going to be like that at all.'

I looked blankly at him and waited.

'Our marriage is already public knowledge,' he said. 'We have acknowledged each other, and I have acknowledged my child. We cannot withdraw from that.'

My hands went out to him again, in a weak imploring gesture. 'Richard . . .' I said uncertainly.

'We shall live here,' he said. 'And when the hall is built, we shall move into it. I shall take the name of Lacey, which we now know I have as much right to claim as you. We shall be Squire Richard Lacey, and his lady.' He smiled at me. 'It sounds well,' he said equably.

'Richard, we *cannot*!' I exclaimed. The sense I had had of an insane world in which my lovely mama could be killed and I could find myself pregnant by my brother was slipping away from me. Coated with Richard's silky tones, the mad mess which was my life sounded utterly reasonable. 'We *cannot!*' I said again.

Richard's chair rocked him gently as he bent and flexed his knees. 'Why not?' he demanded. In a sudden movement he dropped the chair down to stand four-square and turned in his seat to see me better. 'We have announced our marriage; you are pregnant with my child,' he said evenly. 'We both know who it was permitted the conception, who it was insisted on the marriage. I agreed to it, to oblige you. I'm not now going to change tack because of a sudden whim of yours.'

I put my hands to my temples. Richard's view of the world and mine seemed so utterly different. I could not believe we had both been in the room when John had spoken of us with loathing as incestuous bastards who had repeated our parents' black offence. 'I cannot think!' I exclaimed in the whirl of confusion.

Richard stood up and came to me and pulled my hands from my face. 'Be calm,' he said firmly. 'It is your condition which makes you so confused. Be calm, and trust me. I know what I am doing.'

I let my hands stay in his comforting grip and I scanned his face.

'You have no one else but me now, Julia,' he said. 'Don't forget that you have no one else but me. You have to trust me. You can hardly manage on your own.'

I took half a step towards him. I felt so very, very lonely. I leaned my forehead against his shoulder. After the icy touch of the glass his velvet jacket was warm, and I could smell the russet scent of his skin and curly hair.

'Oh, Richard,' I said forlornly. His arm came around my waist and he stroked my back as one would comfort a sick animal.

It was as if the world were a dangerous sea and Richard and I had been wrecked in the storms. All we could do now was to cling to each other and hope to stay afloat.

*

I carried on floating.

I floated through the funerals when we laid the two of them in the Lacey vault. There was some muddle over the burial and they were placed side by side. I was glad of that. In the corner of my floating mind I was glad that they were close together in their death, that their dust would mingle. Grandmama gave a luncheon after the funeral and I received the condolences of the county, standing between her and Richard, speaking to people and hearing them speak as if we were all soundless fish, floating in a deep silky sea.

Only one voice rang clear in the week which followed: Rosie Dench's. She came with a package, not to the front door of the Dower House, but to the kitchen door. Stride showed her into the parlour where I sat, idly looking out. I was looking down the road as though I were waiting to see Mama and John rounding the corner in the gig, light-hearted after a drive.

'I didn't know what to do with them,' Rosie said abruptly. 'They were made for you, Miss Julia. Wideacre gloves for you. Whoever your choice is.'

I turned back to the room. I could scarcely understand her. And then I remembered. Rosie had promised me some gloves. Gloves for my wedding day, for my wedding to James.

She held out the package awkwardly. I tried to smile, but found I could not. I unfolded the wrapping-paper.

They were the most beautiful gloves I had ever seen. Every inch of them glowed with colour. Wideacre colours – the colours of a Wideacre harvest. The background was pale, like the sky at dawn before the sun makes it rosy, to match a cream or a white gown, as my wedding gown should have been. On the back of each glove was a golden sheaf of wheat – yellow and gold – and a handful of wheatfield flowers: the scarlet poppies I love and deep-blue larkspur. Before the sheaf of wheat were crossed a sickle and a hook, as a reminder that wheat is not cut of its own accord. The gloves were longer than I usually wore them – Rosie might be an Acre field-girl now, but she would never lose her eye for fashion – and trimmed with a line of pale gold.

'Rosie, thank you,' I said. 'You have a very great talent. If these were in paint rather than in silk, people would say you were an artist.'

She ducked her head at that, and beamed. 'I hope you'll be happy,' she said doubtfully. 'I hope it was right to bring these.'

'I'm very grateful,' I said. 'I won't be able to wear them while I'm in mourning, but I shall keep them safe and next year, next spring, I shall wear them with my very best dresses.'

She bobbed a curtsy and turned to go. It felt strange that after all that had passed between us there was so little to say. But Rosie could not tell me her true thoughts about my choice of a husband; and I was dead inside and could speak my heart to no one.

'We writes to him,' she said suddenly, turning in the doorway. 'He asked us to write to him from time to time, to tell him that we are well, all of us, the Bath children.'

I nodded. I knew she meant James.

'Can I give him a message from you?' Rosie asked. 'If there was anything you needed to tell him, that wasn't proper for you to write yourself, I could tell him.' She stopped.

I shook my head. I could see again the little coffee-room of the coaching inn and hear the rattle of the wheels on the cobbles as James did not come, and did not come, and did not come.

'No,' I said dully. 'Mr Fortescue and I are no longer friends. And I am now a married woman.'

Rosie nodded, but her eyes were puzzled. 'Goodbye, Miss Julia,' she said. 'We'll see you in the village, won't we?'

'Yes,' I said. But I did not sound sure. 'I will come when I feel better,' I said. I spoke as if I never expected to feel any better. That was true.

I could not weep.

I could not mourn.

I felt I was floating. And there was nothing to do but to carry on floating, and try to get through one day after another and try to forget that each one of these days added up to week after week after week.

In the third week after the funeral my grandmama proposed a

tea-party, to present me to the county as a married woman. I shook my head and said I did not want to go.

'I don't expect you to enjoy it,' my grandmama said tartly. 'I expect you to keep your head up and to answer when you are spoken to, and to remember that I am doing this to save your reputation for the sake of your mama, my daughter.'

So I did as I was bid and floated through the afternoon. With my grandmama in the room no one would tease me about the precise details of the marriage. They might speak slyly behind their gloved hands when I was not there, but no gossip would harm me while I had Grandmama's protection.

When I was lucky I felt that I was floating. Sometimes, when I was alone in my bed at night, I would think that I was not afloat at all, but sinking, drowning, and too foolish to call for help. At the heart of the nightmare of those vague days was my worry that I could not be sure whether I was floating towards a safe harbour, with Richard's love a reality which I should trust, and my grandmama's protection around me, or whether I was sinking slowly into a slime of sin and trouble, ensnared by my own confusion and tricked by everyone around me.

It was Ralph who said it.

'He caught you, then,' he said to me. I was driving to Havering Hall to see Grandmama, and Ralph hailed the carriage in the lane as I turned out of the drive. He had taken a load of Wideacre wheat to Midhurst market and was following the empty wagons slowly home on his black horse.

I pulled down the glass of the window as he reined in alongside. 'I don't know what you mean,' I said steadily. It was pointless to encourage Ralph to speak of Richard as an enemy. We both had to learn to know our master; and Richard was the squire now.

Ralph puffed out his cheeks in impatience. 'He took you, he trapped you into marriage,' he said. 'Now he has Wideacre and no controls over his will, not even parents to protect you, or to protect Acre. All that stands between him and Acre is you and me. And you sit up there in your damned carriage and tell me you don't know what I mean!'

I felt my world shaking, but I said nothing.

'I'm selling wheat in Midhurst as fast as I can,' Ralph said, jerking a thumb at the empty wagons lumbering past us. 'I won't have Wideacre corn sent out of the county while there are poor families who need it at the proper rate. Not while I am manager here.'

'What about the wheat for Acre?' I asked softly.

Ralph gleamed. 'I've hidden it,' he said briefly. 'They can buy it in their penn'orths throughout the year. But young Richard won't find it.'

'It's not at the mill?' I asked.

Ralph's face darkened again. 'I'll not tell you where,' he said. 'You're his wife now. You could be obliged to tell him. I'll keep it safe, never fear. There'll be no hunger in Acre this winter, even if the devil himself was squire.'

I nodded. 'I am sorry, Ralph,' I said.

'You'll be sorrier yet,' he said bleakly. 'When's the baby due?'

'At the end of January,' I said.

'The hardest time of the year,' Ralph said. There was a silence. 'The hardest,' he said. 'You should have come with me to the gypsies that day, Julia.'

I said nothing. It was useless to say anything.

'Could we get the marriage annulled on some legal grounds?' Ralph inquired, his voice as soft as a conspirator's. 'Are you sure it was properly witnessed and all, Julia? You were both minors, remember.'

I thought of my mama and John driving to London to get the marriage annulled and the black secret reason that they had carried with them, the seventeen-year-old secret of the evil lusts of Beatrice and Harry her brother. But those two were my parents, and it was now my secret. I did not have the strength to fight Richard through the courts of the land declaring our marriage invalid. Besides, I needed the marriage as badly as he did.

'No,' I said steadily. 'There is nothing I am able to tell you which could make the marriage invalid.'

Ralph's face under his tricorne hat was black with gloom.

'Remember I'm your friend,' he said dourly. 'You know where to find me if you need me, and anyone in Acre would stand with you. If you need help, you know where to come.'

I nodded. There was a hot mist in my eyes and I could not see him. 'Thank you,' I said softly. 'But I always knew there would come a time when you would not be able to help me, nor I you.'

Ralph put his head on one side, apparently listening for something which I alone could hear. 'Bad time coming for us both?' he asked very low.

I shrugged my shoulders helplessly. 'I have not the sight for it,' I said. 'If I could see as well as they believe in Acre, I'd not be here now. It would all be different – for all of us.'

He nodded grimly, and then he wheeled his horse around. I had seen him ride from me once when he was in a rage and watched him tear down the drive with the mud flying up from his horse's hooves. This time he shambled into the village at walking pace. I watched him go before I pulled the cord to drive on. He rode with a slack bridle; his collar was turned up and his shoulders were as hunched as if he were riding in pouring rain.

I was driving to my grandmama's, for I no longer rode. My pregnancy was showing, and modesty and convention alike would keep me from Sea Mist and in a carriage until the birth. I hoped very much for a dry autumn and a mild winter. The lane was impassable when it got too wet, and if I was not allowed to ride, I should have to stay inside the Dower House for the last long three months of my pregnancy, with no visitors, with no company . . . except Richard.

I was wearing an old black gown of Mama's, hastily adapted for me. My grandmama had called her dressmaker from Chichester to come to Havering and take my measurements, and guess at my likely increase in size, so that I could have some new black gowns ready for the autumn and winter.

I stood still, until I was weary with standing, while she kneeled at my feet and pinned one fold after another. She had a mouthful of pins between her lips, but she was able, by years of practice, to tell my grandmama all the Chichester gossip without dropping one. I watched this, fascinated for a time, but then I grew tired. Grandmama broke into the flow of news when she saw my white face and said abruptly, 'That will do! Julia, you must sit down for a rest.'

So she took my measurements as I sat and then took her leave, promising that the gowns would be ready within the week.

'Are you tired?' Grandmama asked me, and at the kindness in her voice I felt my eyes fill with tears.

'Very tired,' I said piteously. 'And, Grandmama, I do miss Mama so much. It is so lonely at home without her!'

She nodded. 'You were very close, you two,' she said softly. 'It's quite rare to see so much love between a grown girl and her mama. She was very proud of you, you know, Julia. She would not want you to be sad.'

I put the back of my hand to my mouth to bottle up the sobs. I tried to blink back the hot tears which were ready to flow down my cheeks. My grandmama's consoling words helped me not at all, for I knew my mama had been mistaken in me, and that she had died knowing her mistake. She had not loved me when she had cut her dress into ribbons; she had not felt proud of me then. She had known me for what I was – a sensualist like my natural mother, Beatrice. She had hated Beatrice, and I was sure that at the very moment of her death she must have hated me.

'Is Richard kind to you?' my grandmama asked. 'The two of you are so very young to live alone together!'

'Yes,' I said. I said nothing more.

'He is not impatient with you?' she asked. 'When the two of you were children, your mama always used to fear that he bullied you.'

'He does not bully me,' I said steadily.

'And I trust he is . . .' Grandmama broke off and glanced down at her gown, black like mine, mourning like me. 'He is not . . . insistent?' she asked. 'Insistent about your marital duties? At a time like this you would be best sleeping in your own bed.'

I nodded. 'I do, Grandmama,' I said.

She nodded. 'Forgive me,' she said. 'You are a married woman now, and it is the business of your husband and yourself. No business of mine.'

I nodded. Once again we had come to the place where even my powerful grandmama would not support me. Once the door of the Dower House had closed behind me, I was Richard's own. No one could come between the two of us. He owned me as surely as he now owned the land I had once called mine, my land, my horse, my little box of trinkets, my gowns, even my own body. All of them belonged to Richard, because I had once said, 'I do' in the rocking cabin of a dirty little boat.

Acre, and Sea Mist and I might all suffer under his ownership, and there was nothing anyone could do about it.

There was nothing I could do about it.

Richard and Ralph clashed almost daily. I heard about it when I drove into Acre. I heard about it from Grandmama, who had heard it from Lord Havering, who had been present when Richard had told Ralph that he wanted a gamekeeper on the estate and Ralph had said that he would not work with one. I heard about it from the kitchenmaid, who told me that Mr Megson and my husband had shouted at each other in the middle of Acre about whether old Mrs Merry should be evicted or not. 'Terrible scene, it was,' she said in awe.

Ralph had won the gamekeeper question by default, but it was still a victory. He had told Richard that he could not find a man from Acre who would do the job, which was true enough. They knew already, in the way the poorest of the poor sense things early, that the Wideacre experiment had ended almost as soon as it had begun, and that they should rue the day that they went back to work for a Lacey.

They had lost their reputation as the notorious village, the village which had killed its squire, and they had earned county-wide praise for being the fastest team of reapers in the county. If the estate had been for sale, there would have been many, many buyers. Acre had been mastered, and anyone will buy a horse which has been well broken and learned its paces.

They had trusted the Laceys again. They had trusted the Lacey word. It was coincidence that we went back on our word as soon as the wheat was in the barn, on the very day that the harvest was completed, but poor people have little faith in coincidences. Those who still loved me said I was trapped by Richard. Others, who were older and bitter, said it was a skilful ploy by the Laceys to fool Acre once more. The village was back to work, and they had lost their free access to the fields, to the park and to the common, and all around the village were fences they themselves had erected. So the older, wiser ones scented a plot and smiled sourly, and doffed their hats to me with a knowing look in their eyes that recognized a clever victor.

They could not pull down all the fences, all at once. They had learned to hope and they had lost their anger. They could not move against us, they could only mutter and mouth curses against the name of Lacey. They had consulted the Chichester lawyers who drew up the contracts on the land and they had found, as Ralph had once predicted they would, that the law belongs to the landlords. They could not sue us for breach of contract with them, for we had not breached a contract. All we had promised to do was to share profits with them once the costs of running the estate had been subtracted. Richard made sure that the costs cut the Acre share down to a subsistence wage. All the other promises, about loans for seed and equipment and stock, were voluntary offers from the Laceys. They could be withdrawn. Acre needed no one to tell them that they *had* been withdrawn.

There was nothing they could do to bind the Laceys down as they were bound down. All they could do was to look surly and to start poaching. So no one from the village came forward for the job of Richard's gamekeeper, and anyone who set foot on the estate looking for the work was quietly taken to one side by Ralph, or one of the other older men, and warned off. They always went.

It could have been worse for the village where I had once been loved, the village where I had talked of a land-sharing scheme, a share-cropping scheme. They still had rabbits and hares, and even pheasants and venison, and fish from the river. They also had a reliable supply of wheat.

'Where are they buying their wheat?' Richard asked me abruptly one morning at breakfast. The coffee-jug was before me, and I poured myself another cup while I thought what I should say. I was in the fifth month of my pregnancy and I found I had become slow and dreamy as I had grown heavier and broader.

'I saw a great wagon of grain outside Miller Green's, and when I asked him who it was for, he would not answer me,' Richard said with irritation. 'I am sure he was grinding it for the village. I don't understand the returns Megson made from the Midhurst market. I wonder if Acre has hidden some wheat somewhere, to take them through the winter.'

I looked out of the dining-room window, past Richard's head. The trees in the orchard were heavy with fruit, the blackbirds glutted on the windfalls. Through the open window I could sniff the cider-smell of rotting fruit. The branches were bowed to the ground with the crop. The apple trees I had planted were yielding too; Ralph had gangs out every day, picking and packing them for the Chichester fruit market. The land was rich. The Laceys were rich. Acre was dirt poor.

'Where would they hide it, Julia?' Richard demanded. 'You know the estate as well as anyone. If you wanted to hide a couple of wagonloads of wheat where would you put it?'

'I don't know,' I said carelessly. In truth I felt careless. I sipped the coffee and gazed out of the window at that green shoulder of the downs above the orchard. The beech coppice was changing colour already; the green was going and the strong brassy colour was shining through. The cedar tree in the garden was dark purple and the sky was very blue above it. I wondered if all wives have this longing to be elsewhere, a longing which is not even as clear as a wish for freedom or a dislike of one's husband. It is just a vague, wordless sense that there should be something more, something more than being inside a window looking outwards for ever.

'Are you listening to me, Julia?' Richard was sharp. I dragged my eyes from the window and looked at him.

'Of course,' I said. 'I do not know where I would hide a couple of wagonloads of corn on Wideacre. I do not know that anyone has done so.'

'Would you be told if such a theft had taken place?' Richard asked. 'And if you knew,' he continued sweetly, 'would you keep it from me? Would you side with your precious Acre against me? I hope you would not, Julia. But I cannot be entirely sure.'

'I would not, Richard,' I said. I met his eyes without flinching. We had been living in the same house alone for some weeks and I had learned to lie to him. I might not always convince him, but he was often prepared to close his eyes to his uncertainty. Unusually for Richard, he was ready to let things go between us, and I still did not know why that should be.

'Are you sure that Megson has said nothing to you?' he demanded suddenly, as fast as a swooping falcon to my lie.

I shook my head, and half consciously put my hand on my swelling belly.

Richard's face changed at once. 'It does not matter! It does not matter!' he said swiftly. 'Don't think about it, Julia I shall resolve the problem. Do not you trouble yourself with it. The Chichester accoucheur, Mr Saintly, said that of all things you *must* avoid worry. Don't think about it any more.'

'Don't fuss, Richard,' I said. He had risen from his place and come around the table to me. He was looking down at me and his face was filled with concern, but also with some eager hunger that I could not explain.

'Are you thinking of me or the baby?' I asked shrewdly.

'Of you, of course,' he said, but his eyes were on my swollen belly. 'And the baby too, naturally. My son,' he said, and his voice was full of longing. 'My son, the next Lacey, the heir to Wideacre.'

'What about the wheat, then?' I asked, interrupting Richard's meditation on the baby he was certain was a son. 'Even if they have stolen a couple of wagons and hidden it, Richard, that is no more than they were promised by Uncle John and me. It would be difficult to find, and it would cause much bad feeling in Acre if you took it to market now. Surely the best thing to do is to leave things as they are. Acre will need a supply of winter corn, you know. And the price is going up all the time.'

Richard nodded absently. He reached out a gentle hand and touched my rounded belly. 'Yes, yes,' he said softly. 'Don't you trouble yourself with it, Julia. You just stay quiet and at peace, and concentrate on breeding a strong baby for the Wideacre cradle.'

'I can't be at peace if I think you are in conflict with Acre,' I said. 'I know the village seems quiet now, but remember Ralph Megson himself telling us about bread riots and corn riots. It need not always be violent and dangerous, Richard, but the poor believe they have a right to fair-priced wheat, sold and grown locally. I should hate Acre to try to take the law into its own hands.'

Richard nodded at that. 'Yes,' he said, 'and I know that he is still a bread rioter at heart.'

'Maybe,' I said, 'but he would never go against the owners of the land unless he thought they were behaving wrongly. If he has taken some corn, it is to ensure that the contract John and I made with Acre is honoured by you.'

Richard's face was dark. 'Well, don't think of it, Julia,' he said. 'I don't want you worrying about it when you should be resting and making the baby strong.'

'But I *do* worry about it,' I said, and I thought myself very clever to use Richard's passionate concern for our unborn child against his hardness of heart. 'There is only one way I can *stop* worrying, Richard: if you stop giving me cause. Every time there is trouble in the village, I hear of it, and of course it distresses me. If you truly want to save me anxiety, you should take Mr Megson's advice. I don't think Uncle John ever went against him, and it was Mr Megson who got Acre back to work.'

Richard looked hard at me, and his eyes gleamed, but I thought I had a way to rule him and to help Acre. I was not cautioned.

'You admire Megson very much, do you not?' he asked.

'Yes,' I said. 'Indeed I do. If you knew him better, Richard, if you had seen him this spring and summer, you would admire him too. He has done wonders with the estate. Uncle John always said that nothing could have happened without him. And the people of Acre love him and trust him, far more than they would ever love and trust one of us. I do wish you could learn to work with him, even if you cannot like him.'

Richard showed his white even teeth. 'I like him well enough,' he said. 'And I am coming to understand him more and more. I shall ask him directly about the missing corn, Julia. And I shall act on what he says.' The hard brightness left his face and he smoothed my belly again with a proprietory hand. 'So do not upset yourself and upset my son,' he said earnestly. 'Promise me you will rest while I am out this afternoon.'

I did not much like being loved only as the bearer of the heir to Wideacre. And I did not like how Richard was so set on a son. There was some hint of something old and dangerous in the way he so longed for another heir for this land to which the Laceys had clung for so many years.

I hoped very much that the child would be a girl, and that she would be free of the land. I would have her love it as I loved it, as the sweetest best country that anyone could work, not as Richard loved it, with this dark passion for ownership.

I thought I had won my way and won Acre its winter wheat, and so I smiled at Richard and promised I would rest. I would rest quiet while he went out. I kept my promise and went to my bed, which is why I was asleep when the soldiers came for Ralph Megson.

← 28 →

I heard of it from my maid, Jenny Hodgett, the gate-keeper's daughter. She was walking out with Bobby Miles from the village. Bobby had been in the Bush tavern when the two soldiers had ridden down the street with the carriage behind them.

They had pulled up outside Ralph's cottage in the pearly-grey twilight of the Wideacre evening, soft and quiet with the birds going to roost and the stars coming out. An officer with the county militia had got out of the coach and gone into Ralph's cottage without knocking on the door.

By this time everyone who had been drinking in the Bush was outside staring, of course. All the women were at their doorways, and all the children were out in the lane, their mouths agape.

There was no noise inside the cottage, there were no raised voices. Only a few minutes passed before Ralph came out, pulling on his brown jacket, with the gentleman walking very close at his shoulder. Ralph had glanced around at the faces and hesitated, as if he would say something, but then the gentleman tapped his shoulder with his cane – a bit impertinent, Bobby Miles had thought. Ralph had shrugged off the touch, given a little smile to Acre and climbed awkwardly on his wooden legs into the carriage.

'He smiled?' I asked Jenny, for it mattered a great deal to me.

'Bobby said so,' she confirmed. 'He said he gave the little grin he has when something has gone badly wrong on the land, and he says, "Damnation", but does not blame anybody. Begging your pardon, Miss Julia,' she added.

I nodded. 'But what can they have taken him *for*?' I demanded.

She looked at me forlornly as if it was her own lover which had gone. 'Don't you *know*, Miss Julia?' she asked.

I gazed at her blankly. I had a dreadful cold frightened feeling that I did know. I shook my head in denial.

'He was a rioter,' she said, 'when he was young. He led a gang in Kent, and a riot in Portsmouth. Nobody was ever hurt,' she said swiftly. 'It was just to get a fair price, Miss Julia. You know how they used to have riots for a fair price.'

I nodded. I knew.

'And then he went to be a smuggler,' she said softly. 'He was pressed as a sailor too.' She hesitated and looked at me. 'Then he went against the gentry for a while,' she said. 'They called him the Culler.'

'I knew of that,' I said. 'He told me himself.'

Jenny's head was down, and she took one glancing sideways look at me. 'No one in Acre would ever have betrayed him, not if we'd been burned alive,' she said passionately. 'Miss Julia, *who* can have called out the Chichester magistrate to take him in like that? Do you know?'

My hands were as cold as ice.

I knew.

'What will become of him?' I asked, my voice very low.

'They're certain to be able to prove at least some of the riots against him,' she said.

I nodded. There were not many black-haired cripples riding horses in riots. 'But they could not prove he came against the Laceys,' I said as if my loyalty were with him, as if it were not my family he had attacked, as if it were not my own blood-mother he had killed.

'No,' said Jenny. She had her apron up to mop her eyes. 'But just one witness from the other riots will be enough to finish him,' she said with a little wail. 'They'll hang him for sure, Miss Julia!'

'My God,' I said. Jenny sobbed noisily into her pinny, and I sat in my chair with my hand on my belly, feeling the little comforting movement of the baby for which Richard longed as the next squire.

If he was indeed the next squire, he should not have waiting for him this inheritance of hatred and suspicion, and of fear. I could give my baby little indeed when I gave him Wideacre, but I could give him the chance to live on the land without the blood on his head of the best man in the village.

I looked at Jenny with sudden determination. 'I won't have it!' I said. 'I won't have Ralph Megson hanged now for something he did years ago. I won't have him hanged when everyone knows that he did the right thing, the thing that anyone would do if their family and friends were starving. He rid Acre of that generation of Laceys and there is no one who does not think that Beatrice was in the wrong and earned that riot. I won't have Ralph Megson hanged.'

Jenny looked at me. She was in two minds about me. I had held command in Acre and she remembered the days when I was the only heir on the land, and I could call out a ploughing team. But when she looked at me now, she saw a young woman with her belly curving with motherhood. She saw a young wife, newly married, with a husband whom men feared. She saw a girl trapped into marriage and stripped of her wealth. I was no longer a figure of power.

'How can you stop it?' she asked.

'I don't know yet,' I said. 'I'll think of something. I'll think of some way. I'll go out for a walk down the drive to the hall and I'll think of something.'

She bobbed a curtsy and held the door for me, and I went out to take the air and to think. But though I walked all the way to the hall and watched the work there for a while, and though I walked all the way home again, no plan came to me.

When I went to bed that night, I knew that Ralph would see the wide yellow harvest moon criss-crossed with the bars across his window. I thought of his face turned up to the light, and his faint rueful smile as he faced the likelihood of his death. I tossed on the pillows all night until I heard the cocks crowing at dawn. I did not sleep at all.

And while I was thinking, while I was walking and walking,

like a ghost up and down the drive to the hall, walking with faster and faster strides as if my urgency could make a plan come into my head, the Chichester magistrates transferred the case to Winchester, because they feared a riot if Ralph was tried so near to his home. And the Winchester magistrates, no braver than their Chichester colleagues, transferred the case to London, where they said he could be kept more secure while witnesses were found who had seen riots of twenty years ago.

I knew he would need a lawyer, and I knew a London lawyer would cost a great deal of money. I had been poor all my child-hood; I had worn shoes which were too tight as my feet grew, I had patched my gowns, I had done without gloves. But I never knew myself to be poor until I looked out of the window at the rich autumn colours of *my* trees on *my* land, and knew I had no money to help Ralph.

I could have asked Richard for some, but I knew he would guess why I needed it, and I knew he would refuse. I went to my grandmama.

'Two hundred pounds!' she repeated in amazement. 'Julia, whatever can you need two hundred pounds for?'

I stumbled, trying to explain, but as soon as she understood it was men's business she frowned. 'You are no longer in control of Wideacre,' she said. 'And your former manager's concerns are not yours. Have you asked Richard if he would pay for the man's defence?'

'No,' I said quietly.

'I dare say you have your reasons for that,' she said, and there was a world of understanding in her voice. 'But if you cannot ask your husband for a sum of money, it is unlikely you will be able to obtain it anywhere else, Julia. If I had it, I would give it to you. But my own fortune is tied up and his lordship does not provide me with that sort of sum as pin-money.'

She paused, and I saw her swallow her pride like a lump in her throat. 'I have only twenty-five pounds' pin-money a quarter,' she said, her voice very low. 'I have spent this quarter's allow-ance, and I have no savings.'

I nodded. I was blinking hard, for there were tears in my eyes. 'How *do* married women get money if their husbands will not give them enough?' I demanded. I had some vague idea of loans, or of jewellers who would buy a trinket.

Grandma looked at me as if I were a little child once more and she was teaching me how to hold my fish-knife. 'If their husbands do not provide for them, they have no money,' she said blankly. 'Of course, a wife is dependent upon her husband's goodwill.'

I looked at her as if I were a fool who could not understand plain English. I was seventeen years old and I still had not learned that I had no rights in the world. I had no money of my own and I had no land. Everything around me, the water I drank, the food I ate, belonged to Richard, for in marrying him I had made it over to him entire. And whether I wanted three halfpence of what I had once called my own, or whether I wanted two hundred pounds, I had to apply to him. And he could refuse me.

He did refuse me.

I buried my pride and told him I thought Ralph Megson wrongly accused and that I should like to send him some money to pay for a lawyer. Richard looked at me with a sparkle in his eyes as though I had said something most extremely funny.

'Oh, no, Julia,' he said, his voice very warm and indulgent. 'Most certainly not.'

The days got colder, and it was grey when I awoke in the mornings and dark by dinner-time in the afternoon. I did nothing to help Ralph Megson in a prison far away in London. Jenny Hodgett told me they had put their savings together in the village and asked Dr Pearce to send them to him in London. Dr Pearce, torn between his horror at law-breakers and murderers and his pity for the distress of Acre, added to the little fund on his own account, and contacted his own cousin and asked him to see Ralph in gaol and keep the fees low.

I knew then that the time I had seen was here, the time when Ralph would not be able to help me and I would not be able to help him.

I was very lonely.

In autumn the countryside is very beautiful. A Wideacre autumn is a season when the world seems full of colour and you cannot believe that the bright leaves could ever fade. The hedgerows are full of glossy berries: the tulip-shaped scarlet hips and haws, the fat black bobbles of blackberries. The hawthorn trees are dotted with berries of a deep, dark redness, and the ivy flowers with waxy green delicate bouquets.

As the chestnut leaves started falling in great yellow fans on to the drive, I took to walking in the woods opposite the Dower House, going quite far in random sweeps, but staying under the trees as if they could give me some sort of comfort which the empty common lands could not.

Sometimes on my walks I would back against a tree and look up at the blue sky patterned all over with the copper, yellow and orange leaves. I would eat a handful of blackberries or crack beech-nuts open and eat the little sweet kernels. I would put my hands behind me and feel the rough bark of the tree and try to hear the beat of the land. But I could hear nothing at all.

I tried to count my blessings, but something must have been wrong with my arithmetic, for I could not make it come right. I knew I loved Richard with a long love with its roots in my earliest childhood and its flower in my belly, but I could find no happiness in knowing that we were at last where we had longed to be: a married couple on Wideacre.

I thought that was because Wideacre felt like my familiar home no more. Acre had changed already, and would change again when Richard was out on the land with the ploughing teams. I would be indoors with the new baby so there would be no smiles for me, and no calling of 'Speed the plough!'

But I knew also that there would be no smiles for Richard. The special magic of Wideacre – that masters and men could try to work together in unity – had quite gone. Never again would the fastest reaping gang in the country celebrate their triumph in the Bush at Acre. Next year there would be hired hands, paid labourers. Never again would they stand waist-deep in their own corn and laugh for joy at the richness of the land which had grown such a crop, and boast of their own skill in cutting it.

Acre was different, and I was different too.

I was mourning my mama still. Even now it had been less than two months. I was haunted by her in dreams which made me happy while I was asleep, but made me weep and weep when I awoke. I dreamed once that I was sitting before my mirror and pinning on my hat when she walked into the room as though she had been out in the garden picking flowers. In my dream I said, 'Mama! Oh, Mama! I thought you were dead!' and she said with such a sweet smile, 'Oh, no my darling. I'd never leave you in such a pickle!' I was so persuaded that she was alive and loved me still that I could not believe it when I woke in the quiet early-morning house and remembered she would never call me her darling again.

I dreamed she walked into the parlour and asked me where her clothes had gone. I stammered that I had given them away because I had thought she was dead. Then she laughed, a clear easy laugh, and called out of the window to John to share the joke. I gazed from one bright laughing face to another and was as certain as I could be that there had been some foolish mistake and my lovely mama was still alive.

It was pointless for me to try to accept her death. Grandmama Havering urged me to come to terms with it and put it behind me. I smiled vaguely and did not reply.

I did not try to accept it, but neither did I try to escape it. I simply could not believe that I would never see her again. And, although I often wept for her on my long walks and found that I was crying from longing for her hand on my forehead, her smile and the love in her voice, I could think two sad, silly thoughts at once: that I would never see her again, and that it was not possible that she could have left me for ever.

I was very lonely.

She had been my companion and best friend, and I had never noticed before how the autumn kept us so much indoors. When it grew colder and my walks grew shorter, I found I was spending most of the days in the parlour. Sometimes I would sit before the roaring fire and try to be glad that I was inside warming my toes, and sometimes I would sit in the window-seat and press my face to the glass and watch the rain sluicing down the cold windows, and wait for dusk, and wait for night and sleep, and then lie sleepless and wait for morning.

As I grew heavier and more and more tired, I was not glad of the rest, but impatient with this lumpish body which kept me isolated in the little room in the little house while Richard could ride down to Acre or up on the downs, or across the common and drop into any tenant's house and take a pot-luck dinner.

He was popular only with our wealthy neighbours. The poorer farmers saw their interests as at one with Acre. They depended on wage-work to supplement their farming and they needed Wideacre to be a generous employer. They bought much wheat from us, and fodder and straw; and they needed Wideacre to sell at a fair price in the local market. But the bigger farmers nearby were happy to farm hard and sell high, they liked the lordly way Richard condemned 'new-fangled levelling notions'.

There was always a place ready for the handsome young squire at their tables, and Richard came home from these dinners in good humour, tipsy with port, flattered by deference, bursting with charm and conceit.

He had grown so strong since he had become owner of Wideacre. No one had been able to stand against him, and the complaints about him in the village were so soft that only I could hear them.

He had grown so confident. I, who used to laugh at the people who called me Squire Julia, had become a fat tired woman who sat alone in her parlour and longed for her mama who was dead, and for her friend who was in a London gaol, and feared the birth of her child as another Lacey to run the land.

But I had one friend yet.

I thought of him. I had thought of him almost daily since the

death of my mama. I had thought of him without shame. I was
not thinking of a man as a married woman should *not* think. I
was thinking of a young man who was part of my careless childhood when Mama had been happy, and I had been happy, that
short season in Bath.

I was thinking of James.

He was young, he was wealthy, and I knew he would do me a
favour if I asked him.

I left the fireside chair and lit one of the candles at the mantelpiece. I went to the library and opened the drawer for paper, an
envelope and sealing-wax. Then I took pen and ink and went
back into the parlour, the women's room of the house. I had
thought the letter would give me some trouble to write, but I
wrote it as easily and as simply as I had talked to him all those
months ago when we had driven and walked and danced in Bath.

> *Dear James,*
>
> *You will be surprised to hear from me, but I know you will
> understand that I am writing to you because I need your
> friendship. Not for myself, but for a friend of mine who finds
> himself in some trouble.*
>
> *You may remember Ralph Megson, our family's farm
> manager? He was taken up for an old alleged offence of rioting
> and transferred to London before I could aid him. I believe
> he may have a lawyer, but I am anxious for him.*
>
> *You will relieve my mind very much if you could see him
> and ascertain that he has adequate advice and adequate funds
> to secure his acquittal.*
>
> *Any monies he needs I would repay you, as soon as I can, if
> you were to be kind enough to help him now while the case is
> urgent.*
>
> *I beg your pardon for calling on your aid, but there is no
> one else who will help me.*
>
> *Your friend,*
>
> *Julia MacAndrew (née Lacey)*

I could do no better than that in a hurry, in my worry for
Ralph. I sealed the letter with the Lacey seal, and I called Jenny
to the parlour.

'It's about Mr Megson,' I said to her. I knew Richard was out,
but I still kept my voice low. She glanced to see that the door
was shut tight. 'Take this letter down to the village,' I said.
'Take it to Jimmy Dart, and tell him to make sure that Mr James
Fortescue receives it. He'd best take it to their home in Bristol. I
hope that Mr Fortescue will help Ralph Megson.'

Jenny nodded. 'Your young man,' she said wistfully.

'Yes,' I said. Then I drew a deep breath. 'My husband would
not wish me to write to him,' I said. I flushed scarlet with the
shame of what I was saying. 'Keep it hid, Jenny. It's for Ralph's
defence.'

She nodded, her eyes sharp. 'I understand,' she said. 'I'll take
it down now. Mrs Gough won't notice I'm gone if you don't ring
for an hour.'

'I won't,' I said. I went to my writing-desk. 'Give Jimmy this
guinea,' I said, 'for his journey. And tell him to be as quick as he
can.'

She nodded, a little smile behind her grave eyes. 'We'll get
him free, Miss Julia!' she said. 'I'm sure of it!'

I nodded and let her go. A few minutes later I saw her trotting
down the lane, her skirts held in one hand, the other one holding
her shawl, and the letter hidden, if I guessed right, under her
pinny.

Then I set myself to wait for the reply.

I thought James Fortescue might wait until he had seen Ralph
before he wrote back to me, so I warned myself that I must be
patient for at least a week. But I could look forward to the return
of Jimmy. I thought he would come to the Dower House at once
to tell me what James had said. I waited three days patiently. I
waited for the fourth with concern. The fifth day I ordered out
the carriage and went down to Acre.

Ralph Megson's cottage, where Jimmy now lived alone, was
shuttered, the door barred. Jimmy was not yet back, then. With

my hood pulled up against the cold drizzle I crossed the road, walking carefully in the greasy mud, to Rosie's little cottage.

Her door was open, and Nat stood helplessly by a doused fireplace. Rosie was tying a knot in a shawl which was lumpy with what I guessed were all her clothes and perhaps a little food.

'What is happening?' I asked.

They had turned as they heard my foot on the doorstep. Neither of them smiled nor said a word of greeting. Rosie looked through me as if I were not there.

Nat struggled to answer my question.

'It's Jimmy,' he said. His voice was still hoarse from the years of soot, and harsher now with bad news. 'He's been taken up by the Winchester magistrates for vagrancy. They're holding him in the poor house. Rosie's going to get him out.'

I looked blankly from one hard face to the other.

'At Winchester?' I asked. 'When?'

'We don't know,' Nat said. 'He said he had a message to take to Bristol, that he wouldn't tell no one about. He could have been taken on his way home.'

I nodded. 'This is my fault,' I said sorrowfully. 'I sent him with a message. But I gave him a guinea for his fare. They can't arrest a man with a guinea for his fare.'

'He could have refused to be press-ganged,' Nat suggested. 'Or not taken his hat off when bid. They can arrest you for nigh on anything, Miss Julia, if they want to.'

'What will you do, Rosie?' I asked.

She spoke to me for the first time. 'Dr Pearce has given me a letter to show them,' she said. 'And three guineas, which must be enough to get him off whatever charge it is against him.'

'And then you'll bring him back here,' I said. I looked around the room. Rosie's few goods were packed, the hearth was empty of her pan.

'I've been given notice to quit,' she said. 'Jimmy too. I had a letter today, from your husband, the squire. I've to leave at once, and Jimmy's tenancy is cancelled too.'

'Richard is turning you out?' I asked, disbelieving.

She looked at me and her face was hard. I had never seen her look at me like that before. 'Aye,' she said. 'It seems like only yesterday that you brought us here. I was glad of it then, but now it seems almost worse to have been here, to have planned for the future, and now to have to lose it all.'

'I'll speak to him . . .' I said quickly.

Her shrug seemed to suggest my promises were worthless. 'We all know you can do nothing, Miss Julia,' she said. 'You married the wrong man to give your baby a name. We all understand that. I don't expect any good from you now.'

'Rosie!' I said. It was a cry for her forgiveness.

She smiled her weary smile at me and said, 'It's no good, Miss Julia.' And she picked up her kerchief bundle and handed it to Nat, who hefted it over his shoulder and went out before her into the grey dampness.

'Where will you go?' I asked.

She turned in the doorway to answer me. Outside the drizzle had turned to sleet, lancing sheets of wet ice.

'Back to Bath,' she said. 'We can get free passage there, and I can embroider gloves again. I know I can sell them in Bath and we know the city.'

I said nothing. There was nothing I could say.

She nodded at me in silence. Then she pulled her shawl over her bowed head and went out over the threshold into the cold.

I called the carriage over and rode home dryshod.

The weather worsened. We had a long week of fog when not even Richard got out often, and then we had three days of rain. Every day Richard's new groom, George, came trudging through the mire, or rode on his skidding horse, with the post; but he brought no message for me from James.

I thought of everything.

My worst fear was that Jimmy had been arrested on his way to Bristol, that he had been stopped on his way. But I had faith in Jimmy. He would have walked across the Avon for Ralph, and he trusted James as a worker of miracles. He would have gone to great lengths to get the message through. And he had wit enough to get it into the post – even from prison.

But I also feared that the message had come too late. Maybe Ralph was already hanged, and James could not bear to tell me. I hoped desperately that Ralph had escaped, and James was looking for him and not writing until he had clear news. Possibly James and Ralph had met and Ralph had forbidden James to send me news until the case was heard. I even wondered if James would simply ignore my letter. But I put that fear aside. I knew he would not. He had liked and admired Ralph. And he was always generous to me.

I thought I had thought of everything.

I thought of every option except the obvious one. As silly as a child, I did not think of that at all.

I took to rising early in the morning and putting on my wrapper, which enfolded me less and less as I grew broader, and going quietly downstairs to drink my morning chocolate in the parlour so I could watch the drive for George coming from the London stage with the mail.

He never came much before seven or eight, so I could as well have stayed in my room; but in some hopeful corner of my heart I thought I was keeping a sort of vigil. As the grey mist cleared away down the lane, I thought that perhaps Ralph was sitting up on some dirty straw in a London cell and opening his eyes knowing that James Fortescue had engaged a good lawyer for him, and knowing for certain that I had stood his friend and that my friendship could make a difference.

Richard saw me there one morning and asked me what I did. I told him I was just sitting, looking at the misty garden, doing nothing. I smiled deprecatingly to suggest it was a whim of pregnancy, and Richard nodded and went out through the kitchen door to the stable yard.

I heard Mrs Gough laugh as he went through the kitchen and I thought resentfully that she always had liked him best.

The next day he was up early again and saw me at the parlour window.

Again I told him that I felt restless, that I wanted to be sitting in the window-seat watching Jenny light the fire, her routine disarranged by my capriciousness. Richard nodded as if he understood, and his smile was a gleam of white, with a little hint of mischief at the back.

On the third day he was there when George rattled the door-knocker and I heard Stride cross the hall and open the door.

There were letters for the household.

There was a letter for me.

Stride brought it in on the silver salver and Richard paused on his way to the door. 'Who could be writing to you, Julia?' he asked, interested.

I flushed up to my forehead. 'I think Sarah Collis, from Bath,' I said. And the lie slid easily off my tongue, making me blush again.

Richard's eyes were very warm and confident.

'Open it, then,' he said, and his voice was silky.

I should have been warned by that special sweetness of tone, but the letter was thick in my hand and I could only think that it would have news of Ralph.

'I'll open it later,' I said, getting up and going to the door.

As I went past Richard, he caught my wrist and held me, rooted where I stood. I instinctively clutched the letter close to me and caught my breath. His face was not angry; it seemed there was nothing to fear. His smile was as sweet as a May morning.

'Open it here,' he said. 'Read your letter here. I know girls have secrets. I shall not ask to see it, for I am going out now. Sit and read it here, my love.'

My eyes flashed to his face, for I was surprised at the endearment. He pressed me into the chair by the table and stood back, leaning against the wall, as I put my finger under the flap and broke the seal.

I did not look carefully at the seal.

There was no letter inside. There were eight pieces of torn paper and a torn envelope, a bulky package. I forgot Richard was watching and tipped the eight thick jagged scraps out on the table before me, and pieced them together.

It was my writing on the envelope. It read: 'James Fortescue, Esq.'

I slumped against the back of my chair, and my heart pounded so fast I was afraid for the little child who lay quiet inside me and depended on my body for its safety. But this is a dangerous world for little children. It is a dangerous world for grown men. I gave a little moan of distress.

My first thought was that James Fortescue had recognized my hand and had torn up the letter in a temper, and sent it back to me in spite.

But then I hesitated, and I knew I did him a disservice. James would never be spiteful. James was always generous.

I knew only one man who would post scraps of paper to me.

I raised my grey eyes to Richard's face, and saw his deep, dangerous resentment.

'You wrote to another man,' he said.

I said nothing. My thumbs burned. I could hear a humming in my head. I could smell danger like smoke on the wind.

'You wrote to another man. You thought to hide that letter from me,' he said. His voice was soft and infinitely menacing. 'I had to have Jimmy Dart arrested,' he said. 'I had been watching him a long while. I knew you would try and betray me. I was ready for your infidelity.'

I gulped like a landed fish. 'Richard . . .' I said beseechingly.

His eyes were like sapphires. He was my husband and my master. He was the squire, and he knew it. Oh, he knew it.

'I won't have it, Julia,' he said simply.

He could invent rules for Wideacre, for Acre, for me, until the world ended. Richard was the squire and he had the power of God.

'I won't have it,' he said, and I knew his word was law. 'You wanted to be married,' he said, his voice exultant. 'I did as you wished. Now we are married, and you will behave as a proper wife to me. You will not write to other men, and you most certainly will not discuss our business with them. There are means I can take to ensure you do not write to other men, or indeed to anyone.'

He hesitated to see if I would complain. But I said nothing. The scraps of paper lying on the table told me mutely that I was defeated. I looked blankly at them and thought of the little letter inside them which I had hoped would save Ralph. I knew then that nothing could save me, but I had hoped to help Ralph away from the wreck which was Wideacre.

'You must learn your place, Julia.' Richard said softly.

I bowed my head slavishly. I knew I must learn it indeed.

From that moment I rebelled not at all. The Chichester ac-coucheur advised against any long walks, and the weather was bad, so that I looked for no help from the dripping beech trees or the sorrowful burble of the Fenny. I did not mind being confined at home.

I no longer got up early for the post. On some days I did not feel like getting up at all. I lay in Mama's bed in Mama's bed-room, for Richard had insisted that I make the change to the best bedroom in the house, and I watched the grey ceiling turning pale with dawn, and yellow with the midday light, and some days I watched it growing dark again with twilight and never moved the whole day.

No one disturbed me. No one troubled me any more with the news of Acre. I heard nothing of Ralph. I knew nothing about the land. I lay like a whale beached on some desolate shore and I did not stir.

The greatest effort I made was to rise and get down to the parlour in time for Richard's return to dinner so that he would not come to my room. Even then I could not be troubled to ring for candles but sat in firelight, watching the flames flicker, and I would wonder what would become of me when the waiting time was over, and whether this feeling of floating, of drowning, would ever end at all.

'Sitting in darkness?' Richard demanded. The parlour door

had opened so quietly that his voice made me jump and made my heart thud with nervousness.

'I must have dozed off by the fire!' I exclaimed. 'How very dark it is!'

'They say there's a storm coming,' he said.

He came towards the fire and pulled up his riding jacket so he could warm the seat of his fawn breeches. I was sitting in Mama's favourite low chair and he towered above me. His riding and his work had broadened him. He was breathtakingly handsome, with eyes as blue and as careless as a child's, and that dark curly hair as soft and bouncy as a lamb's fleece.

'I met Dr Pearce in the lane,' Richard said. He leaned over me and pulled the bell for them to bring candles. 'He had a young curate friend with him. I asked them both to dinner.'

'Today?' I asked languidly. Mrs Gough had a menu for the week, but she would welcome the opportunity to exert herself to please Richard.

'Yes,' said Richard. 'They said they'd come at about four o'clock and we could have a game of whist afterwards.'

I glanced at the clock over the mantelpiece. It said ten past three. 'I'll tell Mrs Gough,' I said. Richard put a careless hand down to me and hauled me out of my chair. 'And then I'd better change,' I said.

'Do,' he said. 'I'm tired of seeing you in that dull black gown all the time. And the fatter you get the worse it looks.'

I checked on my way to the door. It must have been my condition and the fact that I had just woken, but the hardness in his voice made tears start in my eyes. With Mama gone, and Ralph gone, I could not bear it if Richard was in a mood to bully me.

'Oh, Richard,' I said reproachfully. 'I am not *fat*, it is just the shape of the baby. It is just a large baby.'

Richard stood astride in front of the fireplace. The flickering flames made his shadow leap, large as a giant, on the wall behind me. 'Well, you look damned fat to me,' he said cruelly. 'Run and see Mrs Gough and then put on a proper evening gown, and wear some jewellery to set it off. We're dining at home, after all, and Dr Pearce won't mind.'

'I don't really have any jewellery,' I said in a low voice. I was thinking of Mama's rose-pearl necklace which the highwayman had taken. She told me that she would leave it to me in her will. And now she was dead, and the necklace was probably in some horrid little shop pawned for drink, and I would never see it, or my mama, ever again.

'Wear that nice shiny watered silk anyway,' Richard commanded. 'I'll come up to your room when I'm washed and changed.'

I nodded, as humble as a drudge, and slipped out of the room. I spoke to Mrs Gough and saw her explode into a frenzy of activity. By the way she clattered the pans I knew she would produce a dinner fit for a table of princes, but in the meantime the kitchen was an unsafe territory.

I went upstairs and called Jenny to help me wash. I missed my hot baths, but since my belly had grown so broad it was impossible for me to fit into the tub. Now I stood upright while Jenny tipped water down over my shoulders and let it cascade off the bump of my belly into the hip-bath.

'You surely have your dates wrong, Miss Julia,' she said. 'Such a big child as it is. It surely will be soon.'

'No,' I said. I could hardly have my dates wrong with that May Day morning in my mind. 'It will not be born for another two months at least,' I said. 'It is due at the end of January. I have all of December to get through yet.'

She shook out the black silk gown and helped fasten the buttons at the back. It was rather grand for a dinner party at home with no one invited but the vicar and his friend, but I might as well wear it as Richard had requested. I would not have another chance. No one else visited us in the evenings, and Richard and I never went out to dinner. The roads were so bad, the nights were so dark, and everyone in the county knew that I was pregnant after a marriage which had been announced almost as the baby started to show. I was not disgraced – my grandmama had seen to that – but we certainly were not the most sought-after couple in the county.

That would be remedied when the spring came and we could drive out and around visiting, when the baby was born, and when our great new house was roofed and nearly ready. I had learned enough in Bath to know that no one would ignore us when the estate grew more profitable and we moved into the big house and employed dozens of servants and went to London for the season. I thought for a moment then of what that season would be like with Richard at my side, without my mama to help me, without my girlhood friends to greet me.

Without James.

I shrugged. There was an ache in my heart, a steady constant ache in my heart. I was in mourning for my mama. I was in mourning for the death of my girlhood and the loss of the only man I would ever love. I was happy to wear black, and if I wanted to wear my black evening dress, it would have to be at home. It might as well be tonight.

'Lovely,' said Jenny. 'Just lovely, this dress, Miss Julia.'

I turned and looked at myself in the glass. The deep lustre of the watered silk made my face look shadowed and remote. The folds spread evenly across the front of the high waist concealed the pushing weight of my belly. The only indication of my pregnancy was my plumper breasts, which were pressed into two rounded half-moons at the square neck of the bodice.

I stepped closer to the mirror and looked at myself curiously.

I saw again the girl who had been called the prettiest girl in Bath. In my sadness for my mama, and my loneliness, in my mistrust of my body which had so betrayed me with its fertility, I had forgotten that I was a beautiful girl. But in this hard autumn I had become a beautiful woman.

The curves of my breasts were a sensual promise; even the shifting sliding hints of the prow of my belly were a proof of sweet fertility. The dark mysterious silk accentuated the slimness of my back and the creaminess of my skin, and put shadows in my grey eyes. I smiled at my reflection in genuine surprise. The fine clear lines of my cheek-bones, the lilting upturned corners of my mouth were familiar, but the shadows in the eyes were new, and it was these which had transformed me from a promising girl into a beautiful and desirable woman.

'You do pay dressing,' Jenny said. 'Shall I do your hair?'

'Yes, please,' I said, and I sat down at my mama's dressing-table and watched my face in the glass as she brushed out my light curling hair in long sweeps from the top of my head down almost to my waist, and then started to pile it up in gentle folds.

Behind her, in the darkness of the room, reflected in the glass, I saw the door open and Richard come in. He did not realize I had seen him, for he was watching Jenny carefully brushing and lifting one swath of thick hair after another. There was an expression on his face which made me give a little shiver, although the room was warm. I wondered, even as the hairs all down the nape of my neck lifted in a shuddery life of their own, what imaginary shadow had crossed my mind.

He moved, and Jenny jumped and gave a little squeak. 'Oh! I beg your pardon, sir, I did not know you had come in!'

I heard a note in her voice I had never heard before, and I said nothing for a moment while I considered it. Then I recognized that slightly too quick speech, that slightly too high pitch. She was afraid of Richard. The whole household, the village and the estate were afraid of Richard. And I – his wife, his dependant – I was afraid of him too.

He smiled. 'You can go now, Jenny, if your mistress is finished with you.'

I nodded my head, not turning from my place before the mirror, and Jenny bobbed a curtsy with her hand held to her neck in an odd gesture, strangely protective of her throat. Then she took herself out of the room. Richard walked towards me and stood behind me, where Jenny had stood brushing my hair. I met his eyes in the mirror, and I wondered what he wanted of me.

'I like that gown,' he said. His fingers brushed my neck, the smooth sloping naked line from my shoulder up to the exposed lobe of my ear. I shivered at his touch and I could see in the mirror that the pupils of my eyes had enlarged, making my eyes darker.

'I have brought something for you,' Richard said softly. 'Something I know you will like.'

He smiled.

I considered that smile, watching his face in the mirror which had once reflected my Mama. It was not the smile he used to hide his anger, so I should have nothing to fear. It was not the smile which was his genuine laughing smile. It was affectionate, tender. But there was some joke at the back of it which I thought I would not enjoy.

I nodded warily.

Richard lifted the flap of his pocket and delved in its depths. His jacket was black velvet, his linen cream lawn; the pocket flap was trimmed with black satin ribbon. I was watching his reflection in my mirror so carefully that I noticed how the sheen on the ribbon caught the light from the candles on either side of my mirror.

'I hope you will like it,' Richard said sweetly. His voice quavered on a little giggle of suppressed laughter. 'Indeed,' he said, his voice shaking, 'I *know* you will like it!'

My eyes flew to his reflected face in my mirror. His eyes were dancing with boyish merriment. Then I felt the cool touch of a necklace around my throat.

The cool touch of rounded perfectly matched pearls.

Rose pearls.

Mama's rose pearls.

Mama's rose pearls, which were taken by the highwayman who shot her and left her to die on the highway.

I put my hand up to touch them as if to confirm that they were real. I could not believe they *were* real. I had not thought to see them ever again.

'How well they suit you,' Richard said pleasantly. There was a ripple of amusement under his voice. 'How pretty you look in them, my dear.'

My eyes met his, my grey level stare to his dancing blue twinkle.

'Mama's pearls,' I said, prosaically.

'Mama's pearls,' he confirmed. The joy never left his face. 'Or, at any rate,' he amended, 'something very like them.'

There was a noise of carriage-wheels outside as Dr Pearce and his friend arrived.

'Early!' Richard said, crossing to my window to look out. 'Come then, Julia!' He held out an imperative hand to me as I sat frozen at the glass.

For a moment I thought I could not move. I sat in silence and looked at Mama's rose-pearl necklace and at the matching ear-rings which Richard had tossed down before me.

'Oh, yes!' he said, following my gaze. 'Put the ear-rings on too! You can't imagine the trouble I had getting them!'

It was that nonchalant mention of his trouble in getting them that tipped me from my frozen crystal of disbelief into a well of horror which I recognized.

At last I knew the horror for what it was: Richard's murderous madness.

Richard's hand was held out to me, and Dr Pearce was knocking at the door. I was a woman entirely dependent on one man, that man my brother, seven months pregnant with his child, without a friend in the world who could help me stand against him.

I knew him then as Clary's murderer, the entrapper of Matthew Merry, the betrayer of Ralph Megson, the murderer of Jem the groom, of his own papa, John MacAndrew, and of my beloved mama.

I looked at him as if I had never seen him before; but there was no fear on my face. I was beyond fear, in a pit of such horror that I could think nothing and say nothing.

Mechanically I pushed the studs of the ear-rings through the little holes in my ear-lobes.

They stung.

Then I took Richard's hand and went down the stairs with

him to greet Dr Pearce and Mr Fowler, and sat at the foot of the table, with my husband at the head, while Stride served a dinner of which I could be proud.

Afterwards we played cards, and Dr Pearce and I won. We took tea and then the two of them went home. Richard and I were alone in the parlour.

'It's good to have company,' Richard said, yawning. 'We spend too much time alone. It will make you dull, Julia. You were blooming tonight.'

My hand was at my throat on the necklace. Richard glanced at it.

'It's remarkable how well those pearls set off your skin tones,' he said. 'They make you look like a bowl of warm cream.'

He put out his hand to me to help me to my feet, and out of habit, before I could think what I was doing, I let him pull me up out of the chair and found myself standing close beside him on the hearthrug.

His hand came down under my chin and lifted my face up. For no reason he squeezed my chin until I could feel the strength in his long fingers, killer's fingers. The blood drummed in my head, but I did not speak and my grey eyes on his face never wavered.

'I think I shall come to your room tonight,' he said with a little sigh. 'I think I should like to lie with you.'

There were a few moments of utter silence while my reeling head tried to take in what he was saying.

'You cannot!' I said stupidly. 'Richard! You are my brother!'

Richard's hand left my chin and lingered on my bare shoulder, caressing the slope of my neck, one finger negligently trailing down to touch the warm rounded top of my breast.

'Oh, I don't regard it,' he said idly. 'It was just something they said to frighten us.'

'No,' I said. I tried to step back, but Richard's other arm was around my waist holding me tight beside him. 'No, they meant it, Richard. It was the truth, I am sure of it.'

I was still not afraid – I was too stunned to be afraid. My

brother, and the killer of my mama, had me held tight to his side and was stroking my breast and my neck with confident, blood-stained fingers.

'I don't regard it,' Richard said again. 'I do not think we need regard it. They will not be saying it again, after all!' He gave me one of his most charming smiles, as if that were the wittiest sally he could make, and he put one hard finger under my chin and tipped my face up to receive his kiss.

In the pit of madness which was all that was left of my will, there was nothing to stop him. His mouth came down upon mine and I gritted my teeth to stop myself retching, and I put my hands on his waist to hold myself steady while the world reeled around me.

'Whore,' he said gently, and put me from him. 'Go and get into bed. I shall have you tonight.'

My will was broken and my mind was dead.

I went up the stairs to my bedroom for there was nowhere else I *could* go. Jenny Hodgett undressed me in silence and looked anxiously at my face so pale that it was deathly. I slipped between the sheets of my bed and blew out my candle. Then I lay in the half-darkness with the firelight flickering on the looming furniture of the room; an owl was calling and calling outside.

He was late coming to bed. In my strange calm state I even dozed while I waited for him. I was afraid no longer. I had lost my fear. I was not a virgin – I did not think it would hurt. I could not cry for help and shame Richard, and shame our family name, and shame myself. When he pulled the covers roughly off me, I lay as still as a corpse. Only the little hairs on my arms and my legs lifted and prickled at the cold night air. But I held still.

The bed dipped with his weight as he came in beside me. His night-time candle showed his face still rosy and young. There was the smell of spirits on his breath – brandy. His hair smelled of cigar smoke.

He was at a loss to know how to begin. I opened my eyes and looked at him steadily, expressionless, not moving. He fidgeted with the things on my bedside table, shifted the glass of water, knocked over the little wooden owl Ralph had given me.

'D'you remember Scheherazade?' he asked unexpectedly.

I held my face blank, but my mind was racing.

'You really loved her, didn't you?' he asked. His voice was a little stronger. It held some resonance of his old childhood hectoring tone. 'You were heartbroken when she was killed, weren't you, Julia?'

My silence irritated him.

'Weren't you?' he demanded.

'Yes,' I said. I was unwilling to speak and I did not know why he asked. 'Yes,' I said.

'You cried for her,' Richard reminded me. 'And yet you could never really believe that Dench had cut her.'

I sighed. It was all such a long time ago and the losses then had been mere forerunners of what came later.

'Yes,' I said.

Richard rolled on to one elbow, the better to see my face. 'The horse was cut, then they smashed her in the face with a hammer,' he said. 'And Dench was sacked and had to run for his life. Remember? If Grandpa Havering had caught him, he would have had him hanged for sure.'

'I remember,' I said.

Richard was getting excited, his eyes sparkling, his face bright. 'It was me!' he said exultantly. 'All along! And none of you ever guessed. None of you ever came near to guessing. I cut Scheherazade and I made sure all the blame would fall on Dench. So that stopped you riding my horse all right! And I made sure that I would never have to ride her again, *and* I got rid of Dench who was ganging up with you against me. I did all of that on my own! And I made you cry for weeks, didn't I?'

I lay very still, trying to absorb what Richard was saying. But trying even harder to understand Richard's sudden elation. Then he moved closer towards me and I understood. He fumbled under the covers for the hem of my shift and pulled it up. I checked my movement to grab for it and hold it down. If it came to a struggle, then Richard would win. And I knew, with some secret perverse knowledge which I did not want, that he would like to feel me fighting against him.

'And the goshawk . . .' Richard's breathing was fast; he had pulled his own nightshirt out of the way and was rearing up over me. 'Ralph Megson's precious goshawk. When she bated from my fist, I pulled her back. The first time it was an accident, but she made me so angry when she would not sit still. The second time I wanted to hurt her, and I knew if I pulled her hard enough and quick enough, I would break her legs. D'you remember how they went click, Julia?'

I was sweating, and the inside of my thighs were damp. Richard pushed inexpertly towards me and put a clumsy hand down to part my legs. He clambered, impeded by the bedclothes, on top of me. He giggled like a conceited schoolboy when he pressed down and his hard flesh met mine.

'But you didn't dare touch the sheep,' I said. I spoke almost idly. My mind and my body were numb with fear and disgust and the horror of what Richard had told me, and my acceptance as I recognized the truth at once: that I had, in some deep and guilty way, always known; that I should have said something, done something; that once again I was Richard's unwilling accomplice.

But the sheep had gone against him.

'D'you think they knew you were bad?' I asked.

Richard hesitated.

'They went against you,' I said. 'I've never seen sheep do such a thing. They mobbed you in the barn on the downs. D'you remember *that*, Richard? D'you remember how very afraid you were then?'

'I wasn't . . .' Richard said quickly. 'I've never been afraid.'

'Oh, yes, you were,' I said certainly. 'You were afraid of Scheherazade from the moment you first saw her, and you were afraid of the sheep.'

Richard glared at me, but he was losing his potency. I could feel his hardness melting away and I was filled with elation, with a sense of triumph.

'You were scared to death of Scheherazade,' I said. 'That was why you cut her. Not just because you were jealous of me riding her. But you would have done anything not to ride her yourself. And the sheep were like a nightmare.'

'It's not so . . .' he said. His eyes were sharp with dislike at my tauntings. He looked as he used to look when he was about to explode into one of his childhood rages. I knew I had defeated him and he would not touch me. But I was not ready for his instantaneous spite.

He thrust his forefinger hard into me in a sharp jabbing movement, and I gave a muffled cry of pain and shock. The pain was sharp; it felt as if he were scratching me inside. I bit back the cry and made no sound. I shut my eyes and lay as still as a stone carving. Richard took his hand away and fumbled down to touch himself. He was starting to breathe heavily and I could feel him pulling at himself, rubbing himself against my legs.

I opened my eyes and smiled at him. 'It's no good, Richard,' I said coolly in a voice just like my mama's when she sent him early to bed for spilling jam at the tea table. 'It is no good. You cannot touch me now and you will never be able to touch me. You had much better go to your own bed.'

I pushed his spiteful hands away from me and rolled over on my side to present my back to him, indifferent to whether he stayed or went.

I did not even open my eyes as he left the room.

O nly that one night, only that once did he come to my bed in the months of my pregnancy. And only that once did he speak of the times which had passed, when all the warning signs had been there if we had been able to see them. I knew then what Acre had known, what every animal he had touched had known, what Ralph had seen on meeting him: that Richard was insane. All the clues had been there, but between an indulgent aunt and a weak girl he had managed to pass them off as eccentricity, or talent, or charm.

I blamed myself. I thought of the times that Richard's behaviour had been violent or passionate and I had concealed it from my mama. I thought of the times he had threatened me and I had loyally kept it from everyone, even from Clary and the village children. Ted Tyacke would have been glad enough to waylay Richard and give him a thumping to remind him to be gentle with me. But I had never told anyone. Never told them anything at all.

I blamed myself then. I sat on the window-seat and watched the hoar-frost melt on the lawn under the window as the sunshine warmed it on the last days of autumn, and I blamed myself for living in a sweet girlish pretence, believing that the world was kinder than it was, that adults were cleverer than they were, that Richard was normal.

I leafed through the days of my childhood like old watercolour paintings in a folder. And this time I saw everything quite differently. I saw Richard as an impulsive, uncontrollable bully. I saw my mama as wilfully blind: blind to his cruelty to me, blind to his madness, blind because she knew my parentage and guessed at his. She had not the courage to face the Lacey madness in

Richard's eyes. She should have seen it. I should have warned her. And because I had not warned her, she had died most horridly, and left me to live in a long nightmare from which it seemed that I would never be free.

I did not think about the rose pearls, how Richard came to have them, in that slim box which now lay on my dressing-table. Some days, when the sun was shining and the frost was bright and the air sharp and sweet, I would tell myself that he had seen some pearls in a Chichester shop and bought them for me, thinking that I would like them, to remind me of my mama. But at other times near the end of November when the days grew darker and the nights long, I looked into the embers of the fire and saw Richard in a dirty alehouse, paying a man to kill Mama and John. Richard, with that mad absent-minded smile and his blue eyes shining. Richard, as mad as a rabid dog. My brother, my husband, the father of my child.

I blamed myself for not complaining of him, for not warning my mama, for not alerting my Uncle John. But for one thing I blamed myself no longer: that time in the summer-house. I was not to blame. Richard had raped me, as surely and as wrongly as if he had held a gun in my face to do it. I was in a daydream in the summer-house – but I had been thinking of James, not Richard. I had dreamed of love-making there once before, but that was with the sight, and it had been a dream of being Beatrice with Ralph. I had never thought of Richard as my lover and he had no right to court me, and no right to force me.

It made me icy towards him, those days before Christmas. I knew then that I was trapped just as Ralph had warned me. Richard had raped me and isolated me till I had neither lover, nor friend nor parent to turn to. And the child which I was unwillingly carrying was a product of violence and incest.

I think Richard knew that he had pushed me over the boundary into some cold certainty, for he left me much alone. I think he began to fear me, and indeed, when I caught sight of myself twisting the rose pearls around my throat and of my blank horror-struck eyes in a mirror, I could understand his fear.

Stride and Mrs Gough prepared for a quiet Christmas and Richard ordered George to bring in some boughs of holly and a yule-log. They made their preparations around me as if I were some stone goddess, insensate but powerful, who had to be propitiated with the correct ceremonies. The whole household was aware of my growing strangeness and absence, and conspired to blame it on the pregnancy, on the weather, on my mourning for my mama, on anything, rather than face the fact that I was so sick in my heart that I was barely alive at all.

Only Acre dared to tackle the blackness head-on, but Acre was wise in the madness of the Laceys. They had suffered from Laceys before and they knew the signs. I think they feared for me, for I had once been well loved.

'What ails you, Miss Julia?' Mrs Tyacke asked me. She had come to see Mrs Gough in the kitchen, and had begged leave to pay her respects to me as I sat idly in the parlour. I had called her out of her cottage before it was crushed by the falling spire. I had been her son's friend and playmate, and she had not forgotten. They had not forgotten me in Acre. Her sharp eyes were bright on my face, but I could not summon a smile even for her.

I heard her question. I heard it over and over in my head. Then I recognized it. She had used the same words Ralph had used to Richard that day on the common when Richard had broken the legs of his hawk. 'What ails you?' he had said then. Wise Ralph had seen the madness of the Laceys in Richard. He had not seen it in me.

'Is the baby too much for you?' she asked.

'No,' I said quietly. 'I am quite well.'

'We are all afraid for you,' she said blankly. 'No one in the village has seen you for so long. You do not come to church and we never see you in Acre. When we ask your husband, he just laughs in his merry way.'

I looked up from the flames flickering around the logs. 'Does he?' I said.

'It's all gone wrong again,' she said, and her voice quavered like a disappointed child's. 'It's all gone wrong again.'

I nodded. There was little I could say.

'Other places manage,' she said. 'Other villages have estates which make a profit and keep a village and have a mill which keeps grinding. Why does it never work for Acre?'

'Other places have squires who leave the land alone,' I said listlessly. 'Acre has always had squires who care so much for the land that they cannot leave be. Richard wants Wideacre to be the first estate in the land in the new century. He wants it to be the finest inheritance in the land for the son he is hoping will be born.'

'And you?' she asked me sharply. 'You wanted something special for Acre too. You and Ralph Megson made Acre all sorts of promises.'

'I was a Lacey squire too,' I said dully. 'The future I planned for the place was very different from the future it will have under Richard. But I was still a Lacey squire imposing my will on Acre then. Mrs Tyacke, I believe things will be wrong for Acre until there is no Lacey family on Wideacre and no squire in the hall, and no master over the village. I think Ralph was right all along, but much good that thought does the village now I am no longer the squire, but just the squire's lady. And much good that does Ralph, locked away in some cell in London. And much good that thought does me,' I added, my voice low.

'And you'll be the mother of the next Lacey squire,' she said. 'You'll keep the line going.'

'No,' I said with certainty. 'Not I.'

She nodded at my swelling belly as I sat carelessly, legs half apart to carry the load. 'Too late to be rid of it now,' she said. Her face was hard.

'It'll be born,' I said bitterly. 'I cannot prevent that. But it will never inherit if I can help it.'

She gave a sad, rueful smile, the smile of Acre when it knew it had lost the greatest gamble a landless people can play, when the stakes are land and independence against a servitude of uncertain and low-paid work. It was the smile of a woman legally bound to a master, who cannot prevent conception and cannot stop the birth of a child.

'You cannot help it,' she said sadly. 'We are all trapped now.'

There was silence in the little room, a silence so quiet that the noise of the flames flickering around the logs was quite clear.

'I'll be off,' she said, moving towards the door. 'My son Ted, and many others in the village, wanted to know how you were. I'm sorry to have no better news for them.'

'I'll live,' I said dourly. 'You can tell them I do not ail.'

'I'll tell them you are sick unto death in your heart,' she said plainly. 'And so you are at one with the land again, Miss Julia, and at one with Acre too. For the land is muddy and lifeless, and Acre is cold and hungry and idle and in mourning.'

Our eyes met in one level look which exchanged no warmth except the bleak comfort of shared honesty. Then she was gone.

In all that hard cold month she was my only visitor, Mrs Tyacke, the widow from Acre. No Quality visited me while I sat, idle and plump, in my black mourning. Grandpapa Havering had been taken ill in town and Grandmama had gone up to nurse him. She was afraid she would be away as I neared my time, but I wrote to her that it did not matter, she was not to worry.

Indeed it did not matter.

I thought that nothing mattered very much.

I thought that nothing would ever matter very much again.

The baby grew in my belly, as babies will, unbidden. I slept less and less at nights while the little growing limbs pressed inwards against me, or dug outwards against the soft wall of my belly. Towards the end of December I could sometimes discern a little limb pushing out, and once I felt with my fingertips the outline of a perfect tiny hand as the child flexed against the walls of its soft prison. It put me in mind of Ralph, in a prison where the gates would not open, where it was not warm and dark and safe. But as I sat in my chair, or gazed out of the window, or lay on my back on my bed, I could not even feel that Ralph mattered very much.

Richard was much away from home. I knew that they talked of it, in the kitchen, in the stable. Some nights he did not come home at all but appeared at breakfast, bright-eyed and rumpled, speaking quickly and loudly of a cocking match at Chichester, or once of a bull which someone had brought on to Acre. It had been baited with dogs, and it had killed two fine mastiffs. When Richard told me how it had ripped out the belly of one dog, I turned pale and the breakfast table swam before my eyes. I saw Stride give a quick movement as if he would stop Richard from speaking, but Stride had been in service all his life, and could not stop the squire. No one could stop Richard.

They all feared him, both in our household and on our land. They feared him because he would use the vested legal power of the squire in any way he could. He would cancel their tenancies, stop their wages, throw them out of the parish or have them arrested for insolence. And they feared him because they knew, as all the animals around him had always known, that there was something bad about Richard.

Not I. I had recovered from my fear of him. I feared no one now. I feared neither injury nor death, and if Richard had come to me and tightened his hands around my throat, I would have felt no fear. I would not even have flinched. My mama was dead, Clary was dead, Ralph and Acre were betrayed. I had sworn the baby in my belly should not inherit. If Richard had murdered me on one of the nights he lurched against my door on the way to his own room, he would have done me a favour. I feared him no more. I feared nothing. Everything I had cared for was already gone. If he had opened my door on those nights when I heard him scrabbling on the stairs and giggling drunkenly, if he had stumbled into my room and offered once more to touch me, I think I would have welcomed him and let him lie on me in the hope that he would put his long strong hands around my throat and finish me. But he did not do so. He never touched me again.

He did not like me. He only half knew his own madness; I don't think he ever clearly saw what he had done. I think that chilling little giggle was the closest he ever came to knowing what it was he had done, or what he could do. But on that one occasion when he had touched me and seen my eyes go dark with horror and then grow like pale glass with madness, he had known then that I was crazed. And knowing I was mad was like an enchanted mirror held up to his own face. Our joint corruption was too strong even for him.

Now I no longer feared him, because he feared me. I carried around with me a great strength and a great power: the magic of my growing belly which housed the child he so badly wanted, and the utter potency of not caring whether I lived or died. Richard could never frighten me again.

But nothing could touch him. In the little world which enclosed the Laceys nothing could touch Richard. With Lord Havering away, Richard's word was law for miles in every direction. If he had killed again, there would have been no hue and cry after the murderer. Richard was his own master and was safe from every threat I could imagine.

He feared only one thing. Fool that he was, he let that fear show in front of me.

We were at breakfast and Richard was in one of his sulky tired states. I sat at the foot of the table with a letter from my grandmama by my place, sipping tea. Richard had a hearty meal of cold meat, bread, hot potatoes and eggs and small ale. He was reading the newspaper as he ate, careless of the splattering of fat on the pages.

'Good God!' he said, around a mouthful of food. Some tone in his voice made me jerk up my head like a pointer in August, with the half-forgotten scent of pheasant on the ground. I think I actually sniffed like a dog. There was a sudden smell of fear in the room, unmistakable. Richard was sweating with fright, and the scent was as good to me as frying bacon to a starving pauper. He shot a quick, furtive look at me, and my gaze was blank. I could have been deaf, I could have been insensible. Then he glanced at Stride, whose face was wooden.

'Excuse me,' Richard said, and he crumpled the newspaper in his hand and left the room, his plate abandoned, piled with steaming food, his small ale cold and inviting in his mug.

'Get me a copy of that newspaper, Stride,' I said levelly, my eyes on my letter once more.

'Yes, Miss Julia,' Stride said, his tone equally neutral.

He must have sent to Midhurst at once, for he had it at coffee-time and brought it to me in the parlour with the silver tray and the coffee service.

I did not have to scan the columns. The story which had sent Richard from the room was on the first page inside. It was headed: 'Notorious Rioter Escaped', and it named Ralph Megson as among three men who had broken out of the prison disguised as members of a gypsy family who had been brought in to play for the prison warders. It was thought that the men had fled with the gypsies and would travel with them. There was much lordly huffing and puffing and alerting of the local Justices, but there was also a clear acknowledgement that three men could easily disappear into that secretive underworld and never be seen again. There was a detailed description of Ralph, and of the other two, and a massive reward of two hundred pounds for information leading to the capture of all three.

That reward made me pause and wonder if there could be any safety for Ralph. Then I thought that Ralph was not a man to be taken by surprise, except on that one time when he had been betrayed in Acre. I did not think he would be betrayed by his own people, by his mother's people, his gypsy family. And I had a shrewd idea that Ralph would know exactly how long they could be trusted to resist the lure of such a fortune, and he would be away on a smuggler's vessel the day before temptation became too great.

I squeezed each page of the newspaper into a ball and tossed them one by one on to the fire, and watched each little ball flame and blacken before I took up the poker and mashed up the ashes. I did not want Richard to know that I knew about Ralph.

That was the first time in my life I had effectively conspired against Richard.

He did not come home for dinner, and Stride served me in solitary state at the great mahogany table. I sat with a book beside my plate, a novel from the Chichester circulating library, and between mouthfuls I read about Clarinda's wants and needs, and her unfailing tenderness for the hero. I wondered a little whether I should ever again be a woman who thinks that love, a man's love, is worth the world, or whether from now on I would always feel that one's own freedom, one's own individual pride, is worth so very much more.

I took my novel with me into the parlour, and slouched in my armchair to read it. But I laid it down often and looked into the fire. I had not thought to feel happiness again. But Ralph was free, and some bars had gone from my inner eyes. Ralph could look up at the sky tonight and see the sharp light of the stars which means that it is going to snow. Ralph could see that halo around the moon which warns of frost. Ralph could face north, south, west or east, and go where he willed again.

I hoped he would guess that I had learned my lesson, that although I sat at Richard's fireside on Richard's furniture in Richard's house on Richard's land, I knew at last that I was dispossessed. And that I had become, at this last, a Lacey woman who knew that it was the ownership of the land which mattered more than the chimera of love.

But I thought also that I was a new version of a Lacey, because I rejected the Lacey right to own the land and its crops, and the people themselves. If it had been mine again, I would have given it away at once, without hesitation and mumbling of profits. I would have given the land to Acre, to the people who work it and live on it. And I wished very much that I could see Ralph just once more to tell him that I at last knew what he had been trying to teach me. That there can be no just squires, no kindly masters. For the existence of squires and masters is so deeply unjust that no gentle benevolence can make it right.

I had had to become a servant, Richard's servant, before I knew the injustice of servitude. I had had to be a pauper, Richard's pauper, before I learned that dependence is a death sentence. And the only want that was left me, the only wish I had, was that I might see Ralph once and tell him that I understood, that I too was an outlaw from this greedy world we Quality had made.

Stride tapped at the door and came in with the tea-tray, and Richard walked in behind him. He had been riding and was not dressed for dinner. He asked Stride to bring more candles and sat opposite me on the other side of the fire as though nothing were wrong. But I saw he was as tense as a trip-wire, and he glanced at the curtains when they stirred in the draught.

'I have been to Chichester,' he said without preamble when Stride had set a five-branch candelabra on the table and gone. 'I read some news this morning which disturbed me very much.'

I raised my eyes from the tea things and their gaze was as clear and as warm as the wintry sky.

'There was a report.' Richard spoke with some difficulty. 'There was a report in the paper that some men had broken out of the London prison where Ralph Megson was held. You remember . . .' He broke off. He had been about to ask if I remembered Ralph Megson, but not even Richard had sufficient gall for that. 'I went to Chichester to seek more perfect information,' he said. He took his dish from me and a drop of tea was spilled on the cream hearthrug. Richard's hand was not steady. 'It turns out that the report is true,' he said. I inclined my head, and took up my own dish.

'Magistrates have been warned to be alert for gypsies,' Richard went on. 'Gypsies or travelling folk of any kind. The three men escaped with some gypsy musicians. It's thought they may try to get to the coast travelling with a gypsy family.'

Richard stopped talking and glanced at me. My face was impassive; he could read nothing from it. 'Do you think he would come here, Julia?' he demanded. 'Do you think he would come here with some sort of idea of revenge? Do you think he would come here and hope that Acre would hide him?'

Richard's voice had his old charming appeal. He needed me. I had always been at his side when he needed me. Indeed, it had been the joy of my life to have him need me, to have him ask for my help as he was asking for it now.

'I think he might blame me for his arrest,' he said with driven candour. 'I spoke to the magistrates in Chichester, and they said there was little they could do to protect us, us Laceys, Julia! Unless we had some clear idea of where he might be.'

Richard put down his dish of tea and held out his hand to me. 'Julia?' he asked. It was as if we were small children again and he was in trouble, as if he were a little boy whose scheme of mischief had gone badly wrong, calling for his best friend, his sister, to help him.

I held my tea with both hands. 'Yes?' I asked.

'Do you think he would come here?' Richard withdrew his hand and put both hands together on his knees, ignoring the slight.

'No,' I said honestly. It is not my way to tease and torment a person. And I spoke with regret. I was very sure I would never see Ralph Megson again, and I thought myself the poorer for it.

'Not with the gypsies who winter on the common?' Richard said eagerly. 'They come from London way, don't they? And they are late this year! It would not be them who got him from prison, would it? They are musicians too, remember, Julia! We had them to play at Christmas, do you remember?'

I nodded. I remembered. I thought I remembered everything in a great long tunnel of pain back to my childhood and babyhood when I had loved Richard and loved Wideacre with a great constant rooted love which I thought nothing would ever spoil or change.

'I remember,' I said. 'But I should have thought Mr Megson's safest course would be to take a ship out of London. He had many seafaring friends too.'

'You don't think he would come here?' Richard insisted. His eyes on my face were as urgent as those of a child woken from a nightmare, demanding reassurance.

'No,' I said steadily. I was not rescuing Richard from his fears to oblige him. There was that deathly coldness around my heart still which made me think that I would never again wish to help anyone, least of all Richard. But I was too remote from him to tease him either.

'If he came here, would Acre hide him?' Richard persisted. 'They hid Dench the groom, remember, Julia!'

'I don't know,' I said. 'I never go to Acre these days, Richard, you know I have not been there since the autumn. You must know better than I what the mood of the village is. Would they hide an enemy of yours? Or do they cleave to the Laceys?'

Richard jumped from his chair in sudden impatience, and some cold quiet part of my mind thought yes, you are truly afraid, are you not, Richard? You who have done so much to make so many people afraid of you. All of Acre, and Clary who must have looked in your face before she died in terror, whose fear is so unbearable to me that it is walled away in a rose-pearled corner of my frozen mind. And now you are most bitterly afraid.

'I want you to go to Acre,' Richard said suddenly. 'I want you to go down there tomorrow. I'll order out the carriage for you, and if you cannot get there in the carriage, you will have to go in the gig. Or you will have to ride! It surely would not hurt you to ride if the horse only walked, and the groom could even lead it to make absolutely sure that you were safe. I want you to go down there and tell them that Ralph has escaped and that he is a danger to the public safety. There is a big reward on his head, Julia! I want you to tell them that too. I want you to tell them that if he comes to Acre, I personally will give one hundred pounds to anyone who gives us warning. That should do it! Won't it, Julia?'

'That depends on how poor the village is at present,' I said levelly. 'Are things so bad that they would betray an old friend for a hundred pounds?'

Richard strode impatiently to the windows, but he did not draw the curtains to look out. Ralph was a marksman.

'*You* are supposed to be their great friend,' he said impatiently. 'If you ask them to tell if Megson comes to the village, they would do it as a favour to you, would they not?'

'I cannot say,' I said. I reached to the bell-pull and rang for Stride to clear the tea things away. 'I really cannot say, Richard. I am loath even to consider going. I am only two weeks away from when the baby is due. I am sure Mr Saintly would advise against me going far from the house. He told me to stay indoors some months ago, as you may remember.'

Richard spun on his heel, but bit back his reply as Stride came into the room. Stride glanced curiously at the two of us, and I saw him hesitate to leave me alone with Richard.

'You needn't wait,' Richard said rudely.

Stride's glance went to me, and I nodded. 'It is all right, Stride,' I said. He bowed slightly, and went out.

'You are my wife,' Richard said, and now he had himself under control. 'This is a matter of some importance which affects the good running of our lands and, indeed, my personal safety. You will go to Acre because I wish it, Julia.'

I nodded calmly. 'If you wish it,' I said. I had nothing to lose. If I was taken ill in Acre, I could go to the vicarage or any one of a dozen cottages for the birth of my child. If I had to ride and the baby was damaged, I had hardened my heart to it. I had sworn I would not rear a squire for Wideacre, and I meant it. I might love the little child who rolled and kicked in my womb, but I would not raise another Lacey to lord it in Acre. I prayed that it would die at birth.

To tell the truth, I prayed that I would die too.

So it mattered little to me if I rode or drove, if my child came early at Acre or in a frozen ditch on the way home. Nothing mattered very much any more. Now Ralph was free, there was nothing I had yet to do, except to get this baby born, and then to get it away from Richard and from Wideacre. It must be hidden, or fostered, or killed.

Besides, an appeal to Acre to betray Ralph was hardly worth the breeze which blew my words away. It was a dream of Richard's that *anyone* could turn Acre against Ralph. He was the counterpoint to the discord of the Laceys. He was their black squire. They might give us their loyalty from time to time, they might sell or be robbed of their labour. They might have a season of loving us or of hating us. But Ralph was the man they could trust. If he wanted to stay safe in England, he would come here. There was not enough money minted to buy a betrayal.

The carriage stopped on the village green under the old chestnut tree where the old men gather in the evening, the natural site for a parley. I stood on the steps of the carriage and waited while the cottage doors opened and people came out. I saw the old familiar faces of Acre, and I saw that they were, once more, as I had known them in my girlhood: pinched, wan, cold.

They were not starving – Ralph's hidden wheat would last till spring as he had planned. They were not ill clothed. They had savings which would last them for a while. But the heart was out of them again, and I thought that this time the winter was even worse for them, because for one sweet year they had learned to hope for better.

Poor fools. Poor silly fools. And I the greatest fool of all to have the chance of such happiness for so many people in my hand and to give it away because I was too much of a coward to stand up and say, 'I have been cruelly attacked, and it was *not* my fault.'

They gathered around me in a circle and I knew my face was grim. The child inside my belly stirred and kicked, and I rested one hand on it. I could not help the pang of tenderness I felt every time the little one stirred inside me. But when I saw the eyes of Acre upon me, as leaden as sick cattle, I knew that this child must not be raised here.

This child must not be raised at all.

I should remember what Ralph had said about the French monarchs. I should remember that he said you have to plough before you can sow. The Laceys must be cleaned off Wideacre. The angry ugly French revolutionaries were going to execute their king. I was going to eradicate the Lacey line.

I looked around at the blank faces and I raised my voice. 'My husband has ordered me to come and speak to you,' I said clearly, so that there should be no doubt whose message it was. 'He has learned that Mr Ralph Megson, who was once manager here, has escaped from prison.'

I looked round quickly, but there was no surprise or delight on any face. They knew already, then. I had thought they would.

'A reward of two hundred pounds has been offered for information to bring about the capture of Mr Megson and the men who fled with him,' I said. I was repeating Richard's words by rote and they would all know well enough that this was an empty formality we were enacting. 'My husband wishes you to know that if Mr Megson is taken in Acre, he will reward the village handsomely. He will pay one hundred pounds each to every man who assists in the recapture. There will be free flour and free milk for the whole village until sowing time.'

There was a ripple of interest at that, not because they saw the opportunity for earning such wealth, but because they read from that bribe the extent of Richard's fear. I saw all around me that people were hiding smiles, and I could scarce keep the amused contempt from my own voice.

'My husband asks me to remind you that Mr Megson was a known rioter, and a dangerous man,' I said. 'It is thought that he may be hiding with the gypsies, and you are ordered to report any new gypsy families arriving on the common at once.'

They nodded. I waited a moment, then I turned to go back into the coach. I was unaccountably weary and my back ached. I wanted to drive home as fast as I possibly could and go to bed for the afternoon. I would call for the kitchenmaid to light a fire in my room and watch the flames flicker while the light drained from the window. I just wanted to be in the warm darkness and away from this cold land, and these icy skies and these betrayed people.

'Miss Julia!' someone said. I paused. George had folded up the steps, but he paused and held open the door so I could lean forward and see who wanted me.

It was old Mrs Merry.

I flinched away from her worn face as if I feared she might strike me. All my life I had known that round face, as rosy and as wrinkled as a winter apple. But since the loss of her grandson, all the skin had dropped down, and all the lines around her eyes, around her mouth, had lost their habit of smiling.

She came to the front of the crowd and looked up at me, sitting in the rich high-sprung carriage lined with pink silk which Richard had bought for us to replace the bloodstained one abandoned outside Haslemere. I looked down at her like some fairy princess with an old fortune-teller.

'Yes, Mrs Merry?'

Her pale blue eyes were swimming, and the soft wrinkled skin of her cheeks was wet with her old-woman tears. But I knew that she was not weeping for herself and for her loneliness and the death of her grandson. She was weeping for me. She pitied me.

'You deserved better than this, sweetheart,' she said, and her thin voice was full of compassion. A couple within earshot nodded their support and I saw them all looking at me as if I were a victim, as well as Acre. 'We all hoped for a better world,' she said. 'We have been betrayed by the squire, by the power of the gentry. But even though you are gentry yourself, you were not safe. You're a woman and you have had to learn your master, even as we have learned that lesson again.'

I thought how Richard had mastered me, through my loyalty and love for him, through his violence, and then by the convention of the world which said I *had* to marry the father of my child.

'I hate him, Mrs Merry,' I said. 'I wish he were dead.'

She nodded, her face showing no shock. 'Aye,' she said. 'You would do. But don't waste your courage on hating him. Keep yourself *to* yourself, dearie. And keep up your courage and think of a healthy baby.'

'I won't have another squire for Wideacre,' I said in swift contradiction. I had raised my voice, and a couple of the men turned and listened to what we were saying. 'I won't be the mother of a squire. I won't set a child to have power over the land, nor power over you people. I won't do that.'

She nodded. 'It would be a better world indeed if the masters would refuse to rule,' she said. 'All Acre has ever done is refuse to obey, and we have been tricked and betrayed out of that resolve time after time.'

I hung my head. It was my high hopes and my bright plans and my quickly dishonoured promises which had tricked them this time. Everything around me, my love of the land, my love of Richard, seemed to have been corrupted and made bad.

'I must go,' I said miserably.

Mrs Merry stepped back and George shut the door, his town-bred face impassive. I pulled down the window strap and leaned out. George turned to get up on the back, out of earshot.

'What can I do?' I said urgently to Mrs Merry. 'How can I stop this?'

Her head came up slowly and her eyes met mine and, surprisingly, flowered into a broad sweet smile. 'Do?' she said. '*You* need do nothing, Miss Julia!' George was on the box, smart in his livery, straining his ears, I guessed. 'Ralph will do it,' Mrs Merry said sweetly. 'Ralph is on his way home again.'

'What . . .?' I started, but the horses were moving forward and one of the men had taken Mrs Merry's arm to hold her safely away from the high carriage-wheels. He saw my face, the astonishment, the dawning hope and he grinned at me, the old Acre grin of complete equality.

It was the grin of conspirators who at last have some hopes of victory. The carriage whirled me away and I fell back against Richard's silk cushions. I knew I was smiling too, and my heart suddenly became light.

'What did they say in Acre?' Richard demanded of me. He was at the garden gate, ready to hand me from the carriage.

'Nothing,' I said. I let him lead me up the path and into the hall, but I hesitated when he opened the parlour door. 'I want to rest in my bedroom, Richard. I am very tired.'

He let me go to the stairs, but he wanted more news. 'Did you say what I told you to say?' he asked.

'Yes,' I said.

'And what did they say?' he pressed me.

'They said nothing,' I said.

'Did you speak to no one privately? Did no one mention whether the gypsies were on the common yet? Did no one in particular ask about Megson? What about Ned Smith? – *he* was always very thick with Megson.'

I looked at Richard, standing at the foot of the staircase, and I raised my eyebrows at him. I was insolent and I knew it. But I had a new courage, a new reason for courage, because I knew that there was a clock ticking away under our life in the Dower House, because I knew that soon the hour was going to strike and the clapper would fall and this whole rotten life would smash to pieces. Two events were converging: the child in my belly was moving slowly to be born, and Ralph was travelling the secret ways from London, concealed in a gypsy cart, along little tracks down hidden paths that the gentry did not even know.

'I spoke to no one privately,' I said, ticking off Richard's questions on gloved fingers. 'No one said whether the gypsies had arrived on the common yet, but since they always come around Christmas, I should think they will be there any day now. No one asked about Mr Megson. Ned Smith was there with the rest of them, but he did not speak out.'

Richard took my hand roughly in a tight grip. 'What has got into you?' he demanded. His eyes were sharp, and he looked me over from my suddenly brightened face down to my feet standing squarely on the stair. 'Someone said something which has made you feel that you can challenge me,' he said accurately. 'Someone has made you feel that you can look at me with those impertinent grey eyes. Someone has tried to make you forget what I can do to you.' He broke off and he looked at me measuringly. I could feel his hand tighten on mine, I could feel the bones shift together and the sinews sing in pain.

'No one,' I said. 'I have lost my fear of you because I can see that you are afraid. I can see that you think that Ralph Megson is on his way back home. And you are afraid that he is coming for you.'

I paused. Richard had gone white, and his grip on my hand was suddenly slack. My bones were throbbing with pain, but my heart was pounding in excitement.

'I think you are right,' I said, and my spirits leaped to see how his eyes flashed to my face, alert with fright. 'If Ralph is indeed coming home, then he will be coming to settle his score with you. I know him well,' I continued sweetly. 'And I must say that if I were you and had betrayed him to his death, then I would rather be dead and in the family vault than have Ralph Megson coming after me. For be very sure, Richard, it is the only place you will be safe!'

Richard blenched and dropped his eyes, and I looked at his downcast face for a second before I turned on my heel and went up the stairs to my room. I felt his eyes on my back and I kept my head high as I climbed one weary step after another. Not until I was safe in my room did I lean back against the door and shudder.

I might face Richard down when he was in a twitch of nerves about Ralph, but without the courage given me by one frail old lady I was in a poor state. The baby was heavy in my belly; I was drained by the weight of it and the fatigue of it.

I might talk bravely about ending the line of the squires, but my heart was weak with love for my baby. Knowing its father and our line, I could not help fearing the birth of some dread monstrosity, some freak. Then I thought of the feel of that perfect little hand through my belly wall and I wanted to weep for love of it, a love that I should never be able to show.

The baby had to be sent away and Richard had to be stopped. I had to find some courage from somewhere to face the struggle with Richard, to resist his anger, to resist his corrupt power and somehow to keep free of the sucking madness which Richard had released upon us.

I might talk bravely of dying in childbirth and thus ending the line, but in truth I was very much afraid.

I might talk bravely about fostering the child, or killing it, but my heart was weak for its touch, and I longed to hold its little body.

I might talk bravely about defeating Richard, about hating him, but I had loved him all my life, and I sometimes thought I had imagined the monster which he had become.

I fell into bed like a sickly child and slept while the January sky darkened at my window. I awoke cold, in a darkened room, at neither dawn nor dusk, and I did not know where I was, nor what time it was, and felt afraid.

Richard was not at home for dinner that afternoon. Stride said that he had ridden in to Chichester and would not be back until late. I thought I knew where he had gone. He came into the parlour when Stride brought in the tea, and he confirmed my guess. He had ridden to Chichester and been all day at the barracks. He had brought home with him half a dozen soldiers to be quartered at the Bush in the village.

'I told them that Acre cannot be trusted, and that Ralph may come here and try to start a riot against us,' Richard said. He waved away a dish of tea and rang the bell for a mug of ale.

He had not eaten since breakfast; his eyes were very bright. Richard, the lovely brave child of my girlhood, was a very frightened man. I watched him over my dish and my heart was torn between triumph and sadness for the boy that had gone.

'I had a deal of trouble making them take me seriously,' he said. His face was sulky with worry. 'If it hadn't been for the first riot here, I think they would have refused me,' he said. 'It's too bad! I wish Grandpapa Havering was here; they'd have to listen to him.

'All they would tell me was that they thought it most unlikely that Megson would stay in the country, and that there was good intelligence from London that he and the others had taken ship to the Americas. They simply would not credit the fact that I believe he will come here.'

I nodded and said nothing.

'The gypsies have arrived,' Richard said. 'I told the soldiers to keep close watch on them. It is just the usual families. But you never can tell with those people.'

I nodded again. Richard went to the parlour door and hallooed towards the kitchen for another mug of beer. He was thirsty. I imagined he had been drinking Hollands in Chichester for courage, after his visit to the barracks.

'Why did you lie to me about your visit to Acre?' he said suddenly.

I jumped, and spilled a little tea on my dark gown. 'I didn't,' I said, too quickly.

'You did,' he said. He was smiling slightly now. It always cheered Richard to catch me out. He came back inside the room and went to his favourite chair. Stride, his face a frozen mask of disapproval, brought in the second mug of ale on a silver tray and placed it by Richard's elbow. Now his humiliation at the barracks and his fear of Ralph were half forgotten in the pleasure of bullying his servants and his wife. 'You spoke privately with one of the old women,' he said. 'Who?'

I heard the hectoring tone of the bully of my childhood and my old craven spirit quailed. Then I thought of Ralph coming slowly along the secret paths towards Acre, and my baby coming along the secret tunnels to the world.

And I thought also, at last, of myself. My survival in these lonely times depended on my finding some rock in my own life which I could build on. I had lost Clary and my mama. I had lost Ralph. I had lost my land and the power of being the heir to Wideacre. From somewhere in my own heart I *had* to find some base in my own life. If I trembled every time Richard was crossed, he would master me indeed. He would master me for ever.

'I did speak privately with one of the old women,' I said steadily. 'It was nothing which need concern you. It was not business.'

Richard looked at me askance. 'I hear you mentioned my name,' he said. 'I'm told you spoke against me.' Richard looked shifty. He trusted neither his informant, nor his wife, nor the village which was his own.

I paused with a sudden fear. Surely there could be no friend to

Richard in Acre? No paid informant who had spoken against me? Someone who would inform against Ralph? In all my confidence of Acre's loyalty I had always been certain that Acre could not be suborned. But someone had listened to me talk to Mrs Merry. And someone had reported that speech to Richard.

George.

Richard's smart new groom, George.

It could be no other. He was a newcomer from out of the county, hired by Richard for his sly face and his quick ears to replace Jem. He did not know one old woman of Acre from another, so the report he brought to Richard was vague.

I looked at Richard with contempt. And he, in his morass of suspicion, saw only that I was unafraid and thought that George had lied to him, that he could trust no one, not even his paid spy.

'You listen to servants' tittle-tattle and you'll get false reports,' I said disdainfully. Richard flushed dark red. 'I spoke to no one,' I said coldly. 'But you need not reprimand your spy for getting things wrong. He will not again ride behind me when I drive. Not to Acre, not to a bishop's tea-party. I won't have a dirty little spy in my employ. So you can dismiss him, or, if he is on the box, you will be alone in the carriage.'

My head held as high as a princess's, I swept from the room and did not stop until I reached my bedroom door and shut it tight behind me. It was a gamble. No one knew that better than I.

But if I could face Richard down when he was afraid of the rumour of Ralph's return, if I could look at him with eyes of burning scorn when he had, indeed, caught me out, then I thought I might have some sort of future on the land.

Acre was smiling again. Acre had once more the impertinent grin of a community which knows itself to be badly mastered and recks little what the masters say. I thought that even I, in the big house, in the bed of the squire of Acre, might learn that courage too.

I undressed, but I kept on Mama's rose-pearl necklace and her ear-rings. They comforted me a little as I slid between the cold sheets. Since the baby had grown so large, I had taken to sleeping on my back with my rounded moon-shaped belly pointing at the ceiling. I sprawled out in the bed and sighed as the little kicks and wriggles started, making my own body leap like a net of eels. Sometimes I loathed this child as the misbegotten heir of Wideacre, sometimes I adored it as the fruit of my body, my own child. And sometimes, like now when I was tired, I just sighed like any pregnant woman and wished the hours away and the sleepless night over.

The baby was quieter than usual, and I fell asleep by candle-light, forgetting to blow out the flame. So Richard was in my room, and naked in my bed, before I was awake and before I could stir myself to protest.

He had one hand over my mouth in case I should cry out, and the other, urgently, pulled at my nightgown. I could have bitten his hand, I suppose. The palm was salty against my teeth, and it felt dirty. But I did not think of doing it.

I did not think of doing it.

I was shamed that I did not think.

I thrashed a little, under the sheets, encumbered by the great belly on me and the tucked-in covers. I gave a little smothered moan behind his hard hand, and he saw my eyes widen in distress and darken with horror. But he smiled his blue-eyed devil's smile, and I knew then that the madness was on Richard and that it might – at last, at last – be the end for me tonight.

It was not lust for him. It was not love or desire, nor any hot half-forgivable sin. It was power and cruelty which were driving Richard onward. He had seen the tilt of my head, he had seen the bright courage in my eyes, and he had waited until I was asleep and unguarded, and then he had come for me. He was in my bed, his hand hard on my face, his other hand pulling up my nightdress and his weight coming down on top of me.

He drew the hem of the gown up to my neck, and I froze as his hand brushed across my throat, across the pearls. I knew he was thinking longingly of throttling me as I lay there, eyes wide with fear, beneath him.

When I saw him smile, I knew I was lost.

I was ready. I had promised Mrs Tyacke, I had promised Mrs Merry with all of Acre listening. I would not give them another squire to rule over them. I would end the line of the Laceys. If Richard killed me tonight, that would be the end of me and of Richard's heir – and of Richard too, for they would have to take him up for my murder. I gritted my teeth at the discomfort of the weight of him on top of my rounded belly, and at the distasteful hand against my mouth. And I gritted my teeth for courage and said a swift farewell in my mind to the things I had loved – to James, to Wideacre, to Mama. For I was readying myself for death.

He was heavy. He was half on me, half beside me. The weight of the unborn child kept me pinned to the bed. He put his hand back on the great swelling of my belly and stroked down the slope when his devil-begotten child shifted uneasily as if it knew my fear.

'Oh, Julia,' he said longingly, half to himself. 'I had forgotten this. It is only this that saves your life tonight.'

I tried to keep my face impassive.

'I meant to strangle you,' he said dreamily. 'I am sick of your long face around the house. There are other women I could have here if you were gone. There are other girls I could marry. I wanted you because you had Wideacre, but now it is mine, and I want you no more.'

The candle guttered, throwing menacing shadows on the ceiling above me. But nothing was more menacing than the shadow which was in my bed, which spoke such obscenities in such an intimate whisper.

'I *did* love you once,' he said as if he needed to reassure himself. 'When we were very little children, before we knew who we were, or what we were to inherit. I think I loved you then.' He broke off. He was talking to himself; it seemed he was in a dream of other times.

'I loved Mama-Aunt too,' he said. His voice was suddenly higher in pitch, childlike. I realized with an instinctual shudder that Richard had gone. He was back in the sunlight of his Wide-acre childhood with an aunt who adored him and a cousin who would cross the world for him. The world where he had been the beloved little tyrant.

'I loved Mama-Aunt so much,' he said sweetly. A shadow crossed his face. 'But you were always trying to be first in Acre,' he said, cross as a petulant child. 'Always trying to come between me and Mama-Aunt. You *would* push in where you were not wanted, Julia. And though I could forgive you if you were very, very sorry, I could not help but be so angry, so very angry, with the people you tried to take away from me . . . Are you listening to me, Julia?' Richard said with quick irritation.

I nodded, as obedient as a child in school. His grip had tightened on my mouth again. I feared I was going to retch at the smell of his hand against my teeth and gums, the odour of horse-sweat, cigar smoke, Hollands gin. And beneath it all the heart-wrenching smell of Richard, the cousin I had loved for so many years. So very many years.

'I killed her,' he said, speaking, at last, the unspeakable. 'Your friend Clary. I tried and tried to be friends with her. I even tried pretending I was in love with her. She laughed in my face!' His voice was shocked. 'She said you were worth ten of me.' He paused. 'I knew I'd pay her out for that.'

I watched him, and said nothing. His blue eyes had become hazy.

'She saw us,' he said, 'when I raped you in the summer-house. I looked up and saw her. I think she was going to run towards us, to help you. But she saw my face. She ran off as fast as she could towards Acre. I expect she thought to get help. I caught her at the Fenny,' he said languidly. 'I put my hand around her throat. She was like you, actually, because she was quite strong too. But do you know, she was so afraid, she hardly fought at all. She just choked and then her tongue and her eyes came out. Rather horrible. She looked so nasty I pushed her in the river and went home. I knew it would be all right for me. Everything always is all right for me.'

He sighed quietly. 'I killed your mama too,' he said. A petulant expression crossed his face; I could see the droop of his disappointed mouth in the firelight. 'She was running off with John. That was so horrible for her to do such a thing. She had joined with John against me. She sent me away as soon as he came home. I had thought she was a beautiful woman, a wonderful woman. A woman like an angel. But she was just a whore like all of them. Like you. As soon as my father came home, she was running after him like a bitch in heat. She forgot all about me. It was his idea to disinherit me, and she was going to do anything he wanted. She was going to overturn our marriage, and I would have been disinherited.' He paused. His face became calm again, his words measured, judicious. 'That was a very bad thing to do. You do not understand business, Julia, because you are just a woman, but that was a very meddlesome thing for Mama-Aunt to do.' He paused again. 'I am surprised she dreamed of it,' he said simply, with grave respect. 'She was, apart from that, such a feminine sort of woman.'

I lay as still as stone. I could feel my heart beating and I knew that in a moment the sound would remind Richard that underneath him, in his power, was another woman who had forgotten her place, who had tried to meddle with the ownership of the land.

'It hurt her, I am afraid,' he said regretfully. I half closed my eyes. I had to hang on to some shred of myself, some remnant of sanity not to cry out, not to scream at these words, as Mama's murderer lay on top of me and told me in his sweetest voice the horror that I had tried all these months to evade.

'It hurt her,' he said again. 'I shot Jem at once, you know. And then, with the other pistol, I shot John through the window. He had opened the door and was coming out at me. Rather brave of him, really. He was trying to protect Mama-Aunt, I expect. The shot threw him back into the carriage, over her knees, actually. She screamed. I expect the blood frightened her. But she didn't *do* anything.' He hesitated. 'Well, there was nothing she could do really,' he said fairly. 'I was reloading, but that doesn't take long. Then I waited.'

His hand was slack on my mouth again, his mad blue gaze dreamy in the candlelight. This time I could not have moved. I was frozen with horror and with a macabre fascination at his story.

'I waited,' he said. 'Then I got off the horse and opened the carriage door. The carriage horses were grazing at the verge, quite unafraid, even though there had been two shots. Funny that. I let my horse go beside them. Well, they're usually turned out in the field together. But it looked odd to see the three grazing off the hedge outside Haslemere with Jem dead on the box, and John dead in the carriage, and your mama so silent inside.

'I wanted to know what she was doing. Just that. Nothing more than that, really,' he said confidentially. 'I opened the carriage door with one hand. She was holding John's head in her lap. He had bled all over the carriage floor, and there was blood on her dress too. It made me so angry that she should spoil her dress with his blood. You know, Julia, it just made me so angry that she should be sitting with his dead head in her lap when *I* was in such trouble with you, and the baby, and the marriage, and Wideacre.' He broke off with a little reminiscent smile.

'She knew me at once!' he said, pleased. 'As soon as I opened the carriage door, she said, "Oh, Richard, what have you done!" And I said' – Richard's smile turned into a grin of delight as if he were coming to the enormously amusing conclusion of a tremendously funny story – 'I said, "I've killed you all, Mama-Aunt!" And then I shot her! I shot her right in the face!'

He laughed aloud, the happy laugh of the best-loved child of the household, and then he broke off in the middle of the peal of laughter to look down into my face. 'You're not laughing!' he said, instantly suspicious. 'You don't think it's funny.'

He took his hand from my mouth and my lips were stiff from being pushed back for so long.

'No,' I said, pursing my lips down over my gums again. 'I don't find it very funny, Richard.'

'It *is* funny,' he said, madly insistent.

And I saw then – as bright as a knife-blade in a lightning strike – what I had to do.

I went for my death.

'I don't believe you,' I said softly, provocatively. 'I don't think you did that. I don't think you would dare do that!'

'I did!' said Richard. His voice was that of an aggravated child.

'No,' I said. 'Not you! You like to do things in secret. I know you, Richard. You like dark woods where you strangled Clary. You like breaking the legs of a little hawk. You like night-time stables to cut the tendons of your horse. You'd never hold up a carriage in broad daylight. You're a coward, Richard. And everyone always knew.'

I was taking him up into insanity. I saw his eyes go blank with rage, as bright as sapphires.

'I did it!' he insisted.

'Prove it,' I said instantly. 'Put both hands around my neck and look me straight in the eye. You're a coward and you dare not do it!'

He put his hands at once on my throat, but his grip was slack.

'You are not the favoured child,' I said, goading him. 'You never were! Everyone always loved me, and they loved Mama. You were only ever in second place.'

'No!' he said.

'Oh, yes,' I said sweetly. 'What do you think Grandpapa Havering thinks of you, when everyone saw you could not ride? What d'you think Acre thinks of you, when everyone could see you were afraid of little village children? What d'you think Ralph thought of you? And Uncle John? They all despised you. Clary and I despised you! You killed Clary, but you dare not kill me!'

That did it. His hands on my throat clenched hard in a convulsive spasm of rage, and I shut my eyes and prayed to God that it would be quick and clean and that once I was dead, everyone would know it had been Richard and he would be hanged.

The land would be free of us Laceys for ever.

'Coward,' I croaked through my closing throat. 'Show me you're not a coward!'

Then there was an agonizing pain deep, deep inside me, right up high where I carried the baby who would die inside a dead womb. My whole body quivered like a terrier shaken by a rat. And I knew I had lost my chance to die.

Richard's incestuous rape-conceived bastard was moving on its way to be born. My little girl was ready for her birth.

Richard, heavy on my belly, felt the sudden movement and slackened his grip.

I would have kept silent and let him do it. I thought I had the will for it. I *knew* I had the will for it. But he suddenly released my neck and said in a frightened whisper, 'What is it? Is it the baby?'

And like a fool I nodded and said, as well as I could for a bruised throat, 'Yes.'

He bundled out of my bed at once in real fright, and I smiled wryly at the sight of him looking so like a husband with his bride about to give birth. Then the imperative needs of my body overcame thought, and I could feel and know nothing but the baby making her own potent way to the world. There was a sudden strange feeling, like an explosion of wetness, and the sheet below me was soaked with warm wet liquid, red as blood but clear as good wine.

Richard said, 'Ugh' in utter distaste, and his face was appalled.

'Get dressed,' I said, staring at the spreading stain. 'And go for the accoucheur.'

'I'll send Jenny to stay with you,' Richard said, tearing the door open in his hurry for help and in his hurry to leave my room with its sweet insistent smell of birth.

'No,' I said with quiet, mean cunning.

I knew what I would do next. I think I had known it from the day in Acre when I said I would not give birth to the next squire.

In France they would kill the King and end the line.

I was going to do the same.

But I could not stop the heir being born; I gritted my teeth on my terror of being alone and on my horror at the way my body was suddenly racked with a pain which seemed to last for ever for long unbelievable seconds. Then the pains came as insistently as waves sucking at a shingle bank with an unforgivable undertow. Jenny came in and found me squatting on the floor like some pauper outside an almshouse, and begged me to get back into bed. But then she saw the mess on the sheets and took me to the window-seat. I could see the moonlight ghostly and silver on the tops of the bare trees of the Wideacre woods and I heard an owl cry that seemed to say, 'Whooo, ooooh' for my pain.

In the room behind me I heard the bustle as she changed the sheets and the clang of the brass jug filled with hot water, but I did not look around. Then Stride was at the door with a basket full of wood to make up my bedroom fire. All the ordinary work went on around me and I was a little island of loneliness in the middle of it all with these sudden grips like a savage animal eating me, its teeth in my belly.

I started walking as if I could get away from the pain, walking in the cramped little space of the room along the far wall past the fireplace, into the bow of the window, turning before the dressing-table, and then back again. My nightdress brushed Jenny as I hobbled past her. I had to hold myself very tall not to grab her arm and cling to her and beg her not to leave me, for there were moments when I felt I was nothing but a young girl too small and too slight to give birth, with a terror in her mind and a baby in her belly, both of them tearing her apart.

'I'm afraid!' I said, with a little hopeless gasp.

Jenny looked at me with pity and rose from the fireplace. A thin flickering yellow flame lit the room and made the shadows bounce on the walls. The pain gripped me again and I gave a little gasp and started pacing. I had never felt so alone.

'The master has sent to Chichester,' she said. 'He's in the library. Shall I ask him to come and sit with you?'

I looked at her scathingly. 'I'd rather sit with the devil,' I said fiercely, and then my pain doubled me up with agony for long hard seconds and I could not catch my breath for another word.

'Would you see Mrs Merry from Acre?' Jenny asked diffidently. 'She's old, but she saw my ma through all of us.'

'No,' I said as I straightened up and wiped the sweat off my face with the back of one careless hand. Mrs Merry knew her business too well to leave me alone with the child when I had sworn to end the line. 'No,' I said. 'But go and get things ready, Jenny.'

She shot one scared glance at me and nodded and fled from the room.

Almost as soon as she had gone, the pain came again and I clung to the post of the four-poster bed for a moment. There was another wave of agony which threw me to the floor, my face in the carpet, and then I rolled on my back and felt my belly stand up like a hard box as my child fought its way through corrupt flesh to see the world.

I grabbed the foot of the bed and tried to haul myself into it, but as I reared up towards it, I could feel the passage between my legs opening like some magic cave and a feeling seized me as strong as lust. I sat on the floor with my back to the foot of the bed and pushed as hard as a man setting in fence posts.

I felt its head come out into the world.

Alone, in the darkened bedroom, with half the house running like mad things but no one with the wit to come to me, I held its little head, and then in a rush like thunder, my child, my little baby, slithered out kicking on to the carpet, and I picked it up in my arms.

I felt the cord, purple and slithery, pulsing with my blood. I took the corner of my nightgown and wiped the little mucky eyes and the face and the mouth. The child squirmed and opened its mouth and gave a little wail of protest, and coughed, and began to breath.

It was alive, then.

She was alive.

I held one of the skinny stick legs and saw the little pink female slit, and then I caressed the tiny foot, and ringed the small ankle with my forefinger and thumb.

'Sarah,' I said. And she opened her eyes and looked into my face.

She was *my* child, in that moment. I knew her as well as I knew the horizon around Wideacre. And she was not mad, nor sick, nor corrupt, nor evil. She was just a little baby who needed nothing more than a chance to grow and live and be happy. She had some kind of *right* to that, as surely as every poor child born in Acre had a right to life.

I struggled to my feet, and as I did so a great frightening slithery blob of flesh came away and fell to the floor. I froze, aghast, but I did not seem to be mortally wounded, though there was a great pool of blood where I had been. Then I saw the cord and realized, foolish Quality miss that I was, that it was the afterbirth and I could nibble off the cord in safety. My child was truly born and separate.

I put my mouth down, as natural as a lambing ewe, and nipped away at the cord and put a clean handkerchief over the little trail of blood on her belly. Then I took a woollen shawl from the drawer and wrapped her up like a trussed chicken, and then another shawl on top again, for she and I were going out into the darkness of the night, and I could hear the storm getting up.

Holding her tiny body firmly in the crook of my arm, I opened my cupboard door and pulled out my winter cape, a thick one of navy-dyed wool, and swung it around us both, and pulled the hood up. My bloodstained nightdress flapped at my ankles, but I paid little heed to it. I was barefoot, but it did not trouble me.

The baby, pressed against my warmth, seemed quiet, sleepy. I held her tight, and then I opened my bedroom door and listened.

Stride and Jenny were in the kitchen, for I could hear Jenny's high-pitched anxious voice as they waited for the great brass pans to boil so they could bring more hot water to the room. Mrs Gough was in the bedroom above mine, clumping around in her slippers getting the cradle ready and the fire lit, and the linen aired. I tilted my head to listen, but I could not hear Richard.

I shrugged as if it did not really matter, as if this madness could not be stopped by mischance. I held the precious slight bundle a little tighter under my cloak, and slid like a ghost to the top of the stairs.

Then I heard it. The clink of a decanter against a glass. Richard was in the library, drinking and waiting. Waiting for the accoucheur from Chichester. Waiting for him to come down the stairs with the new heir to Wideacre in his arms and say, 'Squire, your child has been born,' like the last page of a happy novel.

But that would never happen.

I knew I could pay the price. I had faced it when I was ready to die in my own bed with a murderer's hands on me. I was ready even now, with my most precious little girl held close to me. I had to pay a price for being a Lacey. She was the price that had to be paid.

Richard would never see his child.

Wideacre would never have an heir.

Quiet as a shadow I crept down the stairs, my bare feet absolutely silent on the thick carpet. As I stepped delicately and quietly from one stair to another, little drops of blood ran down my legs and stained my feet so I left a spoor like a wounded animal.

The tracks would lead Richard, sniffing blood like some predator, across the hall and to the front door. But outside it was dark and the wind was tossing the trees around. Soon it would rain and all trace of me and my little child would be gone. The Fenny would be up, the waters very high. You can hide anything in the Fenny when it is in flood. Richard, of all people, who had thrown a young woman's body into the river, should have remembered that.

The front-door latch clicked, but the noise was masked by the squeak of the tree branches rubbing together in the wind outside. The gusts of air whipped into the hall, but the library door was tight shut, and Richard did not know his house was wide open to the storm. He did not know that his front door was open to the wind, to anyone. And that the child he longed for was out in the rain, and would never come back.

I gasped as the rain slapped my face like an unforgiving enemy.

A great scud of water, hard as hailstones, smacked me in the face, and stayed like tears on my cheeks. I shook my head like a dog coming out of a river and tucked the baby more securely into my side.

My feet stung with the cold as I crept down the garden path and out of the gate into the drive. I was a fool to go barefoot, but I was not thinking. I was not thinking at all. I was on my way to the Fenny, and neither the stony drive nor the nettles and old brambles of the Wideacre wood footpaths would stop me.

I was biting my lip to stop myself whimpering with the pain as I walked up the drive, stumbling on the chalk stones and splashing in the puddles until the cape and the nightdress were drenched. There was only one dry spot on me and that was the warm little bundle in my left arm. I could feel her breathing softly and sweetly, and some distant thought in my mind said to her, 'This is Wideacre, and you are a Lacey.' But no words crossed my lips. This child, my daughter, would go out of the world as she had come into it – owning nothing.

As I turned under the shelter of the trees, the rain stopped beating in my face and I could breathe a little better. My feet had stopped hurting, for they were numb with cold. When I glanced down at them, I thought they were black with mud in the moonlight, but then I realized that they were cut and bleeding. The birth and the loss of blood, the pain of my feet and the storm had all made me light-headed, and instead of stumbling and struggling down to the Fenny, I felt I was gliding, dancing along the little path. Some old strange magic of Wideacre was singing in my head, and I knew with utter certainty that I was at last in command of myself and in tune with the land around me.

I stumbled over a tree root, and there was the Fenny before me, and I gasped. I had been out so little, I had not seen it since this year's rain had started swelling it and making the waters flow faster and faster. It was frightening. It was boiling like a great dangerous flood, up to the very rim of the steep banks, and threatening to swell over at any moment and drown the whole Wideacre valley. The tree behind me seemed to be trembling with fear at the thought of that flood, and I put my hand out on the trunk to reassure myself that the dry land and the tall trees were safe.

The river roared like some great animal; it was not like the safe waters where I had played. I would hardly dare come to the bank now for fear that it would give way beneath me. Nothing, least of all a little baby, could go into the flood and come out alive.

I looked upstream for the fallen tree which spans the river and serves as a crossing point. I could not see it at all and I thought it must have been swept right away. Then I looked downstream and could see the great spouts of water where the river had overflowed at a weak part of the bank and was engulfing even the trunks of the big trees and slamming against them in great rocking waves. Above the roar of the river and the noise of the creaking branches and the rush of the wind I heard myself give a little sob of fear.

But I knew what I had come to do.

And nothing, now, could stop me.

I knew what I *had* to do: to set myself free, to set Acre free, to finish the Laceys and to destroy Richard.

I left the shelter of the oak tree and went as near as I dared to the bank. I could feel the ground shudder with the water rushing past it and as I watched, a huge lump of riverbank was peeled away and fell with a splash into the torrent. The ground beneath me seemed to be shaking, and I put out a hand to steady myself on the root of a fallen tree.

I balanced myself against the tree and put my cold hand carefully in under my cape. Sarah sighed as I lifted her clear of my protecting warmth and opened her eyes and looked directly at me. I held her to my cold rain-washed face and then I bent down to the flood and lowered her towards it as tenderly as I might have put her in a cradle.

The sound of the river was as deafening as if I were drowned myself and it was flowing through my head, so I heard nothing; but I saw, like a silent ghost, a woman detach herself from the shadow of the trees on the other side of the river.

I froze. Sarah was just inches away from the water, her eyes wide, her mouth opened, crying, but I could hear nothing above the awful roar, roar, roaring of the hungry river.

The woman came to the bank of the river on the other side; she crossed over and came to me. I stared at her as if she were a ghost. From my position, bent low over the water, it looked like she had just walked across the river, walking lightly on the flood as if it were as safe as a dancefloor, but as I straightened up, I saw she had been walking on the tree-bridge. It was half covered with water and in shadow, so I had not seen it properly.

She moved back to the bridge, and then she turned and walked away from me again. I stared after her, and then, not knowing why, I raised Sarah up and tucked her into my side again. I scrambled to my feet and went up river till I came to the bridge. I clung to Sarah with one hand and then stepped cautiously into the swirling, ankle-deep water and picked my way on the slippery wood, clinging to the branches of the tree to keep me steady.

She was waiting for me on the other side. She had glided across as if she knew the bridge and the woods even better than I did, or as if she were indeed a ghost which need not fear death by drowning in a tumbling river.

As soon as I reached the bank, she turned and walked away from me and I followed her in a dream. The storm was still blowing loudly enough, but here in the shelter of the woods I could scarcely hear anything. The noise of the river died away behind us as the deep-green curtains of spruce and pine enfolded us. I followed her, stumbling, but she did not stumble. She walked lightly and did not seem to touch earth.

She was leading me towards the common, and I wondered with sudden hope if she was taking me to Ralph, if Ralph had come back to Wideacre not for vengeance at all but to rescue me. To take me away.

We came out of the shelter of the trees to the little gate in the park wall and she opened it and glided through. As I followed her, I caught a glimpse of her face in the moonlight.

She was beautiful; a young woman, with hair as red as a chestnut horse's mane, and eyes as green as downland grass, set slanting in her oval face. She reminded me of someone, but I could not think who. I stared at her, trying to trace some memory, to find some family resemblance to someone I knew well.

Then she smiled at me, a rueful familiar smile, and I gave a little gasp. She reminded me of myself, and that smile was the one that had called them out in Acre. It was the Lacey smile. It was Beatrice.

I put out a hand to stay her, but she was gone, walking lightly ahead of me as if she could see the path as clear in moonlight as in daytime. I followed her, a ghost like her, a witch like her. I was not even surprised when she led me up the steep cold heather-covered hills and I saw she cast no shadow on the silvery sand.

I had to watch my bruised feet as I staggered up the track. The wet sand was heavy going, and I was afraid of falling with Sarah. Besides, I could feel that I was bleeding more heavily; a warmth was running down the inside of my legs, warning me that I had gone nearly as far as I could go that night. I still had not done what I had come for. When I reached the crest of the hill and struggled to the top, I looked around for her, but she was gone.

There was no slight figure to follow, there was no lingering, inscrutable smile. She had gone as suddenly and as inexplicably as she had come. I had followed a will-o'-the-wisp and was now almost two miles from home and the Fenny; and Sarah was still alive and on Wideacre.

I gave a little sob of despair then, that I should get it all wrong again, and I half turned to go back down the path, back towards the Fenny, to drown Sarah and to drown myself, when a movement caught my eye. It was a ring of carts, loaded up and packed and ready to leave, a ring of gypsy carts in the usual sheltered hollow of the common. I was a few hundred yards from them with my child in my arms and Mama's rose pearls around my neck.

I went down the hill in a sliding dreamlike rush and

approached the nearest cart. A man was at the horse's head, tightening the leathers and adjusting the harness. On the driver's seat there was a woman.

She was a young woman, about my age, with a scarf tied down over her hair and a piece of sacking around her shoulders to keep out the rain. In the cart behind her were the family belongings, with the tent lashed down over them to keep them dry. In her arms, feeding at her breast, was a small baby. She had milk.

I stumbled on my hurt feet up to the side of the cart and she looked down at me without surprise. I fumbled in the fold of my cloak and lifted Sarah up to her, holding her awkwardly so she awoke and cried to find herself suddenly cold, and suddenly in mid-air without an arm around her.

The woman reached out and gathered my baby in to her without a word as if she had been waiting for me. I glanced around at the circle of carts. It seemed like they were all waiting. It seemed like they had packed and readied themselves for one of their unknowable wanderings, and then waited. They had waited in the rain and the dark for someone to come to them out of the shelter of the Wideacre woods.

I put my hands up to my neck and took off Mama's rose-pearl necklace. The woman put her hand out for it and slid it into a pocket hidden in her layers of clothing. As if I had bought my child her rights, she immediately uncovered the other breast and gave my baby suck. The feet of the Lacey heir and the gypsy child kicked in unison as they fed from the same woman.

I stepped back. It was a dream. There was nothing I could say, there was no need to say anything.

The man at the horse's head tightened a final strap and glanced up at the woman sitting high on the cart. At her nod he clicked to the horse and started to walk beside it. The horse lowered its head against the load and pulled hard at the weight of the cart in the softness of the sand. The side of the cart was painted, but in the moonlight and shadow as the storm-clouds blotted out the light, I could not see the patterns nor any colour. The scene was all silver and grey and black; it was a scene out of a dream without colour, in some moonlit landscape as desolate as a white desert.

The other carts had moved away first, the pans swinging at the sides, lashed on with pieces of twine. Many carried baskets of pegs and carved wooden flowers, or little ornaments, all tied on to the sides for easy sale. As the carts jolted away, the pans clinked together, making insane music, and the flowers jogged like dream dancers. The line of six carts moved off, and I suddenly came out of my reverie and realized what I had done.

The woman raised her hand to me and I took a hasty step forward, but the cart stuck, and then lurched too fast for her to hear me call. A horn lantern swinging on the side of the cart illuminated the pure white of the shawl around my baby's head, but even as I stared, the light flickered and went out and I could not see her. The cart was going away from me too fast.

I took half a dozen hasty paces after it, but my blood was flowing and my head was light, and the stars and the storm-clouds seemed to be whirling around between me and my child, between me and my daughter. And I knew that it was no dream. I had given her away and I should never see her again.

'Her name is Sarah!' I screamed towards the back of the cart and I tried to run again, but my knees gave way beneath me and I sank down into the sand, crying and crying, trying to catch my breath so that I might call loud enough for them to hear me. 'Her name is Sarah!' I shouted to the dark jolting cart which was going away so quickly into the night. 'Sarah Lacey of Wideacre!'

I don't know how long I stayed there, after that call to the jolting cart. I watched them go until my eyes were hot with staring into the darkness and so filled with hopeless tears that I could see nothing, not even the whiteness of the shawl around my little girl's head. I stayed kneeling in the wet sand, with the great drops of rain pouring down upon me, and then for a little while I think I pitched forward and wept.

I lifted my head and saw that it was getting lighter. A whole long night had passed. I was free.

Richard had no hold on me that he could ever use again. I had seen him for what he was, and I had conquered my fear of him. Richard was a madman, a cunning charming madman; and he would have killed me last night if I had not begun to give birth to his child.

I had done my duty to Wideacre when I threw away the heir, my lovely, lovely little girl. I would go home and do one further duty. I would face my Grandpapa Havering and tell him that Richard had shot Jem, and Uncle John, and my mama, and I would show him the fraudulent marriage licence as proof of motive, and the rose-pearl ear-rings as evidence. They would take him to Chichester and they would hang him. Then I would pull down the walls of the new Wideacre Hall and live in one of the cottages on the green, alone, mourning, lonely for all I had lost, glad for all I had saved.

I was the squire, the last squire. My last job was to rid Wideacre of Richard.

I pulled my drenched heavy cloak around me and got to my feet. I staggered with weariness and for a moment feared that indeed I might not get home at all. I might collapse out here and be dead of cold and loss of blood before anyone thought to look for me on the common.

Then I gritted my teeth and turned my face for home. I put one bruised and bloody foot before another for a hundred counted paces, and then a hundred more, and then a hundred more. It was the only way to get home I could think of, so I counted my way like a little child. I went back into the dark woods of Wideacre, over the perilous river bridge, where the counted numbers were little gasps of fear as my feet slipped and the river tugged at my heavy cloak and nearly pulled me down to drown, and then, counting, counting, counting, down the little footpath where I had run so easily as a child with my beloved cousin before me. I was counting, counting, counting the paces back to my home where there would be someone – surely there *must* be someone – to help me to bed, so I could rest and ready myself to tell Richard that I had destroyed his heir and that I would destroy him too.

As I came out of the woods on to the drive, it was nearly dawn; the sky was growing pale, though the storm-clouds were still black over the downs. The wind was high, sighing in the treetops. But above the noise of the wind I thought I heard people shouting in the woods.

I supposed they were all out looking for me. I hoped very much Richard was out too, then I could get to my room and sleep and sleep before I had to face him. Richard had to die. Richard had to be utterly destroyed. And I knew I was not yet strong enough to do it.

The front door stood open as I limped up the path, and the house was deserted. It was as I thought: everyone was out in the woods searching for me, and I might be able to creep upstairs and rest before I had to face Richard.

But I was a Lacey, not a silly child, and I thought that the least I could do was to write a note and pin it to the front door so that the men out in the rain could be sent home and would not spend all day looking for me while I lay safe and snug abed. I went into the library to fetch paper and pen to write my note before I went to bed.

Richard was in the carved heavy chair at the head of the table, in his breeches and linen shirt. His chair was tipped back on its two back legs with his weight.

His face was like a skull, his lips drawn back in a terrible piteous grin of fear, his eyes staring, looking to me as his rescuer, as the only person in the world who could save him from certain death.

Ralph was behind the chair, one hand pulling Richard's head back with a tight grip on Richard's curling hair, the other hand holding a long sharp knife against Richard's throat.

They were both watching the doorway. They had heard me come in and the slap, slap, slap of my wet nightgown and cloak as I crossed the hall. I took in the scene in one swift glance and quickly pushed the door shut behind me so that no one else could come in, so that no one but us would know. And I leaned back against it.

Richard's whole face trembled in a pitiful appeal. 'Julia!' he said, and I could hear him trying to put his charm into his voice. 'Julia!'

I looked at him out of my red-rimmed weary eyes. I looked at him, the brother I had loved all my life, and I knew I would never cease loving him. My brother, my blood, my kin.

I raised my head and Ralph's dark, understanding eyes met mine.

Ralph waited in silence for my decision.

'Kill him,' I said.

Ralph's sweep of the knife was as clean as a butcher's.

Dower House
Wideacre
Sussex

Dear Mr Fortescue,

I know you will forgive me for writing to you after all this time has gone by and after my treatment of you, which must have appeared cruel and unloving. I am able now to tell you that I loved you in Bath and that I have never stopped loving you.

I was trapped into becoming a mother, I was trapped into becoming a wife. Now I am a widow and I am ill with a fever, and they have told me that it may prove fatal.

This may sound very brave! Oh, James, I am not at all brave! I am full of anger and regret at the loss of so much and the gain of so little. There is only one little gain. I have a daughter, but in the hallucination of my fever I sent her away with the gypsies, thinking her safer off the estate. I am writing to you to ask you to seek her and to bring her back to her home. I have taken the liberty of naming you as her guardian and as the trustee to hold Wideacre for her until she is of age.

You will find her with the gypsy families who travel in the southern counties and always winter at Wideacre. It is my wish that she be educated to understand her responsibilities on the land. I hope you will tell her that it is my desire that she should sign over all the Lacey rights to the village. I have not the time to change the entail on the estate - only she can do that, and end the power of the squires over this land for ever. Please tell her that it is my determined wish that she should do that.

I am sorry to burden you with the responsibility of caring for my child, but I could think of no one more suitable for caring for the two things closest to my heart - the land and my daughter.

For you, I hope more than anything else that you will find someone to love and marry. I hope she loves you as much as I did. As I still do.

Goodbye, my darling,

Julia Lacey

P.S. Her name is Sarah. Sarah Lacey

Meridon

Philippa Gregory

Meridon, the desolate Romany girl, is determined to escape the hard poverty of her childhood. Riding bareback in a travelling show, while her sister Dandy risks her life on the trapeze, Meridon dedicates herself to freeing them both from danger and want.

But Dandy – beautiful, impatient, thieving Dandy – grabs too much, too quickly. And Meridon finds herself alone, riding in bitter grief through the rich Sussex farmlands towards a house called Wideacre – which awaits the return of the last of the Laceys.

Sweeping, passionate, unique: *Meridon* completes Philippa Gregory's bestselling trilogy which began with *Wideacre* and continued in *The Favoured Child*.

'In other hands this would be a conventional historical romance. But Ms Gregory uses her historical knowledge of the haves and the have-nots of those times to weave a much more subtle and exciting story.'   *Daily Express*

ISBN 0 00 651463 4

Wideacre
Philippa Gregory

Wideacre Hall, set in the heart of the English countryside, is the ancestral home that Beatrice Lacey loves. But as a woman of the eighteenth century, she has no right of inheritance. Corrupted by a world that mistreats women, she sets out to corrupt others. Sexual and wilful, she believes that the only way to achieve control over Wideacre is through a series of horrible crimes, and no-one escapes the consequences of her need to possess the land.

'The eighteenth-century woman is a neglected creature but, in the figure of her heroine, Philippa Gregory has defined a certain kind of witness...This is a novel written from instinct, not out of calculation, and it shows.' PETER ACKROYD, *The Times*

'For single mindedness, tempestuousness, passion, amorality, sensuality and plain old-fashioned evil, [Beatrice Lacey] knocks Scarlett O'Hara into short cotton socks.' *Evening Standard*

ISBN 0 00 651461 8